MW00825384

Marching with Caesar – Rise of Germanicus

By R.W. Peake

Also by R.W Peake

Marching With Caesar®- Birth of the 10th

Marching With Caesar-Conquest of Gaul

Marching With Caesar-Civil War

Marching With Caesar-Antony and Cleopatra, Parts I & II

Marching With Caesar-Rise of Augustus

Marching With Caesar-Last Campaign

Marching With Caesar-Rebellion

Marching With Caesar-A New Era

Marching With Caesar-Pax Romana

Marching With Caesar – Fraternitas

Marching With Caesar--Vengeance

Caesar Ascending - Invasion of Parthia

Caesar Triumphant

Critical praise for the Marching with Caesar series:

Marching With Caesar-Antony and Cleopatra: Part I-Antony

"Peake has become a master of depicting Roman military life and action, and in this latest novel he proves adept at evoking the subtleties of his characters, often with an understated humour and surprising pathos. Very highly recommended."

Marching With Caesar-Civil War

"Fans of the author will be delighted that Peake's writing has gone from strength to strength in this, the second volume...Peake manages to portray Pullus and all his fellow soldiers with a marvelous feeling of reality quite apart from the star historical name... There's history here, and character, and action enough for three novels, and all of it can be enjoyed even if readers haven't seen the first volume yet. Very highly recommended."
~The Historical Novel Society

"The hinge of history pivoted on the career of Julius Caesar, as Rome's Republic became an Empire, but the muscle to swing that gateway came from soldiers like Titus Pullus. What an amazing story from a student now become the master of historical fiction at its best."
~Professor Frank Holt, University of Houston

Marching with Caesar – Rise of Germanicus by R.W. Peake

Copyright © 2016 by R.W. Peake

For A Fan, Kenneth D. Counce

June 26, 1953-March 30, 2016

And His Son, Casey

Thank you for making me aware that my books

Meant so much to your father.

Foreword

No matter what an author has in mind when they start a new project, it rarely, if ever, goes as planned, and this is certainly the case with what, in the beginning, was going to be one book but has now become *Marching With Caesar®-Vengeance* and this, Volume XIII, *Marching With Caesar-Rise of Germanicus.* Oh, when I sat down and began, it was straightforward enough; I was finally at a point where I could begin exploring the life of Germanicus Julius Caesar, something I had been looking forward to for some time, but what I quickly realized is that, if I went directly to young Germanicus, I would be shortchanging my own character's story. Since, from the outset, I have tried to write this series with an eye towards it being as authentic as possible, I could not justify giving Titus II, as I call him, short shrift. And, honestly, since this is a first-person narrative, it was highly unlikely that he would just skip over a huge chunk of his own life, particularly the period that saw the death of his beloved brother, just to get to Germanicus.

However, as is wont to happen, that part of the story developed and took on a life of its own, leaving me with a choice of either condensing this part of the story, or not exploring Germanicus and his role in the Batonian Revolt in a manner that I found acceptable. So, as I tend to do, I chose both, although I will say that I felt some trepidation at the release of Vengeance, since it's "only" 136K words, which, as you readers know, is far short of my norm.

Which brings us to this book, Rise of Germanicus, and before I go any farther, I want to take this time to simultaneously thank, and tout, Lindsay Powell, for his stellar work, *Germanicus-The Magnificent Life and Mysterious Death of Rome's Most Popular General*, published by Pen & Sword. As always, I try to rely on the primary sources, but I found his work informative and extremely helpful in filling in the larger picture of the Pannonian uprising, about which I knew very little detail before beginning this book. Perhaps the only real advantage I had was in my familiarity with the terrain, since this has been the setting for most of the Titus II story, but it also elicits something of a confession.

I would like to say that setting the stage by using the Maezaei tribe as Sextus' killers, and the subsequent drama that played out was part of a master plan that brings Titus full circle when he is marching with Germanicus…but that simply isn't the case. When I wrote the scene that begins Vengeance, I had yet to dive into the Batonian Revolt, so you can imagine my surprise when, once I got to Dio and the other sources I used, I saw that it was the same Maezaei tribe that Germanicus was sent to subdue. Honestly, normally, I would agree that this is a happy accident, except this is not the first time that something like this has happened, and perhaps I am pushing my luck, but I would like to think this is a sign, or even a blessing from the old gods as I continue to tell the story of the Pullus family, whether they be marching with Caesar, Tiberius, or Germanicus.

As always, I want to thank my editor Beth Lynne, particularly for the quick turnaround on this, since, through nobody's fault but my own, I overshot my promised release date by what will be more than three weeks, which is something of a rarity for me. Also, to Marina Shipova for once again bearing with me as I try to communicate what's in my head into a workable cover. And, one note about the cover; the depiction of Germanicus is taken from a combination of the extant busts of his likeness, but it's his cuirass in particular that is a copy of that found in the only full-size rendering of Germanicus in full armor, the one in Perugia, Italy.

R.W. Peake

August 18, 2016

Historical Note

Back when I realized that what has now become the Marching With Caesar® series would be extending past just the life of the first Titus Pullus, there were two specific areas I was extremely interested in covering, and this, *Marching with Caesar-Rise of Germanicus,* is the first. I have long been fascinated with Germanicus Julius Caesar, and I think he is probably the most intriguing "What If" figure, behind the man whose name he took, of course, in Roman history. What if he had survived; would he have succeeded Tiberius, instead of Germanicus' son? If so, would he have been corrupted by the power the way Tiberius was in the latter part of his reign? And, maybe most importantly, would he have realized that his son, "Little Boots," was as crazy as a latrine rat and found someone else as a successor? Who knows, maybe one day I'll do something similar with Germanicus that I did in the Caesar Triumphant series; the possibilities, as they say, are endless. Having said that, there are a few things I would like to point out, clarify, or beg the indulgence of readers for a deviation from the record, and I suppose I'll start with the last one first.

The revolt in Pannonia, referred to by the Romans as the Batonian revolt because of the two leaders sharing the same name, lasted from 6 to 9 A.D. Germanicus arrived with a levy of troops consisting of "free-born citizens" and "freedmen, including those whom he had freed from slavery," according to Dio, the "he" being Augustus, in early 7 A.D. Both for dramatic purposes, and based on what I hope is not an unfounded assumption, I have Germanicus spending most of that year involved in the further recruitment and training of what I called the Germanicus Legion in the book. According to Dio, the campaign against the Maezaei started somewhere around the end of 7; I have postponed it a matter of a few months, and for that I beg the indulgence of the reader.

9

Another *possible* change is the composition of the town of Raetinium, about which little is known; in my story, it starts out as a Roman settlement before being taken by the Maezaei. My reasoning is not just for convenience, but in the name, which aligns with the Roman naming convention for their cities and towns, not with that used by the Pannonian tribes. As far as the locations, Splonum was located roughly where the village of Sanski Most, Bosnia-Herzegovina is located, at 44.843597N, 16.699712E; as nearly as I can determine, the location of where the Barrington Atlas places the iron mines that were the source of Maezaei wealth is around the village of Risovac, Bosnia-Herzegovina, 44°43′30″N 16°13′30″E.

Raetinium's precise location is a mystery, but again, using a combination of Barrington, and "walking the ground" by using Google Earth, I have placed it very near the city of Bihac, Bosnia-Herzegovina, 44.816667N, 15.866667E, but on the eastern side of the Una (ancient Oenus) river, which I did not do arbitrarily. When Dio describes the horrific scene of the fall of Raetinium, he describes the Maezaei retiring to the citadel, then assailing the Romans "from above," which I took literally. Using this as a reference, I found one location where there would be a flat area, in the middle of which is a small hill that would be exactly the kind of place that anyone with an eye to defense would place their strongpoint. The actual boundaries of the town, specifically my placement of the walls on the western side of the river, is strictly my own invention.

Readers well versed in their history may also notice there is one serious omission for anyone who expects a strict adherence to the historical record, and this involves Dio's story about how Splonum fell. Specifically, the idea that, after being unable to make any headway conducting a siege that "Pusio, a German horseman, hurled a stone against the wall and so shook the parapet that it immediately fell and dragged down with it a man who was leaning against it..." and this was what it took to conquer a town is, frankly, something I don't buy at all. To me, it smacks of propaganda, or at the very least, an "urban myth" that Dio used simply because it was easier than trying to determine the truth of the matter. The upshot is that, for those of you looking for Pusio, the Olympic champion stone thrower, you will be disappointed.

What readers may have more of an issue with is the manner in which I characterize the relationship between Tiberius and Germanicus; however, while I do not go along with the theory that Germanicus was poisoned by Piso on the direct, or even indirect order of Tiberius, I do think that Tiberius at the very least viewed Germanicus as a rival.

Essentially, my opinion on Tiberius is that he was one of the most conflicted figures in Roman history. On one hand, he seemed to want all of the prestige, power, and accolades that came with being close to the Princeps, while on the other, my sense is that he loathed himself for that desire for acknowledgment and acceptance. I would point to him as an example of the kind of schizophrenia that haunted more than one of the upper classes of Rome, where one was supposed to aspire to achieve great things, but do so for the advancement of Rome, not the individual. And, being frank, there were more than enough examples of the dangers of what happened when a Roman in the age of Augustus overstepped the limits of what the Princeps deemed acceptable ambition, so it is understandable how this could be, if not confusing, then at least unclear to someone like Tiberius, trying to determine where the line was located. Also, in previous books, I have advanced the idea, through my characters, that Livia was also a powerful influence, albeit behind the scenes, since even today, men are at the least ambivalent about being seen as under the power of their mothers, no matter how ambitious or connected the woman may have been themselves. Putting it in its simplest terms, I think Tiberius was probably the unhappiest man in Roman history, torn between two competing motivations; living his own life, and doing his duty to Rome.

Finally, readers fluent in this early Imperial period may see some names familiar to them, in the form of some of the Tribunes and the men serving as Centurions in the Germanicus Legion. This is not an accident, but I also want to stress that nowhere did I find any evidence that those men actually serve with Germanicus; they were about the right age, and I wanted to present them as possibilities of being involved in some way. Their requisite characters, and their flaws, are again strictly of my own invention.

Chapter 1

I did not tarry in Carnuntum; carrying a pass signed by Tiberius opened up every door, like with the sour quartermaster in the *Quaestorium* there, who tried to slip me a couple of nags as replacements for the mounts I had used to get to Carnuntum as quickly as I did. Latobius had borne the journey well, but he was in his prime, and while he was no Ocelus, he was still a horse well above the average run of mounts used by a man of my status. Which, I supposed, was the reason for the *Immune* in charge of the Legion stables thinking I was a typical man of the Legions who did not know his horseflesh. Parading two specimens that could only charitably be called horses, he initially was resistant to my demand for more suitable animals, until, more out of frustration than any thought it would really work, I produced the scroll that I was to present to Germanicus, turning it so the *Immune* could see the seal and, most importantly, to whom it belonged. This was the first time I would use this scroll in such a fashion, but it was far from the last, which should be understandable, given the results. The horse that would serve as my remount was a smoke-gray, and at first glance resembled Ocelus so strongly that my vision blurred; thankfully, a closer examination showed the differences. For one thing, this horse was not as tall or as broad-chested, and he was a gelding, but when compared to the first offering, he was Bucephalus, and the thought crossed my mind that this might have been a ploy on the part of the *Immune* all along. The pack animal was slightly smaller but was clean-limbed and appeared sound for my purposes, and I was not going nearly as far as I had from Ubiorum to Carnuntum. And, as I had been informed by the Tribune who had caught up with me, sent by Tiberius, once I reached Poetovio, where the 13th was still stationed as their permanent camp, I would be escorted the rest of the way by an *ala* of cavalry. More than anything

13

else, it impressed upon me that this was not a homecoming, and that, for once, nobody was pretending that all was quiet in Pannonia.

Provided that the rebellion had not spread faster and farther than what Tiberius' sources had reported, which, given my experience with the province, was certainly well within the realm of possibility, I was reasonably confident I would be relatively safe riding alone as I made my way south from Carnuntum. I would be paralleling the Danuvius for a stretch, along the edge of the wide plain that is encompassed by the huge loop of the river, making ambushing someone difficult, although as any veteran learns, men whose roots reach so deeply into the soil as those barbarians who called this area home are more than capable of finding a spot that, to the unwary eye, poses no danger. Regardless, I felt confident enough in my experience that I was not overly concerned with the perils of traveling alone, but I did remain alert as I rode, mostly by talking to Latobius. I spent a fair amount of time, particularly the first day out of Carnuntum, trying to unravel the real meaning of some of the things that Tiberius had said, knowing that despite his offhand manner, there was something deeper lurking there. In particular, I wondered about the meaning of his natural son staying in Rome, who I learned was just a year younger than Germanicus, who I thought was about nineteen. As Romans of all classes know, there is a level of expectation present that comes with the privileges of being fortunate enough to be born into one of the rich, powerful, and illustrious families of Rome. Specifically, when it comes to all things martial, despite the level of relative peace, young men of these families are expected to have served under the standard in some capacity, and on the surface, something like this rebellion would seem to be a perfect time for Tiberius to see his son blooded. On the other hand, I felt certain that Tiberius knew, probably better than me and my fellow veterans of the province, how dirty and vicious the fighting can get when suppressing a rebellion, given his broader experience with such. Never far from my own thoughts was the battle with Draxo and the rebelling Taurisci, where I had helplessly watched my first Primus Pilus struck down, and more importantly, the repercussions that had brought down on the heads of the survivors of

14

a town that, even now, no longer exists. One day, it was a thriving place, almost the size of Siscia at the time, and in the space of less than one full day, the entire town was burned to the ground, and we slaughtered every man, woman, and child who had been contained within its walls. No, I decided, it would make sense if Tiberius wanted his son nowhere near the kinds of things that might be part of suppressing this rebellion, although that immediately raised the question about why Germanicus was taking part. To this point, I did not know much of Germanicus, and frankly, the men of the Legions did not either, though I supposed it made sense that, not only was Germanicus older, he was also Tiberius' son by adoption. Of course, my father was adopted by my Avus, and I know Titus Pullus loved my father as a son, and my father returned that love to a degree even higher than he showed his own sire. One thing I had heard from someplace, though I cannot say exactly where, was that Tiberius' adoption of Germanicus had not been his choice, but one forced upon him by the Princeps. And, if the rumors were true, it was one of a series of acts that Augustus had required of Tiberius in exchange for being returned to the favor of the Princeps. The more I thought about it, the more I began to develop the idea that young Drusus, who Tiberius had named in honor of his brother whom, as I had personally witnessed, he loved very much, was being kept in Rome not by Tiberius, but by Augustus. It made sense, on a number of levels; the rehabilitation of Tiberius to favor was still in its formative stage, and of all the things said about Tiberius, one in particular was something with which I had experience, as I learned during the Tribunal of my former Primus Pilus. There was a real fear by a powerful segment of Rome's ruling class that, should he decide to, Tiberius could summon not one, but several Legions, all of them he had personally commanded at one time or another, to wrest the power from Augustus, not perhaps to rule, but to force the Princeps to name Tiberius as his heir. This was problematic, on a number of levels, not least of which is that most of the men under the standard believed this was exactly what he should have done. It was an article of faith that Tiberius had been treated shabbily by the Princeps, and the fact that those Augustus had either named outright, or made it

15

known were his choice as successor kept dying was taken as an omen by the gods themselves. Some men thought this way, at any rate; frankly, I did not then nor do I now think the gods care a whit about the things we do among ourselves, jockeying for power over what I imagine the gods think of as their table scraps. By the time I reached the end of the first day's journey from Carnuntum, I had convinced myself that Tiberius' natural son was being held as a *de facto* hostage, while the adopted son was being sent out to be blooded and, if my instincts were correct, to perhaps stumble in a way that would damage his luster compared to the undamaged young Drusus. As I drifted off to sleep, I had an unsettling realization; here I am, thrown right into the middle of another squabble between my betters. Maybe, I thought miserably, that's the destiny of the Pullus family, to always be at the mercy of powerful men of Rome.

Poetovio was packed full of settlers, although this was not all that uncommon an occurrence, and as I learned within a watch of my arrival, their presence was more of a precaution and not because the violence had spread this far north…yet. Nevertheless, the fact that these settlers were here was telling in itself, since by this point in time, most of them were veterans of the province in their own right, some of them now second generation, and the only time they would uproot themselves and flee was when the prospect for widespread violence and unrest was likely. This was my first tangible sign that this was going to be more than a local uprising of one tribe; by the time I had checked into the *praetorium*, was assigned a set of quarters, and had deposited my baggage there, I learned a fair amount. However, it was that night, when I went out into Poetovio, where I learned the specifics that were the most important to those of us who would be involved in the fighting.

"It was the stupid *cunnus* Praetor, Messallinus," pronounced one of my newfound comrades, who had reintroduced himself as Aulus Corbulo, the Secundus Hastatus Prior of the 13th. "He brought this on." This much I knew, but while I did not know Corbulo all that well, I did know him by sight, from Siscia, and had even been drinking with him before. Consequently, I knew if I just sipped from my cup, I would learn more than I ever wanted about all manner of things, some of which might actually prove useful. Corbulo's tone was always naturally belligerent to my ears, but this time, it was so obviously directed at someone else, I took no offense. "First, he sent out the *publicani* earlier this year than ever before. And," he slammed a hardened palm on the table with sufficient force to make the other patrons glance over at the pair of us, "he tried to make them collect for *two* years instead of one!" This time, he did pause, presumably to give me the time to shake my head in bemused wonderment at the actions of the Praetor, which I suppose I signaled in some way to his satisfaction, since he continued, "*Then*, he holds a *dilectus* for auxiliaries! And you know how much these barbarian bastards *love* being in the auxiliaries." This, I was prepared to argue, to a point at any rate, but he seemed to sense my disagreement, because he allowed, "Now, that's not to say some of these Pannonian tribes don't produce good auxiliaries. They do," he granted, "but you know that they don't like it when we come taking more of their boys than they think they owe us."

That, I had to admit, was certainly true, and without bidding, the memory of the incident that began as an informal, off the books *dilectus* in Draxo's village and ended up as a small riot where a fellow Legionary was killed with a rock to the head leapt to my mind.

"How many did he call for?"

"Ten thousand," Corbulo answered flatly.

"At once?" I was astounded, truly; this was the first time I had ever heard a call for numbers that large at one time.

"Yes, at once," he affirmed with an emphatic nod. "But when they came to Salona, and they got a good look at their numbers," Corbulo shrugged, "and saw by how much they outnumbered the garrison, that bastard Bato convinced them they were better off fighting for their own freedom instead of subduing some Germans."

When put that way, and in conjunction with what Corbulo had said transpired earlier with this Messallinus, it was hard to argue the logic of Bato.

"What about the Breuci?" I asked him, confident that I knew their plans, but I was wrong, and I got my first hint with his reply.

"Last we heard," Corbulo paused to belch, then held his cup out for a refill, reminding me of his combined characteristics of thirst and cheapness, though I did not begrudge him, and he said, "they were marching."

This confused me; even from the farthest edge of Breuci territory, Siscia was no more than three days' march away, and I had learned of the Breuci uprising from Tiberius in more than enough time for the Breuci to cover the distance, even at a leisurely pace.

"Marching where?" I asked, then was struck by a sudden and horrible thought. "They didn't already take Siscia, did they?" I gasped.

Now Corbulo's expression matched mine, as he repeated, "Siscia?" His face cleared then, and he assured me, "Ah. No, they steered well clear of Siscia. It's too well fortified now."

"The camp, yes," I countered, "but not the town."

He cocked his head, squinting at me as he asked, "When's the last time you've been back to Siscia?"

I suppose this was the moment when I realized how quickly the three years had gone by, and I nodded my head in recognition that things had changed.

"So, Pullus," he interrupted my small reverie, "what brings you here to Poetovio?"

I explained briefly what my current duty was, but once I mentioned under whose authority I was acting, there was no mistaking his change in attitude, and suddenly, he did not seem quite so thirsty. Frankly, this was fine with me, and I had become somewhat accustomed to this kind of behavior over the course of the preceding three years when I had been sent on…errands, I suppose is the best word, by Tiberius. Once others knew I was connected to him in some way, I was generally given whatever I asked for, and was avoided, as if there was a fear they were the subject of my interest. And, as much as it pains me to admit, sometimes they were, but not this night. Nevertheless, not long after I explained my presence, Corbulo suddenly remembered he had pressing duties the next morning, leaving me alone to finish the amphora myself.

My stomach was sour, and my head was in a companion state, but I was astride Latobius at the break of dawn, waiting for the Decurion of the *turma* of cavalry that would be escorting me. I was somewhat wary of what to expect; my hope was that they would either be Germans, which was unlikely given how many of the cavalry *ala* had been directed to support Tiberius' planned campaign, or if they were Pannonian, from tribes that were not one of those in revolt. I heard them coming, and when I turned to watch them approach, honestly I could not immediately determine their origins, but what I could see was that they were all born horsemen. The Decurion in command detached himself from his men, trotting over to me astride a coal-black stallion that instantly put Latobius on alert, and to the point I had to curb him.

Grinning at me, the man spoke in heavily accented but clearly understandable Latin as he said cheerfully, "Good morning, Centurion! Are you sure you can handle your mount? I'm sure we can find a remount with a more…suitable temperament!"

Ever since I can remember, I have taken either an instant liking or disliking to most people I have met; that I wanted to punch this man in his grinning mouth within a heartbeat after the words left his mouth still ranks as one of the quickest decisions I have made. It was not just his words, but his complete lack of military bearing or demeanor, or so I told myself; mostly, it was because of his comment on my perceived lack of horsemanship.

"I can handle my horse perfectly well, Decurion." I managed through gritted teeth, but despite knowing it was petty, I nevertheless added, "But apparently in your worry about my horsemanship, you forgot that a Centurion of the Legions outranks a Decurion."

As I hoped, this wiped the grin off his face, yet despite seemingly turning somber, I saw the mirth was still there in his eyes, although he rendered a salute and an apology at the same time.

Somewhat mollified, I handed him the orders meant for him, adding, "I'm extremely familiar with the province, Decurion...?" I let my voice trail off in a way that let him know what I was expecting.

"Ah, yes," he nodded, "again, my apologies, Centurion. My name is Gaesorix of Batavia, which you have Romanized into Batavius."

"Batavians?" I indicated the rest of his *turma* with a nod, and he replied in kind, which made me feel better.

"Every one of them," Gaesorix said proudly, "and I assure you that you will arrive in Siscia, safely and very soon, Centurion...?"

With a fair amount of chagrin, I realized that while he had apologized and was behaving in a proper manner, now I was being the rude one, but I confess I was still nettled by his opening remark.

"Titus Pullus, Quartus Princeps Prior, 1st Legion," I informed him, then added, "but currently on detached duty under orders from Tiberius."

Gaesorix, who I judged to be at least ten years older than I was, with a lean, wiry build and sitting his horse in such a manner that it was difficult to tell where the man ended and the animal began, actually looked startled.

"You're Titus Pullus?" His surprise was such that it sounded to my ears to border on disbelief, one more mark against this Decurion, but at my nod, he turned his head and rattled something off in what I suppose was the Batavian tongue, which sounded Germanic in nature. I heard my name mentioned again, then he turned about to explain, "You're well known in this province, Centurion."

There was something in the way he said it that let me know this was neither meant lightly, nor as a compliment, and for the first time, my escort appeared, if not grim, then sober.

Quite abruptly, he said, "If you're ready, Centurion, we'll leave immediately."

Under ideal circumstances, I would have preferred to delve into this last development, but time was short, so instead, I answered with a nod, and with one of the troopers taking the lead rope of my packhorse, I joined Gaesorix by his side as we trotted out through the gate to Siscia.

Our first disagreement came when we reached a road junction; the Decurion turned to the right, which I ignored and continued straight ahead. As I suspected, I heard a series of shouts of consternation, but I did not turn my head, urging Latobius straight forward. He did so readily enough, but I saw his ears twitching rearward, and my sense was that, if he could have, he would have asked me, "Why are they so upset? What's ahead that I should be worried about?"

"Centurion! Centurion!" Gaesorix's voice rose not only in volume, but pitch, then I heard what sounded like some sort of curse, followed by a drumming of hooves as the Decurion hurried to catch me.

When he pulled alongside, he tried his grin on me as he asked, "Is there any particular reason you want to go this way, Centurion?"

"Other than it's the shortest way?" I countered, keeping my expression as blank as I could manage, then added with a shrug, "Not really."

Although the smile did not leave his lips, I saw his eyes narrow; I suppose he was trying to discern whether there was more to my words than appeared on the surface, and the truth is, there was.

"It's just that," Gaesorix spoke carefully, indicating the steeply rising ridge just about ten miles away in the distance, "that part of the province is very rugged, and it's not made for cavalry. Even," he pointed out, "Batavian cavalry."

I had not planned to maneuver Gaesorix into a spot where I could repay him for his slight about my supposed lack of horsemanship, but I was not about to pass up the opportunity when it presented itself.

"Decurion," now I was the one to grin at him, "I thought you said you knew who I am!"

"I do!" he countered, sounding defensive. "But only in general terms. I know that you were in the First Cohort of the 8th, and that you were in the Legion when Draxo rebelled. And," he paused, which I understood when he finished with, "why you transferred to the 1st Legion."

21

Despite, or perhaps because this was the truth, I felt my stomach tighten, then I forced myself to acknowledge to myself he had every right to bring it up, particularly given the current climate in the province.

I chose to ignore the last part of what he had said, telling him instead, "While all that's true, apparently, you never heard that I grew up here. And," this time, I was the one to point to that particular ridge, "I know that ground very, very well."

Gaesorix was not impressed, but he made another mistake when he persisted. "That's all well and good that you roamed those hills as a boy, Centurion. But these are different times, and," he made a sweeping gesture encompassing our mounts, "we fight from horseback, not on foot."

"So did I," I countered, "fight from horseback," I added, since I saw he was confused.

However, this only deepened it, as he asked in some surprise, "You rode in the cavalry?"

"I didn't say that," I admitted, "I said I've fought on horseback."

As I had hoped, our bickering had taken us a fair distance down the southern road, and by the time I finished telling Gaesorix, and those troopers who were within earshot, about my escape from the Latobici, on the back of Ocelus, it was too late in a practical sense to turn back and retrace our steps. Something, I saw with some amusement, that occurred to Gaesorix immediately after I finished my tale.

"You," he grumbled, "tell a good story. So good that you made me forget where we were." For a long moment, he glared up at me, then he burst out laughing. "But that's my fault, not yours."

I did not detect any falseness in his manner, so I grinned at him and assured him, "Don't worry, Decurion. I know of a cave we can hide in if we have to hide."

Regardless of my tone of levity and my determination to reach Siscia as quickly as possible, I also knew that Gaesorix had cause for concern. We would be crossing the eastern edge of a patch of territory that had caused the Army of Pannonia a great deal of anguish and worry. Not only was the ground itself a nightmare for the cavalry, it was only marginally better for the Legions; that it was located in such a way that parts of it belonged to three different tribes meant that this was one of the first places one of those tribes headed for when they rebelled. Granted, by this point in time, the Legions had been forced into this territory enough times we had a good knowledge of the terrain, but that is a far cry from the kind of familiarity that the barbarian tribes who have inhabited these lands for countless generations. In recognition of this reality, Gaesorix had us riding in an open formation, and with every mile we traveled, I could feel the uneasiness of the troopers who were technically charged with ensuring my safety. I say "technically"; I confess that the thought crossed my mind that, should something occur, these Batavians were very likely to view me as the cause of the problem. And given that they clearly shared Gaesorix's view of a Roman Centurion's horsemanship, I could easily envision a situation whereby they arrived at Siscia, minus their one charge. Like the chance of trouble, I did not think it was likely, yet it was still there in the back of my mind. What I had not thought about was the feeling of apprehension that grew in me with every mile we drew nearer to the landmark that is the easternmost part of the system of ridges and broken ground, where I had been forced to spend a night, using Ocelus for warmth and wondering if my family had been slaughtered. Latobius seemed to sense my growing agitation, and he began twitching, while his large nostrils took in huge gulps of air as he scented the air, searching for any sign of a threat. Meanwhile, Gaesorix and I rode along in, for the first time, an easy silence, although I sensed his eyes on me whenever I was looking straight ahead. Being honest, I probably did as much of the same thing, trying to get a measure on the Decurion, wondering, if we did get ambushed, how he would react. Some might think I should have been less worried about him than the other troopers under his command, but I had long before learned that the value of good leadership, especially during combat, must never be underestimated. The adage "there are no bad Centuries, just bad Centurions" extends to the cavalry *ala* much the

23

same as it does in the Legions, although I suppose it could be argued that adding horses into the mix make matters even more subject to chance.

Turning to Gaesorix, I asked, "Do you have a spare *spatha* I can borrow until we get to Siscia?"

He shot me a peculiar look, part scornful, but I sensed there was an appraising quality to it, but he shrugged and said casually, "Of course. We all carry a spare."

Leaning away from me, I saw his free hand moving, then he tugged at something, producing a scabbarded *spatha* that he had tied to his saddle. He handed it over to me, and while I accepted it, I immediately felt a bit foolish since I could not remain on Latobius and secure the *gladius* to my own saddle.

Seeing this, Gaesorix chuckled but told me, "We were about to stop for a rest break anyway." Glancing about, he pointed to a low knoll with trees on the crest, providing shade. "We'll stop there."

Shouting a command in his own tongue, he kicked his mount into a trot, heading for the knoll, and I turned Latobius to follow. I have had occasion to think about that moment, wondering if my action was simply a lucky, and ultimately happy accident, or if somehow, the land itself sent me a subtle warning about what was about to happen.

The day was drawing to a close, and we were faced with a choice that even before the events that transpired I did not relish making. We had reached the northern base of the ridge, and by my estimate, we had about two parts of a watch of daylight left, but it would take more than a full watch for us to negotiate the low pass that would take us across the ridge and down to the more open country below. Depending on how hard we were willing to push our horses, conceivably we could be descending the opposite side just as the sun went down. Provided, of course, that there was no delay in our progress. Frankly, I take full responsibility for what transpired because I did not spend more than the span of a couple heartbeats considering these issues before making my decision.

"We'll rest the horses a bit," I told Gaesorix, "then we're going to keep going. I know a spot on the other side where we can find water and good forage for the horses. And," I thought to add, "there's a farmhouse where we can get under a roof for the night."

I suppose it was somewhat silly of me to think the idea of sleeping under a roof would be tempting to the Decurion, not to mention that, even if the place was deserted, as it had been when my family took shelter there, there would not be room for the entire *turma*.

Rather than respond immediately, Gaesorix made what seemed to me an exaggerated examination of the area around us, then asked, "What's wrong with stopping right here? No matter if we stop here, or where you're talking about, we won't be in Siscia until tomorrow."

Fighting the urge to make an impatient retort, I answered, "Because if we stay here for the night, we don't make it into Siscia until late in the day tomorrow. If we push on now, we can get there before midday." The Batavian clearly was unconvinced, which prompted me to say something that, while I knew would have an impact, I still felt somewhat ashamed at being so underhanded. "I thought you Batavians weren't scared of anything?" The laugh I gave felt forced, but I pretended it was genuine, pointing up to the wooded slope, and adding, "They're just trees, Gaesorix."

"Yes, they are," he countered, "which could be hiding hundreds of those fucking barbarians." Heaving a sigh, finally, he acquiesced with a resigned shrug, saying only, "Very well, Centurion."

In the moment, I felt the same kind of satisfaction I always did when I got my way, but when Gaesorix insisted that we send out a pair of his men as advance scouts, I was quick to agree, in an attempt to soften the blow the Decurion suffered when I essentially shamed him into taking actions that ran against his instincts. Once we rested the horses, the pair of troopers went trotting ahead, and we waited long enough for them to disappear from sight higher up the slope in the trees, then resumed our journey. For the first several moments, the only noises were the sounds of hooves, the creaking of leather as we all turned and twisted in our saddles, peering through the undergrowth, with only an occasional mutter by one of the men. Inevitably, when nothing happened, and there were no shouts of alarm from our scouts, we all began to relax as we continued up the narrow track. I knew the most likely spot for an ambush, where the track wended its way through a narrow defile and the limestone rock of the ridge was exposed. The defile was perhaps fifty paces wide, and while the rock walls were not that high, perhaps twenty feet on the left side and fifteen on the right, it was still a spot that practically guaranteed it would be viewed as a prime location for an ambush. From what I remembered, this place was about two miles up the slope, making it approximately a third of the way through the pass, and I told Gaesorix about it before we resumed. As we drew nearer, the quiet conversations and banter that had started back up ceased, and I found myself checking the *spatha* in its scabbard to make sure it would slide easily should I need it. More than anything, I watched Latobius, and I saw Gaesorix was doing the same with his own mount, the tension drawing out with every passing moment. The track made a gentle curve, which I recognized as the spot where, once we navigated it, the nearest part of the defile would just be visible, and I told Gaesorix as much. Signaling a halt to the rest of the men, the Decurion nudged his own horse forward, and I felt compelled to go with him, moving at a slow walk farther up the track, navigating the curve until I caught a glimpse of the yellowish-white of the nearest edge where the defile started. At first, that was all that was visible, but as we continued up the track, albeit slowly, we saw the scouts, roughly in the middle of the defile, and while each of them was looking up at the rocks nearest them, neither of them showed any sign of agitation or that they were suspicious. The sight of them prompted a sigh of relief from the both of us, at the same time, which caused us both to chuckle, then Gaesorix turned and yelled for the rest of the *turma*. Moving forward at the trot, we stopped with the scouts, while Gaesorix questioned them in their tongue, then turned to me.

"They haven't seen or heard anything suspicious," he told me, which was obvious just by their body posture, but it still made me feel a bit better to hear it said.

"Once we get through here, we should be all right," I told Gaesorix. "It's mostly downhill, and there's only one spot I can think of where there's a place where anyone can attack from uphill."

I knew that, being a cavalryman, Gaesorix's concern about entering a thickly wooded area was soundly based, since horses need quite a bit more room; entering a wooded area where the path being taken is at a low point is even more dangerous because it gives men on foot the extra impetus of running downhill. Given that the route I had essentially embarrassed him into taking contained both elements, I was as eager to be past this stretch as he was, if for different reasons. Additionally, once we left this area behind, the ground was not only flat, it was largely open, with only strips of forested lands where an ambushing force would have any chance of surprise. And, given how easy these locations were to spot, catching us by surprise would be next to impossible. First, however, we had to finish traversing this stretch, and Gaesorix signaled the scouts to resume their own progress, as we waited for a few moments to give them a head start.

"So, I know you're in a hurry to get to Siscia, but you act like a man who's in a *hurry* to get to Siscia." Gaesorix grinned at me. "As in, you left a woman behind, and now you're worried that someone else might be…" He trailed off, but he had no need to continue; I knew what he was talking about well enough.

Shaking my head, I was surprised at the pang of sorrow I felt at the thought of Giulia, despite our affair and her subsequent death having occurred several years before.

"No," I assured him, "nothing like that. Although I do have friends there. My best friend and former close comrade is an Optio of the Sixth of the First."

"So, you're an ambitious man," he commented but said it in such a way it was difficult for me to tell if this was a compliment, insult, or merely an observation, so I let it pass.

I sensed he was disappointed that I had not risen to his bait, and he changed the subject to something else more mundane and forgettable. As we began descending the opposite side of the ridge, while I still kept my eyes moving, I felt myself relax, and I began thinking ahead, wondering if this youngster Germanicus had not arrived from Rome, how long I would have to wait for him to show up. So absorbed was I in this that I did not immediately notice that Gaesorix had drawn up sharply, making him call to me when I was perhaps two lengths further down the track.

"Centurion!"

His voice was pitched low so it did not carry, and I turned in my saddle to see what he wanted. Later, I wondered if this played a role in events that were a matter of heartbeats from beginning, because I clearly missed the early warning I would have gotten from Latobius that would have made me more alert.

"Where are the scouts?" Gaesorix asked, pointing past me down the track as he did so. "They should be in sight."

It was as I was turning around that two things happened, so closely together it is impossible for me to know which occurred first. One was a sound, a distinctive hissing of a missile streaking past, and I am certain I would have been struck had it not been for the other action, Latobius suddenly rearing, although it is equally possible that the arrow was meant for my horse. I say this because another arrow did not miss its mark, as Gaesorix's mount was struck, letting out a screeching whinny of pain.

"Centurion! Run!" Gaesorix shouted. "Get away while we hold them off!"

For the span of perhaps two normal heartbeats, I was torn by indecision. The way in front was still clear, but men were pouring from the trees on either side of the track, while arrows and the short throwing spears favored by Pannonian tribes came hurtling into the cavalry column from either side. Behind Gaesorix, it was a chaos of plunging horses, many of them struck by arrow or spear, and men either struggling to control their mounts, or falling from them. Gaesorix's horse had an arrow through the neck, although the blood was flowing, not spurting from its wound. Because of my slight separation, I had the perfect opportunity to do as he had urged; naturally, therefore, I did no such thing. Kicking Latobius, hard, at the same time I turned his head back upslope, and for an instant, he shifted his weight under me, onto his hindquarters, before launching himself, going immediately to the gallop. While it was true that I had fought from horseback before, and indeed, had done so on the back of this same animal, before he had a name, attacking a bunch of starving bandits, is vastly different from the hardened warriors of a Pannonian tribe. In the brief span of time I had as Latobius thundered upslope, my inner detached observer noted the warriors now closing with us wore the colors of the Varciani, which made a certain amount of sense since this was their territory, but it also informed me another tribe was in rebellion. Gaesorix had gotten his mount under control and had drawn his *spatha,* but his shield was still lashed to his saddle, so he was unable to protect himself from the spear thrust, launched by a burly, mustachioed warrior attacking from his weak side. Without making a conscious decision to do so, I pushed my left knee into Latobius' side, and in mid-bound, he altered his direction just enough to aim directly for the warrior, just as his arm started to move forward. Catching our movement out of the corner of his eye, the Varciani was faced with the choice of making a kill but being run down in the process, or throwing himself out of the way and regrouping for another attempt. As I hoped, he chose the latter course, yet despite falling backwards to my right, as Latobius inserted his body into the gap between Gaesorix and the Varciani, thanks to the extra length of my *spatha* and my reach being much longer than an average man, I was able to lean over far enough for a thrust, plunging the point of my blade into the man's chest. It was not particularly powerful, for me at any rate, but the warrior let out a bellow of agony, telling me I had at least managed to punch through the boiled leather cuirass he was wearing. Then, my horse's momentum carried me past and directly into the midst of the main body of Varciani who had been hiding in the trees to the left in our original direction of travel. Those Batavian troopers still mounted were now furiously engaged, trying to protect four of their own number whose horses had been brought down, and were now standing in a small knot, backs together, slashing wildly with their longer *gladius,* reminding me that fighting on foot was not something for which these men trained. Fortunately for me, facing in

29

essentially the opposite direction as the rest of our men, meant that my weak side was more or less protected, but I still rued the fact that I had not thought to ask for a shield. Such was my overconfidence that we would not be attacked, I had not thought to ask for one, meaning that now the only protection for both me and Latobius was my *gladius*, which I put to use. I had slowed Latobius down so he did not take us galloping past the column, which was now formed into the mounted version of an *orbis*, as those troopers who had been on the right side of the column were also turned outward to face the warriors attacking our right flank. Out of the corner of my vision, I got the sense that the Varciani numbers had been roughly equally divided between the two attacking forces, but I concerned myself with the warriors I could reach, causing me to bring Latobius to a stop, something I could tell he did not like, which he signaled by jerking his head, pulling the reins from my grasp. I barely took notice, since I was absorbed in blocking a powerful, downward blow from a Varciani wielding a *gladius* even longer than the *spatha*. Between being mounted, and my size, it meant that even raising the blade high over his head, when he brought it down, it would have struck me high on my thigh. This made my block lower than I would have liked, but when his blade landed and drove my own, perpendicular to his, down to my waist level, I anticipated that he would reverse the direction, swinging his *gladius* upward in an attempt to take advantage of the way my body seemed to lean in his direction by the force of his first attack. At least, this was what he thought had happened, but he had underestimated my strength; if I had wished it, my arm would not have budged, nor my body, except this was the impression I wanted to give him. Rather than being off-balance, I had shifted my weight so that, while I was leaning over, I was completely under control, so that when he reversed his blade, trying to slash upwards and catch me in the soft spot under my chin, I simply twisted my wrist outward the instant his blade lost contact with mine. The effect was to sweep his blade aside so that, for an instant it was pointing skyward, as was mine but inside his, and although he had a shield, because of my height advantage, it was a simple matter of bringing the blade down, hard, down onto the top of his helmeted

30

head. Frankly, I was concerned my blade might snap, and the shock was terrific, but the Vinician grip kept the *gladius* securely in my hand, and despite the resistance of metal and bone, I cleaved his skull, down past his eyes. Frankly, wrenching the blade out proved more difficult than the actual kill, but I was aided by Latobius, though I do not believe that was his intention, who suddenly made a small, hopping step forward. This served to jerk the blade free, but Latobius had acted in response to a new threat, one that had appeared on our right rear quarter, which he had seen thanks to the wider field of vision horses possess. I was fumbling for the reins, then was forced to grab instead for the saddle as, suddenly, he dropped his head, shifting his weight once again, this time to transfer to his front legs before launching a powerful kick with his right rear hoof. Lurching forward so that I was looking down the length of my horse's neck directly at the ground, I felt the shudder of his body as he connected with something, the shrill scream telling me that it had been a Varciani, so I risked a glance over my shoulder just in time to see a man staggering backward, his face over his hands, which were covered in blood. I had just gotten grip of the reins when, still behind me but from the opposite side, I recognized the voice of Gaesorix, shouting in alarm.

Signaling the trooper nearest me, whose *spatha* was dripping in blood halfway up its length, but was also bleeding from a leg wound to the thigh, I shouted, "Keep them off me! I'm going to help Gaesorix!"

Without waiting for an acknowledgment, now back in control of Latobius, I spun him about, kicked him again, then just as he leapt into movement the thought struck me, did that Batavian understand a word I said? Nevertheless, I did not turn around to see if he was defending my rear, mainly because I saw that, at last, Gaesorix's mount had finally foundered, and was down on its knees, while Gaesorix was standing next to it, using its body as a makeshift breastwork to protect his back. In front of him were four Varciani, arranged in a rough semicircle, and I turned Latobius, not to head directly for them, but in the general direction of the woods lining the track to my left. I did not attempt to do so with any kind of stealth; I wanted them to see that I

31

was doing so, knowing they would understand that my intention was to get behind them and attack from that direction. The Varciani nearest me, carrying a spear and shield, saw me and shouted something, prompting the warrior on the farther end to snap what I felt certain was an order, because the warrior next to the man nearest me joined the first one to also turn in my direction. I was already moving at this point, but instead of stopping, I forced Latobius into the trees, moving deeper into the cover of the forest, prompting cries of alarm as I plunged through the thick underbrush, something that Latobius clearly did not care for, though he did not hesitate.

Glancing over my shoulder, once I got to a point where I could only hear the fighting but no longer see it, I turned Latobius parallel to the track, then advanced back south, in the direction we had originally been traveling. Even as I did so, I offered a prayer to the gods that my tactic did not end in disaster for Gaesorix; I could only hope he was skillful enough to fend the warriors off long enough for this to work. My hope was that the two Varciani who had been assigned to handle me had at least pursued a few paces deeply into the woods, yet even so, every heartbeat was precious and could not be wasted. Once I reached a spot I thought was far enough, I turned Latobius and moved at a brisk trot, back in the direction of the track. Then, when I saw the faint lightening that signaled the edge of the narrow clearing through which the track traversed, without hesitation, I took my *gladius* and applied the flat of it to Latobius' rear with a resounding smack. Since he cannot talk, there is no way to tell, but I suspect it was a combination of the sound and the fact that this was the first time I had done anything like this to him, as much as the sting of it; whatever the cause was, he shot forward like he had been launched from a scorpion, while I used my left hand to cling not to his reins, but to the saddle. I planned to use my legs to guide him, although this was nigh impossible simply because he was going so fast, by the time we burst from the trees, everything around me was a blur. Thankfully, I had judged correctly, so that when I spotted the four Varciani, the warrior who had been on the far side of their small line was now to our right, while Latobius was heading at a perfect angle for what I had in mind. I caught the barest glimpse of a bearded face, turned upward and towards me, the warrior's mouth opened in what looked like an "O" of surprise, just before Latobius' chest slammed into his shield. As I had hoped, the impact from the thousands of pounds of force created by my horse swept him off his feet, so violently and so fast that for an instant as he flew backward, his legs were splayed in front of him in a perfect mimicry of a man sitting on the ground with his legs straight out. More importantly, his backward momentum propelled him directly into the warrior to his left, but while the second Varciani was not struck with as much force, there was still enough impetus there to knock him off his feet like the first man. Both of them were actually still falling when Latobius, without breaking stride, leapt over them in much the same way we liked to jump hedges and low walls. Unlike those stationary objects, however, his rear hooves did not quite clear one of the Varciani; I did not know which one it was, but I felt the thudding vibration, followed by a choked scream, then my horse's front hooves were touching the ground as I prepared for the impact. Because of his collision, my mount did not land cleanly; indeed, for a brief, heartsick instant, I thought we would both go tumbling headfirst, and I was acutely aware that while I would hit the ground ahead of Latobius, it was a virtual certainty that he would then roll on top of me. Somehow, through no action of my own, he stumbled yet did not fall, but I had no time to marvel at this minor miracle, because our momentum had carried us within spear reach of the two Varciani who had originally been the nearest to me.

I was just turning my head, now certain I would remain astride Latobius and he would stay on all fours, when there was a blur of motion that came slashing across my front, in between my torso and Latobius' neck. Nevertheless, while the point of the spear missed because the Varciani had misjudged our speed, our momentum was such that the shaft slammed into the pit of my stomach, knocking the wind out of me. Making matters worse, somehow, the warrior who had made the thrust managed to maintain his grip on the spear long enough that as Latobius rushed past him, the shaft of the spear across my midsection served to pull me from the saddle. I would like to think that the grip of my left hand on the saddle had been loosened by the jarring impact, but it does not really matter; whatever the cause, I felt it jerked from my grasp, then for an instant, I suppose I experienced the same sensation that the two Varciani we had knocked aside felt, suspended in air, weightless and powerless as I descended to the earth. Which, not surprisingly, I slammed into with a considerable amount of force, on my backside, although my forward momentum of an eyeblink before meant I went skidding along the rocky ground of the track, tearing and gouging chunks of flesh from the back of my legs. Apparently, at the last instant, the Varciani had been forced to let go of his spear or be jerked off his feet as well, while I was scrambling to my feet before I stopped sliding, knowing that now I was back on the ground, the man who loses his feet in a fight usually loses his life. Luckily, the Varciani's only weapon had been the spear, which was now rolling on the ground, but he still had his shield; I still held the *spatha*, except I immediately tossed it aside to draw my normal weapon, feeling it would be more useful for this type of fight.

Gaesorix had been wounded, blood covering his left arm, and he had not had the time to unlash his shield, which was still strapped to his horse, lying immediately behind him at his feet and now on its side, its legs still moving feebly as blood poured from a second wound, made apparent by the sight of a spear shaft embedded in its massive chest. The Batavian was moving well, despite his wound, taking a step forward to make a single, brutal thrust into the body of the Varciani who had been struck by the comrade Latobius had hit and who was already lying motionless in the middle of the track. This was all the attention I paid to the Decurion, and I only spared a glance to locate Latobius who, suddenly relieved of his rider, had immediately slowed to a trot but was even then circling back around towards me. This took perhaps the span of a heartbeat, yet it was long enough for my attention to wander from the Varciani who had managed to unhorse me, allowing him to scramble to the body of his comrade and snatch up the *gladius*. He narrowly evaded a lunge by Gaesorix, but then the Decurion's own attention was diverted by the last of the Varciani still on their feet, besides my new adversary. It was acutely uncomfortable being forced to choose between the fighting that was still going on with the main body of the *turma*, which I could clearly hear, but I saw the movement of several men who were still mounted out of the corner of my eye, as the Batavians fought off our ambushers.

Consequently, I faced this Varciani, instantly discerning that the *gladius* was not his preferred weapon, which he held in an awkward fashion, clearly uncomfortable with it. Determined to take advantage of this, I shuffled forward, holding my blade in the modified first position used by Optios and Centurions who fight without the benefit of a shield, at least in the early stages of a battle. This Varciani was younger than I was, perhaps in his mid-twenties, and he had plaited his beard, I suppose in order to look older, though it did not work to my eyes. Holding his shield out farther in front of him than we do, it also told me that, like most barbarians, he viewed it as a strictly defensive weapon and not as a potent extension of his hand. Therefore, it was at his shield that I aimed my first thrust, catching him by surprise since he understandably assumed I would try to attack from an angle that got around it. That's coming soon enough, I thought grimly, but first I have to soften you up, which was what I proceeded to attempt. Very quickly, I launched a series of thrusts, each of them from a different position, but all of them seemingly with the same target, and I suspect he was beginning to think I planned on besting him by whittling his shield down piece by piece. Finally, he seemed to gain some confidence as this large but obviously clumsy Roman struck his shield at least a half-dozen times in rapid succession. He saw what he thought was his opening, when my third position thrust went even wider than normal, making it easy for him to swing his shield outward from his body to knock my blade even farther to his left. For an eyeblink of time, I understood that what he saw was my body, unprotected by my blade, so I cannot fault his decision to make his own lunge, punching his *gladius* forward and aiming the point just below my breastbone. But, as I had observed, he launched his attack as if he was using a spear, meaning that his hand was holding his *gladius* palm down, with the point angled slightly downward, and more importantly, taking a larger step forward with his lunge than needed for a *gladius*. My own blade, after being knocked aside by his shield, was held almost straight out from my body at my shoulder level, and I kept it in this position, but as he was stepping forward, I was moving as well, in roughly the opposite direction. However, I angled to my left slightly in order to move my torso out of range of his weapon, and I suppose it might have appeared as if we were passing by each other, each in the opposite direction, except that my *gladius* arm was extended out across his path. Between his own momentum, as he made what he thought was a killing lunge, and my own, the edge of the blade, carried by the first Titus Pullus, my father, and now me, was as sharp as always, slicing into the Varciani's throat, showering my arm and right side in a spray of blood. The shout that had been leaving his lips, certainly a cry of victory as he celebrated his kill that would never come, abruptly ended in a gurgling noise as his windpipe was severed and blood filled his mouth. My arm was wrenched backward by the force of his body moving forward, with sufficient force that it spun me about a half-turn so that my back was now to the woods and I was facing the track. Instantly, my eye took in the scene, my mind quickly evaluating what it meant, so that I did not really stop moving, instead simply changing my direction.

Gaesorix was still fighting, but this Varciani, armed with a spear and shield, had been able to force him back so that he was now essentially pinned against the corpse of his horse, which mercifully had stopped thrashing. The lack of shield on the part of the Decurion was causing him to mount a defense that consisted of little more than frantic dodges and the occasional swipe of this *spatha*. Crossing the distance in no more than four strides, the Varciani did not see me until it was too late, warned only by the flickering of Gaesorix's gaze towards me, so the warrior had only partially turned when I thrust the point of my blade under his right arm, driving it deeply into his body before twisting it, then kicking the dying man off my *gladius*.

"You need to learn to fight without a shield," I told Gaesorix, but while I said this with a grin, he did not seem disposed to appreciate the advice.

In fact, he ignored me altogether, turning his attention to his *turma*, though I could have told him that the ambush had failed. Certainly, there was fighting going on, but the Batavians, more or less on their own initiative since Gaesorix had been isolated, had organized themselves. Frankly, it was not the Batavians I worried about, but Latobius, because as I watched in alarm, two Varciani seemed to come to the identical determination that the ambush had failed and were now looking for a means of escape. From where I stood, it seemed obvious that they had laid eyes on my horse at the roughly same time as well, because they both headed for him.

"Latobius!" I shouted, which brought his head up from where, as horses tend to do, he had begun grazing along the edge of the track, seemingly oblivious to the fighting raging just paces away. I tried to use the whistle I had developed that I first used with Ocelus and had trained Latobius to obey, but my mouth was too dry. Instead, I shouted, "Come! Latobius! To me!"

Before he could respond one way or another, one of the Varciani came into his range of vision, and my heart sank as I thought, That bastard is going to steal my horse! I need not have worried; despite never having trained him for war, perhaps it was the fact that this Varciani smelled the same as those he knew were my enemies, my horse suddenly reared, issuing what I could hear was the equivalent of an angry bellow. Understandably, this caused the Varciani to freeze, except now the second man, probably seeing this as his opportunity, tried to dart past my horse's hindquarters, in preparation for leaping into the saddle. With a speed that clearly caught the second Varciani by surprise, Latobius suddenly spun about, but on his front legs, which had just hit the ground, using his massive rear end as a weapon of sorts, swinging it about so his flank smacked into the Varciani with a meaty thudding sound that we both could hear more than a dozen paces away. The second Varciani was sent sprawling, though he rolled to his feet quickly, then without a second attempt, decided fleeing on foot was better than not at all. Meanwhile, just as his counterpart had done, the first Varciani saw his chance and seized it by dashing the last couple of paces, then vaulting up and throwing himself into the saddle. I do not believe his rear end had fully touched the saddle when, with what appeared to me to be with a contemptuous ease, Latobius once more kicked his hindquarters up into the air, launching the Varciani from his back. The warrior, arms flailing, landed heavily but otherwise unharmed, though that did not last long, because the spot where he hit the ground was barely four or five paces away from Gaesorix. Dashing over, the Decurion plunged his *spatha* into the open mouth of the Varciani, who had just pulled himself to his knees, his arms out in a gesture of surrender. Gaesorix was clearly not in the right frame of mind to accept his capitulation, but the warrior would have fared no better with me; he had tried to steal my horse who, now that all the tumult in which he was involved had died down, came trotting over to me, shoving his soft nose into my tunic, as if he expected to be rewarded.

Patting him on the neck, I assured him, "Don't worry, boy. You earned a reward."

Then I swung up on his back, mainly so I could have a better view of what was happening, and I was pleased to see that the only sight I had of Varciani were their heels, as we like to say, as they fled into the surrounding woods. Gaesorix, still afoot, began moving towards his men, bawling out orders to finish off the Varciani wounded and check on our own; at least that was what I assumed, given the manner in which his troopers began behaving. Meanwhile, I dismounted to retrieve the *spatha*, wiping the blood from it using the tunic of one of the dead Varciani, then placed it back in its sheath, then with even more care, cleaned my Gallic blade. As I was doing so, I recall this was the first moment I noticed the length of my shadow, causing me to glance over my shoulder to find the sun. My heart sank when I saw that it was less than two fingers' width above the trees; there was no chance of reaching the safety of open ground before dark at this point. Muttering a curse, I swung back up into the saddle, then went to where Gaesorix was standing, conferring with one of his troopers, while another was kneeling next the prone bodies of three more Batavians. The Decurion obviously heard our approach, but when he turned, his face was a cold mask, and I did not have to know him well to see the barely suppressed fury that radiated from the man.

"Well, Centurion," he said coldly, then indicated the carnage with a gesture, "I hope that this was worth getting you to Siscia a half day earlier."

Now, I was acutely aware that I deserved his censure; it was not difficult for me at all to put myself in his *caligae*, feeling the pain that comes when a leader loses men through the fault of someone else. This did not mean I did not feel the flare of anger at both his words and manner, but I swallowed the biting retort I knew would only make matters worse.

"Decurion," I made sure to address him by his rank, "we still have a way to go before we get off this ridge. And," I gestured at the sun, "you can see we don't have much daylight left. We drove them off, but I don't know that they won't come back."

He did not reply verbally, just giving a curt nod, then turned and rattled off a series of orders to his troopers. As he did so, I was struck by a thought.

"Your horse is dead."

He gave me a look of bitter amusement as he replied, "Don't worry, we have spares now."

Gaesorix turned out to be incorrect; between the horses lost and the casualties, many troopers were forced to ride double, including Gaesorix who, despite my better judgment, I offered to let ride with me. Not more than a furlong later I was regretting it, not because of anything the Decurion said, but what he did not say, in the form of the stony silence. Under normal circumstances, when I am with others, I become uncomfortable with long silences; when one can feel the anger as a palpable force, it is even more so, but somehow, I understood that if I were the one to break it, matters would be worse, not better. Regardless, it was quite a trial, but then the sun dipped below the trees, bathing the track in the low twilight, and for the moment, our lack of communication was less important than the need for vigilance. Because I had never traversed this part of the route in the dark, I had

39

to rely on my memory of the map in my head, which was almost impossible, since judging distances at night or under low light conditions is difficult. By the best calculations I could manage, I estimated we were about two miles from the southern fringe of the trees, which actually extended down onto flat ground perhaps a half mile on this side of the ridge. While we were moving faster than if we had been afoot, it was not by much, as troopers were struggling to keep their wounded comrades in the saddle, most of them choosing to have the injured man in front of them on their overburdened mounts. As far as that went, Latobius was holding up well, but I could hear that his breathing was more labored than was normal for the speed and ground we were covering. Even as this thought crossed my mind, Gaesorix finally broke the silence.

"You," he spoke softly, appropriate given his mouth was near my ear, although I suspect it had more to do with the fear of being overheard, "have a good horse. He's very strong."

"Thank you," I replied, and while I was doing this to be politic, at the same time, I felt a surge of pride. "Yes, he's a good horse. Although," I was suddenly compelled to amend my statement, surprised by the sudden lump in my throat, "he's not like Ocelus."

"Ocelus?" Gaesorix asked quizzically. "Where have I heard that name before?" I explained to him who Ocelus was, or began to do so, but he stopped me by exclaiming, "Oh! Yes! I've heard of this horse! He was gray, yes? And very large?"

"Yes, on both counts," I answered.

"I heard he killed fifty men, all on his own!"

Despite this sudden reminder of loss, I had to laugh, saying, "Well, I wouldn't put it that high. But, yes, he killed a few men in his own right."

"And you rode him?" Gaesorix asked, and there was a note of envy in his voice that, frankly, I had heard before, from other horsemen.

"I more than rode him," I replied, and I did not try to disguise the pride I felt. "My Av...my grandfather left him to me in his will."

There was a silence again, except this was different, then Gaesorix broke it, saying quietly, "That's quite an honor, Centurion. But it does explain why you're a better horseman than I thought you'd be."

Coming from the Batavian, this was high praise, and given all that had transpired, I did not take it lightly.

I was about to offer a response when, from behind us, there was a cry of alarm that was quickly drowned out by the sound of a horse in pain, something that I had heard all too much of in the previous watch. Wheeling Latobius about, while he reacted instantly, his actual movement was sluggish because of the extra weight, but it was not my eyes that identified what was going on; in the midst of the shouts, I heard the soft whishing of a missile, an arrow by the sound of it.

"We have to get out of these woods!" Gaesorix's voice was in my ear, although he managed to refrain from shouting.

I needed no extra incentive; yanking Latobius' head about, I offered a silent apology, even as I kicked him, hard, in the ribs. This time, while he tried to do as he had done before, the extra weight meant he ponderously gained speed, but he gamely went to as much of a gallop as he could manage. Gaesorix was large compared to most Romans, although he was several inches shorter than I was, and Latobius was large in his own right, just a shade shorter than Ocelus and not quite as broad across the chest. Carrying me was a burden in itself, although he handled it well, but with an extra passenger, I could feel him laboring underneath me. However, because it was dark, it was next to impossible to tell how fast we were actually moving; what I did know was that it was highly possible, even likely, that my horse would stumble in the dark, although their vision at night is much better than ours. Behind us, I heard shouts, most of them sounding like one trooper urging on another, but interspersed were cries of pain, both animal and human. Even worse were at least two separate calls for aid, as one of Gaesorix's troopers was presumably unhorsed, then began calling for one of his comrades to come to his rescue. It was a horrifyingly helpless feeling, and they were not my men; I could only imagine the torment Gaesorix was feeling at hearing those under his command in such peril.

More times than I can easily count, I heard, even over the roaring of the wind in my ears, the different sound of a missile slashing through the air, and once I sensed something streak across our front, less than a hand's width in front of Latobius' outstretched nose. Then, without any real warning, we burst out of the trees, into the open area at the southern foot of the ridge, and while it was obviously still dark, the illumination provided by the half moon, which had just appeared in the sky, made it seem much brighter. Despite reaching the safety of the open ground, I urged Latobius to keep moving, though I allowed him to slow to a canter. I felt Gaesorix twisting behind me, checking to see how many men were still following us, then once we were out of range for even the strongest bow, only then did I pull up. Immediately, I slid off Latobius' back, worried by the sound of his breathing, which reminded me of the leather bellows blacksmiths use to fan the flames, and the gleam of the moonlight highlighted the sheen of sweat that covered him. Gaesorix followed suit, but he began striding back in the direction of the woods, watching silently as his men came streaming, single file, out of the woods, their own mounts in similar condition. While I had not taken an accurate count, it was easy to see that not only were their even fewer of them, those men who had been riding double were reduced as well.

Gaesorix swore bitterly, and his voice was thick with despair, but while he was facing away from me, I felt certain his words were meant for me as he said, "I've lost half of my command, maybe more."

We made a rough camp that night, even by cavalry standards, without a fire, the unwounded men first doing what they could for their less fortunate comrades under the circumstances. At first, it appeared that Gaesorix had been incorrect in his estimate; less than half of his men were present, fourteen in total, and of those, six were wounded. The only positive note was that, for the next watch, men came trickling in, along with several unridden cavalry mounts, and, at least for me, the pleasant surprise of three of the pack animals, one of which was mine, carrying my baggage, including my armor. This was small consolation to the Decurion, I knew, and in recognition of that, I gave him a wide berth, choosing to take Latobius a short distance away from the others. Using my *sagum,* which had been lashed to my saddle, I rubbed him down, then strapped the bag with his oats to his nose. Only then did I do anything for myself, although that consisted of little more than reaching into my saddlebag, grabbing a hunk of bread, then throwing myself down onto the ground. Meanwhile, Gaesorix and the trooper who acted as his Optio, whose name I could not recall, were doing what they could to make their men comfortable, moving among them, squatting next to one of the wounded, talking to them in low tones. Sitting there, wrapped in my *sagum*, I was acutely aware that this ultimately did rest on my shoulders; my impatience to get to Siscia had caused the pain and loss that would forever mark these men's lives, and their memory of the first Titus Pullus was now tainted by the actions of the man who might have borne his name, but that was all. My spirits, putting it mildly, were at a low ebb, and they were about to get even lower.

I was barely paying attention, so Gaesorix was just a couple paces away from me when I noticed his approach, and despite my conscious mind chiding me for feeling this way, I nevertheless tensed, waiting for some sort of confrontation. Instead of attacking me, however, the Batavian dropped onto his haunches next to me, though he did not say anything immediately, choosing to stare at his men instead of at me.

Finally, he spoke in a low, flat tone, telling me, "As soon as it's light, we're going back up there."

It took a moment for his words to sink in; when they did, I turned to stare at him incredulously.

"What?" I gasped. "For what purpose?"

"Because," he replied calmly, but he looked directly at me, or so it seemed; it was difficult to see his eyes under the brim of his helmet, "two of my men were captured alive."

Just an instant before, I had felt certain that this situation was as bad as it was possible for it to be, but his statement blew that certainty away like a leaf in a gale, and my stomach clenched in a spasm so hard I thought I would expel my freshly eaten bread. Although it was true that Gaesorix was not normally stationed in Pannonia, I found it impossible to believe he had not heard the tales of what happened to unfortunate men who were either under the standard or associated with Rome as an auxiliary and were captured. They may have been taken alive; the thought that they would live to see another sunrise was close to impossible for anyone with any experience with the province to believe, and I opened my mouth to disabuse Gaesorix of this folly.

But what came out instead was, "I'm going as well. And," I added, "we're not going mounted. And," I swallowed the lump that I suspect was my meal threatening to come back up, "we can't wait until daylight."

I do not know who was more surprised, but Gaesorix opened his mouth, and I felt certain it was going to be a protest against my statement about being afoot, except instead, he simply said, "If we're going to be acting as infantry, then you should be in command, Centurion."

Honestly, I had no idea how to respond, so all I managed was a mumbled, "Well, all right then." I thought for a moment, looking at the moon, then I told Gaesorix, "We should start immediately."

"How many men should we take?" he asked, and I considered for a moment.

"It shouldn't be more than a half-dozen," I decided.

"That's not very many." The Decurion's tone was doubtful, but while I understood his hesitation, I was also certain about this.

"More than that means we're going to be making more noise," I countered, "and we have to move fast. In fact," I thought for a moment, "we're going to ride partway, then leave the horses with a man to guard them. So we'll take seven."

He did not reply for a moment, and I braced for more argument, then he gave an abrupt nod.

"I'll go get the men ready." He rose and started walking back to what remained of his *turma*.

"Gaesorix." I called to him. When he turned to face me, I said, "I know I don't have to tell you, but you need to prepare the men for what we're likely to find. If they are Varciani, they're some mean bastards, and they hate Rome and anyone connected with us."

"I know," he replied grimly. "That's why we're going."

Turning about, he resumed making his way to his men, and I was about to call out to him again, then thought better of it; I was going to advise him to pick men whose ability at stealthy movement was the best, but I realized he would undoubtedly do so without my urging. Climbing to my feet, I walked over to my packhorse, retrieving my armor, though I left my helmet behind. After putting on the armor, I then took a spare tunic and dropped it over my armor; it was snug, but it muted the faint gleam of the metal links, then I strapped my *baltea* on over it. Offering an apology to Latobius, I dropped his saddle back on, and he clearly did not care for this, blowing up his stomach in the manner horses do when they do not want to have a saddle cinched onto them. I had to knee him twice before he gave up, but when I moved to pick up his bridle, my back was turned to him, and he reached out with his long neck, nipping me firmly but not excessively hard, on the back of my lower leg, just below the edge of my armor. While it would not have hurt that much normally, it not only startled me, he bit right on the spot where a part of my flesh had been gouged out when I slid along the track, and I gave an undignified yelp, spinning about to glare at my horse, who did not appear repentant at all.

"All right," I grumbled, "I understand." Walking back to my baggage, I extracted one of the three apples I had left and gave it to him as a peace offering.

It worked, since he munched contentedly as I finished getting him ready, then once he was finished, I slipped his bridle on and vaulted into the saddle. Gaesorix and his men had been doing more or less the same thing, and they were already mounted, so without further delay, I went trotting past them, back in the direction of the woods. Some of the men left behind called out to their friends, wishing them luck and their hope that we would be in time, I felt certain, but I could also feel their cold stare at me as I passed, reinforcing exactly who they blamed for this in the first place.

We moved quickly, then stopped once we were barely two hundred paces inside the forest, before the slope actually started. I had debated with myself for a moment about using our mounts to ascend the ridge a bit, then discarded it, deciding for selfish reasons that I did not want to risk Latobius to being captured any more than I was doing already. We left a trooper behind; he had been wounded, but in the left upper arm, which I forced him to demonstrate would not hinder him in any way, despite Gaesorix's angry insistence that he would not have selected a man who was impaired.

"From here on," I whispered harshly, "I'm in command. You do what I say, when I say. Do you understand me?"

Even without the light filtering through the trees, I saw the Decurion's body stiffen, but he whispered his answer readily enough, assuring me that he understood. Then, when I said nothing more, he correctly interpreted my silent command, turning and relaying the same instructions. Once he was done, I said nothing more, turning to begin moving up the track, deeper into the trees; I was acutely aware that time was against us. Indeed, I honestly did not hold out much hope that we would be in time, and that was even if we did find the two men in the first place, which was not a given. However, I had a hunch I knew where they were headed, in a general sense at least, although I was leading Gaesorix and his men directly to what I considered the most likely spot.

As I had learned when I was a boy, this ridge was riddled with caves, and there was one in particular where, during one of the many minor rebellions, three Legionaries had been taken and tortured to death, this event occurring during my time with the 8th. That time, we had been too late, but what I recalled of this particular cave was that it had been clearly used quite a bit by the Varciani, with what I supposed was a rudimentary altar set up, adorned with human skulls, presumably of slain enemies. The roof was high enough, and it was well ventilated for a fire, which I also knew was likely to be an integral part of what Gaesorix's men would be facing if we did not reach them in time. I shared none of this with Gaesorix, not so much from a desire to shield him from the fate awaiting his men, but because I felt certain he had heard enough tales and that, if even half of them were true, he would do everything within his power to keep it from happening.

46

In the dark, it was extraordinarily difficult to tell much of anything; however, because the rock composing the ridge is limestone, wherever it was exposed, it gave off a pale glow from the reflected moonlight that, while barely discernible, served to let me know where we were. Most importantly, it signaled the point where we turned off the track and began ascending the slope, straight up the western side of the ridge. Under normal circumstances, I would have made my way back and forth across the face of the slope, lessening the grade and thereby saving energy and effort. Not this time, and it did not take long before my lungs were on fire, while my legs were likewise burning with fatigue. It would have been difficult even if I had just risen from my bed at the start of the day; after what had transpired already, I was more tired than I had been in some time, and I wondered how Gaesorix and his men were faring. Riding on horseback is not the slack kind of living one might think, particularly as a cavalryman, but it is not the same as carrying a *furca* with forty pounds of equipment. Nevertheless, when I signaled a stop, Gaesorix, despite panting heavily, shook his head, instead pointing uphill.

"Don't wait on us," he managed, "we'll keep up."

So, I did as he said, despite needing the moment to catch my breath, but I knew these Batavians were fueled by the fear of what might be happening even at that moment. Which, as we were to learn shortly, was every bit as bad as our imaginings.

Groping one's way up a thickly wooded slope, especially one as steep as the ridge got as we neared the top, is quite a nerve-wracking affair, and I was beginning to despair that I could find the spot I had been thinking about. And, I thought miserably, it's possible they aren't even there. But, while I knew this was a strong possibility, there was some small voice inside me that insisted I was on the right path. This feeling was based in my intimate knowledge of how the Pannonian tribes think, and at the heart of this knowledge was understanding what a prize two Romans would be to them. That they were Batavian, and not actually Roman citizens, would be a distinction that made absolutely no difference to their captors, meaning that they would be

47

excited almost beyond reason to have the chance to exact vengeance on men who they thought of as their oppressors, making them eager not to delay in carrying out what they had in mind. This would be true under normal conditions; with the province in rebellion as it was, they would view their three captives as a gift from the gods, providing the perfect way to send a message to us that they were unconquered. It was small comfort, but as far back as I could remember, Romans who were captured were eventually always returned, albeit usually in pieces or, even worse, essentially intact but missing their skin. And, one more thing I did not believe Gaesorix needed to know, the Varciani in particular favored flaying their prisoners. If the stories were to be believed, they were experts in keeping their captives alive for as long as I suppose is possible to do, and that more than anything kept my legs churning, leading the Batavians up the slope. I was searching for another outcropping of limestone, except this one was much larger, practically a cliff that, as I remembered, was at least thirty feet high, and extended a distance of perhaps a hundred fifty paces along a north/south axis, putting it athwart our line of travel. If I had chosen the first landmark correctly, and if I had managed to keep our heading directly west, up the slope, by rights we should have run into the base of the cliff. Yet, as I continued climbing, I did not recall ascending this high, and I was beginning to think that I had veered off so that the cliff was somewhere to our side, but the question was, in which direction? Despite the urgency, I finally was forced to stop, trying to peer up the slope, first to the left, then to the right, and it did not take long for Gaesorix to reach my side, though it took him a moment to catch enough of his breath to speak.

"Well?" he demanded. "Why are we stopping?"

"I'm making sure we're still headed in the right direction."

"You mean we're lost?" His tone was a mixture of incredulity and anger. "I thought you knew where they were going!"

"I do," I snapped, but then I forced myself to be honest, amending my words with, "or at least, I think I do."

"That's not going to…" he began, but then I blindly reached out and grabbed his arm, squeezing it hard.

"*Tacete*!" I whispered harshly, though it was not because I did not want to listen to his recriminations. "I heard something!"

I felt him stiffen, but he remained quiet, and I opened my mouth, turning my ear in the direction from where I thought the noise had come. Several heartbeats passed, then just when I began to relax, the noise was repeated, and this time, there was no mistaking what it was; a man screaming in agony is a hard sound to forget. While I knew it was not meant as such, the tortured man's cries served as a beacon of sorts, because when he screamed again, it told me we had been heading in the right direction all along.

"Let's go." I resumed climbing, and somewhat to my chagrin, not more than a dozen paces farther up the slope, I pushed through a thick stand of underbrush in between some trees, and there before me was the cliff, picking up the moonlight in a ghostly manner that I tried not to think about. Once more, I stopped, except this time, it was to give instructions to Gaesorix and his men.

Crouching down, I pointed to the right side of the cliff, telling the Decurion, "You can get to the cave that way. And," I twisted and pointed to the opposite side, to the left, "that way as well. Going left takes longer, but the way the cave opening is shaped, it's slightly downhill, and the cave actually doesn't extend straight back, but at an angle. You can probably get at least a half-dozen steps into the cave before they'll know it, provided you don't make any noise."

He considered briefly, then gestured to the right side. "What about that?"

"It's shorter," I admitted, "but it's almost the opposite. You'll have to climb up the last twenty feet, and it's too steep to climb with a *gladius* in your hand."

I felt certain which one he would choose, then he instantly proved me wrong, saying, "We'll take both ways. You take the left, with," he turned and indicated three Batavians, "these men, and I'll go to the right."

"But how are we going to coordinate our attack?" I asked, dismayed. "And," I thought to add, "do they understand me at all?"

"Yes, Centurion," one of them answered, in heavily accented but understandable Latin.

"As far as coordinating our attack," Gaesorix was already beginning to move, "don't worry, you'll know."

Biting back a curse, I started moving as well, drawing my blade, wondering what he meant. We had not gone more than another couple of steps when there was another scream; we all broke into a run.

Unfortunately, I never had the chance to catch my breath, even partially, once we scaled the slope to the top of the cliff. There was a natural depression that dipped down from the bare rock at the top, leading directly to the cave opening, and I could see the reflection of the fire within the cavern, its light dancing on the wall opposite from where I was. What caught my eye, however, was a quick blur of motion from the opposite side of the entrance, then chaos broke loose inside the cave as Gaesorix came charging into sight. The movement came from a Varciani who had spotted the Decurion and his men as they scrambled up the short but steep pitch on the far side of the opening. This was the instant I understood Gaesorix's seemingly elliptical comment that I would know when to commence my own attack, since all eyes were on those Batavians, and even in the span of the heartbeat of time from the first alarm, I saw several Varciani rush into my view from deeper within the cave.

Then I was moving, saying over my shoulder, "Follow me!"

As I had recalled, this entrance was slightly downhill, so I went plunging down, *gladius* in hand, navigating the slight bend that served to obscure the Varciani's sighting of me and the three Batavians who were accompanying me. Because all of their attention was on Gaesorix and his men, who had just managed to climb up and stand erect, drawing their *gladius* in preparation to meet what I counted to be about seven Varciani charging at them, I was able to move deeper into the cave than I would have otherwise. Naturally, the attention of all the barbarians was on Gaesorix, including a man standing next to a figure who was strapped to what at first glance appeared to be similar to the frame we use for punishment, a long, thin knife in his hand. Even in the firelight, I saw the blade was dripping blood, and although there were other warriors closer to me, it was towards this man I headed. I did not run, but I nevertheless moved quickly, and I had advanced perhaps four or five paces before a Varciani deeper in the cave was alerted by my movement. He, along with two other warriors, had been standing to my right, but their backs had been turned as they watched their comrades rushing to engage Gaesorix.

Gesturing with my weapon, I snapped over my shoulder, "Take care of them!"

Even as I did so, I was moving, my own blade up and ready in the first position, heading for the man with the knife, who saw me coming for him. Dropping the smaller weapon, he whirled about, reaching for a *gladius* in its scabbard, leaning against the cave wall. I hoped to reach him before he could withdraw it, but I was an instant too late, and he spun back around, swinging his blade as he did so, aiming a typical sweeping blow designed to part my head from my shoulders. Because of the quality of the light from the fire, it made precise judgments of distance difficult, as I learned when I leaned backward to avoid the barbarian's attack, thinking the tip of his *gladius* would miss by the width of a hand. I learned differently when I felt a quick, burning sensation on my chin as the point grazed it, opening it up to the bone, though I did not find this out until later. In the moment, I just experienced the familiar sensation that made me think someone had dragged a burning ember across my chin as the warm blood instantly began flowing. Roaring my anger, mostly at myself, before the barbarian could recover his *gladius*, which was now angled across his body, I leapt forward with the intent of getting inside the arc of his blade, while limiting his own attack to a backhand kind of slash. However, this was an experienced warrior, which he proved by lashing out with his fist, aiming for the newly opened cut on my chin. Because I was moving forward at the same time, it maximized the force of the blow, causing stars of innumerable colors to burst in my vision as my head snapped back, and I felt myself take a staggering step backward. Somehow, I retained enough presence of mind to defend myself in the only manner available to me, by finishing the thrust I had begun, sweeping my blade up from its first position.

The Varciani parried by simply swinging his own *gladius* downward, with enough force that I felt the jarring blow when our weapons clashed, his heavier blade knocking my own downward from where I had aimed it, directly at his groin. Although I did not strike my intended target, I still felt the blade jerk in my hand as the point bit into the meat of his thigh, making it his turn to let out a bellow of pain. More importantly, it caused him to stagger backward as I had done an instant before, except that unlike with me, there was nowhere for him to go, his back coming up hard against the wall of the cave. This clearly gave him the power that comes from desperation, as he seemed to use it as a surface from which to rebound, using his left hand to push himself off to give him extra power to launch himself at me. The other thing his backward movement allowed was him to bring his *gladius* back to its normal position, but while it was better than where it had been, in such close quarters, his longer blade was practically useless. Nevertheless, he lashed out with it in an awkward attempt at the kind of thrust we Romans practice relentlessly, which I knocked aside with an ease that I saw was not lost on my foe, his mouth, framed by a drooping mustache, twisting into a bitter grimace. Before I struck with my blade, however, I balled up my left fist and, stepping into the blow, punched him in the nose, feeling the cartilage give way with a crunching sound I found quite satisfying.

"That's for my chin, you *cunnus*," I snarled, but my *gladius* was already moving, and the point punched through his mail as if was not there. Although his lower face was already a mask of blood, I kept my gaze pinned on his eyes, watching them widen from the pain and shock of impending death, and I said more quietly, "And that's for trying to skin a Roman alive."

Even before he had fallen at my feet, I was turning, my blade up and ready, chastising myself for not maintaining awareness of what was going on around me; fortunately, the battle was all but over. Just as I spun about, I saw Gaesorix use his *spatha* to gut a Varciani with an ax, nimbly stepping outside the arc of the warrior's swing. His men were already either looting the bodies of the barbarians, or hurrying to free their comrade who was bound hand and foot, lying on his side. Not lost on me was the fact that his captors had positioned him so that he could see what awaited him, and it was this reminder that prompted me to turn and hurry to where the first Batavian was bound to the frame. Because of my angle of approach, I saw him from the front, although his head was hanging and obscuring his face, while his arms were outstretched and tied to a horizontal pole, which in turn was lashed to a pair of triangular supports. I noticed the blood pooled on the dirty stone floor of the cave at his feet, but it was not until I stepped around and saw his back that I fully understood why there was so much of it. Bile came rushing up in my throat at the sight before me, and I could not seem to force myself to go to him, despite his soft moans of pain. Instead, I turned to Gaesorix, calling to him. Something must have shown in my expression, or perhaps it was the sight of my own bloody face, because he came running, his eyes alternating between the sight of his trooper and me, clearly searching for some clue, but all I could do was shake my head, ignoring the droplets of blood that spattered on the floor from my movement. Reaching me, I saw him swallow hard, but despite obviously preparing himself, when Gaesorix turned to examine his trooper, he let out a gasp, his face going as pale as I suspect mine had been a moment before. Running down the middle of the trooper's spine was a relatively thin red line that was still trickling blood, but the major source of the ichor still pooling on the floor came from the spot at the base of the man's neck, where his tormentor had begun the process of peeling his skin away. Hanging like a flap, his flesh had been pulled away so that the muscles of his left upper back were exposed, gleaming obscenely from the blood oozing from the spot where the skin had been separated.

"By the gods," Gaesorix whispered, but his quiet tone did not disguise the horror in his voice. "These...*animals.*" The Decurion turned to me, and I still can recall his haunted expression that, while it showed anguish, also contained what I took to be recognition of why I had been so intent on reaching Siscia. "I wish," he finished bitterly, "we hadn't killed them all now."

Using the poles from the frame, Gaesorix's men fashioned a litter, while one of the troopers who had experience with wounds did what he could for his suffering comrade, which consisted of using torn strips from the tunics of the slain barbarians to bind his skin back into a semblance of its original position on his back. As they did so, I used a strip of cloth, cut from the clothes of the Varciani I had slain, trying to bind my own wound, but despite being unsuccessful, the blood finally clotted enough that I felt I could risk not walking about with my mouth essentially tied shut. We had no medicines to help dull the flayed trooper's pain, but I was greatly impressed by the quiet manner in which the man bore his horrible wounds, even managing to joke with his friends, although I suspect their laughter was heartier than his jests merited. As they did what they could, I examined the bodies; there had been twenty Varciani, a number I found troubling, knowing that there had been far more participating in the original ambush, and probably in the second one, although it had been impossible to tell since it had been strictly a missile attack. My surmise was that these men had been left behind to harry us, although I could not discount the possibility that those missing Varciani had gone to summon more help.

"Is he ready to move?" I asked Gaesorix, who nodded, and I told him, "Good, because we have to leave here, now. I think these bastards were left behind while the others went to get reinforcements."

"That," he answered grimly, "is what I was thinking." Taking a breath, he muttered, "Very well."

Barking out orders, four of the troopers picked up the litter, while the wounded man issued a quiet groan at the sudden movement. None of us were happy at the idea of causing him more pain, but when Gaesorix leaned over to offer an apology, he dismissed his Decurion with a weak wave, which I took to be his assurance that he understood it was necessary. Leading the way out of the cave, I chose a more direct route than we had taken, not needing landmarks to know that, as long as we went downhill, we would run into the track. Despite my intentions, we were forced to take a more serpentine route, simply because the grade was too steep for the men carrying the litter, which we discovered when one of the bearers slipped and dropped his end of it. This understandably wrenched a cry of agony from the wounded man, and a short, sharp argument between his comrades, but through Gaesorix, I took responsibility, assuring them that I would choose a gentler route. We made it down to the track perhaps a third of a watch after leaving the cave; by my estimate, it was now around midnight, then perhaps a sixth part later, I heard the nickering of the horses responding to the scent of our approach. Using two mounts, the Batavians lashed the litter between them, and we were on our way shortly thereafter, arriving back at the camp, still without any fires lit. Only then did I begin to relax, feeling the crushing weight of the tension pressing down on my shoulders, practically forcing me to drop straight to the ground to get some rest. Before I saw to my own needs, once more I unsaddled Latobius, although he did not require a rubbing down this time, then went to talk to Gaesorix.

"We need to be on the move before the sun comes up," I told him. "If those missing Varciani did go get help, they're not going to rest trying to catch up with us."

"Will they be mounted, do you think?"

I considered, and while I did not want to, I felt compelled to be honest. "Some of them will be, undoubtedly. Their nobles all have horses, and chieftains and sub-chieftains all mount their bodyguards as well."

Gaesorix grimaced, but he nodded wearily, acknowledging that he understood. He turned to go, then hesitated, looking at me with an intensity that made me wary as I wondered if there were about to be some more recriminations coming.

"Centurion," he spoke quietly, and I heard the fatigue in his voice, the thought striking me that we at least had this in common, "I apologize for my words earlier. It's not your place to worry about us. We were given orders to escort you to Siscia, and you had every right to insist we go by the most direct route. What happened," he shrugged with what I took to be a fatalistic helplessness, "was ordained by the gods."

While I did not know Gaesorix all that well, and we had certainly clashed, I sensed no falseness in either his words or manner, which actually made me feel worse, not better.

"I'm...sorry, Gaesorix," the words came awkwardly, but the gods know they were heartfelt, "I would never have insisted we come this way if I thought this would happen."

"I know," he replied quietly. "And I also want to thank you for coming with us. You didn't need to do that. They aren't your men, but you still risked yourself to help us. And," the Decurion turned slightly to nod in the direction of his men, who I could tell by the series of barely visible oval shapes that they were looking in our direction, "my boys wanted me to let you know they appreciate what you did as well."

"How is he?" I asked, as much to switch the topic, which was making me feel uncomfortable.

"He's a tough man," Gaesorix answered with justifiable pride. "But," as quickly, his confidence seemed to evaporate, "I've never seen anyone hurt that badly survive."

This, I understood, was the simple truth, but I felt compelled to offer some hope.

"If that didn't kill him already," I said with more assurance than I felt, "it's not likely to."

Gaesorix only nodded, then bidding me a good night, he returned to his men, while I finally settled down, rolling up in my *sagum*.

"I'm going to need you to keep an eye out," I told Latobius, who nickered in a seeming response.

This was my last memory before I fell asleep.

Chapter 2

Despite our fears, we were not attacked by a second force of Varciani, and we departed shortly before dawn, carrying the flayed Batavian on the same litter they had made in the cave. The other wounded troopers were forced to ride double with one of their unharmed comrades, while Gaesorix commandeered a horse for his own so that Latobius only had to carry me. For the first watch, we pushed the pace, since we were still not convinced that we were not being pursued, but once the sun came up and we were well beyond the rough, wooded stretch so that any pursuit from behind us could be seen coming for miles, we slowed down to avoid stressing the horses. It was a bit more than thirty miles to Siscia, which meant that under normal conditions, we would arrive in the afternoon, but we were forced to stop when one of the wounded troopers succumbed to his wounds, although to the surprise of all of us, it was not the flayed man, whose name I learned from Gaesorix was Cassicos. As a consequence, we did not arrive in Siscia until about a third of a watch before sundown, but it was in more than enough time for me to see that, as I had been told, there had been significant changes wrought in the place I had called home for a substantial part of my life. Not only had the town grown even more, which I had expected, it was the construction of a wall that protected the town that was the biggest change, although as we circled past it to get to the camp, I saw that it did not enclose the entire population. One neighborhood in particular had been excluded, and I was unsurprised to see that it was the part of Siscia where the natives of the province were settled, although it did make me wonder how they felt about this sign that Rome still viewed them as more barbarian than Roman. When I was a child, my friends and I had been forbidden to go into this quarter of town, which of course we ignored, and I had played with several children, mostly Breuci and Sisciani, whose fathers were serving in the auxiliaries, or were merchants of some sort. Now, with the province in rebellion, I noticed that this

57

neighborhood appeared deserted, making me wonder whether or not these people had been allowed inside the walls, or if they had gone to join their fellow tribesmen in this revolt. Whatever the case, I thought, I'll find out soon enough.

Traveling the short road to the camp, I saw that it was essentially unchanged, although the two towers appeared to have been reinforced, and the gates were closed, something that only occurred under these conditions. Approaching to within shouting distance, we pulled up, waiting only a couple of heartbeats of time before the duty sentry challenged us. Since it was impossible for us to know the watchword, I had prepared for this moment by donning my full uniform at our last rest stop, and I approached alone now, holding up the scroll with Tiberius' seal on it. While it was impossible for them to see it from that height and distance, it was enough to allow me to dismount and walk up to the gate. The small postern door that was inset in the gate opened, and out strode an Optio who, on seeing me, came to a dead stop, his mouth dropping open. Not that I was doing anything differently, although I do recall the stab of pain from the gash in my chin, caused by my mouth opening more widely than normal.

"Titus?" the Optio gasped.

"Is that any way to greet a Centurion, Optio?" I demanded, but despite the pain, I felt the grin spreading into a real smile of pleasure at the sight of Titus Domitius, my best friend.

Naturally, we were allowed into the camp with no more delay than it took for us to embrace.

After promising to come find Domitius as soon as possible, Gaesorix and I made our way to the *Praetorium*, and I noticed that the pennant announcing the presence of the Legate was not the only one slowly flapping in the gentle breeze.

Noticing where I was looking, Gaesorix asked, "Any idea what that means?"

Although I was not certain, I felt confident enough in my guess to answer, "I think it means the man I'm supposed to…advise is already here."

And spy on, I thought miserably; I did my best to keep the despair at this hidden from the Decurion, but I felt his eyes on me for a beat or two longer than normal, although thankfully, he said nothing more. Then, we were walking up the steps to the stone portico and stopping to present the scroll containing my orders to the two men assigned to the provosts who also served as guards for the senior officers and the *Praetorium*. Because of this, they were clearly familiar with the sight of Tiberius' seal, and we were allowed in without delay. Striding to the desk where the duty Tribune was seated, I noticed that the headquarters was unusually busy, and even the Tribune whose only normal duty was to act as the first official point of introduction to the Legate and direct visitors to the appropriate place was deep in conversation with one of the clerks. The two were so engrossed that neither noticed my approach, but whereas this was not all that unusual, it was normally because the Tribune would be gossiping with a fellow nobleman, or pretending to be busy reading a dirty poem, this time, the pair were consulting a wax tablet and seemed to be engaged in some sort of official debate. Therefore, I waited patiently, or as patiently as it was possible for me, while the two concluded their conversation. Sending the clerk off with a shooing motion, only then did the Tribune seem to notice me, and somewhat to my surprise, seemed embarrassed at the delay.

But my slight sense of surprise turned into something deeper when the Tribune, who I had never met before, said, "You must be Princeps Prior Pullus of the 1st Legion."

So rattled that I forgot to render a salute, I blurted out instead, "How did you know that?"

The instant I said it I realized my lapse, and prepared myself for a tongue-lashing, but if anything, the Tribune appeared amused, and he answered readily enough, "Because we've been expecting you, and I was told by your former Primus Pilus to look out for the largest, fiercest Roman in the Legions. But," suddenly, he pointed at my face, and while I cannot say his tone showed concern, he did sound interested, "you're even more so, considering that cut on your chin. That," he said, superfluously in my opinion, "is a right nasty gash."

59

Although I had washed the excess blood from my face, when I had gingerly explored my chin, my fingers told me that the Varciani's *gladius* had sliced a cut that felt as long as the width of my mouth, while it seemed about a half-inch wide open, although this was hard to determine with the blood caked in the wound. And I did not look forward to the visit to the *medici* to have it cleaned out and sewn up, but I knew it had to be done.

"Yes, sir. Well," I fumbled, "we had some...excitement on the way here."

"That's obvious," the Tribune commented dryly, then gave an abrupt shake of his head, as if reminding himself that this was not important, "but I'm supposed to show you immediately to the Legate's office. He's in there now, along with Germanicus, discussing the coming campaign."

"Germanicus is here already?" I asked, despite having reached that conclusion myself, so I cannot say why I did so. Regardless, I followed him readily enough, just barely remembering to turn and give a sign to Gaesorix to wait there.

"Whose pennant did you think that was flying under the Legate's?" the Tribune asked, for the first time displaying what I had learned was the normal attitude of the haughty young men sent from Rome to supposedly learn how to wage war in the Roman fashion. When I did not answer, he went on, "But, yes, he arrived last night."

Before I could think of anything to say, he came to the door, rapped on it twice, and there was a muffled answer immediately. Opening it up, the Tribune stuck his head through the doorway, but I could not make out what he said, although it became obvious when he quickly stepped aside while pushing the door open.

"They're waiting for you," he announced, which once more struck me as unnecessary, given the fact that he had opened the door and beckoned me to enter.

Still, I squared my shoulders, took a quick breath and, with my helmet under my left arm, holding my *vitus* in my left hand and the scroll clutched in my right fist, I marched in with my eyes straight ahead and fixed on a point on the far wall above the desk. Using my peripheral vision, I saw two men at the desk, one slightly shorter than the other, but I noticed that they were not alone, although just from the position of the three other men, I felt certain they were clerks, slaves, or both.

Then, I reached the desk, rendered my best salute, made slightly awkward with the scroll, and rapped out the official response to the summons, "Quartus Princeps Prior Titus Porcinianus Pullus of the 1st Legion, reporting as directed by *Legatus* Tiberius Claudius Nero, sirs."

The man behind the desk, dressed in a tunic but with the purple Senatorial stripe, his hair gleaming from the pomade I suspected cost at least a month's pay for a Gregarius, returned the salute readily enough, but it was the other man, standing to the side of the desk, who was the first to speak.

"This is *wonderful!*" he enthused, completely breaching the proper protocol, and I noticed the man who had to be the nominal Legate grimace, although the second man either missed or ignored this as he stepped around the desk and, in a move that I found slightly uncomfortable, wedged himself in front of me between my body and the desk, putting him extremely close.

Naturally, he was looking up at me, and I had no choice but to look down to meet his eyes; this was how I met Germanicus Julius Caesar.

He was shorter than I was, although so are most men, particularly Romans, and he had an oval face, with a fringe of hair covering his high forehead; more importantly to me, he had a strong jawline and chin. The manner in which he greeted me was nothing short of enthusiastic, but he matched his words by the manner in which he grasped my arm, squeezing it heartily.

"Titus Pullus!" His manner was excited, although I could not discern whether it was feigned or not. "It's a great pleasure to meet the grandson of one of the first Camp Prefects of the Legions! And," he turned to beam at the man I assumed was the Legate Manius Ennius, who looked anything but pleased, "he looks every bit the part, doesn't he?"

"I suppose so," the older man said, but with a sigh that signaled how much of an effort it was to deign to even take notice of such things.

The youth I now knew was Germanicus shook his head enthusiastically, and while his tone was light, his words were mocking as he rejoined, "'You suppose so?' No, I assure you, Ennius, this is exactly what we need for this campaign! Not only is he the grandson of Titus Pullus...just look at him!" Germanicus actually made the effort to turn towards Ennius, "He's the same size! And," he pointed to my chin, which did not seem to concern him in the slightest-- frankly, I did not know how to feel about this--finishing, "he's already bearing a new battle scar! How can we fail now?"

Aside from the instant sense of pressure that I felt, I was compelled to point out to Germanicus, "I'm not quite as tall as my grandfather was, sir."

"Well," he answered cheerfully, "you're tall enough! Now," suddenly the young nobleman's demeanor turned sober, and I caught the first glimpse of the real man under the boyish exterior, "why don't you tell us what you know about Pannonia first? Then I'll tell you what's happening currently. Or," he caught himself, shooting a glance at the man who was supposedly actually in command, his tone turning apologetic, "I'll let Ennius do that, since he's in command."

Ennius still did not look pleased, and that is putting it mildly, but after a long moment, he granted his acquiescence with a grudging nod in my general direction. He still had his air of disinterest, which he maintained as he suddenly dropped into his chair behind the desk, but I instantly understood who held the real power in the room. Do not mistake me; Ennius was a powerful man in his own right, as all Legates are, but Germanicus, despite his youth, was clearly the man in charge, if only of this meeting. Before I could readily comprehend the sudden shift, I had been offered a chair, while one of the clerks brought me a cup of wine that, on my first sip, I discerned was of an excellent vintage. Frankly, I was beginning to enjoy myself; having a youngster the status of Germanicus so interested in me was a heady brew, and I confess I took the time to enjoy it. I did so under the guise of sampling the wine, of course, but it was hard to suppress a grin at the sight of the youngster who, by virtue of his birth, was currently ranked in the third or perhaps fourth position in the Roman hierarchy, sitting with elbows on knees and looking at me eagerly. Finally, realizing that to delay further would be pushing the boundaries Ennius' patience, I began reciting all that I had learned about the tribes of Pannonia, and their politics; frankly, the latter part took up more time than the former, since it is an ever-shifting, living entity of alliances that are sworn for eternity but often last no longer than a season, driven by deeply rooted enmities that go back to a time when Rome was just a dusty little village. Overlaying that dynamic were the rifts, and the agreements fueled as much by the personalities of the chieftains of each tribe as their shared history, whereby every tribe was interconnected in some fashion. Most commonly, it was by marriage, as one chieftain would offer a daughter, or sometimes a son, as a token of sincerity, and at least in this, the Pannonians are not much different from the upper classes of Rome. Naturally, I spent more time on the Breuci, and the Daesitiates, culling every scrap of information that I could think of, until finally, all I could offer up was a shrug.

"And that's about all I know," was how I put it.

Germanicus looked over at Ennius, beaming with pleasure, and I had the sense there had been some sort of disagreement about the value of my knowledge, which was essentially confirmed when he said exultantly, "See, Ennius? I *told* you he'd be helpful in more ways than one!"

For his part, while Ennius did not openly disagree, he did not seem to be nearly as impressed as Germanicus.

Finally, he sniffed, "Yes, you did, although I already knew most of what the Centurion has related." He inclined his head ever so slightly, and despite being somewhat irritated, I confess I also found it secretly amusing how grudgingly the Legate ceded even this to his younger counterpart; I could only imagine what was going through his mind. But then the moment passed, and with an exaggerated courtesy,

63

he asked Germanicus, "Now, with your permission, I'd like to fill the Princeps Prior in on what's happening right now, not the past."

Germanicus' face instantly flushed, but it surprised me to see he seemed more embarrassed than angry at the rebuke that, no matter how veiled, was unmistakable.

"Of course," he replied hurriedly, "by all means."

Ennius then went on to tell me things that, just as he had taken great pains to point out after my report, I had already known, although there was no way I was going to inform him of this, now that I had witnessed how he reacted to someone he clearly thought of as a subordinate behaving like an equal. If I had cut him off, a mere Centurion, I strongly suspected he would feel honor-bound to put me in my place. Therefore, I sat, pretending to listen, waiting for him to finish. My chin was hurting abominably and I was tired and hungry, meaning that all I wanted was to get out of there. When Ennius broached the subject of the supposed cause of all this, the excessively harsh *dilectus* imposed by Valerius Messallinus, acting in his role of neighboring Illyricum, his manner was so offhand that it seemed to me that he merely mentioned the Praetor's actions as an afterthought, as if it had nothing to do with our current situation. Regarding Messallinus, prior to this, I knew that he had a reputation as a competent general, but as any veteran, and every tribe could attest, being a good general does not automatically equate to being a good administrator. In the few letters I had exchanged with Domitius, he had told me of the rampant corruption, which even by Roman standards he viewed as excessive, that had become a feature of Messallinus' administration. Between this, his demand for double the tax revenue the previous year, and the blunder in gathering a force that ended up rebelling against us, I was not impressed with Messallinus, and Ennius' interminable lecture did not raise my opinion of this Legate. Finally, it was over; or, more likely, Ennius was forced to stop so he could wet his throat, which appeared to be the case, judging by his expression when Germanicus finally got the chance to speak.

"Well!" he said brightly, the smile reappearing. "That was *very* thorough, but let's keep in mind the Princeps Prior has just arrived and must be tired!" Ennius, swallowing the mouthful of wine, opened his mouth, and I felt certain he would object, if only at the very idea of seeming to cater to the needs of one of the lower classes, but Germanicus beat him to it, pointing at my face as he continued, "Besides, he must get that wound seen to! We wouldn't want it becoming corrupt, would we?"

"No," Ennius answered readily enough, yet to my ears, it sounded like he was actually saying 'yes,' "we wouldn't want that." Then, I suppose before Germanicus could do it, he said, "You're dismissed, Centurion. Go see to that cut, then report back here at dawn call."

I rendered my salute, turned about and exited, then as I reached the door, I realized that I had not learned the most important piece of information, when we would be marching. As quickly as the thought came, I realized that I could ask Domitius, who, like every other ranker in the army, knew more about when the Legions would be marching than any Legate ever born.

I saw to the needs of Gaesorix and his men, once more marveling at the power of a scroll with the seal of Tiberius. Although I had surrendered it at the *Praetorium*, my association with it still carried the kind of influence that saw Tribunes falling over themselves to take care of the Batavians, I suppose in the slim chance that I would put in a good word with Tiberius for doing so, or at least that was what I imagined. Only then did I head to the hospital, and I had to suppress the sudden rush of memories that assailed me at the sight of the brick building. I had spent a fair amount of time there, and despite the fact that I had always walked out, I do not suppose I am alone in only associating the pain I experienced with this place, and not because they had essentially healed me. There was a new camp physician, which was not unusual, since they are generally attached to the staff of the sitting Legate, and I confess I did have a slight flutter in my stomach as it occurred to me to wonder whether the bone breaker attached to Messallinus would be as incompetent at healing as the Praetor was at running a province.

I was slightly surprised when, rather than being made to wait, the physician himself came to greet me personally, explaining, "We were told to expect you, Centurion." He was fairly tall, was thin, and balding, with a neatly trimmed beard of almost equal parts gray and black, and he eyed my chin critically with a slight frown. "That," he opined, with a refrain I had already heard more times than I cared to, "is a nasty gash."

Curbing my natural inclination towards the sarcastic retort, I reminded myself how unwise it is to antagonize the man who's about to stick a needle into your skin, so instead, I simply replied, "It certainly feels nasty."

"The first thing we need to do is get that cleaned out." He turned and snapped his fingers, whereupon one of the *medici* appeared.

Despite the reason I was there, I found my mouth turning up into a grin, which caused me to wince, prompting the *medicus* to laugh.

"*Salve*, Titus Pullus!" The man, his name Nemedios, was in his late forties, and he had been attached to the hospital since there had been one in Siscia, which meant that he had tended to not just me, but my father. "I see you're up to your same old tricks!" He opened his eyes in exaggerated surprise. "And you're a Centurion now, I see!"

"That I am, you old goat," I laughed, teasing him, "so you need to treat me with the proper respect! Or," I raised my *vitus*, "I'll have to thrash you!"

Nemedios had been dealing with rankers for years, so he was completely unimpressed, and in response, he raised the sponge from the basin, brandishing it in the exact same manner I had with my *vitus*, "You should know better than to speak that way to someone who's about to scrub your wound." For the first time, he seemed to take notice of my chin, and he exclaimed, "Pluto's cock! That's a…"

"Yes," I interrupted with a sigh, "it's a right nasty gash. So I've heard."

"Then sit down and let me do my job," he said grumpily, and I meekly complied. As he approached, he mumbled, "I'd forgotten just how fucking big you are. You're the only man I have to reach up to tend to even when you're sitting down."

"I'll leave Nemedios to his work," the physician interrupted our small reunion, then told Nemedios to fetch him once he was finished.

I waited long enough for the man to get out of earshot, and I whispered, "What kind of butcher is he? I hope he's not a reflection of the Praetor."

"Him?" Nemedios seemed surprised, which was explained when he shook his head and answered, "He's not with Messallinus, or Ennius, for that matter. He just got here last night, with the boy."

"With Germanicus?" I was surprised. "And he's already in charge?"

The old *medicus* gave a quiet snort and said with a satisfaction that was impossible to misinterpret, "He ran that Greek fake of Ennius' out of here within a watch of showing up. He caught him treating a ranker's wound with a dung poultice. His name is Lysippos."

Despite my ignorance concerning the identity of the wounded man, I groaned in sympathy; I knew there was much debate about certain treatments for illnesses, but wounds were the kinds of injuries that were best left to those who had practical experience with such matters. Being a patient as often as I was, I had been exposed to the vigorous arguments between practitioners of the healing arts, and the one thing I had noticed was that the men who were the most vociferous in their opposition to the use of animal excrement as some sort of cure were the men who had the most experience in the field, specifically with battlefield wounds. Most commonly, it would be a newly arrived physician, almost always from Rome, who would try to institute some practice like dung poultices.

"And?" I asked him. "Did it help?"

Nemedios grimaced, but though his words were noncommittal, his tone was not hopeful as he replied with a shrug, "It's too soon to tell. The boy's wound is corrupt already. So…"

"So it's in the hands of the gods," I answered for him, using the trite phrase that seemed to be the favorite phrase of medical professionals who have run out of answers.

"Now shut up and let me work," Nemedios ordered, and I did as he said.

With a freshly stitched chin, I ached for a bath and a meal, but I forewent the first and left camp, knowing there would be food waiting for me at the home of my best friend. I bounded up the steps, and they must have heard me coming because the door was flung open, and out came Petrilla, Domitius' wife, at least in practice, but she was not alone. Next to her was their oldest daughter, and in her arms was a babe of perhaps a year old, while another child, also a girl, clung shyly to her father's leg in the doorway.

"Titus Pullus! You get over here and kiss me!" she demanded, but before I could actually take a step, she had already crossed the space between us, standing on her tiptoes to kiss me on the lips. Then she stepped back, reaching up, and gently fingered the bandage on my chin, scolding me, "What have you gone and done to yourself now?"

"I didn't do anything!" I protested. "What? You think this is a cut from shaving?"

"As clumsy as you are, anything's possible!" Petrilla retorted tartly, then we were both laughing as we easily fell back into our pattern of banter that we had engaged in since we were children growing up together as the children of men of the Legions.

"Should I be worried you're going to steal my wife?" I heard Domitius say, but he was grinning, leaning against the door as he watched the scene, while his other daughter, named Livilla, seemed reassured enough to take a tentative step away from her father's side.

"Are you mad?" I winked at Domitius over Petrilla's head. "I'd never have a moment's peace for the rest of my days! Better you than me!"

Petrilla looked over her shoulder at Domitius, who suddenly behaved with a mock solemnity as he held up his hand in the way we do when making a sacred oath.

"I'm the luckiest man in the world," he intoned, then rolled his eyes, earning a punch from his wife.

Then, we were engaged in a group hug, while the baby, a boy, squirmed mightily and began to protest at being crushed in this manner.

"Meet my son," Domitius said proudly, then gave me a punch on the shoulder and grinned even more broadly, "and guess what his name is?"

"Yes, Uncle Titus! Guess!" Little Domitilla, now almost seven, demanded, showing me a gap-toothed smile.

Playing along, I pretended to think, "Hmmmm, that's a hard one. Gaius?"

"No!" she shouted gleefully.

"Tiberius?"

"No!" This time, she shuddered with an exaggerated horror, causing me to shoot an inquiring glance at Domitius, who reddened slightly. "Guess again!"

"Spartacus!"

This, as I hoped, caused her to howl with laughter, while her parents looked on fondly as we played the game.

"No, silly! It's TITUS!"

"Titus!" I placed a hand over my heart, saying, "Naturally, your father chose wisely, because it's for your Uncle Titus, not your father!"

"Of course," Domitius put in blandly, keeping his face straight, "you were exactly who I had in mind when I gave my son my own name."

"As you should," I countered loftily, "after all, I AM..."

I got no further, drowned out by a chorus of jeers from the family Domitius. Then we went inside and continued our reunion.

"It's bad this time, Titus," was how Domitius broached the subject that we had avoided through the meal, waiting until the children were asleep. "We've both seen rebellions, but this one feels different somehow."

"What makes it different?" I asked seriously, trusting my friend's assessment completely.

"Well," he paused for a moment, frowning as he framed his thoughts, "it sounds like they're actually better organized this time. This Bato..."

"Which one?" I interrupted. "The Daesitiates or the Breuci?"

"Bato of the Breuci," he replied instantly, without hesitation. He made a dismissive gesture. "Yes, the Daesitiates got it started, but you know that the Breuci are more powerful, and while I can't recall laying eyes on him, just from what I've heard, he reminds me of Draxo."

As I am sure he intended, the mention of the Colapiani chieftain got my attention, arresting my hand as it reached for the amphora on the table between us. I knew with total certainty that Domitius was equally aware of that impact, and that I would take him seriously once the name was uttered, so once I recharged my cup, I waved at him to continue.

"He's supposed to be a formidable warrior in his own right, but he's also got the cunning of a fox. And," Domitius added, "he had several daughters, all of whom he married off, and not one of them were to men of the Breuci."

"So he's got blood ties now to other tribes," I mused, then realized I had something to offer. "You may have heard this, but I learned today from the Legate that Bato of the Daesitiates is besieging Salona."

This caught my friend unaware, and I confess I felt a small sense of satisfaction as he sat back, his mouth open.

"*Gerrae!*" he exclaimed. "No, I hadn't heard that! And? What's going to happen now?"

"For who?" I asked, "The Army of Pannonia?" Shaking my head, I said soberly, "I don't think there's much we can do, being honest, at least as far as Salona is concerned. I was surprised to learn that the Breuci hadn't even attacked here, and we're," even in the moment, I caught my use of the word "we," "going to have our hands full with them."

"That's because Bato isn't a fool," Domitius countered. "Instead, he's on his way to Sirmium, which has grown, but it's not as fortified as we are here."

"He needs an easy victory," I guessed, "which means Sirmium makes sense. Once he takes it, tribes will be flocking to his standard."

"Which," Domitius concluded, "is why I'm worried that this time is different. This time, we may not be able to stop this."

Reporting to the *Praetorium* the next morning, I found the headquarters in even more turmoil than it had been the day before, and I learned at least the partial reason from the current duty Tribune.

"A courier arrived a short time ago." His young face was grim. "Praetor Messallinus will be here before the end of the day. And," he took a deep breath, "Tiberius is only two days behind him."

Honestly, I did not really understand why the Tribune seemed so downcast at first, but as I waited for him to announce my presence, I thought about it more, which prompted me to examine the activity going on around me more carefully. As I stood there, I observed that the Tribune was far from alone in looking worried; down to the lowest clerk, everyone attached to the *Praetorium* seemed downcast, as if they were expecting some sort of bad news. Suddenly, an idea formed, as I modified my previous thought a bit. Maybe it was not because they were attached to the *Praetorium*; perhaps their worry stemmed from being tied to the current Legate, Manius Ennius, in some way. Just as this thought began to take shape, the duty Tribune returned from the Legate's office, shaking his head.

"The Legate doesn't have time for you today," he said shortly. "He said you're to tell me where you're staying, and wait there until you're summoned."

I had to bite back my irritation at the idea of just sitting in the inn I had chosen, but then I had a bit of an inspired idea, or so I believed, when I told him, "I'm actually going to the 8th's area. You'll find me in the Primus Pilus' quarters."

Before he could object, I turned about and headed for the exit. Naturally, I had acted on impulse, and suddenly I wondered if Primus Pilus Atticus would be happy to see me at all, let alone unannounced. It had been a bit more than two years since everything that had transpired to prompt my transfer had occurred; surely, I reasoned, enough time had passed. But, I had committed myself, if only because this would be where the Legate, or Germanicus, or whoever sent for me, would look, and given the level of tension that was reverberating throughout the entire army, it would be unwise of me to incur their wrath by not being where I was supposed to be. As I walked across the forum, I observed rankers scurrying about, while men like me, dressed only in their tunic and *baltea*, but carrying the *vitus*, alternately bawled orders or used the twisted vine stick to administer a sound smack across the back of a *Gregarius* he judged to be lagging in his duties, all of this a sign that the Legions were on the march. Reaching the building, the largest such that served as the combination office and private quarters of the Primus Pilus of a Legion, I hesitated outside, mentally preparing myself for any number of receptions. Then, rapping twice with my *vitus*, I did not wait for an answer, swinging the door open. Seated in his usual spot was Crito, and I confess I was a bit disappointed when he looked up and was clearly unsurprised.

"I was wondering when you'd come barging in," was all he said at first, sighing as he did so. Then, he sat back and regarded me for a moment before his face split into a grin, and I saw he had lost a tooth, although otherwise, he was essentially unchanged. "But you're a Centurion now, so I suppose it's understandable."

Only then did he stand up, while I crossed the space as the two junior clerks, neither of them I recognized, gaped at the sight of a man identified as a Centurion offering his arm to a freedman clerk as if they were equals.

"It's good to see you too, old man," I teased, and I was being completely honest. "Are you still stealing us blind?"

"Every chance I get," Crito agreed with a laugh. Then, he leaned back, squinting up at me as he examined me with a critical eye. "And I see you're still stabbing yourself with your *gladius*."

"Every chance I get," I echoed. "You know how much women love scars!" We both shared in the mirth, while the other clerks nervously chuckled, unsure exactly what was taking place. I took a breath, then nodded my head in the direction of the closed door, asking Crito in a lower voice, "Is he in?"

The clerk shook his head, informing me, "No. He's making the rounds right now. You do know we're about to march, don't you?"

"Yes." I was a bit testy in my response. "Why do you think I'm here?"

"Well, according to Domitius, you're on some sort of secret mission. He claims you didn't even tell him why."

This touched me, though I do not know why I was surprised; I had admonished my friend not to divulge the reason for my presence, so naturally, he did no such thing.

"But he didn't need to tell me," Crito went on, and while he kept a straight face, I saw the gleam in his eye. "I already know." Standing on his tiptoes and leaning closer, he whispered, "It's about young Germanicus. You're here to make sure he doesn't end up like that." He pointed at my chin, then in a normal tone of voice, shook his head and said with a mock sadness, "Although why they chose someone as clumsy as you, I have no idea."

Despite my irritation, I was more amused than anything as I ruefully reminded myself how impossible it is to keep a secret in the army, and of all the people, clerks are the most knowledgeable about the internal workings of the Legions.

"I should have known," I admitted, but I still wagged a finger at him, only partially jesting when I warned, "but you need to keep that to yourself."

Crito was completely unimpressed, retorting, "I've been chief clerk before you ever showed up here. You don't need to tell me how to keep a secret."

I had to laugh, since this was nothing less than the truth, and while this was true for all the men acting in the role of the primary clerk for a Legion, for Crito, who had been brought into the position by Urso, he of the secret business of selling armor and weapons to the Pannonian tribes, it was even more the case.

"Well," I said, "I think I'll go stroll over to see how the Sixth is doing. I'll come back later." I was about to leave when I remembered, and I told Crito, "Oh, and I told the *Praetorium* they could find me over here, so if a runner shows up from the Legate, send him to me. Ennius doesn't strike me as the type to forgive someone for being hard to find."

My hand was on the door, but Crito's reply stopped me cold, as he said quietly, "I'll do that, but you don't need to worry about running afoul of Ennius."

Turning about, I raised an inquiring eyebrow, which caused the clerk to look uncomfortable, and I had the feeling he had blurted something out that was better left unsaid, at least in front of others. However, he got up and walked over to me, then followed me outside.

"They don't need to hear this," he said once we were far enough away from the door, although I was certain there was at least one ear pressed to it. "But Ennius isn't going to be Legate much longer."

The instant the words left his mouth, suddenly, the things I had seen in the *Praetorium* made sense, but this prompted an obvious question.

"Who's going to relieve him?" I was struck by a thought, yet I could not credit it. "Certainly not Germanicus! He's too young!"

"No." Crito shook his head, and I felt a sense of relief. "Not Germanicus. Honestly, I'm not sure. It most likely is going to be Messallinus, but you do know Tiberius is coming as well."

"Yes, I do," I replied. I thought for a moment, then shrugged as I realized, "It doesn't really matter, though. Tiberius is the obvious choice, but I know that Messallinus is a competent general. Not," I added, "a good Praetor, though."

"No," Crito agreed. "No, he's not. But either way, I wouldn't be concerned about Ennius. He's a dog with no teeth."

Thanking him for this tidbit, he returned to the office, and I strode over to the combination office and quarters for the Sixth and its Hastatus Posterior. I found Pridaxes in an identical posture as I had found Crito, and like Crito, he was unsurprised at my appearance, although this was more understandable, since Domitius occupied my former post.

"Is he in?" I asked, except this time, I got a nod, but when he got up to go rap on the door and announce me, I stopped him, feeling the urge for some mischief.

I tried to step lightly, moving to the door, then opened it without knocking, strolling in, and without being asked, dropping into the lone chair on the opposite side of the desk from the Primus Hastatus Posterior. Who, while startled at first, quickly regained his composure, leaning back to silently watch as I made the chair creak when I plopped into it, holding my *vitus* in such a way it was impossible to ignore.

"And," Appius Asinius asked dryly, "how long have you been waiting to do that?"

Pleased that he had essentially picked up the game where it had been left off from the last time I was promoted to Optio, while he was still the same rank, I grinned and repeated what I had said the first time, "From the day I showed up."

Only then did his composure crack, and we both stood as he maneuvered around his desk so we could embrace, our faces plastered with the same smile.

Once we had exchanged pleasantries, I blurted out the one thing that had gnawed at me. "So, why did you give up command of a Cohort just to be in the First?"

Asinius laughed outright, a rare enough occasion that I remember it happening, but he answered readily enough, "Sometimes I wonder the same thing. But," he shrugged, "the truth is that I have...plans. Or," he amended, "ambitions might be a better word."

He paused then, presumably to allow the meaning of what he had just said to sink in, and I found myself sitting up straighter as the true import did indeed hit me.

"Wait," I gasped, "are you saying that you might become Primus Pilus?"

Asinius' face gave nothing away, and he gave another shrug, replying, "It's a possibility. Atticus is planning to retire in the next two or three years. Actually, it was his suggestion that I take Galens' spot when he took over the Second. He said it was easier to promote a man into the post if he had commanded both a Cohort and a Century in the First. So," he finished, "that's why I'm here."

"That," I replied, "would be a good thing. Not just for you, but for the 8th."

Whether it was the words themselves or the fact that I meant them sincerely I had no way of discerning, but the flush that came over

75

Asinius' normally placid face was a reward in itself, if only because it was so hard to rattle him in any manner.

I wish I could say that the reception to my homecoming, such as it was, maintained the same level of cordiality and, what I believe was unfeigned happiness, on the part of my former comrades and friends. And, I will say, that it was such with all but one man, although in some ways, that man was the most important. Originally, Asinius had been promoted from being Atticus' Optio to become the Centurion commanding the Second Cohort, while Galens, my first Optio and my first Centurion as Optio myself, was now the Primus Pilus Posterior, as the long-suffering Macerinus, realizing he would never attain the post of Primus Pilus, had retired, thereby opening up a slot in the First Cohort, which Asinius had decided to take, and when he explained why he did so when we met, I could certainly understand why once I learned of his intentions. And, I should add, the intentions of the current Primus Pilus. This is an example of where civilians can become confused when it comes to our system; why would a Centurion commanding an entire Cohort want to then take a posting in a higher Cohort but be back to commanding just a Century? Under normal circumstances, this is actually true, but not in the case of the First Cohort, because while it is not the only path to becoming Primus Pilus, under normal conditions, it is the surest way to attaining the highest posting in a Legion, and the fact that Asinius had taken the Sixth of the First at the urging of Atticus would carry weight with the man who ultimately made the decision, which was still, and always had been during my career at least, the Princeps. Speaking of the Primus Pilus, Atticus was less than thrilled, although he did deign to see me.

"You've got balls, I'll give you that," he had growled, glaring up at me from behind his desk, "but that was never your problem. Brains..." He gave a harsh laugh that I was certain was meant to wound me. "...that's another matter entirely."

I was determined not to lose my temper, nor lose sight of the fact that, when all was said and done, Atticus had been a good Primus

Pilus, both for the Legion and to me as well. Granted, I had volunteered to lie for him at a Tribunal, so it was not like I had done nothing for the man. Nevertheless, I stood there, mute, letting him vent his spleen, and as I learned, there was obviously quite a bit of bile that had built up since my departure.

"Do you know how much trouble you caused us? How much you caused *me*?" he asked, but before I could answer, he went on to tell me, "Plenty! That's how much! The Legate crawled up my ass every day for three months! And now," he pointed at my *vitus*, "I learn that this is how you were *punished*? By being promoted?" He slapped the desk with the flat of his hand, the sound cracking so loudly that I heard a clerk in the outer office give a startled yelp. "It took months before those barbarians settled down!"

"At least this time, it's not my fault," I replied, and while my tone was mild, I had again just blurted out the first thing that came to my mind, and I cringed as I waited for the explosion.

And, at first, I was sure it was coming, because his face darkened as his bushy eyebrows, which were now almost completely iron gray, plunged together in a sign I had long before learned signaled that Mount Atticus was about to erupt.

Suddenly, though, he burst out laughing and agreed, "Well, that much is true. This time," as quickly as it came, his good humor vanished, "but not last time."

I knew very well this was true, yet I also felt like this was plowed ground; fortunately, my presence, in the form of my current status, seemed more important to Atticus than chewing on my hind parts more thoroughly.

"So," he asked bluntly, "why are you here?" I began to recite my orders, but he quickly waved me to silence, the irritation returning to his battered features. "Not that nonsense, Pullus. Remember who you're talking to. So," he repeated, except he leaned forward to glare at me, "I'm asking again. Why are you *really* here?"

I felt trapped; despite my early misgivings about Atticus, and some bumps in our relationship, I did respect the man, and I had never regretted my role in his Tribunal, small as it might have been.

77

Regardless of my personal feelings, my fear of Tiberius' wrath far outweighed my sense of obligation to be honest to Atticus. Consequently, I said nothing, just standing there like a big lump of meat as he continued to pin me with his gaze, and I confess it was quite uncomfortable. Finally, he heaved a sigh, nodding wearily, which I took as his sign of surrender.

"I understand," he said heavily, "you don't want to run afoul of Tiberius. Or," Atticus' eyes narrowed, "are you still working for the Princeps?"

I did not reply, verbally at least, but taking what I considered to be a tiny risk, mainly because I trusted my former Primus Pilus by this point, I gave the tiniest shake of my head at his question.

"Ah," he nodded, as if this confirmed his suspicions, "that makes sense. Better to switch saddles from the old horse to the new before it collapses from under you, neh?"

Although I did not like hearing it put in these terms, I was honest enough with myself to acknowledge I could not argue the truth of the words, but I exacted a tiny revenge by simply shrugging, prompting him to issue another snort.

"Well, whatever it is you're *not* doing," Atticus went on, "I'm guessing Domitius told you that this time is different, that it's..." he seemed to search for a word, finally uttering the same thing my friend had by settling for "...bad. Very, very bad."

The runner from the *Praetorium* found me easily enough, summoning me back to the headquarters building, and even before I reached it, I saw that Messallinus had clearly arrived. And, I was just in time to meet the now-relieved Legate Ennius, accompanied by two cavalrymen who, from appearances, were as much to guard him from bolting as protection, but I rendered my salute as if he still mattered, which he did not bother to acknowledge. Entering, the scene was chaotic, as what was presumably Messallinus' contingent of staff, Tribunes, and clerks who served in functions important to the Praetor, mingled with their counterparts who had been serving under Ennius. The latter were easy to identify by the slightly dazed expressions that come from suddenly no longer mattering, and it was no surprise to see that the Tribunes were the most affected. Their futures, which shortly before had been so bright and seemingly assured, were in doubt, as they wondered if Ennius' disgrace would somehow splatter onto their own nascent, but still shining, reputations. While I had no real way of knowing, if any of them had bothered to ask a lowly Centurion like me, my guess would have been that those Tribunes who had attached themselves the most firmly to Ennius, whether it was through the calculation that diligently performing their assigned duties would attract his favor, or just through simple sycophancy, these would be the men most likely to share in the consequences. Frankly, while I found it interesting, it was not my concern, but when I turned to the runner, whose instructions had simply been to report to the *Praetorium*, he had vanished, probably to find an out of the way spot to hide and wait for the dust to settle. Therefore, I simply stood there, although I did move slightly to stand against the wall next to the doorway, hoping to blend in and not attract attention; my *vitus* might have spared me, but judging from the manner in which everyone present was behaving, that was no guarantee.

The door to the Legate's office was closed, but thankfully, not long after I chose my spot, it opened and Germanicus appeared. I got a glimpse of another man standing behind the desk, looking at the pile of scrolls on it with a disgusted expression on his face, who I assumed to be Messallinus; then Germanicus shut the door and stood for a moment, clearly searching the large room. When his eyes moved to where I was standing, he motioned for me to attend to him, which I did, but frankly, I still felt a little foolish saluting him, thinking that he was just a couple years older than Gaius, my next oldest brother.

"Centurion, I've been assigned a task, and I'm going to need your help," he said immediately after returning my salute. Glancing about, he decided, "Let's go outside. There's too much going on in here."

Following him outside, I was curious, wondering what kind of job Messallinus had given him, and more to the point, whether this was on Messallinus' authority, or if he was just relaying Tiberius' own instructions. While I felt certain Germanicus would not say, I knew where I was placing my imaginary money, but I was in for a surprise.

"My father," Germanicus began straightaway, "sent orders through Messallinus that I'm to perform an impromptu *dilectus* in the province, beginning immediately."

This froze my blood, yet somehow, I managed to avoid blurting out my initial reaction to what sounded like madness to me.

"A...*dilectus*?" I asked cautiously. "Even after what happened with the Daesitiates?"

The surge of relief I felt when Germanicus shook his head was intense, as he went on to explain, "Not of the native tribes. No, what we need to do is call on all the veterans who have settled in the province." He looked up at me intently, and his tone was imploring. "Which means I'm going to need your help, Centurion. I know your name will carry a great deal of influence with these men, and if you're by my side, they'll know how serious this is."

This was extremely flattering, which I suspect he understood, despite his youth; as I would come to learn, underneath his boyish, charming exterior, there was a shrewd mind working there. However, as nice as it was to hear my name praised in such a way; and even in the moment, I did not lose sight of the fact that this was not about me, but about my Avus, I was not quite as certain as he seemed to be about the power of it to attract men out of retirement. My experience with most men who had managed to complete a full enlistment was that, from their viewpoint, they had served their time and earned their rewards, meaning their obligation to Rome was done.

Regardless of my personal feelings on the matter, I also knew what was expected of me, so I merely asked, "When do we leave?"

"Dawn tomorrow," he answered, then hesitated before asking, "Where would you suggest we go first?"

I thought for a moment, then told him, "We need to head in the direction of Emona. That's where the 8th and 13th men are settled. After that," I shrugged, "it depends on how many man we gather." That was when it occurred to me to ask, "And how many men are we supposed to gather up?"

"As many," Germanicus said grimly, "as we can."

Naturally, I spent my last night in Siscia with Domitius and his family; at least, the first part of the night, but then I managed to wrest my friend from the comfort of the bosom of his family to go meet with Galens, Asinius, and some of my other former comrades at the wineshop we had favored back when I was still in Siscia. About the only thing I can say is that, while there was no brawl, this was the only event that did not take place during a night of debauchery, which meant I had a sore head, sour stomach, and a foul disposition when I swung up onto Latobius. In contrast, Germanicus was ebullient, making our contrasting moods a trial for me. We were not going to be traveling alone, naturally; even if Germanicus had not been in the family of the Princeps, it would not have been safe to travel without at least an *ala* of cavalry. As I learned that morning, Germanicus already had a force of five hundred men, although more than half were not cavalry troopers, but infantry who had been given horses, something that was obvious by their clear discomfort as they sat on the back of their beasts. A hundred of them, however, were German troopers, and my assumption was that they were on loan from Tiberius, since I recognized a handful as belonging to his personal bodyguard. One pleasant surprise was the presence of Gaesorix, and those Batavians of his who could ride, although I saw at least two of them were still wearing bandages from the ambush. We greeted each other warmly, our earlier antipathy firmly in the past, sharing a joke about this motley collection of men.

"And this is just the beginning," I warned him. "We're about to go scrape up as many men as we can, and my guess is that the youngest of them will be old enough to be our fathers."

"If they're anything like my father, or your grandfather," Gaesorix laughed, "then I'm not worried."

This struck me as a curious thing to say, since he had specifically mentioned my Avus, but not my father. Surely, I reasoned to myself, if he knew who my grandfather was, he must have known that my father was under the standard as well, but when I asked him about this omission, he gave me a sidelong glance, then a shrug.

"Your father lost his leg, didn't he?"

"How did you know that?" I asked him, curious as to how he learned this.

Gaesorix laughed and replied, "I just sat in one of the wineshops here and learned everything I needed to." The look he gave me was direct as he added, "I knew your grandfather was famous, but here in Siscia, it seems that the Pullus family is very well known."

Now, I had been vaguely aware that this was the case; when my Avus was assigned to the newly formed Army of Pannonia, now more than thirty years earlier, Siscia had been nothing more than a collection of native hovels. Even when I was born, a few years after he brought my parents along with him, finding a spot in the 8th for my father, it was a barely Romanized town, composed of mostly wooden buildings. Still, hearing this Batavian Decurion speak with such familiarity about my family was a bit disconcerting. Then, he said something else.

"In fact," he spoke casually, but I detected something in his voice that caused me to glance over, and he was regarding me with a grin, "I heard that you got some equestrian girl pregnant! Oh," he laughed then, probably the worst thing he could have done, "apparently, it was quite the scandal. She had to disappear and they said she never came back."

I imagine he became aware that he had committed a serious blunder by the way I looked at him, and I did get some satisfaction at seeing the grin vanish from his face, but it was the way he paled that was the most rewarding.

"I-I'm sorry, Pullus," he fumbled, holding up his free hand in a gesture of supplication. "I didn't mean to cause offense, truly! I was just talking." He gave a rueful laugh and finished weakly, "It's a bad habit of mine."

I believed he was sincere, but I held his gaze a bit longer, just to make a point. Once I was satisfied, we continued riding along in silence for a couple miles.

Finally, he broke it by asking quietly, "So you loved her?"

I just gave an abrupt nod, struggling to keep the pain and sense of loss that had burst forth so unexpectedly quelled inside me.

"I'm sorry," Gaesorix said again, then startled me when he added, "I know what it's like to love someone but you can't be together."

This surprised me, and I glanced over at him with a raised eyebrow, still not trusting myself to speak.

Correctly interpreting my expression, the Batavian explained, "In fact, your...situation sounds similar to mine. I was in love, and she loved me, but she," his mouth twisted down into a grimace that I knew all too well, "was the daughter of our chieftain. And he married her off to the chieftain of another branch of our tribe." Sighing, he shrugged, then gave me a sad smile as he indicated the horse underneath him. "So I joined the auxiliaries. That way, I didn't have to be around to bear the shame of not being good enough for her father." He paused for a moment, then asked, "So, what happened to your love?"

For a moment, I was not inclined to answer, but swallowing past the sudden lump in my throat, I replied, "She died." I looked over at him as I added, "Bearing my child." Unbidden, a bitter laugh escaped me, and I told Gaesorix, "That's another thing my family is famous for. We," I indicated myself, "are so big, women who bear us...or our children, are likely to die doing it."

And with that, there was nothing else said between us for the next several miles.

By the time we actually reached Emona, as I had feared, we had not attracted anywhere near the numbers Germanicus was expecting to flock to his standard. The problem, as I saw it, was twofold; the first issue was what I mentioned earlier, that most men considered their obligation to Rome done. The other challenge came in the form of Germanicus himself, specifically his youth. Despite his illustrious name, and the reverence the retired men of the 8th held for his deceased father, the combination of his age, and in my firm opinion, the distance from Rome itself, played against his earnest plea for men to join him. Finally, after we had spent two days in Emona itself and only managed to convince a dozen men, he summoned me to the villa of one of the sitting *Duumviri* where he was staying, near tears from the frustration.

"What am I doing wrong, Pullus?" he cried, pacing back and forth in the *triclinium*. "Why aren't men joining me?"

This was the first real test of our relationship, and I hesitated before answering him, but not for long; nothing I had seen in the time I had spent with him suggested he had any kind of vindictive streak in his nature, something that could not be said for other members of his family, real and adopted.

At last, I offered, "Well, your age doesn't help."

For an instant, I thought I had miscalculated, as the look he gave me was scathing, and I chastised myself for forgetting how sensitive young men are about being young, but he said, "You don't think I know that, Pullus? I knew that already. But I don't think that's it, at least not all of it." He took a breath, calming himself, then asked again, "So, what do you think it is?"

Realizing he was being completely sincere, I did not hesitate, saying, "Your name doesn't mean that much this far from Rome."

This, I saw, surprised him; no, it did more than that; he was shocked at my blunt assessment, but I felt very confident I was right, mainly because I had been told as much by some of the men with whom we had come into contact, one in particular. And, being honest, it was a man I trusted, and had done so on more occasions than I could count, with my life. Servius Metellus, one of the men in my very first section in the First Century, Fourth Cohort of the 8th, had retired and settled on a plot of land he had bought from the widow of another veteran.

He had been the man who scoffed, "Being who he is may matter in Rome, but out here, all that counts is whether or not he can kill the barbarians."

Metellus' attitude was far from unique; what was different was that he was one of the few who made his mark on the document that every veteran was required to sign that stated he would be under the standard for the duration of the rebellion.

When I asked him why, after he had openly disparaged young Germanicus, he was still willing to enlist, he had said cheerfully, "Because you're with him, that's why, you big oaf! Plus," he grinned, displaying a mouth that was notable only because of the paucity of teeth, "I'm fucking bored out of my mind. I hate farming!"

Despite being touched, I had laughed and openly welcomed him into our ranks, as thin as they may have been. However, when a horse was requisitioned for him, he beheld it with undisguised horror, and he looked over at me, an appeal in his eyes, but he had chosen the wrong man to be sympathetic as I merely pointed at the horse, albeit with a grin on my face. For a brief moment, I wondered if he would balk and simply walk away, but then, with a considerable amount of grumbling, he was helped onto the back of the animal. Now, standing in the *triclinium* in Emona, I was trying to explain why men like Metellus, who did not serve with me, were so reluctant to join Germanicus.

"You must understand," I made no attempt to hide how I was imploring this youngster, "the men who you're trying to attract have done more fighting than almost any others who were ever under the standard." Even as I said this, I offered up a silent prayer to the first Titus Pullus as I amended, "Other than the men who marched for Divus Julius, like my grandfather. Otherwise," I warned, "they've been fighting for most of their lives. And, they're tired, Germanicus. Now," I paused, wondering how he would accept this, "here you come, an untried and unproven...man," I chose what I believed would be the less offensive term, "asking them to pick up the *gladius* again and risk their lives once more. Men who," I felt compelled to add, "aren't getting any younger."

"But this is for their own good as much as mine," the younger man cried. "This province is in rebellion!"

"This province," I replied, trying to keep my tone measured, "is always in a state of rebellion. That's just how it is here in Pannonia."

"Not like this!" Germanicus shot back, then he turned to stare at me. "Tell me that this isn't true. That this time is just like all the others."

85

This was something I could not do, not when men like Domitius and Atticus had warned me as much, and I admitted, "That's very true, Germanicus." Despite his status, I could not bring myself to call him "sir," in private at any rate, but he never minded, or at least he never made it an issue. "But they," I gestured in the general direction of the town, "don't know that. As far as they're concerned, this is just like every other time, when the Praetor sent out the alarm and asked for volunteers to quell some revolt that supposedly was the biggest threat to the province in history. Only to find that it was a single tribe, and they were barely needed. Remember also," I reminded him, "that we're up here at the northern edge of the province, and the rebels are tribes farther south. At least," I finished grimly, "so far."

"So," Germanicus asked sensibly, "how do I convince them that it's not like every other time?"

Honestly, nothing came immediately to mind; as it would turn out, we did not need to change our tactics, because the events that occurred proved to be a more powerful incentive than anything we could have said.

Messallinus had not stayed in Siscia long, leaving to join five Cohorts of the 20th Legion that had marched down from Mogontiacum, taking the most direct route to where Bato of the Breuci was headed, Sirmium. Although they stopped the Breuci just a few miles short of Sirmium and met them in open battle, suffering heavy casualties in the process, a short time later, Messallinus' forces ambushed the Breuci, the rebels suffering their own substantial losses in turn, which forced them to retreat from Sirmium. At roughly the same time, Bato of the Daesitiates was badly wounded during the siege of Salona, which he lifted, but then his rebels went raiding up and down the coast of Illyricum, wreaking havoc and leaving a trail of destroyed homes, razed villages, and gods only know how many dead. Returning to Siscia, Messallinus took command of the Legions there and hurried west, engaging the Daesitiates in another battle, but while being outnumbered again, this time, the rebels suffered a resounding defeat, earning Messallinus the award of triumphal ornaments, though not a full triumph. In an odd twist, the news that the Daesitiates were raging north up the coast, while the Breuci were moving back in the general direction of the western part of the province, did more to convince men to join Germanicus than anything we could have said or offered. Regardless of this incentive, by the time Germanicus was satisfied that we had recruited enough men to serve as a potent force, more than four months had passed, and the campaign season was coming to a close. Although in reality, this did not mean all that much; the rebelling tribes would still be active in their depredations, it did mean there would be no large-scale actions initiated by either side. This served as something of a blessing for young Germanicus and his motley force of old veterans, foreign auxiliaries like Gaesorix and his Batavians, and youngsters of the upper class of Roman citizens living in the province who were looking for adventure and a path to glory that they consider to be their birthright, even if they had never laid eyes on Rome itself. With my help, Germanicus organized the men into Centuries first, then Cohorts, although we did not have nearly enough for a full Legion and barely enough for five Cohorts. Even with the increased enthusiasm of the veterans in the province, Germanicus had been forced to relax his requirements; the way I put it to him was to think of it as less than lowering his standards and more as broadening his horizons, which made him laugh when I said it. However he viewed it, in the last month before he was satisfied that we were through and had scoured the countryside, we began accepting freedmen and in a few cases, even the slaves of some of the last of the provincial nobility to join us.

Germanicus, at my suggestion, decided that it was better to winter in Emona; putting it simply, Siscia was already overflowing, both the camp and the town, as Tiberius had arrived with the rest of the 20th and the 9th, while to make room for them, my old Legion, the 8th, was sent eastward to join forces with the Legions of the Army of Moesia, consisting of the 4th, 5th, 7th, and 11th, and led by two men of Consular rank, Caecina Severus and Plautius Silvanus, meeting in Naissus. By the end of the year, and in preparation for the coming campaign season, there was a total of ten Legions, untold numbers of auxiliaries, although only from tribes believed to be loyal to Rome, mostly from Germania and eastern Gaul, while our cavalry arm, distributed across the entire force, numbered around ten *alae*'s worth. Essentially, a huge force of Roman might was now arrayed against the rebelling tribes, and looking at a map, there was one force in Naissus, poised to march west into the very heart of the province, while the one led by Tiberius, in Siscia, was prepared to punch directly south into the heart of Breuci territory. And then, there was the force of Germanicus, numbering a bit more than three thousand mounted infantry, though Germanicus and I were debating on whether they would continue in this manner, and about seven hundred men who were trained as cavalry. If I am being completely honest, the composition of this force between tested veterans like Gaesorix and youngsters like Germanicus was not to my liking; only time and battle would tell how many of these young nobles and their retainers proved to be of any value.

As luck would have it, we actually had a place to not only spend the winter, but to train the men, in the forum of the auxiliary camp just outside of the town walls. The camp itself was almost deserted; the men who had been stationed here were drawn from the Latobici and Varciani tribes of Pannonia, and who had taken their arms and armor to fight with the rebels, along with the Taurisci of Noricum. The latter tribesmen were the only ones who had remained faithful, but there were only a bit more than three Centuries of such men, not even enough for a Cohort. Frankly, I did not care all that much, because I was given the quarters of the Primus Pilus, though they were just a bit smaller than those of their Legionary counterparts. As soon as I learned we would winter in Emona, I immediately sent for Alex and the rest of my baggage, and he arrived as part of a supply train. And when he showed up, he brought me news of more tragedy for the Pullus family.

While it was about a sibling, this time, it was not because of violence, but the one thing that haunted every member of the Pullus family, particularly the men. My sister Valeria, who had been happily married for some time to her merchant Appius Minucius Clustuminus, and had already borne him a daughter, named Antistia, who was now about five years old according to my best guess, was fated to bear a son who, according to my father, was as large as I had been when I was born. Tragically, unlike our mother, my sister was unable to survive the ordeal of bringing him into the world. The boy survived and bears the name Titus, as those of us do who are destined to be born large enough to kill our mothers, although he is not a Pullus, but Titus Clustuminus. Why I did not do so to my own mother, Iras, is a mystery that I have spent a fair amount of time, particularly after all that happened with Giulia, pondering. Whatever the case, I now had another nephew, this one bearing my own name, but in what I can only say is an odd twist, I learned about this from Alex because his mother, Birgit, had become the child's wet nurse. While my father's letter was as cryptic as always, from what I gathered, the babe's father was so distraught over the death of Valeria that he had essentially abandoned the babe at our villa in Arelate, taking my niece and, according to my father, disappearing. This was as much as I learned that winter; only over time would I discover that, from this family tragedy, my father's spirits, which had been flagging since the death of my mother, had been revived by the presence of the babe Titus. As one might expect, I grieved over the death of Valeria, and in our fashion, I cut neither hair nor beard for a month. She had been the closest to me in age, and despite our different genders, in our early years, we had been fast friends and, if my mother were alive, she would attest to this, my partner in the various crimes perpetrated on other members of my family and, more commonly, Diocles, Eumenis, and Simeon. All of whom, it must be said, bore our transgressions with a level of indulgence that went farther than it probably should have, and for that I credit Valeria, who could essentially charm us out of any serious punishment. Now, like Sextus, she was gone, and I confess I raged at the gods for a period of time, wondering why our womenfolk had to pay such an extraordinary price to give us life. My Avus' mother, my great-grandmother, Miriam, and Giulia have been joined by my sister, and to this day, I offer sacrifices to Magna Mater and Bona Dea, asking their intervention to allow them to find each other, where if all that we believe is true, they and my mother will be there to chide their menfolk for eternity.

My personal trials notwithstanding, I spent the winter overseeing the further training of Germanicus' scratch force, and although we did not have to spend time teaching the majority of the newly conscripted men the rudiments of the way in which we wage war, we did have to focus on training as units, beginning with the Century. Also, Germanicus consulted with me on the appointment of men as *de facto* Centurions and Optios, but in this, I am afraid that he exhibited the same behavior one would expect from a raw Tribune who finds himself with that much authority. In other words, he appointed men of his own class as Centurions, although he did allow me to counter this a bit by empowering me to select the Optios. However, I should point out that there was one exception, one for which I fought very hard, badgering the young nobleman until, I suspect more from recognition that I was not going to desist than that I convinced him about the man's qualities. Whatever the cause, I did prevail on him.

"You want me to be a Centurion? *Me?*" Servius Metellus shook his head as if he was trying to wake up from a dream. "But, Pullus, I'm not Centurion material! You of all people should know that!"

I confess I was a bit bemused by his reaction; on reflection, I suppose it was a bit much to expect that a man who had never risen higher than the rank of *Gregarius* would leap at the opportunity to wear a transverse crest, even if it was on a temporary basis.

Nevertheless, I was a bit stung, which prompted me to modify my approach a bit, telling him, "I need a man I can trust, an experienced man. And," I pointed to him, "remember, I've seen you fight! So I know you're up to the job!"

"There's a lot more to being a Centurion than fighting," Metellus retorted, and to my irritation, mimicked my own action by pointing right back at me, "and you know it."

Seeing that I was not making any progress, I decided to appeal to his greed, telling him, "Do you know how much a Centurion makes?"

90

For the first time, his weathered features flashed a sign that I took to be a mixture of doubt and interest, but he still resisted, saying, "But it's a temporary post! We might only be at this a month! Now," he admitted, "that's a fair bit of money, I won't deny, but for a month?" He shook his head, and I got the sense that he was just being stubborn. "It's not worth it."

Sensing an opportunity, I immediately asked him, "If I could guarantee that you would get at least a half year's pay as a Pilus Prior, would you agree?"

"A Pilus Prior's pay?" His mouth dropped open, and I almost believed I could hear the wheels turning in his head as he tried to work out the sum. By some instinct, I said nothing, and finally, he answered, "Well, that's different! But," his expression clouded, and he squinted at me doubtfully, "will the youngster agree to this? I'm not exactly his…" he searched for a word, coming up with, "…one of his own, if you take my meaning."

"I do," I replied, then lied, "and he's already agreed to it."

This clearly caught him by surprise, and I confess I felt a bit ashamed that he did not seem to doubt my veracity.

"Then, Pullus," he said with a wide smile that showed more gums than teeth, "I'm your man to the death! Or," he cackled, "six months at least!"

Honestly, I cannot adequately put into words exactly why it was so important to me for Metellus to be a Centurion, even if it was temporary. It was certainly true that I trusted him implicitly, but he had never exhibited the mental acuity that is required for a man wearing the transverse crest, at least if he wants to be successful. Regardless, I was happy that I had persuaded my old comrade; convincing Germanicus, I thought, shouldn't be that difficult.

"Are you mad, Pullus?"

If only, I thought with a mixture of amusement and unease, I had a *sestertius* for every time I've been asked that, this wouldn't be an issue, and I suppose this was what prompted me to cheerfully answer Germanicus, "So I've been told."

As I hoped, this served to disarm him; I had noticed that he looked for the humorous aspect in any situation, which I suppose is one reason I liked him.

"Well, they were right," the young noble said ruefully, then began rubbing his chin as he paced back and forth in front of his desk. Finally, he shrugged and said, "It's too late now; you gave your word. Didn't you?"

The sidelong glance he gave me was impossible to misinterpret, clearly beseeching me to assure him that I had done no such thing, giving him a way to extricate himself from a predicament not of his making.

"I did," I replied without hesitation, then decided to add, "not only as a Centurion of Rome, but as a Pullus."

This last, I instantly saw, carried more weight, as I had hoped it would, and in answer, he heaved a sigh.

"Very well," he said at last. "I'll deal with my father. But, Pullus," his mouth turned down, and what he said next made my blood freeze, "I'm sure I don't have to tell *you* that Tiberius can be...harsh."

What, I thought with a stab of alarm that bordered on panic, did he mean by that? What did he know about my role as one of Tiberius' men?

Evidently, he saw what he took to be puzzlement, because he went on, "You spent a whole winter with him, didn't you? What was it? Two seasons ago?"

It took quite a bit for me to remain standing erect and not slump with the relief I felt, as I answered, "Three, actually, counting this winter."

"Ah, yes, right." Germanicus seemed embarrassed, then shook his head, clearly ready to move on to another topic, although not nearly as much as I did. "Anyway, I'll handle this business with Metellus, but I just wanted to forewarn you that there's a possibility you'll be standing with me in front of Tiberius, explaining why you made such an extravagant promise."

This, I thought, is something I can live with; as it turned out, I never heard another word about my promise to Metellus, but I suspect that was due more to the fact that Tiberius had his hands full with other matters.

As it turned out, we had a secret ally in the weather. Indeed, if I had not known better, I would have sworn that I never left Germania, as Pannonia experienced one of the harshest winters over the previous decade. Starting the last week of December and extending well into Januarius, we did not experience one day where we saw the sun, and more importantly, it snowed every single day, although some days, it was only for a matter of a watch. Nevertheless, it was enough to severely hamper the abilities of both sides to wage war, as the two Batos were restricted to small raids, while the Legions were confined in their respective camps for the most part. In Emona, with Germanicus' blessing, we used the time to drill the men as much as was possible, given the conditions, still concentrating on Century and Cohort maneuvers, particularly the movements I judged the most likely to occur, namely going from marching column into open line formation, although I also added my own twist. Because so much of Pannonia is rugged terrain, where the only line of march can be up narrow draws that are not wide enough to accommodate our standard open battle formation, I added a slightly different *cornu* call that alerted the men that they were to open up with half the normal spacing. And, as I and every other Pannonian veteran knew, this makes fighting in our fashion extremely awkward, which is what prompted me to institute a training regimen that I had introduced to the Sixth of the First, after our battle by the lake the night the moon disappeared. In its simplest terms, I taught the men how to fight dirty, in the manner I had been taught by Vulso, the *lanista* in Arelate. However, I also had to make some changes to accommodate for the number of men in our ranks like Metellus, although I only did so after two of the older men were injured badly enough to be sent to the hospital with broken bones. Somewhat to my surprise, it was the freedmen and those who had never served under the standard who seemed to adapt to this unconventional training better than the Legionary veterans. Throughout the winter, we worked, while Germanicus traveled back and forth between Siscia whenever the weather allowed, and a sign of how seriously this was being taken by the Princeps was that Tiberius never went back to Rome. Under normal circumstances, I would have insisted on accompanying Germanicus to Siscia, if only for the excuse to visit with Domitius and my other friends, but with the 8th now in Naissus, it made more sense for me to stay behind. Not, I must say, that the men of Germanicus appreciated me staying behind, as Alex, acting as my eyes and ears, reported back to me that, with the help of men like Metellus, they had become convinced that I was possessed by the *numen* of my Avus. That I might have sprinkled a few *sesterces* about to help propagate this belief, in much the same way a farmer spreads his crops with manure, is something that I will neither confirm nor deny; all I cared about at the time was that it seemed to be working. I do not wish to make it sound like I was working alone, nor that Germanicus himself did not contribute significantly to the process of turning what was in truth a motley collection of mismatched parts into something at least resembling a cohesive fighting force worthy of marching for Rome. In the ways that probably mattered more, the young nobleman was the driving force behind giving these men something for which to fight, over and above the nebulous idea of fighting for the glory of Rome, and for the practical consideration of quelling a rebellion in a region in which they made their homes. In its simplest terms, by circulating among the rankers, spending the long watches of winter nights in the huts of the men he was going to lead, sharing cups of wines and listening to their war stories, Germanicus cemented his status as being a leader worthy of these men following, into whatever waited. And, while it seemed impossible when we were in the grips of the deepest part of winter, as is inevitable, the temperature slowly rose, the snows began to melt, and we made the last preparations to begin another campaign season.

It was now the second year of what was already called the Batonian Revolt, in the year of the Consulships of Quintus Caecilius Metellus Creticus Silanus, the adopted son of Caecilius Metellus, but the natural son of Marcus Silanus, who had been a Tribune during the ill-fated Marcus Primus campaign that my Avus had commanded as

Camp Prefect, and Aulus Licinius Nerva Silanus. On a blustery day in early March, I was summoned to meet with Germanicus, who had just returned from Siscia, and I walked into the *Praetorium* of Emona to a scene that, while it was reminiscent of my arrival in Siscia, was on a smaller scale. Germanicus, because of his unique status, did not have the kind of staff that a Legate of a Legion would, relying on a handful of friends he had brought from Rome, most of them around his age, to serve the functions of Tribunes, and it was one of them, who bore the somewhat unusual and simple name of Gaius Silius, who was acting as the duty Tribune. He waved me immediately past him, barely bothering to glance up from what he was doing, which appeared to be scribbling out what I took to be an order of some sort, given there was a man standing next to him, the leather satchel marking him as a courier slung over his neck. Entering Germanicus' office, he was also surrounded by a bevy of clerks, and his youthful features bore the harried look of a man who has suddenly been given some task that he is sure he does not have time to complete.

Instead of saying anything more, he extended a scroll to me, which I took, and the instant I unrolled it, I recognized the hand. It was from Tiberius, but that was not what made my heart feel as if it stopped, and I looked up at Germanicus, trying to determine if he was aware of the implications that were contained in the curtly worded orders.

"The Maezaei?" It did not feel like my mouth forming the words. "He's sending us against the Maezaei?"

Germanicus' expression changed slowly as he studied my face, informing me that he, in fact, did not understand why this was meaningful. The fleeting thought flashed through my mind that perhaps Tiberius had forgotten why I was now with the 1st Legion, but it died quickly. No, I was, and still am certain that he was acutely aware that sending Germanicus into Maezaei lands, when I was serving with him, would be a good way to ensure the most vehement reaction possible from these people. What was next to impossible for me to determine was what his goal was in doing so.

"Pullus," Germanicus asked me, his tone cautious, "what should I know about this?"

How would I explain this? I wondered.

"Perhaps you should clear your office first," I told him, which he immediately did. Sitting down, I pointed to an amphora of wine that was sitting on a stand behind his desk, saying, "And you might want to pour yourself a drink."

"I don't drink wine this early in the day," he answered a bit stiffly, but I only gave a chuckle.

"We'll see how long that lasts," was all I said.

Before I finished, he had consumed two cups.

As if this was not bad enough, that same night, as Alex was hustling about packing my baggage, there was a sharp rap on the door. Since he was busy, I walked to the door, thinking that it was a runner sent by Germanicus with a last moment detail he wanted me to attend. However, when I opened the door, my initial instinct was to slam it shut in the caller's face; that I did not was due to my recognition it would only make matters worse.

"*Salve*, Titus," Tiberius Dolabella greeted me with a cheerfulness that I had learned the agent used specifically with me, knowing how much it irritated me. "May I come in?"

"Do I have any choice?" I asked sourly, but I stepped aside and allowed him to enter the outer office.

"Not really," he replied with a relish I could not miss, reminding me how he liked to reinforce who held the whip hand at every opportunity; all I can say in my own defense is that, on occasion, I would catch him rubbing his neck as he eyed me, and I suspect that he went much further with the others who were of the same status as me.

"What do you want, Dolabella?" I indicated the open door to my private quarters, where Alex was clearly visible, hustling about the room. "I'm sure I don't have to tell you that we're marching in the next couple of days."

"No," he agreed, "you don't." Without my leave, he walked over and set himself down in the chair placed in front of the desk. "But there's something I need from you first."

"From me?" I echoed, and honestly, in that moment, I was not thinking along the same lines as Dolabella. "What could you need from me?"

His face betrayed nothing, but before he answered, he pointed at the opened door that led to my private quarters, and this was when I caught up with Tiberius' primary agent, understanding what he wanted, or being certain that I did. Biting back a curse, I walked over, pulled the door closed, then spun about; in that instant, I decided I was better served to just get this matter out of the way.

Just to be sure we were indeed addressing the same subject, I ventured, "You're here for some sort of report about Germanicus."

Dolabella inclined his head but said nothing; he just looked at me with the one eye he could control, while the other appeared to be looking at a spot somewhere behind me, and I was reminded how I always held the irrational fear that someone was sneaking up on me from behind whenever I talked to the man; only part of that feeling, I understood, came from his wayward eye.

"Well," I said at last, "there's nothing to report."

Once more Dolabella remained silent, just arching an eyebrow as he regarded me silently for several long heartbeats.

Finally, he broke the silence, his tone slightly mocking, "I find that hard to believe, Pullus. Surely the youngster said *something* that was…impolitic."

"Only that he knows that he's under more scrutiny from Tiberius than he is the Princeps," I shot back, and I was pleased to see I had rattled Dolabella, two spots of color coming to his cheeks.

Regardless, his tone was still measured as he countered, "And how would he know this, Pullus? Did someone tell him?" He paused, and I felt my body tense as my right hand began to clench, seemingly of its own volition, and I was grimly amused to see his own hand rise towards his throat, then seemed to notice it, thrusting it down into his lap, but he still went on, "Did you tell him, perhaps?"

97

Despite being certain this was what was coming, I still had to swallow the flare of anger, doing my best to match my tone to that of Dolabella when I replied, "No, Dolabella. I haven't. And," I pressed, "why would I since I'm one of those people? Maybe it's because he's clever enough to know that's the case. Maybe he has two good eyes in his head."

I confess to giving in to the urge for some malicious mischief, and I was pleased to see my jibe about the young Roman possessing two good eyes hit home with the other man.

"Yes." While to an uninformed ear, Dolabella sounded his normal self, I had worked with and provoked the man enough over the years to hear that he was struggling to rein in his anger. "It's probably as you say. But it is...interesting, don't you think? After all," he pointed to our surroundings, "he appointed you as a *de facto* Primus Pilus, didn't he? Some people might take that as a reward for some service you rendered."

"Or, it could be because I'm the most experienced man carrying the *vitus* in this ragged collection of misfits," I replied. Then, realizing this was going nowhere, I said wearily, "Dolabella, believe me or don't, but I didn't breathe a word to Germanicus that I'm supposed to watch him and wait for him to lose his temper and say something that Tiberius can use against him."

For the first time, Dolabella looked uncomfortable; my guess was hearing it put in such bald terms was not the kind of thing a man who works in shadows and whispers wanted put so plainly, especially because it was the truth.

"Very well, Pullus," he said at last. "I'll report back to Tiberius that the boy is minding his manners."

"Why the Maezaei?" I blurted the question out, but unlike most other times, this was calculated on my part. "Why is Tiberius sending Germanicus against the Maezaei when I'm with him?"

Dolabella surprised me then, as a strange expression crossed his face, one with which I did not have much familiarity in connection to him, which I decided was one of bemusement.

98

This seemed to be confirmed by his words when he admitted, "That, I don't know." He hesitated before he finished, "But I've wondered about that as well."

Frankly, I did not know whether or not to feel comforted by the idea that Tiberius was keeping Dolabella in the dark, and a part of me did think that, perhaps, just perhaps the Legate had forgotten about my episode with the Maezaei. Even as the thought crossed my mind, I dismissed it; as I had learned, both through my Avus' account and my own experience, it was always safer to assume the worst when it came to the motives of Rome's upper class. I saw Dolabella out, and perhaps for the first time, our moods seemed to match; both of us were left in states of worried thought.

Three days later, what had become known as the *Legio Germanicus* marched from Emona, heading south towards the territory of the Maezaei tribe. Rather than head southeast and march through Siscia, we took a less developed road that led almost directly south, taking us through Colapiani lands, but more to my dismay, through the western edge of the ground where so many Romans had come to grief, when one or more of the three tribes who shared this territory rebelled, then went scurrying into this nightmare of narrow draws, steep and heavily wooded slopes, and hundreds, probably thousands of caves. Regardless of my direst warnings, Germanicus was determined to take this more direct route, and while I never asked him, I strongly suspect that his decision was based as much in his desire to avoid Siscia, where Tiberius had wintered. Not that Germanicus' adoptive father would have been there, but we did not know that at the time, which meant that men like me, Metellus, and a few hundred other of the old veterans of the Army of Pannonia were especially alert and on edge as we traversed through this area. Thankfully, nothing untoward occurred, other than multiple signs that we were being watched every mile of the way, something that Gaesorix, as one of the cavalry scouts, was never shy to remind me of whenever he stopped by my tent.

"There are as many Pannonians as there are trees," he grumbled one night as we shared a cup of wine. "You can feel their eyes on us every moment." The Batavian actually shuddered, and I wondered why he seemed so shaken, but he explained with his next comment. "Or perhaps they're the spirits of all the men who have died here."

My first reaction was to laugh, then I saw he was not jesting, yet I am afraid I could not completely resist from teasing him when I replied, "But at least a good number of them are Roman spirits."

Gaesorix gave a dismissive snort, then said, "As if that matters! Once a man crosses over into the spirit lands, he is no longer Roman or Colapiani. All he knows is that he is cursed to live in the lands where he died, and that he does not appreciate intruders."

"Except for Batavians?" I grinned as I said this, and he actually glared at me for the span of a couple heartbeats, then laughed.

"Of course!" He raised his cup. "We Batavians are promised a place in Gimlé!"

Although I had heard this place mentioned before and knew that it was a desirable place for a man to go after he died, I asked curiously, "What's that mean exactly?"

The Decurion looked surprised, as if this was obvious, but he answered, "Why, it's the best hall, of course!" He gave me a smug smile as he added, "Just being a Batavian guarantees you this! Everyone knows that!"

Despite myself, I could not resist prodding him by asking with a mock skepticism, "Even the man who stole your woman from you because he was a prince?"

The smile vanished, and he growled, "That dog? That...minion? No," he actually spat on the floor of my quarters, "he's going to Hvergelmir, where the serpent Níðhǫggr will gnaw on his bones for eternity!"

"That," I interjected mildly, "sounds painful."

Gaesorix glared at me for a moment, then once more his normal good humor returned, and he lifted his cup and said as if this was the cheeriest thought of all. "It's a torment beyond belief, Pullus! And the best part is that it lasts forever!"

He left not long after that, and I was just thankful that I had managed to divert him from the gloomy train of thought he had been engaged in when he first arrived; I was nervous enough as it was being where we were.

We all heaved a sigh of relief, to one degree or another, once we descended from the rough country, making camp where the junction of the road we were traveling south intersected with the main road that, if we took it east, would lead us eventually to The Quarry and through the very heart of Colapiani lands. If we took this route, we would intersect with the main road leading south from Siscia that led directly into the geographical center of Maezaei territory, straight to Splonum, where we would approach from the north. For the same reason Atticus had decided we would take the more indirect route that led through Clandate, I urged Germanicus to take the longer but, at least in my judgment, safer route. In order to do this, we had to take a road west and slightly south for about ten miles before we returned to a straight, southerly course. Germanicus, however, was not swayed, but while my initial reaction was that he was just being stubborn for its own sake, he surprised me considerably.

"The reason," he explained to the assembled officers, "we're not taking the route that Pullus suggests is that it would take us through Raetinium, which has been occupied by the Maezaei, and they have strengthened it, which tells me they are expecting us to come that way."

This took me completely by surprise, and it also irritated me that Germanicus had not seen fit to share this with me beforehand, but he clearly saw and correctly interpreted my look, because he offered, "Pullus, I just learned of this from the last courier that caught up with us earlier today."

I was forced to swallow my indignation, realizing that, indeed, a hard-riding courier had come charging up from behind our line of march, delivering a message to Germanicus. Although I had been riding next to the First Cohort, who was marching near the rear of our small column, since I had convinced Germanicus that the feed and attendants needed to support every man being mounted far outweighed the benefit, I did recall this event, even remembering that I reminded myself to ask about it, which I had clearly forgotten to do.

Mollified, I nodded my understanding, and he continued, "As I understand it, there is no way for us to bypass Raetinium without an assault, and even if we could, and approached Clandate by the road from the southwest, we'd have a significant force of Maezaei in our rear. And we would still have to take Splonum. So," he drew a breath, and I caught him glancing in my direction, "I've decided better to take Splonum first, while we're fresh, then decide the best way to attack Raetinium. Which means," he finished, "we're taking the road due east through Colapiani territory, then turning south to Clandate on the road to the west, past Topulcava."

Just the mention of the Colapiani capital, home to their chieftain, now Veco, who had replaced the slain Draxo and managed to remain in power for the past decade, brought forth so many memories that, before I could stop myself, I physically shuddered, something that Gaesorix, standing next to me, clearly did not miss. I felt his eyes on me, regarding me steadily, but I ignored him, studiously keeping my gaze fixed on our young Legate.

Whereas Gaesorix had been wary before, now he was distinctly unsettled, but only part of his discontent was based in the proximity of the Maezaei; the idea of riding directly through the heart of yet another tribe was a good cause for unease, so I did not blame him in the slightest, although I refused to divulge the cause for my display. Speaking of the cavalry, Germanicus was in overall command, of course, as he was the infantry, but at my urging, he had given Gaesorix operational command, although this did not sit well with Germanicus' handful of noble friends, all of whom seemed to feel that they were qualified by their status to lead a veteran cavalry contingent into the lands of hostile rebels. Fortunately, the youngster listened to my counsel, or so I believed, though he may have decided this without my input, since he also directed that a Tribune, who at the time I only knew as Marcus Frugi, serve as Gaesorix's second.

Despite our fears, the Colapiani, to this point, had remained loyal, if by this one means they were not in open rebellion. Since it was impossible to bypass Topulcava, we halted a couple miles west of the town to allow the men to uncover their shields, although Germanicus had ordered us to march in our armor at all times, knowing that uncovered shields are the most potent sign to barbarians that we were not only prepared, we were expecting trouble. Whether or not this was the cause, all that really mattered was that we marched through unmolested, though this is only due to the fact that looks cannot kill men, unless, of course, they are from Medusa. That the men were uncharacteristically silent, so the only real sound was the deep, thudding sound of thousands of hobnailed *caligae*, accompanied by plodding hoof beats and creaking leather, was the most potent sign to me that they were aware of our precarious position. It is impossible for me to say with any certainty, but I would like to think that the time I had spent circulating around the camp the night before we passed through the town, recounting the story of the riot, albeit with some modification, helped make this a reality. Hopefully, the gods will forgive me for omitting certain details, such as the fact that we were there working in what we call an off-the-books capacity, illegally impressing young Colapiani into the auxiliaries, a ruse created by Urso to cover his larger crime of selling old armor to Draxo. As far as the men of the *Legio Germanicus* were concerned, we were engaged in a perfectly legal operation, during a time when there were no open hostilities between the Colapiani and Rome, which meant they were even more on guard this day, years later. Once we passed through Topulcava, we came to the road that leads directly to Clandate from the north, and by the end of that day, we left Colapiani territory when we crossed the Valdasus at a point where it traveled on an east/west axis for a few miles. Making camp with the river serving as protection from any mischief from the Colapiani to the north, we doubled the guard that night, but it passed uneventfully. The next morning dawned bright and clear, and it quickly became obvious that this day would be the warmest we had experienced yet. This made the men happy, until the patches of snow that were still piled high in shaded areas began to

103

melt, making the track muddy. Before the midday break, we reached the first in a series of smaller roads that I knew led up to the first of the mines that were the source of Maezaei wealth.

"Should we send a Century to each mine to destroy it?" he asked, and while he glanced in the direction of his *de facto* staff, his gaze stopped with me.

I did not hesitate, shaking my head and saying, "No, sir." Although I did not relish addressing Germanicus in this way, I had reconciled myself to doing it, seeing it as the best way to support our young commander in front of others. "At least," I amended slightly, "not yet. We should press on to Clandate first and see what the situation is there." Indicating the sun, I reminded him, "We have about two watches of daylight left, and it's going to take two-thirds of one just to get there."

This seemed to clinch the decision, and we resumed shortly after that, but along with Gaesorix and one *turma* ranging ahead, I suggested to Germanicus that he also send a full Century out ahead of us, one from the First Cohort at that. To that end, the Sixth was sent out, under the command of Lucius Cornelius Blasio, who was one of the men to accompany Germanicus from Rome, but between our caution, and the mud from the snow melt, our progress was slower than we would have liked. Then, we negotiated the gentle bend that brought in sight the place that, a bit short of four years before, I had approached, carrying within me a raging sorrow and a savage desire to inflict the same pain I was feeling on anyone and everyone within reach of my *gladius* who was not wearing the uniform of a Roman Legionary. Although that feeling was still there, and has never really gone away, I would liken it to a smoldering fire that has almost died out when one arises in the morning to revive it.

As we expected, the village was deserted, and much to the disappointment of the men, anything and everything of any value had been stripped from it, although that did not stop at least one quarrel from breaking out over what to me appeared to be a carved wooden comb that had several tines splintered from it. Not that the two combatants seemed to think so, and I was forced to wade in with my *vitus*, thrashing the two; when I did, I recognized them not as old veterans, but as part of the contingent of freedmen, whose fighting qualities and, frankly, level of discipline concerned me the most when I considered this motley collection. Otherwise, we took the village without incident, although I did notice that the building I had ordered burned down had been rebuilt, this time of stone, but it was in the same spot and clearly served the same purpose. When I looked at it, I felt nothing but the same feeling of sadness that carried the similar kind of ache as an old wound. Once it was determined that there were no Maezaei present, Germanicus ordered camp to be made as I talked with the men serving as Pili Priores. I say "men," though I use this in the loosest sense; of those appointed by Germanicus as Centurions, Metellus was by far the oldest, but I was actually the second oldest, just days away from my thirty-third birthday. Otherwise, the men selected to serve as leaders of our five full Cohorts would normally have been of Tribune rank drawn from Germanicus' companions, but these were not normal times, and this was not a normal force, meaning they had to accept being considered Centurions. While Germanicus had acquiesced in allowing Metellus to serve as a Centurion, he had balked at making him a Pilus Prior, but being a man of his word, my former comrade was now the highest paid Secundus Pilus Posterior, under the command of one Marcus Asinius Agrippa, who I had learned was actually a friend of Germanicus', not just an acquaintance like some of the others, which made sense given his roots as the grandson of the great Agrippa. His posting as the Secundus Pilus Prior, I had learned through Alex, was not met without opposition, namely from the youngster who was leading the Third Cohort, another nobleman by the name of Publius Cornelius Lentulus Scipio, and who, unsurprisingly, went by the more famous *cognomen* of Scipio. From what Alex had gleaned, through one of Germanicus' personal scribes, Scipio insisted that his name alone served as qualification to not lead not just any Cohort, but the First, and if not the First, then the Second. My nephew, knowing I would undoubtedly be interested, drew from his own precious but small hoard of coins in order to learn the details, and somewhat to my surprise, he found out that Germanicus flatly refused, either to alter the order of his appointments, or more importantly to me, to replace me as the *de facto* Primus Pilus, although I will also say that I was never once referred to by that title whenever Germanicus held a meeting of all the officers. While I was slightly upset that this was the case, I forced myself to think rationally, and I recognized this was an example of the adroit manner in which Germanicus was handling being thrust into an extremely challenging and precarious position. And, ultimately, what mattered to me more than being addressed as such was that I was actually in command of the First Cohort; I could only hope a notation of this fact was entered into my record. Despite the fact that he never said as much, I will cross the river with the belief that Germanicus was acutely aware that his adoptive father had put him in a position to fail, at the very least, or be killed trying to carry out the task he had been assigned, thereby removing another rival to the leadership of our Empire. Now, in Clandate, I was stuck trying to advise the acting Pili Priores on what I was about to suggest to Germanicus, and not surprising me in the least, it was Scipio who not only disagreed, but was openly mocking.

"If we do as you suggest, we're going to be cut to pieces!"

Biting the inside of my cheek, I replied patiently, "It's not without risk, but in my opinion, it gives us the best opportunity to hit the Maezaei and perhaps catch them off guard."

"'Not without risk,'" Scipio mimicked, except before he could say anything more, I cut him off, not by saying anything but suddenly moving closer to him so I could stare down at the haughty bastard.

Then the *bucina* sounded the call that summoned me to attend to Germanicus, and I left a visibly relieved nobleman and his comrades, wondering for the thousandth time how this was supposed to work.

"That," Germanicus' doubt was reflected in his tone, "is very risky, Pullus."

"Yes, it is," I agreed, yet whereas Scipio had been openly dismissive, I could hear by Germanicus' tone he was at least thinking about it. "But if we wait until tomorrow, then march to Splonum, not only will it be in daylight, there's no chance of any surprise. This way, if we move immediately, we can get in position to strike at first light."

"But," he countered, "what are the chances of being able to get close enough in the dark without alerting their sentries? Surely they'll have at least double their normal numbers. And," he pointed out, "I've heard you say more times than you can count that our men are too raw for anything complex like moving at night."

This, I was forced to admit to myself, was absolutely true, but I had thought of little else since we determined that this village was deserted, and as shaky a plan as I was offering, no matter how many times I went over it, I shuddered to think about what would happen if we took the conventional route, which would take us directly underneath the walls of that stone fort. And, even if we made it past the fort without suffering heavy losses, we would have to reduce it before assaulting the edifice on the opposite side of the valley, which served as both royal palace of the Maezaei king and stronghold that guarded the entrance into Splonum from the north. I had at least learned that Dodonis, who had used our reprisal against the Maezaei for the murder of Sextus and two other men as the pretext for deposing Gurgos, was still in power, not that this meant all that much, at least at this point. While I knew the man, back when he had been councilor to Admetos, there was not much to glean from when he was forced to ride a mule under escort, but what little I did recall was the feeling then, which was reinforced when he usurped Gurgos, that while he might not have been a formidable warrior, he possessed a level of cunning that we should not underestimate.

This was what I had in mind when I continued to press the issue, arguing, "While I can't say with any certainty that we won't suffer heavy losses, either because we stumble into their sentries and they raise the alarm, or when the sun rises, we're so disorganized that they can pick us apart one Cohort at a time, what I can promise you is that if we wait until daylight, then take the normal approach from this direction, Dodonis will have all manner of nasty surprises waiting for us."

I saw this had scored with Germanicus, but he was not convinced, signaled by the rubbing of his chin as he frowned at me, then asked, "What if we do something similar to what you're suggesting?"

"Which is?" I asked, unsure what he had in mind.

Once he described his proposed changes, I was forced to admit that, despite his youth, Germanicus had a flair for military matters. Simply put, his idea was better than mine had been.

We left the camp barely a full watch after it was finished, just on the western edge of the village, leaving behind the four Centuries that, if we had more men, would have made for a Sixth Cohort. Two of these Centuries were the Taurisci auxiliaries, with the other two Centuries composed almost completely of the freedmen, slaves of some of the higher-ranking noblemen, and a scattering of veterans. If I am being completely honest, I did not think much of their chances should the Maezaei, thinking along the same vein we were, show up to attack the camp. Despite the fact that we were marching towards Splonum, it was no longer the plan to try and move into position for an attack at first light, at least immediately. Instead, we marched in battle order, with each Century of every Cohort carrying two ladders apiece, and while we began by taking the normal track that led to Splonum, once we covered about five miles, we turned off this, using an even narrower path that led up to one of the mines. It was a narrow, sinuous route, just wide enough for two deep grooves to be worn into the rocky ground by the carts hauling ore, which meant we had to narrow our front. In turn, of course, this made our progress slower, compounded by frequent halts as our scouts saw or heard something suspicious. The cavalry had left the camp with us, but unlike the Cohorts, they had continued towards Splonum, where they were to stop no more than three miles from the village, their approach hopefully muffled by the rags wrapped around the horses' hooves and secured with leather thongs.

Meanwhile, we marched, or more accurately, stumbled upward, deeper into the hills, with Germanicus at our head, something that I had tried to dissuade him from doing, but I suppose I had been too gentle in my admonishment since he clearly did not heed me. To this point, we had not experienced any bumps in our relationship, but this would be the first real test of whether or not he was disposed to listen to me once the initial javelin flew. The mine would be the spot where the main body would wait, while two sections' worth of men, each of whom I had carefully selected, and who I would be leading, continued towards Splonum. Our task would be to climb the last set of hills that separated Splonum from the mine, moving as stealthily as we could, in an attempt to find sentries who Dodonis had likely posted farther out from the town than normal. If we could remove these men, we believed it would be possible to move into a position where we would be above the stone fort, which sat on a shelf of rock about a third of the way up the slope of the hill on the southern side of the road that led to Clandate.

As part of their standard practice, the slope above the fort had been cleared of trees and undergrowth, leaving only the stumps liberally dotting the hillside. However, they had not cleared the slope all the way to the top, although it was more than the standard two hundred paces. Granted, I was going by memory, and I did caution my young Legate that it was entirely possible that, in the light of the recent developments, they had taken further precautions. Regardless, we were going to operate on the idea that the defenses were still in the state I had last seen them, and if there was indeed cover atop the very crest of the hill above the fort, we were going to put a Cohort above it, hidden in the trees, while the other Cohorts would be arrayed along the opposite side of the ridge that overlooks Splonum from the west until shortly before dawn. In my estimation, we had no chance whatsoever of surprising the Maezaei completely; we had seen far too many signs of their warriors watching us from the wooded hills to believe this was possible. Still, I did believe, and I convinced Germanicus, that there was a way to catch them off balance, although only part of it was based in the maneuvers we were undertaking during the night. Ultimately, what I believed would work in our favor was our own practices; Rome is nothing if not predictable, and I felt a modicum of certainty that Dodonis would expect us to come marching down the road, arrayed as we always had before, including the last time I had marched with the 8th. If I was right, the Maezaei chieftain would have arrayed his defenses so that men, tasked with giving early warning, would be spread along the rough road from Clandate; the question was how far out from Splonum they would be located. The mine was a shade less than four miles from Splonum, and I led one group, while Metellus led the second. It should come as no surprise that I had selected only veterans and forbade any of Germanicus' young nobility from even participating, let alone leading something that, predictably, Scipio objected to more strenuously than any of the others. Going further, I only had old veterans from the 8th, for the simple reason of familiarity, not just me with them, but with each other. Not that, aside from Metellus, any of these men had been in any of the Centuries in which I had served, but I knew them all by sight, and a couple by reputation.

As I had done before, I had donned my extra tunic over my *hamata*, except this was where we ran into the first snag, since the rankers' *segmentata*, which in general is superior to the old chain mail, is too bulky to be covered by a tunic. This engendered a last-moment scramble where I went to the acting *Quaestor*, Gaius Fufius, and requisitioned enough *hamatae* for our party, not without swearing on my honor as a Centurion that I would not only return each one, but should they be damaged, pay for the repairs from my own purse. Apparently, what that meant, that blood would probably have to be scrubbed off because the man wearing it was dead, held no real import for him. Under normal circumstances, I would have balked, but I grudgingly agreed, although the delay took time we could ill afford, something for which I took responsibility, knowing this was something I should have thought about beforehand. With our exposed areas rubbed first with oil, then with charcoal, we set out, although at least one of us was still not happy to be part of this.

"I still don't know why you wanted me to come," Metellus grumbled for what I was certain was the tenth time. "I'm…"

"Yes," I sighed, "I know. You're too old for this *cac*."

"Exactly!" he insisted mulishly. "I'm an old, decrepit man! We're not made to go stomping up and down hills, through woods so thick you can't see five feet ahead of you! That's for youngsters!"

That he was saying this as he walked behind me was more important to me than whether he was happy about it or not, yet I did point out, "Remember, I've seen you work at night, which is why I picked you. Besides, you took the money, and you're getting paid as a Pilus Prior at that. Now," I said equably, "shut up and save your breath. We're about to start climbing."

My old comrade only partially complied, muttering under his breath, which I ignored, mainly because I was following my own advice. For the next full watch, we stayed together, climbing the first ridge, descending it, then ascending partway up the second before we stopped for more than a few heartbeats.

I looked to Metellus, who was panting so heavily that I was alarmed he might keel over, making me wonder if he had been right, but when I asked him if he needed more time, he shook his head, so I whispered, "This is where we split up." Turning and pointing directly up the slope, I told Metellus, "You need to work in pairs but spread out as far as you possibly can. If you find any sentries, you know what to do. But," even as I said this, I knew it was wasted breath admonishing these veterans, "do it quick and quiet."

"I just hope the moon doesn't disappear like the last time we were doing something like this," he muttered; surprisingly, this was the first I thought of that night by the lake.

"It won't," I assured him. "That was a once in a lifetime event."

"So is this," he shot back sourly, but he was moving as he said it.

With that, I took my section, moving along the slope in the direction of the stone fort, which, according to my best guess, was more than a mile away, and the crest of this ridge was between us and it, while we also needed to cross the road from Clandate. Somewhere ahead of us, I felt certain, we would find an outpost of some sort, probably more than one. One thing working in our favor was that, although the Maezaei sentries would not betray their presence by the light of a fire or fires that were fully ablaze, they had to have some

111

method to relay signals, which meant that it was highly likely that there was something, either in the form of smoldering coals from a fire they had built during the day, or a shielded lamp they could use to ignite a pyre, and at night that would be more than enough for us to spot, or so I hoped. And, in order to have an unbroken line of sight down to the valley floor where the road was located, they would have to be positioned in a cleared area on the hillside, which would in all likelihood be manmade.

Despite the darkness, the sky was only partially cloudy, and the half-moon provided just enough light that would allow us to see clearings, no matter who made them. This, at least, was my belief, and we were about to find out if I was right. Setting the pace as quickly as I could manage while still maintaining a semblance of stealth, I led the others, peering ahead and occasionally stopping when we reached a thick clump of undergrowth. Then, one of us would creep forward to check on what was on the other side. Every time this happened, I felt certain this would be the time where we would find a clearing with men standing watch, as much as barbarian tribes performed this duty, which is to barely tolerate it and go through the motions. I had learned that this serves true for the tribes of Germania as much as it does for Pannonia, so my assumption is that, in all likelihood, only we Romans approach this duty so diligently; of course, since falling asleep is not only punishable by death, but at the hands of one's own comrades, I suppose it makes sense that we pay attention. As nearly as I could estimate, we traversed more than a mile, and I was growing increasingly anxious, calculating that we should be close to a spot where the road from Clandate would be visible. Although it was a possibility that Dodonis had been content to maintain his normal routine regarding sentries, I did not consider it seriously, so I began to worry that perhaps they were even farther down this hill; or, even worse, they were a mile back in the direction of Clandate. Finally, I whispered a halt, and the section huddled around me as I tried to think what to do.

"I think," I whispered, "you're going to have to split up into four groups. Then," I pointed downhill first, "two groups go farther downhill, one about two hundred paces, the other another two hundred farther than that. And," I indicated the opposite direction, "one group goes another two hundred paces uphill, although that will put you very near the top, so be careful to avoid the skyline." I finished by saying, "And the last keeps moving ahead from here."

"What about you?" Lucius Pulvillus, who I had appointed my second in command, whispered. "Which of us are you going with?"

"None of you," I answered in the same manner. "I'm going on by myself."

I was not surprised at the reaction of the others, who, even in the dim light, I saw stiffen in surprise, but it was Pulvillus who shook his head as he spoke just above a whisper, although he said only, "I hope you know what you're doing. You know there's going to be more than one sentry and probably more than two."

"I know," I assured them. "I'll be careful, but we're running out of time."

With that, we split up, and I began heading directly for one spot in particular.

I cannot say exactly when I recalled something that I had previously forgotten, although it was at some point after we began our search. And, the truth is that my memory was secondhand, something that I learned from someone from another Cohort when I was still marching with the 8th. My defense is that my mind was on other matters at the time, because it was in the aftermath of what had taken place in Splonum after Sextus' death, and I was more worried about my fate than any piece of information that I could possibly use later. It concerned something that men of the Tenth Cohort, who had been sent by Atticus on a search for Maezaei who had fled from Splonum, with orders to round them up and escort them back, found during their task. The only way they discovered it was by literally stumbling on it, because the watchtower was not only not very high, but had been built in an opening just large enough for the tower itself. Not only that, it had been built up against a sheer rock face that, under normal circumstances would have been easily visible from the valley floor, the white travertine ribs of the ridge standing out from the otherwise green hillside. Apparently, the tower had been festooned with cut branches that made it blend into the background perfectly; I imagined that these must be replaced at regular intervals, since the dried, brown branches of evergreen trees would stand out almost as much as the bare rock. Along with this memory, I had recalled a random comment I overheard from one of the rankers who had been charged with guarding me on our march back to Siscia.

"Those bastards put that tower right above that spot where the road snakes around those big fucking boulders, but the only way we found it is from above, because they didn't cover up the roof. Which," the unseen Legionary added, "makes sense since there's no way to see it from below."

Once I recalled this bit of information, I knew the exact spot the ranker had been referring to, and even from high above the valley floor, those two boulders were easy to spot; one of them as large as a section hut, the other on the opposite side of the road only slightly smaller. Since there was no way to remove these obstacles, the road had just wound around them, and it was a simple matter to move to a small bare spot on the hill that allowed me to find them down below. Once I did, I began climbing towards the top of the ridge while cutting across at an angle that placed the boulders directly below me, so that I was almost to the top when I aligned the boulders in my sight. I desperately wanted to pause for breath, but I could not afford the time, telling myself that since I would be going downhill from this point, I could at least not exert myself as much, something I learned was untrue very quickly. Because I was trying to be quiet, before I had gone fifty paces downhill, my legs were shaking uncontrollably, while my arms were beginning to ache from grabbing first one tree trunk, then another as I descended. Seemingly inch by inch, I made my way down the hill, my eyes beginning to water from the strain of looking for the roughly square shape of a watchtower roof, but when I spotted it, I suppose between my fatigue and the tension, it took the span of several heartbeats for my tired body to respond to the command from my equally weary mind to actually stop moving. What this meant in a practical sense was that I was less than a pace away from being directly on top of the watchtower, yet somehow I managed to stop myself, although it was with my foot hovering just above the first rough-hewn log forming the roof of the watchtower. So startled was I that I froze, probably looking quite ridiculous with my foot just hanging out in open space, but it was also to force myself to listen for any sign that my approach had been detected. For a horribly long moment, I was certain that I had been, if only because of the complete silence, except for the wind making the trees whisper their song that is part of the background noise that one learns to ignore. Surely, I thought, they must have heard me, if only because I could not hear any noise coming from the tower, which I took to mean they were listening as intently as I was. Then, I heard a low muttering, and while I could not make out the words, just by the cadence of the speech, I understood a man was speaking in the Maezaei tongue. He's probably warning his comrade to get ready to move, I thought with a stab of fear, which was only heightened when the next thing that came to me was the next worry, or comrades as I reminded myself of the possibility that there were more than just two sentries. Then, there was a low laugh, and I almost collapsed in relief, recognizing that if these men suspected an enemy was nearby, they would not be sharing a joke. I pulled my foot back and placed it on the ground, slowly of course, and began examining the tower more closely, trying to determine the best way to attack. With some difficulty, I made out the parapet that enclosed three sides of the tower, while the back side of it was shielded by the bare rock face, finally leaning over to look down past the edge of the roof, on the right side first, then the left. On the left, I saw a slightly lighter object, and it took a moment to recognize that one of the sentries was resting his arm on the parapet. Judging by the position, I guessed he was leaning against the rock that formed the back of the tower, and while I considered swinging down and attacking from this side, I dismissed it, since his body would be between me and his weapon. Under normal circumstances, this would be my preferred method of attack, but given the cramped quarters in which I would be operating, I calculated that it was more important to instantly reduce the distance to the weapon of my first foe. To that end, I carefully shifted my weight, sliding back to the right side of the tower. My *gladius* was still in its sheath, which I had strapped to my back so that it would not snag on the underbrush, and I knew this would be the most likely moment for me to be detected; the drawing of a blade from its scabbard is a distinctive sound that even a novice warrior will recognize. Consequently, I inched the blade out, moving as slowly as I could manage, while the men below me continued their exchange, which helped mask the noise. Finally, the blade was out, and the feeling of a weapon that was so shaped to my hand that it felt like more of an extension of my own body actually served to calm me. Inching even further to the right, I stared at the opening, where I could just make out a darker bulk that I felt certain was the warrior on the right hand side. This was confirmed when he suddenly reached out with his arm, which was silhouetted against the slightly lighter background. I realized he was pointing at something; I got my answer about what it was when, across the valley floor and roughly directly opposite, there was a sudden flare of light.

The span of heartbeats immediately following the lighting of the signal fire are somewhat jumbled in my mind; what I do recall was that I began moving almost immediately. Hopping down onto the roof, I was on it only long enough to drop into a crouch as I grabbed the edge of the covering with my left hand, then thrust my body out and down so that I could swing feet first into the opening. As I hoped, the hobnail soles of my *caligae* smashed into something substantial, signaled by the shout of alarm that was cut off when my weight drove into the body of the Maezaei nearest to me. That he went sprawling into the warrior to his left had been my plan; that instead of only two, there were three men in the watchtower was something I learned in the span of time it took me to finish landing on the wooden platform of the tower. It was no more than five feet square, making it cramped for three men; with four, it meant I had very little room to use my *gladius*. Despite this, I managed to thrust down into the body of the Maezaei I had knocked sprawling, feeling the spasm of his body vibrating up through my blade, yet even as I did so, the Maezaei on the opposite side of the tower must have used this eyeblink of time to find and grab his own weapon. That it was a spear meant he had to draw his arm back farther than with a *gladius*, which I believe saved my life, as my eyes picked up the movement just in time to twist my torso so that the iron spear point struck a glancing blow, rather than a direct strike that would have punched right through my mail and into my lower left chest. Even so, my breath left me in an explosive gasp, and it felt like Latobius had kicked me in the side. Reaching out blindly, I somehow managed to grab the shaft of the warrior's spear, which he must have sensed because he reacted by yanking violently in the opposite direction, but while I felt the wood slip some in my hand, that was all it did. Even as this was happening, I pulled my own right arm as far back as it would go until I felt it hit the parapet, with the intention of delivering my own thrust while I had this man's spear immobilized. Before I could, the Maezaei I had stabbed first seemed to have a sudden spasm, which I initially thought was a death throe, except that his upper body actually rose up from the floor. All I recall from the moment is the outline of the Maezaei on the opposite side of the tower suddenly being obscured by the body of a man I thought I had, if not killed outright, then mortally wounded, but it was the manner in which the Maezaei was suddenly thrust against me that made me understand that it was because of the third warrior present, who was using his comrade's body as a makeshift shield. Honestly, I do recall the irrational thought that this first Maezaei was somehow possessed by some animating *numen*, and for the first time, I became conscious of a low moaning, although for all I knew, it could have been coming from me, caused by superstitious fear.

Over the span of perhaps two or three heartbeats, I determined that the third man was now pushing against the body of his comrade against me to pin me against the parapet so that he could produce his own weapon. Fortunately, because the parapet only came up to my lower thighs, just under my buttocks, I was able to lean backward out of the tower, though I very quickly felt my body reach the balance point, and I had to begin pushing back to keep from toppling out.

117

Instead of my original target, I extended my arm so I could move my *gladius* out farther from my body, angling the point in something I suppose resembled a third position thrust. The difference was that what I was now sure was a corpse was blocking my ability to pick a spot on the live Maezaei's body in which to plunge my blade rather than the normal defense of a shield. Normally, I did not like just stabbing and flailing about wildly, but not only did I have little choice, I could tell my grip of the second Maezaei's spear was failing as he continued to tug furiously at it. Perhaps the oddest part of this moment was that, other than our harsh breathing and the moan I had heard, none of us were making much noise, something for which I would be thankful later. In that instant, however, with my arm almost fully extended and with the blade parallel to the wooden platform, I was unable to twist my body, thereby relying only on the strength of my arm as I swung it inward, in the direction of my torso while extending it out as far as I was able, until my bicep collided with the body of the dead Maezaei being used to pin me in place. Although it was not as solid a strike as my first thrust had been, I felt the impact, followed less than an eyeblink later by a roar of pain that finally shattered the silence. Just by the manner in which the Maezaei bellowed told me it was a damaging but not mortal blow, yet even before my arm had returned to its original position, my left hand finally failed, and the spear was jerked from my grasp. With my left hand suddenly free, I wasted no time, moving it to a spot between my own body and that of the dead man, my hand immediately becoming covered in blood as I shoved him away from me, using all of my available strength. It was not with the same amount of force generated by my entire body when I swung down into the tower, but it was enough to once more send the man on the other side of the corpse I had just wounded staggering backward, except this time, instead of losing his feet, he inadvertently did me a favor because he caromed into the Maezaei with the spear, whereupon all three of my foes collapsed in a confused heap. In the darkness, I honestly could only make out a jumble of limbs, but I did not waste my time trying to match which pair of legs belonged to which torso, instead using one long stride to stab down into the pile repeatedly, ignoring the sudden eruption of pleas for mercy from the two surviving Maezaei, not stopping until nothing in the pile was moving. Gradually, I became aware that the only sound was my panting, and I am afraid I collapsed onto the platform, ignoring the sticky wetness that I dimly saw was slowly spreading outward in a pool that surrounded first my feet, then reached my buttocks as I sat there, trying to gather myself.

While it could not be considered a particularly neat foray, we managed to find all of Dodonis' sentries, or at least those who could have ruined our plans. As we expected, they had all been in pairs with the exception of the tower and one other spot, strung out along a line that gave them vantage points that extended down the road to Clandate for more than three miles. By the manner in which they had been arranged, it also became clear they had been set up as a series of relay stations, meaning it was only by luck that the tower had been the next and final relay point, and my actions had stopped the sentries from passing along the signal to men stationed in the fort. Although the Maezaei in the nearest post to the tower had managed to light their fire before the pair of veterans, Gnaeus Archias and Tiberius Calidas, both formerly of the 8th, managed to subdue them, that was as far as the attempt to alert their fellow tribesmen had gotten. Metellus' men managed to find all but one outpost, although we did not determine this during the night, but the surviving sentries were too far removed to do anything other than light their fire for the next outpost to pass along, which we had already subdued. Despite being successful overall, it was not without cost; one man of Metellus' section died during their attack on what turned out to be a four-man outpost, with another badly wounded, while the section under my command suffered two men wounded, one of whom died the next day.

Once I had regained my breath, I climbed out of the tower, then as quickly as I could, made my way directly down the hill. Using the pair of boulders once more as a landmark, I trotted back up the road in the direction of where the cavalry was waiting, offering the watchword when I was challenged. Gaesorix was waiting with

Latobius, but I went on alone, as the Batavian and the cavalry waited for the rest of the men of my section, who had been instructed to come down to the road and find the cavalry. Despite my best attempts to time everything perfectly, I was acutely conscious that dawn was rapidly approaching, which forced me to put Latobius almost to the gallop in the darkness, and with every ground-eating stride, I braced myself for him to stumble. Somehow, through no actions of mine, my horse did not fail me, and I reached Germanicus and the Cohorts whole and sound. Informing him of our success, the young Legate did not hesitate, giving the verbal commands necessary to get the men roused from where they had been sitting under strict instructions for total silence. Very quickly, with a speed that would have done no shame to a regular Legion, the Germanicus men formed up, and within no more than a sixth part of a watch after I arrived, we were moving into our final positions. Those slaves and freedmen who served as *medici*, stretcher bearers, and the like were left behind, including Alex, to whom I handed the reins of Latobius, not before thanking my mount with one of the apples that Alex carried.

Germanicus happened to see this, and despite the circumstances, laughed and teased me, "Pullus, I think you have the most spoiled horse I've ever seen!"

This, I knew, was a charge I could not deny, so I did not try, only saying, "That's why I know he'll never fail me! Because if he did," I wagged my finger at my horse, who was munching unconcernedly and completely unfazed, "there'd be no more apples!"

Then, we were off, and I recall the thought as we began ascending the ridge between us and Splonum that I had already done this once tonight, which meant I was feeling my age as my thighs immediately began protesting. Our plan was to reach the top of the final ridge next to Splonum, then descend no more than a couple hundred paces downslope before the sun came up, since the worst possible outcome was that we were still topping the ridge when the sun hit the summit. Even with the trees that lined the length of the ridgeline, there would be no way even the laxest Maezaei sentry could miss that much movement, so it was crucial that we were across and farther downslope when the inevitable occurred. Consequently, we did not allow the men to rest, which made straggling equally inevitable, as we officers were reminded that most of these men were no youngsters. Despite having four months to knock off the accumulated flab from slack living, and rust from years of no longer training of the rankers, the one thing that cannot be defeated is time, and the cumulative toll it takes on a man. As I watched the men laboring up through the trees, I reminded myself that I was complaining, inwardly of course, about the toll my age had taken on me, and I was a decade younger than many of these men, twenty in the case of men like Metellus. Nevertheless, I was no less liberal in my application of the *vitus* as a method of encouragement, despite the sympathy I felt for them. The only men on whom I took the slightest pity were those carrying the ladders, although they switched out several times, but by the time we did reach the top, our cohesion was hopelessly shattered. Even worse, the eastern sky was turning pink, turning the next sixth part of a watch into one of the most exhausting of my life as I alternately pushed, dragged, and swatted any and every man within my reach while exhorting or gasping at the other Centurions and Optios to do the same, doing everything within our power to get our entire force across the ridge before the dawn. And, much to our relief, we made it, although it was as the very last handful of men, not coincidentally the oldest among us, scrambled over the top and began descending into our final positions just as the upper rim of the sun peeked over the horizon.

Our dispositions, which had naturally been worked out beforehand, meant that the First Cohort, which I was with, although Germanicus had insisted on leading it personally, was positioned directly above the stone fort. The Second Cohort, led by Agrippa, was positioned in such a way that, if they descended straight down the hill, they would sweep into the town itself, where their left flank would be anchored on the road that led from Clandate. However, by angling their line of approach slightly, they could support our attack on the stone fort if we needed help; the one drawback being that in order to do so, they would have to cross more open ground, along with ascending the shelf upon which the fort sat. Hopefully, the First, being double the size of the others, would not need the help, but while the stone fort was our first objective, it was not the ultimate prize, which was why Gaesorix and his men were to play what was the most crucial role. Because of the practical impossibility of infantry, even running downhill, to throw their ladders up against the wall of the town, scale the ladders, vanquish what defenders there might be, then make their way through the town to the opposite side to climb the road to take the royal stronghold, we were counting on the speed of the cavalry. The Second Cohort had the main responsibility for securing the Clandate gate as quickly as possible, then opening it to allow the cavalry to come sweeping in and head directly for the stronghold. It was not realistic, nor did we plan for Gaesorix and the seven hundred cavalrymen he was using for this task to try and take the stronghold; their task was to keep the bulk of the Maezaei defenders out.

To any man with experience in such matters, this was a very complicated plan, and in the aftermath, there would be a fair amount of criticism, most of it aimed at Germanicus, with his youth being pointed to as the cause for the difficulties that lay ahead. Although I admit that there were flaws in this plan, the fault did not lay in Germanicus' youth, but the paucity of resources with which he was expected to accomplish his task. Specifically, we had been restricted in the amount of artillery we had been allotted, namely one *ballista* and three scorpions, less than half than that of a Legion. It had been a battle that Germanicus had fought, unsuccessfully, every time he visited Siscia. As to why this was the case, the reason given according to our Legate was that, despite the *Legio Germanicus* being named such, we were not a true Legion, but half of one, and additionally, the rest of the combined army needed every piece themselves. On its surface, I suppose this makes sense, but through Alex I learned that, in fact, Germanicus had been led to believe that his requests would be granted, up until his final meeting with Tiberius in Siscia, which was when he received his final orders. While others might speculate about why this chain of events occurred as they did, I prefer to remain silent, other than to say it was this serious lack of artillery that limited our options.

Now, while the valley in which Splonum was situated remained in darkness, the upper reaches of the ridge became bathed in the early morning sunlight, which Germanicus had decreed would be the signal to begin our final move down to the edge of the cleared area. From this point, it was anyone's guess how close we could get before the alarm was raised by the Maezaei, but Germanicus, walking in the spot I would have occupied, had put me in an unaccustomed position.

"I want you next to me on my right," he had ordered, but I was not disposed to agree, although not for the reason he probably assumed.

"Sir," I shook my head, and as I did I made a gesture indicating our respective sizes, "having me standing next to you is going to draw even more attention from those *cunni* waiting for us as it is. Besides," I saw this was not having an impact, so I switched to a more practical consideration, "if we're both hit, who will be commanding the Legion?"

He hesitated, though only for a moment, saying, "I'll take the risk," he grinned up at me, his face framed by his helmet with the black feather crest fluttering in the light morning breeze, "if you will."

When he put it in this manner, I was forced to realize two things; the first was that I could not back down in front of the men, and that Germanicus knew me better than I thought, even in the short time of our association.

This prompted me to shrug and return his grin, while my answer was louder than it was needed to be so the men could overhear, "I wouldn't be anywhere else!"

Somewhat to my chagrin, I instantly understood I had not thought this through, since some of the men began to cheer this, but the veteran serving as Optio, Vibius Rufius, who had been the same rank in the Seventh Cohort before he retired, was quicker than I was, snarling at the men to shut their mouths. I do not believe that any of us truly believed we would catch the Maezaei completely by surprise, but I certainly did not want to ruin what slight chance we might have had by making too much noise. To that end, we had agreed not to use the *cornu*; instead, the Second Cohort would only begin moving when we in the First appeared from the trees into the cleared area above the stone fort, while the other Cohorts would follow suit. Germanicus mounted his horse, held by one of his slaves behind the Cohort, then went trotting behind each Century before returning to toss the reins to his slave after dismounting. As he strode towards the front, I saw him nod to the man serving as the *Aquilifer*, although instead of a Legion eagle, the standard bore a carved bust of the Princeps and was garlanded with ivy, which the man, Lucius Salonius Arvina, thrust into the air three times. With that serving as the only command, our advance understandably started raggedly, but when we reached the edge of the trees, as I glanced to our left, I saw that our alignment, while not perfect, was acceptable, though this was not destined to last long. Then, we were out in the sunlight, the only obstacles the stumps of the trees that had been cleared, while three hundred paces away, and perhaps a hundred feet lower down, the stone walls of the fort had just been touched by the sun. Although the blazing orb was not perfectly behind us, being more off of our left quarter, it still had to be somewhat difficult to squint up at our advancing line, or so we hoped. If we had been on flat ground, we would have been in range of any artillery the Maezaei might have possessed, although it had been a strict policy of the Princeps that no barbarian tribes were allowed such implements. Which, not surprisingly, was something none of us believed the barbarian tribes obeyed, and despite our best attempts with surprise visits when the province was peaceful, I fully expected to be facing some form of artillery; the only question was the quantity. The irony created by the fact that, before our arrival, the barbarian tribes of Pannonia had not availed themselves of artillery was not lost on any of us, but this was just one more thing beyond my control in the moment, so it was only a passing thought. Because of the grade, we had a bit of breathing room before we would find out if Dodonis had such a surprise waiting for us, but one thing that we could not miss was the sight of men lining the parapet, watching our approach.

"There they are." Germanicus said this in such a way that it might have been to himself, and I glanced over to see that he was trying to make sure his chin thongs were tied, made difficult because he had already drawn his *gladius*.

"Legate," I decided to take the small risk of moving closer to his side since we were still out of range of all but a *ballista* so that I could speak more quietly, "you don't need that just yet." I pointed to his blade, which instead of his normal *spatha* was a Spanish *gladius*, although just the hilt of carved ivory probably cost as much as the blade itself.

Flushing, he did not say anything, though he did sheathe it, then fumbled with the thongs with fingers I knew from experience were made clumsy from the nerves of the moment. Germanicus had no real need to be marching with us, and indeed, in many ways, it was a bad idea, but the simple truth was that I did not even try to dissuade him; as much pressure as I had put on myself to emulate my Avus, I could only imagine what it was like for a youngster who had chosen to bear the name of Caesar. Since we were moving downhill, it was natural that our pace be quicker than normal, but with the obstacles presented by the stumps, we were better served by forcing a slower cadence, except that Germanicus did not seem to realize that, since he had taken my spot, it fell to him to give this command to reduce to half time. Regardless, I share in the blame because I did not speak up quickly enough, so that before we had gone half the distance to the wall, from somewhere behind the men lining the parapet, a sudden blur of dozens of streaking missiles shot up into the sky.

"*Form testudo! Form testudo!*"

Despite the immediate reaction of the officers, the extra dispersion forced on us by the hundreds of protruding stumps cost us dearly, as the men, trying to move as quickly as possible, were either farther apart than normal, or the spot they would have occupied to make a compact *testudo* was already taken by a stump. The result was as inevitable as it was damaging to the First Century in particular, the noise level rising dramatically from the alternating hollow thudding as a man was fortunate to catch the arrow that would have skewered him on his shield, or the sharp, short cry of one who was not blessed by the gods. Within the span of a half-dozen heartbeats, our First Century alone suffered what, from my quick glance, appeared to be at least a dozen losses; only later would we learn how many were dead, although fortunately, most of the time, arrow wounds are not mortal. By the time the other leading Centuries had formed their respective *testudo*, it appeared that their losses equaled that of the First; nevertheless, there was no faltering as the advance continued. Immediately after the first volley, the archers, still hidden from view, were clearly loosing in their own rhythm, unleashing a shower of missiles and thereby continuing the racket, making anything less than a shout impossible to hear.

Keeping one eye on the sky and the other on avoiding one of the stumps that still lay in our path, I was further hampered by my need to make sure that Germanicus was not struck down, though I was aided in this, albeit by the misfortune of a veteran in the front rank. Whether his arm had tired or he had dropped his shield just a bit to have a better look at the ground, which is impossible to avoid doing and was something with which I was extremely familiar as a man who had spent years in the first rank, I do not know. Whatever the cause, I heard the sound that signals a solid strike in a fleshy target, although it was slightly different, with something of a hollower sound that instantly reminded me of someone thumping a gourd or melon, then the ranker on the outermost file, marching next to *Aquilifer* Arvina, instantly dropped, the shield falling from his nerveless hand as his knees simply collapsed. Alerted by the sound first, I was already turning my head just enough to see out of the corner of my eye the havoc that was wrought when the veteran, or more accurately his corpse, with an arrow protruding a bit more than half its length from his right eye, became just another obstacle, and a bigger and more dangerous one than a stump. The man behind him in the second rank, who less than a heartbeat before was holding his shield up above his head, thereby sheltering himself and his now-dead comrade at his feet, not surprisingly stumbled over the body in his attempt to take the extra steps needed to move up to the first rank to replace his dead comrade.

126

Instantly, either some of the archers were standing just behind the defenders nearest to the parapet and could see on their own what was happening, or one of those warriors alerted them where they were located down on the ground inside the fort, so what was probably a half-dozen missiles but seemed to be many more suddenly came streaking down in an arc that converged at roughly this exact point. The next span of time, perhaps ten heartbeats, consisted of a number of separate but equally frantic moves by those of us in the most immediate danger, starting with my own, when I roughly shoved Germanicus aside to snatch up the shield of the man I had immediately seen no longer needed it, my intent being to force my young Legate to take it up. Despite my earlier urging, he had refused to take a shield from one of the ranks, and in my mind, this was a perfect way for him to save face, and himself. However, just as I began moving, I saw one seemingly stray missile, part of the bunch that were plunging down to land within the few feet of area where the front right quarter of our formation was trying to recover, this lone one instead streaking down on a slightly different trajectory. Consequently, while it was certainly not planned, my colliding with Germanicus, which sent him stumbling to his left, meant that the arrow that would have struck him hit me instead. Thankfully, it was a glancing blow, probably because of my own posture, more or less facing the right file of the Century with my torso twisted so my back was facing the fort, yet it still packed a terrific wallop, even though the iron point skipped off the mail of my right shoulder blade before caroming off and sticking in the rocky ground less than a couple feet away, feeling a bit like I had been given a good hard punch. While it was certainly enough to send a man of an average size staggering in the opposite direction from the blow, my own body was heavy enough to allow me to keep moving, so that I snatched up the shield before somehow spinning about to give it to Germanicus; later, whenever I have tried to recall how I did certain things during a battle, I can never remember how I accomplished whatever it was, and this time is no exception. While I move well for a large man, that I was able to perform all of this in the span of no more than a couple heartbeats of time remains a mystery.

"Here!" I thrust it at Germanicus just as he recovered himself, holding it by the top, and as I hoped, he was so startled that his hand reached out automatically, grasping its handle. "Keep it in front of you!"

"But I won't be able to see!" he protested, except I was still moving, this time to jerk the second ranker back up to his feet from where he had fallen to his knees after stumbling on the corpse of the man in the first rank.

"Keep your shield up in front of you!" I repeated, except this time, I was roaring it in the second ranker's ear, although I was admonishing both of them. His left arm actually started to swing the shield back in front of his body from where he had moved it to act as a counterbalance, and I believe he was doing so as quickly as he could, while I grasped his upper right arm to pull him upright; tragically, he was not quick enough. The arrow that struck him carried enough force to punch through a plate of his *segmentata*, burying itself directly in his chest, and I felt the impact vibrate through his body just before his arm was wrenched from my grasp from the force of the strike. He went staggering backward, inevitably colliding with the Legionary in the third rank; fortunately, this ranker had just enough time to not only see but understand what was happening, and most importantly, the threat it posed to the rest of the men immediately around him, meaning that he had already dropped his shield from overhead to down in front of him. Using it to protect himself from what had become an enemy weapon, without my help, he stopped the backward motion of the stricken man by catching him on his shield. The second ranker was still alive but would not remain so much longer—the frothy blood on his lips and the widened eyes as he realized he was stepping into Charon's Boat the telltale signs he was aware of this—then the man in the third rank gave what was a brutal but necessary shove, twisting his shield to the right to deposit his dying comrade outside the formation. Relieved of one obstacle, the third ranker nimbly hopped over the body of the man of the first rank, catching an arrow on his shield even as he was stepping into place, while the fourth ranker had to trot forward, those behind him in the file following suit. It is in this manner

128

that a Century keeps their *testudo* intact, and despite the brief disruption, the First was once more moving forward, but we were now slightly behind the Second and Third Centuries. Meanwhile, I moved back to my spot on the opposite side of Germanicus, but not before I snatched up the shield of the veteran who had finally succumbed to the effects of an arrow through a lung. He had managed to roll over onto his back, yet despite his eyes being open, it only took the length of time to pick up his shield to understand his spirit had fled his body, but it was the fact that I recognized him that I was forced to shove from my mind. What was his name? I tried to think of it even as my body reacted, seemingly without any conscious command from my mind, my arm bringing the shield up just in time to catch an arrow that struck the boss, making a sharp, clanging sound as the arrow caromed off and past me. Before the name came to me, I realized we were now within javelin range, and out of habit, I opened my mouth to give what would be the next order, except the Legate beat me to it.

"Open formation!" Germanicus' voice was more highly pitched than normal, but besides this, I heard no quaver in it, and he paused for the span of a couple heartbeats as the men complied before shouting, "Prepare javelins!"

Now that we were closer to the walls, the Maezaei on the ramparts were not nearly as visible, mainly because they were now crouching down behind the main part of the parapet or hiding behind the crenellations, trying to make themselves as small a target as possible. Thankfully, the only way the archers, who I still had not seen, could continue their own assault on us was by exposing themselves and risking a javelin in their face, and not surprisingly, none of them appeared to be willing to do that. Indeed, they were either already gone from the fort or were in the process of doing so, though we had no way of knowing this in the moment.

"Release!"

There was a blur of motion off to my left, but my attention was still on the wall, watching as our missiles finally exacted vengeance for the punishment we had been absorbing. To my dismay, I saw only two of our missiles find a fleshy target, although it could have been a

129

couple more men judging from the sharp cries I heard, but it was just as likely they had been alarmed shouts at a near miss.

"Prepare javelins!"

"No!" I shouted this to Germanicus, and while it obviously startled him, I was worried that he might drop his shield from its position just a bit above his head, but while he did look over at me, thankfully, it did not budge. "We didn't hit more than a couple of them! We don't want to waste the second volley!"

For an instant, it seemed as if he was disposed to argue, but then he gave a curt nod, and in a slightly quieter tone of voice, asked me, "So what now, Pullus?"

Rather than answer him directly, I shouted, "All but the ladder sections hold steady! If any of those *cunni* show their faces, put a fucking javelin through it!" The response was more in the form of a growl than the kind of verbal response expected, but it was enough, and I immediately followed with, "Ladders! Follow me!"

Even as I was shouting this, I had begun moving, running the last fifteen or so paces to the wall, my own shield above my head. Just as I reached the base of it, my shield was struck a terrific blow that, while it was not torn from my grasp, knocked it from above my head down to my left side, and I glimpsed a rock bounding down the slope back towards the fort. For an instant, I was exposed, and as I gazed upward, I saw a bearded face, contorted with hatred and wearing a high, conical helmet, but it was the rock he held in two hands that arrested my attention. He was just bringing the rock above his head, clearly intent on hurling it down with the maximum force he could muster, then suddenly, as if by some magic, his chest seemed to sprout not one but two javelins, although my eye barely had time to register this before he vanished. Not, I must add, before his blood sprayed down on my upturned face, but then my shield was back in its original position, allowing me to take the opportunity to wipe as much of the sticky fluid off as I could. Before I was finished, I heard more than saw Germanicus, puffing from the tension of the moment, reach my side, mimicking my posture with his own shield. No more than two or three heartbeats after this, the men carrying the ladder nearest to us arrived at the wall, and moving a bit more jerkily than men who have been working together for more than just a few months, the wooden ladder nevertheless went up at roughly the same time as the other ladder for the First. Taking just enough time to look farther down the wall, I saw that the Second and Third had beaten us in putting up their own ladders, and there were already men scaling them.

"We can't let those shiftless bastards in the Second beat us!" I roared, moving towards the nearest ladder, and again my words were affirmed by the shouts of the rankers of the First.

They may be old, I recall thinking, but they reminded me of something my Avus wrote in his account, about how a man's abilities may wane over time, but the desire to be a warrior never does. For a brief moment, I held out the hope that we could still make up the time we had lost to the other Centuries, but then Germanicus inadvertently bungled that chance, and in the process, created the first real test of our relationship. I cannot fault him for his desire to prove to our men he was worthy of being their leader in not only a legal sense but through the valor of his deeds. And neither can I completely dismiss the idea that Tiberius would have been furious with me for what I was about to do because he wanted his adopted son to expose himself, but the truth is, I liked the boy a great deal, and I saw in him a lot of potential to be the kind of leader he wanted to be and, more importantly, what we need from our upper classes. Consequently, when he actually stepped in front of me, clearly intent on moving to the ladder to be the first one up it, I reached out, grabbed him by the back of his cuirass, and none too gently stopped his progress.

Compounding matters, I actually moved him bodily out of my way by shoving him up against the wall, although in contrast to my treatment, I chose my words carefully, saying only, "I apologize, sir. But your chance will come; just not today."

"But…" I heard him protest, then his voice was drowned out as I stepped up onto the ladder as the men behind me lined up, their shields held above their heads, while their comrades supporting with their poised javelins shouted encouragement.

"Gut those bastards!"

"Leave some for us!"

"But it's fine if you decide to kill all those *cunni* for us!"

Even in the moment, I found myself grinning at this last call, thinking that there is always one man who will have something witty to say that, after a battle, will usually be what is remembered more than the fighting itself. Once I was halfway up, I felt the ladder shaking, informing me that I was being followed, but I was more concerned with what was just above me now that I was within a couple rungs from the top. Stopping just long enough to press the bottom of my shield against the ladder to support myself while drawing my *gladius*, I resumed my progress. Fortunately, that brief pause threw off the timing of a Maezaei who must have been just above me, because he took the risk of exposing himself to try and drop another rock onto my shield. Once more, a streaking blur of motion shot past me, coming from behind me and angled upward, then I heard a solid, meaty sound, accompanied by an explosive grunt as the rock went dropping past me, barely missing my shield. Making it to the rung that I would use to launch myself over the parapet, I crouched slightly, coiling my legs as I paused for a heartbeat to gather my strength, preparing to unleash the ferocity that is absolutely essential in a moment like this. Then, I shoved upward with all of my strength, keeping my shield out and to the left above my body and resting my right hand, or actually my knuckles, on the stone of a crenellation as I grasped my Gallic blade, providing the leverage to lift my body up and over the parapet. It is a maneuver that my Avus used, and is one that only those men who are of the same size and bulk as he was can perform without it being more dangerous to the one doing it than to their enemies. The particular danger lies in two factors: the first is that you are doing so essentially blind, since the standard-sized parapet and crenellations mean it is impossible to see the space into which your lower body is moving. Simply put, it means that there might be a man, with a shield, directly in the path of your lower body, and is why this only works for men my size, which naturally excludes most Romans, because there is a real risk that a lighter man will simply bounce off and consequently fall back down to the ground. The second danger is that, for a brief moment, if there is a defender to your right, since all of your weight is on your right arm, while your shield is on the other side of your body, it leaves you completely defenseless. This, at any rate, is the theoretical problem; what I had learned in the half-dozen times I had done this is that, in practical terms, the sudden appearance of a Roman, particularly in this manner, always surprised my foes enough that they hesitated for just the fraction of the moment I needed. This time, although there was, in fact, a Maezaei crouching to the left of the ladder, he was not quite low enough, so that my greaves smashed into his face, and although the collision slowed the momentum of my body, it was not enough to stop me from sweeping him from the parapet. As he flew backward, he cried out, either from the alarm of feeling himself being shoved backward with enough force to send him flying off the rampart or from the pain as the metal of my greaves crushed his nose and knocked out some of his teeth. Whatever the case, my feet came down, more or less on the same spot that had been occupied by the Maezaei an instant before, but my attention was turned to the right, and thank the gods it was, because I barely avoided the sudden thrust of the spear that a warrior aimed at my head from that direction. Honestly, if he had tried to plunge it into my chest, there was nothing I could have done, which means I would not be writing this, but in the bare instant of time I had, I saw the face of a beardless youth, wearing only a boiled leather jerkin with some iron rings sewn to it, with a cap made of the same material, also with iron rings fixed to the crown. Even worse for him was that he did not have a shield, although it is possible that he had one that was now useless because a javelin had pierced it. Not that it mattered why, so that even before he could recover his heavy war spear, which would have been his only defense, it would not have been enough. Bringing my right arm up from the part of the wall I had used to lever myself onto the parapet, I made one smooth motion so that the first few inches of my blade cut into the neck of the Maezaei boy. It was not a decapitating blow, but it was more than enough to turn him into a corpse as the weight of his head, no longer supported by the muscles of his neck, caused it to flop over at an angle and to a degree that it was not meant to go, while blood

133

spurted up in a brief, scarlet fountain. He was still tottering on his feet as I spun back about, meeting the charge of the Maezaei who had been next to the man I had kicked off the rampart, bringing my shield hard up against my shoulder, something I normally did not care to do when I was being attacked.

This warrior, older and clearly more experienced, had thrown himself against my shield, holding his own in a mirror image of mine also up against his body, presumably thinking to send me reeling. However, when I barely budged, only bending backward a bit from the waist, instead of pressing a fruitless attempt, the warrior immediately retreated a couple steps, now extending his own shield out in front of him in the standard position for attack, while raising his *gladius* into a posture that signaled his readiness to launch his own offensive. In the heartbeat of time I had as he stepped away, looking over the top of my shield, I took him in, sizing him up as an opponent. His hair, as black as a crow's wing, had strands of silver and he had the coloring most common to the Maezaei, while his full plaited beard showed even more gray, although this was more the color of iron than the silver of his hair. The helmet he wore was in the Maezaei style, a high cone, except that affixed to it were a pair of wings as black as his hair, and rather than a mail coat, he wore the scaled armor that is popular with the tribes of Thrace. My surmise was that he had taken this from a vanquished foe, my belief supported by the manner in which he handled his blade, holding it so the point was just above his head, except out to his side more than most warriors usually practiced. Even more telling were the slight circles he made with the weapon, with an ease that bespoke the same level of dedication I liked to think I displayed when it came to our common profession. His shield was oval, with three black birds painted on it, which I guessed were ravens, and he held it as easily and with as much familiarity as he did his blade. Our mutual inspection took perhaps a heartbeat, then he was suddenly lunging at me, and normally I would have blocked his attack with ease, except just as he moved, I felt a hand suddenly grasp my harness from behind.

"I'm right behind you, Pullus!"

I recognized the voice as belonging to Germanicus, and while I cannot fault him in any way for doing what we are trained to do, the truth is that this distracted me just enough that, although I brought my shield across my body to block his thrust, this type of attack by a barbarian something of a rarity as it was, I was a shade late, so the point of his *gladius* was already past my defense. Despite the edge of my shield striking his blade to knock it away, it was not before the tip stabbed into the meaty part of my upper arm, eliciting a roar of pain from me, mixed with an equal amount of anger at being caught out. The hurt, while intense, was also of a type that told me that the wound itself was not serious; nevertheless, it was disconcerting to feel the warmth of my own blood suddenly streaming down my arm. Determined not to allow him to continue on the offensive, I leapt forward, unleashing my own attack on him, relying on nothing more than brute strength. Over the span of two or three heartbeats, I rained down blow after blow, all of which he managed to block with his shield, although I was driving it lower and lower with every strike. Consequently, his face became more visible the lower his shield got, enabling me to see the look of desperation as he tried to withstand my onslaught. Once I could see his beard, I began swinging my blade down yet again in the same type of hammering blow, except midway through the stroke, I stopped it while stepping forward as I changed to a thrust, angling it downward. Too late, the warrior tried to bring his shield back up, but the point of my *gladius* was already past his defense, punching into his throat, right in the hollow below the bony lump all men possess. His eyes rolled back in his head, the sign that he was no longer able to fight back, so I looked past him to see that were there men wearing Roman helmets now spreading in both directions on the parapet, towards and away from me, while small battles like the one I had just won were taking place all along the uphill wall of the fort. Only then did I turn to confirm that it had indeed been Germanicus who had been behind me, grabbing my harness. Behind him, more men were streaming up the ladder we had used, which was the one farthest to the right along the uphill wall, so that the rankers following the two of us had begun moving towards the right hand corner of the fort, prepared to meet any Maezaei coming to the aid of their comrades under assault. This was the moment when I first noticed something unusual, which became apparent over the span of the next hundred heartbeats. Those Maezaei waiting for us had fought fiercely and had inflicted some casualties, but as I surveyed the interior of the fort, which was large enough that it contained four large wooden buildings, three of which turned out to be barracks, with the fourth used as a supply building, the only activity was on the wall we had assaulted. Those archers who had tortured us during our approach were nowhere in sight by the time we mounted the wall, so that perhaps a sixth part of a watch after we entered the cleared area, the fort was taken.

"Where," Germanicus asked me a few moments later, after we had descended the rampart and were waiting for the five sections of the First to search one barracks, while the Second and Third did the same for the others, "are the other defenders?"

"I have a feeling," I told Germanicus grimly, "that *cunnus* Dodonis may have played us for fools."

Indeed, the Maezaei chieftain had done that very thing, as we would learn very shortly. Once the fort was secured, Germanicus and I hurried to the opposite end to the side that overlooked the town and gave us a view across the valley to the other, larger stronghold. Ascending this far rampart, it took a moment to observe everything and a bit longer to determine what it meant. Even then, we would not learn the entire scope of what had happened to the *Legio Germanicus* until later in the day. What was impossible to miss was the trail of dust raised by the cavalry, except it was heading in the wrong direction, away from the gates, which we could see were still closed, while the men and horses themselves had already disappeared from our view, hidden by the curve of the road as it moved behind the hill on which the fort was located. Meanwhile, the Second Cohort, under the command of Agrippa, was in a series of *testudo*, under what I saw was a furious assault of missiles, and my first guess was that the archers who had been in the stone fort had scampered down the hillside, then somehow made it inside the town walls before turning their attention on the Second. Looking over towards the long expanse of the western wall on the opposite side of the gate, which the other three Cohorts were assaulting, to our dismay, we saw a disaster in the making. Like the Second, and as we had done, the other three Cohorts had formed in *testudo*, which in itself was not a problem; until, that is, the enemy began using its own artillery. Moving quickly to the corner of the fort that was diametrically opposite where we had gained the uphill wall, even as we were trotting to that corner, I saw with a growing horror that the answer to whether or not Dodonis had artillery, and where at least some of it was positioned, was being answered. Among the barely visible streaking blurs of arrows, suddenly I saw a larger object, moving only slightly slower than the smaller missiles, sweep across my line of vision, where it landed just a couple paces short of what I assumed would be the Second Century of the Third Cohort, positioned in the middle of the three leading Centuries. Despite it going uphill, there was an explosion of dirt and debris when the stone smashed into the ground, but it had enough momentum to bounce up and smash directly into roughly the middle of the Second's *testudo*.

"By the gods!" I heard Germanicus gasping. "They have artillery??"

We reached the corner of the fort before I could answer, waiting only long enough for Germanicus to skid to a stop by my side as we stood on the rampart, watching to see how many of the men who had been knocked down got up. Fortunately, the stone missile had spent enough of its force that, as far as I could tell, every ranker in the Second was still part of the Century as they stepped over the gouge in the hillside. This was good news, but it only lasted long enough for the time it took for another enemy *ballista*, this one further down the wall from where I had spotted the first missile originate, to launch its own deadly cargo, while all we could do was helplessly track its arcing movement, hoping that it would either miss altogether, or do scant damage. Instead, this missile sailed over the first line of three Centuries of the Third Cohort and landed directly in the middle of what I believed was the Fourth of the Third, and even from the distance of well more than a quarter mile, there was no missing the sight of the pieces of one shield flying into the air, while another one that at least appeared whole went spinning crazily off to the side of the formation. It was as if a giant invisible fist had plunged straight down, directly in the middle of the Century, and while we were too far away to see the carnage, I could imagine the sight of one or more men, their skulls crushed, or perhaps eviscerated by the hurtling stone, and a quick glance at Germanicus told me he was no less affected.

"At least," I said aloud, hearing the grim tone, "this should be enough to convince Scipio to give the call to open back up."

"But won't that make them vulnerable to those arrows?" Germanicus pointed at what appeared to be an almost unbroken black line of those missiles arcing down into our men.

I gave him a sidelong glance, wondering if he actually expected an answer, since to me it was obvious, but I saw he meant it seriously.

"Which would you rather be hit by?" I asked him, pointing in the general direction of the top of the arcs formed by the missiles. "Those, or one of those rocks?"

His face colored, but he answered readily enough, muttering, "That's a good point. So," he then asked the correct question, "why isn't Scipio giving the command?"

Seemingly timing it as if the men operating one of the enemy pieces had heard the question, we watched as yet another rock came smashing down, again at the Second Century, except this time, it did not fall short. We were forced to watch a repetition of the punishment absorbed by the Fourth of the Third, as for the span of a few heartbeats, their *testudo* disintegrated, yet still no *cornu* command sounded.

"Pluto's cock," I snarled this, not thinking about the fact that the Pilus Prior was one of Germanicus' own class, "that fucking idiot is going to get his Cohort wiped out!"

Suddenly, I sensed movement to my right, and I glanced over, half expecting the Legate to be rounding on me to chastise me for my intemperate language. Instead, he was clearly looking for someone else, and I saw who it was when he snapped out an order to the *Cornicen* attached the youngster's staff, Publius Natta, ordering him to come to where we were standing. Forced to run up the single set of stone steps, Natta was already puffing by the time he lugged the large horn to our spot, and I wondered if he would have enough breath to immediately do what Germanicus was about to order, and if he did not, how many men would die as a result.

"Sound the call for the Third Cohort to open their formation!" Germanicus snapped, but as I had feared, it took Natta a few heartbeats to gather his breath.

During the delay, I had turned my attention back to see that, this time, it was the Century on the other side of the Third of the Second who was struck, and I deduced that, since the other Cohorts were in a double line, this would be the First of the Fourth Cohort, under the command of another of Germanicus' set, Gnaeus Acerronius Proculus, although he was slightly older than most of the other fine young men who Germanicus had brought with him. This time, not even the greater distance from our vantage point could disguise the horrible damage done to the Century, as the hurtling stone ball wiped a bloody hole right through the two files nearest us. Because of their tight proximity, the *testudo* formation is a juicy target for both cavalry and artillery, although the former can be staved off easily enough, provided the men in it have time to thrust their javelins out in what we call a porcupine. There is no such defense from stone ammunition, or a *ballista* firing iron bolts; even a scorpion can do tremendous damage if the range is close. Natta blew the first series notes that signaled this message was for every Cohort within hearing, then after just enough of a pause to take a breath, sounded the call that commands men to go to a standard open battle formation. At first, I was heartened to see that the leading Centuries of the assault begin to obey, though it did not last long, because no more than ten heartbeats later, the fainter sound of another *cornu* sounded the call that called for *testudo*, the only saving grace being that the first three notes told us the command was meant for only one Cohort.

"What the *fuck* is Scipio doing?" My voice was choked, but while Germanicus' response was lacking my language, his tone was no less vehement.

"Sound the call again!" he snapped, but while I understood why he was disposed to do this, I was afraid that, as confused as matters already were, it was about to get worse.

Regardless, before I could say anything, Natta sounded the call again, even as the rankers of the Third Cohort were once more contracting. Naturally, this series of contradicting orders had stopped the forward progress of the Third Cohort, although the Fourth continued forward, but they were now back in the more open formation. The consequence was that the archers, who from our vantage point we could see positioned a few paces behind the wall down on the street that paralleled the barrier, which enabled them to aim their missiles higher in the sky so that they picked up more speed on the way down, switched their punishment to the Fourth Cohort. At the same time, the Maezaei commanding the artillery clearly decided to switch his entire focus onto the Third Cohort. We had been unable to precisely locate where the *ballistae* were positioned; all I could see was they were not on the wall either, but I just happened to be looking a block deeper into the town when, from between two buildings, a black blur shot into the sky. I had to whip my head around quickly in order to see where it impacted, although I immediately wished I had not, as the missile smashed into the First of the Third again. This time, however, it actually hit in the middle of the formation, but around the eighth rank, as once more shields went flying, I clearly saw a Roman helmet tumbling through the air, with a thick trail of blood and matter that had an instant before been a man's head.

"They're getting slaughtered," Germanicus spoke quietly, but he did not need to shout to communicate the same horror I was feeling. I sensed him turning to look at me, and when I returned it, I saw in his eyes what he was about to do. "Sound the recall," he ordered Natta, although he did not tear his gaze from mine. "We need to regroup."

Our first attempt to take Splonum had failed.

Another flaw in our plan surfaced now; neither Germanicus nor any of the men serving as Tribunes thought about what we would do should the plan fail, but I share as much, if not more responsibility for

140

this than anyone. The attempt to take Splonum was not a complete failure; we left the First Cohort in possession of the fort, also leaving Gaius Silius as the Tribune commanding, while the Primus Pilus Posterior, my ostensible second in command, Lucius Fulvius Veratius, was the true leader of the Cohort. Ironically, the Second Cohort suffered minimal casualties and probably could have succeeded taking the wall, but as we learned from Gaesorix, the presence of Maezaei artillery had driven our cavalry away from the gates before Agrippa and his men could storm and secure it. In order for our plan to work as it was devised, we were counting on the speed of our mounted contingent to sweep through the town to the base of the hill to cut off defenders who we had forced to retreat from the walls. Without the gates being open, Gaesorix was forced to choose between waiting near the walls, just out of range of arrow shot, but after the first set of stone missiles caught them by surprise, and two men and three horses were killed, the Decurion elected to withdraw farther back up the road out of range of the artillery as well. Agrippa's Cohort actually had their ladders up and were about to scale the wall when Germanicus ordered the recall, and I have to credit the young appointed Centurion's cool state of mind, because he actually retrieved the ladders before they marched, in good order, this time using the road to hasten their withdrawal. It was the plight of the Third Cohort that was the worst, because their discipline completely broke down, something that Germanicus had been forced to witness as we stood watching. I did not find it surprising that all three Cohorts obeyed the command with such alacrity, but the Fourth and Fifth Cohorts had managed to withdraw in the manner in which we are trained, essentially maintaining their formation and marching back up the hill, albeit backward, at least until they were out of range. Not so with the Third, starting with the First Century, which simply…disintegrated, for lack of a better word for it. Indeed, it reminded me of the kind of flight we normally put the barbarian tribes to, with no semblance of organization and nobody in command. Oh, Scipio made an attempt, or at least appeared to do so, waving his *gladius* over his head, but when the Cohort *Signifer* is the man leading the retreat, even a good

Centurion has his hands full. The consequence was that, aside from the casualties suffered by the Maezaei stones, perhaps a dozen men were struck by arrows from behind, a truly shameful wound for any Roman. Unfortunately, the young Scipio came away unharmed, but even worse, he was completely unrepentant when Germanicus held his meeting, which was another mistake in a day full of them, because the Legate did not wait for us to return to camp. Instead, completely by happenstance, we reassembled, minus the First Cohort, back at the mines where we had begun what seemed like days before but had been no more than two watches. Morale, which was the one aspect of the *Legio Germanicus* I worried about the most, had taken a serious blow because of our rebuff, and it was compounded by what quickly degenerated into a shouting match between two members of the nobility. Things became so acrimonious between the pair that, when I saw that Sextus Appuleius, another Tribune attached to Germanicus who was standing closest to the pair, was clearly not planning on stepping in, I was forced to, which I did in the most literal sense possible, actually interposing myself between the two.

"This," I was determined to be the calm one for a change, "is neither the time nor the place for this." I turned deliberately away from Scipio to face Germanicus and add, "Sir, what are your orders for the Legion?"

As I expected, I heard Scipio make a hissing sound, since the upper classes of Rome have adopted the idea that I had been told originated in the East, that it is considered an insult for a social inferior to turn one's back to their better. Which, naturally, was most of the reason I did that very thing. Fortunately, I saw I had gotten through to Germanicus, and he might have flushed at this gentle rebuke from me, though it was impossible to say, given that his face was already red.

Still, he took a deep breath before giving a curt nod, saying, "You're right, of course, Pullus." He paused to consider, but I noticed he was eyeing me, giving me the sense he was waiting for me to offer my own input; or more likely, I saw what I wanted to see.

Regardless of the truth of the matter, I took advantage of the pause by saying, "I'd suggest that we go back to camp, break it down, and relocate it now. Our chance of surprise is gone. And," I felt compelled to add, "we need to decide the best way to go about getting those Maezaei out of that town now that they know we're here."

"They have artillery!" Scipio interjected, and my impression there was an implied rebuke was confirmed when he said, "If the Legions sitting in Siscia had been doing their jobs instead of sucking down wine and whoring all the time, there should have been no chance of us being repulsed by barbarian artillery!"

"Just like there should have been no chance of a rebellion because a Praetor chose to double the Pannonians' taxes, then call a *dilectus* of a full ten thousand men!" I shot right back, although the words were barely out of my mouth when I groaned inwardly at my lapse, but I kept going, except my words were more for Germanicus than the other noble. "But that's a broken jug, just like the fact that they have artillery. What we need to do is come up with a plan that takes that into account."

"Agreed," Germanicus answered immediately, then turned and beckoned to the *Cornicen*, ordering, "Natta, sound the assembly. We're marching back to camp."

Natta did as he was told, but I waited to see if Germanicus had thought of something else.

When I saw he had not, I waited for Scipio and the others to walk away to their respective commands before asking, "Sir, what about the wounded?"

"What about them?" he asked, and despite the circumstances, I was amused to see how warily he looked up at me.

"Moving them back to camp, only to pack them up and move them to wherever we make camp is going to kill more men," I told him honestly.

"So we should leave them here?" He shook his head, clearly doubtful. "What happens if the Maezaei send out a warband looking for us and they find them instead?"

Although this was a valid question, I also had my answer prepared.

"Leave the cavalry, the *medici,* and half the men acting as stretcher bearers," I suggested. "The cavalry won't be any help with us pulling up our stakes, and there's enough of them to discourage the Maezaei from trying to fall on our wounded."

Germanicus considered this silently, and as he did, I studied him, thinking that I saw the beginnings of the man he would become in the form of the worry lines that creased his otherwise smooth forehead.

Finally, he nodded again and said, "Go tell the Decurion what their orders are."

Then, he walked to where his horse was waiting for him, while I did the same with Latobius, hopping up into the saddle. Glancing up at the sky, I was shocked to see that it was just past midday. If we hurry, I thought, we can get back, break and make camp, or have it mostly completed by the time dark falls. In the back of my mind, I did worry about the First being essentially abandoned, although it would be for only a short period of time. My hope was that Dodonis, or whoever was in actual command of the Maezaei troops, would decide that the risk outweighed the reward of trying to assault while the rest of the Legion was absent. With their own artillery, there was no doubt they could take their fort back, but at what cost?

As Germanicus and I rode back to the camp, we tried to determine exactly how many artillery pieces the Maezaei had, and more importantly, speculated on whether they had used all of them in repulsing our first assault. Unsurprisingly, Scipio's assessment was the Maezaei possessed at least eight pieces, probably more, but although Quartus Pilus Prior Proculus was a bit more cautious in his estimate, his guess of six pieces still seemed high. The Quintus Pilus Prior, another man from Rome by the name of Gaius Stertinius, had not suffered any casualties from artillery, and in fact, had even fewer losses than the Second Cohort. That this was due to the Fifth lagging well behind the Third and Fourth during the assault was something I decided to bring up with Germanicus at some later time; my sense was that the Legate was nearing the end of his tether when it came to further challenges. Recognizing that we were asking the wrong men,

144

I dropped away from Germanicus' side, using the excuse that I needed to tighten the girth of Latobius' saddle. Once I was finished fiddling with it long enough to appear plausible, instead of remounting, I began to walk Latobius alongside the column, just happening to pick the Third Century of the Third Cohort. They had lost six men, four of them left behind on the slope, while the other two were with the wounded, making them understandably somber.

Spotting a familiar face in the middle of the fourth rank, I called out, "*Salve,* Lurco! Tough day, neh?"

The ranker, another of the old retirees from the 8th, barely glanced over in my direction, giving a bitter laugh as he did so. "That it was, Primus Pilus."

I continued walking with them, silent for a few paces, then I asked quietly, "How many artillery pieces do you think the Maezaei have?"

"No more than three," Lurco answered without hesitation, and when I looked at the faces around him, although none of them spoke, their heads were nodding in agreement. Then, the old veteran added, "If they had had more than that, you wouldn't be talking to any of us."

Despite this aligning with my suspicions, I made sure to ask men from other Centuries, and the answer was more or less the same; there might have been three *ballistae*, but it was more likely two. Once I felt confident, I remounted Latobius, but by this point, we had reached the camp, finding that it had been undisturbed, the four Centuries of mixed forces nevertheless still alert, which made me feel a bit better about them. Because I was ultimately responsible for the First, it was left to me to use the labor I had available to pack up their tents and supervise the loading of the wagons that would normally be used to carry the wounded with the packs of the men, which would drop the baggage at the new site before going to retrieve the men they were supposed to be carrying. Despite trying to be everywhere at once, I knew that, inevitably, rankers in the First would claim that some of their belongings had gone missing, and understandably assigning blame to the slaves and servants who were normally attached to the other Cohorts I had commandeered to help the normal complement of slaves who had been left behind. That many of them would be right was almost beside the point; it was just one more thing to add to the growing list of concerns. My main worry in this regard was what further damage it might do to the morale and relationship between the Cohorts, but there was nothing to be done about it, at least at this moment. Otherwise, the taking down of the camp moved as smoothly as could be expected, and once the First's baggage was taken care of, I went to the *praetorium* to find Germanicus, who was in his office looking at the map created by both the *exploratores* and with my own input. I was curious to see if he had decided on a site, and if so, whether or not it was the one I was planning to suggest. Thankfully, this was one thing that went smoothly, because as soon as he saw me enter, he beckoned to me, then once I was next to him, placed his finger decisively on the exact spot that I was prepared to try to convince him to select.

"I think this is probably the best spot, Pullus. Do you agree?"

"That's the one I had in mind," I told him, which seemed to please the younger man. "Now that we have possession of the fort, we can use the Clandate road, then cut across the slope to the southern side of the town, keeping the fort between us and the town as we move into position. They normally use all that ground for grazing their cattle, so it will be perfect for our purposes. And," I pointed to the thin, serpentine line drawn on the map, "this stream from the mountains feeds into the Valdasus, which actually flows north towards the Savus. Which means that although we're south, we're..."

"Upstream of the town." He nodded, instantly understanding the significance, confirmed by the grimly amused smile he gave me as he added, "Which will serve as our own Cloaca Maxima."

"The men will have to dig a channel," I replied, "but depending on the boundary of the camp, it might not have to be very far."

"Well," he concluded, "at least that's taken care of. But," the smile vanished, "what about taking the town?"

"We're going to need more artillery," I answered instantly.

"But the Legate has turned down all of my requests for more," he protested.

146

This, I knew, was certainly true, but one thing had changed since his last request.

"That was before we knew they had artillery of their own," I pointed out.

"That's true," he granted. "I'll send a dispatch rider to Siscia immediately."

"Perhaps," I suggested, "you might wait until we've relocated the camp, then the rider will know the exact location. And," I actually thought this was the most important point, "you can send him out after it's dark. He'll have a much better chance that way."

I had not meant this as a rebuke in any way, but I saw the sudden rush of red spotting Germanicus' cheeks, his only response a nod.

Returning to the subject at hand, Germanicus turned not to me, but to Appuleius, who had been standing silently, making him one of the better Tribunes with whom I had any congress, and asked him, "Sextus, what do you think we should do now?"

This struck me as a curious thing to ask, not only because of the question, but that Germanicus asked someone other than me, though I managed to stifle a jab of irritation as I waited to hear what Appuleius had to say.

Appuleius did not answer immediately, at least appearing to give the question serious consideration, then said, "Honestly, I think we're going to have to conduct a full siege of the town."

This was actually exactly my thought, but I did not say anything, waiting to hear how Germanicus responded, thinking it might give me some insight into what our Legate was considering.

"And," Germanicus asked conversationally, as if the pair were seated in their *triclinium*, discussing something that was merely an interesting topic of little import, "how would you go about doing this?"

Again, Appuleius considered, then shrugged, saying, "We need to encircle the town somehow. Build up our fortifications. Then use the artillery we're going to get from your fath...from the Legate to create a breach in the wall."

I was listening carefully, both out of curiosity to see how much Appuleius understood, but also in trying to determine why Germanicus had chosen this moment to seemingly conduct a tutoring session with one of his Tribunes.

Appuleius continued, "Once we take the town, we can then decide how to take their stronghold." He looked at Germanicus, and finished, "Do you agree, Germanicus?"

"I do," he replied immediately, then the Legate glanced over at me, and asked, "And what about you, Pullus?"

Although I generally agreed, as far as I was concerned, Appuleius had been extremely skimpy on details, like how we would encircle a town with less than a Legion's worth of men, especially now that we had been bloodied so badly.

Regardless, I answered Germanicus readily enough. "I agree that we need to conduct a siege. How we're going to do that is something I think we should wait to decide until we're settled in the new camp."

As I suspected, Appuleius clearly did not appreciate what I meant as a subtle rebuke, but frankly, I cared only about Germanicus, who I was pleased to see nod his understanding, which was confirmed when he said, "You're right, of course, Pullus. One thing at a time, neh?"

"Absolutely, sir. One thing at a time, as you say."

Thus began what turned out to be a siege that lasted more than two long months.

Chapter 3

The relocation of the camp occurred with a minimum of trouble, especially considering our reduced numbers. Locating it a bit less than a mile from the southern wall of Splonum, Germanicus ordered that the ditch that served as the northern boundary be extended the entire width of the valley, thereby cutting off any Maezaei attempt to encircle or bypass our camp. With that accomplished, the next order of business was to dig a channel between the stream that supplied our fresh water, and another that carried our waste to the Valdasus. I felt certain that there was more than one source of water that the people of the town could draw from, but it is always best to do whatever one can to make the enemy's life more miserable. As Germanicus had ordered, at my suggestion, the dispatch rider was sent that first night, chosen by Gaesorix as one of his most dependable men; that it was the trooper Cassicos, who we had rescued from the cave and who had survived what still ranks as the most gruesome wound I have ever seen, was a testament to the man's toughness. His back was horribly scarred where it had been sewn back into place, but Gaesorix had assured me that the man was not crippled in any way. The fact that he was willing to ride alone through hostile territory, even if it was under the cover of darkness, was further testimony to the quality of the Batavian tribe, which means it comes as no surprise to see how rapidly Rome has assimilated them into the ranks of our auxiliaries and cavalry.

The first week in the new camp was spent almost completely in the strengthening of our fortifications, with most of the effort spent on the construction of a trench that ran directly from the northern edge of the camp and extended in the direction of Splonum, following the contour of the base of the ridge, where it terminated close to the gateway of the stone fort, one of two, this one located on the southern side. Between the slope, the preponderance of stumps, and the amount of buried rock, the ditch ended a bit more than a hundred paces away from the fort, with the end of the ditch tapered upward to form a ramp. While this presented a bit of a challenge, between the relatively short

149

distance and either changing the garrison or sending supplies under the cover of darkness, we were able to ensure the fort stayed in our possession. At first, the ditch was just wide enough to allow a loaded mule, but as our plans progressed, it was widened, and it was the second week before our entire complement of artillery was transferred into the fort.

Speaking of artillery, despite my skepticism, not only did Cassicos reach Siscia, but Tiberius agreed to Germanicus' request for more *ballistae* and scorpions. Better yet, he sent it under the escort of a full Cohort of veterans, detached from Tiberius' own forces, along with two more Centuries of auxiliaries, also from the Taurisci tribe, giving us six full Cohorts of Legionaries, and a Cohort of auxiliaries, freedmen, and slaves. They brought with them three *ballistae* and six more scorpions, with one of the *ballista* being the largest type that could throw rocks of ten pounds and higher, this one being transported in two wagons. The arrival of this bounty created something of a festival atmosphere, although it also was the driving event in the widening of the ditch leading to the stone fort. With these reinforcements, we were able to conduct more of a proper siege, mainly with the construction of another, smaller camp on the opposite, northern side of Splonum. More accurately, it was the improvement of the existing camp where Gaesorix, the bulk of the cavalry, and the four Centuries of auxiliaries were located, which was barely adequate to simply discourage the Maezaei from attempting to either break out or be reinforced.

However, to our cautiously pleased surprise, the barbarians inside the town seemed content to watch us as we prepared for their destruction, which at first I viewed with a fair amount of, if not nervousness, at least caution. My thought was that someone like Dodonis, who had already managed to surprise us, was not likely to be content to sit and watch without attempting some sort of intervening course of action. Not that the Maezaei were idle; quickly understanding our intent, over the course of three nights, they managed to raze every building within artillery range of the stone fort; at least the range of our standard artillery. Perhaps I can be forgiven

150

for believing that I was ultimately the cause for this precaution, given what we had done four years before when we retaliated for Sextus' death. The part of the town we had destroyed by fire had naturally been rebuilt, and I found myself in the unusual position of feeling a twinge of sympathy for those Maezaei who had reconstructed their dwellings and shops, only to see their homes destroyed once again. I suppose my hatred of the Maezaei had cooled over the intervening time, but I certainly never expressed any of this to anyone, not even Alex. Unlike with our permanent Century, Alex did not have much clerical work to do; Germanicus was not a stickler for the kind of record keeping that was expected of a regular Legion, and I suppose his thought was that, once this crisis was over, this command would be disbanded, the men allowed to return to their homes instead of simply marching back to their permanent camp.

The arrival of the artillery, particularly the large *ballista,* rendered the Maezaei precautions at least partially ineffective, simply because the range of the large piece was farther than the distance they had cleared. Provided we used it properly, this could prove to be just the decisive edge we needed, but we had to be careful not to expose the fact that we had possession of such a potent weapon. Our expansion of the ditch was a risk, but it was less so than any attempt to move the large piece to the fort; even under the cover of darkness, there was no way the Maezaei would not hear the sound of a heavily laden wagon, and the pieces were simply too large to be transported by mules. In order to minimize warning, the Maezaei, who had sentries posted along the wall at all times, Germanicus ordered the men to work at night, in complete darkness, and taking even more of a risk, ordered all six Cohorts in the southern camp, minus a single Century in the stone fort, to perform the work, along with every spare slave; even Alex was pressed into service, although I did restrict him to hauling the spoil up out of the ditch with a rope attached to a wicker basket. All through the night the men worked, and it was understandably one of the sloppiest jobs I had ever seen, with the spoil simply hauled up and dumped in an untidy pile, while the Centurions strode up and down the finished portion of the ditch, smacking the laggards as a reminder of the urgency. And I was right among them, though for once I spared the *vitus*, preferring to use more positive encouragement in the form of reminding the men of all the loot that lay on the other side of that wall. A dozen slaves were assigned another task, wrapping the wheels of the wagon in rags, oiling the axles, and tying down the loose bits of tack that would be attached to the oxen that were the only beasts strong enough to pull the wagons.

By the time it was midnight, the men were still working hard, but had made it barely halfway to the fort, prompting the Legate to command that the wagon be driven into the completed portion of the ditch, then move inch by inch towards the stone fort. As the freedmen responsible for the wagons skillfully guided the oxen, using the combination of the reins and a goad with a long strip of braided leather attached to the end that they snapped just above the heads of the beasts, despite all the precautions that had been taken to muffle the movement, I winced at the level of noise, not believing it possible that the Maezaei on the wall could miss hearing it. My hope was that it was because I was standing nearby, next to Germanicus, Silius, and Appuleius as we watched what we hoped would be the maneuver that would give us the advantage we needed to make certain this siege was as short as possible.

More to pass the time than anything, I turned to Germanicus and jokingly said, "I'm surprised you didn't order a circumvallation like Divus Julius did at Alesia, instead of trying to use a ruse like this."

"I thought about it," Germanicus admitted ruefully, "and if we had a bigger army, I'd have done it."

"I imagine you've read his Commentaries a time or two," I commented offhandedly, more to pass the time than for any other purpose.

"Read them?" Germanicus laughed, although there was what might have been a bitter edge to it as he said, "My adoptive grandfather made me memorize them, just like with The Iliad and Odyssey." I shot a glance at him, thinking he was jesting, but his face was dead serious, and he made a face that reminded me of the times I had balked when Diocles had been my tutor as he continued, "In fact, if he has his way, memorizing Caesar's Commentaries is going to be considered a cornerstone of a patrician's education."

This prompted a laugh from me, and Germanicus shot me a look that, even in the darkness, I interpreted as if he was trying to decide whether to say something. Finally, he seemed to come to some decision, because with a jerk of his head, he indicated I should follow him, and we walked a short distance away from the Tribunes. I saw them watching us, but slightly surprisingly, neither Silius nor Appuleius made any move to follow. Once we were more than a dozen paces away, Germanicus took what I believe was the further precaution by turning so his back was to them before he spoke.

"You know, Pullus," he began, his voice just above a whisper and pitched low, "I've given a lot of thought about why I trust you so much." He paused before saying something that made my blood run cold. "If I'm being honest, I was warned against doing that very thing, by men I also trust. Or," he amended slightly, "mostly trust. But," he shook his head, "I think you and I have a lot more in common than I do with those men who are whispering in my ear about the danger of putting my trust in someone of the lower classes in general. And," I must credit him for looking up at me, meeting my gaze directly as he finished, "someone bearing the Pullus name."

Honestly, it was quite difficult for me to keep my mind focused on what was ultimately a compliment as I wondered who exactly had been disparaging my family, but I forced myself to do so, asking instead, "And, what is it we have in common?"

"We both have so much pressure to live up to the legacy of our fathers and grandfathers," Germanicus replied instantly. "In his own way, and with the Head Count, your grandfather is as famous in his own way as mine. And," he said earnestly, "you've been under the same kind of pressure that I feel."

This, I thought, was something that had crossed my own mind long before and was a reason why I felt the way I did about this young noble. Despite feeling the same way, it was a bit awkward for me to say as much, and I experienced a flash of insight in that instant, that even in this Germanicus and I were similar. He had been warned about my family, and I confess his stating that this was the case had ignited a flare of anger in me, yet I forced myself not only to tamp it down, but to acknowledge that I had been warned by both my family and those of my class about trusting someone of his status, in both class, blood, and more importantly, by someone connected with the Princeps. Ultimately, I realized as we stood there that this was something else we had in common; if we were to heed the warnings of our kin, neither of us would trust the other man at all. Yet, I did, and here he was saying essentially the same thing.

"That," I finally managed, "is certainly true. Now," frankly, I was quite uncomfortable, "let's see if we both can live up to the expectations." I pointed in the direction of the fort, seeing a flurry of movement as men scrambled up ladders, out of the ditch. "It looks like they're finished."

Turning, Germanicus saw the same thing, then trotted to his horse, leaping into the saddle without help, as I followed suit on Latobius. The Tribunes hurried to catch up, but when we reached the spot where the ramp up out of the ditch began, we saw that our troubles were not over. Although it was true the wagon had reached the point where the ramp out of the ditch started, the grade was too steep for the oxen to drag out the wagon. The only positive note was that the wagon itself was still down in the ditch, the top of it just inches below the lip of the ditch. This, unfortunately, was where the good news ended; even in the darkness, there was no way that the Maezaei just a few hundred paces away could miss the mass of movement next to the stone fort. No, they could not make out details in the darkness, but it would not take much of an imagination for them to determine the likely cause.

"We need to get the men back into the ditch so they can head back to camp that way," I urged Germanicus. "There's too many of them standing around up here!"

He did not reply—to me, at any rate—but he kicked his mount into a trot, pulling up in front of someone wearing the transverse crest whose back was to me. Since Germanicus was approaching from the same direction, it meant the Centurion had to turn around, yet even before he did, I suspected I knew who it would be, and I was right. I was still a bit too far away to hear, particularly since Germanicus had his voice pitched low, but I could make out Scipio shaking his head; more importantly, men were still milling about next to the ditch. Rather than wait for our Legate to handle a man who was his subordinate so gently, I kicked Latobius hard, and he leapt forward.

"Get into the fucking ditch," I snarled at the men, and while most of them obeyed immediately, I saw a handful of them, nearest to Scipio, look at him uncertainly.

"Those men are under my command, Pullus!" Scipio snapped, his face suddenly gone pale with rage.

"No," I shot back, "they're not. They're under his," I pointed to Germanicus, who looked extremely nonplussed, "and under mine as Primus Pilus."

"You're *not* the Primus Pilus!" Scipio shot back. "You're just a Princeps Prior, and not even of the First Cohort! You have no right to command me!"

Here it is, out in the open, I thought. Now Germanicus was forced to deal with the one thing that he had been avoiding, although I bear just as much responsibility for not forcing our Legate to make my role more defined than it had been to this point. Not surprisingly, both Scipio and I looked to Germanicus, and not even the darkness could hide his unhappy expression at being put on the spot.

However, if he hesitated, it was for no more than a heartbeat or two, and Germanicus turned to Scipio and said quietly, "Pullus is the *de facto* Primus Pilus, Scipio, and I apologize if I didn't make that clear before. But," now he turned to me, and his expression became, or at least he attempted to look, severe, "Pullus, I had this handled."

"I protest this...this..." Scipio spluttered, and while he was gesturing up at me, I would like to think that whatever was going to come out of his mouth, he thought better of it, settling on, "...decision of yours, Germanicus."

"I believe," Germanicus replied, but while his voice was pitched low, there was iron in it, "you're supposed to address your superior by their proper rank, Pilus Prior."

Scipio's mouth dropped open, looking as if he had been slapped, then he snapped it shut, and without a word or rendering a salute, he turned and stalked off. Now it was my turn to gape in shock, except this was aimed at Germanicus, who sat his horse without saying a word, his face suddenly like a stone mask, and I was struck that this would be what his statue looked like.

"You're not going to stop him?" I blurted this out, and this seemed to snap the Legate out of whatever state he was in as he glared at me for a heartbeat.

Then, his shoulders slumped, and he said tiredly, "Not right now, Pullus. We have other things to do. Besides," he added this softly, almost as if he was trying to convince himself, "dealing with Scipio is...complicated." Before I could comment, he shook his head and said briskly, "Get the men down into the ditch while I try to figure out what to do."

"That," I promised him, "isn't going to be a problem. In fact," I decided to make myself sound cheerful, grinning over at him, "we're going to kill two problems at one time."

While I did not ask, my suspicion was that Germanicus had envisioned some incredibly complex solution for the stuck wagon, involving block and tackle, the kind of engineering solution for which we Romans are rightfully famous. Instead, I solved the problem by having those men outside the ditch hop back down, then with some of them pushing, others of them using makeshift harnesses that they attached to the oxen, used brute force to drag the first wagon up and out of the ditch, followed by the second one, which was set up in the exact same manner. Once both wagons were out, however, we did not allow neither men nor beasts to rest, using the last of their strength to move the wagons as quickly as possible into the fort, driving them through the open gateway. The sky began lightening not long after the gates were closed, while only the oxen were taken back up the ditch back to the southern camp, leaving the wagons in the fort. The smaller artillery had been broken down and packed on mules, which had already been taken into the fort, except for the scorpions, for which

Germanicus said he had other plans. According to the *Immune,* Aulus Bibaculus, who was in charge of the large piece and who had come with it along with his crew, they would not be ready until well after midday the next day, while the smaller pieces, although still unassembled, could be put together very rapidly. After we discussed it, Germanicus decided to use the cover of darkness to drag the small pieces up to the rampart, then assemble them there; however, there would not be time to do it on this night.

"We begin the assault at first light, day after tomorrow," he announced to the assembled officers back in the *praetorium.* "But we're going to start with the smaller *ballistae* first, and we're going to concentrate on creating a breach." Unrolling a large piece of vellum and placing it atop the map that showed the surrounding vicinity, he pointed to the spot he had selected. "This is the closest point the wall comes to the stronghold, which makes it the obvious choice for us to concentrate."

"Which will be just as obvious to the barbarians inside the walls," Scipio sniffed, his patrician nose tilting up at just the proper degree to express his disdain for his commander's plan. "It seems to me to be better to spread our effort out with four different spots, since that's the number of the small *ballistae* we have in our possession. Although," he gave our Legate a smile that was as insincere as his words, "if we used that large beast, we'd make such short work of that wall, we could be inside the town before they could muster their forces to meet us in the breach."

Somewhat surprisingly, Germanicus did not seem offended; if anything, he appeared to be pleased that Scipio had raised this objection.

"Scipio," he returned the man's smile, and I saw it was just as false a coin as the one he had been offered, "that's exactly why I want us to concentrate our effort to one spot. I *want* the Maezaei to come rushing to defend that breach."

I sensed the eyes of some of the other Centurions on me, but I could only give a slight shake of my head; Germanicus had not

157

confided in me beforehand, making me just as interested in his plan as any of them.

Clearly enjoying the atmosphere of suspenseful anticipation he had created, Germanicus went on to explain, "We're going to force the Maezaei to make a choice."

Once more pointing down to the vellum, he indicated the series of squares that had been created in a rough approximation of the layout of the buildings of the town. Although they were not to scale, most importantly, using our vantage point from the stone fort, and from high up the western ridge, the intersection and direction of the dirt streets had been drawn with meticulous care, so that at a glance, we could see the best and shortest direction to take to get to the stronghold once we took the outer wall.

Going on, Germanicus said, "Once they've assembled the bulk of their troops near the breach, that's when we use the large piece." Glancing up, he moved his gaze from one face to another, apparently waiting for questions; when there were none, he continued, "*Immune* Bibaculus has informed me that the stronghold is about two hundred paces short of the large piece, at least from where it is currently positioned inside the stone fort. The problem is that he has to change the trajectory to clear the wall of the fort, which shortens the range. So," his finger had been resting on the square representing the stronghold, and he suddenly moved it, tapping the map, "instead of going for the stronghold, we're going to aim for this line of buildings here."

Predictably, it was Scipio who, with a frown, shook his head, saying in a brusque manner that bordered on outright rudeness, "How will knocking down some of their hovels help us?"

My eyes had stayed on Germanicus, so I believe I was the first man present to get a presentiment of what he was about to say.

"Because we're not going to be just knocking them down," Germanicus said quietly, "we're going to be firing them."

I experienced a sudden wave of...something; not fear, exactly, but dread, as the memory of another town going up in flames leapt into the forefront of my mind, suddenly remembering the intense heat, and

158

worse, the smells of men burning to death. That some of them, like Bestia, had been comrades, only made the emotional impact worse; as I learned that night, there is no difference in the smell of men burning to death, whether they be Roman or barbarian.

The silence around the table stretched out, and the other men began exchanging glances, silently urging someone else to speak, but finally, it was Agrippa who asked, "And then what?"

"Then," Germanicus replied, "the defenders are going to be forced to make a choice between stopping us or saving their homes. Also," he drew our attention back to the map, "if you notice, where I've directed Bibaculus to target will cut off any defenders who stay at the wall from either retreating back to the stronghold, or any reinforcements coming from the stronghold to help them at the breach."

This, we all could see, was true, but I, for one, was not sanguine that the fire could be controlled that easily. After all, I reasoned, it had been the swirling wind that had created the conditions that consumed the Varciani town during Draxo's rebellion. It was true that, while there were similarities between that town that no longer existed and Splonum, the differences between the two were significant. Namely, while Splonum is surrounded on two sides by higher ground, because the Valdasus had created the valley in which the town sat, the northern and southern sides of the town are open, while the other town had been completely surrounded by heights. Also, the prevailing wind, now in the beginning of April, had begun blowing from the south, at least most days. The problem was that we were still in the time of year when, for a day, or even two, whatever gods control the winds would capriciously change the direction, meaning it was not out of the realm of possibility that the entire town could be consumed. That said, the real question was whether or not this was important to Germanicus, but rather than ask, I bit my tongue, probably because I did not want to know the answer.

Preparations continued the next day, including the transfer of most of the cavalry from the northern camp, leaving behind two *turmae* to hold it with the Cohort of auxiliaries, and the two Centuries of freedmen. After some discussion, Germanicus agreed to give the northern camp two scorpions; I had pressed for more, but he was unwilling to give more than two. Moving between the two camps was somewhat difficult, because we had to stay above the cleared area now that we knew the Maezaei had artillery, but the transfer was made with minimal problems. Meanwhile, at the request of the *Immune* Bibaculus, a tough, grizzled veteran who normally belonged to the 15th Legion, the ironworking *immunes* created a special device, something like a bucket made of strips of latticed iron. Its purpose was to hold the ammunition that, at the same time, men were busy preparing inside the stone fort. Under normal circumstances, flammable ammunition is nothing more than small clay pots with stoppered lids that are secured to the pot with wax, and from a hole in the lid, an oil-soaked twisted rag protrudes, or sometimes a length of rope, also soaked in oil. The pots, even full of the combustible material, do not weigh much, but they are designed this way in order to shatter and thereby spread the flames over a wider area. Consequently, they don't do much physical damage from the impact, but while I never learned whose idea it was, the ammunition we would be using was an ingenious combination of the two types. Sheets of leather of the type carried by every Legion, usually used to replace *caligae,* or other bits of leather gear, were softened by soaking, but rather than in water, as would be normal, these sheets were soaked in oil. Once they were pliable, men were busy wrapping them around the stock of both fifteen- and some of the ten-pound stones, securing the skins with rawhide thongs.

"That's why we need an iron basket, instead of the leather sling," Bibaculus had explained to Germanicus and me. "It shortens the range a bit, since the leather is elastic and adds a bit of power when the missile is launched. But," he gave a cackling laugh, "we can't take too long once we light the stones. It's going to scorch the *ballista* as it is, but if we're slow, that seasoned wood will go up like that." He snapped his fingers to demonstrate. "But," he finished, "one of those stones will tear through a roof or wall and bury itself inside a building, which

160

will make it difficult for them to put it out before the fire fully catches."

I had to admit I was impressed, and I wondered why I had never seen this used before, but when I asked Bibaculus this, he looked slightly uncomfortable as he admitted, "Because only a crack crew can make this work without burning up their piece. But," the *Immune* boasted, "you won't find a better crew than my boys!"

Shooting a glance over at Germanicus, I saw he was, if not unsettled, then at least somewhat concerned, though he did not say anything about the challenge, only offering the veteran encouragement. It was when we were walking away and out of earshot that I felt compelled to speak.

"Are you sure you want to do this?"

He did not look up at me, choosing to stare straight ahead as we strode towards the southern gate of the fort where our mounts were waiting.

"Am I sure?" he echoed, then surprised me by admitting, "No, I'm not sure. But," his voice turned grim, "I'm not going to fail to take Splonum. And I think this is the best way to do it." Finally, he shot me a sidelong glance, asking lightly, "What do you think?"

"I think," I said grimly, "that given the manpower available to us, I don't think this is the right thing." I paused just long enough for him to react before I finished, "I think it's about the only thing we can do."

Shortly before dawn of the next day, I led the First Cohort from the camp, followed by the other four of the originals of the *Legio Germanicus*; Germanicus had decided to leave our newest Cohort, the Sixth, in reserve in the camp, although they would move to the fort once we began the assault on the breach. I had performed my normal pre-battle ritual of sharpening my Gallic *gladius*, taking comfort in the monotony of a task that I had done so often before. Once that was accomplished, I had Alex send for the Centurions of the First, offering them watered wine, ignoring the sour looks and muttered comments, particularly from Metellus, who I had decided belonged with the First. Somewhat surprisingly, Agrippa had fought this move; I had assumed, incorrectly, that the young Secundus Pilus Prior would chafe at having a grubby ranker as his second in command of his Cohort. However, it had been Metellus who informed me that the nobleman had often sought Metellus' counsel, and while he never came out and said as much, I could tell my old comrade actually respected Agrippa a great deal. What I also learned, mainly through observation, was that Germanicus had not been happy with the arrangement, and with Alex's help, I learned that it had to with the fact he had actually promised the post of Secundus Pilus Posterior to one of the young nobles he had brought with him from Rome, which was ruined because of my big mouth making promises he felt honor bound to uphold. Consequently, this transfer served Germanicus' purposes as neatly as my own, leading to his presence in my tent.

"He's not normally this stingy." Metellus whispered this, but loudly enough that I would hear.

"That's not going to work," I told him, though I grinned at him for trying. "I'd rather hear you complaining now than listen to you bitch and moan tomorrow about sore heads and sour stomachs."

"Better than spending the night before battle with a dry throat," he shot back, but when he saw I was still unmoved, he lapsed into a grumbling acquiescence of this reality.

"I suppose we're going to be first through the breach."

This came from Lucius Veratius, my newly demoted Princeps Prior, the news of which he had taken with surprisingly good grace, or at least had pretended to do so.

"Yes," I answered simply, not seeing any reason to add anything.

Veratius nodded, as did the others, but I saw by their expressions that, with one exception, the prospect of storming a newly opened breach in a wall was not how they would have chosen to spend their day. That Metellus was the exception was not due to any excess of martial ardor or dreams of glory—he was too old for that—but he was more occupied with eyeing the amphora sitting on the table next to my desk, gazing at it with a longing that made it difficult for me to concentrate.

Finally, I could take it no more, grumbling, "Fine. The rest of you can thank Metellus for this." I signaled to Alex, who had been trying to make himself inconspicuous by standing against the wall of the tent, and he hurried over, producing extra cups from the small cabinet under the table. Pouring six cups, he offered each Centurion one, but when he handed Metellus his, the old veteran squinted down at the contents, then looked back up at my nephew with a lifted eyebrow, though he said nothing.

Alex looked over at me, but I was impatient to continue, so I contented myself with a look of disgust, telling the boy, "Go ahead. Fill it to the brim. If you don't, I'll never hear the end of it."

Metellus was anything but chastised, smacking his lips as he watched Alex fill his cup as I had directed, then once it was fully charged, said, "You are a truly fine and noble lad, and your generosity will earn you favor from the gods!"

Although I was mostly amused, I was also not above exacting a petty vengeance of my own, so that when Metellus lifted the cup to his lips, I cleared my throat, stopping him before he could take a swallow.

"Since we're drinking," I said this with a straight face, "I think it's appropriate to raise a toast to the success of the First."

"The First!"

The men repeated this, raising their cups, and it was actually quite ragged and not nearly with the unison I expected, but although I was struck by the urge to make them repeat it, I stifled the impulse. There was a moment of silence as the men drank, and I was cautiously pleased that the only man who appeared to need the fortification from Bacchus was Metellus, while the others took small, almost cautious sips of the unwatered wine. However, I was unworried about Servius Metellus' performance the next morning; he had always been fond of his wine, back when we marched together in the First of the Fourth, and it had never affected his performance.

It was Blasio, the Hastatus Posterior, who broke the silence by asking me, "How long do you think it will take to create the breach, Primus Pilus?"

163

The only answer I could provide was one that I knew was unlikely to satisfy him and the others, but I was only being honest when I replied, "It's almost impossible to say. It depends on the wall and what it's made of."

"Made of?" Numerius Tubertus, the Princeps Posterior, was openly skeptical, shaking his head as he said, "It's made of stone; anyone can see that!"

I could have used this opportunity to put Tubertus in his place; he had been one of the more troublesome of my Centurions, and I did not think it was a coincidence that he was a close friend of Scipio, but instead of exposing his ignorance directly, I chose another approach. Glancing over at Metellus, who predictably was tilting the cup back to get every last drop, I had to wait for him to lower his head and see that I was looking at him in a manner that told him I was expecting him to contribute. It should have come as no surprise that my old comrade expected recompense, but when he thrust his empty cup out in Alex's direction, I had to bite back a curse, though I gave my nephew a nod.

Thankfully, Metellus began talking before his cup was filled, allowing Alex to refill it while he turned to address Tubertus, saying, "Just because you see stones on the outer part of the wall, that doesn't mean that it's stone all the way through." Glancing over, he saw his cup was full, so naturally he had to take a sip, which I was sure was just to torment me before he continued, "The way these barbarians like to build walls is that they normally all start out as wooden walls, but as the town gets bigger and the tribe gets richer, instead of tearing the wall down, they build an outer wall of stone, except on both the outside and inside."

Deciding Metellus had carried this far enough, I interrupted, finishing by explaining, "So if Splonum is fortified in this way, while knocking down the outer stone part of the wall won't take long, if there are logs as a second layer," I shook my head, "that means we have to burn through that layer. And that," I looked directly at Tubertus, who I was pleased to see looked chastened, "could take several watches."

As I expected, this did not sit well, not only with Tubertus, but with the other three young Centurions, something I could see by the manner in which they took a sudden interest in their own cups of wine. A silence descended, and I had to content myself with glaring at Metellus, who I blamed for setting a bad example.

Finally, I decided that it would be rude not to join my Centurions, although I did mutter, "Just remember I warned you about being hungover tomorrow."

With the four *ballistae* arrayed on the rampart, Bibaculus, who had been appointed the overall commander of the artillery, ordered that the torsion arms be winched back the night before and over a longer period of time than normal.

"The sound of the winch carries, especially at night," he had explained, "so if we want to catch these *cunni* by surprise with the first volley, we should do it gradually."

"But won't that hurt the accuracy?" Germanicus asked, and I saw that Bibaculus was impressed.

"Yes, sir, it will," Bibaculus agreed. "But even if we winched them and loosed immediately, the first volley is never accurate. But it will give us a reference for the next series of shots." He paused to think for a moment, then added, "It may mean an extra volley before we have the range and direction perfect."

"I can live with that," Germanicus replied, though he did glance over at me, but since I agreed, I simply nodded as he continued, "and any advantage we can get I'll take. The surprise may not last long, but it's still better than nothing."

Waiting for the sun to illuminate the section of the southern wall that Bibaculus had calculated was not only within range of the stone fort, but at the proper angle that would enhance the difficulty of the warriors inside the walls reaching the stronghold once the second part of our plan went into effect, I took a moment to examine everything inside our walls. A fire was stoked and ready, while a series of tubs containing the wrapped stones were arranged in a circular pattern around the large piece, which now had the iron basket attached. In short, all was ready; the men of the First Cohort positioned next to the gateway that faced the southern wall, while the other Cohorts were either still in the camp, or concealed by the ditch, since there was not room for all of our force inside the fort. After what seemed to be a full watch, but I knew was barely a third of one, the wall came bursting into the full light of the sun as it rose above the eastern ridge.

"All right, boys!" I turned from my examination of the wall at the sound of Bibaculus' voice. "Let's introduce these *cunni* to what their future home will look like!" He paused only long enough to check that every man responsible for yanking the cord attached to the pin holding the *ballista* was looking in his direction, waiting for his next command. Seeing all was ready, the *Immune* actually turned to Germanicus. "Legate, we are ready for your order."

While this had not been discussed beforehand, Germanicus did not hesitate, raising his arm, holding it for an instant before sweeping it downward while calling out in a loud, commanding tone, "*Ballistae*...loose!"

The sudden cracking sound was the loudest noise that had been made to this point, prompting me to return my attention to the wall in the instant after the command. At this moment, there were only about two dozen Maezaei visible on the parapet within the vicinity of the spot that had been selected, but even from this distance, I saw their heads jerk up sharply, telling me they at least understood what the echoing sound meant. It was the fate of one of them, however, that I most vividly remember, because he either misjudged how close the stone missile would come to where he was standing or decided to risk sacrificing himself in order to shout a warning. As I watched, this one Maezaei spun about, and although I could not hear the call itself, I could see his arms move as he cupped his hands around his mouth in order to amplify the sound of his voice. Whether or not he actually managed to alert his comrades presumably housed in the buildings nearest to the wall I would never know, because faster than my mind could comprehend the sight my eyes took in, one of the four stones of the first volley plummeted down out of the sky to sweep him from the rampart. My last glimpse was of his body, or the pieces of it, tumbling out of sight behind the wall; otherwise, the other stones were spread across a span of what appeared to be at least fifty paces, with another one sailing high and crashing into the roof of the nearest building, while the final two hit the wall, but so far from each other that they would be useless for the purpose of breaching. Bibaculus, watching from his spot in between the inner *ballistae*, turned and snapped out a series of corrections, addressing the crews of each piece in turn, even as the pair of men responsible were cranking the winch that drew the arms of their *ballista* back into position.

"This," I told Germanicus, "could take a while. May I give my men the order that they can sit down and break out something to eat?"

The Legate did not respond, but he did nod distractedly, his eyes never leaving the wall, as if by his willpower alone it would tumble down. Leaving him, I went and called down to Metellus, telling him to spread the word, and by the time I was back next to Germanicus, I could follow the progress of my second in command by the cheers of the men. For a moment, I considered also ordering the Centurions to inspect each ranker's canteen to ensure that it was filled with water, but I quickly thought better of it. If these men had not been old veterans, I would have gone through with this, except these rankers had centuries of combined experience in fighting Rome's wars, and I was not about to run the risk of exposing them to a punishment that is extremely harsh, not when some of my Centurions were men like Scipio. Speaking of the Tertius Pilus Prior, although he had shown up for Germanicus' final meeting more than a third of a watch before dawn, he had since disappeared; my guess was that he had returned to his tent to sulk. Agrippa, however, was down in the fort with some of his Cohort, and I paused just long enough to watch as he circulated among his men, apparently sharing a joke with one, then patting another man on the back. Seeing this made me wonder just how much of what makes a leader comes from what one learns, and how much is simply passed through the blood. Recognizing this as one of those random thoughts that, ultimately, have no value in moments such as this, I returned to Germanicus' side just in time to see the second volley. All four stones not only hit the wall, but within a matter of feet from each other, forming a rough, circular indentation in the stones of the wall. Despite this positive sign, I felt compelled to point out to

Germanicus something that I had noticed earlier but did not feel sufficiently confident about to bring it up until this moment.

It was due to the Legate turning and giving me a triumphant grin as he crowed, "It doesn't look like it's going to take nearly as long as you think, Pullus!" Suddenly, he slapped his forehead, which startled me, but he explained his act when he said, "I *knew* I forgot something! I should have bet you on how quickly the wall comes down!"

This made me laugh, despite myself, but then I remembered what I was about to say, so in answer, I pointed down to the wall, saying, "Before you lose your money, can I point something out to you?"

The way his face changed so quickly was more than worth it, and he asked suspiciously, "What is it?"

"See how their wall is made of native, not dressed stone?" I asked him, but he was nothing if not dismissive.

"Yes, yes," he scoffed, "we already discussed this! And," he pressed, "the fact that they didn't dress the stones but used rocks and just filled in the spaces with mortar is why it won't take long to bring down!"

"That," I answered carefully, "is true. Except that," I did pause for a moment, mainly because I was still trying to recall exactly from where this piece of knowledge I had suddenly remembered came, but I still could not place it, so I continued, "most of the time barbarians use this method, it's because they're building around something that's already there."

Germanicus' expression faltered, and I watched as he glanced back at the wall, studying it for a moment before turning back to me, saying only, "Go on."

"You're absolutely right that it doesn't take as long to bring down a wall made of native rock, simply because, as you know," I felt it would not hurt to stroke his pride a bit, "a crack will travel down through the mortar, and with irregularly shaped rocks, that means there could be a couple of feet before the crack is stopped because it runs into another stone. But with shaped and dressed rocks, which are offset as well, a crack will only travel the height of two, or maybe three stones." Pointing back at the wall, I finished by saying, "That's why I feel fairly certain that this wall was built around an existing wooden one."

"That," Germanicus sighed, "is what I thought you were going to say. But," he shrugged, his tone turning, if not resigned, then at least as if he was preparing himself for the possibility, "we'll see if you're right."

As matters turned out, I was indeed correct, but it is to Germanicus the credit must go for turning what could have been a setback into what was ultimately a positive event that aided us in our efforts. Actually, it took barely a third of a watch to penetrate the outer stone shell, aided by the thing I had pointed out, as large cracks began developing around the third or fourth volley, moving several feet in multiple directions because there was only mortar and not rock in the way. Once that happened, huge chunks of the wall fell away in large, intact sections, quickly exposing the vertical wooden logs of the original wall.

"I don't see why we can't just batter those down as easily as we did the rock."

Scipio, to my disgust, had finally reappeared, joining what had become a small party of officers on the rampart as we watched Bibaculus and his men do their work, and he was the one to make this uninformed comment. However, rather than being the one to put the boy in his place, I managed to keep my mouth shut, so that it fell to Germanicus, although from my perspective, he seemed eager enough.

"Well," the Legate responded coolly, "I see why we can't. It's because while the rock is brittle; strong," he allowed, "but brittle wood has more give in it, so it can absorb the strike of a rock more easily. Which," he finished, pointing at Bibaculus, "is why we need to change the ammunition."

This was the point where several of his officers urged him to change our plan, and I confess I was one of them.

"We can use the large *ballista*," I believe it was Silius who said this, "and the extra weight should do it."

"It would," Bibaculus was the one who spoke up, having arrived just in time to hear what the Tribune had said, "although it would ruin the surprise we have planned. Still," he shrugged, "that would be the fastest way to knock those fucking," his weathered features flushed, and he stammered, "er, I mean, those cursed logs down."

"No," Germanicus replied mildly, "I think 'fucking logs' is appropriate."

This, as I was guessing he wanted, elicited a laugh from most of us, except for Scipio and Stertinius, who I had noticed seemed to mimic Scipio in his attitude towards those of us they considered beneath them.

Then, Germanicus surprised us when he continued, "But I don't want to use the large piece." Turning to Bibaculus, he asked, "Pretend we didn't have the large piece. How would you attack the wooden part of the wall?"

"That's simple," the *Immune* answered immediately. "We'd use the small pieces, but we'd use the flammable ammunition." He shrugged as he added, "It will take longer, but as long as we keep hitting the exposed wood, they'll try to douse the flames, and they'll be successful. For a while," he said pointedly. "But once it catches and gets hot enough, there's no way they can stop it. Then," he finished with another shrug, "there's no telling how long it will take."

"Won't we have to knock down the other part of the stone wall?" I asked, but while I was surprised he shook his head, Bibaculus did not hesitate at all.

"No," he replied firmly, "because the fire will be so hot that the stones on the other side will basically explode. Actually," he amended slightly, "what will happen is that it won't be the rocks, but the mortar. It may not seem like it, but there's moisture in mortar, and the heat from the fire will make the mortar basically crumble. And," he finished, "unlike a normal wall made of finished stones that are offset, a wall with all those differently shaped rocks will never stand on its own without being anchored in some way."

"If," Germanicus interjected, his tone thoughtful, "we use the small pieces, it will take more time, but it will also convince the barbarians that this is all the artillery we have. After all," he favored us with a grim smile, "if we had that," he pointed down to where the large *ballista* sat, poised and waiting, "we'd surely use it, neh? So if we don't, it will never occur to them that we have it."

Once he explained his reasoning, I instantly understood he was right. Fortunately, while some were disposed to argue, most of the other officers clearly saw the sense in what Germanicus had said. The result was that Bibaculus ordered his men to switch the type of ammunition, and while men began carrying the stoppered jars up to the rampart, the *Immune* gave his crews the necessary information to adjust for the lighter load each *ballista* would be flinging. As he did this, lit oil lamps were also brought up to the rampart, so that in a short space of time, all was ready, and the attack resumed. Just as Bibaculus had predicted, the Maezaei worked frantically to try and douse the flames, and the first few times they were successful, but finally, a pot hit right at the base of the wall, well out of the reach of any of the warriors, unless they were willing to be lowered down with a rope, which did not happen. Well before midday, the wall was blazing fiercely, but this was the point where not even Bibaculus and his experience could tell us how long it might take. Most of the others, including the Tribunes, grew bored waiting for the inevitable, essentially doing nothing more than watching as the smoke rose high into the sky; I remember wondering if the Maezaei in Raetinium would be able to see it, and if they would know what it meant if they did see it. My guess was that, since they were almost forty miles away it was unlikely, and even if they were somehow able to see this beacon of their fellow tribesmen's distress, the chances of them sending a relief column in time was extremely small. Growing hungry, I sent for Alex, and he brought a loaf of bread that was almost fresh, a stoppered flask of oil, and a small cheese. I offered some to Germanicus, mainly out of politeness, but when he actually accepted it, I had to hide my irritation at having to split my meal. Fortunately, my grumpiness passed, and we stood, leaning forward on the parapet, watching the fire burning away the wooden portion of the wall as we consumed our food. By the time we finished, one of the logs that had been exposed had been burned sufficiently that, suddenly, it toppled over, falling away from the wall in an explosion of sparks and roiling smoke. Not wanting to read too much into this, I walked to Bibaculus and asked him if he had a better idea about when it would be ready.

"Unfortunately," he answered me readily enough, but I could see he was unhappy, "I think this is going to burn through before dark, then by the time it's cool enough that your boys can enter the breach, it will probably be around midnight."

"Which means," I finished for him, fighting the dismay that felt like it would choke me, "they would have time to repair the breach."

"It wouldn't be a really solid job." The *Immune* seemed to be looking for some reason for optimism, but I was not swayed.

I trotted over and told Germanicus the bad news, but he gave yet another demonstration that, despite his age, he had the makings of a true general. Truly, an expression of dismay flashed across his face, except as quickly as it came it was gone, and he shook his head.

"No," he said firmly, "we're not going to let them do that." Leaning over, he looked past me to call to Bibaculus, who came quickly, whereupon Germanicus ordered him, "We're going to need the scorpions."

When we marched out of the northern gate, darkness had just fallen, while the light of the burning breach served as a beacon that threw a lurid light well more than a hundred paces beyond the wall. I was at the head of the First Cohort, while Germanicus was still on the rampart, waiting to join us until the last moment before we began the assault. With the First was our entire complement of scorpions, along with the crews who would man them, minus the two in the northern camp. Their task was straightforward; stop the Maezaei from attempting to block the breach, while we waited for the fire to die out and cool enough for us to charge through it. There was a risk, one that was not all that great while it was dark, but once the dawn came, there would be a real threat from the two, or three, enemy *ballistae*. Before daylight, we had nothing to fear from their archers, if they even tried to stop us, since the range of a scorpion extends well beyond even the

172

strongest bow. Also aiding us was the light of the fire, which illuminated the area around the breach, not only in front of the wall, but on the town side as well.

Bibaculus' prediction had come true, as the mortar holding the stones that composed the shell enclosing the old wall burned away, allowing the irregularly shaped rocks to collapse in a pile. In all likelihood, this pile of stones on the inside part of the wall would have to be cleared away by the Maezaei, particularly since they would not have the time to do anything elaborate, like construct another wall around the breach. My guess was that they would drive two heavily laden wagons across the opening, lining them end to end, which was about the width of the breach, then take the removed rubble and pile it around the wheels to prevent us from sliding them out of the way. Their only other alternative would be to attempt to build that second wall during the night, except in order to do so, they would have to expose themselves, which is why we arrayed the scorpions, in a single line, that allowed the widest coverage of the breach. The angle of the scorpions on each end of the line was such that we could actually see any Maezaei approaching the breach from either side of it, to a distance of about fifty paces, making it impossible for the barbarians to catch us by surprise. One Century, the Third, was posted around the scorpions for protection, while the rest of the First were allowed to sit higher up the slope, acting more as spectators, and in the event that the Maezaei tried a sortie. This was an even more remote possibility than their attempting to build a second wall, in my opinion, simply because of the spot we had chosen along the wall to create the breach. Not only was it the closest point to the stronghold, it also put it far away from the gate, where the warriors would have to run across in front of the stone fort for a distance of more than three furlongs, well within range of our *ballistae*. Additionally, it would not take more than a moment's work to reposition the scorpions in enough time to rake the Maezaei and tear them to pieces. Consequently, what most of the men did was curl up in their *sagum*, making themselves as comfortable on the hard ground as possible, leaving it to their Centurions and Optios, along with the Century guarding the scorpions, to remain alert. Then, about a third of a watch past midnight, the last of the large flames flickered out, although the glowing coals were plainly visible, while the smoke continued trailing into the air. This, I thought, was happening faster than we thought it would, so I sent a runner to ask Germanicus for his orders. Rather than send a message, the Legate chose to come down himself, trotting up to where I was standing with Metellus, my Optio Rufius, and Veratius.

"Are we going to wait for dawn?" I asked Germanicus, only after offering my salute.

He did not hesitate, shaking his head, saying only, "No. Once it looks as if we can cross over without men being injured from the fire, we are going through that breach."

When he said this, while I had expected it, I felt my stomach clench even tighter than normal; this would be the first nighttime assault in which I had ever participated in, not to mention in any kind of leadership position, and I wondered if I would be up to the task. As if sensing my thoughts, the young nobleman turned so he could face me directly, and despite being forced to look up at me, Germanicus' tone was that of a commander giving his subordinate an order that he expects to be obeyed.

"And, Pullus, I'm leading our men through that breach this time. Nothing will stop me." He did not say this loudly, but the words hit me with an impact I believed was like those stones that had been flung down on me when assaulting the fort. "Not you or Tiberius. This is my command. Do you understand?"

Despite the sudden lump in my throat that threatened to keep the words from coming out, I managed to say, "I understand, Legate." I had to swallow not once, but twice before I could get out the part I knew was most important to Germanicus. "And I will obey."

Rousing the First, we did so as quietly as possible, not wanting the racket that is a normal part of waking men up and ordering them to get into formation to reach the ears of the Maezaei who were waiting for us. As I busied myself with this, Germanicus returned once more to the fort, presumably to give Bibaculus his final instructions, and to make sure that the other Cohorts were ready to follow us. However, when he returned, despite the coming trial, he was grinning broadly.

"I had an idea," he said, "and when I told Bibaculus about it, he thought it couldn't hurt."

Despite my respect for Germanicus and his budding abilities as a commander, perhaps I can be forgiven for the twinge of unease I felt, wondering why he seemed so pleased with himself and, more importantly, what it meant for the First Cohort.

However, when I asked him, he refused to say, though he kept that damnable smile on his face, telling me only, "Just watch."

Fortunately, I did not have to wait long, as no more than a dozen heartbeats later, the crashing sound of our artillery resumed from behind me, and in a reflex action, I spun about to look up at the rampart, so I missed the first of the missiles striking their target. Or, more accurately, missing their target, but by the time I returned my attention to the wall, it was impossible to see any damage, despite hearing the distinctive, higher pitched cracking sound that I identified as being from the clay pot ammunition. Except, I noted dismally, there's no fire; once my ears heard that sound, my assumption was simply that Germanicus had ordered Bibaculus to try and douse the defenders on the walls, most likely the missile troops, with flaming oil. When nothing of the sort happened, I turned and gave an inquiring look to the Legate, but he seemed unmoved.

"Just wait," was all he said. "It will take a couple of volleys before you see what we're doing."

And, true to his word, it was the third volley when three of the four *ballistae* hit their target, which turned out to be the breach itself, but the result confused me, and it took me the span of several heartbeats to understand the meaning of the sudden billowing of what seemed to be smoke.

Except that it was not smoke, and I glanced over at Germanicus as I guessed, "Is that…steam?"

He gave a short, delighted laugh, nodding as he confirmed, "Yes! I asked Bibaculus what would happen if we filled those pots with water and flung them at the breach!"

175

Turning back to the wall, which was still glowing, it must be said, but perhaps not quite as brightly, all I could think to say was, "Well, he obviously thought it was a good idea."

Germanicus laughed again, but more ruefully, admitting, "Actually, he said he'd never heard of anything like that before. I think he was just humoring me."

That, I thought, is something men of my class do most of the time when dealing with those like Germanicus; somehow, I managed to keep this contained within my skull, for once.

"Well," I tried not to sound grudging, since I would have agreed with Bibaculus, and I would have been as wrong as the *Immune* had been, "all that matters is that it seems to be working."

Germanicus' smile vanished, making me think he had been offended by my admittedly lukewarm praise, but he dispelled my belief by saying, "Which means we'll be able to start the assault sooner than we thought."

For the first time, I saw the young Legate show the kind of nerves that would be expected of a man about to lead other men through a breach, and somewhat paradoxically, this served to make me feel better about the youngster.

"I need to let the others know." Germanicus was already moving as he said this, swinging back up onto his horse before telling me, "Primus Pilus, have the men stand ready. As soon as I get back, we're going to begin."

I saluted, but he was already kicking his horse into a trot back up to the fort, leaving me to ready the Cohort.

Assembling in a line of Centuries, with the exception of the Third, already guarding the scorpions, which only had to send a dozen or so bolts towards the breach to discourage the Maezaei from attempting to block the breach, we marched down to where they were positioned. After I took the report from Veratius, he led me to the scorpion farthest to the right, pointing to a darker bulky shape, just behind the wall.

"They tried to pull a wagon across the breach, just like you expected," he explained, "but we killed the oxen, then the warriors who tried to drag them off and hitch new ones. It only took a few to convince them it was a bad idea."

By this point in time, although there was still a sullen glow along the bottom of the breach, along with some flickering flames around the edges of the breach where the logs that were still encased by stone had caught fire, one could see that the fire had been almost completely quenched, although there was still a fair amount of smoke. Because estimating the width of a breach from a distance of three furlongs is as much of an art as it is a skill, we would have to compensate by reducing the front of our formation, but only by two men; even without the threat of open flames on each side, the breach was only wide enough that we would be in a thirty-man front, meaning it would be six instead of the normal five ranks deep. With a thirty-man front, it would also give us a narrower sixth rank, while it made it somewhat awkward since we had to split sections up, something that no Primus Pilus would normally do with a Legion technically as green as the *Legio Germanicus*. Arraying the First Century with the extra rank, although I did not whisper the command to begin moving, I kept my voice pitched low, making for a ragged start, but we were not moving far, advancing just enough to allow the other Centuries to align behind us.

Once the actual assault began, it would come down to our ability to feed as many men through the breach as quickly as possible, but even more importantly, our assault had to draw as many of the Maezaei to defend the breach as they had available. In its simplest terms, the Maezaei had to be convinced that this was not just our main, but our only effort to take Splonum. Only then would Germanicus' surprise have the desired effect of both cutting off their line of retreat, and gathering the defenders in one place where we could crush them. Such was the hope, at least, yet despite the fact that I could think of several ways in which this could go wrong, I believed then, as I do now, that this was the best available option open to Germanicus. Never far from the forefront of my thoughts was the very real possibility that,

177

from Tiberius' perspective, Germanicus was not supposed to succeed, despite the fervent desire of the Princeps to blood the younger man and, presumably, give him the opportunity to shine. Regardless of the Princeps' intentions, the reality was that he was far away, though not in Rome, but Ariminum, where he had relocated because of his concern with this Batonian revolt. Certainly it was true that Tiberius was also physically distant, but it was by a matter of degree, and as much as I loathed myself for being one of them, I had to acknowledge that it was a likelihood bordering on a certainty that I was far from the only one of Tiberius' men surrounding the young Legate, keeping an eye on him. Or, I thought miserably as I stood there, waiting for him to assume command, maybe they have been given orders that are worse than just watching him, a thought that seemed to take on a life of its own, wrapping me in its embrace, and I glanced over at Arvina, trying to remember where he had come from and the possibility he might have been one of Tiberius' own. Of all the times for this to enter my mind, I could hardly have selected a worse one than this moment; all that I could be certain of was that Dolabella had never even hinted that I might be expected to do Germanicus some sort of physical harm, and while it was highly probable that Tiberius was more than content to simply make the challenges Germanicus was facing even greater and that was all, I could not shake this sudden feeling that dogged me.

"Primus Pilus! I see the men are ready!"

So absorbed was I in my miserable train of thought that Germanicus' voice actually made me jump a bit, something that I saw Arvina did not miss, though he tried to keep his face turned towards the front and pretend otherwise.

"Yes, sir," I nevertheless answered him readily enough, but even as I did, I was stepping a couple of paces to the side in order to give him the position of Primus Pilus. "We're awaiting your command."

This time when Germanicus drew his *gladius*, I did not bother stopping him; we would be approaching under the cover of darkness and moving more slowly than normal, but I also knew we would be breaking into a run the instant the alarm was raised. And, I noticed, this time he already had his chin thong tied; even better, he was holding a shield in his left hand, and I observed how he kept wiping his hand on the edge of his tunic before renewing his grip on his shield. There had been a low-pitched, rustling type of sound as men used whispers to communicate with each other, but all Germanicus had to do was clear his throat a bit more loudly than normal for all the noise to cease.

"I suppose I should have given the speech I prepared before we left the fort." He muttered this, and honestly, I do not know if he was speaking to me or to himself, but then he took a deep breath, and with what was more than a conversational tone, yet not quite a shout, ordered, "First Cohort...march!"

The men stepped off more smoothly than they had earlier, and I tried to tell myself this was a good omen, but then I was more concerned with matching my pace to that prescribed by our Legate, and thinking it would have been a good idea if I had wiped my own hands dry. Immediately on the heels of this realization I was struck by the thought that as wet and slick as my palms were, my mouth was correspondingly dry, and I wondered why that was. Then, a man stumbled somewhere in the middle of the formation, creating a noise that was probably not nearly as loud as it seemed, though it did serve to jerk my attention back to the moment at hand. Thankfully, we were still far enough away that something like that would not alert the Maezaei who, frankly, we could not distinguish from the bulk of the stones forming the rampart. Only the breach was distinguishable, and that was just because it was outlined by the still glowing embers, seemingly shimmering and winking, which I knew from years spent around fires meant there was still smoke rising from the remains. Beyond that was a darker mass, barely distinct itself, and certainly not defined to a point where we could see if it was something like the wagon that the Maezaei had attempted to block the breach with, or a mass of warriors quietly waiting for us. Step by step, we quickly settled into a rhythmic walk that, while we were not hurrying, still ate up the ground at a rate that seemed much faster than normal. We had begun by using the road that led from the town up to the fort as the anchor for our left flank, but according to our plan, when we were

179

approximately two hundred paces away, we pivoted slightly, where the end of the formation where Germanicus and I were at noticeably slowed our pace, while the men at the far end began taking slightly larger steps. In its conception, I suppose it could be likened to a door swinging open, where the Centurion, or Germanicus in this case, serves as the hinge, and even during the daylight this can be a tricky maneuver; in darkness, and on a fairly steep slope, frankly, I was more surprised once I saw that it had worked than I would have been if our cohesion had fallen apart. However, it also meant that once our angle was adjusted, our end of the Century increased our pace to match the speed of the men on the other end, rather than their slowing down, the final preparation before we broke into a full run. Despite knowing it was inevitable it would happen at some point, the sudden shout coming from the direction of the wall, followed by a thin, wailing cry from the horn of the type I had long before learned was used by the Maezaei, evoked a ragged chorus of curses.

Germanicus, however, did not hesitate and understanding the need for silence was over, shouted as loudly as I believe he could, "Men of the First, follow me! For the Princeps! For Rome! For our families!..."

The rest was drowned out by the answering roar of the more than one hundred forty able men of the First Cohort; I know he said something else because I was looking at his mouth moving, even as he broke into a run. Then I had to pay attention to myself, but what I can say is that, as old as most of the men of the First Cohort may have been, their full-throated answer to Germanicus would have done any Legion justice. As always, I had to be careful not to outrun the rest of the Cohort because of my longer legs, but this time it was even more important than usual, because this time I was going to let Germanicus have the honor of being the first officer to the breach. Honestly, my decision was based less in my desire to give a young man with whom I had much in common the chance to live up to the illustrious nature of his name and more to do with the hope that, once he got a taste of what it was like, in the future he would be more circumspect about placing himself at such risk. But, no matter the reason, I slowed enough so that I could fall in behind the Legate, who was holding his shield out and to the side as I had advised him, his *gladius* thrust high and waving about in the other hand. Just as I did this, there was a short, shrill cry from deep in the formation, followed by the sound of men colliding with each other, but it was the hissing sound, along with the barest glimpse of a streaking object that passed to my right no more than an arm's length away that informed me what was happening.

"Archers!"

Someone had beaten me to it, but I shouted, "They're loosing blind, boys! Keep going!"

The ground leveled out, just as I was beginning to feel the effort from our exertion to this point, so I could only imagine how the men older than me were feeling, and for an instant, I was worried that Germanicus might forget to give the command to slow back to a normal march to allow the men to regain some of their breath and to hurl our javelins. Fortunately, as soon as the thought crossed my mind, I heard his voice ring out, but his breathing was so ragged that I added my own voice, and while it was not forum perfect, the men slowed.

"Pullus," he called over his shoulder, "what do you think? Should we go launch our javelins or go straight to the *gladius*?"

Now that we were within about seventy paces from the wall, I used my height to peer ahead, above Germanicus' crest, into the darker recess of the breach, and I saw the rippling of movement that were the Maezaei warriors, undoubtedly hurrying to arrange themselves into a position to fend off our coming attack. Dousing that fire, I thought, worked both ways; I could see that the enemy warriors, while not actually standing in the middle of the breach, had been able to get closer to it than I would have liked.

"Use the javelins," I answered immediately, "but we're going to need to get closer than normal because we can't see *cac*."

He did not reply verbally, though I thought I saw his head bob, and I reminded myself to talk to him about how doing something like nodding in the dark is not a good idea for an officer. That he did not order us to draw our blades informed me that my guess had been correct, and it was about this time that, suddenly, a roar issued from the Maezaei, who were now standing ready, waiting for us.

"Century, halt! Prepare javelins!"

Germanicus gave the order so quickly that I did not have a chance to stop him; he had halted us too far away, I was certain, but it was too late to do anything about it, other than mutter a curse under my breath.

"Release!"

The sound of well more than a hundred arms sweeping forward, one rank following the other, temporarily dampened the noise coming from the Maezaei, but in that brief moment after the javelins had begun their flight, I was heartened to hear the absence of the kind of noise one hears when barbarians know that our most potent weapon is hurtling their way. Usually, it sounds something like a low, collective moan, though sometimes one hears a hoarse voice shouting what is likely a prayer to one of their gods for protection, but this time there was none of that. Unfortunately, the thunderous noise that should have followed—a series of slightly hollow thudding sounds, packed so tightly together it sounds to the ear as if it is one continuous noise, as the hardened points punch into enemy shields, interspersed with screams and shouts of pain—while they did happen, it was not with the same volume that I knew there should have been if many, if not most, of our javelins had not fallen short.

"Resume the march, then have them launch on the run." I had stepped forward so I could say this to Germanicus without being overheard by anyone other than Arvina, and thankfully, answering with only a grunt, Germanicus then shouted the appropriate order.

We only went about four steps at the march, then Germanicus ordered us to the trot, then about the same number of paces later. "Prepare javelins...release!" Then, in the same breath, the young Legate bellowed, *"Porro!"*

The assault on Splonum had begun in earnest.

Charging into a defended breach was something I had heard about from other veterans, and I certainly had read about it in my Avus' account, although I can never recall having a conversation with my father about what it was like. This, I must confess, is rather odd, given that he won two *Coronae Murales*, the last for the assault on Naissus, not all that far from Splonum. However, I had never done it personally, and even the veterans among the First who possessed relevant experience had never done this at night, and I cannot say I look forward to doing it again, although I had one more coming in my immediate future, for which I am thankful I knew nothing about. The first challenge is the footing; while there was not a high rubble pile, both because the wall was made of two materials, one of which had been reduced to a pile of ash and charred remnants, it was still treacherous. I suspect it would have been so, even under ideal circumstances, but with the addition of the heat, still radiating from the dying embers of the fire caused by Bibaculus and his crews, it created a distinctly unusual and painful sensation as the hotness transferred up through the soles of our *caligae*. Perhaps it was something of a blessing, since it encouraged men to shove their foes backward with even more vigor and savagery than normal, or whatever passes for normal in a situation where one man is trying to enter another's town with the express purpose of killing everyone and destroying everything within its walls.

I only stayed behind Germanicus long enough for him to claim the honor of being the first man into the breach, before taking advantage of my longer stride to step up next to him on his right immediately after our front rank collided with the leading warriors waiting for us, the most eager among them leaping forward into the smoky space, braving the heat and the likelihood they would be the first to die. It was not only a tight fit, but as I quickly learned, the heat from the burning logs on the edge of the breach that were still in place and vertical was intense, and later I saw that the hair on my right arm had been singed off. I turned my back to the source of the heat, although I would have preferred to press my back against the uneven surface, but I had to content myself with knowing that any Maezaei trying to get behind me would be scorched. As quickly as I moved up next to him, the young Legate had already punched the warrior across from him with his shield by the time I had my own up into a position

183

to protect him, and the warrior demonstrated that the hazardous footing was not just our problem, his stumbling backward only partially caused by Germanicus' action. Before this Maezaei could regain his footing, another warrior, this one tall but very lean and wielding an ax, shoved the first man aside, apparently intent on being the first to claim the honor of not only killing a Roman, but one who was wearing the crest of a high-ranking officer at that. Shouting something, barely distinguishable from all the other noise, the warrior who had been deprived turned his attention to me, getting his feet under him while thrusting a spear at me at the same time, which was probably the mistake that cost him his life. Despite the darkness, we were still able to see each other well enough that I could tell he had taken too large of a step as he lunged at me. Rather than deflect the blow off my shield by angling it slightly outward, I instead caught it square, feeling the point bite deeply into the wood before shoving the shield downward with most of my strength, and as I hoped, it jerked the warrior off balance, helped by both his widened stance and his foot slipping on one of the irregularly shaped rocks. When one suddenly loses their balance to one side, a person will throw their opposite extremity out as a counterbalance; it is an unconscious reaction, and almost impossible to stop oneself from doing, something I had first learned at the hands of my father, who had inflicted a fair number of bruises in teaching me, and such was the case with this Maezaei. Stumbling to his right caused him to move his left arm, upon which was a round wooden shield held in place by two leather loops around his forearm, slightly out from his body, not much, but enough. And in much less time it takes to describe it, I ended this Maezaei with a simple thrust to the chest, inside his shield, before turning my attention back to Germanicus, even as this dispatched warrior was collapsing at the feet of his comrades, one of whom tried to hop over the body to fill the newly created gap. Forced to divide my attention between Germanicus and my own well-being, I made what was a half-hearted thrust with my blade, using only the length of my arm, though it was enough to momentarily arrest the new Maezaei's attack.

The Legate, a bit to my surprise, already had a body at his feet, but he was clearly in some trouble because he had pressed his advantage, stepping forward without the support of the men around him, something I had done in my first battle. In my case, my intemperate action had ended up working out well, and indeed it had been my current Legate's father who had rewarded me for what ultimately had been my disobedience. Even if this had not been the case, I would not have behaved any differently, but I concede that, perhaps I took an extra risk because of that familial connection to Germanicus. Almost too late, I realized that those Maezaei to our immediate front had been working in concert together, the man who had replaced the warrior I had just dispatched clearly given the task of keeping me occupied. I do not like to imagine what might have transpired if I had actually launched a true attack, rather than a feint to buy me some breathing space, but whatever the case, I was barely in time to thrust my shield out and away from my body to the left in order to deflect the hard thrust of a heavy, leaf-bladed war spear that a large Maezaei had aimed directly at Germanicus' unprotected side. This time, I actually used my shield in a manner more similar to my *gladius*, swinging it as if I might a blade to deflect a thrust by knocking it aside, and I was rewarded by the sharp cracking sound as the wood of my shield slammed into the hard oak shaft of his spear, although the point missed Germanicus by only a matter of inches. It had been a faint hope because of the sound of my shield colliding with it, but I was still disappointed to see that when the warrior recovered the spear, it was whole and I had not managed to snap it.

Meanwhile, I could hear Germanicus grunting with the effort that came from taking a heavy blow to his shield by another Maezaei armed with an ax, attacking from Germanicus' left, but the glance I gave the Legate was all I could spare as the spearman renewed his attack. This time, however, he did so with the clear intention of trying to shove me into Germanicus, and for this misjudgment I blame the darkness, because he must not have gotten a true glimpse of my size, or perhaps the fever of the moment induced him to believe he possessed the strength to do what he intended. Rather than lunge again

185

and recover, this time when he lunged, I did not even have to move my shield, giving me the idea that he had aimed for it specifically, which in turn gave me an instant's warning of what to expect when, once more, a spear buried itself in my shield, this time immediately below the boss. Consequently, rather than pull back on my shield to dislodge his spear, the normal action, I did the opposite by brutally shoving the shield forward, matching my strength to his, thereby catching him by surprise instead of the other way around. For the briefest instant, perhaps a matter of less than a heartbeat, we matched each other so I suppose it might have appeared we were frozen in our respective positions as if we were posing for a sculptor creating a statue, though this would have been belied by the contorted face of the Maezaei as he pushed against me with all his might. Through the spear, I felt him trying to steer me to my left, but I was not budging; at least, not until the man immediately behind him, seeing our deadlock, added his weight to his comrade by throwing himself against the first warrior's back, and suddenly, I felt my rear foot slipping. If I had been younger, and this was my first campaign, I suspect I would have taken this as a challenge to my strength, but thankfully, I no longer felt the need to meet every one of them with brute force; instead, I moved my blade as quickly as I could, sweeping it down a few inches in front of my shield, using every bit of the power in my arm to slice through the shaft just behind the head. The spearman, having put all of his weight into his attempt to use me to unbalance Germanicus and who also had the full weight of the comrade behind him pressing against his back, ultimately was the one who lost both his footing and his life. Suddenly stumbling forward within easy reach of my blade when the tremendous pressure he had been putting on his spear unexpectedly no longer met my corresponding resistance, I quickly plunged the point down into his back. Just as I withdrew my blade, two things happened, roughly simultaneously; Germanicus was knocked sideways, colliding with me, and there was the sound of a horn once more, except this time, it was a Roman horn. Natta, obeying Germanicus' orders, had clearly reached one hundred in his counting and sounded the signal to alert

Bibaculus, unleashing the surprise that Germanicus, and certainly I, hoped would prove to be the decisive factor in the taking of Splonum.

At first, my fear was that Germanicus had staggered into me because he was wounded, but while I could see the sheen of a liquid that I knew was blood covering the front of his finely worked cuirass, seeing my glance downward, he assured me, "It's not mine."

I have nobody to blame but myself for paying too much attention to Germanicus, reaching across and using my *gladius* hand to steady him, which turned my back to a warrior on the very outer fringe of the mass still fighting our attempt to clear the breach. Thankfully, Germanicus was facing me, and being as close as we were, I saw his eyes widen as he seemed to be looking at a point above my shoulder, but while I know he shouted something, the sudden, crashing blow that struck my left shoulder blade seemed to create so much noise that whatever it was got drowned out, though I imagine most of that was inside my head. I cannot say it was particularly painful at first, but my initial indication that I had absorbed a serious blow was when my legs suddenly gave way, which surprised me considerably, and my initial reaction was the thought that I had been struck in roughly the same spot a Latobici arrow had inflicted my first wound when I was a boy. Ironically, while I could feel a dull throbbing along my left shoulder blade, the first real pain I experienced was when my knees hit what served as the ground, in the form of the charred logs and embers that had composed the wooden interior of the wall. Someone let out a roar of real pain; I was only dimly aware it came from me, but I reacted immediately by trying to climb to my feet, not thinking about anything other than trying to stop the searing agony as the still-smoldering coals cooked my flesh.

"Stay down!"

I cannot say with any certainty how I managed to obey the command; whether it was because, even in my moment of distress I recognized the voice of Germanicus, and I reacted from years of habitual discipline, or that I was aware of the mortal danger I was in and understood I had to rely on our young Legate, only the gods know.

Nevertheless, I managed to comply, enduring what was not only extraordinarily painful, but one of the more frightening moments of my life, trying to follow the progress of the small battle that would decide my fate taking place just above me. Germanicus' legs filled my field of vision, so I could only track the fight by listening as there was the hollow report of a weapon of some sort striking a shield, but when I saw Germanicus' left leg slide backward, simultaneously accompanied by an explosive grunt, I knew he had just blocked a blow. Then, his waist suddenly twisted, telling me he had countered with an attack of his own, except I was nearing the end of my tether, feeling the sweat streaming down my face as I clenched my teeth as tightly as I believe I ever have, the agony now reaching an excruciating level. So deeply did I have to dig into my reserves of strength in order to avoid leaping to my feet, even knowing that it would undoubtedly lead to my death, I actually lost track of what was taking place above me. As far as I knew, I could have been kneeling there for a watch, only vaguely aware of the blows being exchanged, and while I clearly heard the short, choked cry from a voice immediately behind me, it barely registered in my consciousness.

Then, I heard someone ask, "Can you get up, Pullus?"

That, I thought, is a good question, yet somehow I managed to climb to my feet, although I could not contain the bellow of pain when, in doing so, I left some of the flesh of my knees sticking to the smoldering remnants of the wooden portion of the wall. Such was the agony that I actually staggered, but then a hand grabbed my arm to steady me.

"You shouldn't have sheathed your *gladius*," I mumbled; frankly, my vision was so clouded with the tears from the pain I could not really make out who had helped me, but I assumed it was Germanicus. "Or," a sharp stab of concern actually helped clear my head a bit, "your shield!"

"We're fine." It was Germanicus' voice, surely enough, except that it came from a spot that told me he could not have been the one to steady me.

Finally, after wiping my eyes with the back of my *gladius* hand, which I was oddly proud had never left my grasp, my vision cleared enough to see that it had been Arvina who was supporting me, and although Germanicus was also standing there, somehow we were now standing inside the wall by a couple of paces. While I did not remember it happening, the *Aquilifer* must have guided me the half-dozen paces away from the middle of the breach, but my thinking was still a step behind what my newly cleared vision was taking in, for which I blame the throbbing agony of my knees. Gritting my teeth, I forced myself to actually absorb the meaning of this new set of circumstances, even as I became aware that Germanicus, who had not sheathed his *gladius* after all, was staring at me, even as I slowly became aware that the sounds of the fighting were still going on, but had moved. Only then did I turn my head to the right, seeing that the back rank of the First was now a dozen paces away from where we were standing; obviously, they had pushed the Maezaei out of the breach. Even in the moment, I sensed that I was moving as slowly as my mind was working, but before I could give any indication that I was aware that the situation had changed, I first heard a sound that, while familiar, was strange at the same time. Then, streaking above my head, I saw what looked like a small, flaming sun that passed over us, trailing smoke and sparks that went floating down for a few feet before they died out. Before I could turn to track where it landed, there was a crashing sound, and for the first time I actually looked beyond the First Century, past the buildings that marked the far edge of the area the Maezaei had razed to keep our artillery from doing what it was doing now, where I saw that a sullen glow was already turning the sky above the rooftops orange.

"That's the third volley," Germanicus explained. "The fire started with the very first one. Bibaculus' crew is working faster than I've ever seen!"

This was good, but before I could comment, there was a shouted warning, this time from our left, and Germanicus, Arvina, and I were forced to scramble to one side of the breach as the Second Century appeared from the darkness beyond the wall. In an odd way, I felt relieved; I could not have been insensible that long if the Second of the First was just arriving, but despite this technically being my duty, I was content to listen as Germanicus directed Metellus and his men.

"You and the Third head for the gate." The Legate's tone was decisive, and I noticed that he did not even glance in my direction as he normally did, which ignited an unusual and conflicting mix of feelings, which I would liken to a proud father whose son has demonstrated for the first time his counsel is no longer needed. "Get it open as quickly as you can."

Metellus saluted readily enough, but I was close enough that the darkness did not hide his glance over at me, which prompted me to say, probably too harshly, "You heard the Legate, Centurion!"

My old comrade stiffened to a quick *intente*, though that was his only hesitation, then the Second pivoted so that their left flank was next to the inside of the wall before they went forward at a shuffling run. They were followed by Veratius and his Century, then it was Tubertus' Century, which Germanicus directed to support us in the First, while the Fifth and Sixth were also sent along the wall, but in the opposite direction of Metellus and his men. Arriving with the rest of the First were the Tribunes, Frugi and Silius, who Germanicus ordered to stand there to direct the next Cohorts, and only then did the Legate move back towards the fighting.

Stopping where I was standing, he eyed me with what I took to be a mixture of concern and skepticism as he asked me, "Pullus, are you able to continue the fight?" When he pointed down at my knees, I did not miss the sudden grimace, though he at least tried to keep his tone from expressing his true opinion about the severity of what he was seeing. "Those are some nasty burns, Primus Pilus." Looking back up, he dropped his voice. "If you want to go see the *medici*, you have my permission. In fact," he glanced back down, and shook his head, "it might be best if you call it a night."

"Nonsense." The word came out quickly enough, then I thought to add "sir." Shifting my weight, I tried to demonstrate by flexing one leg, but when I said, "I'm fine," it came out as more groan than anything. Nevertheless, I forced myself to do the same to the other, trying to pretend that the stab of agony was a trifling business. "Besides, you saved my life, so now I'm honor bound to return the favor."

The look of what I interpreted as relief that crossed the younger man's features told me that, despite his outward confidence, he was still growing into the role he was trying to portray, though my sense was that he at least tried to sound reluctant when he replied, "Very well. If you're sure you're up to it."

Once more, I was struck by the thought that, despite his youth, this young Roman nobleman was a shrewd judge of character. Or, my pride is that obvious to even callow youths; frankly, I prefer to believe it was more the former, while a part of me, the brutally honest part, knows it was likely the latter. Whatever the cause, I indicated that he should lead the way, mainly because I was not altogether sure that when I took my first step, my leg would not collapse under me. Somewhat to my surprise, walking was no more painful than just standing there, so I hobbled behind him as we made our way to the back of the First. The Fourth Century had aligned itself to the left of the First, but at an angle that was now pressing the right flank of the mob of warriors, while just behind the First there were well more than two hundred enemy bodies, along with what I counted to be a dozen men wearing our armor. Mingled among them were *medici*, alternately kneeling next to one of our own, bandaging a wound, or leaning down to check for life among the other Romans who had fallen. It was typical Roman efficiency, but I gave it only a passing glance, more intent on keeping up with Germanicus, who had broken into a trot to reach the front of the formation. My initial concern with our situation was that, while the Fourth Century had bolstered our left flank, our right was still hanging in the air, unsupported, but for a reason I could not initially understand, the Maezaei had not simply extended their own line to wrap around us. Only when we drew closer could I see that, if the enemy warriors had done that, the Fifth and Sixth Centuries would be in a perfect position to fall on their unprotected rear, but it was why I was able to determine this that was probably the most important factor. What had been a dull orange glow just above the

191

rooftops of the first row of the houses that were still standing had grown in intensity to the point that, just in the glance I gave it, I saw the tips of flames leaping up into the sky. Most crucially, the line the fire made now extended across our front and right quarter, cutting off access to the stronghold, meaning that the Fifth and Sixth did not have to concern itself with attack from that direction, allowing them to align themselves at an oblique angle, ready to pounce on any Maezaei attempt to flank the First.

Even as I was taking this in, another blazing rock came hurtling overhead, and this time I was able to watch it land, farther to the right of the extreme edge of the area that was already on fire. Bibaculus and his crew were placing each burning stone ball in an arcing line that, slowly but surely, had cut off access to the stronghold; the only question was how long it would take the Maezaei we were currently battling to understand this, and what they would do in reaction to this threat. Then, Germanicus was back up with the first rank, and I was pleased to see that, in the absence of both Germanicus and me, Optio Rufius had maintained the presence of mind to sound the relief three times as I recognized that it was the fourth rank that was now doing the fighting. This was the point in the battle where, while it is still noisy, most of the din is created from actual combat, not the shouts, curses, and calls to the gods for strength, as men need to conserve their breath. Not that there are no cries, except these are invariably when a man is either defeated, or victorious, and this is the only moment where, in my experience, all men speak the same language; a scream of anguish or a bellow by the victorious at the sight of his enemy falling at his feet needs no translator. Germanicus, reaching the front rank, seemed to hesitate, but a barbarian warrior a few paces away from him, obviously seeing his crest of black feathers that ran front to back, did not, making a short hop to his left to get around a comrade in the front rank who was engaged with the Gregarius of the first file, then took a bounding step while raising his long *gladius* high above his head. I began moving, the sudden motion and the impact of my own jumping step forward sending a bolt of pain shooting up from first one knee then the other, but Germanicus was not caught unaware.

Even as I closed the distance, I saw him pivot, and for an instant, I thought he was trying to bring his shield over across his body, which would have taken too long. Instead, the Legate was only partially turning to give his *gladius* arm a better angle, and he swung his blade up to collide with the descending barbarian *gladius*, which created a small shower of sparks that was made more visible because of the darkness, punctuated by the clashing, ringing sound of metal on metal. While the Maezaei's *gladius* had the advantage of weight and momentum and Germanicus' shorter blade was driven downward, it was not before, by twisting his wrist inward, the Legate was able to deflect the blow off to his left, shield side. I was still moving, but even as I reached his side, Germanicus showed the advantage provided by the shorter blade that is made as a stabbing weapon as he executed what the weapons instructor in me appreciated as a well-tutored counterthrust, aiming directly for the space created between the edge of the Maezaei's shield and his *gladius* arm. The enemy warrior did try to bring his shield across his body, but Germanicus' point was already past, punching into and beyond the chain mail shirt the Maezaei was wearing. It was not a killing blow; I saw that only two or three inches of his blade penetrated, but it was damaging enough to force the warrior to go reeling backward, bellowing from the pain. For an instant, he acted as if he was intent on renewing his attack, then apparently thought better of it, and my last sight of him was as he was roughly shoved aside by another Maezaei, except rather than step into the spot vacated by Germanicus' original foe, this man seemed content to wait for the young Roman to come to him. Which, I was alarmed to see, Germanicus planned on doing, but just as he was taking a step forward, I was forced to drop my shield and stretch out to grab the back of his harness, which I did, just barely. Yanking backward, I clearly caught him by surprise, the sharp, yelping sound that came from him being most undignified, but I was not concerned.

"That's how you got in trouble the last time," I growled at him as he came stumbling back next to me.

Turning towards me, his mouth opened and I prepared for some sort of reprimand, but he surprised me by saying, "You're right."

Before he could say anything else, I reached down for the bone whistle that by rights I should have given to the Legate; the reason I had not was that I was certain he had no idea what to do with it. Filling my lungs, I blew three short blasts, the signal for a line shift, then waited long enough for the men in the front rank to either finish the barbarian across from them, or more likely, give him a good, solid bash with the shield that knocked his opponent back a step, before taking a single step to the left, while the man in the second rank stepped forward. When one does this enough, both in training during a mock combat, or in actual battle, it is possible to tell by the sound as easily by sight when the relief has been performed, so once my ears informed me, I gave another blast, one long one that we use to sound the advance.

"Push, boys, push! Make 'em crack!" Germanicus shouted this, and the fact that he was right there with the men of the first rank was probably the most powerful incentive he could have provided, and I think back to this moment as the one where my regard and respect for Germanicus was first shared by the men in the ranks.

And these old veterans of the First, most of them who had spent even more time complaining about their aches and pains, and how they were too old for what is ultimately a young man's pursuit, responded as if the years, the wounds, and the wear and tear of so many campaign seasons had suddenly just fallen away. The only way I can think to explain it is that they somehow drew on Germanicus' vitality, taking his youthful strength as their own, because our progress, which had been foot by foot, suddenly increased to a pace or two at a time as the Maezaei, who had been stubbornly giving up ground, seemed to lose heart. Behind them, the flames had finally come bursting forth, catching the last row of buildings afire, creating a lurid backdrop that outlined the remaining warriors. I suppose it was inevitable that, when this happened, I was suddenly transported back to another moment, to a town that once belonged to the Varciani, but even in the moment, I understood that this was the only thing that this assault on Splonum shared with the night both Urso and Draxo were killed. There was not the air of killing madness on our part, and while the Maezaei had been

194

putting up a stiff fight, there was something missing on their part, although I could not really place what it was in the moment. At some point as we continued pushing the barbarians back, I was dimly aware of the noise of thrumming hooves behind us, the sound swinging around to our right, but it was not until Gaesorix and his cavalry traveled far enough along the wall in the direction of the stronghold that I saw them, illuminated by the growing flames to their left. For some reason, I thought of Latobius, and how much horses hated fire, which in turn made me wonder how much difficulty the Batavian and his cavalrymen would have forcing their animals in a direction that took them closer to the flames instead of their instinctive preference to be running away from them.

Off to our far left, the sound of a *cornu* sounded, alerting us that the other Cohorts had arrived, which in turn informed us that Metellus and Veratius had been successful in opening the gate. This part of Germanicus' plan called for the Second and Third Cohort to hurry along the road following the wall to the northern gate, cutting off escape in that direction, while the Fourth Cohort was following behind the cavalry, heading towards the stronghold. The last Cohort not in reserve, the Fifth, came through the breach to support the First Cohort, while we were rejoined by the Second, Third, Fifth, and Sixth Centuries, collapsing down onto the increasingly small pocket of Maezaei warriors from three sides, the rearmost ranks of their force now less than a hundred paces from what was now a fully involved fire that was consuming their town. It was in the midst of the second full rotation of the First Century, the men of the fourth rank currently engaged when, from somewhere in the middle of the enemy mob, a single piercing note on a horn suddenly began sounding, and while the pitch of the note did not change, whoever was blowing the horn began repeating the note, over and over. Not surprisingly, this caught our attention and the men in the front rank eased or ceased whatever offensive maneuver they were engaged in when the horn started sounding, but they were veterans, so they did nothing intemperate like drop their shields. The Maezaei across from them did more or less the same, quickly stepping back from the Roman across from them, making the predominant sound the harsh panting from both sides, along with the moans of wounded men, and cries for a *medicus* to help attend someone. For the span of perhaps a half-dozen heartbeats, both sides were content to glare at each other, and this confused Germanicus, or at least this was what I read in his expression when he turned and gave me a quick glance. Even as he was doing so, I saw a stir of movement across from where the Legate and I were standing, then a single Maezaei pushed his way to the front. He was young, though he was older than Germanicus, but he had the long drooping mustache favored by some men of the Pannonian tribes, and while he held his *gladius*, it was lying across both palms, with his arms extended out in front of him.

"I am," his Latin was surprisingly good, "Donnado, son of Dodonis, chieftain of the Maezaei. And," he paused, his mouth twisting into a bitter grimace, "as the commander here, I offer you our surrender."

To my surprise, Germanicus did not respond, at least immediately, and when I glanced over at him, I had the disturbing sense that he was thinking of refusing. That his face was now fully illuminated, although with the dancing shadows created by a large fire not more than two hundred paces away from where we were standing, made me think that perhaps I was misreading his expression.

"And why," the Legate's tone was cold, but it was his words that seemed to support my feeling that at least Germanicus' bloodlust had not been sated, "should I accept your surrender?"

The newly identified Donnado surprised me by replying, "Because if you kill us all, who will be left to fight that?" Since he was still holding his blade across his upturned palms, he jerked his helmeted head back in the direction of the fire, which for the first time began dominating the sounds; the crackling, popping, and hissing it made growing with every passing moment. "And if Splonum is destroyed, how long will it take Rome to start receiving the iron it needs to," despite the mustache there was no missing the bitter twisting of his mouth, "keep us barbarian tribes under your control?"

196

"We have other iron mines," Germanicus retorted, but there was a subtle difference from his earlier tone, though I did not look over to see if his expression indicated he was having a change of heart, "so you're going to have to give me a better reason than that not to order my Primus Pilus," with this, he actually turned away from Donnado to make a pointing gesture with his blade, directly at me, "to blow his whistle and finish this." Our eyes met as he was saying this, and his face gave no indication that he was thinking about what he was about to say, yet when he turned back to face the Maezaei, although his tone was casual, the words were anything but as he asked, "And I suppose you know who my Primus Pilus is?"

For the first time, Donnado seemed to turn his attention towards me, though I realized in this moment that his seeming disinterest was not by accident, and even with the fire to his back, throwing his face into shadow, there was no mistaking the glare of utter, complete hatred as he stared at me.

"Yes," it was as if he bit the word off, "I know who that..." although his eyes were locked with mine, I suppose we were far enough apart that he did not miss what, frankly, had become a habit of mine that I did without thinking, as I began swinging my Gallic blade, which I was holding loosely by my side, point down, forming easy, perfect circles with it as I kept my arm loose, because he seemed to have a change of heart, saying instead, "...Roman is." Tearing his eyes away from me, he returned his attention to Germanicus, and now he made no attempt to hide his frustrated rage. "And I must commend you, Legate, on your choice in bringing this man with you. He is certainly well known to those of us you call the Maezaei." The bony lump in his throat bobbed once, and he asked something that I know had to hurt his pride. "But will you accept our surrender and allow us to stop this fire?"

The silence that followed dragged out—in my opinion, unnecessarily—but again, this was Germanicus' first victory as a commander, and I suppose he wanted to savor it. At least, so he, and I confess I did as well, believed, that this surrender by Donnado signaled the fall of Splonum.

197

Finally, Germanicus spoke, raising his voice so that as many men could hear as possible, "Very well, I accept your surrender. And," this he seemed to seriously consider, or perhaps he was just enjoying the moment, even with a roaring blaze that was close to becoming an uncontrollable inferno, "yes, once your men surrender your weapons, we will allow you to do what is necessary to save the rest of Splonum. Now," I suppose he could not resist behaving dramatically, pointing down at the ground with his own blade and raising his voice to its fullest, ordered, *"drop your weapons!"*

The clattering sound briefly drowned out the other noise, even the hissing, dull roar of the fire, which was beginning to make me sweat, but every remaining Maezaei complied with Germanicus' order, then stood there uncertainly, exchanging glances with each other, while I saw out of the edge of my vision our men were behaving in a similar fashion, everyone unsure what to do next.

"Pullus," Germanicus called me to his side, which required me to walk a few paces, but despite my best attempt not to hobble, I saw that Donnado noticed, and his eyes dropped to my legs.

It was the twisted, hate-filled smile he gave me that told me he saw, and understood, the cause for my infirmity, but I chose to ignore him for the moment in the same manner I was trying to shut out the pain.

Germanicus had turned, and seeing my distress, actually met me halfway, then whispered, "Now what should we do? How do we handle this?"

"Bring up the Fifth Cohort to take over for my boys," was my first response. "Then form up a Century on each side in a double file, and make these bastards pass through and be searched. One man does the searching, the one behind him ready and waiting to kill any of these *cunni* who try to be clever and smuggle a weapon past us." I had formed this part of the plan in the span of heartbeats after Germanicus accepted the surrender, but now I had to think ahead past this to what would come next. "Send a runner to the Cohorts by the northern gate and have them shake themselves out along one of the streets that run east and west, from one wall to the other." It was difficult to concentrate because of the throbbing in my knees, but I tried to remember my mental image of the map of Splonum, remembering. "There are only two streets that actually span the town in that direction, but they should take the one that runs through the village square. That way, they can stop any of these bastards who try to escape."

"We do have the auxiliaries already doing that just outside the walls," the Legate pointed out, but I was unmoved.

"These men," I argued, "have lived here their entire lives, or if they're from villages like Clandate, they've been here more times than we can count. They'll know all the little cracks and secret passages out of this place. And," I assured him, "trust me, every one of these barbarian towns have more than one secret way past the walls."

I was relieved to see that he immediately accepted this without resistance, and he turned, found Natta, then gave him the necessary orders that would summon the Fifth Cohort forward at the double quick, though not before blowing the signal to Bibaculus and his crew to cease their activities, but just not quite in time to stop one last, blazing ball from soaring overhead. Fortunately, it landed in an area of the town that was already fully involved, yet this did not keep our newly surrendered foes from shouting curses at us, obviously thinking they had been betrayed, which Germanicus wisely ignored. Once he heard Natta sound the appropriate series of commands, he called for Silius, who had been standing ready, holding the reins of his horse a few dozen paces behind where we had been fighting, issuing the Tribune orders to ride to the northern gate and instruct them in what to do next. Appuleius, who had been standing next to Silius, was next, and he was sent to find Gaesorix and inform him that the town had been taken. By this point, the Fifth had arrived, and it was a bit chaotic, Stertinius fumbling by issuing orders that, perhaps if we had been assembled in the forum, might have worked to maneuver his Centuries into their proper position, but not in the middle of a town, over ground strewn with bodies and debris. Finally, I was forced to order the First Century to perform a rearward march, though naturally without requiring them to turn their backs to the Maezaei; they seemed defeated, it was true, but I was not taking the risk that Donnado might view our retreating rear as an opportunity to at least take as many of us with him to Hades as he could. Finally, after a span of a few hundred heartbeats, there was something like a gauntlet, of the type that is formed by a Century when one of their own has been sentenced to death at the hands of his comrades, and the Maezaei, led by Donnado were paraded past. Only Dodonis' son was spared the indignity of being thoroughly searched, at the order of Germanicus, reminding me that, when all was said and done, the truism that nobility always look out for each other no matter their origin held for this occasion. The chieftain's son was actually led to where Germanicus and I were standing, but in a gesture of defiance, when the ranker pushed him towards a spot that would place him closer to me than Germanicus, the Maezaei refused, changing direction so that he was on the opposite side of the Legate than I was, glaring at me the whole time.

Germanicus, far from being offended, seemed greatly amused, and he turned to me and joked, "By the gods, Pullus! He *really* doesn't like you!"

While I understood that the younger man meant no harm, I suppose it was impossible for me not to associate the cause for Donnado's antipathy towards me with the event that originally caused it in the death of Sextus, which prompted me to snap, "These *cunni* murdered my brother, so I can assure you, sir, the feeling's mutual."

"Oh," Germanicus' expression clouded, and I recognized by his look that he had forgotten this, "…right. Yes, I'm…I'm sorry, Pullus."

"No need to apologize, sir," I sighed. "It was…" I had to actually calculate how much time had passed, and it was with a shock that I realized, "…almost five years ago."

I shook my head, a wave of sadness so strong that, for the span of a few heartbeats, I did not notice the physical pain I was feeling as it was replaced with one of a different kind, although that was not much of a relief. But it was something else that occurred to me that was almost as surprising; I had been with Germanicus almost a year by this point. How much longer would I be expected to serve with him? And, probably more importantly, had I been officially replaced

200

as a Princeps Prior in the 1st Legion? What, exactly, was my status? These thoughts formed, like a chain, one link upon another, with a rapidity that threatened to completely overwhelm and occupy my attention, and it took a real effort, albeit internally, to force myself back to the present, reminding myself that nothing could be gained by this train of thought, not at this moment. Obviously, not much time had passed, because the same warriors were still being searched by the same rankers just in front of us, before being shoved to join the group who had already been searched. Only when that was done were our new prisoners escorted away, following along the wall, under guard by three Centuries of the Fifth, to get in position to create a fire break. I do not recall it happening, but Germanicus had obviously sent word back to our southern camp, because perhaps a sixth of a watch after the prisoners were set to work, several wagons came through the southern gate, moving at the trot.

"They're bringing our heavy tools to help tear the buildings down," Germanicus explained when I inquired about them. "The faster we can stop the fire, the sooner we can go to the stronghold and accept Dodonis' surrender."

"Dodonis?" This was the first time Donnado spoke, and we both turned to where he was standing, flanked by two Gregarii who were eyeing him suspiciously, despite Germanicus deciding, at my urging, to have the Maezaei prince's hands bound, though he was allowed to have them in front of his body. "What did you say about my father?"

"That we'll wait until the fire is out before we go and accept your father's surrender."

I suspect that Donnado did not even make an attempt to hide his reaction, his mouth forming what appeared to my eyes to be a mocking smile, but there was no mistaking the note of satisfaction when he informed us, "My father isn't here in Splonum. And," he turned towards the stronghold, jerking his head to indicate it, "that is being held by my brother." Looking over at Germanicus, he actually laughed, and the sound of it was lacerating as he finished, "If you think he's going to surrender, you're sadly mistaken, Roman."

The brother's name, we learned, was Decebalus, and despite being younger than Donnado, from what we could determine, there was a bitter rivalry between the two of them, something we would learn more about, but only later after it was too late to make good use of the information, and in a manner that was beyond debate. Germanicus decided to continue with his original plan to wait until daylight before approaching the stronghold, except that it was as much to prepare for the next phase of an assault in the event that Donnado was not lying to us.

The smaller *ballistae* were broken down and placed on mules and brought from the stone fort, as was the large piece, though it took longer, and the wagons were required. Meanwhile, the surrendered Maezaei at least worked diligently to save their town, and with the help of our heavy equipment, working through the night, they managed to quell the fire. That it was at the expense of a strip three blocks wide, extending across the entire town, meant that well more than a third of Splonum was destroyed, and when I had a chance to examine the damage, I could not help noticing that a significant portion of the ruined area was the same that had been burned down when I had last been here with my old Legion. While all this activity was going on, Germanicus ordered me to be attended by a *medicus*, the end result being two heavy bandages around my knees that gave me a stilted, stiff-legged gait that did not take long for some of the rankers to begin imitating behind my back, though I pretended not to notice, mainly because even in my state, I could see the humor of their Primus Pilus waddling about like a giant stork. The ointment that the *medicus* applied stank to high heaven, but he swore it was the most effective treatment for burns, which, as odd as it may sound, I had still refused to look at, and frankly, I was thankful that they were bandaged, despite the lack of mobility.

"You're done fighting, Primus Pilus," Germanicus had ordered, and perhaps more than anything else I can offer, the fact that I did not argue this is the best proof that I was not my normal self. I know he did not do this to assuage my pride, but he had gone on, "I'm going to need your experience more than I need your *gladius*."

The fire might have been out for the most part, but there was still a heavy pall of smoke that hung over the burned portion of the town as the smoldering embers consumed what was left. There was something in the early morning air that kept the smoke from rising very high, some invisible force creating an illusion that the stronghold was actually floating on a dirty, gray cloud. That this was something of a blessing for us was explained by, of all people, Silius.

"We found out from some of the prisoners that the barbarians only have two artillery pieces, and they were dragged to the stronghold just after dark yesterday. They knew the assault was about to start and I suppose they weren't confident that they wouldn't lose them in the process," the Tribune reported when he came back from his own tasks.

"Then why aren't they loosing rocks down on our heads?" Germanicus wondered, something I had thought about as well.

"Probably because they can't see through the smoke clearly enough and they can't be sure they won't hit some of their own men," Silius suggested.

Once he said it, I could see Germanicus immediately accepted this, but he mused, "That's probably true, but how can we use it to our advantage?"

The only thing I saw that we could do was use the smoke to maneuver our *ballista* into a better situation.

"Right now, we're only going to be attacking the stronghold from the southern side with our artillery," I suggested. "It would take too long to get the big piece on the other side of the town, but what about taking a page from their own book by setting up two of the smaller pieces on the other side, but keep them hidden between the buildings that are still standing?"

I was slightly surprised when Germanicus did not seem enthused by the idea, which he explained by asking, "But wouldn't they be firing blind if we did that?"

"They would," I admitted, then pointed out, "but Bibaculus is the best artilleryman I've ever seen. I'd have faith that he can figure out a way to hit that stronghold pretty quickly. Besides, that thing is a big target, and even if it just keeps their heads down, that only helps us."

203

This made up his mind, because he turned to Silius, "Gaius, since you're the man who gave us the answer, I'm putting you in charge of getting two pieces moved." He glanced up at the lightening sky; the sun had not yet cleared the eastern ridge, but we probably had less than a third of a watch. "See to it, and hurry!"

Silius was clearly pleased, and he vaulted into the saddle, kicking his mount into a trot, leaving Germanicus, the remaining Tribunes standing together, me and two of the Pili Priores Stertinius and Proculus of the Fourth, discussing what else needed to be done. As we were talking, Bibaculus came trotting up, puffing so much that he had to stop and put his hands on his knees before catching his breath. While waiting for the man to do so, Germanicus informed him of the change in tactics, but while the artilleryman clearly thought it was a good idea, he had another suggestion.

"I'd like to do that with the other two five pounders," he explained, referring to the *ballista* by the size of the rock it threw. "If we array them over there like we originally planned," he turned and indicated a part of the town in which there was only smoking ruins, "we'll certainly be in range of the stronghold. But," he said grimly, "now that we know they moved the pieces, that means we'll be in range of their artillery. In fact," he turned and made an arcing motion from the stronghold to a point relatively close to where we were standing, "because of their height advantage, they'll actually have further range than our pieces. I could build some *plutei* to protect them, but there's no guarantee that those bastards won't just bash them to pieces."

"Where do you want to put them?" I asked, and as I expected, he pointed in the direction of the northern gate.

"More or less along the same line that the other two will go," he squatted down and sketched in the dirt a shallow arc, then made four "x" marks at different points on the line, before drawing the relative position of the stronghold. "This way, we'll be able to cover the northern and western sides of that stronghold with the small pieces. And Bellona can handle the southern wall."

"Bellona?" Germanicus asked, puzzled, but despite the pain I was feeling, I had to chuckle.

"Yes, Bellona!" Bibaculus' eyes widened as if the answer was obvious. "She's the goddess of war, isn't she? And," the *Immune* said with pride, "she's the queen of this battlefield!"

The Legate's face cleared, and he appeared slightly embarrassed, either because he had not realized that Bibaculus was referring to the large *ballista* sooner, or more likely, that one of his implements of war had a name.

However, all he said was, "Ah, yes. Understood. So," his voice turned brisk, "will your...Bellona be ready by dawn?"

"No, Legate," Bibaculus at least seemed a bit chagrined, "that's what I wanted to tell you. It will take almost a watch before we're ready, and even then, it won't be secured as well as I'd like it. So," he finished, "I'll be able to launch two, maybe three stones at most, but we'll have to reposition it."

"How long does that take?" Germanicus asked, then recognizing he had not been clear, amended, "To properly secure it?"

"No more than a sixth part of a watch more," Bibaculus answered immediately.

"Then take the time," Germanicus replied. "We can afford that much."

Saluting, Bibaculus went trotting off in the direction of southern gate, where the wagons carrying the pieces of the *ballista* were waiting. Because of its range, there was no need to hide the placement of the piece, and Germanicus had been of the opinion that perhaps seeing what awaited them, Decebalus would recognize the futility of further resistance, which caused his brother, who had been allowed to sit on the ground, to issue a derisive snort, though he did nothing more than that. He had been less than forthcoming about the strength of the garrison, their level of supply, and probably of equal importance, how many of the town's inhabitants were crammed inside the stronghold. It was a good size, much larger than the stone fort, but Splonum had about ten thousand inhabitants, and we had seen the steady stream of terrified tribespeople ascending the winding road to find refuge once we had taken the stone fort. What we had no way of knowing was how many of those people, using the cover of darkness and the fact that we did not have the manpower to completely encircle the town, had slipped out of the fortress in the night, fleeing east into the hills surrounding the town on that side. Never far from my mind was the recognition that, with every passing watch, the chances of Maezaei reinforcements arriving grew, while we could expect no such succor, at least as far as I had been informed. Although I had expressed my concerns to Germanicus already, I did not see the point in constantly reminding him about it, since he already had his hands full, but he seemed to grow in confidence with every passing day. The sun finally rose high enough to illuminate the town, just in time for the Tribune and acting Quaestor Gaius Fufius to trot up, holding a wax tablet.

"I have the figures you requested." He extended the tablet to Germanicus, who had summoned his horse so that he could at least sit in the saddle, something for which I envied him, since I had yet to figure out how I would be able to sit down in a chair, let alone climb aboard Latobius.

Germanicus took the proffered tablet, studying it with a frown, but when he said nothing, I was forced to clear my throat to remind him that we all had a vested interest in what was written on it.

Glancing up and seeing we were all looking at him, he reddened slightly but understood why we were doing so, saying, "These are our casualty figures, which are very light, considering. Pullus," he turned to me, "the First Century took the brunt of it. You've got six men dead and fifteen wounded; the Second Century, two dead and five wounded." He continued on, but while I was concerned about our casualties, there was another piece of information that was more important to our immediate situation. "Now," he turned to examine the other side of the tablet, "as far as the Maezaei, we took nine hundred-odd prisoners, and they lost a bit more than that dead, almost a thousand."

"And the wounded?" I believe it was Silius who asked this question, which prompted what could be called an uncomfortable silence, and I saw Germanicus' eyes move to where Donnado was sitting, clearly within earshot, and judging from his expression, was listening.

"We don't treat enemy wounded, Tribune," I spoke up, then allowed, "at least most of the time. If they're like him," I jerked my thumb at the Maezaei noble, knowing he would take it as an insult, "and are worth something alive as a hostage, then we will. But otherwise..." I finished with a simple shake of the head.

"Oh," Silius replied, "I see." He looked down at the man who was, presumably, the crown prince of the Maezaei, then said only, "That makes sense."

"More importantly," Germanicus interjected, and I had the feeling he wanted to move on, making me wonder if he was trying to spare the feelings of our vanquished foe, "that means there are around three thousand warriors unaccounted for. Which in turn means," he twisted to point back to the stronghold, "they're likely in there."

Honestly, this seemed high to me, but from the moment of our arrival outside Splonum, somehow the number of five thousand defenders was taken as fact, and I never learned exactly from where this estimate had originated. In my judgment, based on what I saw when we took the stone fort, where there had only been five hundred warriors holding it, less than half the number it could hold, if there were four thousand warriors holding the town, it was unlikely to be more than twenty or thirty more men over that number. However, when I had expressed my reservations about our estimates, Germanicus had pointed out, correctly I knew, that it was better to overestimate than the opposite.

"There's not much more we can do," Germanicus announced, "and I want to give the men the chance to rest. Which," he turned and pointed directly at me, "includes you, Pullus."

"I can't ride," I protested, looking down at my knees, "and by the time I walk to camp, it would be time to turn around and come back!"

"Which is why," he was unmoved, "you're going to go lie down in one of the wagons over there."

He was referring to the wagons that had finished transporting the wounded back to the hospital tent and had been driven back inside the gates, where they were arrayed by the gate, out of enemy *ballista* range, and were waiting for fresh cargo should they be needed. Despite myself, I shuddered, knowing what the inside of a wagon carrying the wounded looked like, and I felt certain that the slaves responsible for them had neither cleaned up the mess of soaked bandages nor washed out the blood that had saturated the planks of the bed. Nevertheless, I was so exhausted that I simply saluted, then hobbled over, finding that my fears had been justified, so I selected the least filthy, and with the help of the pair of slaves assigned to the wagon, crawled into the wagon and only pulled off my helmet while falling onto my back, thinking that the pain would keep me from sleeping.

Chapter 4

"Primus Pilus! *Uncle Titus!*"

Jerking awake sent a spasm of agony up my thighs, which certainly blew away the cobwebs in one's mind that come from a deep sleep, although I would have preferred another method. Forcing myself to sit up, I saw Alex standing there, wide-eyed and seemingly torn between the sight of my heavily bandaged legs and whatever it was that had caused him to rouse me. My initial thought was that it was simply because enough time had passed for all our preparations to be made and Germanicus was ready for whatever was to come next, but once I slid out of the wagon, needing Alex's help down onto the ground, I instantly saw that more than that was going on.

"What happened?" I asked Alex, then thought of something else, and I confess I was a bit grumpy when I added, "And how did you get here? Why aren't you back in camp where you belong?"

"I was helping load the wounded into the wagons," he informed me, which seemed odd to me.

"I didn't see you earlier," I am not sure why this seemed important, but when Alex shifted uneasily, rocking back and forth from one leg to another, something he had done since he was walking, it served to make me even more alert and suspicious.

"It was dark," he said evasively, though he refused to meet my eyes. "That's probably why you missed seeing me."

"Or," I was not fooled in the least, "you made sure to stay as far away from me as you could." I sighed, realizing this was pointless, so I asked him, "Now what's going on?"

"I'm not sure," Alex replied and this time, he did meet my gaze, "but something happened. So," he shrugged, "I thought you would want to know."

I was about to tell him that he had done the right thing, but we were interrupted by the sound of a horse moving at a canter, causing me to hobble around the side of the wagon, giving me an unobstructed view of the area.

"Primus Pilus!" Appuleius hailed me, but he had headed for the wrong wagon, then seeing me, turned his mount, slowing only to a trot. "The Legate needs you to attend to him immediately!"

"Where is he?" I asked, noticing that neither he nor any of the other officers were in the spot they had been when I had been banished. "And what's happening?"

"We've been betrayed!" The Tribune said this with an emphasis that seemed a bit dramatic to me, although I had to acknowledge that, depending how bad it was, he might have been justified. Appuleius twisted and pointed in the general direction of the town square, prompting a groan from me. "He's put his headquarters in a building on the west side of their forum, just out of range of the savages' artillery."

"Tell him I'm coming," I told Appuleius, whose face darkened and he seemed to consider making an issue that I had not addressed him in the manner in which he deemed proper from a grubby ranker, even if he was a Centurion.

Instead, he gave an abrupt nod, and without saying a word, turned and immediately kicked his horse into a gallop, while I followed behind him. I saw that Bellona was fully assembled, but while Bibaculus and his crew were present, they appeared to have finished making preparations to begin assaulting the stronghold. The Second Cohort, minus Agrippa, was in formation next to the western wall, although they had been allowed to sit in place, their shields and javelins stacked in neat rows, while some of the men were consuming their morning meal, while others were stretched out, doing what I had been, trying to grab some sleep. Next to them was the First Cohort in the same posture, and I took the time to find Metellus, whose face was drawn and looking near collapse himself.

"I'm fine." He waved my concern off, then pointed down at my legs, saying, "I'm just tired. At least I don't look like that!"

We chatted for a matter of a few heartbeats, and I promised that as soon as I knew what was going on, I would return and let him know.

"Something happened up there," Metellus pointed across the town to the stronghold, which was now clearly visible, most of the smoke now blown away by a brisk morning breeze from the south. "There was some sort of commotion, then I saw horsemen tearing down the road like Cerberus himself was taking a chunk out of their asses."

Despite myself, I had to chuckle at my old comrade's colorful description, and clapping him on the shoulder, I left him to make my way to the center of the town.

It was easy to find Germanicus, who had appropriated the low, squat building that, in area, was one of the largest in Splonum, and was a remnant of the time when this had been a barbarian town whose inhabitants had not been under Roman control. Originally the chieftain's hall, it was now used as a storehouse, or at least had been, although whatever it held had been removed, leaving only a few broken jugs, some discarded sacks, and the like. Lamps had been hung, since like most such structures, there were only two windows, along with the double doors, which were open, and through which I hobbled. A makeshift table had been created from what looked like doors from other buildings, and some crates, and around which I saw Germanicus, the Tribunes, the other Pili Priores, and Gaesorix, who gave me a cryptic shake of his head that I could not readily interpret.

Germanicus looked up from what I assumed was the map of the stronghold, and seeing me, echoed Appuleius, crying out, "Pullus, we were betrayed!"

"So I heard," was all I could think to say, "but I don't know the specifics."

This was the moment I learned that, as much as young Germanicus had grown into an able commander, he was still as green as spring grass, particularly when it came to understanding the enemy he was fighting.

"I decided that it would mean more to send Donnado to parley with his brother..." he began, but got no further, probably because of my spontaneous curse, which caused him to flush a deep red.

211

"Pluto's cock," I groaned, forgetting that this was an impolitic manner in which to behave in front of my Legate. "So now that bastard is up there with his brother?"

My first indication that my assumption had been erroneous occurred when Germanicus gave a laugh, but it was with a combination of bitterness and disgust to my ears.

"No," he shook his head, confusing me, "the brother didn't do that. *That* I would have understood."

When he said nothing else, choosing to stare down at the map, it was Gaesorix who supplied the answer.

"Apparently," even with his thick accent, there was no mistaking the heavy humor present, "Decebalus didn't like his brother very much. Or," he shrugged, "he decided he should be the heir and not his brother."

"Wait." I held up a hand as I tried to absorb this. "You're saying that he *killed* Donnado?"

"Threw a spear down from the rampart and it went right through the poor bastard's chest," Gaesorix confirmed.

This elicited a groan from me, but not from any sense of grief; the truth was as soon as the words were out of Gaesorix's mouth, I realized that this was something I should have foreseen. Knowing these tribes as I did, and particularly all that had transpired when Dodonis had snatched power from his predecessor Gurgos, it was obvious how likely it would be that the sons of a man who had schemed his way to power would be like their father.

All I could think to say was, "Well, I suppose that means that Decebalus isn't considering surrender."

Despite the circumstances, something in the way I said it must have struck a humorous note, because Germanicus chuckled along with Gaesorix and a couple of the others around the table.

Scipio, of course, did not see anything humorous in the moment, but he went even further, because he rounded on me, and while his words were respectful, it was not matched by his tone as he said stiffly, "Forgive me, Primus Pilus, but you reacted as if this was something you expected. If you had known this was the likely outcome, shouldn't you have stopped the Legate from making this error in judgment? After all," he pointed out, albeit with what I suppose he thought was a smile, though it was as false as the man himself, "our Legate has made it clear that he relies on you a great deal for advice. Even more than," Scipio raised a hand to indicate his fellow nobles, but to my eyes it was the same languid gesture he might have made to a slave to bring him his wine, in a jeweled cup, of course, "men who are his peers?"

Now I was not disposed nor was I in the right frame of mind to let this pass, but this clearly had been aimed at Germanicus as much as me, and it was he who offered a rebuttal, snapping, "The Primus Pilus wasn't present when I made my decision, Scipio, so he can hardly be blamed for my error!"

"Neither was I," Scipio fired right back, but I saw by the rapid rise of color to his face that he recognized his mistake, while the other nobles, particularly those of Tribune rank, regarded him with looks that ranged from cool disapproval to outright hostility, the latter of those raising a great deal in my esteem. "I mean," Scipio amended lamely, "neither were we."

"I was here," Gaius Silius, whose expression fell into the second category, said quietly.

"So was I," offered Marcus Frugi, who went even further by adding, "and we didn't think there was anything wrong with Germanicus' decision. Why?" His voice, still quiet, nevertheless became pointed, as he pressed, "Do you? Is there something you want to say, here in front of all of us?"

As I suspected Frugi knew it would, this shut Scipio's mouth more than an open rebuke from Germanicus could have accomplished, to the point that the arrogant young bastard acquiesced with only a shake of his head. A silence hung over the group as Germanicus studied Scipio long enough to not only make the man uncomfortable, but sent a potent message of its own.

Finally, Germanicus turned away from Scipio, dismissing him in more than one way as he looked down at the charcoal lines drawn on vellum that served as our map.

"Now," he spoke, finally, "we need to decide the best way to attack this stronghold."

With that, we began preparing for the final assault on Splonum.

With all but the royal stronghold taken, what it meant in a larger sense was that, for the first time in months, the road from Siscia south that connected the upper and lower half of the province was now open. Consequently, communication with the wider province was resumed, which meant that the stream of orders, dispatches, and all other manner of messages recommenced as quickly as it took for Germanicus to send a rider to Siscia to inform Tiberius of the gains we had made. I have had occasion to wonder if my Legate would have been better served to wait until Splonum was taken in its entirety, despite the reality that there was nothing that Decebalus could do to exert any pressure on us and influence our efforts to reclaim the Maezaei territory in the immediate vicinity of the town. In the larger world, specifically concerning the rest of the Maezaei, we had learned from the prisoners that it was true that Dodonis was not present because he had been leading the force that took Raetinium. When viewed in retrospect, I suppose those critics who said that we should have taken Raetinium first have a valid objection, but the truth is we simply did not know Dodonis was at the head of the force holding Raetinium, and it was not a leap to assume that he would remain where his power and his defenses were the most potent. Once it became clear that there would be no surrender by Decebalus, Germanicus decided that it was in the best interest of the Legion that we postpone trying to take the stronghold, which he explained had two purposes.

"The men can use the rest," he informed us, "but I'm also releasing the cavalry. I need to have a better idea of the situation in Raetinium." Pointing to Silius, he said, "I'm sending Silius along with Gaesorix to be my eyes and ears. Once they've scouted Raetinium, I'm ordering them to take the southerly route to swing through the province." He assumed a grim expression as he finished by speaking directly to the Decurion and Tribune. "And if you meet any resistance, you have my permission to burn the nearest village to the ground. It's still too early to raze their crops, but maybe if they have no home for this coming winter, they'll think better of throwing in with those other rebels."

From where I stood—I had learned that leaning against the nearest wall was the best I could do—Gaesorix did not look happy, and I made a mental note to speak to him privately, since I was certain his unease had to do with Silius. Normally, I would have shared his sentiments, but I had spent enough time around Silius to see that he was the steadiest of Germanicus' staff of Tribunes and seemed to have the least problem with being ordered about by a man who technically outranked him.

"I'm going to allocate the part of town that can't be touched by their *ballistae* to serve as quarters for the men." Germanicus moved on to the next subject, and his words prompted me to limp back to the center of the room.

That this was the first I had heard him mention anything about this idea was bad enough; that he had uttered it aloud in front of others put me in a damnably awkward situation, because I thought this was an extremely bad idea.

Trying to forestall him, I asked Germanicus, "Have the houses been searched yet? Because I know the First didn't do it."

Germanicus shrugged, and despite clearly not wanting to, he asked cautiously, "I don't know, but why does it matter?"

"Because while it's probable that the townspeople took everything of value, the men aren't going to believe that until they've torn each home apart, and if you have them sleeping there, it gives them the time to do just that."

"So you're saying that the rankers would deprive themselves of a roof and place to sleep just because there might be a few coins buried under a hearth or hidden in the rafters?" Scipio, who predictably had been the man who spoke, sniffed, muttered something under his breath that sounded like "animals," but continued in a normal tone, "Why doesn't that surprise me?"

Germanicus, looking unhappy, finally broke in, asking me, "Is there anything else we should consider? I mean, besides that?"

I nodded, and as I did, I said simply, "Mead."

"Mead?" For an instant, the Legate looked confused, then his face cleared. "Ah, you mean that drink the Germans love so much. I thought that was just drunk by the tribes across the Rhenus."

"That might have been true at one time," I replied, "but once Pannonia became part of Rome, it means they have access to our roads, our transport system, and our merchants. They love the stuff. And," I finished with this warning, "unless you want drunken rankers brawling in the streets, you're going to want to search those houses if you do that."

Sighing, Germanicus shook his head, saying, "No, we wouldn't want that." He hesitated for a moment, then seemed to come to a decision. "They stay in camp, then."

Now it was my turn to sigh, but it was of relief, and I suppressed it as Germanicus returned to the business at hand. Bibaculus had been summoned, and it was to the *Immune* he turned, asking, "Bibaculus, how long do you think it would take to create a breach in that stronghold?"

Having obviously given it thought, the old veteran answered immediately, "It will take longer than it did the wall, because as you saw, it's made of dressed stones, laid in an offset pattern. But," he cautioned, "what I don't know is how thick the walls are. If the wall is the thickness of the rampart, it could take at least a week."

"A week?" Germanicus was clearly dismayed. "That long?"

Bibaculus actually shook his head to the question, which I confess confused me as much as it seemed to confound Germanicus, but the *Immune* explained, "But we couldn't do that anyway, not right now, because we don't have enough of a supply of ten-pound stones."

Not surprisingly, it was Scipio who once more offered his opinion, and thereby exposed his ignorance, scoffing, "No stones?" He gave a mocking laugh. "There's a river full of stones out there. Surely you can fish a few out of the river and use those."

"We very well could do that, Tribune," Bibaculus answered evenly, but I dropped my head so my expression would not give away my anticipation at what was coming. "And if we did, I would have to change my estimate to two weeks."

Scipio gasped, obviously disbelieving, but before he could argue this any further, Germanicus raised a hand, saying wearily, "Those aren't just any stones, Scipio." As he glanced over at Bibaculus, it seemed that he was asking permission of the *Immune* to continue the Tribune's education, and out of the edge of my vision, I saw the man give a faint nod. This prompted the Legate to go on, "The stones have to be carefully shaped so that they're perfectly round. Otherwise, they're wildly inaccurate, which means that we would have to throw many, many more stones in the hopes that some of them hit the spot we're trying to break through. Is," Germanicus returned his attention to Bibaculus, "that about the size of it?"

"Exactly right, sir," Bibaculus replied happily, and I was certain part of his good mood came from Scipio being taken down a peg, but not by him. "And they can be just as dangerous to us as they are the enemy. Why," he suddenly became enthusiastic, "I saw once when a poorly shaped stone took the head right off one of our own who was standing well out of the way! As I recall," there was a slight change in his voice as he finished, "it was a Tribune that happened to. Sir."

Muted snickers rippled around the gathering, and even Germanicus had to smile; for some reason, Scipio did not seem amused in the slightest.

"So," Germanicus asked, "what do we need to do?"

For the next three days, any Maezaei who was willing to brave a scorpion bolt through the face would have seen what I am certain they would think was an odd sight, as Romans waded into the Valdasus, dragging out rocks to be inspected by the *Immunes* who were responsible for using a hammer and chisel to carefully shape stones of the proper dimensions and weight. While this stockpile was being replenished, we were busy with other matters as well, including completing an encirclement of the town, with a Century sent to the eastern hill overlooking both the town and stronghold, with orders to scout for a suitable site for an outpost. Not only did Germanicus direct

217

it be large enough to hold a Century, he also wanted the ability to drag one of the small *ballistae* up there as well. It was not a circumvallation of Alesian proportions, but in what I still believe was a form of tribute to Divus Julius, Germanicus did order the construction of a line of entrenchments that made a curving line from the southern wall to the eastern, something that the Maezaei did make an attempt to stop by using their two pieces. This was done despite the construction of *plutei* and *fascines* that were erected to protect the men digging, but if it was not a half-hearted attempt, it was at least short-lived. By the time they lobbed their third stone, our large and small pieces went into action themselves, and even from a distance, the cracking sound as our missiles smashed into the parapet was impossible to miss, with the ten-pound stone shattering a crenellation, leaving only a jagged stump that reminded me of the teeth along my lower jaw. More importantly, we inflicted massive damage on one of their two *ballistae*, and I was hopeful that it was beyond repair, although Germanicus announced that we would still behave as if it was still operational. With the construction of a ditch first, which took two full days, the next step was to erect a series of small towers in which a scorpion was placed, while the Maezaei could only look on helplessly from their rampart. The Century that was sent out to find a good location for an outpost, the Second of the First led by Metellus, who was the only man I trusted to have the necessary experience to accomplish the task set for them, returned with two alternatives for consideration. Like everything else I have ever experienced as a man of the Legions, neither was a clear-cut choice, with both advantages and disadvantages for each.

"There's a flat spot right near the top of the hill directly above the stronghold," Metellus reported, "but we'd have to cut down a fair number of trees and saw the stumps flat." Pointing to the spot, he went on, "With the height advantage, Sacerdos says we would have the range with one of the small *ballistae*."

Gnaeus Sacerdos, another old veteran, had previously served as an artillery *Immune*, though I cannot recall which Legion, and while Germanicus made it clear he would have preferred that Bibaculus or one of his men accompany the Second, they were too busy with other tasks.

"Then what's the problem with it?" Germanicus asked, reminding Metellus, "You said that there's a problem with it as well."

"The problem," I was secretly proud of the manner in which Metellus was conducting himself; as reluctant as he had been in taking this post, he had risen to the occasion, although anyone with eyes could see it was taking a toll on him, and he did not hesitate in answering, "is that the southeast edge of the fort isn't visible from that spot." He paused, then added what I knew was the most important aspect, "Including the gate."

"Which means that they could slip out under the cover of darkness and cause us all manner of trouble." I was pleased to see that Germanicus instantly grasped this, which I took as another example of his growing grasp of military matters. Nodding his head in acceptance, he moved on, "So what about the second spot?"

"That one," Metellus moved his finger, not far, but it instantly became clear what the issue would be, "puts us in a position to see the gate, but too far for the *ballista* to reach."

The Legate's brow furrowed, but it appeared he made up his mind when he said, "Then I suppose it's obvious which spot we choose."

"Not necessarily."

Marcus Asinius Agrippa did not speak in these councils often, but I had noticed before this that when he did, it was usually to our benefit, and this time was no exception.

Placing his finger on the spot where Metellus had indicated, he gazed at the map for a moment before asking my Centurion, "You can see the gate, but it's out of range of the *ballista*?" When Metellus confirmed with a simple nod, the young Pilus Prior asked, "But according to the map, you have a clear view of that road that leads to their mines to the east?"

"Yes, Pilus Prior," Metellus confirmed, and there was something in his tone that made me shoot a glance in his direction, surprised to see the beginning of a grin on his battered face, as if he understood where Agrippa was headed.

"If this spot isn't able to reach the stronghold, can it reach the road?" Agrippa asked, prompting what could only be described as an emphatic nod from my old comrade.

"Yes, sir," Metellus answered, and if it had been appropriate, I would have informed Agrippa that Metellus was conferring what, for him, was a rare honor in deigning to show this level of respect to someone of not just Agrippa's age, but his status.

Germanicus, who had been listening to this exchange, resumed control of the conversation, saying, "So we could stop them from either sneaking away, or more importantly, being reinforced?" His tone was doubtful, which surprised me somewhat, but it was explained when he went on, "One *ballista* wouldn't be enough to stop a determined force, either one trying to get away or one coming."

This was an accurate assessment, but I decided to point out, "That's true, but any damage we can inflict in either case is to our benefit." Germanicus listened, then after a pause, nodded, except I was not quite through, aiming this question at Metellus. "Did Sacerdos say whether or not it was within range of the *ballista* if it wasn't throwing stones, but firepots?"

"No," Metellus admitted, which prompted me to try and hurry past by addressing Germanicus.

"If we can lob fire down on their heads, we can maximize the damage," I stated.

"Then we need to find out if that's the case," Germanicus decided, "and if it is, I don't think we can pass up the chance."

"So," I asked, more as a formality, "if that second spot is within range for firepots, we build an outpost there?"

"No," Germanicus replied, but before any of us could react, said with a broad smile, "we're going to do both. Now," he turned to Metellus, "I thank you, Pilus Posterior Metellus. You may return to your men and give them a ration of wine as my thanks."

The look on Metellus' face was akin to that of my nephew, young Gaius, when he was given an extra candied plum after dinner, and I thought ruefully that Germanicus was either lucky or knew more about my old friend than I would have thought.

"Send for Bibaculus," Germanicus ordered, then turned to Frugi and Appuleius to instruct them, "Find a horse for him and take my personal bodyguard. Have him examine this spot personally so he can determine if it meets our needs for what Pullus suggested. You have enough daylight to be there and back before dark. If it's suitable, we start out first thing in the morning."

My purpose for bringing this up is that, along with the other decisions and activities that derived from them, this was another situation that was used against Germanicus, and as I would only learn later, I was the unwitting author of these troubles.

The worst part of this final phase of taking Splonum was not the tension that is an inherent part of a siege, particularly when there is the possibility that a relieving force will be sent to help, although I had a great deal of faith in Gaesorix to alert us, which I would not have thought possible in the watch after we first met. No, for me, it was the fact that I was left with very little to do, other than stand in one spot and look like I supposed my Avus did when he was a Primus Pilus, imposing and as if I knew what every man was thinking. On the fourth day, the Sixth Cohort was busy building two fortified outposts, since Bibaculus had been confident that even the small piece could hurl a firepot, although it had to be slightly larger than the normal size, and I was in a truly sour mood. Finally, shortly after midday, I could take it no longer, and I hobbled back to my quarters, which were still in the camp, although Germanicus, the Tribunes, and three of the men serving as Pili Priores had chosen the comfort of one of the abandoned houses; naturally, Germanicus had appropriated the largest one, consisting of several rooms, which was appropriate for his rank. Growling for Alex to follow me as I moved through the outer part of my tent, I sat down on the edge of my cot, my legs splayed out in front of me. Despite having the bandages changed on the second day and ordering the *medici* not to make the dressing as bulky, bending my

221

knees was something that was not only difficult because of the wrappings, but it was terribly painful.

Although Alex complied, the manner in which he pushed the partition aside to enter my private quarters I would liken to a man who's been told there is a lifetime's fortune in a cave, but there is a ravenous bear guarding it. Which, I suppose, was not that far from the reality.

Pointing down to the bandages, I growled, "Cut these off of me. I'm fucking done with them."

My nephew did not look surprised, but he did look as if he would rather have been anywhere else, and he spoke cautiously, "But you're supposed to have them on for a full week. That's what…"

"I know what that butcher said," I snapped, "but they're wrong as often as they're right." I pointed again, but this time to the blade that Alex used to shave me. "Now get to cutting."

Sighing, he did as I directed but moved slowly enough that there was no mistaking the message he was sending that he was doing this against his will, then squatted down next to me.

Suddenly, he looked up at me with narrowed eyes and asked suspiciously, "And you're not going to hit me?"

"No," I assured him, "I'm not going to hit you."

He, however, was not swayed and insisted, "Swear it on the black stone you're not going to smack me because I did what you said."

"Juno's *cunnus*," I groaned, but he was still not moving, so I gave in. "I swear on the black stone I won't hit you."

Even then, he hesitated, and I suppose if I had been in a better frame of mind, I would have found it amusing how he tried to concentrate on sliding the thin blade under the bandages and keep an eye on my left hand, which was the nearest one to his head.

"Don't take all day," I grumbled, but he would not be hurried, shooting back, "I'll take all the time I need so I don't cut you."

"I promised I wouldn't hit you," I protested.

"We'll see," he mumbled, but he had just finished slicing through the bandage, yet when he reached down with his free hand to peel the bandage away, I stopped him.

"It's going to hurt like Dis," I told him, "so go ahead and slice the other one, then you pull one off and I'll pull the other one at the same time."

Alex looked up at me, horrified, and he gasped, "That is a *terrible* idea, Uncle Titus!"

I confess that I was not altogether convinced he was wrong, but my rationale was that if it was going to be agonizing, doing it all at once seemed like a better alternative. This is an opinion I no longer hold, but hopefully, I will never be in a position where I need to perform a similar act again. Once Alex saw I was not budging, he moved to the other side, and I saw that his hand was shaking more noticeably than it had for the left leg, yet he managed to slice through the bandage without inflicting more damage. Then, he laid the blade down, and there was no further cause for delay.

"We'll do it on three," I told him, then took a deep breath before saying, "One...two...three!"

The best thing I can say about the experience is that I at least was true to my word and did not strike Alex, but it was a close run thing. Afterward, I was told by more than one man that my bellow had been heard in Splonum; as I said, if I had to do it all over again, I would have chosen differently.

Now that the bandages were off, I was able to get around better, albeit marginally, but the tradeoff was that I could not avoid looking at my knees. Neither, it appeared, could anyone else who saw them, and I would have donned a pair of *bracae*, except they would have been stuck to the oozing, blistered skin, which would have been a repeat of the ordeal of taking the bandages off. Now, all these years later, the scars are so similar in appearance to those on my left arm that one who was unaware of the cause would think both were from the same kind of wound. Then, however, there were large blisters that would burst, then overnight would reappear, only to open again when I flexed my knees, something I forced myself to do. It probably is not surprising that this did not do my frame of mind or my temperament any good, and I am ashamed to say that poor Alex bore the brunt of my surly disposition, exacerbated by the constant and growing friction within the command group, as Scipio became more and more vocal in his opposition to, seemingly, anything and everything Germanicus decided. As so often happens in matters such as this, what was the cause of this change only became apparent later, once more information came to light, and most importantly, I had the time to think about it and compare it to the bits and pieces of the picture I already knew. In the moment, however, it was nothing more than a source of irritation until a week to the day after we had taken the town. We were supposed to resume the siege in earnest the next day, with every preparation that we could think of making being accomplished, which included the creation of a huge pen in which the captive Maezaei were held, and in doing so, Germanicus demonstrated that there was, in fact, a streak of cold iron in his makeup. It was not the pen itself, it was where he located it, in the section of town inside the wall that had been razed, either by the Maezaei or by the fire, the rubble of which had been cleared out as part of the process. By locating it where he did, if the Maezaei still inside the stronghold were to try and use their *ballistae* on us, the chances were good they would kill some of their own tribesmen. In itself this was enough to make even the most hard-bitten rankers take notice, but it was in the Legate's other decision concerning the prisoners that caused even more of a sensation.

"They're going to be fed and watered," Germanicus informed us, his face not only grim, but there was what I took to be a certain air of unease as he added, "but only just enough to keep them alive."

This caused a stir among the others, with the exception of Scipio, who looked pleased with himself, but it was actually Quartus Pilus Prior Proculus who raised the question, "To what end, if I may ask?"

"Because," Germanicus replied, his face registering nothing that would indicate his personal feelings, "if the barbarians in the stronghold see men who are their friends, husbands, and sons suffering, it only puts more pressure on Decebalus. We don't know what conditions are like in the stronghold, but they're going to be better than what those men out there are going through, because at least they have shelter. And," he concluded, "more food than our prisoners will."

There was a silence as the officers, all of them younger than me and without a fraction of the experience that not only I but the men marching in the ranks of the *Legio Germanicus*, absorbed this, each to a varying degree. Judging by the manner in which Scipio was smiling, it led me to believe that this idea had either originated with him, or at a minimum he had been an enthusiastic supporter, while men like Proculus and, a bit to my surprise, young Agrippa looked distinctly uncomfortable, something that I shared with the pair, but not for the same reason. The truth was that, while I could not say I heartily endorsed Germanicus' decision, I understood and agreed with it, barring some practical considerations; no, the real source of my own discomfort was that I found myself aligned with the pompous bastard Scipio, and this more than any other reason gave me pause, wondering if this was indeed the right path to take. Otherwise, my one real reservation was based in the practical consideration of how we would cope with the stench created by almost a thousand men's *cac* when it was not being washed downstream. Ironically enough, sanitation became an issue with the Maezaei, but not with our prisoners first.

We knew that the stronghold had to have been built on a site where there was an underground spring, since there were no watercourses visible anywhere around the stronghold. As hard as I tried to remember, I could not recall if, the one time I had actually been just a few feet away from the only gate, I had seen a stream or glimpsed a well through the open double doors. Back then, we had been ordered to take the now-dead Admetos into custody, so perhaps I can be forgiven for not paying attention to my surroundings with an eye towards a time when we would besiege this place. However, while it turned out that the royal palace did have that very thing, in the form of a spring, what it lacked was proper facilities to handle the waste created by a few thousand inhabitants. Without the aid of a truly experienced man in the capacity of *Praefectus Fabrorum* to perform their calculations using formulae that, even with Diocles' tutelage, I could never master, our estimates of the number of people who were enclosed within the stronghold varied widely. Regardless, what became clear was that, whatever number of people were stuck inside those walls, it was more than their latrines could handle, which became apparent when the Maezaei began dumping their waste outside their walls, under the cover of darkness. And, given where they dumped it, over the eastern wall on the opposite side from the town below, it would not be until it had accumulated over enough time that not even a strong southern breeze could dissipate the stench. Inevitably, there were further delays, this caused by Germanicus' decision to create two outposts, both of them manned by a Century and one of the small *ballistae*, something that drew even further comment and criticism, since we would have one quarter of our available small *ballistae* not active and just waiting in the event there was some sort of activity down on the road, while one of the other *ballista* could harass the defenders but was not in a position to contribute to creating a breach since it was located on the northern side. All of these things are small items, but as I would learn, they would be tallied up and used against Germanicus, though not by the Princeps, who sent a message of his own to his adoptive grandson that, judging by the demeanor of our Legate, who, for the first time in days, had a spring in his step, had been of a positive nature. The arrival of the letter, carried by courier from Ariminum by way of Siscia, coincided with the day when, at last, Bibaculus and his crew manning the ten-pounder, yanked the pin to send the first stone flying. As befitting such a moment, Germanicus had the small team of priests and augurs who came with him from Rome and who, by and large, were huge wastes of food and wine, perform a sacrifice, although we did not possess the most sacred animal, a white bull. Instead, we had to make do with a large ram, which would be yet another thing held against Germanicus by certain parties; that the liver was clean, the animal did not do anything unusual like fight its way to the altar which, being frank, I have always believed is anything but normal behavior, did not appear to matter as much as the creature used. The fact that by the end of a third part of a watch, Bibaculus had been unable to send two stones in a row to hit the spot that had been selected to create the breach did not help matters, as some of the more religious men began muttering about how it was a bad omen that we used a ram, although Bibaculus' assertion was that the river stones were imperfectly shaped. As for the breach itself, the place we had selected was the western wall, the side facing the town, but farther towards the northern end than the southern, where the gate was located. Once we were down to only two smaller pieces in the town, the decision was made to move them so they could add their weight to pounding against the stone walls. By midday, my ears had become accustomed to the steady, rhythmic sound of a *ballista* crashing forward violently enough to fling its cargo at a speed that was impossible to track with the eye if one tried to follow it anywhere near the piece. Only if one gazed at a spot in the air, roughly midway to the fort, was there any chance to catch it during its flight, yet even then, I missed a fair number of them. Stone after stone, from three different angles, once Bibaculus had created enough of an indentation that it could be seen by the other crews, we worked on the wall. Once, but only once, did a Maezaei warrior take a risk to lean out over the parapet to try and inspect the damage; one scorpion bolt, perfectly aimed to pass through the chest of the curious barbarian, was enough to dissuade the other defenders. By the end of the first full day, there was a noticeable crater that, according to Bibaculus, was about my height and perhaps three men wide, but despite this progress, when the *Immune* gave his report to the rest of us, he was not happy.

"We should be making more progress than we are so far," was how he put it. "I may have made a bad assumption; that's the only reason I can think of why we haven't gotten farther."

"Which is?" Germanicus asked, and while we were all interested, there was an avidity to the manner in which Scipio was listening, leaning forward on his elbows as if he needed to get closer.

"I assumed that the rock used for the stronghold is of the same type that composed the outer shell of the town wall." As he said this, he lifted a chunk of rock that he tossed down onto the table, the sound making those closest start a bit, while tiny bits of the mortar that still

227

clung to the stone crumbled onto the table, leaving a circle of crumbs. Pointing down at it, he continued, "This is the native rock, and as you can see, it's the same kind of limestone that's used everywhere around here and even in Rome. And," he demonstrated by pulling an iron-headed hammer of the kind used by the metalworking *immunes* from the pouch he always wore slung around his neck that contained the tools of his trade and gave the rock a single swing with the hammer, which fractured it in more than a dozen pieces, "that's what it should do every time it's hit with the force that even a five-pound stone holds. But," he shook his head again, "that's not what's happening."

There was a silence, then Germanicus asked the next logical question. "So, what's the wall made of, if it's not limestone?"

"I don't know." Bibaculus' frustration was obvious. "And naturally, we can't walk up to the wall and say, 'Excuse me, would you we mind if I pick up some fragments from your wall so we can see what they are?'. What I *can* tell you is that it's a bit darker than the travertine, but I originally thought that was because it had just been weathered. Now that we've knocked off that outer layer, we've seen it's the same color throughout the rock. It *could* be travertine," he shook his head again, "but I've never seen a variety this tough..." He did not finish verbally, just offering a shrug.

"Wait." Our newest addition, the man serving as Sextus Pilus Prior, Numerius Salvius Cethegus, who, according to Germanicus, had served as a Centurion in the Praetorians, said, "I thought travertine and limestone are the same?"

"They're similar," Bibaculus answered, "but travertine is a bit denser, which is why a builder who has the choice will always choose travertine. And," he waved a hand in the general direction of the rugged line of mountains to the west that serve as the barrier between the coastal strip and the inland of the region, "those mountains are full of the stuff."

"What does this mean?" Germanicus' lips thinned down at Cethegus' interjection, and I was reminded that Cethegus had originally been part of the contingent that accompanied Germanicus from Rome, but Tiberius had kept him back as part of his own force before sending him and the Cohort of veterans to reinforce us, although Germanicus said nothing, which I supposed was because it was a valid question.

"It means that it's going to take longer than I originally thought," Bibaculus answered calmly, then hesitated before he added, "and we might need one of two things."

"Which is?" Germanicus' question came so quickly that I felt certain it was his way of reasserting control of the meeting.

"Either we go out and gather more rocks that can be shaped," the *Immune* replied, then paused, which I understood when he finished grimly, "or you can persuade Tiberius to send us more artillery."

Later that very night, I learned firsthand that, despite my urging, Germanicus had not ordered a thorough search performed on all the remaining structures in Splonum, in the worst manner possible.

"Uncle Titus."

I was in my quarters, still in the camp and not in the town, something that only all of the Centurions of the First Cohort still did, eschewing the comforts of a real roof, solid bedstead, and a shelter more substantial than canvas, reading something that young Agrippa, also an avid reader had lent me. Not, I must say, without obvious reservations, undoubtedly because those like Scipio, Appuleius, and several of the others serving with Germanicus took such a dim view of men like me doing anything that smacked of ambition. Still, the fact that he did was something that, along with all the other moments I had observed, most of them having nothing to do with battle, recommended the grandson of one of Rome's greatest generals to my esteem. Now I was in the middle of a particularly fascinating account by Xenophon, titled The Anabasis, when Alex appeared, pushing through the partition.

"What is it?" I asked him, but I did not look up from the scroll, so it was not until I looked up at him that I felt the first rustling of disquiet.

"I...I...You should just come with me and see for yourself," was how he put it, but before I could even chastise him for his elliptical summons, he was already gone, and I heard him push aside the outer flap to our tent.

Grumbling, I pushed myself up to my feet and hobbled out into what was the Legion office, seeing that my nephew, while holding the flap aside, was actually still standing in what served as the doorway, looking out onto the forum of the southern camp.

"There better be a good reason for this," I muttered, except Alex did not answer verbally, instead stepping aside to allow me an unobstructed view of the center of the camp.

At first, I did not see anything untoward, seeing only a half-dozen men on the opposite side of the forum who seemed to be walking towards the Porta Praetoria, the shortest way to Splonum, although there was no guarantee they intended to actually leave the camp. However, when I continued watching, I noticed something unusual, but even before I could process what I was seeing, let alone comment, there was a shout from another direction, back around behind my tent. This forced me to leave the tent to step around it, yet when I did, to my shock and dismay, the sight that greeted me was two rankers rolling around in the dirt of the Cohort street. Over the span of heartbeats, I watched before I started moving; one of the combatants managed to wrestle his opponent so that, with one motion, the stronger man was straddling the other man's chest, whereupon he began pummeling the pinned ranker in the face. This, more than anything else, shook me from my astonished shock, and I roared at the pair to stop, which was completely ignored, forcing me to go limping over to them. Without any warning, I grabbed the man on top by the back of his tunic, then, applying my strength, threw him aside in much the same way I had seen little Scribonia fling aside her rag doll after she had grown tired of it.

"What the fuck do you think you're doing?" I roared this, and while even I could tell it was not with the same power I used when we ripped the bandages from my knees, it served its purpose.

The beaten man struggled to his feet at roughly the same time as the other combatant did, both of them trying to come to at least a semblance of *intente*, but it did not take more than the span of a

230

heartbeat or two for me to understand that the reason both men were weaving about had nothing to do with their fight. Suddenly, the memory of what I had seen no more than twenty heartbeats earlier, where I witnessed the six rankers shambling along with the equivalent sideward motion as they walked that these two were exhibiting as they tried to stand still, came back to me, my mystification evaporating. Reaching the nearest man, the defeated Gregarius, I only had to get within two paces of him to smell the telltale combination of sweet from the honey and the sour from the fermentation process to know what had happened.

"Where," I demanded, "did you get mead?"

"Plius Prior?" The ranker, a man I recognized as an old veteran from the 13th, was so inebriated that not only could he not address me by my proper rank, however temporary, he mangled it.

"It's Primus Pilus, idiot," I snapped, though I realized with some chagrin that I had forgotten to snatch up my *vitus*, so I had to content myself with using my open hand, applying it to the side of his head with enough force to restore a semblance of sobriety but not render him insensible.

Unfortunately, I underestimated not the strength of my blow but the level of his intoxication, because he went stumbling in the opposite direction from my slap, his arms swinging wildly in the kind of overcorrection that one sees in drunks of every kind, and like most drunks, it was to no avail as he went crashing to the ground. While he attempted to scramble to his feet, his legs refused to cooperate, so he finally gave up, seemingly content to at least sit upright and resigned to a beating at my hands. He looked up at me blearily, but even his torso was weaving about, and with a disgusted snort, I offered him my hand to pull him up. The ranker might have been drunk, but he was not so far gone that he viewed my extended hand with a suspicion that, frankly, did more to dispel my anger than anything else.

Sighing, I said, "I'm done hitting you, Gregarius. I just need to know where you got the mead from."

This served its purpose, and he took my hand, but while he tried to help, I more or less hauled his dead weight to his feet, then had to steady him from falling again. It was about this moment I became aware of a sound that, while common enough in a military camp, was unusual because of the circumstances, so it was with a sense of disbelief that I glanced over my shoulder. And, surely enough, there was the other combatant who, a matter of heartbeats before, had been snarling and rolling around on the ground like an animal, now lying on his back in the middle of the Cohort street, snoring as if he was on his cot.

"Pluto's cock." I could really only shake my head, but I returned my attention to the first ranker, just in time to reach out and keep him from falling over again. "Now," I did not yell, knowing it would no more harm than good, "where did you get the mead?"

I was expecting the ranker to continue regarding me with some suspicion, wondering where the hidden trap was in my gentle tone and soft words; instead, he stared me with a bleary-eyed surprise, as if it was the most obvious answer in the world.

"Why, we got it in town, Pil..." He blinked several times, his face screwed up as he struggled to correct himself, finally coming out with, "Primus Pilus."

"No," Germanicus was at least forthcoming, "I didn't search the town." He regarded me for a long moment before he went on, and I suspect it was the fact that we were alone, in his private quarters, that encouraged him to admit, "I forgot to give the order, Pullus." As he studied my face for some clue, I suppose I gave enough away that it prompted him to sigh and ask, "How bad is it?"

"It's not good," I admitted, "but I have my Centurions and Optios out right now, searching for whatever's left of the mead." I paused, because I had serious misgivings over what I was about to suggest, mainly because of who would have to be included. "But the search would go faster if we had all the Centurions involved."

"Done." Germanicus did not hesitate, and he opened his mouth, I assumed to summon a clerk to issue the order, but I held up a cautioning hand.

"It's just that," I tried to frame my words in such a way that it would convey the message I was trying to impart but not in a blatant manner, "it might be a problem if we have all the officers of the Legion tied up. Maybe," I at least tried to make it sound as if the thought had just come to me, "we should leave the Centurions of one Cohort out of this, in the event that the Maezaei choose this moment to try something."

His mouth closed as he sat back in his chair, folding his hands together across his chest, a mannerism I had seen one other time, and I have often wondered if this was an accident, or if the gods were somehow sending me a sign about what they had planned for this young Legate.

"Which," Germanicus' tone was neutral, but there was no missing the keen interest in his gaze, "Centurions would you suggest aren't involved in this search?"

Keeping up the pretense, I paused long enough that, if someone had their ear pressed to the wall that separated his private quarters from the outer world, they would perhaps be fooled into thinking that I was actually considering the question.

"I think," I said thoughtfully, "that the Third would probably be the best."

"I see," Germanicus replied, but rather than approve, he completely threw me by disagreeing with me, offering instead, "But I think it should be the Sixth's officers."

"The Sixth?"

This caught me by such a complete surprise that I wondered if Germanicus had misread my implicit reason for offering up the Third, believing that Scipio was the worst person to have involved in any incident that could put Germanicus in a bad light. For an instant, I was about to press my case for Scipio, even though in doing so it would force me to articulate my suspicions, but when I opened my mouth to argue, the young nobleman gave me a faint but perceptible shake of his head. It was a subtle but unmistakable message, or I took it to be such, although I am afraid that I was now completely confused.

Regardless, I tried to recover, saying briskly, "Then the Sixth it is, sir."

Only then did Germanicus call to the clerk, and when the door was opened so quickly that it told me how impossible it would have been for the man not to be listening at the door, I shot a glance over at the Legate, but he only gave a faint smile that told me he knew this would be the case. I left with the clerk, wondering if I would get any sleep this night, and how many of our men would be suffering the kind of morning that only a night with mead can provide. If only that had been the worst that came out of this incident; the best that I can say is that I did not have long to wait to find out what it would be.

More than twelve casks of mead were found in a building a block from the village square that had clearly been the home and storehouse of a local merchant. This was the good news; the bad was that, from what we could tell, there had been a supply of more than thirty casks originally contained within. Despite an all-night search, with a Centurion and his Optio responsible for thoroughly searching the tents of their Century, which roused the men who were sober while identifying the miscreants, most of whom tried, unsuccessfully, to pretend they were as sober as their tentmates, we could only account for fifteen casks. Or, being accurate, the remnants of fifteen casks, most of them only containing the dregs. This was done as quietly as possible; by Germanicus' order, the men were not paraded outside their tents, or for those Centuries who had been moved inside the town, which was all of the Third and part of the Fourth, out in the street next to the houses they occupied. Despite our precautions, I understood it was a bit much to expect that it would go unnoticed by the Sextus Pilus Prior, but it was still a surprise when he showed up at my tent.

"Primus Pilus," Alex announced, the use of my title alerting me that this was an official matter, "Sextus Pilus Prior Cethegus requests to speak with you."

I had to stifle the curse that almost burst from me, then I used my normal voice to give permission. The partition opened, and I could not fault the manner in which the man entered, his helmet under his arm, while his *hamata* was immaculate, his leathers varnished until they gleamed. Despite the fact that the man had been with us for weeks, and I had certainly been around him, this was the first occasion where I took the time to examine him closely. Cethegus was medium height, with a slightly stocky build but not with a muscularity that one would associate with a Centurion of a Legion; instead, it bespoke a life led in a place like Rome, with its rich variety of food and copious supply of wine. More than that, however, was the lack of weathering to the man's features, along with a round face, something that I only took notice of at this moment, wondering why I had not made this observation before. That, I thought, was before I was made aware of Germanicus' worries about the man, yet despite this, I also admonished myself not to color my examination of the man with those suspicions. The salute he rendered, like everything else about the man, was perfectly proper, though I thought I detected a flair in it that I assumed was a Praetorian touch, but I returned it, then despite not wanting to, I indicated the chair opposite the desk.

"What can I do for you, Pilus Prior?" I asked him. "Since your Cohort had duty watching the prisoners and the stronghold overnight, I would have thought you'd be taking a well-deserved rest."

Cethegus gave what, to the ear, sounded like a rueful laugh, but I was carefully observing him, and I noticed that it never reached his eyes.

"You know as well as I do that Centurions never sleep," he replied, then added what I believed was an attempt to disarm my suspicion, "not in the real Legions, anyway. In the Praetorians..." He shrugged, and I gave what I hoped was a polite laugh but said nothing, which seemed to force him to come to the point, which he did by saying casually, "Quite a bit of excitement last night, neh, Primus Pilus?"

"I'm not sure what you mean," I replied blandly, and for an instant, I saw the flash of irritation cross Cethegus' face, but he recovered quickly.

"Really? Well, some of my boys apparently were talking to friends in other Cohorts, and they heard that some lucky bastards stumbled across a huge supply of that drink these barbarians love so much. The way I heard it, half the men in the Legion were stumbling around drunk!"

He said this with a smile, which I matched so that both of us were being equally false, replying lightly, "Oh, you know how rankers love to exaggerate. Yes," I granted, "there was an incident, but it was a single cask, and the men who got drunk were from the same Cohort." Suddenly inspired, I opened up a wax tablet that actually contained the morning's sick and punishment list, which by rights should have been completely full but only had the most egregious offenders from the night before, and I pretended to study it. "Yes, here it is. It was a total of a half-dozen men, from three Centuries of my Cohort."

"Your Cohort?" He lifted an eyebrow, then joked, "Well I can't imagine you cared for that very much! The men of a First Cohort are supposed to set an example, am I right?"

"That you are," I confirmed, "and these men did." I grinned at him. "They managed to find a single cask of mead that was overlooked by every other Cohort, and I suspect they got drunker than anyone else would have. And," I stopped smiling, "they're going to pay for it in a way that upholds the honor of the First."

Cethegus gave a brief dip of his head, which I took to be an acknowledgment of my words, and for a moment, I thought I had ended this, but he was not through.

"Still," he insisted stubbornly, though he clearly tried to remain good-natured about it, "that's not what I heard, and I trust the men who told me. So," that grin came back, and he leaned forward to whisper conspiratorially, "between us Centurions. What *really* happened?"

Realizing that he was not going to take the hint, I decided to put him off with another tactic, and it was actually a relief to drop the mask of pretense as I asked coldly, "And why do you want to know so badly, Cethegus?" This seemed to uncork the growing anger that had been building inside me, and without thinking, I stood from behind my desk to lean over it. "What business is it of the Sextus Pilus Prior, and who the *fuck* do you think you are to question me about a matter that didn't have anything to do with you or your Cohort?"

My sudden change in demeanor clearly caught him off guard, and I was happy to see a look of, if not fear, then concern, but there was a hint of anger as well.

"I'm not questioning you, Primus Pilus." He held up a hand that, when he did so, I noticed that his nails were manicured, deepening my suspicion and loathing of the man. "At least," he allowed, "not in the manner in which you seem to have taken it. I was just…"

"Yes, you were just curious," I interrupted, "and I answered you. Which," I pointed at him then, "you clearly didn't accept. Which means that you're at least implying that I'm not telling you the truth."

"Not at all," he protested, holding both hands up in a placating gesture, but he did it so quickly that it caused his helmet to fall from his lap, which made a sharp, crashing noise, and in turn caused him to visibly jump in his chair.

Apparently, this served the purpose of ending his attempt, because when he bent down to retrieve his helmet, once he did, he sat there and said nothing more.

Finally, I said as pleasantly as I could manage, trying to impart the message that I was not holding anything against him, "Now that we've cleared that up, if that's all, then I have some matters to attend to before I go meet with Germanicus."

As I hoped, the mention of the Legate's name caused a flash of alarm, and as he stood up, he said, "Thank you, Primus Pilus, and I apologize for giving offense. I was just…"

"Yes, you were just curious," I finished for him, but even after I dismissed him with a wave, he lingered for a moment.

"Primus Pilus," he spoke hesitantly, "I would ask a favor of you."

"Oh?" I knew exactly what he was going to ask but wanted him to say it aloud.

"There's no real need to mention this to the Legate, is there?"

I pretended to consider, then shrugged as I told him, "He's got enough on his mind, so I don't see any reason why I should."

Cethegus' body sagged a bit, and he wasted no time leaving my quarters. As I stared at his retreating back, I wondered if he knew I was lying; I suspected that, being from the Praetorians, he was not fooled in the slightest.

Despite all the excitement, the actual business of the siege had resumed as soon as it was light, but in the southern camp, we were far enough away that we could not hear the echoing reports of the stones smashing into the wall. One had to be within about three furlongs before the noise reached the ears, only growing in volume after entering the walls of the town. Sound might not have traveled that far, but smell did, and even with a wind from the south, the stench from the prisoners was growing, seemingly by the watch, or so I believed that to be the source. I had waited for Cethegus to leave my quarters and given him enough time to clear the area before I set out for the town. My Optio Rufius had roused the Century earlier to join the rest of the Cohort who were back out on the river, searching for more rocks, and I was pleased to see that it was shaping up to be one of the hottest days to this point, thinking that it would be a good way for those men who had overindulged to sweat the mead out of their bodies, and their comrades who had maintained their discipline to take the opportunity to inflict their own punishment on the drunkards. Otherwise, it was a routine day; the Centuries who were manning the outposts were relieved as soon after first light as it took for the relieving Centuries to climb the hill, using the route that kept them out of sight of the stronghold, and the relieved men were just marching through the village square on their way back to the southern camp when I arrived at what was now referred to as the *praetorium*. Germanicus, naturally, was already present, and he was deep in conversation with Frugi, but when I stopped, not wanting to intrude, the Legate waved me over.

"We were talking about this." Germanicus waved a wax tablet, but rather than make me ask, he extended it to me.

Opening it, I read what turned out to be a report sent by Silius, who was out with Gaesorix and the cavalry; they had reached

Raetinium, and the news was mixed. There was no sign that the Maezaei showed any inclination of sending reinforcements to Splonum, there being no activities inside the formerly Roman town that indicated preparations were being made. However, the number of Maezaei present in Raetinium was daunting, and that was putting it mildly, but beyond this, it was the repairs and improvements they had made in the defenses that had been in place when they took the town that was the most troubling.

"Do you think those numbers are correct, Pullus?" Germanicus' question broke into my growing concern as I re-read the report. "Do you think they have almost ten thousand spears waiting for us?"

"I think," I had to admit, "that it's possible." I looked over at Germanicus, slightly worried that he would take what I was about to say next as a rebuke. "I've never made it a secret I don't think there's as many defenders up there in that stronghold as we estimate, and if that's right, they have to be somewhere."

Thankfully, he did not seem offended, merely nodding his recognition, and he agreed to an extent. "This would seem to support your belief. But," he shook his head, "ten thousand men are too many for anyone to expect us to subdue!" Springing up from his chair, he began pacing, rubbing the back of his neck, and the worry he was feeling was palpable, but when I glanced at Frugi, who I knew Germanicus trusted, he seemed no less worried.

Suddenly, without thinking, I blurted out something that I never would have divulged otherwise. "You know, my grandfather left an account behind of his time with Caesar."

Germanicus stopped pacing, spinning about to face me, the worry I had seen replaced with an intense interest.

"Really?"

While it was a predictable response, that it had not come from Germanicus, but from Frugi, who was off to the side of where I was standing, caused me to turn and see that, while he was still seated, he was now leaning forward, clearly as intent as Germanicus.

"Y-yes," I cursed myself for stammering, although a part of my mind chided me for being surprised at their reaction. Despite my intention of using something I had recalled reading in his account to help wrest Germanicus' attention away from a future event that had no bearing on our present situation, I was compelled now to address Frugi. "I didn't realize you were familiar with my grandfather, Tribune."

"Why wouldn't I be?" He was clearly surprised, but I can promise it was a shade compared to my shock, which blossomed when he said, "Your grandfather served with my father in Moesia."

This, naturally was interesting, but it was Germanicus who, divining that I was missing a piece of the puzzle, spoke up to ask, "You do know who his father was, don't you, Pullus?"

"Sorry," I shook my head, "but I don't remember hearing my grandfather mention a Frugi. Or," I added, "my father either, since he was an Optio in the 8th at the time and he was in Moesia."

"That's because," the Tribune's mouth suddenly quirked, twisting into what seemed to be a bitter grimace, which I understood when he said, "I don't go by my full name. I'm Marcus Licinius Crassus Frugi."

The gasp that escaped my mouth was unfeigned, and it was heartfelt, as I instantly recalled the regard with which my Avus held the grandson of the first Triumvir Marcus Crassus, and now I was learning that this Tribune was the great-grandson.

"That," I finally managed, "is a surprise."

"Yes, I can see that," the Tribune remarked, "but my father thought a great deal of your grandfather, you know."

"The feeling was mutual," I assured him, and I hoped he believed my sincerity, since this was the case. Then I committed a blunder by automatically asking, "And how is your father?"

"Dead," Frugi replied instantly, and for the barest moment, his features betrayed his true feelings when he added, "He never saw Rome again, after..." Suddenly, he obviously became aware of the company, because his face composed itself as he said neutrally, "...after he had to retire from public life because of his health."

Shooting a glance over at Germanicus, I saw he was no less uncomfortable than I was, and for a brief moment, I thought I might have escaped my own indiscretion, but I suppose that was a bit much to hope for, because Germanicus used the moment to return back to the topic.

"You were saying something about your grandfather's account, Pullus," Germanicus said, "and I suspect you didn't bring it up without some purpose in mind."

Well, I brought it up to yank you from your self-pity, I thought; what I said aloud was, "No, I didn't. What I was going to say is that, as you know, the first Titus Pullus marched with Caesar, and I remember how my grandfather would always talk about one of Caesar's greatest abilities was to focus all of his attention on a problem in the moment, and not let worries about other issues that weren't as pressing distract him."

Now, what I can say in truth is that, having read my Avus' account more than once by that time, he had never said any such thing, at least not in those words, but I did not believe I was playing Germanicus falsely. If what I related to the Legate was my interpretation of the mindset of Divus Julius when he was still a man and not a god, I came by it honestly, that much I can promise.

Taking a breath, Germanicus offered, "So what you're saying is don't borrow trouble, eh, Pullus? Because that's how Divus Julius did it?"

Nodding, I confirmed, "Yes, sir. That's exactly what I'm saying."

"You're right," he said at last, then walked back to the table, picked up the tablet, and studied it for a moment before saying, "And the news isn't all bad." He paused, then gave a laugh as he tossed the tablet back down. "At least none of those bastards are heading our direction." His spirits seemingly restored, he clapped his hands together and said, "Now let's go see Bibaculus and see what kind of progress he's made so far."

I waited for the pair to pick up their helmets, then we left the room, but I took a moment to grab Germanicus by the elbow to whisper to him, "You were right, sir."

"About?"

He looked at me with a raised eyebrow, but while Frugi was walking ahead of us, I slowed just to make sure I would not be overheard when I told him, "About Cethegus. He came nosing around earlier this morning, wanting to know all about last night."

There was a rush of color to the Legate's face, but that was his only reaction, other than to give a curt nod and say, "Thank you for telling me, Primus Pilus." His voice returned to normal and he called out, "Remember, Marcus, we have a wager about today!"

"I haven't forgotten," Frugi assured him, looking back over his shoulder to grin at Germanicus. "Your money is as good as mine!"

With that, we returned to the larger war going on.

With a replenished stock of ammunition and replacing the torsion ropes for the three pieces left in the town, our attack on the wall of the stronghold continued, Bibaculus giving us his report. After this, Germanicus announced that we would also conduct an inspection of the line of outposts where the scorpions were emplaced, but he stopped more than a hundred paces short, suddenly gagging.

"By the gods," he covered his mouth with one hand, "is that stench coming from the prisoners?"

Although my first inclination was to answer in the affirmative, I actually forced myself to stand and sniff the air, turning as I did. It took quite an effort not to mimic Germanicus' reaction, but I somehow managed to avoid retching when I replied, "Actually, I don't believe it is." Pointing back to the enclosed pen where the prisoners sat in their misery, roped together by the neck in groups of ten, I said, "The way the wind is blowing right now makes it impossible for it to be them, sir." Turning back around, I pointed up to the stronghold. "I think that smell is coming from up there."

Germanicus considered, mimicking what I had done, then despite looking a bit sick, he offered a wan smile and said, "If it's this bad down here, I can't imagine how bad it is up there. Which can only help us."

When we reached the outposts, each one manned by a section, along with two men trained in the use of the scorpion if the section did not contain men with that knowledge, every single man had their neckerchiefs tied around their noses.

"This is our first day on this post," the voice of the Sergeant of the section was slightly muffled, "but the boys in the Second of the Fourth, who we relieved, say it's getting worse by the watch. They were here all day yesterday."

"Any activity?" I asked, regretting my decision that, as a Centurion, it would not do well to display a sensitive stomach by doing the smart thing, as were these men, along with Germanicus.

The Sergeant shook his head. "No, Primus Pilus. Oh," he admitted, "they take a peek every now and again, but they do it damnably quickly, and never from the same spot." Turning to gaze up at the western wall of the stronghold, a bit less than two hundred paces away but well more than a hundred feet higher from this, the nearest outpost, the Sergeant said, "It's almost like the place only has a handful of defenders who are trying to make us think there's more of them than there are."

This, I confess, had occurred to me, but I now understood this was not the case, but I held my tongue in the hope that Germanicus would be the one who refuted this, which he did by pointing out, "That's an awful lot of *cac* for just a handful of people, wouldn't you say, Sergeant? Even if they are barbarians."

Germanicus' neckerchief was, naturally, of a much higher quality than ours, but while it hid his lower face, the smile in his voice was clearly communicated, and the Sergeant chuckled, as did the others.

"Very true, sir," he admitted with good grace, "even for barbarians, that's a lot of *cac*."

Even as this conversation was going on, I believe it is important to note that the rhythmic noise of arms slamming forward, followed by a sharp cracking sound, albeit of varying pitches depending on which machine had sent its stone, as we chipped away at the wall, continued. From our vantage point, the damage was clearly visible, but it seemed that we had barely gotten halfway through the wall at the deepest point of penetration. I suppose it was inevitable that, despite Bibaculus and his crews targeting an expanse of wall wide

243

enough to allow a section of men to assault, the edges of what would become the breach had not been developed as much as the center. When we left to visit the next outpost, I whispered a reminder to Frugi to have Germanicus ask Bibaculus if this was intentional, or was just another in the series of problems that had been plaguing this siege. One by one, Germanicus made the rounds, and while I do not believe he became accustomed to the smell, he was inured to it enough to take his neckerchief off his nose. Watching him as we moved from one outpost to the next, what I saw in him was a common touch that was completely missing in Tiberius, a way about him that appealed to the men and made them want to do their best for him. Now, I am not saying that this was not the case with Tiberius, but with the older man, the respect we had for him was based in the fact that he shared our hardships, he was a tough but fair disciplinarian, and a highly competent general, which as all veterans of the Legions know, is more a matter of happenstance when it comes to our Legates. With Germanicus, he had all of that; even with the mistakes he had made to this point, none of them were viewed by those of us in the ranks, at any level, as being caused by his irredeemable stupidity or ineptitude, but as a matter of his youth. However, what I saw that day, as he joked with the rankers and laughed at their own clumsy attempts to match his jocularity with them, was an early example of the strong bond the young noble had with the men he commanded. Even as they bantered back and forth, I was interested to see that the men seemed to know where the invisible line was between being friendly but not overly familiar; thinking about it later, I ascribed it to the fact that these men were all older, having performed at least one full enlistment, which meant they had served under a seemingly endless procession of patricians and high-ranking plebeian men, sent from Rome by the Princeps. It was as we were leaving the last outpost that the *bucinator,* one of whom was always posted on the northern wall of Splonum now that Germanicus had moved the *praetorium* into the town, played the call that announced a rider, or riders approaching, although it was with the series of notes that told us whoever was approaching was friendly.

"Probably something from Tiberius," Germanicus sighed, "wondering why we haven't taken this cursed place yet." I was about to offer something, then realized that I actually agreed this was the likely cause, but he glanced up at me and said with a mock annoyance, "You know, Pullus, it would help if you said it could be something else!"

"Oh." At first, I thought he was truly upset, but he was smiling, so I offered, "It could be something else."

He gave a groan, rolled his eyes, and then turned to Frugi, who was on the other side of him and who was grinning broadly, prompting Germanicus to grumble, "You're no more help than he is."

The three of us were laughing now, which I have cause to remember, because it was when we turned the corner and entered the village square that we saw the riders just dismounting outside the *praetorium*, and even with the distance, I could see solely by the manner in which the man carried himself that not only did I know one of these new arrivals, I also understood this was not a matter of a routine message from Tiberius.

Despite myself, I muttered a curse, though I tried to bite it off immediately, but not before Germanicus heard, and I sensed him turn to examine me.

My face must have shown him something, because he asked guardedly, "What is it, Pullus? Do you recognize any of those men?"

I was tempted to lie to him, but I did not, nodding as I replied, "Yes, one of them. His name's Dolabella."

Germanicus' face clouded, telling me he was at least familiar with the name, which he confirmed by saying softly, "And why would Tiberius' spymaster be visiting us, I wonder?"

I came very, very close in that moment to telling Germanicus the truth then; that I did not is something that, while I can rationalize it, I cannot truly defend my decision to instead simply shrug and say, "I have no idea."

That Tiberius Dolabella waited until it was dark to come find me was not only appropriate, given his line of work, but as much as I loathed the man, I appreciated his discretion. The thought had occurred to me that Germanicus might have him followed, but when I asked him about it, Dolabella regarded me with an ironic amusement.

"So you're asking me if I'm so bumbling that I can't spot someone following me?" He shook his head sadly and said, "I thought we had reached a point in our time together where you'd appreciate my skills."

"Oh, I appreciate them," I said sourly. "I just don't know if your confidence in yourself is warranted."

"Would I still be alive if I overestimated my abilities?" he asked quietly.

"Fair enough," I allowed, though I hated to cede anything to the man. But, while I was happy he had taken precautions, I did not want him in my tent any longer than necessary, so I came right to the point, asking him bluntly, "Why are you here and what do you want?"

"Ah, that's the Pullus I know," he replied genially; I had deduced over the last few years that it was a tactic of Dolabella's, at least when dealing with me, to be correspondingly cordial to my surly rudeness, which I suspected was done strictly for the amusement he derived from getting under my skin. Pointing to the amphora, he asked, "May I have a cup of wine first, though? The road from Siscia is quite dusty, and this is the first chance I've had to refresh myself since I've gotten here."

"Been busy with your other spies?" I asked bitterly, but once more, he took no offense, simply shrugging and saying, "Something like that."

Since I did not want Alex involved in this, the moment Dolabella had arrived, I sent him on an errand to the *praetorium*, whispering to him not to come back any time soon. This meant it fell to me to get up and pour a cup, or two, deciding it could not hurt to fortify myself for what was coming. Offering it to him, I resumed my seat, forcing myself to be patient while he sipped from his cup, making a face at the first sip.

"It's watered," he complained.

"We're in a marching camp, besieging an enemy stronghold," I countered, "so of course it's watered."

I should have known better; I should have remembered that Dolabella was a clever man, something I was reminded of when he pounced, "Not everything is watered. At least," he offered me a smug smile, "not from what I heard."

It took an effort not to reward Dolabella with a reaction of my own, which would not have been a smile.

Instead, I shrugged, saying only, "I'm not sure what you're talking about."

This at least served to wipe the smile from the agent's face, replaced with a look that could have been irritation, and he countered, "I think you do know, Pullus. And," he paused, "Tiberius was very concerned about the state of this army before this. Now?" He shook his head, and while I know he tried to pin me with his gaze, as usual, it was marred by the fact that only one eye was looking at me, which meant I was more focused on the other eye that was staring over my shoulder; I suppose just as Dolabella had his little games he played with me, I returned the favor in kind, because I knew this irritated him immensely. "What possessed Germanicus to give the men mead?"

"He didn't give it to them!" I protested, alarmed that this was how it was being characterized, but again, I should have known better. "They found it on their own!"

"That's even worse," Dolabella said so quickly that it made me realize he had known this beforehand; he was simply building his case. "If he had allowed the men a ration of mead, it would have been imprudent, but the fact that he wasn't aware there was a supply of the stuff is even worse, because it's incompetence. At least," he amended as he held up a hand, and I suspect it was the look on my face that caused him to alter his words, "that's how some will perceive it."

"Some?" I shot back sarcastically. "Or just one?"

"If it is just one," Dolabella said evenly, "it's the one that matters."

"Not necessarily," I shook my head, tiring of the careful language, "unless you're referring to the Princeps. But," now it was my turn to pin Dolabella with my own gaze, pleased I could do so with both eyes, "you're not talking about Augustus being the one who matters, are you, Dolabella?" I paused just long enough for the words to sink in before I finished, "I wonder how the Princeps would take being considered irrelevant now?"

I was rewarded by the sight of Dolabella's face suddenly going pale, but his voice was even, and there was an undercurrent of menace I had learned to recognize when he replied, "This is a very dangerous game for you to be playing, Pullus. And," he reminded me, "Augustus is an old dog now."

"An old dog," I agreed, then added, "but he's still got teeth."

"The only thing you would be guaranteeing should you decide to do something…imprudent," Dolabella acted as if he had not heard me, "is that we'd both be destroyed. You do know that, don't you?"

"I do," I saw no point in dissembling about this, because I knew it was true, "but you forget something, Dolabella. I deal with death every day." I pointed in the general direction of the stronghold as I continued, "Any day now, there's going to be a breach, and I'm probably going to be one of the first through it again. This is my business, Dolabella, so threatening me with death doesn't mean much."

"Who said," he said this in almost a whisper and with a look of real fear on his face, "anything about you, Pullus?"

Unlike the last time he had threatened my family, I did not launch myself across my desk, but standing up as suddenly as I did caused him to flinch, and once more, without seeming to think about it, he reached up to his neck.

"I'm not talking about me, Pullus! I swear it by all the gods! I learned the last time not to say anything like that!"

Only then did I realize how tightly my jaw was clenched, and it took an effort for me to sit back down, saying only, "Go on."

Clearly relieved he had gotten this reprieve, Dolabella asked, "Do you think I'm the only man who works in my capacity for Tiberius?"

Honestly, I had not given it much thought, but while I did not particularly want to, I shook my head and admitted, "No, I suppose you're not."

"And do you think, given our history, that I would be stupid enough to come here and threaten your family? Or," he hurried on, "that if anything happened to your family, I don't know that I'd be the first man you'd come looking for? Pullus," he said this with almost a beseeching tone, "I know you hate me, but at least grant that I'm not a stupid man."

For a moment, I said nothing, then I allowed, "No, you're not stupid. So," I returned back to the subject, "you're saying that this mess with Germanicus is something Tiberius really wants?"

"Pullus," Dolabella answered, "if I'm being honest, I don't know what Tiberius wants when it comes to Germanicus. And," he shook his head, "I don't think Tiberius knows what *he* wants. He's a...complicated man, Pullus. I think that he's genuinely torn about whether or not he wants to be the man who follows in the Princeps' boots."

Somehow, I sensed that, for once, Dolabella was being as candid and forthcoming as a man in his line of work could be, and I considered what he had said. There was something about his assessment that resonated with me. Of all the moments I had spent in Tiberius' company, few as they were, or had been close enough to observe him during our winter across the Rhenus, if I had to reduce my summation of the man to just one characteristic, it would be that he did not seem to ever be happy. As odd as this may sound when talking about a military man, especially of the status and with the responsibilities of a man like Tiberius, even the most serious, sober, and professional among us have moments of levity or even happiness, because if we did not, ours would be a grim existence indeed. And yet, not once did I ever see anything in Tiberius where I could ascribe even a moment where he seemed to be genuinely happy, or even content with himself and those around him. Nevertheless, I realized in the moment that Tiberius' outlook on life, while having an impact on all of us who were within his power to one degree or another, there was

249

nothing to be gained by continuing this line of discussion with Dolabella.

"All right," I granted, "so you're not the one who would harm my family." Seeing Dolabella's shoulders slump in relief was somewhat gratifying, and I asked, "What is it that you're looking for from me?"

"Something about Germanicus that will satisfy Tiberius," Dolabella replied instantly. "Something that will convince him that you're still loyal to him and acting in his interests."

Despite suspecting that something like this was coming, it did not stop my stomach from suddenly flipping over, but I was more curious about one thing, and I brought it up, asking Dolabella bluntly, "Why does it matter to you that I stay in Tiberius' good graces? After all," I pointed out, more as a matter of fact than in an attempt to sound menacing, "if everything is as you say, then having Tiberius use someone else to remove me at least means you don't have to worry about my hands being wrapped around your neck again."

While he clearly did not like being reminded of this, Dolabella did not flinch or react in some other way; neither did he hesitate in answering, "Because I'm the one who suggested to Tiberius that you could be a useful man to have in his service. If it turns out that he believes you're now more loyal to Germanicus than to him," he paused for a moment, then finished, "let's say that he's the type to hold me as responsible for what he would see as a betrayal as he would you."

Now it was my turn not to like what I was hearing, but at the same time, I could not deny the sense of what Dolabella said. As I sat there, my mind raced, yet, despite knowing how important it was, I could not think my way out of the predicament in which I found myself.

Sighing aloud, I said, "I'm not going to give you anything that can be used by Tiberius as an excuse to humiliate the boy, Dolabella."

Somewhat surprisingly, the other man shook his head and replied, "Nor would I want you to, although probably not for the same reason." Raising my eyebrow, I stared at him, not saying a word, until finally he relented. "As you said, Augustus may be an old dog, but he still has teeth, and I'm afraid that Tiberius may underestimate just how much the Princeps values Germanicus as part of his plans for the future."

"Or," I countered, "Tiberius does, and he's not willing to allow Germanicus to get to a point where he's too much in favor to do anything about it."

Dolabella did not reply verbally, but he inclined his head in what I took to be a confirmation, leaving me to try and decide what I could offer that would satisfy Tiberius but not give him enough justification to send someone to relieve my Legate and thereby publicly humiliate the youth, and in doing so, causing a stain on Germanicus' honor and reputation that he would never be able to erase.

Finally, I broke the silence by saying, "Germanicus has made some errors, it's true, but he's young, and," this was a point I felt it important to emphasize, "men who are supposedly a lot more experienced than he is have made more mistakes than he has." Taking a breath, I felt truly horrible, but this was one time where I believed, or chose to believe that Dolabella had correctly assessed our predicament, and I told him, "We could have taken Splonum, all of Splonum by now."

"But?" Dolabella asked after I remained silent for a span of heartbeats as my conscience made a last-gasp attempt to stop me.

"But he's so worried about having to take Raetinium next that he's trying to be cautious."

"How so?"

Swallowing the lump down, I plunged ahead, saying, "We don't need to breach the wall. We could use our wagons to make mantlets, then we could push them up the road to the stronghold, while the men inside the mantlets would be carrying ladders. That's one way to do it."

"But I thought the barbarians have artillery," Dolabella objected.

"They do," I agreed, "but we've got the ten-pounder, and two five-pounders down here, and one of the other five-pounders is in a position above the stronghold. If the Maezaei roll their artillery out to try and stop the mantlets, we could squash them like a bug. Or," I

251

added, "we could also go at night, but if we did, that's when we would need the cavalry. We'd take fewer men, just with the ladders, on the first moonless night, then get over the wall to the gate and open it for the cavalry. That night," I finished, "is in three days' time, so if he were to do this, he needs to recall the cavalry immediately."

Dolabella considered this, then pointed out, "That sounds like it could get bloody. According to Germanicus, he's certain there's three thousand men inside that stronghold."

"That's where he's wrong." I said it before I thought it through, but of all the small things where I truly believed Germanicus was mistaken, it was in this assessment, because I had never been able to narrow down exactly how this estimate had become accepted. "There's not nearly that many men in there." Taking a breath, I finally said, "I'd be surprised if there's more than a thousand, at most fifteen hundred warriors inside that place."

"Well," Dolabella seemed doubtful, which increased my irritation and made me start to wonder if he was intent on forcing me to offer something more damaging, "Germanicus made a point to mention that the barbarians have been resorting to dumping their *cac* outside the walls, which he seems to think is proof that his estimate is correct."

"There are a lot of people inside that place," I agreed, only partially, however, "but most of them aren't warriors."

"Why do you say that?"

Honestly, I had not spent much time trying to determine why I was so certain, but once I did, it was actually easy.

"This town has ten thousand inhabitants," I answered, "and it's no different from any other barbarian town, which means that just of the townspeople, only about three thousand of the population would be warriors. Now," I continued, "since we've been here, and before Gaesorix took the cavalry to Raetinium, he and his men scoured the countryside, and there's been no trace of large groups of any civilians, which means that either seven thousand people vanished...or," I finished by pointing at the stronghold, "they're penned up in there."

"Would that place hold that many people?" Dolabella still did not seem convinced, but this was one thing I had been puzzling over as well, but I thought I had the answer.

"No," I admitted, "at least, no, not if there were three thousand warriors as well. And to be honest, I don't think there are seven thousand civilians up there either. I think that it's likely that maybe about two thousand of the townspeople have either fled, or died. Finding a couple thousand people, especially split up into small groups, is a lot harder than finding seven."

There was a long silence, then Dolabella sighed and said, "I think that will satisfy Tiberius." He paused, then said the one thing I dreaded more than anything, "For now, anyway."

"I have a suggestion," I told Germanicus the next morning after both Dolabella and his escort departed, and we received what was the same gloomy report from Bibaculus.

Normally, I would not have broached this topic in front of others, but time was so critical that I did not want to take the risk of letting a watch, or two, go by before I could get the Legate alone.

Germanicus, his demeanor more or less a match to his chief artilleryman, seemed to be more apathetic than anything else, and this in itself was a disturbing development, but he lifted a listless hand from where it was resting on his chair to signal his permission, accompanying it by saying, "Of course, Pullus. Hopefully, your suggestion will be better than the news we've gotten so far."

"I think," I responded, but I was carefully choosing my words, acutely aware that the eyes of all the officers, particularly those of Cethegus now that I knew he was working for Tiberius in some capacity, were on me, "it might be. Provided, of course," I thought to add, "you approve."

Now the young man shifted in his chair, sitting up straighter, which in itself was an improvement over the manner in which he had been slumped down in it, although I could hear the caution in his voice as he urged, "There's only one way to find out, neh? What do you have in mind, Primus Pilus?"

253

"I suggest that we don't wait for a breach," I began, which served to instantly deflate Germanicus' initial show of hopeful enthusiasm.

I did not need more than the sight of him slumping back down in his chair, but he still said, "Pullus, we discussed this a couple weeks ago, and we decided that it would be too risky."

"We did," I agreed, but I was far from through, "but the situation has changed."

"Oh?" Scipio, proving he was always ready to pounce, asked mockingly, "And what's changed? They still have the same three thousand spears waiting for us that they did two weeks ago. Or," he laughed at his own humor, his eyes darting to the others in what I supposed was an attempt to gauge how his counterparts viewed his wit, "are you suggesting that somehow their warriors have sprouted wings and flown away without our noticing?"

I must admit there were a couple of chuckles at his jibe, but not from Germanicus, and he was the man who mattered, so I was facing him when I countered, "I'm certain there aren't nearly that many warriors in the stronghold. In fact," I did hesitate but decided that this was not the time to try covering myself by modifying my assessment in such a way that I could have something to fall back on if I was wrong, "I'm so certain of it that I'm volunteering to prove it."

Once more, Germanicus became interested, his expression sharpening, but his tone remained neutral, "And how do you propose to do that, Pullus?"

I answered him, going into the plan I had concocted with Dolabella the night before, although I had modified it somewhat, mainly by recognizing how unlikely it would be that Germanicus would be willing to recall Gaesorix. However, I still believed that we would need a mounted force to accomplish taking the stronghold, and this was the part of the plan that I knew would appeal to Germanicus, or at least the part of Germanicus that, like most of our young nobles, is in a constant search for glory.

"Between your personal bodyguard, and those belonging to the Tribunes, and the *turma* that Gaesorix and Silius left behind as scouts, we can muster about a hundred men," I explained. "They'll use the cover of darkness to move into position at the bottom of the slope, and once I give the signal that the gate's been taken, they'll come at the gallop to help us hold it long enough for the rest of the Legion to come up the road. Although," I decided to add, "I'm certain we won't need more than a Cohort."

"That's a good way to get slaughtered." Scipio muttered this; I say "mutter" because he said it in such a way that it was clearly meant to be overheard, but I was cautiously pleased to see the look of irritation cross Germanicus' face.

That feeling lasted all of a heartbeat, as the Legate spoke up, and even before the words were out, I heard in his tone how he would view my proposal. "Well, as much as it pains me to say it, I'm afraid that, while Scipio was out of place for saying so," he shot his ostensible subordinate a warning glare, who appeared to my eyes to be anything but chastened, "I tend to agree that this would be a bloody exercise." He paused, then finished quietly, "And one that's not likely to succeed."

Even before I had opened my mouth, I knew my plan would be met with resistance; that it came from Germanicus himself was not something I expected.

"Legate," I admonished myself to avoid saying something that would damage my chances to help Germanicus, and even more importantly, expose the real reason why I was standing in front of him at this moment, "I understand why you'd be skeptical. But, consider this. We know there are a few thousand people penned up in that stronghold."

"There are," Germanicus agreed, "but that doesn't mean there isn't a significant portion of those barbarians who are warriors."

"That's true," I countered, "except that doesn't account for the fact that we've never found any sign of a large number of civilians outside of Splonum." For the first time, I saw what I took to be a glimmer of doubt in Germanicus' face, but it was the manner in which he glanced around at the others that I found interesting and troubling in equal measure; nevertheless, I pressed on, "This town held at least seven thousand inhabitants who aren't warriors, and even if they split up into multiple smaller parties, that many people can't vanish without a trace. And," I reminded him, "remember that even before we sent the cavalry away, they scoured the countryside for miles and only found tracks of a few groups, but none of those were of a size large enough to account for that many people to be missing."

I stopped speaking, and there was a silence that dragged out for several heartbeats, then Germanicus asked, "How many men are you talking about taking? If," he held up a hand to cut off the protests of some of the others, "I allow you to do this?"

"No more than two sections of men," I answered him, "and naturally, I'd choose them. All we would do is open the gate, then hold it for," I shrugged since I honestly had no idea, "what, a hundred heartbeats? Two hundred at the most?"

"And if you're not successful?" Germanicus stared at me intently. "If you're wrong about how many men are in there and you can't make it to the gate?"

"Then," I said simply, "we die. And you're out sixteen men."

"But one of them would be you," Germanicus countered, "and I'm not sure I'm willing to risk that."

He sat silently for a moment, which I suppose was what prompted Scipio to say something that I felt certain would ruin my chances, if only because it came from him.

"Pullus has a good point," he said, shooting me a malicious smile. "All we'd lose is a handful of men."

Germanicus shot him a furious look, but he addressed me and asked, "Are you proposing that we stop trying to affect a breach?"

"No," I answered immediately, "because it would arouse their suspicion, for one thing. And," I admitted, "if I'm wrong, then you'll need to assault the stronghold according to our original plan."

Germanicus did not respond to this, choosing to stare down at some point in his lap, while the rest of the officers remained silent.

Finally, he looked back up at me, his gaze level, and with a sober tone, he nodded. "Very well, Pullus. I grant your request. We'll try it your way."

"Why me?" Metellus protested again. "Why do you always pick on me?"

"Because I trust you," I answered him truthfully. Then, feeling a stab of remorse at my presumption, I did say, "But if you'd rather not, I won't hold it against you."

My old comrade stared at me suspiciously, clearly not buying my sincerity and sure there was some hidden barb in my words. Which, I admit, was understandable, but at least this time, I was being completely honest.

"Well," he grumbled, "now that you said that, there's no way I can refuse." Sighing dramatically, a gap-toothed grin split his face, and he held his cup out. "So if I'm going to my death, you need to make sure I'm properly fortified!"

"We're not going tonight!" I protested. "It's going to be tomorrow night."

"And I intend to have a full cup until then," Metellus retorted, completely unrepentant; indeed, he looked at me defiantly. "If I'm going to die, I want to be drunk!"

Sighing, I relented, pouring him another drink, but only because I knew that, words aside, when the moment came, I would be able to count on the man, understanding that he enjoyed the reputation that came from his supposedly prodigious appetite for wine more than the wine itself. The rest of our time was spent picking the men who would accompany us, which frankly created more disagreement between us than Metellus' drinking. Although I understood his reasoning, the brutal truth was that this task would require men who were stronger than most of the older veterans that Metellus put forward for consideration. Consequently, my first requirement was that only men who had retired after a single enlistment would be considered, not two, like Metellus himself. The second in some ways was more difficult to fulfill than the first; however, they had to be men who were stronger than average, but who also were not clumsy on their feet. Finally, though it went without saying, I wanted men whose skill with just a *gladius* was sufficient to handle themselves, and more importantly, protect the other men who would be participating in this sortie, because none of us would be carrying shields. A *gladius* and *pugio* was all that we would be bringing, along with two ladders, which we would be transporting from where this attack would originate, the outpost on top of the hill. This was all fairly straightforward, but as I expected, it was when I revealed to Metellus the more detailed specifics that was the cause of the most vociferous debate between us, which lasted well more than a third of a watch.

"If I'd known this was what you had planned," he actually shouted this, standing up on unsteady legs to point an equally wobbly finger at me, something I detest; that I did not reach out and snap that finger off was only because I needed Metellus to be part of my plan, "I never would have agreed to it! And," he warned, and in this I realized he was right, "those men you want need to know what you're asking!"

"If I do that," I protested, though it was half-hearted, "I might be doing this by myself!"

"Better to tell them now than when we're under the wall," he retorted, but my ears picked up one word in particular.

"So you're saying you're going to do it anyway?" I asked him, hearing the note of pleading in my voice but not caring. "Even now that you know what's involved?"

"I said I would, didn't I?" Metellus answered, somewhat belligerently. There was a moment of silence as he remained standing, or weaving, staring down at me, then his weathered features softened, and he grunted, "But I'm going to need even more wine now."

That, I believed, was a small price to pay. Once Metellus was fully informed, he agreed to come with me to ask those men who we had decided should be part of this small force that would give our Legate the final fall of Splonum. Honestly, I had the strong feeling that one reason Metellus wanted to be present was less to lend his name and credibility, which was certainly important with men like those in the *Legio Germanicus*, but to ensure I did not renege on my pledge to inform each man what they would be facing. However, I cannot say who was more surprised, Metellus or me when, even after I did so, only two men on our original list refused to participate.

Fortunately, we had a longer roster of men who were our second choices, and both of those we approached agreed, which kept us from going even further down the list. By nightfall, I had the complement of men who would be going with me to attempt to take the Maezaei stronghold with stealth and guile.

What caused Metellus to have such a dramatic reaction, once I explained to him the full details of what I had planned, was understandable given what would be involved. Simply put, I was planning to approach the Maezaei stronghold from a direction that, if I was right, our enemy would never expect. The seed of the idea was planted when, two days before, as part of the daily situation report, we were informed of a change in enemy habits that was, frankly, horrific.

"They're not just dumping their *cac* over the eastern wall anymore," was how I recall it was put by Germanicus, when he was reading the wax tablet submitted by the Centurion who had been in command of the outpost that overlooked the stronghold the day before. "They've started throwing bodies over the wall."

"They're trying to stop an outbreak of some sort of plague," Germanicus had guessed, and he read further to comment, "But so far, it appears that it's either small children or old people."

Although this was met with a considerable amount of revulsion among all of us, as I recall, it was Agrippa who made the observation. "They're clearly not close to surrendering if they're trying to stop an outbreak."

This assessment was met with acceptance as probably being the case, and I was one of those who agreed with the young noble. Regardless of the cause of it, this was something that I planned to capitalize on, despite how unpleasant and trying an ordeal it would be. Therefore, my decision was that, between the utter darkness of a night when there was no moon, and the horrific presence of the combination of the fecal output and corpses that were in a spreading heap outside the eastern, or uphill, wall, this would be our best avenue of approach. Moving downhill, we would advance to the eastern wall, place ladders against it, scale the wall, and then, using the rampart, would move to the only gate, overpower whoever was guarding it, then open it. Once opened, I would send a man to a spot where the mounted force, presumably led by Germanicus, would be visible where they were waiting below, whereupon my ranker would wave a torch to signal them to come at the gallop. Where, hopefully, my two sections of men, fourteen rankers, Metellus, and me would be able to hold off the Maezaei defenders long enough to be reinforced by Germanicus and his horsemen. Then, according to the plan, thus bolstered, we would hold off the Maezaei warriors long enough for every Cohort, starting with the First, to ascend the road up to the stronghold and overwhelm the defenders. I was counting on the Maezaei's knowledge of Romans' well-known abhorrence of filth, along with our revulsion of the barbarian custom involving the dead that did not involve burning the corpse, to convince Decebalus, provided he was still in command, there was no need to post sentries along the eastern wall. That it would have been a trying ordeal for any man, barbarian or Roman, to remain alert and at his post and stand above what was a horror to view, not to mention the overwhelming stench, had convinced me that it was extremely improbable that there were sentries posted along that expanse of the wall. Such was my reasoning, at any rate; only undergoing the trial would tell us if I was right.

Shortly before dark, allowing for enough daylight to enable us to reach it without undue problems, I led the men we had selected up to the outpost, carrying the two ladders we would be using to scale the wall. Once again, I had prevailed upon Fufius to provide every man with a *hamata*, rather than the *segmentata*, although I allowed the men to just wear this, without an extra tunic. There would be no moonlight this night, but as the sun began to set, I was heartened to see that not only was it going to be moonless, there was a thick cover of clouds. Each man would rub oil on his exposed skin before taking the charcoal from one of the fires used by the Century who had the responsibility for manning the outpost, rubbing it over his body, before being examined by a comrade. In this way, by the time we were finished, I was certain that, even if there had been a moon, we would have been as close to as invisible as possible. Whether this was actually the case, however, we would only learn one way.

We had spent the remaining period of daylight in the outpost in the manner most Legionaries of all ranks do; chatting about small, mundane things, arguing about which chariot team was the best, or regaling others with exploits of debauchery that grew more lurid and fantastic with every telling. Meanwhile, the steady punctuation of the three *ballistae* that had resumed their assault came rolling up the hill to us, and I appreciated the different perspective our vantage point afforded.

"That started late yesterday." The Centurion in command of the Century, from the Fourth Cohort as I recall, pointed to the small cloud of dust roiling up from inside the fort. "At least," he allowed, "that's what Priscus told me when we relieved his boys this morning."

Even as we watched, an object, originating from where I knew the ten-pounder was located, came streaking through the sky, descending in a blurred line to smash into the western wall. It was somewhat odd being above the highest arc of the missile, and we could not actually view the exterior portion of the wall, but there was a small explosion of dust to add to the hovering cloud already there, kept within the confines of the stronghold by the rampart, or so I supposed. The sound of the stone smashing into the wall followed perhaps a heartbeat later, and I noticed that the report sounded slightly different up here than the noise to which we had become accustomed down in the town.

"We're getting close to breaking through," I commented, and I felt the eyes of the Centurion on me, studying me intently, while I tried to remember his name.

"We are," he agreed but said no more for a brief span of time. Standing where we were, on the dirt rampart, and being the only two standing next to each other, I heard him draw a breath, knowing what would come next. "So, knowing that and seeing it for yourself, why would you want to run the risk of what you're planning tonight?"

It was a fair question, I knew; as understandable as it might have been, there was no way that I could explain my real reasoning for what I was about to do, if only because I was not completely certain about it myself. Why, indeed, would I essentially give Dolabella information that would satisfy Tiberius but harm Germanicus' budding reputation, then turn around and try to affect a taking of the stronghold that would render that information no longer relevant? If I was being true to Tiberius, who I never forgot was the man to whom I had sworn my loyalty, no matter how it happened, it would be in his best interest to allow Germanicus to move as slowly as he was, which in turn would help me by extension. After all, I reasoned to myself, it wasn't like I was actually *doing* anything to Germanicus and his fortunes if I simply allowed him to continue as he had been doing in regard to this siege. Even now, many years later, I still cannot fully articulate why I was unwilling to do so; perhaps, in some small way, there is more of my Avus in me than I had come to believe. Whatever the cause of my decision, the choice I made was what found me standing on the dirt rampart of this outpost, and I realized I had to provide an answer of some sort to what was, ultimately, a reasonable question.

"I don't know about you," I turned and gave the Centurion a grin, who I had finally remembered was the Quartus Hastatus Prior Marcus Junius Pacilus, hoping that it did not look as false as it felt, "but I'm tired of this fucking place. I want to get out of here, don't you?"

As I hoped, Pacilus laughed, shrugged his shoulders, and said only, "Fair enough." Then, he offered his arm, which I took, giving me the soldier's traditional blessing. "May Mars and Fortuna guide you."

Returning to my small group of men, I roused them from where they were sitting, ignoring the grumbling as I made yet another inspection of them. When the bottom rim of the sun touched the top of the hill on the other side of Splonum, I deemed it time to rub on the oil, then apply the charcoal to ourselves, each man teaming with another.

"It seems that ever since I said yes to you, I'm always covered in this *cac*," Metellus grumbled, standing with his arms out as I applied the darkening substance to his exposed skin.

"Oh, quit crying," I told him. "You sound like an old woman, not an old Legionary."

"Like there's any difference between the two once you get to his age," one of the others standing nearby quipped, prompting a round of hearty laughter, which I took to be a good sign.

"Shut your mouth," Metellus muttered, the whites of his eyes showing as he peered over in the direction of where the comment originated. "You're just lucky I can't recognize you, you bastard."

Then, we were done and ready, and all there was to do was settle back down for another two parts of a watch as the glow of the setting sun grew fainter. I did the same as the men, settling back down and leaning against the *ballista*, which had only been used perhaps a half-dozen times until the Maezaei learned which parts of their sanctuary were exposed. And, as the others did, I retreated within myself, except in the case of a Centurion, he does not have the luxury of introspection; there are far too many things for which he must account, both planned and unplanned, and this was what occupied my mind as I sat there. Or, so I thought, until someone kicked one of my feet; only then did I realize I must have dozed off, and I felt a stab of guilt.

"It's the time you set to leave, Primus Pilus."

I certainly recognized the voice, but I was cautiously pleased that, when I looked up in the direction from where the voice had come, I could barely make out the darker outline of Pacilus, and there was no way I could have seen his face. Climbing to my feet, I was happy for the darkness so that nobody could see the grimace from the pain I still felt when I made a sudden move, thinking that at least my knees were no longer constantly weeping from the blisters. For the first time since I had been burned, I had decided to wear *bracae*, choosing a dark brown pair that covered my damaged knees, and while I felt confident I was no longer hindered in my movement, I did have a nagging worry at what might happen if I was forced to kneel. Regardless of my own issues, I tried to imbue my voice with the kind of confidence a leader must display when he is asking men to do something as dangerous as this undoubtedly would prove to be. It had gotten so dark that there was a bit of fumbling for the ladders, and one of them was dropped, causing me to wince, along with inciting a round of curses, despite knowing that we were too far away to be heard. Very quickly, I determined that we would have to move so closely bunched together that, whenever I whispered the command, each man would reach out and try to touch the back of the man in front of him. Naturally, this was even more difficult because of the ladders, yet somehow we managed to navigate our way out of the outpost, then steering clear of the ditch, we allowed whatever force it is that makes all things move downhill to guide us. Leading the way, I literally moved one foot at a time, pausing every fifth step to both listen to and to whisper the command for the men to reach out and grab hold of their comrade. Originally, I had thought to move in a double file, with Metellus leading the other file, but very quickly discarded this, fearing that one or both of us would veer off at an angle that placed us too far apart to mutually support the other file. Instead, we were in one long line, with the four men carrying a ladder roughly in the middle of the long column; or, so I hoped. Because of the clouds, we did not even have starlight, and as I discovered within the first few moments, without even this faint illumination, we were guided more by the combination of moving downhill and the stench. Honestly, with every single step, the air grew fouler, although I had thought to take precautions, appropriating several sprigs of whatever fragrant herbs Germanicus' personal cook used to flavor the Legate's food, distributing it among the men, which they pinned to their neckerchief. Pulling up my own, one of my spares, I inhaled the sage, yet it only helped marginally, and my estimate was we were still more than two hundred paces away from the wall if my counting had been correct. Moving another fifty paces downward, I stopped, but this was planned, turning uphill to hold my hands out, whereupon Metellus, who was the second man in the line, almost walked into me. I suppose that, under other circumstances, it was probably very humorous, the two of us facing each other, each waving our arms wildly about trying to make contact, but the first thing my hand touched was my old comrade's chest. The instant I made contact with him, Metellus exhaled in surprise, blasting me in the face with his breath, and the thought that crossed my mind was that perhaps I might have misjudged how much of my friend's talk about his love for wine was just that. Fortunately, he did not make any noise, but behind him, as each man, who had been warned by me beforehand that we would be stopping, more or less collided with their halted comrade, I suppose it was inevitable that there was some noise. I held my breath, waiting for a shout of alarm or some other sign we had been heard, but nothing happened, and slowly I relaxed, relatively speaking. Now we would wait, and this time we were the ones listening for something that had become a regular event on the part of the Maezaei.

Without exception, in the first full night watch, the defenders took advantage of the darkness to perform a ritual that had started with just their waste, but had become more than that. Judging by the slight rustling, I assumed the other men had squatted down on their haunches, but I was not willing to risk that because of my knees. Therefore, I stood, one ear turned in the direction of the stronghold, mouth open since that helps one's hearing, though I have no idea why, and waited. In what I hoped was a good omen, we actually did not have long to wait; my estimate was that in well less than a sixth part of a watch, I heard a faint series of noises, accompanied by a low hum that I knew from experience were voices; men's voices, judging from the pitch. The sounds grew in strength and became more distinct, and I was certain I heard the heavy, scraping tread of men climbing the stairs up to the rampart along the eastern wall. Listening intently, I felt certain I could make out that, just by the sound, the stairs were not wooden but stone, lacking the hollow, echoing noise one associates with the former. The accompanying voices grew stronger, but while they spoke in low tones, just above a whisper, it was impossible for me to determine how many men were involved. That they had reached the rampart only became clear when there was a scraping sound, followed immediately by another one, this sounding like a substance that was at least partially liquid but also composed of solids. Almost instantly, I guessed what it was, confirmed first by the slightly lower position of the source of the noise, but it was the sudden increase of the stench of *cac*, which I would not have thought possible, rolling uphill and slapping us in the face with an almost palpable force. Behind me, I heard a man gag, and while I could not blame him, I braced myself for the inevitable alarm that I was sure would come. However, nothing happened, at least of a nature that would indicate we had been heard, although we were forced to endure what sounded like three more barrels being dumped. This, I thought, can't get any worse, as for the first time, I began to have real reservations about this plan which, in the comfort of my quarters, seemed that it would be unpleasant, certainly, but nothing that we could not overcome. Now, I was confronted with the reality, which only got worse when, after a brief cessation of the noise accompanying the dumping of their barrels, the first body was dropped from the rampart. That it was a body was evident by the sound it made when it landed, a much more solid, meatier impact that, even if I had not known what it was, would have made me uneasy.

Although it might have been my imagination, I was fairly certain that I could detect a different odor, one that as a soldier we become all too familiar with, starting in the immediate aftermath of battle, the stench of the decay of a human body. As we stood there, I determined that however many Maezaei were involved in this unpleasant task, they were dumping more than one corpse at a time, making it practically impossible to count. Whether it was thirty, or sixty, or even more, all I could say definitively was that it was in the double figures, and the only way I could tell they were finished was in the retreating nature of the voices, followed by their descending footsteps on the stairs. Just to make sure, I slowly counted to a hundred, still listening for any Maezaei who might be lingering, though I could think of no plausible reason anyone, hardened warrior or not, would want to spend a heartbeat longer near this horror than necessary. Or, if I am being honest, I was simply trying to avoid what came next, but then I felt a gentle but solid nudge from behind as Metellus silently urged me to forge ahead. I had given up trying to take anything more than the shallowest breaths, but as bad as it was, I knew it was only going to get worse, and that waiting was not going to accomplish anything, so I resumed moving. Repeating my slow pace, I did alter the manner in which I was walking; instead of lifting my feet higher than normal to avoid tripping over things like roots or exposed rock, I began sliding forward. My biggest fear was that I would step down into one of the corpses, which naturally meant this is exactly what happened, and to make matters even worse, judging from how easily my foot plunged through what felt like a small ribcage, it was one of the earliest casualties, the small bones snapping under my weight. All of my resolve, the use of the herb pinned to my neckerchief, and the fact that I had put nothing in my stomach, none of that mattered, and I barely got the cloth out from around my face before I retched, loudly, realizing in that moment there were no preparations one could make for something like this. Behind me, I heard a muffled gasp, which was quickly replaced by a sound similar to the one I had just made, and was immediately joined by other noises like mine, and I was certain that, in a matter of a few more heartbeats, we would be running for our lives; there was no way the sound of what had to be at least eight or nine men vomiting could go unnoticed. And, I thought miserably, I'm the one who started it all.

In moments such as this, it is usually not until well after the event before any kind of sense is made of what seems to be nonsensical, and even then, it is extremely unusual that matters are fully explained. All I knew at the time was that, somehow, there were no shouts, no challenges, nothing that indicated the sound of several Romans puking their guts out had been heard. Nevertheless, rather than taking the risk of a renewed bout of retching, I retreated back a step, then turned and groped for Metellus, somehow grabbing his arm.

Expelling my air, I whispered, "We're only using one ladder, and we're going to place it further out from the wall than we planned."

I felt his body tense, and in the same way he asked, "Will it be tall enough to reach if we do that?"

267

"No idea," I replied honestly, "but if it isn't, I'll pull everyone up myself."

While there was no way to tell, my sense was that he shrugged, but more importantly, I heard him relay my order to the man behind him. There was more rustling, and I heard the sound of the men responsible for the first ladder sliding it forward on the ground, and I leaned down, and after some fumbling, my hand brushed against it. Once I had a firm grasp, I began pulling it forward, then lifted it above my head while, clenching my jaws so tightly that, while I was still retching, I did it with my mouth closed, I extended it in front of me, using the rungs to control it. Assault ladders, as their name implies, are purposely made to be heavy, both to support more than one heavily armored man and to make it difficult for defenders to push away from the wall. Naturally, the steeper the angle of ladder against wall, the easier it is to dislodge, but despite the fact that our woodworking *immunes* had assembled ladders based on the height of the stronghold wall, which was a bit over twelve feet, I was attempting to place it at a much shallower angle than normal. My arms were beginning to ache from the strain, and it is not a boast when I say that I doubt there was another man currently with Germanicus who could have done what I was doing then, yet just when I was sure my arms would give way and the ladder would come crashing down onto my helmeted head, I felt it touch something solid. Giving just one shove, more to assure myself that it was indeed touching the wall, I lowered my end of the ladder to the ground, stepping backward to allow it to touch.

Despite my intention to avoid placing the bottom of the ladder in the midst of the indescribable horror of this combination sewer and barbarian graveyard, I found I could not, discovering this the hard way when my hands, gripping the bottommost rung, plunged into a cold, slimy semi-solid mass that made me thankful it was too dark to see what it was. My stomach, however, was not to be denied its own protest, and no amount of fighting it kept my mouth from opening as the sour taste of bile filled it. Perhaps one can get a sense of how awful it was when I say that I actually welcomed the taste of my own stomach fluids compared to the foulness of the air that filled our noses and mouths when we were forced to breathe. Nevertheless, I pushed down hard against the base of the ladder, trying to ensure it was solidly connected to the ground, though there was only one way to find out. Before I took the first step, I pulled my neckerchief out from under my armor, thinking chafing was a small price to pay for cleaning my hands before throwing it aside, happy only in the sense that I was unable to see what I had removed from them, though there was still a sticky feeling I tried not to think about.

Turning, I whispered to Metellus, "I'm going up. Wait until you hear this." Using the hilt of my *pugio*, I tapped against the wood three times. "Then you follow. And," I thought of something else, "only one man at a time."

"That will take too long!" Metellus' voice was at the same whisper as mine, but I could clearly hear the protest in his words, despite how quietly they were uttered. "We were supposed to use two ladders, and we were going to climb one after the other like we always do."

This was certainly true, but I was not changing my mind as, out of a reflex, I shook my head before realizing he could not see, so I replied, "It can't be helped. One. At. A. Time."

He made a soft hissing sound that I supposed was his way of expressing his disagreement, then he answered, "Fine. One at a time."

Then, I was moving, crouching down in what I instantly felt was an extremely awkward position, essentially moving on all fours, except instead of on my knees as a young babe does before learning to walk, I was forced to use my feet. It was one of the times where I did not appreciate my height, and I can only imagine how ridiculous I must have looked as I felt my way up the ladder. Moving slowly, because of the shallower angle, I could clearly feel the ladder sagging under my weight as my bulk pressed down against the wood in a manner it was never designed to withstand, and twice I had to stop when I was certain I heard a cracking sound. Even more than the idea of discovery, the thought that I could plunge down into the morass of filth and rotting flesh convinced me to discard caution for haste, so that I scrambled the last half-dozen rungs then, without even taking the time to listen for signs of an enemy presence, pulled myself up onto the rampart, just happy when my feet touched the stone surface. Only then did I pause, dropping into a crouch while telling myself that the sound of my panting was loud only to my ears and could not be heard down below on ground level, no matter how sure I was that it could. It was probably no more than a dozen heartbeats' worth of time before, not only remembering what I had told Metellus, I realized I had been forced to reach up above my head to grasp the stone ledge to pull myself up. Even worse, as I felt for the ladder while drawing my *pugio*, I determined that, since we had been working in the blind, this end of the ladder was aligned not with the lowest part of the parapet, but one of the crenellations. I debated moving my end over so that it was between two crenellations, enabling the other men, all of whom were shorter than I was by several inches, to more easily pull themselves up and onto the rampart, but the thought of dislodging it and thereby causing one of the others to fall into that horrific mess because it would be at an angle, I decided against it. Rapping three times, I was immediately rewarded by the vibration as the ladder began to move slightly in response to the motion of who I presumed was Metellus making his way towards me. I heard his raspy breathing faster than my eyes could make out his bulk, and I cautiously extended my hand; the last thing any of us wanted was to be knocked off the ladder by someone trying to help. Fortunately, my hand brushed the links of his *hamata*, whereupon he reached up in response, his hand grabbing my forearm with a strength that, particularly with his age, was impressive.

Using my strength, I hauled him up onto the rampart, then while I still had him in my grasp, whispered, "You help the next man up. Send him after me."

"Where are you going?"

I sensed the taut nerves, but I assured him, "I'm only going in the direction of the stairs. I won't go any farther."

He gave a grunt that, frankly, did not tell me anything, but I assumed it meant he would at least comply, even if he did not agree, and I moved away from him. For a brief instant, I considered crawling, but quickly decided to walk on my haunches, which I suppose made me look like some huge, armored duck as I waddled forward, using my left hand in front of me to feel my way down the rampart. Although I am certain that it had been going on for the entire time I arrived inside the stronghold, it was not until I separated from Metellus before I became conscious of a sound. Naturally, I stopped, straining to listen, staring down into the center of the stronghold as I realized for the first time that I had never actually ever been inside. Frankly, it was all blackness, but I thought I could discern the outline of the parapet as it extended to the southeast corner, then just barely making out the edge as it extended from my left to right front, forming the southern rampart. Roughly in the middle of that, I knew, directly beneath the rampart, was the single gate, our objective, but before I did anything, I wanted to determine the source, and most importantly, the meaning of this noise. It was akin to the kind of buzzing sound we had heard earlier, when the Maezaei who had drawn the unfortunate task of disposing of their own dead had held muttered conversation, but it was distinctly different because it was uninterrupted, without the pauses that are the pattern of normal speech. Finally, it came to me, the answer coming from my own memory of the times when I had been wounded after battle, and was confined with other wounded men, some so grievously that their lives could be measured in watches. This, I recognized, was the sound I was hearing, I was certain; people were moaning from pain. While this helped in one sense, in another, it was mystifying; had we really wounded that many Maezaei that they made enough noise I could hear them? I tried to think through the previous days and weeks, but aside from the occasional lapse by one of their sentries, I was certain that what I was hearing were the civilians who had believed their best hope lay in seeking sanctuary. All in all, it seemed to support my belief that there were many more civilians inside this stronghold than Germanicus and his other officers believed.

When I felt a light tap on my shoulder, I came very close to letting out a startled yelp, but then I heard Metellus whisper, "We're all here."

"I'm going for the stairs," I told him, except that when I began moving, I forced myself to stand at least partially erect, yet while I expected my knees to protest, I do not remember noticing them.

Moving slowly, holding my *pugio*, I slid along the rampart, crouched over so that I could feel along the edge of the stone ledge to find the stairs. When I did, I lowered myself, one step at a time, stopping on each one before taking the next, reaching the bottom, and it was only then I caught the first glimmering of light. Not much, but after such complete darkness, it allowed me to see more of the interior of the stronghold, and most importantly, where we needed to head. As it turned out, the stairway, which was open to the air, was located directly next to a passageway that I quickly determined followed underneath the stone parapet. I discovered this by sticking my head into the doorway, taking a quick peek in both directions, but while in some ways it helped me make sense of the layout, it also gave me a very strong sign that we were fucked, since I also found the source of the noise. The light came from a spot down a long stone corridor, and the flickering light illuminated that there was a chamber of some sort, perhaps thirty paces down from where I was standing, the light coming from within the chamber. But it was not what dangers lay in the chamber that made me stifle a curse; it was that every inch of the corridor, even beyond that chamber, was crammed with bodies, some sitting with their backs to either wall, but most in a supine position.

"We're going to have to find another way to get to the gate," I whispered to the men, all of them waiting for me on the rampart. "The shortest route is that corridor, but there's no way we can make our way to the gateway in that direction. Not," I added this, not meaning it seriously, "without cutting our way through all those people."

"What does that mean?" I did not recognize the voice, so all I could say was that it was not Metellus.

"It means that we're going to have to go another way and find another route." I thought it was obvious, but my questioner had something else in mind.

"And who's to say that we don't have the same problem?"

I was about to reply, but then the other man pointed out, "And if you're right, that most of those *cunni* townspeople are penned up in here, it's more likely than not that we'll just run into more of the same."

"And we might be farther from the gate." This time, I recognized Metellus' distinctive whisper; more accurately, I smelled his breath and knew it was him. "Isn't it better to take the shortest path?"

When put this way, I could not deny they were both right; perhaps this is just a convenient lie I tell myself, but I honestly believe that both men had made important points. Yes, we would end up putting civilians to the *gladius*; I cannot say this bothered me all that much, but it was enough of a concern that I considered it. However, when all was said and done, if we spent more time sneaking about, somewhere there were defenders, meaning the chances we would be discovered increased dramatically. What it boiled down to was the certainty of having to kill most of however many Maezaei civilians were crammed into the corridor that was the shortest route to the gate, or the possibility of bypassing this group and finding another path, balanced against the likelihood that we would either be discovered or blunder into the stronghold garrison. And, even if it was not the three thousand warriors Germanicus believed, one thing was certain; they would outnumber the sixteen of us substantially.

Consequently, I took a breath, then said only, "All right. We're going the short way. Follow me."

Choosing speed over stealth this time, I descended the stairs again, so I suppose it was inevitable that, between this and the sound made by being followed by the others, I heard a voice cry out in alarm. Then I was in the corridor, and without hesitating, I thrust down into the first body blocking my path. Naturally, it was not a killing blow; given everything that had happened to this point, I suppose it was too much to ask for the gods to guide my *gladius* straight and true. The shriek that issued from this first victim, a woman by the sound of it, instantly ignited complete and utter chaos, as bodies that had been lying prone suddenly leapt up, screaming with terror. My comrades, though I could not identify which ones, were immediately by my side, and we roared our own battle cries that only added to the tumult. In the semi-darkness, I indiscriminately thrust at anyone and everyone before me, blocking out of my mind that some of those who fell before me were undoubtedly female; all I can offer in my defense is that, by restricting my attacks to a certain height, the few smaller bodies who tried to scramble out of our path, their high-pitched shrieks piercing my ears like an invisible awl, escaped death at my hands. I will kill whoever I must, whenever it is necessary, but this is another way where I suppose I am similar to the first Titus Pullus in that I try to avoid slaughtering children, and this night was no different. How does one describe such a scene, where a passageway that was only wide enough for three of us to stand abreast, and even then, close enough to each other that I felt the sudden drafts of air created by the *gladius* of the man to my left, which contained well more than three or four hundred people who had gone from some form of sleep or rest, no matter how fitful, to a state of screaming terror?

The warm blood of my victims flew freely, and I felt it spattering onto my hand, my arm, and my face, yet we moved steadily forward, those civilians at the far end being the lucky ones, given just enough warning to scramble to their feet to make their escape. Not, I will admit, that their reprieve would last long; only the span of time it would take for us to reach the gate and open it, then however long it took for Germanicus and his mounted force to reach us. The noise was such that it was impossible to hear, or in my case to be heard, so I did not try to give any commands, while I felt the hand of the man behind me grasping my harness, not that one needs much support slaughtering helpless people. While it is impossible to say with any certainty, my best estimate is that perhaps fifty heartbeats after I stabbed my first victim, we had pushed well more than halfway down the corridor, it was only about this time that I heard what could be described as any sign that the garrison had been roused, hearing completely masculine bellows of alarm and rage from the opposite end of the corridor. Naturally, the people who were able to had leapt to their feet and, almost without exception, began fleeing away from us, directly into the arms of the Maezaei warriors, apparently literally because there was a counterpoint of shrieks, screams, and curses that for the most part matched the same sounds being made by those we were cutting down. I say almost without exception, because in what I felt certain was a state of panic, at least one man; I had the sense of a bearded face, but atop a body bent with age, came at me with outstretched arms, yelling something unintelligible at me as he, for all intents and purposes, ran himself directly onto my *gladius*, the sharp Gallic blade slicing into his body with an almost ridiculous ease. For the span of a couple heartbeats, we were just inches away from each other, but it was because of the sudden glisten caused by the faint light that told me blood was pouring from his mouth, yet his mouth kept working and even in the darkness, I saw his almost frantic gaze fixed on mine.

"Don't…" was the first word in our tongue that I could pick out, but he continued babbling, then I heard the words, "…we surrender! We don't…."

Then he died, on the end of my *gladius*, and I shoved him away from it, while I felt a hand pushing me forward, a directive I naturally obeyed, especially now that I could see the recessed area to the left that I knew was the interior portion of the gateway and at the end of which lay our objective. From around a corner at the farthest end of the corridor, where I assumed the southern and western walls met, I saw a cluster of figures, two of them carrying torches and leading the way, flooding the corridor with a light that, in contrast to the dimness a moment before, seemed to be as bright as if the sun was shining. This illumination enabled me to see something that, even now, I cannot really explain, but it was only after taking in the sight before me that the words of the man I had killed a few heartbeats earlier started to make any sense. That a group of what were clearly warriors finally appeared was not surprising; that those civilians we had thought were fleeing from us and looking for a refuge from our onslaught immediately threw themselves on their supposed defenders, their fellow tribesmen, was one of the most shocking things I have ever witnessed.

It is impossible to say with any certainty, but what I can say with a fair amount of assurance was that, less than a sixth part of a watch after I first set foot on the rampart, the stronghold of Splonum fell. Yes, it fell, not at Roman hands, but at the hands of those Maezaei townspeople who, we learned in the aftermath, had been kept more as prisoners than as fellow tribesmen to be protected. Once they were given the slightest excuse, these poor people had risen up and in their fury, and through the strength of their numbers, killed more Maezaei warriors in less than a third of a watch than, as we would learn, we had during our entire siege of the stronghold. Honestly, I only felt partially vindicated when we learned that, far from three thousand warriors, there were only about five hundred, and of those, only about a tenth part of the three thousand Germanicus had been convinced were contained within were healthy enough to lift a weapon. As we had witnessed, the inhabitants of the stronghold had been stricken with the plague, but we learned from survivors, when Decebalus, who was somehow still alive, was approached by the remaining elders and they beseeched him to surrender, those tribal elders had been put to the *gladius* at his command. This had happened some ten days prior to our scaling the wall, and in the intervening time, the son of Dodonis' hold over his father's subjects had become simultaneously more brutal and more tenuous. Our arrival had simply precipitated what had been brewing for days, and of all the unusual, odd moments, the fact that we had to protect Decebalus, who we had found cowering behind the precious few remaining sacks of grain, kept behind lock and key in an underground storeroom, not from Romans but from his own people, stands out in particular.

Next morning, when the sun rose, it fully exposed the horror inside what had begun as the pride of the Maezaei king, this large stone structure that served as both fortress and palace, but was now nothing more than a large tomb for most of those unfortunate to have been penned inside. Not surprisingly, it was quite the chaotic scene, as the men of Metellus' section shoved open the gates and people went staggering out into the night, not caring in the slightest about anything other than getting away from the horrors behind them. Inevitably, when Germanicus led his horsemen, moving as quickly as was prudent under such dark conditions, up the road, and they encountered the first of the Maezaei villagers fleeing from the stronghold, these unfortunates were cut down before I could inform the Legate of all that had occurred. Even then, it was a terrifically disorganized mess, and rather than make matters better, the arrival of the First Cohort, with Rufius leading my Century, made them worse, at least at first. Not until we got dozens of torches lit, and Germanicus himself started issuing orders, was a semblance of order restored. As equally inevitable as the accidental and needless slaughter of those civilians who only wanted to escape, some of the more enterprising Maezaei warriors tried to slip past us by shedding their weapons, armor, and most importantly, the *animus* of warriors, mixing in with the townspeople who, on Germanicus' order, we treated with mercy, trying to blend in by acting as frightened and cowed as those people they had been terrorizing. But in yet another surprise in a night and day full of them, we did not need to examine each male Maezaei to try and determine if they were merchant or warrior, because the true civilians among the survivors did not hesitate to betray those men who tried this. Before the night was through, perhaps thirty or more men were betrayed by their own people, and there was not a shred of mercy to be found among those civilians. Indeed, I firmly believe that, when all was said and done, we did those warriors offered up by their own a favor by giving them a merciful and quick death, given the fate of one man who the mob fell upon before we could get to him and who was literally torn apart. It was the second watch after dawn before there was at least partial order restored, while the prisoners who had been penned up down in the town were marched up the road under guard to join the less than three hundred able-bodied warriors remaining to begin the grisly but necessary task of cleaning up the mess created by the enforced resistance of the Maezaei.

"Pullus," Germanicus was standing, upwind, on the rampart of the stronghold, watching as the first part of the grim cleanup began, "you were right. I should have listened to you sooner."

Yes, you should have; naturally, this was what I thought, not what I said, but despite this success, I was dubious about how much good it would do as far as Tiberius was concerned. Which, of course, I could not say; or more accurately, I was unwilling to take the risk of what might happen to not just me but my entire family.

Consequently, all I said was, "Don't worry about it, sir. This was your first siege." Shaking my head, I consoled myself that in this I was at least being sincere when I went on, "And every siege is different. Honestly, I've never seen anything like this."

My young Legate responded with a laugh, but I heard a shaky note in it as he rejoined, "By the gods, I hope not! I'd hate to think this was a normal siege." He paused for such an interval that I thought he was finished, but when he spoke, it was almost as if he was talking to himself when he mentioned what I understood was still preying on his mind. "And Raetinium isn't going to be any easier."

Sensing another opportunity, I pointed out to him, "We won't know exactly what to expect until we lay eyes on the town itself."

"True," Germanicus granted, then added, "But it's a Roman town, with a Roman wall and not one of those," he waved a hand in the direction of the original breach, "things."

"That's so," it was not only my turn to accede to his observation but to try and score a point of my own, reminding him, "but we also know how a Roman town is laid out. There won't be any real surprises."

He did give a slight nod at this, yet I could see he was far from convinced. We watched the grisly work below as prisoners continued to find bodies; it seemed that for every corpse that had been dumped over the wall, there was at least one or more that had been tucked away in some corner of the fortress.

"Have you gotten any idea of many of those poor people are dead?"

This, frankly, surprised me; it was the first time I had heard Germanicus refer to them as anything other than "barbarians" or "savages," the normal terms Roman noblemen use for anyone not Roman or Greek.

278

Regardless of this hint of compassion, I answered him by producing a tablet tucked in my *baltea* and saying, "We decided that the first thing we should do is count the number of people still living, figuring it would be easier. Which, so far, is a bit more than three thousand."

"So far?" He frowned, turning to look up at me. "Are you expecting to find some more people still hiding?"

"No," I replied. "According to the *medici* who looked them over, they estimate that two or three hundred aren't likely to live more than another day. They're too far gone."

He did not reply, just gave a grim nod, and we returned our attention to the work below, which we continued to watch for a bit, then he turned and said abruptly, "We're meeting at dark in the *praetorium*. We need to talk about moving to Raetinium."

This, to me, seemed premature, yet I was tentative when I asked, "Can't we take a day or two to regroup?"

Staring straight ahead, not even glancing at me, Germanicus' tone was abrupt. "No, Primus Pilus, we can't." Perhaps the words came out more harshly than he intended them, because he added, "Under ideal circumstances, yes, Pullus, we would take some time to reorganize ourselves. But," at this, he reached down and produced a tightly rolled scroll that he had tucked into his *baltea*, though he waved it in my direction rather than allow me to read it, "the Legate has expressed his…frustration with how long we've been bogged down here in Splonum." For the first time since I had been associated with Germanicus, I saw a flash of real anger, which I understood when he said, "And my father made it clear that I erred in taking Splonum first. He says we, no," he amended and as he did he looked up at me, "*I* should have known better than to be talked into taking," Germanicus actually unrolled the scroll, and I saw enough to recognize by the tiny, oddly slanted writing that this came from Tiberius' own hand, "what did he call it? Oh, yes, here it is. 'A miserable collection of hovels and muddy streets,' and not marching on Raetinium and taking it back for Rome first."

This was, and still is, grossly unfair, particularly since I had been certain that Germanicus marching to Splonum first had been at the very least because of implicit orders from Tiberius. As we stood there, I tried to recall every conversation and moment we had been together, from the time we were in Emona and had received orders, yet nowhere in my memory was there any recollection that Raetinium had been mentioned as a priority, either in the form of a courier or by reference from Germanicus. I thought to tell Germanicus this, but when I opened my mouth, still without looking at me, he gave the tiniest shake of his head.

"No, Pullus," he spoke quietly, "if this is what Tiberius says happened, then that's what happened." Giving a wan smile, he finished, "Now all that matters is taking Raetinium."

Chapter 5

The meeting that night was a strange affair, particularly considering we had managed to complete our conquest of Splonum just a few watches before; the mood was anything but celebratory. Perhaps the most telling sign of the unusual circumstances was that, for once, Scipio seemed to be of a like mind as Germanicus, although I suppose this had as much, or more, to do with the prospect of being forced to share in the censure of Tiberius. And, as bad as it was starting out, by the time we were through, if anything, the mood was even more, if not despondent, then grim, as we took stock of the current state of the *Legio Germanicus*. While it was true that we had managed to avoid taking more casualties assaulting the stronghold according to the original plan, the presence of so few defenders meant that we still had yet to face the bulk of the Maezaei warriors, and barring a serious overestimation of their numbers, we would be heavily outnumbered when we marched to Raetinium. That this would have been so even when we were full strength meant that it was a matter of degree now that we had taken casualties, but as much as I trusted Gaesorix, and to a lesser extent the Tribune Silius, who had been sending constant reports, until we were actually at the walls of Raetinium, we would not really know how much of an ordeal awaited us.

"We march tomorrow," Germanicus announced his decision, which was met with a few mutters but no real resistance. Then, he took a deep breath before he continued, "And we're leaving a Cohort behind to guard Splonum, and the prisoners until I receive instructions about what to do with them." This, again, elicited some comment among the Pili Priores and the Tribunes, but to this point, there had been no real surprises. Just wait, I thought with a sense of satisfaction, though I aimed this at one man in particular, who I was happy to see looked unsuspecting. Germanicus shot me a quick glance, then turned to Cethegus and, in a neutral tone, informed the former Praetorian,

"Pilus Prior Cethegus, your Cohort will be staying behind in Splonum."

This at least had the effect of rousing stronger emotions around the makeshift table, but while I was not surprised that, aside from Cethegus of course, other Pili Priores leapt to their feet to protest this, one of them was Agrippa. To be accurate, he did not react with quite the same amount of vigor as Scipio, Proculus, and the Tribune Appuleius, remaining seated, but I saw his mouth moving as part of the chorus of disagreement with their Legate's decision.

"Sir!" Cethegus, naturally, was the man who was the most strenuous, but I found it interesting that I saw something else in his manner aside from indignation. Was it fear? I wondered. Whatever it was, it seemed to be what fueled him to say, "I must protest this decision! It's a…" He paused as if searching for the right way to characterize his objection, but what he came up with was, "…a slur on my honor! And," he added in an obvious afterthought, "the honor of the men of my Cohort as well!"

I had to admire the manner in which Germanicus, despite being more than fifteen years younger than Cethegus, going by looks, at any rate, responded, keeping a cool head as he widened his eyes in what I knew was mock surprise, though it did serve to remind me that this youngster, despite his years, undoubtedly had a great deal of practice in duplicity.

"Nonsense, Pilus Prior!" He gave the Praetorian his most winning smile as he assured Cethegus, "In fact, it's the opposite! I need a man I can trust here in Splonum, someone with experience and judgment who will know how to handle these barbarian prisoners and the townspeople."

When put that way, I did not see how Cethegus could argue the point, and I saw that he instantly realized this, although his mouth opened to say something; unfortunately, before he could speak, someone else interjected, and in doing so, changed everything.

"Sir," Marcus Agrippa spoke up, "while I certainly understand the need to leave someone here who you can rely on to keep Splonum pacified, I'd simply point out that leaving the Sixth behind means that we'll have to rely on the Cohort of auxiliaries, including two Centuries composed of those slaves and freedmen." Turning to the man who commanded this Cohort, ostensibly a Pilus Prior by rank, a member of the Vindelici tribe who had once been a hostage of Rome, back when they had been part of the rebellion of Rhaetian tribes, and who like so many other barbarians, had adopted our ways, giving himself the *praenomen* Tiberius while keeping his original name as his *cognomen*, which was Cotto, Agrippa said apologetically, "I mean no offense, Pilus Prior Cotto, but the Sixth is composed of men of the Legions."

Cotto, who was not normally part of these meetings, managed to keep his face impassive, but I was seated near enough to him to see the way his knuckles, gripping the side of his chair, turned white.

When he spoke, his Latin was almost flawless, carrying barely a hint of his original tongue, but his tone was a closer match to his body than his face as he replied tightly, "While I take no offense, Pilus Prior Agrippa, I would also respectfully disagree with your assessment that the men of the Sixth, just by virtue of having been in the Legions once, are superior to mine. My men," he pointed out, correctly, "are not men who have retired, and we have been in service to Rome for more than a decade now. During which time," for the first time Cotto seemed to become, if not agitated, at least animated in his defense, "they have been involved in no less than eighteen engagements with enemies of Rome."

Cotto paused, which Cethegus took as an opportunity to weigh in, and he was not shy about boasting, "That doesn't matter! My boys can whip any bunch of auxiliaries ever born!"

I was not a bit surprised when Cotto, leaping to his feet, glared at Cethegus across the table, and for an instant, I thought the Vindelici would do more than just glare at the Praetorian, but he contented himself with words, and I will say they were well chosen.

"And what would a Praetorian know about real fighting men?" Cotto sneered, pointing a finger at Cethegus, and this was the first I noticed that the Vindelici was missing the tip of his pointing finger down to the first knuckle, making it look quite odd. "If I need advice on the best way to polish awards I earned for drunkenness and whoring, I'll ask a Praetorian!"

Cethegus bellowed in outrage, and unlike Cotto, he actually reached down to his *baltea*; this was the sign it was time for me to intervene, although I confess a part of me was tempted to allow the two men to have a go at each other, if only because I felt certain Cotto would cut the Praetorian into bloody meat. Regardless of my personal feelings, by the time Cethegus' hand had grasped the hilt of his *pugio*, not only was I up on my feet, ignoring the stab of pain from my knees, I already had my own blade drawn and, in one continuing motion, stabbed it down into the table. That it was my *gladius* was a dramatic gesture, but I was also counting on the nature of the blade itself, the dark, gleaming grain of a weapon that had cost my Avus a year's salary and was almost as famous as Titus Pullus himself, to make a statement on its own. It did serve to stop the racket of noise, and I was pleased to see that neither Cotto nor Cethegus seemed disposed to continue arguing, but it was Germanicus who actually spoke next.

"I believe that the Primus Pilus has made his point."

As I am sure he intended, this immediately caused everyone around the table to burst into laughter at the Legate's pun, a reminder that we Romans love a play on words more than anyone, perhaps save the Greeks. Even Cotto's face split into a grin that, if I am any judge, was also somewhat sheepish; the same cannot be said for Cethegus, who was still glaring at the Vindelici.

"However," Germanicus' voice raised and changed inflection, reminding us this was a serious matter, "Pilus Prior Agrippa makes a good point as well, although not as dramatically as Primus Pilus Pullus'."

This only elicited some chuckles, but Germanicus' face did not give a hint of what he was thinking, and since we had not discussed anything beyond his intention to leave Cethegus behind, I was as interested as everyone else to hear what our Legate had to say next.

"Thinking about it," Germanicus went on, "I can see both sides of the argument. With no disrespect to Pilus Prior Cotto or to his men," he looked to where the Vindelici, who had just sat back down and

284

dipped his head in recognition of the man, "the truth is that, rightly or wrongly, I suppose I'm like the rest of the men here that I'm simply more...comfortable with men of the Legions." I glanced over at Cotto, but his face had gone back to its same immobile state, while his hands were not gripping the chair in the same manner. "But," Germanicus continued, "I do need a man who I trust implicitly and who has the experience in dealing with what is a delicate situation by any measure. As we learned today, there's a fair amount of tension and hostility, not just aimed at us, which is understandable, but at the ruling class of the Maezaei on the part of the townspeople. At least," he amended, his tone grave, "those townspeople who survive." Pausing—I personally felt certain he was doing it just to draw out the tension—before he said, "So I'm taking the Sixth Cohort with us to Raetinium." Another pause, as naturally our eyes turned to Cethegus who was looking triumphantly at Cotto, which meant we could all see his reaction when Germanicus finished with, "But it will be under the command of Pilus Prior Cotto, while you, Pilus Prior Cethegus, will stay here and oversee matters in Splonum."

For an instant, Cethegus' face remained frozen with the same expression of victory before Germanicus' words sank in, whereupon his mouth dropped open in shock, although he was not the only one caught by surprise.

Finally, he managed a protest, albeit only to say, "But...why?"

"As I said, I need a man I can trust here, but Agrippa does make a fair point. Which," Germanicus turned and apologized to Cotto, "neither he nor I mean as a sign of disrespect, Cotto. But remember, two of your Centuries aren't pure auxiliary as it is. So," he shrugged as he turned back to the Praetorian and gave him the kind of smile that I imagine candidates for offices along the *cursus honorum* offer potential voters, "I'm compromising by putting a man I trust in command here, while taking the men who are best suited for what comes next."

When put this way, it was clear to see that Cethegus had been outmaneuvered, and it was equally obvious to anyone with eyes that he knew it.

"Thank you, sir." His round face expressed his bitter frustration, though he managed to keep his voice from matching his demeanor. "You do me a tremendous honor."

With that settled, Germanicus turned to the more practical matters, and in this, it was our chief artilleryman who had some good news.

"We captured their two pieces intact, more or less," Bibaculus began, but Germanicus interrupted him, holding up a hand.

"I thought we had put one out of commission," he said. "Is that not the case?"

"Oh," Bibaculus agreed, "it's true that one was damaged beyond the ability of the barbarians to repair it. But not," he finished with a disdainful sniff, "beyond ours to fix it right up."

"That *is* good news," Germanicus commented, "though we need to find some men who can crew them."

"That won't be hard," Bibaculus assured him. "There's a fair number of old *immunes* scattered about the Cohorts. Now," he allowed, "that also depends on something else, sir."

"Something else?" Germanicus asked cautiously, though this turned out to be good news of a sort.

"Yes, sir," Bibaculus nodded, "it concerns something we found inside the stronghold. There's a supply of seasoned wood that will serve as material for three, or maybe even four more scorpions."

"Scorpions?" Germanicus seemed, if not disappointed, a bit let down. "The pieces aren't big enough for a *ballista*?"

"I'm afraid not, sir," Bibaculus told him, then I suppose felt the need to offer some encouragement. "But as it is, once we make those scorpions, we'll have a full Legion's complement of artillery when we add in the *ballistae*."

That did seem to cheer Germanicus, but only for a moment, as he returned to the other challenge facing us.

"We're still going to need more men," he said gloomily.

And that, I believed, was simply the truth. What remained to be seen was whether or not we would get them.

When we marched away from Splonum, while I cannot speak for the other men, I knew I was more than happy to be away from this place, as much for the memories it still held for me as all that had transpired with the *Legio Germanicus*. Accompanying us, in a wagon and in chains was Dodonis' son Decebalus; whether or not he was the last surviving son of the Maezaei chieftain we did not know, but the reason he was with us was not only as a bargaining chip. Given all that had taken place, from the murder of his brother to the manner in which he had treated his fellow tribesmen, essentially keeping them in captivity inside the stronghold, Germanicus also believed it was likely that the young barbarian nobleman was safer with us than he was left behind. Not, I can attest, that Decebalus was appreciative of this decision, judging from the raving and cursing that was issuing from inside the wagon where he was also chained up as a further precaution. Thankfully, he was at the tail end of our column, and while we might not have been a complete Legion, he was far enough away that we could not hear his ranting where we were in the vanguard, though we certainly heard about it secondhand, when the Centurion commanding the Century marching drag took advantage of our first rest period to make his way to the front.

"That barbarian *cunnus* has been screeching his gibberish at us every step of the way," he complained to Germanicus, somewhat to the amusement of not only the Legate, but the rest of us in earshot. "So I'm requesting permission to gag the bastard for the rest of the day."

Germanicus, laughingly, gave his permission, and a pleased Centurion went stalking back down the column, causing the Legate to call after him, "Be gentle with him, Centurion! We need him alive!"

"Oh, he will be, sir," the Centurion called over his shoulder, "but he might be a bit bruised."

Under other circumstances, I might have felt a bit of sympathy for Decebalus; having been confined against my will for more than a month had awakened me to the plight of those in similar conditions, but for the captive Maezaei prince, I felt not a flicker of pity. The man had murdered his own brother and had treated his tribespeople

287

horrifically, although this was less a consideration for me than the former reason. Although none of us could hear, since we did not receive another visit from the Centurion, I assume that Decebalus spent the rest of the time gagged as we marched through Clandate, reaching the mining village at midday. From appearances, it was in the same condition as we left it, indicating that no Maezaei had returned to it while we were at Splonum. Marching north from the village, we reached the junction where the road that followed along a narrow river valley in a roughly southwesterly direction leading to Raetinium, Germanicus gave the order to make camp about four miles from the junction, where a stream provided water from the beginning of the hills that formed the northeast mouth of the valley we would be following.

"We should be hearing from the cavalry tonight, or first thing tomorrow," he informed us. "Then we'll know the latest on what's happening in Raetinium."

"What have we heard from Tiberius?"

I do not recall who asked this, but I was as interested in the answer as anyone; a courier had caught up to us, having ridden through Splonum first, but Germanicus had been very close-mouthed about what was contained in the dispatch that I saw the rider hand to our Legate.

And, now in the *praetorium*, which was back to a tent for all of us, he was clearly unhappy at being asked, and for a long moment, I felt certain he would not answer. However, as I was already beginning to learn, this was not something that came naturally to Germanicus; he is, by nature, an open person who is easy to read, and I suppose that is one reason why we got along so well, since I am the same.

Finally, he answered, "As you all know, I've sent several dispatches to my father, asking for reinforcements. And," I could see he was struggling to keep a neutral expression on his face as he went on, "I sent him a message as recently as last night, letting him know that now that Splonum was taken and that I was forced to leave a Cohort behind to secure the town. Now it's too early for him to have gotten that message and to send instructions back."

"Why?" Scipio interrupted. "It's barely a half-day's ride from Splonum to Siscia."

The edges of Germanicus' mouth turned down, although he did answer, saying tightly, "That's because Tiberius isn't in Siscia. He hasn't been in Siscia for weeks."

This was news, not only to the rest of the officers, but to me in particular, because on his last visit, just a matter of days before, Dolabella had said that Tiberius was still directing the campaign from Siscia. Or, I suddenly thought, had he actually said that? Trying to recall every moment of our time together was not only frustrating, it was fruitless; that I could not remember Tiberius' spymaster ever coming out and saying Tiberius was in Siscia did not make me feel certain he had not done so. There was something tugging at my memory, where it was as if I was overhearing a conversation that was indistinguishable, except for the word "Siscia." Then, it finally came to me, and I remembered that, while Dolabella had said he came from Siscia, he had not specifically said that Tiberius was there. Now, despite Scipio's pressing, Germanicus refused to say anything more about this revelation concerning Tiberius' whereabouts. Apparently satisfied, Germanicus dismissed the officers, but when I rose to leave, he signaled for me to stay, something that caused Scipio, Appuleius and Proculus, who had taken to sitting together in the officers' mess, and in meetings like this, to exchange some whispers as they exited. Our Legate ignored them, waiting until they, quite slowly, shuffled out of the room, but they were gone no more than a matter of a few heartbeats when Germanicus, beckoning to one of the clerks who took notes, but who I had learned was one of Germanicus' personal slaves, whispered something to the man once the slave came to his side. Nodding, I noticed the slave was grinning slightly, but he walked to the partition, except did so in a manner that meant he made no noise. Pausing for an instant, he suddenly pushed through the hanging leather partition, and while that partially obscured the scene, I was seated facing that direction, so I saw at least two bodies, standing closely together, who had clearly been positioned just opposite the partition. There was the sound of bodies colliding, accompanied by a rather undignified yelp of fear and surprise; although I could not swear to it, to my ears, it sounded like Scipio's voice.

"Pardon me, masters," I heard Germanicus' slave say apologetically, "I didn't realize you were there!"

What the two interlopers said I could not hear because, as I am certain Germanicus intended, his slave's appearance served to herd the pair away from the partition, and most importantly, out of earshot. Sitting with his head cocked, Germanicus waited a moment before deciding it was safe to tell me whatever he intended, but while I did not really know what to expect, it certainly was not what I heard.

"The reason Tiberius isn't in Siscia is because he's been visiting the armies under Silvanus and Severus," he began, but it was what came next that shocked me, as he continued, his expression grave, "because there have been…problems with the Legions."

"Problems?" I echoed, though it was more to give me an instant to understand what he might mean.

"They're on the verge of mutiny, Pullus," Germanicus said quietly. "And Tiberius has been forced to make some…concessions to them."

While my initial reaction was one of shock, as I sat there in the silence that followed, with Germanicus seemingly content to watch me, I realized that, once I thought about it, there had been discontent growing with my old comrades in the 8th. I recalled the last letter I had received from Titus Domitius, who expressed his frustration with the manner in which the 8th, still under the command of Silvanus, was being used. Somewhat skimpy on the details, between what my best friend had described, and other bits and pieces that I had picked up from a number of different sources, it sounded like what at least was part of the problem was the fact that Silvanus was trying to force the rebelling tribes to face his army of five Legions into a set-piece battle. One thing that stuck with me from Domitius' missives was his quip that he believed Silvanus saw himself as the embodiment of Divus Julius, back when he was conquering Gaul, but even men as uneducated as we were, at least as far as how the patricians viewed us as such, we know there is a difference between conquest and pacification. Consequently, Silvanus' army was marching from one place to the next, chasing phantoms, although being fair this is a feature of life in Pannonia for the Legions. However, he had exacerbated matters with his policy of indiscriminate reprisals, not bothering to do even a modicum of investigation into whether an ambush in one tribe's territory was actually perpetrated by that tribe, or, as was a common practice by the tribes, by a roving warband who were essentially accomplishing two goals at the same time, attacking Rome, and when we retaliated against the tribe in whose territory in which the ambush occurred, weakening a rival tribe. I bring this up as explanation as to why, when Germanicus informed me of this, it only took a matter of a few heartbeats for me to realize that this was not unexpected.

Despite recognizing this, I was struck with a pang of worry, which prompted me to ask cautiously, "Have any specific Legions been mentioned as being the most trouble?"

Germanicus shook his head, but he did not seem to notice me slumping back in relief as he answered verbally, "No, or at least I haven't been told. But that's kept Tiberius moving about as he tries to appease the Legions." Suddenly, he gave me a direct look that, while not challenging, was at least direct as he said, "Pullus, this is the wrong time for the men to start airing their grievances. You do know that, don't you? That there is too much at stake right now?"

This, I understood, was true, yet I also felt a bit nettled that this young man was taking the part of the Princeps, which caused me to retort, "I don't remember it ever being a right time, sir. And maybe if the Princeps had taken the time to allow rankers to adjust to having their enlistments arbitrarily extended four years before he began talking about adding another five, Tiberius wouldn't have his hands full now!"

For the first time in our relationship, I clearly angered Germanicus, because he leapt to his feet and retorted hotly, "And he was right to do so! The army is the biggest drain on Rome's resources, more than feeding the Head Count! And we spend a great deal of money on training you men! Not to mention how well fed you are compared to every other citizen of your class! Are we not entitled to see an adequate return on that investment?"

"*Investment?*" I was, frankly, too flabbergasted to be angry. "That's how you nobles view us in the ranks? As you would when you buy a slave that you train for a certain skill, and you only look at him or her as a means to make you even more money than you already have?"

As surprising as it was, this seemed to rattle Germanicus, because while his mouth was opened to issue some retort, or so I believe, nothing came out for a long moment.

Then, taking a deep breath, he held up a hand in a gesture of placation, saying, "I…I never thought about it from that viewpoint, Pullus." He paused again, and frankly, I could understand his hesitation, remembering what it is to be young, but he seemed sincere when he offered, "I apologize, Pullus. And, I thank you for your honesty."

This prompted a laugh from me, and I was practicing that quality when I assured him, "That's only because I let my mouth get ahead of my brain, Legate."

As I had hoped, he smiled at this, but insisted, "Nevertheless, I'm happy that you speak your mind, Pullus. The gods know that someone in my position learns fairly quickly that most of the time, the men around you are telling you what they either think you want to hear, or what they want you to hear to further their own aims."

"That must be hard," I allowed, and I meant it, "never being sure whether or not people are telling you the truth."

"You," he answered fervently with a rueful smile, "have no idea."

I suspect he decided that nothing was to be gained by continuing this conversation, and if he had asked me, I would have agreed.

"We have another big day tomorrow," was how he put it. "We should be near Raetinium by the end of the day, and I'd like you to accompany me when we go take a look and get an idea of what's ahead."

Assuring him that I was more than happy to do so, I saluted, then left his presence, walking to my tent in a thoughtful mood, although it was more about the larger situation and not our own. I cannot help thinking that, if I had kept my mind on our own challenges, I might have foreseen what was about to come.

Destroying the marching camp the next morning was something that, predictably, some of the rankers felt was a waste of time, simply because of the probability that we would be marching back through this valley. The feeling, which I cannot say I disagreed with entirely, was that the Cohort left behind in Splonum was not going to be sufficient in the event that there was another Maezaei warband skulking about. For that was still the one thing that nagged at most of us, of all ranks, the idea that our belief that the entirety of the warriors that could be mustered by the Maezaei were now penned up in Splonum or contained within the walls of Raetinium, essentially waiting for us, could have been mistaken. Certainly, it was possible, but if it was, that would imply that Dodonis, after deposing Cebrenas, had a personal grip over the various branches of the tribes similar to that of the famed Vercingetorix of the past, or a German whose name was known to us but had yet to betray Rome in an act of treachery that will survive through the ages. Again, all I had to go on with this Dodonis was my one brief contact with the man, but there was nothing about him at the time that struck me as a man who possessed the kind of force of personality that would persuade the handful of sub-chieftains of the different branches of the Maezaei to set aside their personal ambitions to follow him. As much as they hated Rome, my observation was that it was only a matter of a degree more than they hated each other, and in their constant infighting, backstabbing, and maneuvering as they struggled for power, they reminded me of our own upper class. I would argue that the fact that we were approaching a fortified position that could contain up to ten thousand defenders with a force of a bit more than three thousand infantry and less than a thousand cavalry, even with the artillery, would support my assertion that, when it came to our respective leaders, Romans were not that different than those we call barbarians.

Regardless of our feelings, the men marched along in reasonably good spirits, although in retrospect, I believe a more accurate description would be they were resigned to the belief we would have to conquer Raetinium with the men we had with us at the moment. The first half of the march was uneventful, reaching the westernmost iron mines belonging to the Maezaei, the small village that served the three mines located on the southern bank of the Oeneus predictably deserted. This did not stop the men from taking advantage of the midday rest break to descend on the cluster of huts and rip them apart in their search for something valuable. Which, equally predictably, was fruitless, and caused the men to take out their frustrations on the couple of dozen huts that could be pulled down without a huge effort. The village was not razed, but it sustained a massive amount of damage, which Germanicus allowed as he conferred with his Tribunes, while munching on a repast of bread and cheese.

On this day, it was the turn of the Fourth Cohort to be the vanguard, and while the First was not marching drag, we were in the spot immediately ahead of the baggage train, which consisted of more than twenty wagons, along with eight or nine of the two-wheeled carts that the Pannonians favor, which we had appropriated at one time or another. I spent the break with Metellus, my Optio Rufius, and Veratius, quietly discussing what to expect in the next phase of the day's march. To this point, we had been marching almost due west, but the site of the mines also marked where the road, still following the river, curved south; more crucially, the valley through which we were marching narrowed considerably, while the angle of the slope of the ridges on both sides that paralleled the river steepened as well. Resuming the march, I marched alongside my Century for a short bit, then decided to stop to wait for the tail end of the Cohort, where Tubertus, the Hastatus Prior Lucius Novellus, and Blasio were with their Centuries. I had become accustomed to their avoiding me whenever possible, but considering what was ahead of us, I had hoped they would overlook their disdain for me and my lowborn ways, since they were all from Rome and were part of Germanicus' set. Because of the possibility of contact, I had ordered the Cohort to march in Century order, meaning that the first to reach where I was standing was Tubertus, who eyed me warily as he approached, though he did render a salute.

"We're about to turn south, and the valley narrows, so keep your eyes open," I told him.

"I'm aware of that, Primus Pilus," he replied stiffly. "I've already ordered the men to be especially alert."

Ignoring the edge of insolence in his voice, I merely nodded, then deliberately looked past him at the approaching Fifth Century; as I expected, he did not react well to the slight, although whatever he said as he stalked off he kept to a low mutter that I could not make out. Watching Novellus approach, I confess to mixed feelings about my Hastatus Prior. Despite the fact that he was a Praetorian, like Cethegus, he at least did not appear to be cut of the same cloth as the Pilus Prior we left in Splonum, not only in the manner in which he conducted himself and led his men, but in his physical demeanor. Whereas Cethegus was soft and round, Novellus was whip-thin, with a narrow face that accentuated the countenance of a man who was perpetually hungry. What, exactly, he was hungry for was the thing that had eluded me to this point, but while he kept himself aloof from me, as did Tubertus and Blasio, I did not sense the hostility in the man that seemed to radiate from the other two. Therefore, I had to admit, if only to myself, that perhaps the man just did not care for me because of some personal reason of which I was unaware. Frankly, I did not care all that much, provided he did his job, and even I was forced to acknowledge that he was extremely competent. Unlike Tubertus, he did not seem offended by my admonition, though he did the minimum to acknowledge my warning, then he was marching away, leaving only Blasio. His reaction was, if anything, even stronger than Tubertus', and I had the sense that he just barely avoided saying something intemperate to me that I would be unable to ignore. Rather than make an issue of it, I decided to trot Latobius back up to my spot, and this was the first time I recall that my knees did not pain me enough to notice when I leapt back into the saddle, despite their still being an angry pink.

The rhythmic sounds of an army on the march began to echo more as we navigated the gentle but noticeable curve to our left, turning southward, and up ahead, I saw where the track narrowed. Since we were marching along the southern bank, our right flank was somewhat protected by the river, but before we had traveled more than a mile into this narrowing part of the valley, not lost on any of us was that we were well within the range of missiles, if a force was hidden somewhere along the wooded slopes on the opposite bank. Nevertheless, it was to our left that we kept under observation more than our right, and for the next third of a watch, it was extremely tense. Inevitably, however, with every passing furlong, with no sign of any kind of trouble, men began to relax, and I include myself among them. Judging from the angle of the sun, I calculated that we would exit this narrowed stretch about a watch before sunset, giving us just enough time to make camp. Looking ahead, I began thinking about what came next, rather than paying attention to what was happening in the moment, which meant I missed something significant.

When I say I missed something, this is not exactly true; I immediately recalled passing by a spot that I noted as being a likely place from which an enterprising enemy could launch an ambush. However, it was our place in the column that worked against me when I first spotted it, since the majority of the *Legio Germanicus* had gone past it. And, if these warriors had been behaving normally, they would have sprung their ambush by the time the First Cohort came marching past, aiming for the command group ahead of us. Unfortunately for us, the aim of their ambush was not to inflict casualties; no, they had a very specific target, which were carried in several wagons. I first became aware when, from a good distance behind me, I heard a series of shouts, and while I was too far away to distinguish what they were shouting, just the tone of it alerted me that it was something bad. Only after I had turned about, taking a couple steps out to the side of the column so I could get a better view did there come a blast of sound that, while not from a human voice, informed us what was happening, as the *cornu* belonging to one of the Centuries marching drag sounded a series of notes.

"Ambush!"

Several men shouted this at roughly the same moment, even before the last note of the *cornu* died down, but what was difficult to judge was exactly from where it had sounded. My view was obscured by a slight curve, but I was already climbing aboard Latobius, who I had been leading most of the day, thinking it important that the men see their Primus Pilus afoot like they were. For his part, my horse was already leaping forward, back along the column, even before I was firmly in the saddle, and I felt his body almost vibrating under me with the nervous energy. I recall wondering, how does he know what that *cornu* call meant, because he was clearly excited in the same way he had been when we fought off the bandits trying to attack Birgit and the children, back before he had a name and he was just a horse I rented, and the ambush by the Taurisci, with Gaesorix and his Batavians. I shoved this thought aside, and we went thundering past the other Centuries, all of them already turned about, having dropped their *furcae* in preparation for an order from the highest ranking officer in the area. Which was me, but before I was willing to commit them to a course of action, I wanted to see for myself what was happening. No more than twenty heartbeats after I had leapt into the saddle, Latobius had made enough distance that, for the first time, I could see the entire column, and what I saw unfortunately caused me to jerk the reins of my horse, something I knew he did not appreciate.

"They're attacking the baggage train!"

This came from Blasio, but while it was certainly true, what astounded, and infuriated me in equal measure was that, of all the Centuries of the First Cohort, he was the closest to the wagons, but his men had not even discarded their *furcae*, and those who were facing in the right direction had clearly done so on their own, which meant that I had a Century of men, half of them facing the wrong direction.

"Century, drop your *furcae!* About turn! Ready! Advance at the double!"

297

In rapid succession, I bellowed the orders that Blasio should have already given, now more than thirty or forty heartbeats before. Thankfully, his Century responded quickly, but Blasio himself seemed content to stand there, gaping at what was already beginning to be obscured by dust, the sight of what appeared to be a couple hundred Maezaei grabbing terrified wagon drivers and their assistants, pulling them down off the wagons and slaughtering them. My first instinct was to kick Latobius and go galloping forward in an attempt to stop the Maezaei from exterminating our complement of drivers, but as quickly as the notion came, I discarded it; a lone horseman, unsupported, charging into a mass of other cavalry, is a dead man.

Instead, I swung down and grabbed the nearest ranker, handing him the reins and ordering him, "Stay here and protect my horse." I looked down at the man, who appeared happy at the prospect of being excused from what was about to happen, until that is, I snapped, "And if anything happens to him, I'll fucking kill you myself!"

Before he could respond, I was already moving, and this time, I shoved Blasio, none too gently, out of the way, and effectively took command of his Century, bellowing the order to follow me. Judging from the noise, they obeyed instantly, a reminder about there being no truly bad Centuries, but this was not foremost in my mind as I forced myself to move at a brisk walk, rather than going barreling into a scene I could barely make sense of already. Before me, the scene was chaotic, as the oxen reacted to this sudden onrush of strange men, plunging and bucking against their harnesses, and even in the brief span of time during which I was trying to get a sense of the best course of action, no less than two of the wagons lurched out of the column, their animals driven mad with fear. Not surprisingly, both wagons were pulled towards the river, directly away from the barbarian onslaught, and I caught a bare glimpse of a flailing body, apparently one of the drivers or attendants who had been unseated from their wagon, trying to scramble out of the way but was unable to do so, one of the wagon wheels rolling over him as he let out a shrill scream. Even as this was happening, I reached the first wagon, which to this point was being ignored by the Maezaei warriors who, from what I could see, were not paying the slightest bit of attention to the approach of not just the Century with me, but one of the three Centuries of the Fifth Cohort who had drawn the short straw and were marching drag, one of whose standards I could just see through the dust. The answer as to why this was the case became apparent when, suddenly, arcing through the air were objects that my eye immediately identified as not being spears, being much smaller, but more substantial. It was the trail of black smoke trailing from each object that gave me the eyeblink of warning when, in rapid succession, they slammed into five of the wagons.

"They're going after the artillery!" I do not remember if I was the one who said this, but I definitely was the one who, turning to check that my ears had not deceived me that Blasio's Century was just behind me, shouted at the men, "Prepare javelins!"

Returning my attention to the front, I saw that perhaps two dozen Maezaei, seeing our approach, had pivoted and formed a rough line, but they were still just out of javelin range, so I continued forward, waving my *gladius* in the signal for the men to follow me, accounting for the space between where I was and the Sixth was located behind me, thereby closing the gap even further than normal before I gave the next order. "Release!"

There is no way to know with any certainty, whether it was an accident or by design on the part of one of the Maezaei, though I heard no shouted command, but rather than wait for our javelins to land, they came charging towards us. Or, more accurately, towards me, since I was about a dozen paces ahead of the Century. Their precipitate movement meant that a fair number of the javelins launched by the Sixth came hurtling down in the spot where they had been an instant before; fortunately for me, when there are about a hundred fifty of the missiles launched, more than thirty of them hit their targets, either in the form of bodies or shields. Whatever the case, it was as if an invisible hand casually swept aside the bulk of the Maezaei who were trying to buy their comrades the time to accomplish their real objective. And, it pains me to say, in this they were successful, so that by the time we disposed of the remnants of those Maezaei who interposed themselves between the Sixth and the bulk of the barbarian warriors, four wagons were fully ablaze and beyond any chance of salvaging. Even as I was thrusting my blade into the chest of the last warrior, I first felt, then heard the pounding of hooves from behind me, and I turned just in time to see Germanicus, at the head of the fifty men of his bodyguard, come thundering past, sweeping up those Maezaei who, for whatever reason, had lingered a moment too long. Perhaps they were admiring their handiwork, but the only consolation was that, after Germanicus and his mounted contingent were done, there were well more than a hundred bodies of barbarians littering the ground, while our casualties were negligible. If, that is, one only counted the cost in humans. Otherwise, I suspect that whoever had ordered this attack would be satisfied in the knowledge that half of our artillery, contained in those wagons, were completely destroyed.

"How could they have known which wagons were carrying the artillery?"

Germanicus, who had asked the question, was still mounted, but was viewing the still flaming hulks of the wagons, while I, despite myself, was forced to admire the guile and skill of whoever had engineered this attack.

Pointing to one of the blackened hulks, I could only offer a guess. "Probably from the way they rode, sir. They were heavier than the other wagons."

What I did not say was that, like so many things we Romans do, we predictably place our most valuable items, like artillery, in the middle of a baggage train; I decided that there was no need to make Germanicus feel worse than he already did. The men of his bodyguard had gone off in pursuit of the fleeing Maezaei, who had stayed only long enough to ensure the wagons were fully aflame and beyond saving before trying to reach the relative safety of the wooded slopes. Bibaculus had been summoned from where he marched just behind the command group, since he was the one man who could identify which pieces had been destroyed by their position in the column. Once the Maezaei were repelled, if it could be described in this way, I had

300

ordered Blasio's Century to at least try and save some of the oxen, although the Maezaei had been equally thorough in this regard, making sure to kill at least one of a team in order to immobilize the wagons for the men who doused them in flaming oil. The two wagons that had been dragged into the river by their panicked animals once the drivers had been slain had to be hauled out, which was still being done while we waited for Bibaculus' assessment.

Breaking the silence that had fallen, it was Tribune Frugi who asked what I believed was the more important question. "How did a force that large get past the cavalry? I thought they had Raetinium under observation."

I opened my mouth, but Germanicus beat me to it, pointing out, "Who says they came from Raetinium?" Giving what appeared to me to be a fatalistic shrug, he was nevertheless speaking truly when he said, "These could be some men from Splonum for all we know."

"Splonum?" Appuleius echoed doubtfully. "How could that be? We had it surrounded."

"Only after we took the town," Germanicus replied. "And even then, we only had two Centuries on the eastern side. They could have easily slipped out."

"Well," Frugi interrupted, and when we looked to him, he was pointing back in the direction from which the ambush had come, "it looks like we might get some answers about that at least."

Following his finger, we saw three of Germanicus' bodyguards, and behind each one came a stumbling prisoner, hands tied in front of them and secured with a rope to the saddle. The mounted men kept their horses to a walk, but it was a fast one, and even as we watched, one of the Maezaei stumbled and fell heavily, though he was able to partially break his fall with his bound hands. Rather than stop, or even slow down, this man, a German by the looks of him, continued his progress, resulting in the prisoner being dragged a few paces before he somehow managed to regain his footing.

Reaching us, they drew to a halt, and one of the Germans reported to Germanicus, "The rest of the men are finishing their search for more like these." He gestured contemptuously to the three men, two of them bearing expressions that were easy to read as they glared up at us defiantly.

The third man's face was unreadable only because it was covered in blood, and I saw that when he had fallen, he clearly had been dragged on his face for a few paces. Germanicus only gave a curt nod, then nudged his horse towards the trio, staring down at them from his horse.

"I suppose it's a waste of time to ask them politely," he mused aloud, prompting a couple of chuckles. Turning to the man who had reported to him, Germanicus ordered, "Take them to the wagon with Decebalus for now; he can use the company. Make sure," he added, "their hands are bound behind their backs, and with chains, not rope."

I just happened to be watching the trio when Germanicus was speaking, so I saw their reaction when the name of Dodonis' son was mentioned, and the two unhurt men exchanged a glance that, while I did not know its meaning, knew that it did mean something. Before I could say anything, though, the German horsemen were already moving, then Bibaculus came trotting up, and I confess it slipped my mind to bring this up.

The grizzled *Immune* looked suitably grave, but he did not appear to be devastated, which was explained when he said, "The news is bad, sir, but it could be worse." Flipping open his tablet, he consulted the notes he had made. "We still have the ten-pound piece; that's the most important thing. One wagon held the two captured pieces, and we also lost one of our own five-pounders."

"I thought you said it could be worse!" Germanicus burst out, clearly dismayed.

"While we lost most of our scorpions, the wagon carrying the wood we took from Splonum was untouched." Bibaculus' voice remained calm, which I, for one, appreciated, having noticed Germanicus' tendency to become agitated in the face of setbacks, to which I attributed his youth. "So we can at least replace the scorpions that were lost."

"So our final tally is going to be, what, one ten-pounder, one five-pounder, and a half-dozen scorpions?" Frugi was the one who asked this, and Bibaculus nodded.

"We could barely take Splonum with what we had," Germanicus said bitterly. "Now we're going to take Raetinium with less?" Shaking his head, he balled up a fist and hit his thigh repeatedly, obviously frustrated at this setback. "How," he finished miserably, "are we going to do that?"

It was a vexing situation, to be certain, but I also decided that this was not a scene that needed to be continued in front of the men, so I nudged Latobius and moved next to Germanicus, turning so my back was to them. Most were still busy, it was true, but I also understood that the men could do their jobs and listen at the same time.

"Sir," I suggested quietly, "perhaps we should reconvene this meeting later, after we're finished for the day. Besides," I pointed out, "you're going to want to let one of your men have a go at those three in the wagon, and that's best done after we stop."

For a moment, I thought he would argue, but then he gave a curt nod, saying only, "You're right."

Turning to the others, he loudly commanded, "Once this mess is cleaned up, we're resuming the march. We'll discuss this later tonight."

Without another word, he kicked his horse into a trot and, with the Tribunes trailing behind him, made his way back to the front of the column, while I returned my attention to the tasks at hand. No more than a third of a watch after the ambush, the column resumed moving; we left the bodies of the Maezaei for the carrion birds.

The delay meant the men completed the camp in the dark, and because of our proximity to Raetinium, Germanicus ordered an alert of half-strength, which only served to further dampen the mood. Naturally, there was no way to hide what had happened, and as the *de facto* commander of the First Cohort, I bore the responsibility for the fact that it was my men who quickly relayed all that had transpired to their friends in the other Cohorts, waiting only long enough for the

303

next rest stop. Frankly, I was not looking forward to entering the *praetorium*, and I even briefly considered instructing Alex to come and fetch me for some imaginary emergency before thinking better of it. What caused me to discard this idea was not as much from a sense of duty or my regard for Germanicus as it was from the question; would my Avus do something like that, back when he was in roughly the same position I was, when he was the *de facto* Primus Pilus of the 6th with Caesar in Alexandria? Regardless of this, however, I was still not in the best frame of mind when I made my way to the *praetorium* once I had ensured the men of the First were performing their assigned task to my satisfaction. Entering, I got something of a pleasant surprise when I spotted a familiar figure, dressed as a Roman cavalryman, but with long braids and a full beard.

Gaesorix saw me at roughly the same time, and we met each other halfway, exchanging a firm handshake while sharing the same grin.

"You're not dead yet?" he asked with a laugh.

"Have you enjoyed yourself lounging about while the real men did all the work?" I shot back, something of a normal taunt men of the infantry reserve for cavalrymen.

"Of course I have," he said equably. "Why wouldn't I?"

While I would have been content to keep matters lighthearted, considering I was about to go face Germanicus, I changed the topic, asking seriously, "So, when did you get here? And what's your report?"

His cheerful demeanor vanished in the time it took for me to blink, and he replied soberly, "We arrived just now; Silius is already in with the Legate. And," he hesitated, "as far as the report, it's not good, Pullus. The Maezaei have not only completely invested Raetinium, they've improved the defenses. Although," he shook his head, "I have to admit that, while we've watched them working hard along the walls, we haven't really figured out what they're doing."

This was puzzling, but before I could press him, the partition was thrust aside, and it was Silius who, seeing the both of us, beckoned to us. Following him back into the officers' mess, I saw that all of the Tribunes were present, along with Bibaculus, but none of the other

Centurions were there, which Germanicus explained as soon as he saw me enter.

"I'm not asking the Pili Priores to be here for this," he informed me, "because I don't need the aggravation and second-guessing right now."

This was something I understood, but I also thought it was a troubling sign of how close Germanicus was to cracking under the pressure. Germanicus turned to Silius, nodding at him to go ahead with his report, and in preparation for this, he unrolled a large piece of vellum, then produced a stack of wax tablets from a satchel he had slung over his shoulder.

"This," he began, "is everything we've learned from our observation of Raetinium."

For the next third of a watch, we examined the sketch of the town he had drawn, and I must say I was impressed with his eye and ability to create such a complete picture of what awaited us. Accompanying this was his assessment of the numbers of Maezaei warriors, although for this I surreptitiously glanced over at Gaesorix, but the Batavian gave a small nod to confirm his agreement with Silius' report.

"As far as the number of defenders," he began, and his face became grim, "I'm afraid the news isn't good. By our count," at this, he turned to indicate Gaesorix, who did not say anything but nodded to indicate his agreement, "there are at least four thousand defenders inside the walls." Despite expecting something like this, there was a collective sound from all of us that I suppose could best be described as a gasp. "What's hard to tell," he went on, "is the composition of the force. There's no need for cavalry, but Gaesorix believes that almost a thousand men are cavalry. Isn't that correct, Decurion?"

Gaesorix held up a hand as he cautioned, "Yes...and no, Tribune. What I believe is that there are that many men who are mounted, but that they're composed of the upper nobility of the Maezaei. My guess is that the bulk of these men serve as the bodyguard for their king."

"That," I interjected, "sounds like a lot of men for just Dodonis."

Gaesorix considered this and opened his mouth to reply, but it was Germanicus who beat him to it, asking me, "What are you saying, Pullus?"

"I'm saying," I replied, speaking more slowly than normal because, frankly, I was thinking it through as I said it, "that, as we know with every tribe, while there's a high chieftain, there are men who are considered sub-chieftains and leaders of a particular clan of that tribe. So I think it's more likely that what Gaesorix saw was the combined total of all the bodyguards for all the tribal nobility."

"Which means," Germanicus, I was pleased to see, instantly picked up on the point I was trying to make, "that if," he quickly amended, "I mean, *when* we take Raetinium, we'll be able to completely crush the Maezaei's rebellion because there won't be anyone left to lead it."

I suppose it was too much to expect, but despite Germanicus excluding the Pili Priores, Tribune Appuleius clearly felt that since he was the only representative of the faction that seemed determined to either thwart or belittle Germanicus in some way, he felt compelled to do so, because he sniffed, "That's a nice idea, Legate. But I wouldn't put much stock in that. You know," he smiled at the rest of us, as if he expected us to appreciate his insight, "that there's not a barbarian born who has enough sense to know when they're beaten."

The silence that followed seemed to signal to Appuleius that he had said something that was, if not offensive to one of our party, at the very least awkward, but it was when we all, myself included, glanced over at Gaesorix that he seemed to realize that one of us might take exception to the kind of thing men of Appuleius' status like to bandy about their *triclinium* back in Rome as they eat their delicacies and sip their wine. For his part, the Batavian was stone-faced, but someone came to his defense, and it was not me.

"I've just spent the last few weeks with one of those 'barbarians,' Appuleius," Silius did not raise his voice, but there was no missing the anger in it, "and all I can say is that I wish we had more men like him with us right now. Particularly," he finished by staring directly at Appuleius, "among my fellow Tribunes."

Appuleius, not surprisingly, stiffened at this insult, but before he could utter a retort, Germanicus intervened, saying wearily, "Let's get back to the business at hand." He turned to Gaesorix, and while I never brought it up with him later, I suspected that Germanicus was not only ameliorating the offense given to Gaesorix, he was sending a scorpion bolt of his own at Appuleius, "But I want to thank the Decurion for his assessment and for the excellent job he and Silius have done. I'm lucky to have men like you under my command. Even if," despite his eyes never leaving Gaesorix, there was no mistaking who he meant as he finished, "I don't have enough of them like you among my officers. Now, let's talk about the rest of the defenders."

From where I stood, Appuleius seemed as if he was considering making a hasty exit, his face a bright red, but he remained rooted to his spot. Probably, I thought sourly, to make sure he doesn't miss anything so he can share it with Scipio.

"They have men on the walls throughout the watches," Silius resumed his report, "and they have bundles of hurdles, along with lamps they keep lit, ready to throw down off the walls in case we try something at night." Glancing down at his tablet again, he read, "We saw at least two hundred men carrying bows, but there may be more. It was hard to make out whether the men we were counting were different people or not." This, to me at least, seemed a bit unusual to mention, but I learned why when Silius said, "The one thing we do know is that they've looted every single house, warehouse, merchant's shop, and the like, and a lot of them have swapped their clothing for things they found somewhere in the town." The Tribune shrugged, "So we may be seeing the same men just wearing different clothes."

Once more, I felt compelled to point something out, despite my hesitance to do so more than once, but I reminded myself this, at least as far as Germanicus knew, was the reason I was with him and not back in Ubiorum with my Legion.

"Actually," I offered, "I think your numbers for the archers are probably correct."

"Oh?" Germanicus regarded me with a raised eyebrow, and there was something at that moment in the manner in which he did it that reminded me of his father Drusus. "Why do you say that, Pullus?"

"Because their warriors don't use bows," I explained. "That's considered beneath them. So those men you saw are likely the hunters from the various villages, either pressed into service. Or," I shrugged, "they volunteered. But either way, there's no more than ten or twenty per settlement."

Our young Legate considered this for a moment, then nodded his acceptance, but then he said offhandedly, "So they don't have many missile troops, then. That's a good thing."

"Not necessarily," I warned, "because the youngsters of their warrior class start out as javelineers." Looking to Silius, I did not need to say anything more, because he correctly interpreted my glance.

"Pullus is correct," Silius said, glancing down at his tablet again. "According to our estimate, we saw about five hundred men who were very lightly armored and were carrying sheaves of javelins."

"They're going to be on the walls, then," Germanicus mused, tacitly accepting what I had said, then asked, "Were you able to determine how many of the remainder are spearmen and how many are *gladius* men? Or," he amended, "axmen?"

"At least a thousand spearmen," Silius replied immediately, "and a bit less than two hundred are carrying axes. The rest are *gladius* men, but that includes those mounted men I already mentioned."

Silius dropped one tablet to pick up another, but Gaesorix cleared his throat in such a way that it seemed to be a signal, which it clearly was, because Silius looked over at the Decurion and gave a quick nod of acknowledgment.

"Yes, right," he muttered, then offered apologetically, "I'm sorry, sir. Gaesorix reminded me of something else that involves the defenders." Moving his pointing finger, he found what he was looking for, but he then hesitated for an instant, perhaps to try and frame his thoughts, then said, "As I recall, when we left Splonum to come here, there was still some questions about the number of civilians inside

Splonum." Glancing over at Germanicus, he asked, "Did you find them?"

"No," the Legate shook his head. "At least, not all of them."

"Well," Silius actually extended the tablet towards Germanicus to show him, "I believe we did."

Germanicus, who was examining the tablet, let out a small gasp, looking up sharply to ask the Tribune, "And this is an accurate count? How certain are you of this?"

Not surprisingly, Silius seemed to become cautious, but his tone was firm as he answered, "While I can't guarantee it, I feel very strongly that we did a thorough job of counting heads." Glancing over at Gaesorix, he asked the Decurion, "Would you agree with that, Gaesorix?"

"Yes, Tribune." The Batavian did not hesitate. "I think we're as close as we can get."

Since none of us could see the tablet, it was left to Germanicus to inform us, "There are at least three thousand people inside Raetinium who aren't warriors. Which," only then did he look up at the rest of us, "makes sense. The barbarians have had more than ten months since they took the town." He laughed, but there was a bitter edge to it as he observed, "I suppose they liked the comforts we provide in our cities better than their own homes."

While I was certain he offered this as somewhat flippantly, I also believed, and still do, that he was more right than he knew. All one had to do was visit a barbarian town, then a Roman one, and the differences were so obvious, and the advantages so numerous, that it made one wonder why they were so resistant to our rule. Nevertheless, I did feel somewhat relieved that we had located the missing Maezaei civilians.

There was a brief silence as we all absorbed this, and more importantly, what impact it would have on our planning, then Germanicus took a deep breath before asking the dreaded question, "And what about artillery?"

Although Silius answered readily enough, I, for one, saw before Germanicus did that none of us would like what was coming.

But, rather than answer directly, Silius asked, "Sir, were you aware of the improvements that were made by one of the *Duumviri* of Raetinium in the beginning of this rebellion?" Germanicus' expression became somewhat guarded, but he only shook his head in reply, and Silius continued, "Apparently, they either requested permission or took it upon themselves to emplace some artillery pieces on the ramparts." He pointed to the drawing and explained, "Those X's you see are *ballistae*, and the Deltas are scorpions."

Naturally, this was not good news, but there was one positive, which Germanicus pointed out. "They're only on the eastern and southern walls?" When Silius confirmed this, he mused, "I wonder why?"

"Our belief," Silius answered, glancing over at Gaesorix, who nodded his confirmation, "is that they ran out of time before the town was taken. And," he pointed to the oblong circle, through which was the line designating the southern wall, "the best place to start was because of this hill that overlooks the town. I'm afraid that trying to emplace our own artillery on the slope will give us a height advantage, but we'll be within range of those fixed positions."

"Which leads to the question," I asked aloud, though I had not meant to, "how was the town taken? Was there an obvious breach?"

"No," this came from Gaesorix, "there are no signs of any kind of assault. No repairs to the wall, not even scorch marks." Shaking his head, he finished flatly, "Nothing."

"So it was taken by some sort of ruse," Germanicus opined. "Either by guile or," he added grimly, clearly not liking to think along these lines, "some sort of treachery."

It would not be until after the fact that we learned that Raetinium had fallen by the latter means, when someone whose identity was never learned opened one of the four gates into the town in the middle of the night. The Maezaei flooded in, but in a slightly unusual act, rather than slaughter the inhabitants, the Roman inhabitants were allowed to flee, and the reason we had not been informed was that, since they were cut off from going north, and Salona was under siege, they had gone the only direction they could, west through the Dinaric mountains, all the way to the coast to the settlement of Vegium. My personal belief for this relatively rare show of mercy on the part of the Maezaei was because this occurred very early in the rebellion, the year before.

"Can those pieces be moved?" Frugi asked, which prompted us to look to Bibaculus, who, despite having been included in these meetings for some time, always appeared uncomfortable.

At least, until he was asked a question like this, and he answered, "Yes, but not without some difficulty. And," he finished, "they can't do it quickly."

"So, if we can keep them guessing about where we're going to attack, we might be able to get to and up the wall before they can do anything about it." Germanicus nodded thoughtfully. Turning to Silius, he offered, "Thank you, Silius. And," he turned to Gaesorix, "to you, Decurion. You've given a first rate report. Now," he concluded, "we move to Raetinium tomorrow, and I can see for myself what's waiting." Once Silius was done, he spent the next few moments answering questions, mostly from Germanicus, while I added a couple of my own. Only then did the Tribune, with a tentative glance over at the Legate, bring something up that, only in hindsight, was probably the most crucial bit of information.

"The Maezaei inside the town have been busy working on something, but they only do it at night, so we don't know exactly what they're doing, but it has something to do with the outer wall. Our guess is that they're trying to strengthen it in some way."

Despite the fact that Silius was wrong, I do not want to give the impression that I fault him in any way, even knowing what was to come.

Approaching from the north as we followed the Oenus upstream, once the town came within view, I realized that since we had bypassed it on the way to Splonum, I had not laid eyes on Raetinium for some years, and even from a distance, I could see much had changed. It was bigger, certainly, and the outer wall had been extended to the west so that the river now ran directly through the town, while the northern wall had been pushed out so that it now ran along the crest of a low hill, and the forum had been relocated in the low point between this one and the one around which the town had been built in the first place. My guess, once I laid eyes on it, was that the Romans running the town had liked the idea of locating the central point in between two hills, in much the same manner as the city from which we claim our heritage, although there were only two here instead of seven. Because Raetinium began as a frontier settlement, and it straddled the only road running east/west to the coast and the road that served as the westernmost north/south road in the province, it had been deemed strategically important from its first days. What this meant to us in a practical sense was that, perched atop the one large hill completely enclosed within the walls, located on the east side of the town was a building, made of stone, that was more than a *Praetorium* but not quite a fortress. The southern wall, the only part of the town that had not been expanded, was about three hundred paces from the foot of the hill, running at an angle in the low point between the hill inside the town, and a hill that was slightly higher that was located at the junction of the southern and eastern walls. One did not need to possess any knowledge of strategy to grasp why the *Duumviri* in charge of the town made the decision to emplace their artillery pieces in this location, and as tempting as it was, the idea of trying to take advantage of the height was rendered ineffective because of this fact. The best we could manage was to observe from the very crest of that hill, because it was about a hundred-fifty paces beyond the range of the mounted *ballista,* but this was a small comfort.

Because of the unusual nature of the river flowing northward, we took the long way around, crossing the Oeneus a couple miles north of Raetinium, then, taking advantage of a large hill that was not quite a mountain just to the west to screen our movement, we swung around the town, coming back within sight of the southern wall. This detour meant it was early afternoon when Germanicus gave the order to halt and begin the main camp, and as the men were constructing it, he took all of the officers on a scouting mission, heading directly for the hill overlooking the town. Riding up the opposite slope, we reached the crest and, sitting our horses, observed the scene below, protected from easy detection by our enemy by the trees that were still standing, although what had once been a thick forest had been considerably thinned by the men who built the town. Similarly to Splonum, the slope directly opposite both the southern and eastern wall had been cleared, but unlike the Maezaei, we Romans were more thorough, either uprooting and dragging away the stumps, or sawing them flat, depriving any attacker of even a modicum of cover. I say that it was a hill, but it was more of a ridge that curved slightly, somewhat like a backward letter "L" wrapping around part of the southern and the entire eastern wall. Taking care to remain well out of range, we rode along the crest of the ridge, stopping every few moments to not only take in the defenses, but to observe our enemies.

If one did not know about the rebellion, it would appear to be a normal day in a town in one of the frontier provinces, with people going about their business; there was even a market of a sorts in the forum, at least judging by the throng of people present. Perhaps a sharp-eyed observer would have noticed that the style of clothing worn by the people did not match the layout of the town, which had the Roman forum somewhat in the center, although in order to place it in between the two hills, it had been relocated farther east than its original location, and while the streets were arranged in symmetrical lines, crisscrossing each other, the current occupants going about their business were exclusively barbarian. Despite the circumstances, I confess I chuckled, inwardly of course, at how outraged the Roman citizens of Raetinium would be to learn that some smelly barbarians were sleeping in their beds and fouling up their private latrines with their stench. However, it was clear that the Maezaei civilians who were now the occupants of Raetinium preferred this settlement, which was on a modest scale by Roman standards, over their former homes in Splonum, and I idly wondered if they were laboring under the delusion that this swap would be permanent in any way. Maybe, I thought, Dodonis thinks he can negotiate some sort of peace where everything will stay as it is, and Splonum will be occupied by the Roman inhabitants who formerly called Raetinium their home. If so, this Dodonis was not nearly as clever as one might otherwise think, given his actions to this point.

"Any ideas, Pullus?" Germanicus asked as we sat our horses, looking down at the town, as warriors arrayed along the southeast corner looked back up at us, their faces merely tiny lighter-colored dots framed by hair and beards.

"No," I answered him honestly, "nothing comes to mind. I mean," I made sure to look directly at him, "nothing other than getting us more men. And artillery."

"I've sent a dispatch to Tiberius," Germanicus' tone was not surly, though he was shorter than normal, "but I don't know how long it will take to find him, and whether or not he'll even agree to send more men. And if he doesn't send the men," he concluded, "it's not likely he's going to send us more artillery."

"Well then," I tried to sound cheerful, but it was not easy, "we need to come up with a truly clever plan."

He did not seem to appreciate my effort to sound optimistic, shooting me a dour look that was more reminiscent of his adoptive father than his real one, saying, "We can start by depriving them of clean water."

"That can't hurt," I agreed, but I suspected that it would not have the impact he thought it would, since I felt fairly certain there was a source of fresh water other than the river.

Turning to Bibaculus, who was on one of the spare horses, Germanicus' tone turned plaintive as he asked, "And you're certain we can't drag the artillery up here and they'd be safe from those pieces down there? I would think with this height advantage, we could do some real damage."

"We could," Bibaculus allowed, "now that I've seen everything with my own eyes." I glanced over at Germanicus, who immediately brightened, but the *Immune* tempered this piece of news by pointing out, "But only the ten-pounder will work up here, at least to the extent I suspect you would want it to. The small *ballistae*," he said, "will be able to hit the wall, that's true, but the slope of this hill isn't as great as I'd hoped it would be, which means that to get them close enough

314

to do more than that would put them within range of their own pieces. And," he went on, clearly not happy at being the one to convey this to Germanicus, "the scorpions are useless because their range is shorter. Also," he concluded by pointing down at the section of the rampart that was visible and said, "now that I've seen that their rampart isn't all stone, but looks like it's mostly wood, that means they can pry loose those pieces and move them more quickly than I thought."

Germanicus did not respond to Bibaculus, nor did he utter a word for a long stretch of time, but I saw how tightly clenched his fist was, and once more, I saw him beating it against his thigh; I was learning that this was a habit of his that was a good way to gauge his frustration.

Finally, he gave a curt nod, then glanced over at me and said tightly, "Then I suppose we need to come up with a different plan." An expression crossed his countenance that I did not recall seeing before, on him at any rate, and when he spoke next, I realized that it was a look of, for lack of a better term, cunning.

"I think we need to find out just how much this barbarian loves his son."

Given our situation, I certainly cannot fault Germanicus' thinking, particularly considering the amount of time it was likely to take to get an answer back from Tiberius. If there is one thing with which I can find fault with Germanicus, it is that he did not seem to think it important to keep us apprised of the situation in the rest of the province. At first, I suspected that he was simply not telling me, but I was assured by Frugi, then Silius after he rejoined us, that they were as uninformed as I was about what was taking place elsewhere. Only if I managed to be in the vicinity when a dispatch rider came trotting up and found Germanicus, then waited until after the message was delivered to our Legate could I surreptitiously press the courier for information. Not surprisingly, the quality of the information I got was not the best, and I soon determined that it was more rumor than anything, since on more than one occasion, I would question a messenger who would inform me that Tiberius was with Silanus, then later the same day another man would insist that he was back in Siscia, then the next day. the courier would claim he was in Sirmium. What was obvious was that we were essentially on our own for the foreseeable future, so Germanicus had to try something, and I supported the general idea, although I did feel compelled to point something out when the topic was broached in the *praetorium*.

"Dodonis might know that this son killed the other one," I pointed out, but if anything, it seemed to strengthen Germanicus' resolve.

"Which means he can't afford to lose another one," he replied without hesitation, indicating he had thought about this as well. "So we just need to impress on him that his son's life rests in his hands."

Now, I admit that for a moment I struggled with the urge to point out that, in all reality, we had no idea how many sons Dodonis had; for all we knew, he had another four or five spares, but I sensed that Germanicus was going to go through with this no matter what I might have said.

What did surprise me, or so I believed, was when he announced, "I am going to be escorting Decebalus under a flag of truce up to the walls." This elicited an uproar, as all the Tribunes and the Pili Priores, who had finally been allowed to attend a meeting, began shouting what a bad idea this was. Which, I believe, is why I did not hear what came next; it was only when I noticed that, while they were still protesting, a couple of the men were looking in my direction that I became conscious I was somehow involved. I suppose that, since I did not react, Germanicus must have realized I had not heard him, so he repeated, "And you're coming with me, Pullus."

"I am?"

This got out before I could stop it, my surprise such that I was not particularly alarmed, but he confirmed I had not misheard him, nodding emphatically as he explained, "I need someone who speaks their tongue better than I do…"

"I don't speak their tongue," I protested, but I realized this was not exactly the truth, so I did amend my statement, "at least not very well. I understand it better than I can speak it."

"Then you'll at least know if they try to fool us by switching into their language," Germanicus said. "Plus, you know this Dodonis." He held up a hand, clearly seeing that I was about to dispute, once again, that my familiarity with Dodonis extended to perhaps being able to pick him out of a group, cutting this off by saying, "You've laid eyes on him before, and again, that's more than I've done." Turning to Gaesorix, Germanicus asked delicately, "Decurion, I'm about to ask you a question, but know that I wish no offense. It's just that, to our ear, the Germanic tongue sounds similar to what these bar...natives use."

Gaesorix shifted uncomfortably but cautiously allowed, "There are similarities, that's true, sir. But that doesn't mean that I'd be any better than Pullus. In fact," he finished, "he can probably understand more of it than I can."

Again, Germanicus made it clear that he was not going to be swayed, but rather than pursue the language idea, he switched tactics by saying, "I also need a good horseman, in case Decebalus gets it in his head to try and ride off." He surprised me then by flashing me an apologetic smile as he said, "Sorry, Pullus. I know you're proud of your horsemanship, and I confess I was surprised at how well you ride for," he stumbled, "well, for a man of your size. But," he concluded with a simple truth that even I could not deny, "Gaesorix is a born horseman."

"Sir," Silius spoke up, and while he clearly wanted to remain respectful, he also was obviously alarmed at Germanicus' decision, "please forgive me for questioning your order, but..."

"Then don't," Germanicus said this amiably enough, but he was not smiling as he spoke.

Silius, however, seemed determined to bring up his objection, and he repeated, "...but is it wise to have both the Legate and the Primus Pilus put themselves at risk like that?" The Tribune was speaking quietly, but there was a force behind his words as he pressed on, "If I were this Dodonis, I'd have to think very carefully about the chance of killing the two commanders of this army, even if it did mean his son would die. He could think it was a bargain he couldn't pass up."

Now I did agree with Silius' reasoning, but what struck me more than that was how it takes a nobly born man to think like another noble, even if they are of different nations. Only a patrician, I thought with morbid amusement, would think losing a son in exchange for two men because they were of a high rank would be something to consider.

"That's true," Germanicus allowed this, though I could see he was doing so reluctantly, "but I think it's a small risk." His own words seemed to bolster his determination, because he shook his head and said with a tone that we had learned meant his decision was made, "No, Pullus, Gaesorix and I are going to go speak to Dodonis and make him see reason."

Despite my understanding that he would not be swayed on the decision itself, I did think it was a good idea to try and persuade him to consider something else.

"Sir, will you at least allow Gaesorix to pick a half-dozen of his men he trusts to come with us? That's not unusual in moments like this."

It was clear he did not like the idea all that much, but I suppose the looks his subordinates were giving him convinced him to acquiesce, though without much grace.

"Fine," he grumped. "Decurion, pick the men."

"And," I asked, trying to sound light-hearted about it, "when are we going on this horseback ride?"

Somewhat to my relief, this seemed to soothe Germanicus' temper, because he grinned at my characterization and said, "As soon as it's light tomorrow." Suddenly, the smile faded, and I understood why when he turned to Frugi. "Which reminds me. Has your man had any luck with the prisoners?"

Because the *Legio Germanicus* was an *ad hoc* force, not only did we not have a full complement of men, or artillery, we did not have the men who serve as both provosts and as interrogators of prisoners. In its simplest terms, we did not have anyone skilled in torture, or at least, so I believed, but I had been informed by Germanicus that one of Frugi's personal contingent, which no Tribune would leave Rome without, even if they were of a status lower than the great-grandson of Marcus Crassus, possessed skills at this arcane and bloody art. What, exactly, a Tribune was doing with such a man in his employ was something that I found intriguing and disturbing in equal measure, but when Germanicus had informed me of this, I immediately recalled that Frugi's father had employed gladiators as his personal bodyguard, and one of them had bitten off my Avus' little finger. Naturally, Titus Pullus had killed not just the man who had done it, but all of the gladiators, including their leader Prixus, and when I remembered this, it made a bit more sense that Frugi would have similar types in his employ. Now Frugi answered Germanicus' question, nodding as he produced a tablet, and I wondered if I was seeing things, because the wooden cover looked as if it had been stained with something, but judging by the manner in which the others were staring at it, I knew I was not imagining it, and I wondered just how close that tablet had been to the prisoner as he was being tortured.

"Scarax," Frugi began, "that's my man, said that he's not through, but he got information from one of them before he died." Even though we were talking about barbarians, I noticed the faces around the table got a shade whiter. "The party that attacked us were men who escaped Splonum before we took their royal fortress, and they were on their way to Raetinium. But," he pursed his lips as his eyes moved down the tablet, "they spotted us, and one of them who was something of their leader, I suppose, convinced them that it would help their cause if they destroyed our artillery." Frugi paused then, but did it in such a way that we all sensed there was something else that he was trying to frame the right way, but it was Germanicus who spoke.

"What aren't you telling us, Frugi? Does it have something to do with how they knew which wagons to attack?"

"Yes, sir," Frugi answered, reluctantly. "But it hasn't been confirmed yet. So far, only the first barbarian has made this claim, and frankly, it sounds somewhat far-fetched. I wouldn't want to claim it as fact until we can confirm from the others that this is what happened."

319

"Go ahead and tell me what he said," Germanicus told him, making it clear it was an order.

"Yes, sir. Well," Frugi cleared his throat, "according to this first man, when they saw us marching here, they decided to follow. Then, when we made camp, this barbarian claims that two of their number managed to sneak into the camp, and they got the information from Decebalus, who apparently had been paying attention to our order of march. He was the one who told them where the wagons hauling the artillery would be located in the train."

"That's impossible!" Scipio snorted. "He's lying! It's obvious!"

On the surface, this seemed to be a time when Scipio was right, but I raised a hand to catch Frugi's attention, then asked him, "And when did this happen?"

"The night before last," Frugi answered, which confirmed my suspicion, both about the likelihood and why Scipio was so dismissive.

For once, I decided not to bring this up, but somewhat to my surprise, Silius was the one who asked, "Who was the duty Cohort during the night watch the night before last? Does anyone remember?"

Just by the way he said it, I felt certain Silius already knew the answer, but while I did not want to be the one to bring it up, ultimately, I was the one who answered after nobody spoke up, "Third Cohort, Tribune."

Scipio, unsurprisingly, did not care for where this was headed, and his face turned a bright red.

Leaping to his feet, he actually shouted, "That's a lie! No barbarian could have gotten past my men, and I resent the implication!"

This was met by a long silence, but we all turned to Germanicus, since this was now his problem to deal with, and he looked at Scipio coldly for a moment.

Then, in a manner that was in direct contrast to Scipio's bluster, he said quietly, "Nobody has implied anything, Scipio." He paused, then added, "Yet. But," he leaned forward and his eyes narrowed as he regarded his fellow nobleman who had been a rock in his *caliga* since the first day, "it does raise an interesting question. If this does turn out to be true, and it's confirmed that it happened night before last," for the first time, Germanicus gestured, pointing a finger directly at Scipio as he finished, "then ultimately it's your responsibility, and your failure." Turning to me suddenly, Germanicus asked, "Pullus, what's the punishment for an offense like this? I mean," he added, "for a man of the ranks?"

"For allowing someone to infiltrate a marching camp during a time of war?" I deliberately drew it out; frankly, I was enjoying the sweat that suddenly began running down Scipio's face. Shaking my head, I said flatly, "Death. But," I added, "at the hands of his own comrades in his Century."

"That sounds like a rather bad way to die." Germanicus, I could see, was enjoying this as much as I was. Turning back to Scipio, he said, "Luckily for you, Pilus Prior, your status means that you won't be executed. Your career, on the other hand," he shrugged, "would be what ended up dead."

"I...I," all of Scipio's bluster had gone, "I don't believe that things happened as this savage says."

Clearly tired of the game, Germanicus said brusquely, "Well, we'll put that to the side for now." Standing, he concluded, "We have a big day ahead of us, so let's get some sleep, eh?"

There were no clouds in the sky when dawn came, but Germanicus changed his mind about when we would leave the camp, deciding to wait for the sun to be fully up above the horizon. Alex put extra effort into polishing my helmet, armor, and awards, which Germanicus insisted I wear, though I think he might have had second thoughts when I drew alongside him on Latobius, considering that despite wearing the helmet of a Legate, his cuirass was bare. Not that the cuirass itself was anything to sneer at, and I found myself admiring it; that we caught each other doing the same thing prompted a laugh from both of us.

"Want to trade, Pullus?" Germanicus quipped, then laughed. "Although I think we'd look ridiculous. The only way this," he indicated his cuirass, "would fit is if you flattened it out. And I," he finished ruefully, "would look like I was a boy wearing his father's armor."

"Maybe we should then." I grinned at him. "Maybe that will make Dodonis laugh so hard he falls over the wall and breaks his neck, then the barbarians will give up!"

As I hoped, this prompted him to laugh again, then he said, "Believe me, Pullus, if I thought that might work, I'd do it." The mirth vanished from his countenance, and he lowered his voice so only I could hear him say, "I just want to get all this over with."

"It's not what you thought, is it?" I asked him, my voice pitched to match his own near-whisper.

Shaking his head, he admitted, "Nothing like what I thought it would be. Oh," he allowed, "there have been some moments that were close to what I imagined. But only a few."

Not liking this morose turn in the conversation, I said only, "Well, let's go see what we can do to end it now."

Germanicus turned to give me a level look, and for a moment, I thought he might take exception to my attempt to steer the conversation, but he simply gave a nod, then pulled on his helmet, the black feathers having been replaced by one of his slaves after they had been singed during our assault on the breach, tying his chin thong. As he did this, Gaesorix and one of the troopers he had selected came walking up, with the prisoner mounted in between them, but with his hands tied behind his back.

When I glanced over, I recognized the other Batavian, and called to him, "Oy, Cassicos! Haven't you gotten close enough to these bastards once already?"

The trooper grinned, saying in a Latin that had been steadily improving, "Bah! Primus Pilus, I still owe these *cunni*," I had to chuckle at his use of one of the most common pejoratives men under the standard use, "for that!" He continued smiling, but it changed in its character as he glared over at Decebalus, saying, "Maybe I should start with him?"

"Well," I gave Germanicus a surreptitious sign I was not serious, "maybe if this doesn't work out and his father doesn't want him, we'll give him to you." Twisting in the saddle so that I was looking directly at the Maezaei prince, I asked him, "Do you know what we're talking about, boy?"

Apparently, being chained in the back of a jouncing wagon and having your own piss and *cac* splashing over you with every bump, had cured the youngster of his haughtiness, at least temporarily. Now his eyes shifted back and forth from me to Cassicos, who was on the opposite side from where I sat on Latobius, and he licked his lips nervously, then only shook his head.

"The Taurisci tried to skin him," I told him, this causing him to blanch, but I was not through, "but he's too tough to die from it. So now he's just asked for a chance to return the favor." Although I did want to rattle the boy, it was not for its own sake, which was why I warned him, "Keep that in mind. If you have any thoughts of misbehaving in any way," I pointed at Cassicos, whose face split into a wide grin as I promised Decebalus, "I'm going to grant his wish. With you. Understood?"

Even if he had been disposed to do so, I got the sense that the young barbarian would have been unable to reply verbally, judging from the way the lump under his chin was bobbing up and down, yet he did manage to give a nod.

While this exchange was taking place, the other men Gaesorix had selected arrayed themselves in a column of twos, while the odd man out was directed by Gaesorix to lead us out, carrying the white banner that signaled a truce. The men of the *Legio Germanicus* who were not on watch had been given leave by their Centurions to gather around the gate, and they called out their wishes for our mission to be successful, though I had to wonder how many had their hearts in it. This had been a singularly unprofitable campaign in terms of loot, and the status of the captives we had taken was still undecided, Germanicus informing us that one of Tiberius' messages had taken the power to decide from our Legate's hands. Honestly, this was not surprising in the slightest, and in this at least I do not believe there was any underhanded motive on the part of Tiberius to reserve the right to decide about their fate himself. Just behind our small party, our entire force of cavalry that remained with the main body had saddled their mounts and were standing ready. As soon as we cleared the camp, they would take our place, while men on the ramparts would watch for a signal on our part that we needed help. We had briefly discussed having them exit the camp as well but decided that the sight of several hundred cavalry just a few paces longer than a mile away from the walls would seriously damage what chance we had of convincing the Maezaei we wanted to talk.

Trotting out of our northern gate, we moved quickly at first, until we got just out of *ballista* range, where Germanicus ordered us to a halt.

"I should have brought Natta," Germanicus muttered, and I suppose he had been prompted to say this after he twisted in the saddle and seen how much farther a mile seems when one is in the kind of situation we were at the moment.

Although I understood his reasoning, I assured him, "The men we've got watching are going to see our signal faster than the sound of a *cornu*."

"Provided they see it," he muttered.

"They will, sir," I promised, but then I did think to call to the Batavian just ahead of us who was holding the truce pennant aloft on the point of a javelin. "Be sure and keep your arm up if you have to give the signal."

I saw his head bob in acknowledgment, but before anything else could be said, the southern gate, which I had been examining carefully, began to open, creating a cascade of dust while the hinges squealed in protest. It did not open wide, just enough for a single mounted man to exit through it, his hands held out wide as he guided his horse with his knees at a trot, stopping a dozen paces in front of our trooper. Who, as he had been told, moved slightly aside so that Germanicus, flanked by me to his right and Gaesorix to his left, had an unobstructed view.

"Yes, Roman?" The man's Latin, I was somewhat surprised to hear, was nearly flawless, and it made me wonder if he had once been a hostage to Rome as a youngster. "What is it that you wish?"

"I am Germanicus Julius Caesar," our Legate began. "I am the Legate of the…"

"We know who you are, Germanicus," the Maezaei cut him off. "There's no need for you to recite all of your titles and all the powers granted to you by Rome." Then he pointed at me, and his mouth twisted into a sneer as he added, "And I know who this is. Titus Pullus, the Roman who butchered some of our innocent people."

I was certain that the Maezaei had said this to disconcert Germanicus, and me, I suppose, but to my surprise, not only did he not seem offended, Germanicus' tone indicated that he was happy to dispense with the formalities, but I quickly learned that the Maezaei was not the only one who could play such games.

"That's good," Germanicus replied genially. "I don't care to waste time any more than you do. Which is why," his voice hardened, "I'm not going to waste my breath discussing matters with Dodonis' lackey."

It was instantly clear this had hit home, and I bit back a smile at the sudden change of the barbarian's demeanor, his face flushing at being described in such a way.

"I am no lackey," he hissed, but Germanicus, now that he had the upper hand, was not about to relinquish it, raising a hand as if he was issuing an order.

"Frankly, I don't care what or who you are," Germanicus sounded almost bored, "but I have something of Dodonis' that I think he wants returned."

This was the signal to Cassicos, who put his horse in motion while pulling on the lead rope of the horse on which Decebalus sat. I heard this rather than saw it, since I was watching, not the lone Maezaei, but the gate, waiting for the first sign of treachery, and I suppose my tension must have communicated itself to Latobius, who I had to curb while Cassicos guided our captive's mount to my right. Only then did Cassicos reach over and yank the hood off Decebalus' head, which we had put on him just before we left the camp. My eyes never left what lay in front, so I heard the prince gasp, and at first I thought it was because of the sudden glare pained his eyes, but I quickly learned differently.

"You?" Decebalus' voice was hoarse; whether it was from surprise or lack of use I do not know, but I saw him shake his head out of the corner of my vision, as he blurted out, "What are you doing here, Suadanos?"

The now-named Suadanos, who by my judgment was almost as surprised as Decebalus but recovered more quickly, replied coldly, "I'm serving my king, Decebalus. The real question is," he raised his hand, and before I thought about it, I had reached for my *gladius*, though it was the Gallic blade and not the *spatha* that I still carried strapped to my saddle, but Suadanos only pointed, "how did you let yourself be captured?"

"We were betrayed." Decebalus, for the first time since his captivity, showed a spark of his old haughty defiance. "They had help from some of our own. That's the only reason I'm here right now."

Suadanos actually glanced over at Germanicus, as if he trusted our Legate to either confirm or deny this, and for a moment, I was afraid that, in the moment, the Legate would forget that it was not even remotely in our interest at this point to let our enemy know the true circumstances behind Decebalus' claim.

Fortunately, I did not need to worry, because Germanicus gave a shrug, and over his shoulder said only, "This is a war of rebellion, so you're not protected by any of the rules of warfare."

It took a bit of effort not to sigh in relief, but what mattered was whether Suadanos believed this, and while he stared hard at Germanicus, after a few heartbeats, he gave a barely perceptible nod.

Then, he said simply, "Wait here."

Wheeling his horse about, this time he went to the gallop, and his shouted command to open the gate was barely audible as it drifted back to us through the cloud of dust, though he was instantly obeyed.

"Now," Germanicus said lightly, "we wait."

It quickly grew hot, the sun beating down on us without a respite from even a small cloud, and it did not take long before my tunic was

326

soaked through. Germanicus seemed to fare better, if not by that much, but it was the Batavians who were the most miserable. Gaesorix's face was a bright red, glistening from the sweat, which prompted me to lean over and catch his eye.

"I'd think you'd be used to this," I said honestly. "You're out in the elements all the time, and you've been here long enough to know how hot it can get."

He glared at me for a moment, then muttered, "When we're riding, at least we have a breeze to cool us. Just sitting here like statues?"

Shaking his head, he leaned over, spat in the dust, and mumbled something in his tongue that I could not hear. Germanicus, in between us as he was, had kept his attention on the southern gate; I had ordered our escorts to spread out in a line behind us, mainly so they could scan the rampart, which not surprisingly was crowded with Maezaei staring down at our small party. We were too far away to hear them doing so, but I felt certain that there would be a steady buzzing as their warriors did essentially the same thing Legionaries would have if the circumstances were reversed. Guessing at what it meant, speculating on how one of their royalty had managed to get himself captured, the only thing I was unsure about was whether or not they would be wagering on the outcome, something that is a given with Romans. Finally, about a full third of a watch after Suadanos disappeared, the gates opened, the only difference being that there was not as much dust, although there was even more noise as both doors were pushed open, each one by a single man. For the first time, we had an unobstructed view into Raetinium from ground level, but honestly, there was not that much to see, then the gateway was obscured by a party of horsemen, these coming not at a trot but a walk. Doing a quick count, as I had suspected they would, the Maezaei had chosen the exact same number of men to come to meet us; whether the composition was the same was not as clear. However, I instantly saw that Suadanos was part of the party, but it took a moment longer for me to recognize the figure of Dodonis, riding directly in the middle of a column that was five-wide, matching our own now that Decebalus was sitting next to me. One reason that I did not recognize him immediately was that the chieftain had lost a considerable amount of weight; as I recalled, he was quite portly, but I suppose rebellion is a good way to curb one's appetite.

As they approached, I took the chance to look over at the youth, and his face was not only pale, it seemed to convey a mixture of hope, and more than a little fear, making me wonder about the nature of the relationship between father and son. Or, I thought, he knows he's going to have to explain what happened to his brother, whom he had slain with his own hand. Personally, I could not imagine any version of events where Dodonis would excuse one son for murdering another, but then I could not fathom a circumstance where I would entertain the idea of murdering my brother, unless it was in one of my fits. Before I could dwell on this, the Maezaei party drew up about twenty paces away, but Dodonis barely cast a glance at Germanicus; nor did he look at his son, more than a similarly cursory examination. No, it was me he stared at, one that I returned, trying to keep my expression as impassive as I could manage.

"The last time I saw you," he spoke at last, and his accent was more noticeable than that of Suadanos, but he was still clearly understandable, "you were just a Legionary." He showed his teeth then, but because of the beard that was now an iron gray, I could not tell whether he was smiling or grimacing. "And your Centurion assured me that you could rip our chieftain's head off with your bare hands." Tilting his head, he asked curiously, "Have you ever actually done that, Pullus?"

"Not yet," I answered him, "but I'm still young."

"Not that young," he countered, but as he did so, he pointed at my arm. "And I suspect that doesn't help." Pausing, he said, "As I recall, you got that during the rebellion of the Colapiani? Is that right? Back when your Legion lost its, what do you call them, Primus Pilus?"

Now that I understood what he was trying to do, I did not hesitate, shooting back, "You mean when I gutted Draxo personally? And," I only bobbed my head to indicate my scar, "I had that when we came and hauled Admetos away."

"As much as I would love to hear more about old war stories," Germanicus interrupted, "perhaps we should talk about this one."

Normally, I would have shut up then and allowed our two leaders to verbally spar, but I felt certain I knew what Dodonis was up to, so before he could say anything, I said, "Sir, I think Dodonis is trying to make a point about the inevitability of this province always being in rebellion by one tribe or another."

This time, Dodonis did smile, and I believe it was unfeigned as he congratulated me. "You're correct, Pullus. It's about time you Romans realize that this is, as you say, inevitable." The smile vanished, and he finished harshly, "We will never stop fighting!"

I do not believe Germanicus expected to be handed such a neat way to reassert control of this conversation, but he did not hesitate, saying in an oddly gentle voice, "Even if that means your son will die because of that decision?"

For a moment, I thought that the Legate had aimed true and scored a telling blow, because Dodonis' face completely lost its animation, becoming immobile, while he did not say a word for an uncomfortably long span.

Finally, he said coldly, "Son? I have no sons left." Only then did he finally turn his gaze directly on Decebalus, his mouth completely disappearing in his beard, although the only sign that his emotions were being tightly contained was in the slight tremor of the finger he pointed at the youth. "This…this *thing* is no son of mine!"

"*Bashta*!" Decebalus cried out, using the native term for "father," but he went on not in his native tongue or Latin, but Greek, though I do not know if he thought none of us would understand him. "Please, I beg you! I am your son! Why would you deny me now?"

Dodonis looked as if he had been slapped, gasping, "Why? *Why?*" His finger curled back to join the rest of his hand, and he shook his fist at Decebalus, shouting, "You think I don't know what you did? You killed Donnado! You slew your own brother!"

Naturally, we were intensely interested in this exchange, since it would play a huge role in our own collective fates, but I, for one, was certainly unprepared for Decebalus, matching his father's volume, insist, "That's a lie, *Bashta*! I did no such thing! Who is telling these lies about me?" Since his hands were bound, he had to use his head to indicate Suadanos, asking scornfully, "Him? My beloved cousin? You know he's had designs on your crown! What better way to remove me than to spread these lies?"

"And you don't?" Suadanos sneered. "That's why you killed Donnado!"

"I did no such thing!" Decebalus insisted, then he turned his head, leaned past me to look directly at Germanicus, and said loudly, "Ask this Roman! He'll tell you!"

And, just that quickly, I realized we had been duped, and judging from Germanicus' expression, he was as aware as I was that this cunning little bastard had put us in an extremely awkward, not to mention unusual situation. In order to achieve our own aims, Germanicus had to make a choice, over the span of a couple heartbeats, about whether he went along with Decebalus' fiction in the hope that Dodonis would accept it, thereby keeping Germanicus' hope that we could achieve taking Raetinium without bloodshed alive. During that interminably long period that, in reality, did not last long at all, I glanced over at Decebalus, and I was sure I saw a look of cunning there, as if he was still manipulating others, using us as pieces to buy another day or more of life, and after that? Who knew what he had planned.

"Is that true, Legate?" The fact that Dodonis used Germanicus' title was unusual, but there was no missing the pleading tone in the man's voice as, despite his self-control, for a moment he was just a father who was hoping that he was mistaken about his son. "Is Decebalus telling it truly?"

When I think back to those days, this is a moment I recall as one where Germanicus' natural tendency towards honesty actually harmed us, because while he said, "Yes, he's telling the truth," he looked so uncomfortable doing it that Dodonis immediately detected the Legate was not being honest.

"You're lying," was how the Maezaei put it, flatly and without a hint of doubt.

Next to Dodonis, I saw Suadanos' body suddenly slump in relief, reminding me that for a brief instant, his own fate hung in the balance. Germanicus opened his mouth, then he clearly realized there was no point, shrugging instead as Dodonis now returned his attention to his son, who must have realized his gambit had failed, judging from the sudden loss of color from his face.

"As I said," the Maezaei chieftain's voice became cold again, "I have no sons. So," now he looked at Germanicus, "you're free to do whatever you want with your prisoner. Now," he returned his attention to the larger subject, "as far as your reason for asking for this truce. I suppose you believed that I would be...persuaded to leave Raetinium in exchange for a son. But, as you can see, I have no son." His smile reappeared then, a grim one, as he finished, "What else are you prepared to offer?"

Germanicus had been thwarted, but I got the sense that he had not placed much hope in this, because he did not hesitate, responding, "Just this. If you surrender now, you won't be executed, nor will any of your nobility." He paused, then went on, "You *will* be expected to compensate Rome for the damages you have inflicted..."

"The damages we have inflicted?" Dodonis gave a barking laugh that held no humor. "You see for yourself," he turned and made a sweeping gesture towards the town, "that we took this town without inflicting any damage or with much bloodshed. We allowed the Romans who lived here to leave..."

It was Germanicus' turn to interrupt. "With only the clothes they were wearing! You robbed them of everything else."

Rather than argue this point, Dodonis countered by asking, "And what happened to Splonum? How did my people's homes fare when you took it?" Once more, he returned his attention to me, asking mockingly, "Did you let Pullus rape our women, kill our men, and burn everything down again, like he did the last time?"

Before I was aware I was doing it, I kicked Latobius forward, snarling, "You savages fucking killed my brother, you *cunnus!* You cut him down from behind! He didn't stand a chance!"

"Pullus! Pullus! *Primus Pilus!*"

Germanicus' voice cut through my rage, and I calmed down just enough to realize that I was now ahead of my own party, while Suadanos on one side and another Maezaei on the other of Dodonis had drawn their *gladii*, each of them moving their horses at an angle that placed them in a position to protect their king. Despite my return to a semblance of normal, I was still angry enough that I seriously considered cutting my way through the pair of warriors, certain that I could kill Dodonis before he could escape. It was the knowledge that in doing so, I would be placing Germanicus, Gaesorix, and the rest of the party in danger that stayed my hand, but it was a difficult choice.

Dodonis, I was grimly pleased to see, no longer looked angry; indeed, he looked a bit worried, and he held up a placating hand as he said, "Pullus, it was not the Maezaei who slew your brother. We tried to tell you this when it happened, but you wouldn't listen."

"Like you'd tell the truth?" I shot back scornfully. "Knowing what we would do?" Shaking my head, I did not then, nor do I now believe him, or any of them.

Only then did I urge Latobius backward, which he did, though I know he did not like it, but I kept my eyes on the Maezaei, returning to Germanicus' side, muttering an apology.

"Legate, Centurion," Dodonis spoke loudly enough for everyone to hear, "know this. We do not yield, and if you try to take this town by force, I swear to you, by the gods of both our people, and those you Romans worship, that I will burn this town down around all of us!"

Germanicus did not immediately respond, so both sides were content to glare at each other for several long moments, then finally, our Legate said, "So be it. But, Dodonis," he was the one pointing now, "when this is all over, and if you survive, I will take you to Rome in chains personally, and you'll be executed as part of my father's triumph over all the barbarian tribes of this province who have rebelled. Remember that."

Without waiting for an answer, he spun about and put his horse into a trot immediately, but both Gaesorix and I waited, as the troopers originally assigned to guard Decebalus led him away, then the rest of our party peeled off to head to camp.

332

Before I turned Latobius, I locked eyes with Dodonis, and I meant it when I told him, "You asked if I was going to rape your women, kill your men, and burn your homes again. The answer is yes, and I hope you live long enough to watch." I confess I was a bit surprised that he did not have a mocking reply, or challenge of some sort, instead just looking at me steadily, which spurred me to try to say something else that would rattle him in some manner. I was about to give up, then I had an inspiration, saying loudly, "But if you do happen to survive us taking our town back, one thing I'll make sure will happen; you'll be entering Rome on a Legion mule, just like the last time we met."

This, I was happy to see, angered him, but it also seemed to embarrass him, judging from the way his face colored, though again, he did not reply, and I turned and kicked Latobius to a gallop, just as a way to make it more difficult for one of the barbarians to end me like they had my brother. Nevertheless, my shoulders tensed tightly as my horse carried me away, and frankly, I was surprised that nothing happened. Since I had let my horse run, I kept up the pace to catch up to Germanicus, only slowing as I drew alongside him.

Glancing over, he asked with a tight smile, "Do I even want to know what you had to say to them back there after I left?"

"Just made a promise of my own," I said casually, but he did not seem disposed to press me for details.

Instead, he asked me, "So, do you believe him?"

"Believe who? Dodonis?" I shrugged. "About which part? That the tribes are going to always fight Rome?"

"No," he replied, shaking his head, "not that. About burning the town down if we try to take it."

I snorted and did not hide the scorn I felt, assuring him, "Not very likely, sir. That's just typical barbarian bragging." Seeing he was not convinced, I added, "Besides, it doesn't make much sense, does it? That they'd try to burn us alive, because that means they'd suffer the same fate."

He considered, then after a moment, he replied, "I suppose you're right."

"I am," I promised him.

This time, however, I was wrong.

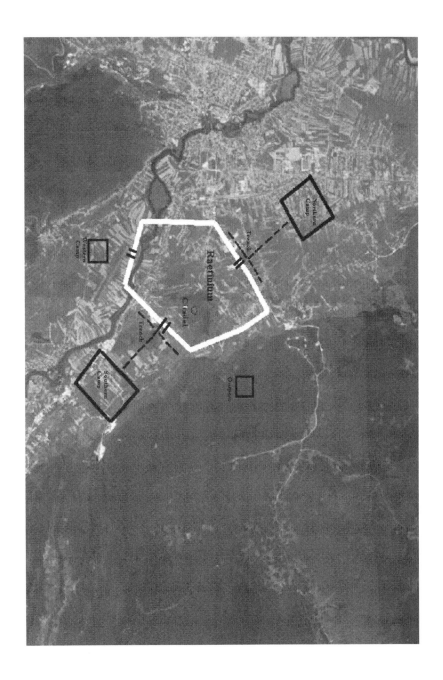

Chapter 6

Now that we had tried the gambit of using Decebalus to no avail, work began in earnest on taking Raetinium by storm. To that end, all but one Cohort was marched out and back across the river, carrying their tools and accompanied by a number of carts, going to the lone hill on the opposite side of the river from our camp, where their first task was to procure timber, which was done by midday. From there, they marched north, then crossed back over the river, stopping at a spot exactly the same distance from the walls as the southern camp, whereupon they set to work to create another camp. Once completed, the slaves attached to the even numbered Cohorts, having packed up the tents and loaded up their mules, left the original camp, while the two odd numbered Cohorts returned to our camp. The First, because of our numbers, had drawn the easy duty of watching from the southern camp and providing security for the artillery wagons, although the Sixth Century was given the task of creating a channel from our latrines to the river. While all this took place, the Tribunes, Bibaculus, and I remained with Germanicus in the southern camp, discussing what we would do the next day, or more accurately, what would continue into the night; specifically, it was agreed that the ten-pounder would be moved up to the hill overlooking the southeast wall under the cover of night, with a Century accompanying them, along with extra oxen to pull the two wagons up the slope. Something else that was decided, not without a fair amount of debate, was to create a line of entrenchments, with a single trench running from the southern camp in the direction of the southern wall of Raetinium, to a spot where it would then extend in both directions and parallel the town's southern rampart. The bone of contention was whether or not to build a series of fortified positions to house the scorpions, which was Germanicus' idea and one that was extremely difficult to overcome.

Finally, in exasperation, I blurted out, "How many men do you think we'll lose trying to create those positions, and how many do you think we'll kill with our scorpions? They have a numerical advantage of more than two men for every one of ours, so unless we can guarantee that it will be worth the cost in blood, I'm begging you to reconsider!"

Germanicus, seated at the head of the table, did not reply at first, choosing to glare at me for a span, before finally waving a hand and saying, "Fine, Pullus. But," his voice sharpened, "we need to use every available resource at our disposal. So I'm charging you to come up with a way to employ the scorpions!"

"Take them to the northern camp, and do what you're planning to do on this side," I said immediately.

His expression softened somewhat, though it was clear he was doubtful, because he turned to Bibaculus and asked the *Immune*, "Didn't you say that those pieces can be moved?" When Bibaculus nodded, he pointed out, "Then they'll just haul the pieces on the southern wall over to the northern side."

"And when they do, that's when we can create those positions you want on this side," I put in.

Germanicus' expression turned to annoyance, and I thought that it was aimed at me; instead, he said ruefully, "I should have thought of that."

"You have more than enough to worry about."

That I was the one blurting this out, while it was sincere, sounded to my ears like the kind of sycophantic flattery that I have observed is one of the real dangers facing men in Germanicus' position. That he seemed pleased at my words was somewhat troubling, and I promised myself that I would resist the temptation to utter anything similar in the future. After a bit more discussion about how we would handle the possible reactions of the defenders to our own actions, we moved on to the most important phase, how we would actually assault Raetinium. Unlike Splonum, the walls of this town were stone throughout, but they were not as thick as Splonum since they had not been built around a wooden core. A consequence was that, since it was not as thick, the rampart was widened with a wooden scaffold, something that we had not known until our scouting the day before.

At the time, it was merely a piece of information that did not impact our tactical considerations all that much, other than the idea that, perhaps, we could ignite the wood somehow, although this would only be as a last, desperate resort. Like my promise to Germanicus, this would prove to be quite significant in what was to come; at the time, it was simply a thought. We briefly discussed undermining the wall, but quickly discarded it, mainly because there was no one among us, of any rank, who possessed the highly specific skills that are required, particularly when it would be so close to a river. Ladders were considered, but in order to employ them, we would have to create enough of a subterfuge that did not give the Maezaei time to move their artillery to our point of attack, particularly those scorpions. Concerning the artillery, one thing that Bibaculus continued to insist was that, while the barbarians might be able to use those pieces, their lack of experience would be a crucial factor.

"Those scorpions in particular," he assured Germanicus, "are finicky bastards, and it's easy for an inexperienced man to work the crank too much and overtighten the torsion ropes."

"What happens then?" Germanicus had asked him, and I listened closely because I wanted to know as well.

"Oh, it'll work for two, maybe three bolts, but it'll start losing velocity, which means the man working the crank will think cranking it even tighter is going to fix the problem. Then," he snapped his fingers to demonstrate, "that rope snaps just like that. And sometimes," his grin was, if not malicious, then at least was unmerciful, "it'll kill the stupid bastard."

"I'm sure they'll have spare ropes," Germanicus pointed out, but I could tell he was feeling better, and Bibaculus' snort of derision at this idea only helped his confidence.

"Oh," the *Immune* agreed, "they'll have at least two spare sets per piece, for both the scorpions and the *ballista*. But there's a reason we give men like me *Immunes* status. Not just anyone can replace those ropes; there's a trick to it that I'm sure those *cunni* in there don't have any idea about." This made sense, not just to Germanicus but to me. And, I do not know whether or not what Bibaculus said next is true, but it sounded credible then. "There's a reason for that, though, and it's for this very kind of situation. It's just like our javelins," with every word, he seemed to become more enthused, and it served to remind me that there were men for whom such matters are more than just of passing interest, "that were part of the Marian Reforms. You know how the shafts are cold forged and not tempered, so they'll bend? This is the same idea. We make it hard for our enemies to turn our own weapons against us."

Again, I do not know if this is actually the case, but it does make sense. Regardless of Bibaculus' assurances, we had to accept that, should we try an assault on the walls using ladders, we would lose men to artillery; the question was how many. If Bibaculus was correct, our losses would be acceptable, but this was a risk, which prompted more discussion.

"What about a two-pronged attack," Silius suggested, "but with rams? One at the northern gate, one at the southern?"

My initial response was to dismiss it, but Germanicus was not as quick to do so, and I saw he was at least seriously considering it.

"With rams?"

"Yes," Silius replied, "we should attack from two directions, but at a spot where they're the farthest apart."

I decided to wait, watching Germanicus as he considered this, but my relief at seeing him shake his head was short-lived, because instead of putting a stop to it, he said, "The problem with the northern gate is that their artillery is along the entire length of the eastern wall." Silius looked somewhat confused, and the Legate explained, "That means they wouldn't have to go very far to move the pieces at the northeastern corner straight down the rampart towards the northern gate. And given how far away the camp is, they'll have plenty of warning that this is our tactic, and while I agree with Bibaculus that their crews aren't likely to move as quickly as we Romans, I think they'll move quickly enough." Turning to the *Immune*, Germanicus asked, "Bibaculus, could we build a ram that's mobile but strong enough to withstand a beating from *ballistae* of the size they have on the walls?"

"No, sir," Bibaculus replied without hesitation. "Oh," he allowed, "we could build something sturdy enough that it would take a fair bit of punishment, but over a span of four hundred paces, we would have to create something so large that it wouldn't be able to be moved quickly enough as they pound us. And that," he finished, "would be with one *ballista*. If they got two of the three they have on the eastern wall, over to the northern rampart in time?"

He did not finish verbally; the shake of his head left no doubt. I was about to heave a sigh of relief that this idea seemed to be discarded, but then Germanicus mused aloud, "Still..." Falling silent, he stared down at the vellum on which the layout of the town was drawn, and I felt my stomach tighten as I realized he had not given up yet. Suddenly, his eyes narrowed, and he leapt to his feet to lean over and point, "What about here?"

I looked down at the spot, and as soon as I saw it, I felt better, but when nobody else spoke up, I offered, "The only problem with the western gate is how far we'd have to push the ram, and from either camp, we'd have to cross the river with it." Shaking my head, I dismissed this alternative, but I did feel badly about destroying Silius' suggestion, so I tried to offer some encouragement, saying, "I agree that if we had a camp over there, and we came up with a ruse to draw the defenders away, that gate would be the best choice."

In this, I was being sincere. When Raetinium had expanded, they had pushed the walls out far enough they actually crossed the river, while there was about three hundred paces of space between the western bank and the new wall. During our scouting of the town from the eastern hill, we had paid some attention to the far end of the town, but from our vantage point, not much was visible, although it appeared that the new strip of land on the western side had been taken over by some sort of buildings dealing with commerce. Without getting closer, the guess I ventured when Germanicus asked me was that I believed it was probably the businesses that are considered unpleasant for other townspeople, whether they be malodorous, like cloth makers and the urine they use, or unsightly, like a large meat rendering business, or were involved in some enterprise that required a copious supply of water. Whatever it was, the one thing I felt certain about was that there were not pure residences on that side of the river, aside perhaps from the proprietors living above their business.

My final remark had barely left my mouth when Germanicus said excitedly, "That's it! You're right, Pullus!" Turning to Silius, he explained, "Your plan is good, Silius, but it needs one modification." Pointing at another spot, he announced, "We're going to build a third camp here, which will make sense to the Maezaei, especially since we'll have a position on the eastern hill by the end of today. This is something they will expect us to do, to have a presence on all four sides." Glancing up, presumably to see how we were absorbing his words, I noticed he looked from one face to the next...but stopped before he got to me, and continued, "And we're going to build rams, three of them. But," he again stopped, except this time, I felt certain it was to build the tension, "two of them are going to be decoys. Very, very heavily built decoys," it was when he flashed his grin, as he did now, that his youth was still apparent, "but decoys nonetheless, because it will be the third ram that is going to get us into Raetinium."

He continued explaining, and I had to admit that, once he was through, while I was not thoroughly convinced, neither could I argue that Germanicus' plan did not have merit. Risky, yes, but given the realities of our situation, the more I thought about it, the harder it was for me to continue thinking that this was not the best plan. Essentially, we would be sending two rams out as bait, hoping that the enemy took it, and focused their entire effort on stopping them. Meanwhile, we would be moving a third ram, this one with minimal protection, and therefore more mobile, to the western gate, and it was the composition of this gate that would actually aid our cause. Since this gate was a new one, and the road west that led through the mountains to the coast was still not a well-developed or traveled route, it was not as high or as wide as the other two gates for the simple reason it was not used as heavily as the originals. Now all that remained was doing the work to make all this happen.

Germanicus' first challenge came when the men of the ranks learned that the camp they would be constructing on the western bank of the river was not going to be used by them, but the cavalry.

"They can fucking dig just like the rest of us!"

This, and other comments of a similar nature, rang out from the rear ranks of the three Cohorts assembled on the forum, and I did wonder if Frugi, who had been appointed the camp commander of the northern camp, was hearing the same kinds of things. More importantly, I worried that young Agrippa, the Secundus Pilus Prior, would be unwilling to do what I did, turning and striding through the ranks, lashing out with my *vitus*, snarling at men to keep their mouths shut and obey orders. The men of the First were the most incensed, because it was their turn to do some of the dirty work that is part and parcel of our lot, but as I reminded them, usually with an accompanying swipe, they had been standing watch when the northern camp was constructed. Once matters settled down, we marched out of the gate, taking the Third with us, mainly because Germanicus did not want to leave Scipio behind unsupervised, since the Legate had insisted on going with us, and even leaving Silius in command might not have been enough to stop the arrogant bastard from doing something stupid. Using what had become our normal fording spot, we waded across, then marched the short distance north, while Gaesorix and half the cavalry accompanied us, arraying themselves across the road leading to the town, where they were allowed to dismount, but stood ready to intercept any Maezaei sortie. Working without interruption, the camp was created rather speedily, mostly because it was not a large camp, having to fit a bit less than two *alae* of cavalry, and we left it to Gaesorix and his men to configure it to their needs. The site we selected placed it so that the western road aligned with the Porta Praetoria and Porta Decumana, and we took advantage of the presence of a small stream that came down from the large hill as the water supply, which was used by the men in the northern camp as well, since the river beyond the town was fouled, although in their case, they had to make daily trips across the big river to replenish their supply.

342

Using the construction of the camp as a plausible reason, I sent Veratius' Century the four hundred paces to the hill to chop down the trees that, as far as the Maezaei were concerned, would be used to construct two towers, which were to be erected at the northeastern and southeastern corners of this new camp. The fact that Blasio's men were felling enough trees to make more than just these two towers was a gamble, but it was a small one in the estimation of Germanicus, and I agreed, not that it mattered. One thing I had observed over the course of my time with Germanicus was that he sought my counsel less and less, almost with every passing day. However, I was not upset about this, though I am honest enough with myself to acknowledge that this had more to do with the fact that he was not seeking the opinion and advice of anyone else among the officers instead of me. Petty, perhaps, but I would like to think that it was also at least partially due to the idea that he did not fall under the influence of Scipio, or more likely because of his rank, Tribune Appuleius. In every other way, however, Germanicus remained unchanged as far as his treatment of me, which meant that I stood next to him, me afoot and him mounted, watching as men handed up wicker baskets full of dirt to their comrades, who dumped the spoil onto the steadily growing pile of dirt that would become the wall of the camp, and we chatted as amiably as we always did. Naturally, while the tone was pleasant, the subject was serious, as we discussed all the things that still needed to be done to accomplish what he was determined to do, which he actually revealed to me while we were on the western side of the river.

"Pullus," he said quietly, and I realized that he had deliberately waited until nobody was within earshot before he broached the subject, "I've made a decision, and I want you to know what it is so there's no surprises or doubt."

This understandably sharpened my attention on him, but since I did not know exactly what I was expected to say in response, I simply waited for what he had to tell me.

"We're not waiting," he informed me. "I intend to take this city with what we have, now." Pausing, he glanced down at me, and I read in his expression that he was feeling me out, waiting to see what my reaction would be; it was not good, I must confess.

I did manage to bite back the first thing that almost came out of my mouth, which would be to raise the possibility that he had been rendered mad by all the pressure he was under.

Instead, what came out was more measured, and I chose my words carefully, "Sir, I understand how you feel, and why you'd think that this is the best approach. But," I held up a finger as I began counting off the reasons it was such a bad idea, "not only are we substantially outnumbered, those bastards inside those walls have artillery. And," I hurried to get this out to quell the objection I knew was coming, "while I agree with Bibaculus that they're not going to be nearly as effective in the use of it, we're still going to have a fair number of scorpion bolts coming our way, not to mention those five-pound rocks." I held up another finger. "Another thing to remember is that our plan, as it's been conceived right now, means we're going to spread our forces out, into three different groups, which spreads out what power we can bring to bear even more." Shaking my head, I did not raise my voice, but I tried to sound firm as I admonished, "Sir, I'm sorry, but we're going to need more men."

I think it was the manner in which Germanicus glanced around, still making sure that nobody was listening, that alerted me somewhat, so I was not completely taken by surprise when he said, even more quietly, "Pullus, we're not going to be getting any more men." He did have the grace to look somewhat guilty as he explained, "I've already heard from Tiberius. A rider came in late last night bringing me his answer, and he said he can't spare anything, especially men."

He was lying; I knew it with utmost certainty, because there was no way I would not have heard about a strange rider approaching the camp in the darkness, but I tried very hard to keep the knowledge that he was doing so from showing in my expression.

"That," my voice sounded strange to my ears, I suppose because I was trying so hard to make it devoid of any emotion, "is certainly a shame to hear." For an instant, I debated about saying anything more, but I needed to do something for the men, make some sort of resistance, and this prompted me to ask, "Did he give you any particular reason why?"

Germanicus' own face remained unchanged, still looking uncomfortable, but he answered readily enough, sighing as he said, "Not in so many words, Pullus, other than to say that his campaign isn't going particularly well. Both Silanus' and Severus' armies have suffered setbacks, that much he did say, although," he held up a hand to preempt my next obvious question, "he didn't give any details beyond that."

If I am being completely honest, I have to admit I had heard bits and pieces from the various couriers, so I knew this was likely the truth, as far as the difficulties the main armies were encountering; what I doubted was the timing of this piece of information.

Seeing I was not disposed to say anything else, Germanicus continued, "Which is why we're going to have to take Raetinium with what we have and as quickly as possible. Because," once more, he paused, "we need to finish this so that we can join the main effort."

"As far as these men are concerned," this I could not keep behind my teeth, indicating them with my *vitus* in a sweep of my arm, "*this* is the main effort, sir. Remember," I reminded him, "none of these men are your age anymore. Or even mine. They want to succeed, certainly, but more than that, they just want to survive to go back to their homes."

I saw Germanicus did not like this one bit, and he stared down at me, his lips pressed tightly together, and he replied coldly, "You don't have to remind me of that, Pullus. But," he mimicked my gesture from a moment before, "these men still owe a duty to Rome, and that duty isn't finished yet."

For the first time since we had been together, now well more than a year, I felt the tightening in my gut that signaled the arousal of my anger towards my Legate, but more than being irritated, I was disappointed that, despite seeming unlike the others of his class, Germanicus now appeared to be no different, viewing men of my social rank as little more than tools to be used to advance their own fortunes. My young Legate, it seemed to me in that particular moment, was not so different from the Scipios and Appuleiuses after all, and it took quite an effort of will for me to remain calm.

I stiffened to *intente* and rendered a salute, keeping my voice flat as I asked, "If that's all, sir, I'd like permission to go check on the progress of the camp."

Germanicus, suddenly looking as if he was regretful, nevertheless returned my salute, though he only nodded his permission, and I turned about, stalking away in a direction where he could not see my face.

Our personal trials notwithstanding, the camp was built without incident, though by the time we were through, the western wall of Raetinium was crowded with onlookers who had come to see for themselves what we were doing. Using the mules we had brought from our camp, the Sixth Century dragged the felled trees, now stripped down to just their trunks, although the bark was still on, down from the hill, and the two towers were constructed, leaving behind well more than a dozen large trimmed trees behind, where they were placed as close to the eastern wall of the camp as possible, which acted as a shield that obstructed the view of any nosy Maezaei. Once our job was completed, we marched back to our own camp, retracing our steps and thereby giving the town a wide berth. Not that the Maezaei could not see exactly what we were doing, since the whole valley floor was naturally flat, and like the area around Splonum, had been cleared for cultivation. And, like with Splonum, the Maezaei had made no attempt to grow any crops, which, when one thought about it, made sense. Why waste the time and effort to grow food when you know that it will either be destroyed, or even worse, consumed by your enemies? On the subject of supplies, this was one area in which we did not suffer from shortage, but that was only because we raided the granaries of Splonum, taking the substantial reserve they had built up, and of which I felt certain was due to the management of Dodonis. He was clearly a capable man, and I did recall forming that impression the first time we met, and nothing I had seen since dispelled it.

The only excitement came in the form of a sortie by the Maezaei, when a force of some five hundred warriors attempted to leave the town, climb the eastern hill, and either capture or destroy our ten-pounder, which they had finally spotted. Thanks to young Agrippa, although he credited Frugi, since there was no eastern gate out of the town, the Maezaei had chosen to leave by the northern one, and when they did, the Secundus Pilus Prior, whose Cohort had the duty, did not hesitate, ordering his men to march out from their camp immediately. That they moved so quickly meant that the barbarian attempt to destroy our valuable artillery piece was repelled without a single javelin being thrown, because whoever was commanding this contingent of warriors instantly understood that, while they might be able to climb the eastern hill, then deal with our *ballista* and the Century guarding it, they would have to descend the slope after that, where a Cohort of Romans would be waiting for them. Their timing, or lack thereof, did not help, because this happened immediately after the First and Third crossed the river, and we were marching back to our camp. It was within the realm of possibility that they could have climbed the slope, then instead of retracing their steps and reenter through the northern gate, they could have simply changed their angle of march, and descend on the southern side of the town. Fortunately for the Maezaei, and for us, albeit for different reasons, their commander quickly turned his men about, even before they reached the northeast corner, reentering the town. Otherwise, the men who had been left behind had been equally busy, sent by Bibaculus to perform an identical task to Veratius' Century, except they were farther along when we marched through the Porta Principalis Sinistra. Turning over my Century to Rufius, who was running the First Century in everything but name and doing a magnificent job of it, I sought out the *Immune*, ostensibly to get a progress report, but also to get a sense of his true feelings for what we were doing. I was not contemplating mutiny, exactly, though I did harbor the hope that, if I could get enough of the officers to prevail on Germanicus to reconsider his current plan, it would be in the best interests of all of us, except, perhaps, Germanicus himself. I found Bibaculus in the forum, where the men were working on the ram. Unlike me, he was in a good mood, and he explained why by pointing to the pile of logs.

"They found some really green wood, full of sap," he told me, smiling as he did so.

"Obviously that's a good thing," I observed, then said honestly, "but I have no idea why."

"Because," he explained, "we're not using these for artillery, which means the wood has to be seasoned properly. Too much moisture in the wood makes for a piss-poor *ballista*." Hooting at his depiction, once he saw I was not sharing in his mirth, he hurried on, "Yes, well, the thing is, we want these rams to be as soft and pliable as we can make them, because that way, they'll absorb the punishment better."

"Does that change your opinion about whether or not they'll stand up to the punishment they're likely to get?"

He considered the question for a moment, then somewhat to my disappointment, instead of saying no, he shrugged and said, "It's possible." The *Immune* must have seen something in my expression, because he hurriedly added, "I know what I said before, but I hadn't seen the wood yet. Now," he pointed again to the pile of finished lumber, and I admit I could smell it from where we stood, the fragrant scent of evergreen quite strong, "I'm not saying it's impossible, Primus Pilus, but I have to say that our chances are a lot better with this kind of lumber. That," his tone turned cautious, "is a good thing, isn't it?"

"Yes," I lied, "it's a good thing." I thought of something else, and asked him, "But doesn't that mean these rams will be even heavier?"

"It does," he agreed, "but it also means that the actual ram is going to be carrying more weight, which will make each blow more damaging." I felt him glancing up at me, I supposed to see if I understood his point, but while I did, I remained silent, which caused him to go ahead and explain, "So, while we're going to take more punishment on our approach, once we're against the wall, our boys won't be under there as long, and you know as well as I do that that's when things get really nasty."

"I do," I agreed, suppressing a shudder at the thought of the vats of boiling oil, or pitch, being dumped down onto the ram.

Although I had never experienced it myself, one of the more vivid memories from my Avus' account was how his first Optio, Aulus Vinicius, the man whose name is associated with the manner in which I, and a fair number of other men, grip my *gladius*, was burned to death in Titus Pullus' first campaign. It was true that Vinicius had been scaling a ladder, but I do not think that any man who suffers what is a horrible death by any standard would really care about the distinction; whether it was while battering down a gate or climbing a wall, burning to death would not alter the level of pain they felt. This ram did not yet have the covering, which actually looks like a small roof, peaked in the same manner except pitched much more steeply in order to make it difficult for missiles to strike it solidly, but the frame was finished. It was the size of a small wagon, while the timbers making up the rectangular frame were more than a foot wide on all four sides, with the vertical supports that would hold up the roof that was a bit wider than the ram, thereby providing protection to the men who would be tasked with moving the ram into position. Despite the fact that I did not have much experience with devices like these; honestly, there were only two or three barbarian towns whose walls and defenses were such that a ram was needed, and I had never been involved in assaulting any of them, I still felt certain that this machine was larger than normal. I felt the first glimmer of, if not optimism, then by the idea that perhaps this could perform its main purpose, which as far as I was concerned, was to keep the poor bastards who would be the ones to push this towards the walls alive.

As if he was reading my mind, Bibaculus assured me, "And I'm extending the edges of the cover out two more feet than normal, so whoever's pushing it will have more cover."

"Will the other one be the same?"

"Exactly," he confirmed, "I made a sketch and included the dimensions. I sent a courier with it as soon as I was done."

"What about the other one? The real one?" I asked him.

349

"It's going to be half this size," Bibaculus replied quickly, but then an uneasy look crossed his weathered face, alerting me there was something I would probably not like. "But," he confirmed my suspicion, "the Legate decided that it's not going be roofed. It's going to just be a frame, the ram, and wheels."

He said something else, but I did not hear, because I was already walking quickly to the *praetorium*.

"That's my decision, Primus Pilus, and it's final."

I had found Germanicus in his private quarters, which is configured in the same manner as a Centurion's tent, with a leather partition dividing the office from the private quarters. The one difference between my quarters and those of the Legate's was simply a matter of scale, and Germanicus was behind his desk, writing something on vellum, meaning that it was of some importance. He had bid me entry readily enough, but now I had the feeling he was regretting his decision, judging by the manner in which he regarded me, arms crossed, after I had bluntly asked him to reconsider. Which, I instantly realized, was a tactical error on my part, though it was too late to go back now, and I also sensed that arguing further would only make matters worse.

Consequently, I said instead, "Then, I have a request, sir."

"Which is?" he asked cautiously.

"That I be allowed to lead the assault on the western gate."

"Actually, Pullus," he smiled, "I'll be leading that effort." Silent for a moment, he seemed to be considering something, and I learned what it was when he offered, "But I would be honored if you'd be by my side again." This surprised me enough that I did not reply immediately, causing Germanicus to assume an intense expression, as he continued earnestly, "Pullus, I know we've had our...differences over the last couple of days. But, I assure you, I still value your counsel, but even more than that, there's no man I'd rather have at my side during something like this is likely to be." If only he had not flashed that damn boyish grin as he added, "Besides, you're still a bigger target than me."

Despite myself, I laughed, and once more I was reminded that I was as susceptible to Germanicus' charm and ability to appeal to my own vanity as any man. By the time I left his office, I was back to being an admirer of the young nobleman, although I was also somewhat confused as to how it had all happened.

The operation to emplace the ten-pounder was accomplished without any complications; the one slight disappointment was that, even with the height advantage and the longer range, we could not quite reach the stone *praetorium*. Speaking of that building, another frustration on our part was that, since we did not know the whereabouts of the Romans who had been living there, we could only guess about the layout of the building. Under normal circumstances, these structures are identical, since we Romans appreciate regularity in all things, but just from its external appearance, we could see that there had been alterations to the design. That some of these seemed to be done in order to make it fit on the side of a hill, so that there was something like a stone porch that supported the building as it jutted from the hillside, this much was obvious. Equally visible was that there had been additions made to the building, but done in a radically different style, which I took as a sign that Dodonis had ordered some of his skilled workers to improve the structure from a defensive standpoint, which included the addition of a stone parapet lining the roof. The only thing that we felt certain about was that the Maezaei clearly planned for this building to play a role in what was to come. The rest of the hill was covered with buildings intended to support the local government, including a *quaestorium*, where stockpiles of supplies, and more importantly from our perspective, armor and weapons that were supposed to be used by the men who formed the levy of Roman citizens who were the last line of defense for the inhabitants, were located. Since those supposed defenders had fled, which was all we knew at the time, now those mail shirts, *gladii*, shields, and siege spears would be used to try and repel our attempt to take the town. The only real question was the quantity; our guess was that it was around five hundred, given the population of the town, which was around five thousand. What had been done to the *praetorium* to make it more defensible was certainly a concern, but it was far from the only one, and over the course of the next days, as final preparations were made, we spent a significant amount of time standing atop the eastern hill, carefully studying every foot of the outer wall first, then moving on to other likely spots where we could expect resistance. It was during this period we spotted something that we knew was significant, the presence of what we could tell were heavily loaded wagons, placed at a number of intersections. No animals were hitched to them, but the Maezaei had made no attempt to disguise the fact that all of the wagons we could see were loaded down with rocks.

"Why rocks?" Germanicus asked, when we made the discovery.

"My guess," I told him, "is to make them extremely heavy." This prompted a snort of amusement on the part of Germanicus, presumably because of my statement of the obvious, which I ignored as I thought about it more, and I added, "I think their plan is to use these to block our progress as they fall back to the *praetorium*."

"That," he allowed, "makes sense."

And it still does, but while I was partially correct, this was only part of the puzzle, which we would not learn until a few nights later.

Using the surplus ten-pound stones we still had after Splonum, the men crewing the large *ballista* managed to destroy two pieces on the eastern wall before the defenders removed the other two, one *ballista* and one scorpion, which, predictably, they placed on the northern wall. Germanicus, still intent on employing the scorpions somehow, was extremely frustrated at this delay, and it fell to Bibaculus, who had become not only our artillery expert, but our *Praefectus Fabrorum* as well, despite never receiving formal training, to come up with a solution. His proposal was that, but not one that pleased Germanicus in the slightest.

"There is a way we can extend that trench in each direction," Bibaculus informed us at our evening briefing, after, it should be noted, we had lost three men from a *ballista* stone when they were just beginning the digging of the stretch that would run parallel, "but you won't like it."

"If it gets those trenches finished, why wouldn't I like it?" Germanicus asked peevishly. "So, what is it you're proposing, Bibaculus?"

"We work from the bottom up," the *Immune* answered, but like Germanicus, I was mystified about what this meant until he explained further. "Our trench is twelve feet wide, which means four men can work side by side. We put them down in the trench, and they start digging into the wall at the end, four in each direction, but from the bottom. The dirt above where they're shoveling will collapse down into the space, which they shovel out. Then the men who are charged with piling the spoil will do so, but by using a ladder inside the trench, and dumping it out on the wall side."

There was a silence as Germanicus and the rest of us absorbed this, then he burst out in dismay, "But that will take forever! Only four men working at a time? There has to be a better way!"

"I told you, you wouldn't like it," Bibaculus replied, but in a murmur that only I could hear, his tone such that I had to duck my head to hide my smile. More loudly, he answered Germanicus, and while he was not defiant, he was firm in defending his idea, "Legate, if anyone has a better suggestion, I'm more than happy to hear it. This may not be the best way, but it's the only way that I can come up with."

I, too, had an objection, but mine was based in a different consideration, and I asked him, "Won't that be dangerous to the men who are doing the digging? They could dig deep enough before the dirt above them collapses that they'd be buried alive."

"That's a risk," Bibaculus admitted, but he clearly had thought about this, because he went on without hesitation, "which is why we'd have a man behind each of them, holding a rope that's tied around the waists of the men doing the digging. If it does collapse, they'll be pulled out, quicker than Pan."

Although this was true, speaking for myself, I was not quite so sanguine that the poor bastards who drew the short stick to do the digging would be happy to know that, in the almost inevitable event of a collapse, their entombment would not last long. I could easily imagine, knowing the tensions within a typical Century, that there would be men who might take this opportunity to even an old score or send some sort of warning to a comrade by being a bit leisurely in hauling them out of danger. However, I had to acknowledge to myself that it was likely my initial reaction stemmed from my own fear of enduring such a fate myself; like my Avus, I have a huge fear of being in enclosed spaces, something that never seemed to bother my father. I suppose it has to do with our respective sizes.

After his outburst, Germanicus seemed to settle down and give Bibaculus' proposal serious consideration, and I took it as his tacit acceptance when he grumbled, "And how long will this take?"

"At least a week," Bibaculus answered unflinchingly, no doubt prepared for the gasp of dismay from our Legate, who accompanied this with pounding his thigh, while Bibaculus continued with the specifics, "and that's if we work through the watches." I know he was trying to be helpful when he pointed out, "The Cohort that has the night watch can actually do both, since you're only going to be using two sections of men for both directions."

"And even doing that, it will take a week," Germanicus muttered.

This prompted me to point out, "Sir, this can be avoided if you abandon the idea that we have to have the scorpions in place for the assault."

This earned me a glare from Germanicus, but I took some heart from the way the other officers were looking at him expectantly, giving me the strong impression they were silently willing him to concede the point.

Stubbornly, however, he shook his head and insisted, "No, we're going to need that support when we make our assault."

"Sir," I decided on another approach, using the one bit of information that I thought might have the greatest impact, "I'd just like to remind you of something."

"Oh?" He eyed me warily. "What's that?"

"In three days, it will be a month since we took Splonum's citadel," I said, "and I thought we'd decided to use the same approach we did there."

Instantly, I saw I had aimed true, as Germanicus' expression changed with the realization that I was right; if we were going to take advantage of a moonless night, and he prevailed in this insistence on the scorpions, we were talking about waiting another month.

Hissing in frustration, he did turn to Bibaculus and ask, "How far do you think we can get in three days?"

Thinking for an instant, Bibaculus answered cautiously, "Probably more than a hundred paces in each direction, maybe between a hundred fifty and a hundred seventy-five, but," he shook his head firmly, "that's the absolute farthest we could expect. And that," he warned, "is only if we work through the watches."

Clearly disappointed, Germanicus nevertheless did his best to put a positive face on matters, saying, "That's better than nothing, I suppose. It will give us at least partial coverage of both walls, and if we can make them move their own pieces farther away from the gates, that only helps the men who are working as decoys as it is."

This was true, certainly; hopefully, the men who would be assigned this task would appreciate this.

Germanicus' decision to perform the assault on another moonless night was based in many factors, I believe, but one of them that encouraged him was due to something the Maezaei were doing, yet like so many things in warfare, it was a *gladius* that cut both ways. Even if there was cloud cover on the night there was no moon, we would not be as literally in the dark as when I led our foray against the citadel at Splonum, because Dodonis clearly expected us to do something under the cover of night. The way we knew this was by the presence of what, judging by the amount of light they gave off, were lamps, placed at regular intervals along the walls on every side, ready to ignite large bundles of flammable material that would be launched from the wall. Even shielded, once it became dark, they were impossible to hide, the reflection of the light helping delineate the outline of the parapet, which would be crucial on the night of the assault. Bibaculus' plan for extending the parallel trenches worked, not without several collapses, where men were yanked from the crushing weight of several hundred pounds of dirt, and we suffered some injuries as a result that were serious enough to confine men to the sick and injured list, though most of them were bruised but unharmed. During this period, we refined the plan, deciding on a number of changes, including the decision to withhold trying to emplace the scorpions the day of the assault. Instead, they would be carried down the trench from both camps after it was dark, then placed on the spoil, ready to send their bolts at targets that would hopefully present themselves when the enemy started lighting the hurdles we knew they would be flinging out as far as they could to aid their own artillery. Also, it was actually Frugi who pointed out something that, quite frankly, was an embarrassing oversight on the part of all of us who were supposedly more experienced, including me.

"If you create the parallel trenches, when it's time for the rams, how are they going to get across?"

The result of this was that a change was made in how we would align the rams, where they would be pushed outside of their camps and moved to a point where they would clear the end of the parallel trench, using a stake that we placed at a point where the ram could be pushed in a straight line, except once again at an angle. This would be awkward, because the men pushing the ram would have been forced to muscle these huge beasts to hit their assigned gate straight on, once they were on the other side of the trench. For a matter of a watch, there was pandemonium in the *praetorium* as it appeared that all of our plans were for naught, but once more, it fell to Bibaculus to come up with a solution.

"We're going to have to use the entire front assembly of two wagons," he told us, "but we're going to have reinforce it somehow because the way the ram is balanced, there's a lot more weight bearing down on the front than one of even the heaviest wagons. Which," Bibaculus turned and addressed Germanicus, speaking apologetically, "will have to come from your personal wagons, sir. They're the heaviest of all the baggage wagons as it is, so they're the only ones with a chance of bearing up under the weight, even with an extra crosspiece."

Germanicus colored slightly at this reminder that, despite his trying to live rough, like all noblemen, even Tiberius, he had arrived with pieces of furniture, rugs, and of course the obligatory bust of Augustus that adorned his private office, but he gave a curt nod and said only, "Of course. Get started immediately." Bibaculus saluted and did as he was bid, but before he got more than a couple steps, Germanicus called to him. "Bibaculus, will this delay the assault?" he asked anxiously.

To the relief of almost everyone in the room, to one degree or another, Bibaculus assured him it would not; from where I sat, only Scipio looked unhappy.

An unintended benefit of the problem posed by the slower excavation meant that there would be no change in what was becoming routine, because Germanicus decided to keep the men working into the night. When it was quiet, once the inhabitants inside Raetinium were settled down for the night, leaving only the men standing watch, we were confident that they could hear the sounds of our own men, still digging away. Finally, the night before the assault, we detailed men to watch the walls carefully, starting shortly before sundown, their task to locate precisely the position of the lamps on each side. Of particular importance was their relation to the location of the gates on each of the three sides, because we would be using these beacons to guide our entire effort, both the two feints on the northern and southern wall, along with the real one, that the First Cohort would be making, led by Germanicus. In short, we did absolutely everything we could think of that would give us the edge we would need to overcome our disparity in numbers. By midday before the moonless night, everything was essentially done and ready, including the modifications to the two decoy rams, and there was nothing left to do but wait. When I think back on this interval, I cannot help but wonder if we had still been trying to think of every possible action, might we have stumbled across the one outcome that Dodonis

357

actually had planned. I would like to think that this was not the case, but it has haunted me for years now, just another event in what has become a long list where I question myself about what I could have done to prevent it, and inevitably, comparing myself to my Avus and coming up short yet again.

We would not be using the beacons provided by the lamps, as faint as they were, just for the purpose of guiding the men pushing each ram. In a last-moment decision, rather than depart the southern camp at dusk to move to the newest one, still occupied by whatever portion of Gaesorix and the cavalry that was not out patrolling, Germanicus decided we would wait until it was fully dark. This decision would not have been possible without the knowledge provided by the foresight of Tribune Silius, who had been the man who came up with the idea of mapping out the locations of each lamp, which we used in the same manner as the stars above to navigate our way, using them as reference points in relation to the walls. I made all of the officers of the Cohort, including the Optios, look at the marks that had been inscribed onto the map of the town denoting the position of each lamp and memorize it, stressing that they try to visualize how it would look when we were actually moving. Although it was not a great distance, barely more than a mile and a half taking what was now a well-worn path from the southern camp and the western, we did have to ford the river again, which was now at least somewhat firm underfoot from all the traffic, so Germanicus allotted two parts of a watch for the movement of the Cohort. This, or so we hoped, would give us the time we would need to move as quietly as possible, although I was worried less about the noise than the idea that, even in the dark, the movement of more than eight hundred men would attract attention of one of the sentries on the wall. Working in our favor was the fact that, as undisciplined as barbarians are about matters such as sentry duty, I was fairly confident that, just like most such tribes, the Maezaei considered standing watch beneath the higher status warriors. What this meant in a practical sense was their practice of putting their most inexperienced and lowest ranking men on what is, no matter who one marches for, almost always an excruciatingly boring time, staring out into the darkness, waiting for something that is unlikely to happen, and does not ninety-nine nights out of one hundred. And, during their period, it is equally inevitable that, even if it was shielded, the beardless youth standing watch would first glance, then finally give in to gazing into the flames. It is something I have seen more times than I can count, both when involved in an operation at night like this one and the time by the lake when the moon disappeared; there is something about fire that draws men's attention, in much the same way one can see moths dancing about the flames, despite the fact that it spells their destruction when they invariably get too close. I suppose it is inescapably reminiscent of other fires, like the ones that are in barbarian homes, usually in the middle of their dwelling, and evokes memories of long winter nights filled with tales told by an elder, or the smell of roasting meat for an upcoming feast. This is why it is a natural tendency for men to gaze into the flames, but is also why truly professional fighting men, like we Romans of the Legions, know not to do so, because if and when something does happen beyond their post, at night, they are as blind as Homer when they tear their attention away from the comforting fire. Was it an absolute certainty this was the case? No, which was why I did not bring it up to Germanicus; a quiet reminder to my Centurions to offer this gentle reassurance to our men was sufficient.

Nevertheless, we took the usual precautions for moving at night, but we restricted the men to making their preparations inside their tents and only summoned them, without the use of the *cornu*, once it was dark, using another practice that serves to our advantage. I know that this is not the main reason behind our practice, but the fact that our camps, both permanent and temporary like this one, are identical in layout, means that even a four-month *tiro* can find his way to his proper place, no matter how dark it is, as it was this night. There was partial cloud cover, but between the few stars that were showing and the fact that we had been keeping the camp darkened, without lighting the normal number of torches, since our enemy could look down into our camp from their higher vantage point on their walls, the men were accustomed to it so that we had no delays in forming up. Our inspection was perfunctory, and frankly, a bit strange, since it consisted mostly of walking up to a ranker, then fumbling around on his body to check by feel that his gear was properly tied down or muffled with a wrapping. We did not whisper, but neither did I, or any of the Centurions, bellow at the top of our lungs, since we knew that, for reasons I do not know, sounds carry much farther at night than they do in the day. The one problem I encountered that, had it been lighter and the men had the ability to see it, was in trying to locate where Germanicus was standing in front of the *praetorium*, and I am sure it would have given the moment quite a bit of levity seeing me stumbling around, both arms out and blindly groping for my Legate. Who, I will say, gave quite an undignified yelp of surprise when I literally fumbled into him, and because of my height, my hands struck his helmet.

"By the gods, Pullus!" he gasped, once he determined that I was not a *numen* from the shades coming to claim him. "Did you have to do that?"

"Look at the bright side, sir," I said cheerfully. "I just proved I can move about in the dark pretty well for a big man."

"Yes, you can," he grumbled, "but how about you save that for those bastards inside the town?"

"Yes, sir." I do not know if he saw me grinning, mostly at his use of the profanity, because to my ears it sounded like I am sure I did when I was a boy, trying out my first use of "*cunnus*" in front of my friends. "I just wanted to let you know that the Cohort is ready to move."

"Then," his voice instantly changed, clearly communicating the tension of the moment, "let's get started."

Calling the command loudly enough for my Century and probably the Second to hear, we began the march, and my ears told me that, while there was a bit of stumbling, for the most part, our departure was about as smooth as could be expected. The men were carrying only their javelins and shields, though they still had their leather covers on, both to muffle the sound when there was the inevitable banging against each other, but to cover the metal boss, which was the largest reflective material outside of the men's helmets, which were similarly wrapped. Most men used a spare neckerchief, but I had noticed something during my brief inspection, that a large number of men had chosen to use something else. Normally, this would have not meant much, but once I determined that those men who were using something other than a neckerchief were all using the exact same thing, I had to smother a grin as I thought, You thieving bastards. What I felt certain would turn out to be one man in every section was using on their helmets was an empty sack, of the type that carried our grain, or under other circumstances, loot of the portable variety. This was no accident and was just a sign of rankers planning ahead, looking forward to the moment they lived for, running rampant in a newly conquered town. The fact that they would essentially be stealing possessions that had originally belonged to fellow citizens, despite the fact that they were originally stolen by our enemies, I knew would not make one whit of difference to them. I hoped that Germanicus would not be idealistic and inexperienced to the point where he tried to keep the men from looting, or even worse, tried to make them give their plunder back, but that was a problem for later.

Reaching the river, we halted, and after a short discussion, Germanicus decided that each Century would wade across, then wait for a short period of time, trying to determine if there was any change on the walls that would indicate the alarm had been raised. Personally, I chafed at this delay, but Germanicus was firm in his decision, and I only made one attempt to change his mind. Naturally, we were the first across, and while the First Century moved a short distance away, then stood silently, the water dripping from their tunics, I kept my attention riveted on the town, not just to see if there was any change, but finding the landmarks of the lamps to help guide us straight to the western camp, mentally rehearsing the route we would take to it. Finally, Germanicus called across the river, and the Second, led by Metellus, entered the water, and I realized that the sound was louder than it seemed when we were the ones crossing, but again, there was no change. One by one, over perhaps a sixth part of a watch, the Cohort crossed, and once I was informed of this, I pivoted so that the glow of the lamp I had selected as my guide was in the proper spot to my right front quarter, then we resumed moving. The ground was not particularly rough, so I did not hear anyone stumble or collide with a comrade, and we had no delays in reaching the camp, though I discovered I had almost walked into the ditch before I realized we had arrived. Fortunately, I was warned by the low-pitched challenge of the sentry, except his voice came from an unexpected direction, and somewhat to my embarrassment, I realized I had not been quite as inerrant in my guiding as I had thought, because we were at the rearmost corner, between the Porta Principalis Dextra and Porta Decumana, instead of arriving in front of the Porta Praetoria as I expected. Despite my personal chagrin, I reminded myself that, if this was as bad as things got, we would have an endeavor blessed by Fortuna. Once I was oriented, instead of turning to the right and trying to navigate, I instead led the Cohort around to the back gate, whereupon we entered the camp. Because of its tiny size, it instantly became crowded, between the horses and the cavalrymen, all of whom appeared to be out of their own tents and making preparations. I found Gaesorix standing outside his tent, his horse already saddled, but after a brief clasp of arms, I went instead to a much larger, dark bulk standing next to Gaesorix's mount, hearing Latobius blowing as he took in my scent, then gave a soft nicker as he nosed me, gently at first but then more insistently.

"I'm wearing my armor, you big oaf." I laughed. "You're not going to find anything." But then I produced the apple I had in the small bag I had slung across my body, and he unerringly followed his nose, his big teeth scraping my palm as he snatched the fruit. I kept my other hand on his neck, taking comfort in the crunching sound as my horse munched his treat, and not for the first time the thought crossed my mind, if only that was all it took to make me content. Turning to Gaesorix, I said, "Be sure and bring him once you get the signal."

"I will," he promised, and for the first time, the Batavian was not his normal, bantering self, while his tone was solemn. Suddenly, he blurted out, "And, Titus, be careful. I have a...feeling about this."

Not only was it the first time Gaesorix had used my *praenomen*, despite the fact that we had become good friends—and next to Metellus, he was my closest one of this time period—he had never said anything like this. This means I should not have been so dismissive, but honestly, I was more confident about this assault in these last moments than I had been in the entire time leading up to it.

"Are you becoming one of your old wise women?" I teased, but rather than offer a retort, I barely made out him shaking his head.

"Just be careful," was all he said.

"I will," I lied.

Then, it was time to make the final dispositions, which involved manning the ram and pushing it from its spot on the edge of the small forum of the camp, to the Porta Praetoria and out through the gate. Our plan was to assemble just outside the camp, confident that the sound of the ram, which was using wheels from one of the wagons that were wrapped with both a thickness of leather, then with strips of thick woolen cloth as well, would not carry all the way to the walls. The First, Second, and Third Centuries were outside the camp, and the men were allowed to sit, while we waited for the next phase of the assault, which would originate from both northern and southern camps. Despite Scipio's constant objections, whining and acting like a coward, Germanicus had remained firm in it being the Third Cohort that would be manning the ram from the southern camp, while the Second would be doing the same on the other side. Germanicus had also made a point to order that it be the First of the Third that would be responsible for the ram, but while Scipio was clearly unhappy about the idea he was required to be in the most danger, he gave no indication he would disobey the order. As for Agrippa, neither Germanicus nor I held any doubt that the steadiest and most competent of the nobly born Centurions would do his utmost to carry out his own orders. Regardless of our beliefs, there would only be one way to find out, and the Legate and I stood together, him watching to the north, me to the south, looking for any sign of movement. Each Pilus Prior in command of the ram had been given a watch candle in order to synchronize their movement, and by our calculation, the time had come for them to emerge from their camps, and we were both searching for any sign of movement. My eyes began to ache from the strain, but I could not pick up any kind of movement, at least for some time. It was my ears that alerted me first, and I untied my chin strap to raise the flap of my helmet as I turned one ear in the direction of the camp. I was just beginning to think I had been hearing things, then I heard it again: a deep-pitched, rattling, rumbling sound.

"The ram's moving on this side," I told Germanicus.

"I don't hear anything on my side," he replied, his frustration clear, and I happened to glance over at him.

"Sir," I suggested, "untie your chin strap and hold up a flap. Or," I thought, realizing how ridiculous it looks when a man does that, "you could take your helmet off right now. It will help you hear better."

"Oh," he mumbled, then I made out his hands reaching up and the outline of his feathered helmet disappeared. Not more than a half-dozen heartbeats passed, he said excitedly, "Now I hear them!"

With the knowledge that both Cohorts were moving, we waited to a count of five hundred, then I turned towards the men, calling them to their feet. The noise they made seemed louder than it was, but it still forced me to wince; fortunately, the men were settled quickly, standing in their formations, while their comrades assigned to pushing the ram moved to it, taking their respective places. Because of its construction, while our hope and plan was that between the speed of our movement, the fact that we were attacking the western wall, and the defenders inside, particularly those manning the artillery, would be focused on the other two rams so that we would escape being pounded by rocks and bolts, I had offered the men a bonus of two hundred *sesterces*, along with the first choice of any loot their Century took, as an incentive. Even then, it was two days after the announcement was made before we had a full complement of men, one full section, with another section trailing immediately behind to serve as replacements; the other two Cohorts were reduced to drawing lots for those assignments. Once everyone was ready, I gave the command, and with a rumbling sound, the ram began moving. Almost immediately, we learned something; without a roof and all the extra weight, while it certainly rolled easier, it sounded to my ears that it made more noise than one would have thought as it rattled and jounced over the ground. At first, I thought it was because we were on rougher ground, but when the ram reached the road that was the purpose of this western gate, it did not get much better. Granted, this was a road in the sense of being a worn path, the ground beaten smoother than the rest of this swathe of ground, and it was not paved, but I could detect no appreciable difference. Regardless of my fear, when we gave the order to stop at precisely two hundred paces, which put us a bit more than five hundred away from the gate, no shouts or, worse, horns were sounding the alarm, though this was not destined to last long.

It was the sentries along the northern wall who were the first to alert the defenders within Raetinium that, at last, the Romans were coming. As we stood, waiting and watching, a series of events occurred, more or less simultaneously, the first being a sudden flare of brighter light, partially obscured by the bulk of the parapet between our position and the northern wall. Before we could even comment on what it might mean, a blazing ball suddenly shot out from the wall, in a tumbling arc that trailed sparks as it sailed out from the rampart before plunging down towards the ground. Even before the first object impacted, there was another one of the same size, and more importantly, behaving in the same manner as the first, which was not in the normal way of a solid missile, or even a firepot. It was when the first one hit, but short of the parallel trench, and seemed to remain intact, that we understood what was happening.

"They're shooting flaming hurdles." I said this aloud, in the event that Germanicus was unsure. "They're trying to see what's coming."

It was just about then that the thin, undulating single note wail, made by the horn used by the barbarians in the same way we use our *cornu*, drifted across the distance to our ears, followed by the sound of barely audible shouts, though it was impossible to know if they came from our men or theirs. Another hurdle arced out, but it became apparent fairly quickly that the Maezaei had not perfected the ability of tying the bundles tightly enough and making the sticks of uniform length and size to give them greater range, because none of them went beyond the parallel trench. Still, after a half-dozen of these objects were strewn in a rough line less than two hundred paces away from and paralleling the wall, we could see not only the trench, but the ram, making its own rumbling progress towards the northern gate. Now the only question would be if the Maezaei waited to let it draw closer, both to the wall and to the hurdles, except my attention was drawn away by an almost identical series of events, this happening on the southern side. Before the span of fifty heartbeats passed from when the alarm first sounded, the artillery pieces on both walls had launched blazing bundles of sticks, serving as large torches to try and turn night into day. Not surprisingly, it was the *ballistae* on the northern wall that changed their ammunition and sent the first stones streaking towards our ram, which was barely visible since it was still more than a hundred paces away from the northern lip of the parallel trench. Speaking of which, it did not take more than another couple of missiles for our own surprise, in the form of the four scorpions and their crews who had been hiding in the trench, to climb ladders and drag their weapons up onto the spoil. Being just within the circles of light created by the hurdles, we had a relatively clear view of them as they hurriedly tried to secure the weapons, but before we could spend any more time with this, essentially the same sequence of events took place with the southern side. However, very quickly we saw that, while the hurdles used by the crews provided the same area of illumination, they had managed to send their hurdles just beyond the parallel trench, yet despite this, the ram pushed by Scipio's men was nowhere to be seen.

At least, not until we peered into the darkness, when the movement made their location known, but it was Germanicus who beat me to it. "They're barely a hundred paces out of the camp! They should be the same distance away as Agrippa's men!"

"If they left at the right time," I replied grimly, and while I did not want to add to his burden, I also felt compelled to point out what I had seen in the few heartbeats of time, "and weren't going a lot slower."

"I'm going to ruin him for this," Germanicus muttered, and while I appreciated the idea, there were more pressing concerns. By our respective positions, he was now outlined by the light provided by the hurdles, and I saw him turn his head towards me. "Primus Pilus, should we start now?"

"No, sir," I replied immediately; this had been the one challenge I was certain I would be facing, Germanicus' eagerness to start what would be the real assault. "We need to let both those rams get as close to the walls as possible. They need to be convinced this is our real effort."

"I knew you would say that," he muttered, then after a pause, "but I know you're right."

Although I was grateful for his acknowledgement, nothing had happened yet, other than a few rocks being lobbed, none of which had hit their target. Just wait, I thought to myself, until one of those rams takes a hit; I might have to hold him down to keep him from charging the walls all by himself. I suppose it was inevitable that, since I was thinking this very thing, it would be the moment where we heard the first solid hit on the northern ram, a hollow reverberating crash that, by the time we turned our heads in that direction, the stone had already hit the ram. With it being so dark, there was simply no way to determine what, if any, damage had been done to the ram; all we could tell was that it had come to a stop. Only when it began moving again did I realize I had been holding my breath, but before it traveled another dozen paces, the same sound repeated, causing it to stop again.

"What if it doesn't make it all the way to the wall?" Germanicus asked, and it was a valid question, forcing me to think before an answer came to me.

"Let's wait just long enough for it to get where the light gives us a chance to see for ourselves," I suggested.

"All right," he agreed, "but get the men ready now."

Turning about, I strode back and called the Centuries to their feet; it was as I was returning to the ram to resume my spot next to Germanicus that, for the first time, one of the pieces on the southern wall launched a rock. Whether their crew was just blessed by Fortuna or was better at their job, as with the northern ram, it was our ears that told us they scored a hit, although this one sounded slightly different, and to me, it sounded as if the ram might have been struck on the rebound. Now that my attention had been returned to Scipio's side, I could not contain the curse that burst from me; not only were they behind Agrippa's men of the Second, even in the darkness it was easy to see that they were still moving more slowly. The only positive was that, like their counterparts on the northern side, the scorpion crews used the first real missile as the signal to climb up out of the ditch, then make their own preparations to either pick off the Maezaei manning the wall *ballista* and scorpions, or failing that, at least keep their heads down and prevent them from loosing their own ammunition. Once I was satisfied I had seen all there was to see, I turned back north and saw that, at last, the northern ram's front edge was just entering the circle of light, and I was somewhat heartened that at least the roof of the ram retained its original shape. Otherwise, it was impossible to tell anything other than it was still moving.

"All right," Germanicus said abruptly, "we've waited long enough."

Just by the tone of his voice, I understood that it would be a waste of breath to try and convince him to wait, and if I am being honest, I was as tired of it as he was. Consequently, I trotted up to the man at the left rear of the ram, my Optio Rufius, and patted him on the shoulder.

"It's time," was all I said, and in kind, he only replied with a nod before calling out, "All right, you bastards. Let's go get rich!"

For an instant, I was afraid that the Optio had made a horrible mistake, but the men remembered our strict orders about not shouting until they were given the order, so it was an oddly muted response. More importantly, the ram began moving again, and I knew this time, we would not be stopping again until we reached the wall.

While we were beginning our approach, Agrippa's men had advanced inside the shortened trench running parallel to the wall, moving at a slight angle that they would have to correct to square themselves on the gate. Now that they were well inside the illuminated area, and within range of the smaller scorpions, the Maezaei wasted no time in unleashing everything they had in an attempt to stop the ram, which we could now see better because we were closing the distance. The ram was moving still, that much was true, but there was a dip in the center of the roofed portion, the sign that a *ballista* stone had cracked the center beam that served as the spine of the roof; if that completely collapsed down onto the ram, Agrippa's assault would be over. However, nothing could be done about that, and frankly, now that we were moving, I was becoming less concerned with them and more focused on our own effort. Germanicus, holding a shield drawn from stores as I was, strode a half-dozen paces behind the section following the ram, while I essentially tried to be everywhere, stopping to talk to our *Aquilifer* Arvina, to whom I had given the responsibility for maintaining the cohesion of our formation. I had ordered the men into the narrower eight-man front but with fifteen ranks deep instead of the twenty it would have been had we been at full strength, which would enable us to storm through the gateway more efficiently, and a quick glance assured me that the men were properly spaced. Most crucially, nobody was saying a word, meaning the night air was dominated by the sound of the ram, rattling along at a much quicker pace than the other two had been maintaining. Speaking of the other rams, the southern one had finally entered into the lit area, but was still about twenty paces short of the spot where the trench terminated and turned parallel. This, however, was not the problem; Scipio had either ordered or allowed his men to move in a straight line and not at an angle that would take him beyond the extended trench. In short, the path of the ram was now blocked, given its trajectory, and would have to be turned at a much sharper angle than it was designed to go, even with the new front wheel assembly that allowed them to steer the ram.

"You *stupid*, arrogant, useless..." I cannot remember all the things that came out of my mouth, but naturally it caught the attention of Germanicus, who had been keeping his eye on the western wall, now looming ahead of us, but so far with only the dull glow of the lamps and with no sign we had been spotted.

369

"What is it?"

I pointed first, then remembered it was still too dark, especially when looking towards the blazing hurdles, then back towards the darkness, so I said only, "Look at Scipio."

He did, and somewhat humorously, he essentially repeated the same string of descriptive words I had an instant before.

"How is he going to get out of that?" Germanicus asked, but before we could discuss this any further, from ahead and slightly above, we both clearly heard a shout that was loud enough to be heard over the din of our ram. Without hesitation, and before I could do so, Germanicus ordered loudly enough for the men pushing the ram, "It's time to pick up the pace, men! They know we're here, so let's get to the wall!"

Instantly, the ram picked up speed, while I now called over my shoulder, "Make ready for *testudo* but wait for my command!"

Then I had to actually pick up my own pace, over and above just lengthening my stride, catching up to Germanicus by trotting a few paces forward. His head was tilted upward, as was mine, but while I saw movement in at least two spots, both of them immediately next to where one of the lamps was located, there was no sudden increase in the level of illumination like we had witnessed when the hurdles were ignited just before they were launched. I did not want to say anything, I suppose because I was afraid I would curse us, and I am glad I did not, because after we had traveled another fifty paces, there was a flurry of movement along the wall to the right of the gate, then a series of what looked a bit like tiny torches appeared from between the crenellations.

"Fire arrows!" I bellowed, now that there was no need for silence. "Keep your eye on them, boys!"

This was a moment I had struggled with, because the normal order would be to form *testudo*, but until I was certain there were no *ballistae* or scorpions, I was not going to give that command. Even before I could have given the order, the first volley was loosed and came arcing down from an angle, which I suppose was why Germanicus hesitated.

"Get your shield up!" I snapped, which he did, just in time, although neither of us were the targets. "They're aiming for the ram!"

This was the moment where the tradeoff between security and speed showed itself, and in a tragic way, when most of the more than fifty arrows that came plunging down missed, but while a dozen that struck something stuck in the wooden frame or the shields of the men pushing the ram that were essentially the only protection they had, or in one case, in the wheel, one of them plunged into the chest of the ranker at the front right, coming in at an angle just above his shield. The scream he let out as he had to endure both the sensation of an iron point slicing into his vitals and the agony of fire was horrible to hear, and so rending was it that, for the first time, it caused the others to falter. Even worse, none of the group of men immediately behind the ram moved to replace him.

"Get up there, you gutless *cunni*!" I roared this, hating myself for doing it, despite knowing it was necessary. "We can't stop now or we're all going to suffer his fate!"

This served its purpose, but our hesitation was costly, because it allowed the archers on the wall to nock another arrow, dip the flammable material wrapped around shaft in the nearest flame, then loose a second volley. In what I can only think of as the kind of cruel joke the gods like to play, the man who had moved to replace the fallen ranker, whose body was now lying directly at my feet, was struck, in almost exactly the same spot, making almost exactly the same last shriek of agony.

"Keep moving! Keep moving! Keep moving!"

Germanicus began shouting this over and over, but despite what had just happened, this time, I did not have to order anyone to move, as another man darted from the spare section, nimbly hopping the second fallen victim. This volley managed to place more arrows in the wooden frame of the ram, while each man on the right side now had at least one arrow piercing their shields, which they were holding in their right hands while pushing on the horizontal bar in front of them with their left. Now I could see that in at least two places, the arrows had not flickered out before catching the wood, and smoke was

371

beginning to curl up from it. Despite all this, we continued moving, and I was torn between the need to keep an ear tuned to the sound of a *ballista* crossbar crashing forward, an eye to any visual sign that this was about to happen, and worrying that the ram would begin burning in earnest. But then, a very strange thing happened; we were suddenly at the gate, the ram less than a half-dozen paces away from the double wooden doors, and I have absolutely no memory of the last hundred paces. Really, the only sign that this had happened was that I noticed the ram was now burning in more than the two spots, but to this point, nobody had thought to do anything about it.

"Go to work!" Germanicus ordered, and I frankly was more embarrassed that he was the one who maintained his presence of mind, but also grateful because nobody hesitated.

Seeing this crucial matter was being attended to, I spun about and ordered loudly enough for my Century to hear, "Form *testudo*!" Then, I called to the *Cornicen* of the First, Lucius Salinator, "Sound the command for the entire Cohort to form *testudo*!"

The First, Second, and Third were the only Centuries within range of the archers, but I now was certain that we had managed to fool the defenders, there was no artillery on the western wall, and there was not enough time for them to shift their pieces, nor would it have done any good since we were under their range. Now that we were against the wall, what was taking place elsewhere, namely with the northern and southern efforts, was essentially occurring in another world; indeed, the noise of their struggle was almost completely masked by the walls and by the shouts and clamor taking place where we were standing. There was a huge crash, and I could feel the impact of the ram against the gate all the way up through my legs, prompting me to turn to watch. Because of our *ad hoc* nature, there was only one of the iron heads that are affixed to a ram available to us from stores, and Germanicus had used his prerogative as commander to have it affixed to our own. This one, as most are, was in the shape of a ram's head, but it is not purely decorative in nature, because there is a definite point to this piece, both literally and figuratively, and it had already created a solid dent in the right door. Once more, the men who had survived pushing it grabbed the twin ropes attached to the back of the ram, while the men who were to be their replacements moved into their comrades' former positions and pressed their entire combined weight against the ram in order to create the greatest impact, holding their position while the others hauled the huge log back as far as the ropes would allow, then released. As before, the noise was terrific, but there was a distinctive cracking sound, one that was clearly heard by the men behind us, because for the first time, they unleashed a mighty roar at this sign we were making progress.

"Keep it up! We're about to get inside this town, and we'll make these fucking savages pay!"

With exhortations of this nature, the men working the ram began picking up their pace, the metal head smashing again, and again, into the right hand of the double gate, each time the splintering sound becoming louder as well. I do not want to give the impression that the Maezaei were not resisting, but it was still solely in the form of flaming missiles, which we were now taking from both sides. Whether or not this was because the archers had split into two groups to attack from two directions or others had arrived, it was impossible to tell. Although I tried to keep my attention on the gate, waiting for the moment we would be able to force it open using our muscle, I could not help glancing over my shoulder, and I was slightly worried at the number of arrows that protruded from the shields of my Century, several of them still flickering, with at least three of them having caught the leather covers on fire. My hope was that we would have time for the men to knock these missiles from their shields, but much depended on what awaited us on the other side of the gate.

As best as I can remember, it took about fifteen strikes from the ram before, finally, the iron head snapped the locking bar with a higher-pitched splintering crack, but it was the way in which the right door suddenly sagged slightly inward that was the most potent sign we had broken through. Naturally, this raised a cheer from the men on the ram, which in turn incited a roar from their comrades behind us, though it was slightly muffled by their raised shields. My own shield had been struck twice by flaming arrows, while Germanicus' was understandably hit more than a half-dozen times, but it was now time to switch to the offensive. The ram battered the door two more times before it was clear that the locking bar had at least been completely broken and separated.

"Pull the ram out of the way," Germanicus ordered, which was done immediately, but just as it was pushed aside, the young Legate went striding forward towards the now partially opened gate, clearly intent on pushing it open.

Once more, I found myself forced to take a leaping step forward, just barely managing to grab the back of Germanicus' cuirass at the collar with my free hand, not having drawn my blade yet, but not before he kicked the right door open, or at least tried to do so. Thankfully for him, for Rome, and for my own career, he remembered to keep his shield up in front of him. The door was too heavy to swing aside from just a kick, so that the gap only widened perhaps a foot, but it was enough for a single short throwing spear to come slashing through, burying itself in Germanicus' shield with such force that he was hurled backward into me. Before he could react, with my hand still firmly grasping the collar of his cuirass, I flung him aside to my right, my intention being to swing my shield across into the space where his body was an eyeblink before to use it as protection instead of my Legate. While I got the first part right, and he lost his footing from the force with which I tossed him out of the way, careening into one of the men assigned to the ram who had just finished pushing it aside, I was an instant too slow in bringing my own shield up in front of me. I had the barest sense of a blurred line moving directly at me faster than my eye could track, but I definitely felt a tremendous impact on the extreme right side of my lower chest, and for the first time in my adult life, I was knocked cleanly off my feet. There was a brief sensation of falling backward, then my back slammed into the hard surface of the road with a force that drove what little breath was left from the initial impact from my body, and when the back of my helmet slammed into the same surface, my world turned as bright as if a thousand lights exploded inside my head. The span of what I suppose was the next several heartbeats is extremely fuzzy, but I do recall the beginning of a horrific pain along the right side of my chest, though there was competition from the throbbing in my head for the honors of what hurt most. Making matters worse was that, when I tried to take in a breath, I could not, which oddly enough triggered in my addled mind a memory of the only other time I had had the wind knocked from me, when I had been ten and thought I was ready to face the dwarf Spartacus back at the *ludus* in Arelate. And, just like that time, I saw a face suddenly above me, not Vulso this time, but my Optio Rufius, although he had a similar look of concern on his face.

"Primus Pilus!" he shouted. "Primus Pilus! Can you hear me?"

I felt my mouth working, but nothing was coming out, and it took quite an effort of will to remember that the only way to get my breath back was to relax rather than struggle to suck air into my lungs.

As I did, Rufius continued to shout at me before, finally, I was able to half-gasp, "I'm not deaf, idiot. I can hear you and so can everyone for a mile around."

I held up my arm, which he took, though I was about to admonish him for turning his back to the enemy, but when he managed to drag me to my feet, with a fair amount of effort, I saw that both sections of men around the ram had formed a makeshift *testudo* in between us and the gate, allowing us to shelter behind their protection. My head was spinning, but it was the ribs of my right side that were sending sharp stabs of pain, which made raising my right arm in order to examine myself difficult, although I was relieved to see that there was not a spear shaft protruding from my body.

At some point, Germanicus appeared next to me, and he pointed down at my side, under my upraised arm and, like Rufius, shouted at me, "The gods love you, Pullus! That spear just grazed you!"

He was correct, as I could see that several links along my side had been broken, and I could actually see my skin, under the padded shirt and tunic, with a thick, red line marking where the Maezaei spear had sliced into me. It hurt like Dis, and it pained me to lift my arm, but this was not the time to worry about what ultimately was a trifling matter, though I felt certain that I had at least one broken rib. Now that my Legate had wasted time making sure I was still in action, I was more worried about what was happening on the other side of the gate, but when he made no move to give any kind of command, I temporarily forgot our respective ranks.

"Don't just stand there, boy! Order the First up and have the men on the ram make ready to push open the gates," I snapped.

The instant the words were out of my mouth, I regretted them, but while Germanicus' jawline tightened, rather than rebuke me, he gave a curt nod, then turned about, and with the kind of roar that would have done no Centurion any shame, he ordered, "First Century, forward!" Turning to the men who had just yanked the ram out of the way, he indicated, "One section on the left hand gate, another on the right! Use your shields to push against it and for the love of Jupiter, keep them up in front of you once you push them open! Wait for my command!" Then, turning back to the men of the First, he saw they had moved forward but were still holding their *testudo*, and I saw a glimmer of doubt on his face, which I suppose was why he looked to me for what came next.

Rather than waste time, I called over my shoulder, "First Century, wait for my command!...Open formation!" Pausing the least amount of time I was willing to spare, knowing the archers would instantly pounce on this opportunity, even before our men finished sidestepping, I bellowed, "Prepare javelins!" No more than a heartbeat later, I gave them the order but slightly modified it, counting on these men as veterans to be aware. "Pick a target!...Release!"

It was inevitable that, in the crisscrossing of missiles, some arrows found their marks, particularly because men who were hurling their own javelins were particularly vulnerable, and behind me, there were screams from the First as arrows found fleshy targets, the one small consolation that the archers had foregone lighting their missiles now, exchanging the extra damage caused by fire for greater accuracy. The punishment was not one way, however, and above us, I heard cries and shouts similar in nature to those issued by the fallen men of the First, indicating we had inflicted our own punishment, but as tempting as it was, I wanted their next javelin sent to a different target.

For this, I told Germanicus, "Give the order to open the gates!" Turning my head only enough so I could be heard, I shouted the order, "Prepare javelins!"

Germanicus had immediately done so, but when the men instantly obeyed, and I saw that Germanicus was not stepping aside, I had no time to reach him, so I could only shout, "Germanicus, kneel down!"

Thank the gods he did so, because the gates were pushed open even as this came out of my mouth, and I caught my first glimpse of a solid line of Maezaei warriors, their own short throwing spears poised for release. Dropping down into a crouch, I did not even need to give the order, and I will cross into the shades thankful that those hoary old veterans of the First Century took it upon themselves, because in doing so, they beat the Maezaei to the punch. I heard the deeper-throated whishing sound of our javelins, larger and traveling slower than arrows but hitting with greater force, passing over my head, followed instantly by the punching sound as dozens of our javelins struck Maezaei shields, while the sharp cries and curses of men whose shields had not managed to block them sounded above it all. It was time to move, and for the first time, I drew my *gladius*, but Germanicus, who had resumed his standing posture, exchanged a glance with me, and I nodded my encouragement.

"*Legio Germanicus!*" he cried out, thrusting his own *gladius* into the air, but he was already beginning to run, which caught me by surprise and forced me to scramble to catch up with him as he shouted, "For the Princeps! For Tiberius! FOR ROME!"

The full-throated cries of the First Century felt like an invisible hand pushing me along, but I had to run even faster than I would have normally to catch up with Germanicus, intent on doing the same thing I had done in Splonum, protect his weak side. And I will swear on Jupiter's stone that I did try to come abreast of him, but he was too fast, and I could only look on helplessly as he literally threw himself at the Maezaei. What saved his life, and probably mine as well, was that there was a young warrior who, seeing this Roman of obviously high rank rushing ahead of the rest of us, was determined to be the first to meet the challenge, and he leaped from the mass of Maezaei who were arrayed at the far end of the gateway in what looked like their version of a formation at least as deep as our own. This barbarian was unable to get up to the same kind of speed as Germanicus, who thankfully led with his shield, and in that eyeblink of an instant, I felt a flush of relief that the Legate had at least thought to cut away all the arrows that had been studding it, although in that instant, I saw it was still smoldering. Then, with a tremendous impact, he smashed his shield into that of the Maezaei, who appeared to be perhaps four or five years older than Germanicus, wearing a beard and equipped with a high, conical helmet, which was all I caught a glimpse of as he went reeling backward, his own round shield waving wildly as he tried to keep his balance. This time, thankfully, Germanicus did not repeat his mistake of plunging after this Maezaei, who took advantage of the Legate's blow to choose to essentially reintegrate himself back into the Maezaei line, but Germanicus managed to stop himself only a hand's breadth away from the reach of a barbarian spear, thrust at him by the same warrior he had knocked backward. Then, before anything else could happen, I was next to Germanicus, though we were alone for no more than an eyeblink as, like a wall of rushing water, our men came surging around us, and they were not hesitant about throwing themselves, behind their shields of course, against the solid line of defenders. The crash of body, metal and wood colliding was amplified by the interior of the gateway, creating an echoing sound that made it even louder and more chaotic than normal. Now that Germanicus was not isolated, both of us turned our attention to our foes across from us, as the Legate clearly had chosen the young Maezaei as his personal adversary, which I had learned long before, through my Avus first, then my father, and finally through my own observation, was a particular habit of our upper classmen, who tend to view these matters much more idealistically and personally than we rankers do. I never asked, and I would not be surprised if Germanicus claimed to have no memory, but I felt certain that he had taken the young warrior's stepping forward, ahead of his own line, as a personal challenge and affront.

Indeed, it appeared as if Germanicus had selected this warrior as his private target, because when a man of the First Section to the Legate's left saw that his commander had created an opening, I heard Germanicus roar, "Leave him be! He's mine! Tend to your own!"

Despite hearing the exchange, I was not distracted from the sudden spear thrust, launched by the Maezaei directly opposite me, an older warrior with a milky eye that, in another odd moment, reminded me of Caecina. While I cannot say so definitively, I suspect that it was that association I made with my old foe that helped me there in Raetinium, because I did not wait for the warrior to finish his recovery, his spear not fully withdrawn when I punched my shield forward, preventing him from generating any force for a second thrust. Since he had partially brought his shield over to keep my boss from striking his body, I pressed hard, bracing my elbow against my hip while twisting my body to keep up the pressure, then feinted a high second position thrust before dropping my elbow and switching to a third position attack that was in earnest. It was without the force generated by my body twisting from the hips as we are trained, but it was enough for the point to slice into his throat just under his jaw. Instantly, this Maezaei fell backward, except I had anticipated this, so I did not stumble forward with the sudden disappearance of the pressure against my shield. I did, however, take advantage of the sudden gap, taking not a full but half-step forward, which put me in a perfect position to end Germanicus' private battle with the young warrior, with one well-aimed thrust that took advantage of the Maezaei shifting his shield to block yet another attack by the Legate.

Not surprising me in the least, Germanicus did not take this assistance gratefully, but when he turned his head towards me, before he could open his mouth, I snapped, "Keep your eyes in front of you!"

Since I was viewing him out of the corner of my eye, all I saw was him doing as I ordered, just in time to block a smashing overhand blow from a Maezaei ax, wielded by a man who was just an inch or two shorter than I was, with a long black beard that was plaited with what appeared to be more than a dozen small bones, proclaiming his prowess as a warrior. Germanicus got his shield up in time, but despite

379

catching the blow as evenly as he could, there was no mistaking the sharp crack that accompanied the heavier thud as the ax chopped down into the shield. Neither of us had covers for our shields, since they had come from the *quaestorium*, and the thought flashed through my mind that, perhaps if I had thought to find a couple, his shield would not have cracked. Then, I was absorbed in my own problems as another warrior stepped over the body of the man I had dispatched no more than a couple of heartbeats before, swinging a long *gladius* down in an overhead blow. On its own, my arm swept up, the shield tilting to match the angle of his blade in order to distribute the impact more evenly, then the iron edge of his blade smashed down onto the painted wood, in a blow that shivered all the way down my arm and into my shoulder, turning my arm numb, which served to warn me that this man was stronger than average. But, before I could respond, the Gregarius of the First who had placed himself to my right, did essentially the same thing I had done to Germanicus, taking advantage of the manner in which the Maezaei was thrown slightly off-balance, I believe because of the way his blade rebounded from my shield, or perhaps he was anticipating me repeating the same kind of maneuver I had used on the warrior who had been immediately in front of him and was now at his feet. Whatever the cause, his shield was farther across his body towards his right side than was prudent, and the ranker did not hesitate to take advantage of this lapse, his own *gladius* striking out so quickly that not only I barely saw it, but clearly his foe never did either, judging by the look of shocked surprise on his face. He opened his mouth, presumably to cry out from the pain of a *gladius* punching behind his left arm and slicing deep into his body, except all that came out was a gout of blood; if he made a sound, I could not hear it.

In the brief moment I had as the Maezaei's knees collapsed, I shot a quick glance to my right, seeing a grinning face and I did hear the ranker shout, "You're welcome, Primus Pilus!"

The man's name was Glabius, one of the younger old veterans, having only done one enlistment; as I recall, he had been in the 13th, but just as I was about to growl something about not needing his help,

I managed to catch myself, thinking that it would be hypocritical to chastise the man. Instead, I gave him a returning grin, and that was all the time either of us had, because the Maezaei across from Glabius had stepped past a figure that was crawling away from the fighting, who I presumed Glabius had just taken out of the fight, this new man holding a spear shoulder-high, while there was another enemy warrior who took the time to reach down, and grabbing a leg of the dead man directly to my front, dragged the corpse back a few feet. The reason I recall this is because it was an unusual thing to do, but I quickly realized it was because we were still confined within the gateway. It was true that everything I have just described from our first collision with the defenders to this moment was not much more than fifty heartbeats of time, but we were severely hampered. The problem was the width of the gateway, which was wide enough for an eight-man front, but not with the space we needed to properly do the job of killing the men trying to keep us out. Taking advantage of the momentary respite where I did not have to be concerned with defending myself, I took quick stock of our situation. To this point, it appeared as if we had slain a dozen Maezaei, and when I glanced past Germanicus, who even then was continuing a furious attack on a warrior who was frantically parrying the Legate's thrusts, I saw we had one Roman down, right next to the far inner wall of the gateway, while on my right side, I saw two men down, but one was doing essentially the same thing as Glabius' foe, crawling back in between the files. That he was dragging his shield was a good sign that he might be back in the fight; this was something that was beyond my control, and I had more pressing concerns.

"Push these *cunni* back!" I shouted. "We need to get out of this gate!"

This was the moment where the composition of the *Legio Germanicus* showed itself, because, while the men answered with a ragged chorus of shouts, and they did try shoving their opponents backward with their shields, putting their shoulders into it, nothing happened. Despite their best efforts, these men were simply not strong enough, particularly now that they were already worn down from the beginning of our battle. In retrospect, I should have ordered a shift relief, so the men of the second rank, who would be fresh, would have at least had a better chance of dislodging these Maezaei. It did not surprise me that the Maezaei were fighting so furiously; I was shocked that we could not seem to dislodge them from the gateway. True, it was within the realm of possibility that either Agrippa, or much less likely in my estimation, Scipio's men could have made it to their gate and battered it down, but it was not something I took as a serious possibility. Consequently, I felt certain that it was down to us, and I was equally sure that Germanicus felt the same way. Hoping that it would help matters, I blew my whistle to signal that it was time for a shift, despite the fact that we were closer together than normal. Instantly, six of the eight men acknowledged the order by either knocking their foes back before stepping quickly aside or by using their weapon to do essentially the same thing, forcing the enemy back with a hard thrust. However, Germanicus did not move, which in turn meant neither could I, since I was not about to let the youngster out of my sight. The rest of the relief went more smoothly than I would have thought, but when I gave these fresh men the order to physically shove our enemies all the way out of the gateway, once more, the Maezaei stiffened their own resistance. I could clearly see over my shield that the men of the front rank were actually being braced, in much the same manner as we did, and it was another example of how our own tactics were being turned against us. Stealing a glance at Germanicus, I saw that his face was shining in the low light from the sweat that was streaming down it in rivulets, and he was panting from his exertions, despite his youth, but in the less than a heartbeat's time, I observed him I saw something more alarming than his fatigue. He had just made a follow-up thrust with his blade after using the boss of his shield to try and knock aside his foe's own kite-shaped shield, which was unsuccessful, so the Maezaei neatly caught the point of Germanicus' *gladius* up high. However, when Germanicus had recovered his own shield, drawing it back in front of his body, he held it at a lower position than it should have been, which, as we learn when we are *tiros*, is a sign to anyone with experience that fatigue is starting to set in. And, I could tell his opponent saw this and understood the meaning as well as I did, so that he did not hesitate in testing Germanicus' reflexes with what turned out to be a feint, except somewhat unusually, he performed a jabbing type of thrust, more like our own preferred method of attack. Germanicus managed to block this, though I could see how late he did so, but this was the last attention I could pay to him; turning one's attention away from one's own immediate situation, even if it is for the span of just a heartbeat, as my glance was, can be fatal, something I almost learned the hard way. This time, it was my shield that was slow in blocking a thrust, except this was from a spear; that it was so not because I was fatigued but I was more worried about Germanicus ultimately did not matter. What did was that I caught the point of this Maezaei's spear very high on my shield, no more than a couple inches from the top. Not only was it a sign I had been tardy in reacting, but it created a problem when, rather than recover his spear for another attempt, this bastard instead extended his arm out, pushing hard against my shield, which in turn caused the bottom to tilt upward. Barely in time did I realize that, whether he was capitalizing on the situation or this was a planned move, the man next to him had already dropped into a crouch, and I sensed more than saw the flash of a movement that was so quick that, even now, I have no idea how I responded the way I did. This second man had aimed his Thracian *gladius* for the area around my knees in a backhand slash, but at such an angle that I understood he was trying to hamstring me, except that somehow, my right arm was moving before my mind commanded it, in a downward, sweeping blow that clashed against his blade as I knocked it aside, instantly making not only my hand, but my arm below the elbow numb once more. Shouting something that I imagine was uncomplimentary to my mother, his curse quickly turned into a scream of pain as, making one motion, I reversed the direction of my *gladius*, the edge slicing into his arm about midway up his forearm, severing the appendage in less than an eyeblink. Because I severed the major vessel that carries blood to the hand, I was rewarded for my effort by the feel of a warm spray as his blood shot out like a geyser, splashing over my right leg, and as I would only learn later

383

when others thought I had been wounded, completely covering every inch of my exposed skin with his blood.

The spearman, meanwhile, had yanked his spear back at roughly the same instant that his comrade had launched his own attack, I am sure in the hope that the feeling of him doing so would distract me and force me to concentrate on retaining hold of my shield. My slash had been performed at an awkward angle, but at the end of that movement, my *gladius* was actually back to an almost ideal spot for a first position thrust, which was what I did, executing the kind of attack that, had it been at the stakes, I would have judged perfect. But this was not at the stakes; my aim was spoiled when I lifted my right foot slightly, the preparatory move for twisting my hips, then when I took my step forward, my foot came down not onto the hard surface of the roadway, but the arm of the man I had just taken it from in the most painful and dramatic manner. The consequence was that, instead of punching up under the spearman's shield, the point hit it squarely, just below the boss. Thankfully, it was a solid blow that might not have been the killing one I had intended, but served to send the Maezaei reeling back a step, falling against the man behind him, and taking him out of the fight for a brief instant.

And, thank the gods, because just then, a panicked voice to my left rear quarter shouted, "Germanicus is down!"

Because of everything that took place this night, I never learned exactly what the sequence of events were that ended with Germanicus being knocked off his feet, but I strongly suspect he made a mistake that was caused by his fatigue. The reason, of course, did not matter; what did was that, completely forgetting I had been involved in my own fight, I pivoted to my left, and in doing so, I inadvertently kicked the arm that I had stepped on, sending it spinning towards the Maezaei. I vaguely recall hearing a shout of disgust, and even with all that was happening, I felt a grin crease my face, another of the odd little moments that men vividly remember later, for whatever reason. I immediately saw that the ranker who had shouted, a man of the Third Section, had not been exaggerating. Germanicus was indeed sitting on his ass, but rather than taking a respite, he was holding his shield up above him with an arm that I could clearly see was trembling, while he swung his *gladius* wildly about, just a foot or so off the ground. Perhaps this was intended, though I tend to think it was accidental, but the result was fortuitous for both Germanicus and Rome, because when he did flail about, his blade cut deeply into the lower leg of a warrior who at that instant was drawing his arm back, preparing to thrust his spear down into the young Legate. I could not miss the savage grin on that Maezaei's face, his lips peeled back in a sneer of hatred and triumph, and how that expression vanished as Germanicus' *gladius* sliced into the man's calf, stopping only because it hit bone. His mouth transformed, opening wide in a scream of agony, but I suppose even through his pain, he must have sensed me moving the less than two paces that separated us, because his head turned, just in time for me to thrust my *gladius* into his open mouth. I felt the extra resistance as the point hit the bone, but as I had learned long before, when you kill a man in this manner, severing his spine like that, you have to be prepared for your enemy to simply collapse straight down. As difficult as it is to describe, the best I can come up with is to ask them to imagine what would happen if they could instantly remove every bone from a man's body, which was what occurred now as his body sagged lifelessly to the roadway, transforming into a mass of dead weight. Fortunately, I was prepared, managing to yank the *gladius* out before it and my arm could be dragged down, thereby enabling me to take another step in time to perform a punching blow with my shield, just as the other Maezaei who had thought he had easy prey in this young Roman noble was bringing his *gladius* down from the high overhead position that, had it landed, would have at the very least broken Germanicus' shield. This time, it was someone else's aim that was ruined, as the boss of my shield struck his own rounder and smaller protection with enough force to send him staggering to his right. I did not bother following up, because my immediate concern was Germanicus, so I stood over him, essentially straddling his body as I pivoted and faced the Maezaei in one motion, keeping my shield up.

"Help him up!" I barked without turning my head, but the man I had just knocked aside was no longer a threat, because when he stumbled, the ranker to Germanicus' left did not hesitate, taking advantage of his loss of equilibrium with what I saw out of the corner of my eye was a slashing blow.

Once Germanicus was back on his feet, I decided it was time I step aside as well; I had sensed the man behind me move into my spot when I had come to Germanicus' aid, so I alerted the ranker in this file, who had helped Germanicus back to his feet, by calling over my shoulder to prepare to move. Rather than being forced to shove the Maezaei across from me away, the bodies of the two freshly dead warriors enabled me to simply step aside as they were rudely dragged out of the way by their comrades while simultaneously, I took a step backward, still with my shield up.

Germanicus, now standing, holding his shield, which I saw had several cracks and gouges where it had been struck, seemed ready to try and resume his spot, but I called to him, "We need to go to the rear, sir. I need your help."

I guessed this would be the better way to entice him to extricate himself, and it seemed to work because he nodded, then like me, walked backward a couple of ranks deeper in the formation before turning about and making his way down his file, while I did the same.

Meeting at the rear, before we spoke, we had to catch our breath, but there was no time to waste, so I suppose I was gasping more than speaking when I told Germanicus, "We have to push these bastards out of the gateway, but it doesn't look like we're strong enough."

"I know," Germanicus panted, his face still glistening. "So what do we do?"

"I think we need to…"

Before the words were out, there was a sudden roar from the front of the formation, echoing back out of the gateway to where we were standing, immediately next to the wall. Turning back towards the gateway, two things occurred at roughly the same time.

"The *cunni* are retreating!"

Even as whoever it was shouted this, I saw the front ranks suddenly begin to push forward, and I immediately began moving back in that direction, with Germanicus right behind me, trying to determine what was happening. Although it was true that it seemed as if we had been fighting for a full watch, I knew from experience that much less time had elapsed from the moment we opened the gate, yet it still did not seem as if we had been at it long enough to make the Maezaei crack. Before I made my way back to the front, the first three or four ranks had clearly exited from under the wall and out into the open area inside the town. We were inside the city! This was the first thought that flashed through my mind, yet while I knew I should be happy about this, there was something that did not make sense, but I shoved that nagging worry aside, chiding myself for being so pessimistic. Exiting the gateway arch out into the town, I took notice that there were at least fifty Maezaei bodies, though I was pleased to see that the men trailing behind the leading rank had taken the time to make sure none of these barbarians suddenly came back to life. Despite this being a positive development, it did not mean we had won or were even out of danger, but I was pleased to see that, without being told, Rufius had directed two sections of men to climb the set of stairs that were placed on both sides of the gateway. I took the time to check to see those men, who were in a rank only three abreast because of the width of the parapet, were advancing quickly towards the force of archers, some of whom were still absorbed in loosing as many missiles down on the rest of the First Cohort who were still waiting outside the walls. Those were the first men to die in this second phase, though I only saw the first couple struck down before I returned my attention to the situation on the ground. The Maezaei had actually retreated in good order, again behaving with more discipline than I had witnessed previously, withdrawing back to the first block of buildings, but while doing so, they had separated into smaller bands in order to block every street with at least a hundred men. For the time being, they were content to watch us as I hurried our own men into position, shouting at them for moving too slowly as we spread out. Not only did we return to our more normal spacing between files, but we were forced to increase to a rank of more than forty men across in order to cover the width of the town, which meant we had to bring more than just the First Century into position. Germanicus was apparently content to allow me to do this part of my job without interruption, at least until the moment he called to me to attend to him, which I did, reluctantly.

However, he surprised me when he pointed out, correctly, "Pullus, the First is out of javelins. Are we just going straight to the *gladius*?"

The curse I bit back was aimed at myself, because he was absolutely correct. Fortunately, I spotted Veratius, but my Century was not far enough away from the wall to allow his men of the Third to align behind us, so they were left to stand jammed inside the gateway, waiting for their oaf of a Primus Pilus to sort things out.

Running over to the Princeps Prior, I ignored his salute, telling him, "Have your boys pass up one of their javelins." Then, without waiting for him to acknowledge the order, knowing he would carry it out, I turned and called the men of my rearmost rank nearest to me, "Come here, grab these javelins, then pass them down and forward to the men up front." Giving them a grin that promised nothing good for our foes, I said, "They'll send them at those *cunni* for you, and that way, your *gladius* arms won't be tired for all the wet work ahead!"

They responded with a cheer, but I was already turning back to Veratius.

Pointing in the direction of the northern wall, I ordered him, "Take your boys down that direction to support the Second Century."

As soon as Veratius acknowledged, I was moving back to the front, where Rufius was waiting, standing next to Arvina, and ordered him to move down to the far end of the Century on the left to oversee our push forward from that spot. Now that we were within the walls and out from the gloom of the gateway, the reflection of the torches that the Maezaei had placed in the brackets made it seem as if it was daylight when compared to the darkness of a just a few moments before, and it was one more unusual thing, or so I believed. The truth was that I had only been involved in a couple of assaults on a fortified town, and this was only the second time I had done so at night, so I did not have enough experience to know any differently, but that is said with the clarity of hindsight. Before another fifty heartbeats had passed, javelins were being passed forward, and I know I was not alone in being grimly pleased at the sudden shifting of the previously stolid bunch of warriors directly across from where I stood at the corner of the western and southern wall.

"Look at 'em, boys!" I roared. "They're not so confident now, are they?" The answer came in the form of a low-pitched growling sound, sprinkled with muttered curses, but I was already bellowing, "Prepare javelins!" Then, "Release!" Even as the missiles were in the air, I gave the command to draw *gladii*.

I did not waste a moment of time looking over my shoulder, instead shouting something completely unremarkable as I began running at the barbarians across from me. My first forward step coincided with the impact of the missiles, but I was disappointed to see how relatively few of the javelins hit something substantial, in enemy flesh ideally, or at least the wood of a shield. This did not seem to matter, however; aiming for the largest Maezaei of the front rank, rather than put my shoulder behind my shield to smash into him as I had earlier, this time, I feinted the action, drawing my protection hard against my body and lowering my shoulder as if readying for the impact, then came sliding to a stop instead. My hope was that I had fooled my adversary into thinking this was going to be my first attack, then take advantage of whatever his reaction was, and it was a maneuver I had used to good effect before and have since. And, I suppose in a sense, what happened was good, or so it seemed in the moment, even as I cursed bitterly when, instead of my foe lashing out in some manner, he suddenly began scrambling backwards, holding his shield up in front of him and his spear up on top of it. That he did so at the precise instant when the rest of my men came slamming into the defensive line around him is what I attributed his action to; I can only blame all the turmoil and confusion that is a normal part of an action like this, heightened by the darkness and the larger circumstances for making me miss the significance of something. The idea that the men behind him instantly gave way, and not only that, copied his action, backing down the street between the outer wall and the first row of buildings of the town back to the next block seemed somewhat unusual, but not to the point where it triggered an alarm call inside my head.

"Keep pressing!" I shouted, though I actually stopped, doing this to look left down the road that intersected with the one we were traveling, peering into the dimness as I saw what took a moment for my eyes to identify as men wearing our uniforms moving through the intersection at roughly the same pace as my Century the first few blocks down from where I was standing.

Beyond them, although this was a Roman town, laid out in the standard grid pattern, the road curved slightly as it followed the contour of the ground upon which Raetinium was built, making it impossible to see more than three blocks further. Between this and the darkness, I was forced to rely on just the sensation of movement, about the only thing a human eye can track well at night, though there were a handful of torches that remained lit at odd points deeper in the town. Once I got a better sense of where things stood, my next worry was Germanicus, and where he was, but I got my answer when, from among the cluster of figures the block over, one detached itself to come trotting in my direction.

"Pullus!" The voice enabled me to answer that question, and I stood waiting as he came trotting up. His face still shined, but he had clearly recovered his energy, and his brush with an ignominious death seemed to be a thing of the distant past as he shouted exultantly, "We've got them on the run!"

"It seems that way," I agreed, then pointed out, "which is why we need to keep pushing." Indicating behind him, I asked, "Was Rufius with your group, sir?"

He shook his head. "He's with the boys the next block over. Why?"

"Because I'm trying to figure out how wide an area of coverage we need," I explained. "Right now, they're falling back, but I suspect they're going to have to stop and fight at some point, and since we're separated like this into smaller groups, I want to have enough men for each group for when that happens."

"That makes sense." He nodded, then after a moment of thought, offered, "What if we have a Century for two streets? Half in one," Germanicus used his *gladius* to indicate the one nearest to where we were now standing, then turned to indicate the one from which he had come, "and half in the other."

"That should be enough," I agreed, then saluted as I went looking for the nearest *Cornicen*.

Our push into the town was paused as we rearranged our forces, immediately after the First crossed the only bridge across the river within our assigned area, where we were forced to collapse back into a single formation before using the street that paralleled the river on the eastern side, cutting down the barbarians who elected to stand. The Second and Third did the same, though they actually had to share a bridge, and that was after a bitter fight for Maezaei who blocked it, inflicting a half-dozen casualties of our own. After a quick conference with the Centurions of the Cohort, we then made our dispositions for what we felt certain in the moment would be our final push towards the base of the hill, where what had once been the *praetorium* but now served as the focal point of the Maezaei defenses loomed above us. I can only surmise that during this lull, Dodonis was equally busy, except we honestly could not tell, other than in the form of the defenders just a few dozen paces down each street who were still standing ready to resist us. During this pause, we also rearranged ourselves somewhat, by placing the Fourth and Fifth Centuries to the right of the First, with the Fifth now arrayed so their right flank was hard up against the southern wall. We were still at least three hundred paces from the two main gates on the northern and southern side, and during the period of time when Germanicus and I shook out the First Cohort into its alignment to continue our sweep east, I took a few moments to try and see beyond the Maezaei who were arrayed to prevent us from penetrating deeper into the town, but nothing I saw indicated in any way that the Third Cohort was anywhere close to penetrating their gate.

Up on the rampart, there was only a darkened mass that was hard to delineate, until I happened to see the sudden flare of a hurdle illuminating the *ballista*, its crew and the Maezaei immediately around them. It did not last long, but there was enough light that enabled me to see that either at least some of the archers who we had swept from the western wall had run to join the defenders on the southern side, or they were part of the force Dodonis had apportioned for the defense of that gate. For a moment, I did toy with the idea of sending the one Century I was keeping in reserve, the Sixth, to sweep around the wall, using the parapet, but along with the archers, I had noticed there were more than twice the number of warriors up there as well. It was not much of a stretch to think that they were indeed waiting for this very thing, so rather than pursue it, I decided it would be better not to bring it to Germanicus' attention. The amount of time spent in shuffling Centuries about and preparing for what would now be this next effort took perhaps the span of a few hundred heartbeats; enough time for men to catch their collective breath, but not enough time for us to stop and really think things through, because when I rejoined Germanicus, he did not hesitate to turn to his *Cornicen* Natta and order we resume the advance. Across the space of no more than thirty paces, the Maezaei were standing, and their spirits seemed to be somewhat revived, as many of them were clashing their blades against their shields or making some sort of taunting gesture, daring us to step forward. Naturally, we did just that, except this time, I prevailed on Germanicus not to be in the front rank, but just behind them.

"You'll be in a better position to direct the battle, and you'll be able to be reached by a runner from the other Centuries," I told him, but while he clearly did not like it, he nodded his head in agreement.

Pausing only long enough to allow men to launch the handful of javelins remaining, it was now the men of our Fourth Section who led the way, the first three ranks already having performed a rotation. Once more, there was the crashing sound, while I stood one file apart from Germanicus, and for once, both of us were equally unhappy. I felt as if I was abandoning my duties; ironically, I was actually performing them, really for the first time, because it is not the job of the Primus Pilus to always be in the thick of the fighting, for the same reason I had given to Germanicus. This case was slightly different, because Germanicus was in command, but I was certain that if I rejoined the fighting, no more than a few heartbeats would pass before I would see him up there with me. Fortunately, fairly quickly, a half-dozen of the front rank of Maezaei were cut down and were soon underfoot as we pressed them even farther backward. Our alignment was such that, given my spot in the middle of our ranks, I could see straight down the street that led further east, but it was what I saw that was important; the beginning of the slope of that hill upon which the *praetorium* stood, was just ahead of us. The road itself took a sharp bend to the left, following the contour of the foot of the hill, but the upper part of buildings lining the street blocked the view of all but the highest part of the hill except for where we stood in the middle of the street. Towering above us was the *praetorium*, and it was brightly illuminated, which gave me the ability to see how it was completely surrounded and the front porch was jammed full of people, giving me the first hint of where the Maezaei civilians had fled to once the assault began. Up to this point, I did not recall seeing any Maezaei civilians darting about, nor did the buildings we passed show any sign that they were occupied by tribespeople who were huddled together in some room, shaking in terror as Rome came to exact vengeance. They could be dealt with later; at least, this was my thought as we continued our pressure on the warriors of the Maezaei, who gave ground, but not quite at the cost I would have expected from a people for whom this was the last gasp of their rebellion. I do recall at some point in the process, as I watched the enemy suddenly begin shuffling backward after only suffering two or three casualties, thinking that their hearts did not seem to really be in this defense. In the moment, it was odd, but I ascribed it to a variety of different factors, none of which turned out to be anywhere near their real reason for yielding. What mattered was that we penetrated more deeply into Raetinium, until we were at the foot of the hill, where the Second and Third Centuries made something of a pivot to their right as they pushed the Maezaei back towards the northern flank of the small hill inside the walls. At my suggestion, Germanicus dispatched the Sixth Century to make their way to the northern gate, where Blasio was instructed to help Agrippa and the Second Cohort to achieve their goal of battering it down. Under ideal circumstances, I would have ordered the Fifth Century to do essentially the same thing, but it was clear that Scipio's ram had not even reached the gate; there were no shattering crashes that would signal the heavy log of the ram was battering at the heavy wooden doors. Whether it was destroyed or it was just because of Scipio's ineptitude did not really matter, and I paid no more mind to the Third Cohort. By the time our Tenth Section took their place at the front, we had cleared the streets all the way up to the first perpendicular street located at the very base of the hill, the one that continued around the base of the northern side of the hill, but again, it seemed as if the casualties we were inflicting were lighter than it would seem the Maezaei should be willing to endure before giving ground. Our situation was far from ideal; the First and Second Centuries, roughly in the middle of our line, were now pushed out ahead of the other Centuries, as runners from each came and informed us of their status. This prompted another quick conference between Germanicus, Metellus, who he summoned from his Century, and me as we discussed the next steps.

"If we keep pushing, we're going to have to start climbing that hill, and we can see they're falling back to the *praetorium*," Germanicus began, and I was heartened, because I was afraid his blood would be up to the point where he would throw caution aside. "But," my heart skipped, knowing there is almost always something bad coming behind a "but," "we don't want to let up our pressure on them. We can't give them time to get organized."

"They're already organized."

That it was Metellus who blurted this out caught both Germanicus and me by surprise, but when I turned to look at my old comrade, I realized he was no less caught off guard than we were, and he suddenly looked as if he wanted to be somewhere else.

"What do you mean by that, Pilus Posterior?" Germanicus asked, and I heard the stiffness there.

Metellus hesitated, then glanced over at me, and I gave him a nod, so he said, "We're not killing enough of these *cunni* to justify them falling back like this. They're up to something."

Rather than respond, Germanicus glanced over at me, and while I did not relish the idea, I felt compelled to agree. "It does seem strange, sir." To support our case, I turned and pointed to the intersection through which we had just passed. "There are only a dozen men down there. Out of the, what, two or three hundred we're facing?"

"They've been dragging their wounded with them," Germanicus pointed out, and that was certainly true. Then, he turned to Metellus and demanded, "So, what are they up to?"

"That," Metellus' face was even more seamed than normal, to which I attributed the torches creating enough illumination to provide the stark contrast between light and shadow, "I don't know, sir. I just have a...feeling."

"Well," Germanicus' tone turned dismissive, "I'm afraid I can't make a decision based on your feeling, Metellus." Turning back to me, he began issuing his orders. "We're going to keep our current orientation but start pushing up this side of the hill." Leaning over to peer past me, he pointed at the nearest street that ran in an east/west direction athwart our current facing. "We'll use that street." Lifting his finger, he indicated the next perpendicular street, perhaps a hundred paces up from the bottom of the slope that ran north/south and ran across our front. "Metellus, I want you to push to the next block, then take the road up the hill from the north. The First and Second will meet at where the two streets intersect, and then we'll decide from there what's next. I want to get on this hill, now."

I opened my mouth to try one more time to argue for a more prudent course, but Germanicus preempted me with a firm shake of his head, though he said nothing. So, Metellus and I saluted, and we hurried to pass the word to our respective Centuries.

As soon as the two parallel streets the First was using turned upward to begin climbing the hill, the Maezaei took this as a signal to stiffen their resistance, meaning that it took us longer to reach the intersection where we were to link back up with the Second Century. I managed to refrain from joining in the fighting, though it was difficult, particularly after I had blown my whistle for the fifth relief and we were still a half-block away from the next intersection. Germanicus was clearly of a similar mind, but fortunately, he was sufficiently distracted by the series of men sent by the other Centuries, apprising the Legate of their particular situation. It was shortly after we began pushing up the hill that Blasio sent a man to inform Germanicus of the status of the Sixth.

"Agrippa's Cohort just breached the gate," the Gregarius got out as he panted for breath. "Centurion Blasio wants to know what the Sixth is to do now that we've done our part."

"Tell him to come join us," Germanicus ordered. "We can use your Century to keep the men fresh as we get nearer to the *praetorium.*"

Saluting, the runner departed, but before we could return our attention to our own battle, there was a shout from our right flank, where a section of men had been detached to face towards the southern wall, presumably where the Fourth and Fifth Century were located. Since Scipio and his men were still outside Raetinium, I did not think it likely that the barbarian in command of the contingent defending the southern gate would be willing to take the risk to detach warriors to come and fall on our right flank, particularly when the Fourth Century was somewhere out there between us and the Fifth. I say "somewhere," and I am not exaggerating; we had not heard anything from Tubertus, although there were sounds of fighting in the general direction where his Century was supposed to be, but it was yet another problem that is inherent in a night action. This disturbance was caused by another runner, except this one was from Novellus, and the news he brought was unsurprising, though that did not make it any less disturbing.

"Centurion Novellus reports that the Third Cohort's ram has been destroyed, and that they've retreated out of range of the artillery. He wants instructions about what to do next. Should he try to force the gate so the Third can come in?"

Before he answered, Germanicus glanced at me, and I shook my head, saying without hesitation, "A Century won't be enough."

The Legate nodded his agreement, but then he asked me, "What about with the Sixth? Once Blasio is here, we can send him straight on to help Novellus."

Frankly, I would have preferred to send someone to find Tubertus, but I could not deny that it made sense to use two of our Centuries to assault the southern gate from the inside, so I merely nodded my agreement. Honestly, my attention was only partially on Germanicus and what was taking place immediately around us, because higher up the hill, illuminated by a series of torches that were placed along the roof of the *praetorium*, I saw a flurry of movement of a nature that attracted my eye. It was not merely the presence of men, because they had been there from the moment we got close enough to see them. Before I could make sense of it, one of the Maezaei on the roof loosed an arrow, directly up into the sky. It was easy to track because it was a fire missile, and it streaked skyward, trailing tiny sparks as whatever flammable material they had attached burned away, and I could not help myself from standing there, my mouth open, as I watched it reach the apex of its flight, seem to pause for a fraction of a heartbeat, before turning to hurtle down to the earth.

"They're sending a signal," Germanicus' voice sounded calm, but I was certain I heard the tension there, as it was the unspoken part that was the cause for concern.

My initial thought was that, somehow, Dodonis had managed to coordinate with another band of Maezaei outside the walls, and this was their signal to attack one of the camps. It did not take long to dismiss this; I had too much faith in Gaesorix and his cavalry to believe that a force of a substantial enough size had managed to get close enough to us to do any such thing. This left the Maezaei inside Raetinium, and while it was possible that this was some sort of signal

397

to the men with whom we were currently engaged, trying to push them up the hill before we closed in and finished them off, I did not believe this was the case. Whatever it was, Germanicus was clearly not disposed to spend more than a handful of heartbeats discussing it, and he ordered me to resume command of the effort.

"We don't want to let up," he instructed, "so you go ahead. I'm going to wait here for the Sixth Century and tell them what I want them to do."

Consequently, the riddle of the signal remained unanswered, and I rejoined the First, directing Rufius back to his normal spot, stopping only to check on the half-dozen wounded rankers who had fallen in the latest round of fighting. Pleased to see none of them were mortally injured, in the moment, the fact that two of them were unable to move without help, suffering leg wounds, was merely one of those myriad details that a Centurion must tuck away in the back of his mind. Fairly quickly, I was back in the front rank, and it was not much longer after that I personally dispatched two Maezaei and sent one crawling back between the legs of his comrades who were still fighting. But, as we had been doing since we exited the gateway, we pushed the barbarians back, and the fighting had entered that phase where the initial wild frenzy had worn off, with men saving their collective breath as they grimly tried to either stop their foe, or in our case, tried to drive them back into a smaller area where we could bring to bear our entire force.

The Second Cohort, according to the plan, was going to sweep south from the northern gate, arranged on an east/west axis, pushing whatever resistance they met back to the hill, and while it was difficult to judge, in the momentary lulls of our own fight, I heard sounds coming from our left front quarter, which was the general vicinity of Agrippa and the Second, with Proculus and his Fourth Cohort following closely behind. Scipio's Cohort had been charged with sweeping up the southern, or back side of the hill, but since they had not even penetrated the gate, this was a major component of Germanicus' plan that was going unfulfilled, which also meant that Stertinius and his Fifth Cohort were still presumably standing outside the southern camp. Again, it is impossible to know with any certainty, but it was not very long after we saw the Maezaei fire arrow when our front rank cut their way to the intersection with the street that the Second Century was following. A handful of Maezaei either sacrificed themselves, or more likely, lost track of their overall situation, because once we gained the access to the perpendicular street, I sent two sections to our left, where they fell upon the rear of those barbarians who had been battling Metellus and his boys. Once more, the Maezaei, seeing they had lost control of yet another block, backed up the hill, except this time, rather than stopping midway in the next block, they retreated all the way to the next street.

"Ha!" Metellus pointed his blade, which looked black in the flickering light from the blood covering it. "They're finally figuring it out!"

This was certainly possible, yet the nagging thought that had been dogging me almost since we entered the gateway caused me to simply shrug and say, "It looks that way."

Metellus opened his mouth, I assumed to chide me for being so pessimistic, but he suddenly stopped, then tilted his head back and, quite strangely, began sniffing the air.

The sight of his great beak of a nose, quivering as he sniffed the night air, made me laugh, and I teased him, "Are you already trying to sniff out their mead supply, you old goat?"

For the only time since I had known him, Metellus did not reply with a joke of his own, and his frown only deepened as he turned his head. Finally, he asked, "Do you smell smoke?"

Biting back a cutting reply, pointing out that since the Maezaei had decided to illuminate the night, it was hardly noteworthy; instead, I forced myself to follow suit. It only took me a couple of breaths for whatever humor I was feeling to vanish. But it was not until we actually turned to face in the opposite direction, so that we were looking in the same direction as our enemies, back the way we had come, that both of us saw the same thing.

Our eyes met, and I imagine his eyes, widened as they were in shock and the very beginning of fear, mirrored mine.

"They fired the rampart!" I gasped. "They're trying to trap us in the town!"

We were only able to see this new threat because we had ascended the hill to a point where we could see over the roofs of the buildings, and I have often wondered if this was perhaps the only mistake Dodonis made in his fiendish plan. If his warriors had put up a stiffer fight just for a few blocks away from the hill, by the time we reached a spot where we could see what was happening, it would probably have been too late for any of us to survive. As it was, I only took long enough to turn almost directly left, to about where the southern gate was located, then turn and scan the horizon to see the sullen glow of fire that encompassed almost everything in my view. Only after I determined that this was not isolated to one part of the wall did I go running down the street, back two blocks to where Germanicus was just then talking to Blasio, giving him his orders.

"You need to see this." I did not even salute nor did I wait for Germanicus, turning and running back up the hill, trying to ignore my lungs screaming for mercy.

Thankfully, he was right behind me, but he was clearly irritated as he snapped, "This better be good."

Grasping his shoulder, I turned him around and simply pointed, then, using my hand, I turned his body so that he could see the entire scope of what was happening. I felt his body stiffen under my grip, and when he spun around, I did not need light to see his face go white with shock.

"He...he," Germanicus seemed to have trouble forming the words, "he wasn't bluffing! He's burning the town down!"

"And with us in it," I answered grimly. "Legate, we need to withdraw. Now."

As I had feared, the look of shock was replaced by what I had learned to recognize as his obstinate expression, when he was prepared to use his rank to ensure his will was done, but our cause was aided by a sudden crackling noise that prompted us to both to spin and stare in the direction of the southern wall, where a sudden gout of flame leapt high into the air, far above the rooftops or the wall. For a brief instant, the entire hillside facing the southern wall was illuminated, giving us a glimpse of dozens of figures, all of them moving uphill, towards the *praetorium.* From there, we turned a bit more to the right to face the southern gate, and while it was impossible to know, from appearances, it seemed as if the Maezaei had either started the fire from that spot or they had placed even more flammables than normal, because the flames were already several feet above the rooftops nearest the gate. .

This served to convince Germanicus more than anything I could have said, and he gave an abrupt nod, saying only, "You're right." Then, he turned to call to his *Cornicen* and ordered him, "Sound the call to withdraw."

The notes of the command rang out, and I ran the short distance to my spot, then waited for Metellus to reach the Second Century, which I was informed of by his own *Cornicen* sounding a single low note. Watching the rankers of the front rank who were currently engaged, I tried to time my next command properly, but there were still men either thrusting with their blades, or using their shields, which I could not avoid.

"Century! Prepare to withdraw!" I shouted the order, but I ignored the mutters of surprise and dismay, thinking to myself that since they could not turn around, the rankers had no idea what was happening behind us.

Then I gave the blast of my whistle, whereupon the men of the first rank shoved the Maezaei with whom they were engaged backward, then stepped to their left in the normal manner, except instead of stepping forward, the men of the second rank now became the first. In this manner, we were able to retreat, albeit slowly, giving up the ground we had gained. By the time we reached the first block of buildings on the bottom of the hill, the smell of smoke was unmistakable and could no longer be dismissed as coming from a handful of torches. The Maezaei seemed content to let us retreat without putting any pressure on us, other than an occasional hurling of a short spear when one of our men got careless and dropped their shield a bit too much. Thankfully, we did not take any casualties, while the men who had been wounded earlier had been dragged back behind the Century, or so I ordered. Meanwhile, Germanicus shouted to me that he had sent runners to all of the other Centuries, along with the Second Cohort, but none of them had returned. While this was certainly important, at the moment, I was more concerned with our immediate situation, and I hoped that the five other Centurions in command of the First Cohort had heard the loud call of the *cornu* already and recognized it for what it was. If there was hesitation or confusion, that would only complicate matters. Particularly worrying was the recognition that the Third and Fourth Centuries, whose section of the town did not include the hill, would not have the view of the now raging fire blocked by the buildings surrounding them because they were on ground level. This was especially true for Veratius' Century, because he and his men were essentially in the middle of the town, where most of the buildings had two stories, and a couple had three, but at this moment, there was nothing I could do about them. Until we got closer to the western gateway, which was the most direct way out of the town, and judging by the raging fire around the southern gate the safest, only then did I feel we could spare the time to ascertain where everyone else was, except as we were about to learn, Dodonis had been nothing if not thorough.

"The street is blocked!"

"We can't go any farther! Those fucking savages have trapped us!"

This and shouts like this reached my ears, but before I removed myself from the front rank, I blew a blast to signal a relief, then watched to ensure it happened without mishap. Only then did I back away three or four ranks before spinning about and trotting back to where the rearmost ranks of our Century were standing, while the wounded were either lying or sitting at their feet, as Rufius was trying to keep a lid on what I could hear was a simmering panic. Germanicus waved me past him to go check on the problem, shouting to me he would stay put and direct the fighting.

"At least we know what those wagons were for," I muttered to my Optio once I reached his side, shoving men out of the way, and got close enough to touch the wagon, giving it a cursory examination. This was dismaying, to say the least, and I forced myself to try and think about our progress to that moment, and how many of these wagons there had been, at least that I had noticed. The chatter of the men, the moaning of the wounded, and the growing glow of the fire threatened to overwhelm my ability to think, and it was this moment I recalled how a town on fire had triggered this feeling before. Forcing myself to concentrate, I did snap an order for the men to shut their mouths, then first tried to wedge myself between the wagon and the corner of the building, but quickly determined I was too big. Instead, I clambered over, landing in the intersection, which was when I saw that the Maezaei had done the same thing to the next three blocks over, all the way to where the Second Century with Metellus was located. Hearing the shouting from that direction, I ran quickly the two blocks over and hopped up onto the wagon, almost causing a panic from the men who were behaving in almost an identical manner, seemingly content to bemoan the perfidy of our enemies.

"Shut your mouths," I roared, "and someone go find Metellus!" A ranker turned to go, while I directed a section of men, "Climb over on this side and hurry! You can see for yourself the fire's spreading!"

Without waiting to see if they obeyed, I ran back to my own Century, but I was happy to see that Rufius had ordered the men to do essentially the same thing, and without waiting, they had climbed over to begin trying to move the wagon out of the way. Putting their shoulders into it, the wagon barely budged, so I came over and growled, "Watch how it's done," as I grabbed a ranker and pulled him aside. Bracing my shoulder against the wagon, I dropped my hips, then called to the others, "All right, on three…"

It did not move quickly, but it moved, and we continued scrabbling against the pavement stones, our hobnails making it hard to get a purchase, not stopping until the wagon was in the original spot it had been in when we passed it the first time.

"Go to the front and take over the relief," I ordered Rufius. "Keep them moving! And tell Germanicus the way is open, but we're going to have to collapse down and just use this street! We don't have time to move every fucking wagon!"

Saluting, he disappeared through the ranks of men, while I ordered the men who had helped with the wagon to stay nearby before running over to find that Metellus had arrived, and was already organizing the men to move the wagon that was in the identical spot.

"Do you remember how many of these wagons we passed?" he asked me, but I was somewhat ashamed to tell him I did not, then I added superfluously, "But we can be sure we're going to run into this again."

He shot me a sour look, then we spent a moment taking advantage of being in the middle of an intersection, giving us a slightly better view of our overall situation. Almost immediately, I was not sure this had been wise, because the fire had clearly engulfed the entire length of the wall that was within our range of vision, excepting only that part obscured by the bulk of the hill in the middle of the town, which included most of the eastern wall and about half of the southern. Meanwhile, up on the hill, the glow of the fire was such that it reflected onto the slopes, giving us a better view of the mass of people who were standing in the streets surrounding the *praetorium*. Too far away to tell whether they were warriors or civilians, what was clear was that Dodonis and his people were counting on the height of the hill to protect them from the growing fire, and I was struck by the grim thought that they had gathered to watch the spectacle of Romans burning to death.

"That fire spread awfully fucking fast," Metellus commented; we exchanged a glance, and I could see our thoughts were aligned.

"They had to have been planning this," I agreed, then felt a frown tug my mouth downward as I realized, with even more chagrin, that I had indeed noticed the barrels that had been arranged against the wall next to the western gate, underneath the wooden rampart, prompting me to groan, "Those barrels must have been at least partially filled with oil for the flames to reach the wood rampart so fast."

Whatever Metellus was about to say was interrupted by the blast of the whistle by his Optio, Gnaeus Cerrinius, and we turned to see the rest of his Century emerge out into the intersection, backing up in good order, although the rearmost ranks were dragging four freshly wounded men along with them. Before either of us could react, the men of the First, also in good order, retreated into the intersection a few blocks over, so I left Metellus, to return to my command. Germanicus was back in the front rank, lunging at a Maezaei who, in a fit of boldness, had dashed forward a couple of paces into the more open intersection, swinging a long *gladius* in a wild circle over his head, before bringing it crashing down onto Germanicus' shield.

"Pluto's cock," I am afraid I said this more loudly than I intended, "we don't have time for him to play Horatius!"

Rufius had been forced to place himself next to Germanicus, protecting his weak side, but fortunately, only this one Maezaei seemed to be interested in trying to smite our Legate, while the others stood, just in between the buildings on the eastern side of this intersection, using them as protection for their flanks. Striding up between the files, I snapped an order to a ranker to hand me his shield, and without hesitating, moved through the ranks, stepping out into the spot to Germanicus' left, just as Germanicus, having weathered the attack from his opponent, was launching his own assault. It was not planned, certainly, but the fact that he performed a third position thrust, trying to get behind the left side of the Maezaei's shield, forced the warrior to bring his protection farther out from his body than was prudent, especially when I was in a perfect position to end this private battle with a single thrust. My blade was already back in first position before the Maezaei, mouth sagging open in shock, staggered backward and fell against the raised shields of his comrades.

Ignoring Germanicus' glare, I snapped, "We don't have time for heroics." Then I backed away, returning to the safety of the formation, with Germanicus, clearly reluctant, following suit, leaving Rufius to wait until we were out of immediate danger. Reaching my side, the youth opened his mouth to say something, but I pointed with my *gladius*, still dripping, sweeping it across the expanse of the rampart, saying, "This fire has already caught along the entire rampart. If we don't hurry, that wood is going to collapse, and it's going to spread to the buildings."

This served its purpose, because he shut his mouth, giving a curt nod instead. By this point, the rearmost ranks of both the First and Second were already a few paces down the next block, while the men of the last section had already hurried down the street towards the next intersection.

"There's another wagon!" Rufius, who had resumed his original post, came to report, but even as he was doing so, another ranker, this one from the Second, ran up to us, gasping out the same information.

This is the first moment where I can remember noticing that it was distinctly warmer, while the smoke was now thick enough that men were beginning to cough.

Turning to Rufius, I ordered him, "Take a section and head that direction," I pointed towards the southern gate. "I need you to do two things. First, check and see if every street west is blocked by those wagons, and second, see if you can find Tubertus and his Century. If you find a way through, send a man back to tell me." Without waiting for him to acknowledge, I addressed the ranker of the Second, telling him essentially the same thing, other than naming Veratius' Century as the one for which they were looking. Once this was done, rather than wait to see if there was another way through as I originally intended, I changed my mind and sent the same section that had moved the first wagon down the block to the next intersection and who had just returned from checking for the presence of a wagon, telling them to repeat what they had done a couple moments earlier, ignoring the muttered complaints about their Centurion making them run back and forth. Returning my attention to the front, I saw I was still a couple ranks short of the leading edge, where I could see that the Maezaei had apparently decided to renew their own attack. The men in the front rank were now furiously engaged, and Germanicus had taken up a spot immediately behind them, exhorting the rankers, and I moved to join him. I only got within a couple paces when, from behind us, there was a sudden cacophony of shouts, the ringing sound of metal striking metal, and worse, at least one scream of a kind that only comes from a mortal wound. Whirling about, I began running, but before I made it back through the ranks, I spied a lone figure, with only a *gladius*, dashing towards us from the direction I had just sent the section to move the next wagon.

I slid to a stop, the fire now providing enough light that I saw the blood that turned the plates of his *segmentata* black, though it was the wild-eyed expression that matched his words as he shouted at me, "They were waiting for us! They were waiting for us! My section's under attack! They're probably all dead already!"

Shoving him aside, despite knowing I had no choice, I reluctantly called for two sections to accompany me, mentally doing the math as I tried to determine just how deep a formation we had left, keeping the Maezaei, who were now pressing from our east, at bay. Even with the most optimistic assessment, the numbers were not good; they had no choice but to hold, and I began pinning my hopes that either Tubertus or Veratius, or better yet, both of them and their Centuries would show up.

I instantly saw that the Maezaei had timed their attack well, waiting until our men were involved with pushing the wagon out of the way, and they had been thorough, cutting down all but two of the eight men, though four of the fallen were wounded. Rather than stand and fight, the band of Maezaei vanished into the smoky darkness, heading in the general direction of the western gate.

"They were hiding in that warehouse," the most lightly wounded of the section informed me, trying to suppress a groan as one of his comrades of the sections who had come with me used the man's neckerchief to bind a nasty wound to his upper left arm. "They caught us good, Primus Pilus." Glancing down at the corpse of one of his comrades, the ranker's face twisted into a mask of bitter but impotent anger. "And that stupid bastard Pusio, I don't know what he was thinking." Only then did he look up at me, and I pretended not to notice the tears in his eyes as his voice broke. "He threw himself in front of me, Primus Pilus! He took a spear right through the lungs for me! Why did he do that?"

What does one say to that? I certainly do not know now, nor did I then, so I mumbled something about how he would have done the same thing for the dead Pusio, but honestly, my mind was already elsewhere. Perhaps a sixth part of a watch had now elapsed since we began our withdrawal, and we were still at least five blocks away from the western gate and one block away from the small stone bridge over the part of the river enclosed by the western wall that we had used, but I was at least close enough now that, provided I moved to the proper spot, I could look down the street we were using to retreat to catch a glimpse of the western wall. Not surprisingly, it was fully involved, blazing fiercely, and I could see that, at this moment, the rampart was still intact and had not collapsed, but I also could see that there was another wagon, this one drawn across the bridge. The fact that the fire had not yet spread was something that could not last, I knew, and I was forced to make a decision. I had just lost almost a full section of men, added to those casualties we had already suffered, totaling almost thirty men of the one hundred forty of the First Century who assaulted the western gate what seemed days before. The Second was in slightly better shape, and as I stood there, I saw a section of Metellus' men come clambering over the wagon that was blocking their way, but unlike our men, they were unmolested as they grunted and strained, pushing the rock-laden wagon out of the way. Facing back east, I saw that about half of the remainder of the Century was now into the intersection, with the front rank still roughly halfway down the street, while the barbarians were once more content to stand just out of reach, and occasionally darting forward in pairs or threes to maintain some sort of pressure. One did not have to be a veteran to understand that their intentions were to keep us from simply turning around and retreating with any haste, but what puzzled me was how long they were willing to keep up this pressure, because one thing I was certain about was that these men did not have any intention of burning to death. At some point, I reasoned, they would certainly retreat back to the safety of the hilltop, which was obviously serving as their refuge; the real question was whether or not they were, in fact, safe from the spreading flames. From what little I could tell, down among the buildings, while the entire rampart was now involved, I had no way of knowing whether the fire had spread to the buildings nearest to the wall. However, I had more pressing concerns, namely that wagon drawn across the eastern approach to the bridge. Although I could not see it, I also felt certain that the only other bridge in that direction that the Second and Third had used and connected the newer part of Raetinium with the original town was also blocked. The river was a bit more than fifty paces wide, but I had to assume it was too deep to wade across, and even if it was not, now that we knew there were an unknown number of Maezaei in between us and the gateway, I was not about to risk sending men into the water where they would be their most vulnerable.

Even though it went against my instinct to move as quickly as possible, I forced myself to refrain from sending men to begin moving the wagon blocking the bridge, choosing instead to wait in the more open space of the intersection for Germanicus to reach me. Fortunately, he emerged from in between the buildings of the previous block a matter of heartbeats later, just ahead of the first two ranks of the Century, who backed into the intersection. The fact that Germanicus was half-dragging yet another wounded man, the arm of the ranker draped over his shoulder as he did what he could to help his Legate bring him to the parlous safety of the rear of the Century was yet another worry. As he deposited the man gently on the street, I could not hear Germanicus' words to the wounded man, though I saw the ranker, who I recognized as Gnaeus Siculus, one of the two-enlistment veterans from the 8th, nod his head in response, even as he resumed using both hands to press down on his thigh, although I could see it was doing little good. Germanicus called to one of Siculus' comrades to help the old veteran, but I could tell by his expression as he walked up to me that he understood it was a forlorn hope.

Saluting, I kept an eye on the Maezaei, who, once more, seemed content to stop just short of the intersection and keep their flanks protected by the walls of the structures, as I explained the situation to our Legate.

"They've blocked the bridge we crossed, and while I can't see the other ones, I'm willing to bet they're blocked too," I began.

Germanicus' face was once more glistening from sweat, except now I could feel the moisture on my own face and, this time, it was because it had become noticeably hotter; his expression was grave, but it was the fact that he asked, "What should we do?" that told me he was sufficiently rattled that he was falling back into the old habit of our relationship when it first began.

"We're going to have to coordinate with the Second, because we're going to need more than a section or two to move that wagon. I'm about as sure as I can be that those Maezaei who ambushed us when we moved the last one are waiting to attack whoever we send out there."

He considered this for a brief span, then nodded, but asked, "Should we wait to find out about the other Centuries? And what about the Second Cohort?"

Those were certainly valid questions, but while I was willing to entertain the idea of waiting for word of the rest of the First Cohort, on the Second, I was not sanguine about the wisdom of wasting time trying to link up, and I said as much.

"We can wait a bit longer," I agreed, though I was keeping my eye on the enemy, who were standing there, watching us, "for the other Centuries. But the Second," I shrugged, and said only, "I don't think we can afford the time it would take to try and link up with them."

Whether it was by accident, or the gods decided to help my case, for the first time that night, we felt the beginning of a breeze, coming from our left and funneled a bit by the buildings lining the north/south street where we were standing, but it was the appearance of a flare of flame over and above the current dim light that caused us to turn and look to the north just in time to catch what looked like a roiling ball of fire that poked upward above the rooftops that settled matters.

"I think that bastard Dodonis has placed barrels of oil all over this town," I told Germanicus, nodding my head where the flames were just then subsiding, "and that was one of them going up. That," I finished grimly, "is about where Agrippa and his men should be."

Germanicus' mouth was hanging open in what I took to be a combination of shock and dismay, but he did not argue, simply nodding and saying, "Let's find the rest of the Cohort. The Second's fate is in the hands of the gods now."

Perhaps the only positive development was that it was not more than a hundred heartbeats after this when there was a shout from the men on our right flank, who had been facing south along the north/south street, and we turned to see a handful of figures trotting in our direction. The light of the fire had grown to the point I did not need to wait for Rufio to come within a few paces to recognize him, but it was the ones wearing the transverse crest who were a more welcome sight. Novellus and Blasio saluted, which prompted a shout of alarm when a trio of Maezaei, seeing a cluster of high-ranking Romans, hurled the barbarian version of javelins in our direction, although they were all blocked by our men in the ranks arrayed between us and the enemy. It did serve to make me suggest we move a bit farther away, just within the shelter of the next block to the west, the last one between us and the bridge. I had sent two sections partway down the street, and they were now facing the bridge, while our wounded had been moved to a spot a few paces away in between them and our impromptu conference. We now had fifteen men out of action but were still alive, although Siculus was one of them and was likely to be dead by the time we resumed moving, and that was not counting those who were already dead and we had been forced to leave behind.

"The barbarians on the southern wall just ran east along the rampart until they were behind the hill, then they jumped down and went up there," Novellus pointed back in the direction of the *praetorium*, then finished bitterly, "but not before they set fire to the rampart."

"How did they do it?" I asked, though even as I did, I understood it did not really matter. "Did they set fire to the rampart itself? Or did they light some barrels underneath it?"

Somewhat to my surprise, Novellus replied, "They did both. We didn't notice until it was too late, but they had a bunch of crates and

411

barrels and the like on the rampart, and they put the torch to them, but when they ran east and climbed down, I saw a handful of the *cunni* go underneath the rampart. Then," he snapped his fingers to illustrate the rapidity, "there was a fire blazing high enough to touch the bottom of the rampart, quicker than Pan."

"But," Germanicus blurted out, "why? Why would Dodonis want to burn the town down while they're still inside it?"

This was a valid question, but I did not think it mattered all that much, though I was not willing to say this openly, so I changed the subject instead, asking Novellus, "Where's your Century?"

He turned and pointed south. "They're three blocks that way, but right now, I have them in between the buildings out of sight."

"On which side of this street?" I asked and was relieved when he answered that it was on the western side, while I also tried to recall where the other bridges were in relation to our position, but while I knew there was one to the north, or right of where we were currently standing, I could not remember whether it was a matter of three or four blocks away, or farther. Turning to Blasio, he informed us, "My boys are with Novellus' Century."

That gave us two Centuries whose casualties were much lighter than those of the First and Second's, and I deferred to Germanicus, who gave the order for them to march in force down their street to place themselves on the north/south street that was next to the river, with the Fifth facing east where the bulk of the Maezaei were still more or less standing there watching us, and the Sixth facing the southern wall in the event that there was a force of Maezaei hidden somewhere in the remaining three blocks between them and the southern wall. Tubertus' Century was still missing, but I was beginning to suspect I knew where they were; my suspicion was that they had already retreated back across the river, and for all I knew, were already outside the walls. All that remained was the whereabouts of Veratius, but this was solved even before we broke up our quick conference, when Metellus arrived and brought the Princeps Prior with him.

"We could see that the fire has made it to the first block next to the wall," Veratius informed us grimly, and while we were all sweating profusely now, we could see that there was a fine film of soot coating his helmet, while the grime on his face was marked by the rivulets of sweat cascading down it. "It's at that section of the northern wall before it turns straight," he explained. "It was only that first block, but that's not going to last, not with this wind blowing."

The spot he was referring to was the addition to the northern wall that extended out to meet the newer western wall, creating a kink in an otherwise straight line, and when Veratius brought it up, I did remember noticing that the row of homes and shops were actually closer to the wall at that point than anywhere else, though I thought no more about it at the time. Now that we had all but one Century of the First accounted for, Germanicus quickly amended the plan, essentially having Veratius' Century mirror that of the Sixth, facing north, while the First and Second continued to withdraw to the bridge. It was a solid plan; indeed, given the circumstances, I believe it was the best plan with which we could come up, but as always, the enemy has plans of their own, and in the case of Dodonis, his was not only fiendishly clever, but involved an aspect of the character of the Maezaei that heretofore I had never witnessed.

Our first hint, though only in retrospect, was that for the first time, the Maezaei did not follow our leading ranks of either the First or Second as we backed down the streets leading to the bridges. In the moment, I ascribed it to the idea that by doing so, they were getting closer to the band of fire that was now encircling all of us and threatening to trap my Cohort. As far as the blaze, even those of us facing east could feel the heat transferring itself to either the plates of our *segmentata*, or in my case, the *hamata*, quickly becoming bearable but distinctly uncomfortable. When facing in the direction of the fire, it felt as if one was staring into an open oven, but even worse, the flames were now clearly visible, leaping into the air above the wall, though it was still impossible for me to determine if the fire involved the buildings of the nearest block. Judging just by the heat, I found it impossible to believe that at least one block was not aflame, and I was clearly not alone in this belief, the men moving as quickly as possible under the conditions. Stepping out into the intersection, I led five sections across the street to the bridge, regretting the fact that we had expended all of our javelins, but I only designated one to actually push the wagon aside, and one section picked up the yoke to pull, while the other men arrayed themselves at the rear and side away from the bridge to push. Even with the brighter light from the growing fire, none of us, myself included, saw the hail of arrows that came arcing from across the river until they were less than an eyeblink from plunging down into the essentially defenseless men around the wagon. The fact that more than half of the missiles missed, striking either the side of the wagon, or skittering across the paving stones, was little consolation from the sudden shouts and cries of pain as a half-dozen men were struck.

"Get around them and get your shields up!" I roared, cursing myself for not thinking of it before.

There was no hesitation on the part of the comrades of the fallen men, but neither was there time for them to get into place before another volley came slashing down, although it did give me the opportunity to see the figures of what appeared to be perhaps thirty archers positioned on the roofs of the first row of buildings on the western side of the river, now outlined against the flames behind them after they stood up. Fortunately, the men who escaped injury from the first arrows had scrambled to the opposite side of the wagon, dragging their injured comrades with them, and they were now crouched within the shelter of the wooden sides of the wagon, so there were no further casualties. Once enough men had arrayed themselves so they presented their shields to protect the rankers tasked with moving the wagon, they resumed their task, albeit with four less men. In addition, it was extremely awkward for the men protecting their comrades, as they were forced to sidestep at the same pace as the moving wagon. As this was taking place, I backed away, trying to keep a wary eye on the archers as I backed away to check on the rest of the First. Continuing their recent behavior, the enemy warriors were not only content to watch us retreat, they did not even leave the intersection at the eastern end of the block we were in, instead just watching as Germanicus, with Rufius calling out the count we use for withdrawing, and the rest of the First exited from between the buildings. With the fire now burning in a rough circle all around us, as the wooden rampart was now fully involved and the flames were clearly visible everywhere except where the hill blocked our view, it provided a level of illumination that enabled both sides in the fight to see more clearly than at any other point, and the archers took advantage of that by shifting their aim to begin raining arrows down on the bulk of the First Century. Since the first four ranks were still facing east, observing the Maezaei we had been battling for what I guessed was now a full watch, this exposed their backs, and despite the brighter light, it was still extraordinarily difficult to track the missiles once they left the bows of the archers. This meant it was our turn to suffer from what I had estimated as thirty missiles slashing down from the darkness above us, and whether it was fortune or skill, some of them arced over the shields of those men who had turned about to face the bridge, which, an instant before, had been the rear of our formation but was now the front, at least from this missile attack. Once again, my ears were assailed by the sounds of the iron-tipped heads punching into shields, or worse, the solid meaty noise as some of them either found a gap in a man's armor or, in one case, penetrated it. I know this last to be so because I was the one struck, only seeing the arrow hurtling down in the fraction of an eyeblink before it punched through the chainmail protecting my left upper arm. Honestly, it did not hurt at first, instead feeling like some invisible man with my own strength had suddenly punched me in the arm, causing me to take a staggering step backward. And, I am somewhat ashamed to admit, my immediate reaction was to stare dumbly at the shaft that had seemingly just sprouted from my arm; what I recall most vividly was noticing that it was still quivering, although I suppose that could have been because of my body shaking in reaction to being struck.

"You've been hit!"

I do not know whether or not hearing Rufius shout this had anything to do with it, but the words were barely out of his mouth when the pain hit, and I was unable to stop myself from groaning aloud.

Crossly responding to Rufius as I felt an irrational stab of anger, I snapped, "Don't you think I know that?"

Without waiting for a response, I thoughtlessly pointed, or tried to, in the direction of two men I could see had been struck from behind, their comrades facing the opposite direction unable to raise their shields high enough above their heads to block the plunging missiles, and my groan turned into a bellow of pain because, out of habit, I had used the hand that normally carried my *vitus*.

Consequently, I could only speak through gritted teeth as I ordered Rufius, "Help those two first."

Rufius hesitated, but my glare was enough to get him moving, and as it happened, Germanicus as well, his attention on the eastern Maezaei force diverted by the sounds of the arrows striking behind him. When he turned, he saw me standing there as I was frankly trying to determine what to do about the cursed arrow sticking out of my upper arm, while I tentatively flexed my left hand and forearm.

"You've been hit!"

This time, I managed to refrain from a surly retort, given that it was my Legate, so I said nothing, simply nodding in response. He reached my side at almost the exact instant there was a shout from the westward facing men, warning us the archers had loosed another volley. Thankfully, now they were more prepared, so the only sounds were those of arrowheads striking shields, or the sharper sound as the iron points struck the street and went caroming off, except these ricochets can be as dangerous as a direct strike, although that did not happen this time. Nevertheless, both of us flinched, dropping into a semi-crouch and, without saying anything, I shuffled closer to the men who were protecting us, getting immediately behind them, and Germanicus followed suit.

"Is it bad?"

"I don't think so," I answered cautiously, then hesitated, not relishing what I was about to ask. "But, sir, I need you to break the shaft off as close to the head as you can."

As I expected, his expression fairly screamed that he had no desire to do anything of the sort, which I suppose prompted him to ask, "Shouldn't we pull it out? Or," he amended, "push it through?"

"Yes, we should," I agreed, noticing that the blood was now flowing down from under my *hamata* and down onto my upper arm, "but we don't have time. I'll have to wait until we get out of here."

The light was strong enough to see the younger man turn pale, but he did not argue, nor did he hesitate, stepping close enough to reach out and grasp the shaft; just that was enough for me to have second thoughts, but I was committed now, more out of pride than anything else, and I clenched my teeth together. Giving him a curt nod, I braced myself, or at least I thought I did, but the pain was horrific, and suddenly, I was transported to a completely different place and time, because this was a type of agony I had experienced before, albeit when I was ten years old. Somehow, I cannot say how, I managed to stay still, though I could not stifle the cry as Germanicus managed, with one brutally strong motion, to snap the shaft of the arrow.

"Pluto's thorny cock," I think I gasped, and for a horrifying moment, everything began spinning, which Germanicus must have noticed, because he suddenly grabbed my arm, taking care to grasp it just above the elbow, ignoring the fact that it was covered in blood.

"Steady, Pullus," he spoke lightly, or attempted to, "I'm going to need you."

This was the best thing he could have said to me, and in the moment, I wondered if he had divined this was the case, or it was just a happy accident. Either way, what mattered was that it gave me what I needed to regain my self-control.

"I'm fine now," I assured him, but then thought of something. Grabbing my neckerchief, I pulled it free and asked him, "Will you bind it, sir?"

"Part of the shaft is sticking out," he pointed out, but while I had seen this, I was undeterred.

"I can't afford to lose more blood," I told him honestly, then with a bit of difficulty, awkwardly lifted my free arm and indicated my right side, where the spear had sliced through the links of my mail. It had stopped bleeding, but I could feel that my tunic around the wound was now wet, although it was beginning to stiffen as the blood dried. My hope was that the moisture I was feeling was sweat, but I was not willing to take the chance. "So, just tie it up tight enough to stop the bleeding."

Germanicus did as I asked, and this time, I could not avoid letting out another rather undignified yelp as the cloth tightened over the splintered inch of the protruding shaft.

Stepping away, the Legate eyed his work critically, but when he reached up to rearrange it, I stopped him.

"This will do fine, sir. And," I tried to make a joke, "at least I don't notice my side as much."

Whether Germanicus' laugh was forced or not, what I could discern was that he understood why I had spoken louder than was necessary and that it was meant for the ears of the men around us, and he played his role well, saying with a cheerfulness that sounded genuine to my ears, "Good! Then, let's get out of here, shall we?"

"Yes…"

Before the words were out, there were shouts from the men around the bridge, and we both stepped around the rankers still holding up their shields, risking exposure to more arrows in order to see the cause. Much to the relief of both of us, we saw that the wagon was now moved to the side, opening the way across the bridge.

"Perfect timing," Germanicus remarked, and he grinned up at me, which I at least tried to return.

"Let's get out of here, boys!" I called out loudly enough for at least the First and Second to hear me, while Germanicus called Natta, who had suffered the indignity of an arrow through the wide mouth of the horn, and ordered him to sound the call so that the other Centuries could hear.

"Right," Germanicus practically shouted as the notes were being sounded. "I think the Second should lead the way across the bridge. They're in better shape than your Century."

I hesitated in answering, waiting for him to ask if I agreed, but once more, he had resumed his role as the commander, and I understood there was only one thing to say. Luckily, I actually agreed, so I saluted and fell back into my job as a Centurion in command of his Century, recognizing that Germanicus was now making the decisions regarding the Cohort. Since they had not been given any orders beyond moving the wagon, the men involved picked up their shields, joining their comrades who had been protecting them. I suppose it makes sense that this was the moment that we noticed something else had changed, realizing that the arrows were no longer flying at us, and I looked up to the rooftops to see that the archers had disappeared.

Germanicus did as well, and he commented, "I suppose they decided they'd done enough damage and they want to save themselves from being roasted."

This certainly appeared to be the case, and we did not waste any time taking advantage of the first respite from fighting we had experienced. Summoning the sections of the First and sending them to reintegrate back into our formation, I did keep half of the Century facing east, with the other half watching the bridge and the buildings across the river. Metellus had quickly answered the command from our Legate, but I was not within earshot of Germanicus when he gave my old comrade his orders, though I did move closer to the bridge so that I could exchange a word with Metellus as his Century began crossing the bridge.

For the first time certainly this night, and one of the only times I could recall, the old Pilus Posterior did not seem disposed to make a joke, nor was he even smiling as he saluted me. "It's time we get out of here, eh, Pullus?"

"It is," I agreed, "and we're counting on you and your boys to lead the way."

"We'll do that," he assured me, but then he did something completely unexpected, suddenly thrusting out his arm as he said, "and may the gods go with you, Titus."

Frankly, I was more bemused than anything, because this was extremely unusual behavior for Metellus, who never behaved or talked as if it was anything but a foregone conclusion that we would be victorious and see another sunrise.

Regardless, I took his arm and said, "And with you, Servius. Now," I jerked my head in the direction of where the Second was waiting, "get us out of here."

And he and the Second did as he promised, or at least tried to, but we were a matter of heartbeats away from learning of the final trick Dodonis had to play on us.

As befitted his status as a Centurion, Metellus was at the head of his Century as they crossed the narrow bridge, their helmets outlined against the fire that was now clearly out of control and moving more rapidly than even a few moments earlier. It had been decided by Germanicus that the First would be more or less taken out of the fight, our task to carry the wounded and those dead who had fallen over the course of our withdrawal, having been dragged along with us by their comrades still effective. Our wounded were quickly divided into three categories; those who could walk on their own, those who were either unconscious or wounded in a spot whereby one man could carry him over his shoulder, and those who could only be carried on a shield. The dead, however, we were forced to treat in a manner that could be construed as disrespectful, but we had no real choice in the matter, and those charged with this grisly task took the leather thongs or lengths of thin rope that they all carried when we went into battle, usually for use as a method of securing captured prisoners, instead tying them around the feet of their dead comrades and using this as a means to drag them along. It was a horrible sight, but the circumstances left us with no choice; this was the fastest way to take our dead with us, and by the time the First had gathered up the wounded and dead, and arranged them in the manner I described, I was left with a total of fifteen men who were unburdened. I was so absorbed in this task that I was caught completely by surprise, as were we all, by the sudden explosion of sound in the form of roaring shouts and the kind of shrill cries that some barbarians use when they are sprinting into battle. My back was turned to the river as I stood with Rufius, supervising our men, forcing me to spin about so abruptly that I felt a tearing sensation of the wound along my ribs, taking my breath away. What I saw when I looked beyond the bridge was so horrifying that I believe it was the sight as much as the pain that wrenched a gasp from my lips. Pouring out of each of the structures of the first block on the other side of the river were what seemed to be several hundred Maezaei warriors, converging on Metellus' Century from three sides. The noise was deafening, and I am afraid that the rest of the Cohort, still on the eastern side of the bridge, stood there in shock for the span of a few precious heartbeats, forced to watch as Metellus and his Century were surrounded by a swarming, snarling horde of barbarians who did not seem frightened in the least at the prospect of burning to death, not if it meant they could take Romans with them.

"Third Century! Advance across the bridge! NOW!"

It was only because Germanicus was actually standing next to the Third, who had just begun to move across the bridge that Veratius and his men heard our Legate's command, although his tone was the shrillest I had ever heard, and tinged with a panic that, frankly, every one of us shared, and I include myself.

"Follow me, boys!" Veratius, despite his overall youth and the fact that he had been one of the contingent of young upper class Romans who had shown up with Germanicus more than a year earlier, did not hesitate, and behaved exactly as a Centurion of Rome is expected to and should, leading his men while holding his *gladius* aloft, crossing the bridge at a dead run.

The voices of the Third Century added to the din, but in a practical sense, their move onto the bridge itself obscured my view of what was happening to the Second; the last glimpse I had gotten, it appeared that Metellus was attempting to get them into a sort of *orbis*, as the Maezaei came rushing at them like a flood, surging around them to cut them off from the bridge. Just an instant before Veratius and his Century crossed the final stretch of the span to slam into the Maezaei, I saw the lighter blur of faces now turning to meet our attempt to help the Second. Then there was yet another crashing sound that briefly overpowered the din of the fighting, and as proof of the tremendous collision, a lone helmet suddenly flew up at least three or four feet in the air, tumbling over and over. Fortunately, I could see that it was not one of ours, and it quickly disappeared, but there was a sudden high-pitched shout in Latin that never bodes well, as a long Gallic *gladius* suddenly thrust up into the air, the fire making the blood on the blade glisten. Before I could react, Germanicus was next to me, the good humor of just moments before now vanished, and to my eyes, it seemed as if he had aged ten years in the span of heartbeats.

"We're going to need to feed more men over there to help Metellus," he spoke quickly, "but how? The bridge is already packed," we both turned to see that Veratius' men were still fighting furiously but had yet to shove their way off the bridge, "so we can't send the Fifth or Sixth across, it won't do any good." He turned his head slightly, and I followed his gaze, but before I could stop him, he pointed. "What about wading across the river, downstream a hundred paces or so?" Then, to my relief, he answered his own question. "No, that would be suicide, especially since we don't know how deep it is."

"I think we're going to have to send men that way," I pointed north, "to that other bridge."

Germanicus turned and peered in that direction, but I could have told him he was wasting his time since the river curved slightly, not much, but just enough so the bridge was obscured by the buildings lining the river.

"We don't know if there are any of these bastards waiting for us," he spoke doubtfully, but again, his hesitation did not last long enough for me to intervene, "but we don't have any choice, I suppose." Without pausing, he wheeled about, scanned the cluster of men nearby, then found who he was looking for, calling Novellus, who came at the run.

Without bothering to return the Centurion's salute, Germanicus pointed back in the direction we had just been looking. "Take your Century, at the double, to that second bridge. Get across it, and then," he looked at Novellus, his face a grim mask, "hit those fucking savages over there as hard as you can."

Novellus' eyes widened, but he did not hesitate in saluting and repeating the orders he had just been given before returning to his Century, then leading them at a quick trot north along the street paralleling the river. I watched just long enough to see them round the slight bend and disappear behind the series of temples that were in the outlying section around the forum, which was located at the northern foot of the hill. As I recalled, the second bridge was more or less aligned with the southern edge of the forum, but about three blocks west of it. What I did not remember was whether one could see the bridge from the forum, and the reason for my concern was this was a large open area where Dodonis could be waiting with part of the Maezaei force, prepared for the very move we were making, although in theory Agrippa's Cohort would have been there instead. It was a horrible feeling, being so helpless to influence the outcome and forced to rely on others, and once more, I felt the cold grip of panic creeping around the edges of my conscious mind, like the wolves that had once lurked outside our camp when we marched for Germanicus' father Drusus. Only being responsible for our dead and wounded did not help, except that it was due more to the pressure I felt from trying to protect them than any feeling I had been slighted, and just from a scan of the expressions of the rankers of my Century, I saw I was not alone. Perhaps the worst part was in being spectators to a fight that would ultimately seal our fate, and despite not really needing to do so, it was with some surprise that I realized I had my *gladius* in my hand, the point down and moving in the circles that I had copied from my Avus from the moment I held my first *rudis*. It was an odd moment, but I was struck by the memory of a story my father liked to tell about how, while I watched my Avus sparring with those few men willing to face him, I would stand to the side with my own small *rudis*, mimicking his every move, including that circling motion.

423

It took several long moments, but Veratius and his Century were finally able to vanquish those Maezaei warriors who were interposed between them and Metellus' men. With the light as strong as it was, we could see the fighting very clearly, including when one of our own men was struck down, though most of the time, they came crawling back in between their comrades supporting those doing the actual fighting. Fairly quickly, I found myself ordering Rufius and the few spare men we had left to dash across the bridge and bring the wounded back, which in turn meant I was running out of able-bodied rankers. Germanicus had positioned himself in the middle of the bridge, with Natta next to him, although at this point, he was as much of a spectator as I was, his contribution being shouting his encouragement and exhorting his fellow Romans to destroy our enemies. I divided my time between watching the fight directly across from me and squinting to the north, praying to every god I thought might have some sort of interest in what we were doing, asking them for their intercession. Naturally, they gave no sign they were listening, unless it was in the form of the movement that I caught in the general direction of the second bridge. Without any thought, I felt my body tense, half-expecting this to be some other Maezaei force that their cunning bastard of a chieftain was sending to try and finish us off. It made for a tense dozen heartbeats as I squinted against the stinging smoke, cursing how it was making my eyes water so much I could feel tears on my cheeks.

"It's Novellus! He must have gotten across with no trouble!"

Rufius shouted this, and even with the overall sense of foreboding that hung across the shoulders of my men almost as heavily as the wounded they were carrying, they nonetheless managed a cheer. Which, I realized too late, served as a warning to the Maezaei, who were now pressing the advantage they had gained from their surprise attack, specifically those on the northern side. Even with the noise generated by the fighting, I could only watch helplessly as the warriors of the rear ranks suddenly turned their heads, first in our direction across the river. For the span of a heartbeat, I entertained the hope that they would be satisfied with just looking our way to try and determine why their foes were letting out a cheer, then simply dismiss it as something unimportant. And it seemed as if they would do just that, as all but one of them returned their attention to what was happening in front of them, waiting their turn to strike a blow at us, except only one man was needed to raise the alarm. It was simply a matter of luck that I was actually gazing at the man who did that very thing, turning all the way around to stare north, and I knew that our chance of surprise had been lost. Obviously, Novellus understood this as well, because the man had barely turned to face him when I heard a faint shout, followed quickly by the sound of Novellus' *Cornicen* trying to blow the right notes to signal that his Century was to go immediately to the run. In short, it was the kind of noise one expects from a man just learning to play the horn, but it served its purpose, and thankfully was drowned out by the full-throated roar of Novellus' Century as they went pounding down the street. Shifting my gaze, I saw that, while the Maezaei had indeed been warned earlier than was ideal, there was only a thin line no more than two men deep who were facing north, preparing themselves for what was to come. It came quickly, with Novellus leading the way, barely slowing down as he threw himself against the hastily raised shields of the barbarians, and I confess I winced at his hubris, since I had watched him working the stakes and had seen he did not have the skills necessary to perform a maneuver like that, but before I could see how matters turned out with him, he was obscured from my sight by the bodies and shields of the rest of the Fifth Century.

Before I could count to ten, the noises emanating from the fight across the river changed in tenor and volume, and I experienced a sudden surge of, if not hope, then at least relief, as my experience in battle informed me that the battle was now changing, and in our favor. It was a combination of things that I did not even need to lift the ear flap of my helmet to interpret, a mixture of alarmed shouts that for once were not in our tongue, a shrill voice calling out a name that I recognized as a Maezaei god, and underlying it, a guttural growling sound that we Romans use to inspire fear in our enemies. By a count of twenty, my eyes were taking in a scene that matched my ears, as the front rank of the Fifth cut through their foes with a ruthless efficiency, hacking and stabbing their way ever closer to the point where there would be no barbarians left standing that could prevent them linking up with the beleaguered Second, although the Third had managed to do essentially the same thing from the bridge side.

"That'll teach those fucking savages." Rufius had come to stand next to me, and I heard the ferocious satisfaction in his voice, which I shared wholeheartedly.

"I hope Dodonis is seeing this from up there," I commented, and as I said this, I turned to check on the *praetorium*, and I saw that, if anything, there were more people thronged around the building, milling about.

The flames were so intense now that the reflected light bounced off the buildings lining the slope of the hill, creating dancing shadows that were reminiscent of the last time I found myself in a town burning down around me. That the previous time had been by accident only made our current circumstances seem even direr than that night years before, and it was only with an effort that I yanked my thoughts away from this fruitless line, returning my attention to the fighting. Even in the short span of time my attention had been turned away, we had made progress, and for the first time since Metellus crossed the bridge, I could see farther down the street. Almost immediately, a part of me wished I had not done so, because what I saw I would liken to a tunnel whose sides and top seemed composed of fire, with the tunnel itself filled with smoke.

Once I saw what awaited us, for the first time I moved, running out onto the span of the bridge, crossing almost to the other side to reach Germanicus, who was advancing his position as the three Centuries hacked out a bloody path. The Maezaei had not quite given up, but even as I was running, I saw the rearmost ranks of the southern part of their force beginning to first back away, before turning about and fleeing in the general direction of the southern wall. They were not my concern, but out of the corner of my vision, just as I reached Germanicus, I saw a disturbance in the surface of the river, which informed me that those Maezaei were either seeking the sanctuary of the water from the intense heat and smoke, or more likely, trying to cross it to get to the hill. I felt a glimmer of satisfaction at the thought that Blasio's Century would be standing there, waiting, but that was the last I thought of it because Germanicus, either hearing or sensing my approach, had spun about to face me.

"We're going to be ready to push through those savages very soon." He did not bother to return my salute, but while I understood his assessment, I also realized that because of his proximity, his view of anything beyond the mass of our own men and the remaining Maezaei was blocked.

Consequently, I only said, "Come with me; you need to see this."

This clearly irritated him, but he moved with me without hesitation nonetheless, following closely behind until we returned to my former vantage point, a few paces away from and to one side of the bridge. Simply turning around, I only pointed, but I was watching his face, and I heard the gasp of dismay that went with his expression as he saw what still lay between us and safety.

"How are we going to get through that?"

For once, I actually had an idea, and I explained it to him.

After hearing me out, he looked doubtful but said, "I suppose it's our best chance." His jaw tightened, reinforcing my impression that Germanicus had aged more than ten years in one night, and he ordered, "You better get started."

Again, I saluted, more out of force of habit, but did not bother waiting until it was returned, trotting over to Rufius. In as few words as possible, I outlined the plan, and like Germanicus, he did not look hopeful, but all I cared about was his obedience, which I could not fault. Bawling out his orders, section by section, men peeled off and ran down to the river, carrying their shields, which they dropped into the water, then took off their helmets, which they filled with water from the river. Rufius supervised this, while I ran over to where the only other Century left was standing, half of them now covering two streets facing east, and the rest facing the southern wall. As I suspected, there were more than a half-dozen bodies lying directly in front of the part of the Sixth facing south, all of them in a pool that was a mixture of water and blood.

"We caught those *cunni* coming out of the river," Blasio said proudly, but I was not going to indulge in the time to praise him; I had more pressing concerns.

All I said was, "Good," then without pause, I pointed back at the men of the First. "You need to get your men ready for when we have to make it to the gate. Have them soak their shields. Since we wore our covers, the leather will retain more water and that should help. Then have them fill their helmets and douse themselves until their tunics are soaked." I paused just long enough to see that he understood, then finished, "Then their neckerchiefs, which they're going to tie around their faces." As I spoke, I saw the look of real fear cloud Blasio's face, but while this was understandable, neither could I allow it to infect his men; this was a moment where Blasio had to act like a real Centurion of Rome. However, I ignored my first instinct to snarl at him and use threats, certain it would do no good, so instead, I moderated my tone to reflect an encouragement I did not feel. "You know I've had my doubts about you Blasio. But," I lied, "I can see I was wrong. Now," I grasped him by the shoulder, offering a prayer that I did not sound as false to his ears as I did to my own, "I'm depending on you to lead your men like the Centurion I know you are." Pausing to gauge the effect my words had, I asked encouragingly, "So, can I count on you?"

For a brief moment, he stared up at me blankly, making me wonder if he had lost his wits because of his fear, but thankfully, I saw him swallow once, then he nodded his head.

"Y-yes, Primus Pilus." His voice was hoarse, but I heard a determination there that I had never experienced before with Blasio; or, perhaps, I was hearing what I wanted to hear. "I won't let you down."

"Good." I clapped him on the shoulder, then said briskly, "Now, get them moving. We don't have much time."

Watching just long enough to make sure he was intent on living up to his promise, once I saw his men beginning to move, with the kind of alacrity I knew the moment required, I returned back to the First. Germanicus had returned to the opposite side of the bridge, while by the time I returned, I saw that Metellus' Century had pushed those Maezaei who were still fighting and had not fled, and there were a fair number of them, back more than fifty paces south of the bridge, while Veratius had moved into Metellus' original spot, except farther west, just up to the edge of the first block of buildings. At that precise moment, the nearest block was not yet fully aflame, but there was smoke rising from the rooftops where, not long before, the enemy archers had launched the surprise attack. Stopping only long enough to ensure that the men of the First were making sure to douse the wounded, most of whom who were still conscious did not appreciate it very much, I made my way to Germanicus and informed him that we would be ready to move in a matter of heartbeats.

"I hope this works," the Legate muttered, then he seemed to realize how that could be taken by the man who had suggested it, because he added, "but I think this is the best thing we can do." Turning to face west, much in the same way the dancing flames played on the larger surface of the hill, the same movement of the fire reflected on the features of Germanicus, his mouth set in a thin line as he observed the situation. After a moment, he asked me, "Should we begin?"

"Yes, sir," I replied without hesitation, but then suggested, "Novellus' Century is in the best shape to lead the way, then we'll come through with the wounded." Before I went on, I spent a moment carefully watching the fighting still taking place, first to my right, where the combined force of Veratius and Novellus' Centuries had reduced the opposition down to a small knot of now-trapped warriors, numbering no more than a hundred men who had been forced into the barbarian version of an *orbis*. Judging from appearances, they would finish cutting this remnant down very quickly, but it was Metellus' Century that I worried about the most, because although they were pressing the barbarians, they still numbered at least three hundred strong, and there was an untidy pile of bodies wearing our uniform just a matter of a couple steps away from where the bridge met the street we would be using to escape. It was impossible to determine with any certainty, but there were clearly wounded scattered among the dead, and because of the circumstances, I was struck by how this was the only moment where men who were foes just heartbeats before now lay side by side, suffering equally and no longer worried about killing the stricken enemy who was lying less than an arm's length away.

"I think we're going to have to switch out the Second," I told Germanicus, but when I heard no reply from the Legate, I glanced down at him; that he was not looking in my direction gave me an instant's warning.

"I disagree, Pullus." Germanicus said this quietly, though that is a relative term, since it was just that he did not shout. "The Second is too hotly engaged to try and relieve them. Besides," this was the moment he turned to look at me, his expression frank as he finished, "it would take time we don't have."

He was right, I knew that then, but this was a moment where I was unwilling to acknowledge this, which prompted me to argue, "The Second has done their part and then some! They deserve to be relieved!"

Rather than argue, Germanicus actually nodded his head sadly, agreeing, "You're right, Pullus. They do deserve it. They're fighting like the heroes of Troy. But," his voice hardened, and now he looked up at me, "you know I'm right."

There was really nothing to argue about, so I only saluted and asked, "Shall I give the orders, sir?"

He nodded, and I trotted the rest of the way across the bridge west, then skirted the rear ranks of Veratius' Century, walking parallel to the riverbank for a few paces, looking for the standard of the Fifth Century. As I had expected, the grim work of putting the last survivors of the warriors that had been isolated by Novellus' surprise attack was essentially over, with no more than a half-dozen panting Maezaei, standing back to back, snarling and spitting their defiance to the very last. Before I was able to reach the Hastatus Prior, I heard him blow his bone whistle, and like a pack of wolves, the leading rank of both the Third and Fifth Centuries descended on them. I barely glanced at the scene, only catching a glimpse of a long Gallic *gladius* raised high in the air, its blade slick with blood that came from my men, but my ears told me everything I needed know. Screaming, first in defiance, then in their final agonies, the cries of the barbarians were met by the savage howls and shouted curses of the Legionaries. I found Novellus, standing just behind the men doing the work, exhorting them to finish their job of butchering these men who dared to stand against us, and I had to shout his name twice before he heard me. He came quickly once he heard and stood before me, the sweat literally dripping in a stream from his chin and nose, which I understood now that I was closer to the fire, feeling the sudden increase of my own perspiration, so I wasted no time.

"Once you're finished here, march back to the bridge. Your Century is going to lead the way, but before you do…" I went on to explain the precautions we were taking, and once more, I saw the doubt at my tactic reflected in his face, but he saluted and assured me he would do as I ordered.

I went to Veratius next, and while they had suffered a bit more losses than the Fourth, they were still in much better shape than the Second, something I was finding difficult to shove out of my thoughts. Because they were actually nearest to the river, and since the last Maezaei were slaughtered by the time I reached Veratius, I ordered him to start preparations immediately, and his men went splashing into the water, carrying their shields and doffing their helmets. Then, I could delay no longer, and I made my way, stepping carefully over the bodies, following the course of the Second's fight, until I reached the rearmost rank, then skirted the outer file to reach a point where I could call to Metellus. I waited as he finished off his opponent with a strong thrust that caught the warrior in his mouth, going down immediately at Metellus' feet, though he landed on top of another body. Only then did I shout to get his attention, but while he did not hear me, his *Signifer* did, turning around then nodding to me. Taking a step, he tapped Metellus on the hip, then when my old friend leaned backward without taking his eyes off the enemy, informed him that I was waiting, whereupon he simply nodded, then backed away from the front rank. Before he turned to come to me, however, I saw him scan the ranks of his Century, then lift the whistle to his lips to signal a relief, which he watched to make sure occurred smoothly before turning to come to me. I could see he was trying to come at the trot, but it was more of a stumbling, staggering walk, and I could not help noticing that Metellus looked more exhausted than I had ever seen before.

Nevertheless, despite his fatigue, he straightened to render a proper salute, and this simple gesture threatened my composure more than anything he could have said, which was only, "Hot work, Pullus. Hot work."

"Servius," I had to force the words past the lump that had formed in my throat, and I hated myself for what I was about to say, "you and the Second have saved the Cohort, and I won't ever forget it, and neither will Germanicus."

While I do not know exactly what effect I had hoped my words would have, I was completely unprepared for him to simply nod, then say flatly, "But you need us to stay here and hold these *cunni* off so you and the rest of the Cohort get out of here before the rest of this fucking town burns down around us."

Now I did open my mouth, then when nothing would come out, I was forced to simply nod, but for one of the few times in my life, I was neither ashamed nor did I try to pretend that the tears that had been streaming from my eyes were no longer caused by the smoke.

Only then did Metellus give me a grin, but it was one I will always remember because there was none of the normal cheerfulness in it, and he said, "Then you better get out of here, Titus. My boys and me won't let you down."

Somehow, I could not seem to move, standing there like a useless lump of meat, and suddenly the thought came to me that I would rather stay here, next to one of my oldest comrades, facing whatever came, than live with the shame of the knowledge that I had abandoned a man I considered a friend. I do not know if this in some way showed in my expression, because the grim smile vanished from Metellus' face, and despite our disparity in size, the shove he gave me was such that it sent me staggering back two or three steps.

"Don't you fucking dare," he snarled. "You're not staying here, and if you try, I'll cut you down myself!" This was a Servius Metellus I had never seen before, a look of savage anger contorting his features into a mask that I barely recognized. "Now, get the *fuck* out of here, Titus! My fate is in the hands of the gods, and nobody, not even you, is going to change it!"

Still mute, once more, the only response I could summon was a nod, but I did as he said, and turned to go.

"Titus!" Whirling back around, I saw that Metellus' face had lost its harsh edge, and there was something of his old self in the smile as he called out, "You better pay for a huge fucking tombstone, you cheap bastard!"

It will always be to my shame and pain that, again, all I could do was nod, then I turned around and hurried away, trying to tell myself that what I was doing was for the greater good of the First Cohort of the *Legio Germanicus*.

By the time I got back, Novellus' Century was already moving and was more than halfway down the first of the four blocks we had to travel to get to the western gate. Rufius, in my place, had roused the First, and gotten the men as organized as possible when all but a handful were either carrying one end of a shield with a wounded comrade, standing with a wounded comrade whose armor had been stripped from him to lighten the load slung over his shoulder, or was standing with a length of thong held in their hand with the other end tied around the ankles of a dead comrade who had been similarly stripped. Putting it in its simplest terms, it was a sight I had never seen, or even heard of before, and one I hope to never see again in my life; if I had known that this was simply the first of the unprecedented events of what had already been an eventful night, perhaps I would have returned to stand by Metellus' side, no matter how angry it made him. Germanicus was now off the bridge, standing to the side of it in the middle of the street paralleling the river on the western bank, but when I reached his side and suggested he accompany me at the rear of the First Century while Rufius led the way behind Novellus' men, he refused.

"I'm going to be the last man of my command out of here," he told me flatly, and I understood it would be fruitless to argue, though again, I only nodded. This prompted him to try to joke, "But by the gods, don't leave me behind!"

"We won't," I assured him, then made a half-hearted attempt to match his own weak jest. "What kind of trouble would I get into if I did?"

It pleased me that this actually seemed to make him genuinely laugh, and he acknowledged, "That's true! So keep that in mind."

"I'll see you at the gate," I promised him, then left him to follow after my Century.

Almost immediately, I realized that in my haste and worry about trying to prepare the rankers for the coming and literal trial by fire, I had forgotten to make my own preparations. I had neither a shield nor was my tunic soaked with anything more than my perspiration and blood, while my neckerchief was wrapped around my shoulder, which had at least become a dull throbbing pain that was bearable. I do not know exactly what it says about me, but despite this realization causing my bowels to turn to water, exacerbated by the sudden increase in the heat as I walked past the first set of buildings, I did not turn around and go scrounge up a shield, even though there were several that our wounded and dead no longer needed. Probably it was that stubborn pride that had gotten me into so much trouble throughout my life, yet at that moment, I told myself the time I lost doing so meant that the fire would only be worse. Although the buildings in this first block had not yet caught fire, they were smoldering, and smoke was streaming through the windows out into the street. Very quickly, almost every man was coughing and hacking, and it was a constant battle to keep wiping my eyes to clear my vision enough to walk a few more feet before having to repeat the process. And, I thought fearfully, this is as good as it gets. Novellus' Century was now entering the second block, moving in something like a *testudo*, except their shields were all turned outward to at least partially deflect the effect of the flames, with the men in the center of the Century carrying their own wounded, and thankfully just a section of men at the rear dragging their dead. It was a maneuver I would have loved to be able to order my own Century to perform, but I did not have enough spare men, so we had to make do with six men holding their shields outward on one side and seven on the other. This was the only protection from the heat and flames we had, and before we reached the end of the first block, the steam that had been rising from the soaked leather of the shield covers had vanished as the moisture was quickly evaporated. My face, arms, and legs felt as if I was standing directly next to an open flame, making it difficult to concentrate on making sure none of my men stumbled, stopped, or worst of all, panicked. Only occasionally did I turn around to check and see that Veratius was behind us, while he and the Third were followed in turn by Blasio and the Sixth, but because of the thicket of men and shields, I could never catch a glimpse of Germanicus. The third block was even worse, since the buildings were burning, but the one saving grace was that every structure in this block was made of stone, although this did not stop everything inside from going up in flames. What this meant was that whereas before there was certainly heavy smoke, now there were columns of black, choking clouds pouring from every open window, while the wooden doors into each building were aflame. Not only did it make it extremely difficult to breathe, it was practically impossible to see more than a pace ahead, which caused men to stumble into each other, and judging from the sounds, dropped their wounded charges, who understandably howled with pain. Inadvertently, I made matters worse by stepping on the leg of one of them, though I tried to ameliorate my blunder.

"I'll carry him," I told the ranker who had been carrying him and was staggering back to his feet, his eyes streaming and coughing so violently that I was worried he would be unable to regain his breath, which was partly the reason I offered.

I bent over the wounded man, who I recognized as the Sergeant of the Fifth Section, Lucius Floras. He stared up at me as he held the *baltea* that either he or more likely his comrade had tied just below his elbow to stop the rest of his blood from leaking out through the

435

severed vessels where his hand and most of his forearm had been. What this meant in a practical sense was that he could not be any help in his own cause as I lifted him, but somehow I managed, even as it wrenched a gasp from my lips from the sudden sharp flash of pain as the wound along my ribs re-opened.

"Sorry, Primus Pilus," Floras mumbled apologetically, causing another stab of pain that, while it was different in nature from what I had just experienced, was no less acute.

"No, I'm the one who's sorry, Floras." This came out as more of a gasping cough, but to his credit, although he groaned in the same manner I had, tried to assure me, "It's all right, Primus Pilus. There's nothing ol' Floras can't bear."

"I know that." I tried to make myself sound as if I was not struggling with his weight. "That's why you're in my Century."

Only after making sure the man who had dropped him was recovered enough to move under his own power, we resumed moving down the street, reaching the end of the block. Whereupon we discovered that Rufius, leading the way, was forced to stop because Novellus' Century had come to a halt. This was the moment where the men of the First Cohort came the closest to breaking, since the Fifth Century had been forced to stop because every structure in the final block was fully ablaze, creating a maelstrom of fire that filled the street that no mortal man could pass through and live. Suddenly, Rufius appeared out of the smoke at a staggering run, almost passing me by, either because he did not recognize his Primus Pilus with a man slung over his shoulder, or he could not see because his eyes were streaming so heavily.

"Over here," I called to him, then listened as he informed me, "This street is blocked, but Centurion Novellus sent some men in both directions to see if he can find a way out."

"What?"

"We're trapped! By the gods, we're trapped!"

"We're going to fucking burn to death!"

Finally, the discipline of the First Century, my Century, broke down as men gave in to the panic that, frankly, I was fighting against with every fiber of my being, just as scared of dying in the most horrible way imaginable as the men around me. That black beast that I had always managed to keep at bay was now gnawing at the door that confines it in that part of a man's mind where he keeps such things locked away, with a fury and intensity that surpassed every other time it had tried to rouse itself and break loose. Not the ambush at The Quarry, or the only other time I had been in a similar situation the night Urso had been slain, and I in turn killed Draxo, Caecina, and Mela; neither of these compared to this moment. As the men around me, most of them hurt, some grievously, and all of them now witless with fear, shouted in despair, called to the gods for their intercession, or cursed the fates that brought them to this place, for a span of heartbeats, I was frozen in a state similar to those around me. But then, as clearly as if he was standing next to me, my Avus came to my rescue, as I heard his voice, speaking to me with that deep, gravelly tone that might have made other men tremble in fear, but remains to this day one of my fondest memories of the first Titus Pullus, if only because he never spoke to me in the manner for which he is still famed throughout the Legions.

"We're all afraid when we're in battle, and any man who tells you differently is either a liar or a fool, and you should avoid being anywhere near him. But it's the man who can stay the master of his fear and control it, rather than letting it control him, who will always have the best chance at seeing another sunrise."

My one regret was that this visit by my Avus was only with the sound of his voice; I would have given all of our family fortune if I could have seen him standing there next to me at that moment, ready to stand by my side, the only mortal man who could possibly defeat the savage force of a raging inferno.

Nevertheless, just his words were enough to prompt me to roar as loudly as I could manage, "*SHUT YOUR FUCKING MOUTHS, YOU GUTLESS, WHINING CUNNI!*"

Honestly, I was surprised I managed to generate a volume at least close to the level as if we were standing in the forum of camp, and even more so that this worked as quickly as it did, even as I realized

437

that I had not thought of what I was going to say next since I was certain I would have to shout this or something like it over and over.

Consequently, when the men stopped their shouting for the most part, there was a pause before I continued at only a slightly lower volume, "We're not dead yet, and we're not going to be unless you lose your heads and start acting like those barbarians do whenever we gut a few of them and they turn tail and run!" Pausing, this time deliberately, to check to see that they were at least listening, I finished, "Right now, Novellus has sent men looking for another way out, and…"

It would be nice to think that the gods arranged for this very moment to be when I was interrupted by what was clearly a cheer, coming from the direction of the western gate, followed quickly by an excited shout from someone. "They found a way out!"

"All right, you bastards," I tried to avoid letting the relief I felt creep into my voice, though I do not think I was successful, "let's stop wasting time!"

Resuming our withdrawal, we were met by a Gregarius from Novellus' Century who directed us to turn left at the intersecting street, heading in the direction of the southern wall, then continuing for two blocks, where another man was waiting, pointing west.

"This is it, boys!" I believe it was Rufius who called out, or it sounded like him. "We're almost out of here!"

I saw him, still leading the way, reach Novellus' man, but although I could not hear what was said, I saw my Optio take a staggering step backward as his jaw dropped open. More tellingly, he did not start down this last block before the western gate, instead standing next to the other ranker, simply looking west but doing nothing more than that.

"This can't be good," I muttered, prompting a groan from Floras, or I assumed this was what prompted it, since he had been mostly quiet to this point.

The men ahead of me similarly came to a stop, except this time, there was no panic; if anything, what I saw in them was a sense of resignation, in their demeanor and posture, as men set their wounded charges down and stood there with slumped shoulders and hanging heads, something I only understood once I reached Rufius' side. Despite being somewhat forewarned that there was more bad news just by what I was witnessing in the men who had reached this intersection before me, once I reached Rufius' side and looked down the street, what little energy I had left seemed to drain from my body, and I just barely managed to warn Floras that I was putting him down. I did try to be gentle, but while I saw that he was only semi-conscious, depositing him on the paving stones elicited another groan and a fluttering of eyelids. Novellus had found a street where the buildings were not only stone construction, but were low, squat structures of the type where the roofs were made of stone as well, although the smoke from all the other burning structures was still black, thick, and choking. But it was the sight of the gate that had stopped our progress again, as Novellus came trotting back from where his men were standing, just two dozen paces away from what should have meant our escape but now looked to be the cause of our collective doom.

"The rampart above the gate's collapsed," he said needlessly, since I had eyes, but I barely noticed, and I remember that, for the span of three or four heartbeats, I had the absurd thought that, because my vision was so blurry, with my eyes stinging and still weeping, perhaps I was not seeing things correctly.

Of course I was, since everyone around me was standing there, similarly in a state of numbed shock and despair, and while I knew that I was supposed to say or do something as I had just a few moments before, I simply had no idea what that was. This was how Germanicus found us, standing there in a bunch not even remotely resembling a Roman formation, but when he strode up, then saw the fiercely blazing pile of timber that blocked our path, even he did not seem to know what to do, at least at first.

Suddenly, after a morose silence that stretched for some time, I sensed Germanicus stiffen, whereupon he reached out, touched me on the arm, and with a gesture of his head, beckoned me to follow him. By this point, both Veratius and Blasio's Centuries were packed on the north/south street, but while they could not actually see the blockage, their friends and comrades who could were not shy about letting them know. This was when the panic that had infected the First came the closest to enclosing the entire Cohort in its grip, yet Germanicus did not seem to notice, so intent was he on speaking with me.

"I have an idea," he spoke in a low voice, with an urgency that was impossible to miss, "but it's not..." Suddenly, he seemed at a loss for words, and I waited impatiently, and he finally seemed to settle on, "...going to be easy for the men."

I said nothing, which forced him to blurt out the idea that had come to him, and I will say that I understood why he had been so hesitant, and why he had a hard time finding the right words.

Even as I felt my stomach lurch, I forced myself to consider his proposal, yet despite the gruesome aspect of it, I realized that what he was proposing was the only way that we had any chance of avoiding burning to death. And, I realized, as I felt his eyes on me, this was a decision that Germanicus was not willing to make on his own.

"I think," I finally managed, "that's our only hope."

There are really no words that can adequately describe the final horror that the First Cohort, save one Century, had to endure that night in Raetinium, so I will not even attempt to do so, except in the barest terms. What Germanicus ordered the men to do, if it can be called an order, was to perform an act that, in an extremely morbid way, was simply accelerating the manner in which we Romans honor our dead, by purifying them through flames. Using our dead, we threw them onto the burning lumber that blocked our path, their bodies smothering the flames just enough to enable us to use them as grisly stepping stones. Putting it simply, it was the most horrific thing I or any man of the *Legio Germanicus* had ever seen, let alone been forced to do. But when it came down to our survival, I am still utterly certain this was the only course open to us, and I have never heard any other survivor from that night say otherwise. The remnants, for that is what we were, of the First Cohort of the *Legio Germanicus* staggered out of Raetinium, and we only traveled just far enough from the walls before, without any orders being given, by Germanicus, me, or any other Centurion, the men came to a halt, dropping to the ground in their utter exhaustion and benumbed horror. Not, I must add, before those carrying the wounded, deposited their charges carefully on the ground before collapsing next to their unfortunate comrades, an action that I copied myself when I finally lowered Floras off my shoulder. He had been quiet during the last part of our ordeal, and I assumed that he had finally lost full consciousness. It was when I laid him a gently as I could on the ground, I saw that he had indeed done so, but in a permanent sense; I had been carrying a dead man for only the gods knew how long.

"I'm sorry," I heard myself whisper, yet I could not seem to summon any real emotion as I said the words, though I did fumble for the small purse tucked inside my *baltea* and personally placed the coin in my dead comrade's mouth.

All around me, men were mostly silent, though I heard occasional muttered questions and equally terse responses. The most common action, however, was to sit, sprawled out on the ground, and stare blankly at the sight of Raetinium, the lower part of the town now completely consumed in flames that reached forty or fifty feet above the stone walls, which were the only part that seemed unaffected. One consequence of this inferno was that it was now almost as if it was daylight, illuminating the scene in a manner that meant it was impossible to ignore the shattered state of what had marched across this very spot two watches before, a tough, veteran Cohort of men who, despite being long in the tooth, was the match of any First Cohort under the standard, something that I will maintain and defend until my last breath. Now, what I saw all around me was a collection of old, broken men, men who had been forced to confront in the most brutal fashion imaginable that they were no longer what they used to be, both in the immediate and larger sense. I finished with Floras, arranging his body so that he was stretched out as if he was simply asleep, though as is our custom, I took his neckerchief to cover his face, which also is the signal to the *medici* there is a man who does not need their attention. Speaking of those men, it was when I happened to turn my back to Raetinium that I saw a large group of mounted men coming at the trot from the western camp, and behind them I glimpsed another, smaller contingent, though none of them were in uniform and many of them were leading mules. Returning my attention to the town, I stared at the gateway with a forlorn but stubborn hope that I would see the Second Century emerge, or what was left of it, but the bodies we had used to affect our escape had finally succumbed to the greedy flames. Even as I stood there watching, the opened passage we had created in the grisliest manner possible closed back up as the flames reclaimed the space, making it practically impossible to see beyond them, even if there had been anything to see.

"Maybe they got in the river."

Germanicus had managed to come to my side unnoticed, but my fatigue and grief was such that I did not even start in surprise. Honestly, that had never occurred to me, yet this seemed to be such an unlikely proposition that I barely even considered it.

"Maybe," I said unenthusiastically, then pointed out, "but I doubt those barbarians would let them. And," I added, "if they did, they'd be dead men in the water."

Germanicus did not seem dissuaded and insisted, "But the only way they could do that is to risk getting cut off by the fire."

This, I recognized, was true, but my overall mood would not allow for any optimism, though I refrained from arguing further, mostly because I was too tired, so I simply nodded. Then, the sound of the cavalry arriving at the trot interrupted us, and we both turned just as Gaesorix drew up next to us. Frankly, I barely noticed him, my eyes instead fixed on who was following him, albeit led by his reins. Without saying a word to my Batavian friend, I only walked up and took the reins from him before going to Latobius. I cannot say why with any certainty, yet just by leaning my head against his neck, it made me feel not only better in a general sense, but restored a sense of calm that enabled me to return my mind to the fact that, while we were safe, our night was not over. This recognition was what forced me to turn away from the comfort and security I found with my horse and walk over to where Germanicus had already climbed aboard his

442

own mount that had been brought along with Latobius by one of Gaesorix's troopers.

Saluting, I said, "With your permission, I'd like to get the men assembled so I can get a butcher's bill. And I need to find out where Tubertus' Century disappeared to."

"I know where they are." This came from Gaesorix, who was still mounted but within earshot. Naturally, we both turned to the Decurion, whose expression of contempt belied his flat tone as he informed us, "We saw them marching back to the southern camp." He paused, then added, "They're with the Third and Fifth Cohort."

This, at least the last part, was no surprise, but the fact that one of the Centurions of the First Cohort had essentially abandoned the rest of us to our fate caused, for the first time in a long time, the sudden rousing of that thing I think of as the beast that slumbers inside me. I could see that Germanicus was no less angry, although I doubted that he had residing within him the kind volcanic rage that had alternately plagued me but also proved to be my salvation on more than one occasion.

"We'll deal with Tubertus later," was all the Legate said firmly, making it clear that this was an order. Then, returning to the original request, he nodded and said, "Yes, Pullus, that's a good idea. Get the Cohort formed up and let's see who we lost."

I saluted, and began the work of returning my Cohort to a semblance of its former self. By this point, a large party, formed of the *medici* and clerks who worked as medical orderlies, along with the slaves who worked as stretcher bearers, spotting us with the help provided by the light of the blazing inferno, had waded across the river, heading our direction. The men responsible for carrying our wounded had laid them in a number of rows, prompting the thought how unlikely it would be for barbarians to have the discipline to arrange their wounded in a neat formation, mimicking the same arrangement that I was calling the able-bodied men of the Centuries to fall into just a dozen paces away. My one quibble was that I noticed the wounded had not been arranged by Century, which is what normally happens, but this was such a minor consideration at this point it only crossed my mind without me speaking about it. As those men who were either unwounded, few that they were, or whose wounds were minor enough that they had been bound up, quickly arranged themselves, they used the spot where I had stationed myself as the reference point, just as if we were in the forum, with Arvina placing himself to my left, or the far right of the formation. This was when the savaging we had endured became apparent, as I watched the men of my Century arrange themselves by taking into account our losses, shuffling into a new spot from their normal one. Once they had finished, I vaguely heard a gasp, which I suppose came from me, prompted by the sight of what would be less than a Century of men in all but the First Cohort.

"I've got barely sixty men left," I said to myself, though I forced my expression to remain as immobile as I could make it, but that proved impossible.

Because of the years of ingrained habit, the Century *Signiferi*, using Arvina as their guide, positioned themselves with their normal spacing, which meant there were two huge gaps in an already shrunken formation. The sight of it proved to be the unmanning of me, and I was forced to spin about as if I was suddenly interested in the destruction of Raetinium, but I barely noticed that, although the walls partially obscured the view, one could tell by the leaping flames that the entire town below the hill was now consumed by fire. Blinking away the tears, I composed myself and was about to turn around to face the remnants of my Cohort when, out of the corner of my vision, there was a sudden flurry of movement to my right, but closer to the southwest corner of the wall than the fording spot we had been using. My initial reaction was to reach down for my *gladius*, drawing it as I began the process of turning back about to shout a warning that the Maezaei had somehow managed to escape the trap of their own making and were sortieing out from the doomed town. Something arrested me from completing this, and I stared, hard, at the figures, appearing to be a few dozen strong, understanding that there was something unusual about them but not quite recognizing what it was for the span of several heartbeats.

"It's the Second," I heard someone shout behind me, and I glanced back to see that Germanicus had ridden up behind me without me sensing it, and even in the moment, I felt irritation mingled with the sudden blooming of relief as my mind accepted this was indeed what I was seeing. "And," he said exultantly, "there's their standard! They didn't leave it behind!"

"Of course they didn't leave it behind," I snapped without thinking, nor did I turn my head and at least face Germanicus when I made my surly retort, so I cannot say how he took it, nor did I care in the moment.

I actually took a tentative step towards the straggling group who, further proving they were not attackers, never increased their speed, then decided it would not be seemly for the Primus Pilus of the Legion, or what remained of it, to run and greet returning comrades, no matter what the circumstances. None of the men were wearing their helmets, and once they got within a hundred paces, we saw they had shed their armor as well. Because of this, I could not differentiate between the men by their facial features since they were still too far away, so for an all too brief span of time, I harbored a pathetic hope that Servius Metellus was among these survivors. That expectation only lasted the length of time it took for me to recognize that, while not in a perfect formation, they were being led, and it was when that man drew close enough that I felt the strength drain from my legs.

"Primus Pilus," Optio Gnaeus Cerrinius' salute was properly rendered, though it was hard to ignore the fact his tunic was still dripping from the river, or the rough blood-soaked bandage that obscured one eye, "Optio Cerrinius reporting that the Second Century, First Cohort, has returned…"

He could get no further, and I had to rush forward to catch him as he collapsed, laying him gently on the ground, and I crouched down next to him, my heart feeling as if it had somehow turned leaden and threatened to tear itself from my chest as I leaned over Cerrinius.

"Thank you," I managed to whisper, but before I could say anything else, a shadow interposed itself, and I glanced up to see

Germanicus had dismounted, and was dropping to his knees on the other side of the Optio.

"Optio Cerrinius," Germanicus' voice was choked with an emotion that I sensed was heartfelt, though I chose to believe it was about this specific moment and not the larger situation and the impact it would have on his career, "the men of the First Cohort owe you a debt that can never be repaid, as do I." He hesitated, which caused me to glance away from Cerrinius, whose one visible eye was open but seemed fixed on the skies above us, and I saw Germanicus was looking at me and not the Optio, a questioning expression on his face.

Thinking I understood, I took a deep breath, but before I continued our questioning of Cerrinius, I realized there was another piece of business, and I stood up and addressed the survivors, "Go past the formation," I pointed, "on the other side you'll find the *medici*, and the slaves have brought food and water." More out of habit, I tried to joke, "And there'll be enough wine to drown in when you get back to camp." That there was not the slightest reaction from the men verbally, and their expressions were a uniform blank stare, gave me a deeper insight into the horrors they had faced than any description could. Nevertheless, I dropped back down, where Cerrinius had been helped to a sitting position by Germanicus, who was steadying him with a hand on the shoulder, and took a breath before I asked him gently, "What happened, Cerrinius? Where's Pilus Posterior Metellus?"

The Optio did not answer immediately; he had turned his head and was seemingly absorbed in staring at the roaring flames, which I could see reflected in his one visible eye, but when I was about to repeat the question, he finally said hoarsely, "The Pilus Posterior stayed behind with a section of men to keep those..." suddenly, his face contorted with a savage hatred, "...*animals* away from the rest of us while we got away." Only then did he tear his gaze away from Raetinium, looking me unblinkingly in the eyes as he continued, "He saved all of us, Primus Pilus. We wouldn't have gotten out of there if he hadn't done what he did."

This proved to be too much for my composure, and before I could stop it, a sob burst from me as Cerrinius' face dissolved into a shimmering image only recognizable by its outline, yet for one of the few times in my life, I did not care if I was behaving in an un-Roman fashion, or the fact my Legate was there to witness it. And, very quickly, I was joined by Cerrinius, and despite our differences in rank and that I did not know him well, we fell against each other, expressing our grief at the loss of a man who I had known since my first day under the standard.

Chapter 7

Germanicus made the decision that nothing could be gained by keeping the First Cohort outside Raetinium, and he sent for the Cohorts who had not gotten involved in the assault out from the camps to join the cavalry, surrounding the town on three sides, while reinforcing the Century on the eastern hill with two more Centuries of auxiliaries. Once this was seen to, we returned to the southern camp, carrying the wounded on proper stretchers, while comrades helped those walking wounded, usually by supporting them with an arm around the waist, although some men were too proud to accept the help and limped along, making our progress even slower than normal. Just before we reached the Porta Sinistra, we met the Third Cohort marching the other way, which prompted a very tense moment as the First passed the men who, rightly, we all viewed as abandoning us. What became instantly obvious was that, as far as the rankers of the Third were concerned, they felt the same way, because there was absolutely no interaction between the two groups, but more importantly, the men of the Third looked ashamed, none of them even looking in our direction. For my part, I was on Latobius, and I veered him slightly so that I was within arm's length of Scipio, who I was pleased to see look terrified at seeing me approach. However, I contented myself with a contemptuous stare at him, but in one of the few instances where he was of a like mind with the men of his command, he refused to meet my eyes.

"There'll be time enough for him later," I consoled myself, though only Latobius heard me, and he did twitch an ear.

Immediately after we entered the camp, I did not bother to lead the men to the forum, heading directly to our Cohort area, whereupon the surviving Centurions and Optios took command, including Rufius.

Oddly, though, when I informed him to see to the men, he did not move for a moment, but when I just wearily looked at him, I was

448

unprepared for him to blurt out, "Primus Pilus, you need to go see the camp physician to take care of that!"

He pointed up at my shoulder, reminding me that I had been wounded myself, not once but twice. That it was not until he pointed it out that I remembered, and then as soon as I did, I became aware of the throbbing pain that I suppose I had somehow blocked out of my mind, meant that I was not exactly gracious with Rufius.

"You go take care of the men," I growled at him, "and let me worry about myself."

A look of anger flashed across his face, but he was wise enough not to press the issue, saluting and replying stiffly, "I understand, Primus Pilus, and I will obey."

Turning about before I acknowledged his words and salute was the kind of tiny insult that lower ranks use, but I did not even consider making an issue of it. Then, when I turned around and entered my tent, or at least, I attempted to do so, I was confronted by Alex, whose expression I would liken to someone who has been told to dig a ditch, but with his spoon.

"Uncle Titus," his voice, I noticed, did not have the usual quaver in it that would have been normal when he risked my wrath by using my familial title, "Rufius is right. And," I actually noticed the hard bump in his throat as it bobbed, "I'm not letting you in the tent. We're going to the *quaestorium* and you're getting that," like Rufius, he indicated my wound by pointing to it, "seen to. And," he spoke so firmly that any thought of resisting was banished, "by the physician and not just a *medicus*."

Whereupon I meekly acquiesced, letting my nephew escort me to the large tent that, as I knew it would be, was packed with our wounded men, which was the main reason I did not want to go inside. Guiding me by the elbow, Alex led me to a bench that sat next to the partition that separated the combination small office and supply room that the chief physician usually uses as his own.

"Wait here," he actually ordered me, pointing to the bench, "I'll be right back."

That I actually docilely did as he said without comment was perhaps the most potent sign of my overall fatigue, though there was a fair amount of bemusement at the manner in which my young nephew had taken charge. Fortunately, I did not have to wait long; sitting where I was, I had a good view of the suffering, and even in the lamplight, the sight before me of so much agony was hard to bear.

"Primus Pilus." I turned to see a man standing there, but it was not the camp physician, and he informed me, "Master Germanicus sent me to personally see to your wounds again."

This actually did not make me feel better, but worse, and I extended my right arm, wincing at the stab of pain, sharper than the dull ache of which I had become conscious, though I persisted in pointing at the large room that was completely full, saying, "I think you'd be of more use helping those men than me. I can wait."

The Greek, whose name I recalled was Lysippos, did not seem surprised at my demurral, making me wonder if Germanicus had warned him I might try to put him off, which seemed to be confirmed when he replied, "I'm sorry, Primus Pilus, but our Legate gave me very specific orders to attend to you first, and then I'm to report back to him on your condition. Until I do that," he shrugged as he gestured at the scene around us, "I'm not allowed to lend my services to your men."

Knowing better than to argue, I gave my grumbling consent, and only then did he step closer to examine me, taking my right arm gently in his grasp, yet despite his slow and careful movement of it, I had to suppress a gasp of pain. It seemed to me, as I was sitting there, that I was actually feeling worse with every passing watch, and it made me wonder if this was an effect of growing old. Bending over, he thankfully did not actually touch the long slashing wound along my ribs, nor did he make any comment. Satisfied, he turned his attention to my left shoulder, which I frankly had been dreading more than my side. During his examination, Alex had returned with an expression that seemed composed of equal parts dejection and anger; that nobody was with him explained why, and the physician glanced over at his arrival before returning his attention to me.

"Is your slave trained as a *medicus*?"

I managed to catch Alex's eye before he responded, his face flushed and lips pressed tightly together, a sign I had learned that he was struggling to control himself, so I answered quickly, "No, my slave's not. But my nephew and the First Cohort clerk is."

Lysippos redeemed himself somewhat, because he not only looked embarrassed, he turned to Alex and said quietly, "My apologies, young man." Then, returning back to business, he beckoned to the youth, "I'm going to need your help unwrapping this bandage. Which," now that he had examined it, he frowned, "I must say wasn't applied very well. I thought all Legionaries received at least some training in how to properly bind a wound."

"I'll be sure and tell the Legate he made a mess of the job," I replied pleasantly, and now the physician's discomfort visibly increased.

"There's no need for that," he said hastily. "I'll make sure he's properly instructed as soon as there's time."

His talking done, I tensed when he and Alex, working together, began unwrapping Germanicus' handiwork, but as I feared, it was when they were extricating the cloth from around the splintered shaft of the arrow that I could no longer keep my composure, groaning aloud. Which, I immediately realized with some chagrin, went completely unnoticed, mingling as it did with the same sounds, and worse, as the *medici* worked around us on men whose wounds were far more severe than mine.

"That," Lysippos pronounced with a grave expression, "is not going to be easy to get out. At least," he added, superfluously in my opinion, "not without doing more damage."

Unclenching my teeth, I thought it a good idea to point out, "Well, isn't that why Germanicus sent you to tend to me? Surely you've got experience at this."

"I do," the Greek agreed cautiously, "but each wound is slightly different. So," his tone turned brisk, and now he turned and called a *medicus* who appeared to be unoccupied, "we're going to need some room. And some help."

"He can help," I indicated Alex, whose face had exhibited quite an array of colors just since we entered the *quaestorium*, but I tried to ignore his paleness as he stared down at my shoulder, "and I told you, he knows what to do."

"Oh," the physician assured me, "he will. But," he actually finished as he turned away to give the newly arrived man some instructions, "he's going to need help holding down a man your size."

The physician was telling nothing more than the truth. Indeed, it took Alex and the second *medicus* to hold me down just to allow Lysippos to get my armor off. Complicating matters was that in doing so, the wound on my side was reopened, though it was seeing him using a pair of shears to cut my tunic away that hurt almost as much, causing me to complain about the expense.

"Primus Pilus Pullus," Lysippos' tone was weary, and as far as I knew, I was the first man he had worked on, making me wonder if it was me causing his fatigue, "I'm sure you can afford a new tunic."

"He can." Alex chose that moment to speak up for the first time. "He just doesn't like spending money."

This prompted a glare from me, but he did not seem fazed in the slightest, actually grinning at me. Perhaps he was trying to distract me, or it was a coincidence that this was the moment when, the tunic now having been cut all the way through, the *medicus* peeled it from my side, where the dried blood and sweat made it feel as if it had been glued to me. The act elicited a half-yelp, half-bellow of pain, and I felt the sudden rush of warm fluid streaming down my side, and despite the promise I made to myself, I looked down, peeking under my arm. And, of course, I immediately cursed myself for not keeping my vow, but while I quickly looked away, there was no way I could erase the image of the dull white of what were at least two ribs. Since I had been wounded before, I at least knew that Lysippos and the *medicus* standing there watching my blood leaking out of my body was normal, not that it made it any easier to keep my patience. Once he was satisfied, Lysippos told me it was time to lie down, having moved me from the bench to one of the tables upon which men are laid to enable the *medici* to work on them, and as I did so, gingerly, I noticed that he picked up a long, thin probe, made of bronze, with a hook at the end.

"You're not sticking me with that!" I declared, but despite myself, I amended, "Are you?"

"If you're willing to leave it up to the gods that there isn't any foreign matter left in your wound," the Greek answered.

When put that way, I could not really disagree, though this was when Alex and the *medicus* were put to the test, since, despite my best attempts, I found it impossible for my body not to react when Lysippos inserted the probe into the wound. For what seemed like a third of a watch but was likely no more than a handful of heartbeats, the physician gently ran the probe the length of my wound, starting from the end closest to my back. Then, when he was what felt like a matter of an inch or two from where the slash terminated near the front of my chest, I both felt and heard it when his probe came in contact with something metallic. Alex and the other man were forced to lay their bodies across me for the blessedly brief span of time it took for Lysippos to fish out what turned out to be a single link of mail, which he proceeded to thrust in front of my face.

"You see?" he said triumphantly. "Aren't you glad you didn't leave it up to the gods? With this inside you," the Greek shook his head, "you would be dead in no more than three or four days."

Nodding my head to let Alex and the *medicus* know it was safe for them to get off of me, I could only gasp my agreement, but the physician was already preparing for the next step.

"Now," he told me soberly, "comes the hard part."

"Aren't you going to sew that up first?" I used my head to nod in the direction of my side, but he gave a decisive shake of his head.

"No," he answered instantly, "because it's almost a certainty that you would tear the stitches apart when we started working on your shoulder."

"It's going to be that bad?" I tried to make it sound like a joke, but either I failed or he missed it, because his expression turned grim, although he allowed, "Well, that depends on how badly embedded that arrowhead is, Primus Pilus. But," he nodded gravely, "yes, it could be that bad." This seemed to remind him of something, which I understood when he twisted about, muttered something to the *medicus*, who nodded, then reached into his bag that they all carry slung over their shoulder. Handing the object he extracted from it to the physician, in turn, Lysippos faced me again, but this time, he said only, "Open your mouth."

I complied, understanding an instant before from his words what he was offering, and I bit down on the thick wooden dowel wrapped in leather, forcing myself to ignore the unsettling feeling of all the indentations from clenching teeth that my tongue felt. Nodding that I was ready, the physician picked up a highly polished, and I hoped very sharp, bronze knife, but with a short, thin blade that is the standard tool for those charged with tending to Rome's wounded. All I can offer in my defense is that the third man did not need to be summoned with the first cut that Lysippos made, nor the second, but when he took what looked a bit like a pair of shears, except the ends were blunt, and as I was about to learn, actually worked in the opposite fashion, where pressing the two ends with the loops for fingers together actually makes the opposite end widen, that proved to be too much for me. And, when that end is in your flesh, I will only say this was the moment where Lysippos yelled for help to keep me down. I suppose it was quite a sight, Alex draped across my chest, with the other two men essentially laying their own bodies across mine from my waist down, even if I did not appreciate it in the moment. Alex never confirmed it, and frankly I did not press him, but I feel certain I fainted at some point, albeit not for very long, because I do not remember anything immediately after Lysippos opened my wound to extract the arrow.

My next memory was Lysippos speaking with what almost sounded like a cheerful tone as he informed me, "Well, Primus Pilus, it appears that at least one of the gods must love you."

Now, in the moment, this did not seem very likely, and I said as much, but he held up an object and moved it so I could see it, yet while it was still covered in blood, I saw that it was what remained of the arrow, which the physician was holding by the splintered end.

"See this?" He pointed to the iron head, and I did indeed see, and understand, though he explained anyway, "Whoever loosed this at you either grabbed the wrong kind of arrow in the heat of the moment or they ran out of the other type, because this is a hunting arrow."

This, I understood, was good news, yet I still felt compelled to ask him, "So it didn't do much damage."

"Oh," he replied, "it did a fair amount, but it didn't hit the bone, nor did I have to cut away much muscle to extract it."

He stopped then, but after a moment when he did not seem disposed to tell me on his own, I asked impatiently, "So I'll recover and be as good as new?"

"I wouldn't go quite that far," the Greek cautioned, then somewhat surprisingly, pointed to the knotted mass of scar tissue that covers my lower left arm. "But it won't be as bad as that clearly was."

Having this confirmed made me sink back in relief, although it was short-lived; now that the wounds had been cleaned, it was time to stitch them up, but I managed to endure this. I was made to sit up so that my ribcage could be bound, which one *medicus* did, while Alex, under the supervision of Lysippos, wrapped my upper arm, which was not stitched shut because the hole was too big. Then, I was essentially done, but the men who tended to me were not, and the *medici* quickly returned to the other wounded, leaving Alex and me alone.

"Now," I told him, "we're going to my quarters. If," I added, only partially in jest, "that's all right with you."

Alex made a face that told me he understood I was teasing, although he complied readily enough. Leaving the tent, however, I was in for a surprise; the sun was coming up, and I knew that Germanicus would not want to delay in finishing this business with the Maezaei. Speaking of the town, a thick column of black, greasy smoke was now towering several hundred feet above the northern wall of our camp, but more importantly, I saw that the hill had, in fact, not provided the barbarians protection, or at least not to the extent that they probably hoped it would. Easily half of those buildings that I could see above our wall were either smoldering, or still afire, albeit in the final stages. Only the *praetorium*, perched on the very top, being

455

made of brick, seemed untouched, except it was now almost completely black from soot, telling me that the flames had to have come fairly close. And, considering how intense the heat had been, I did not think it likely that Dodonis' people had escaped unscathed by fire. Regardless, I understood that, despite the crushing fatigue I was feeling, our day was not over; the idea that I would not be present when Germanicus did whatever he planned on doing next never occurred to me.

Somewhat regretfully, I handed Alex the small, stoppered bottle of poppy syrup that Lysippos had discreetly given to me, telling him, "You're going to need to go back to the *quaestorium* and get me another *hamata*." Thinking for a moment, I asked him, "Did you pack a spare crest?"

"Yes." This came out as a gasp. "But why?" When I did not answer, he groaned and said, "Surely you're not expecting to go back out there again! You're hurt too badly!"

While I was slightly annoyed, I was more touched at the clear passion he displayed, though I resisted the temptation to ruffle his hair, both because I knew it annoyed him, and honestly, I was not altogether sure I could lift either arm.

"I'm not hurt so badly that I can't sit on Latobius," I began, then groaned. "Pluto's cock! I forgot..."

"He's been fed, watered, and rubbed down," Alex answered, but while this was welcome news, I was confused.

"When did you have time to do that?"

"I didn't," he replied, then added vaguely, "I got someone else to help."

This, I thought, was interesting, and frankly, I welcomed the brief diversion, so I asked curiously, "And how did you do that?" A stab of concern prompted me to add, "You didn't pay someone, did you?"

Alex gave me a look that, in the moment, reminded me of his mother, a scornful amusement that I had seen her give my brother, and if I am being honest, me on more than one occasion.

"No," he assured me, "I didn't pay anyone." Again, he paused, then shrugged as he said, "I didn't have to."

Now I was almost consumed by curiosity, so I pressed him, "So? Are you going to tell me how you did it?"

"Why?" he demanded, then he threw his shoulders back, I suppose in an attempt to make himself look more imposing, which seemed to be confirmed when he said, "What if I told you that I threatened to thrash someone if they didn't obey me?"

Before I could stop myself, a chuckle burst out of me, or that was how it started, quickly turning into a groan of pain from the stabbing sensation from my ribs. Unfortunately, the look Alex gave me only exacerbated my mirth, prompting a painful span that finally forced me to stop to catch my breath and recover somewhat. Naturally, without thinking, I leaned over to put my hands on my knees, and just that quickly my shoulder added to my discomfort, although this seemed to assuage Alex's own distemper, so before long, he had begun laughing.

"All right," he mock-grumbled, "I'll tell you." He grinned at me and said, "I just told them that I was going to tell you I caught them whipping him."

Staring at him for a moment, I tried to determine whether he was speaking in jest, but it did not seem so, and I did not know how to feel exactly.

"That," I finally allowed, "is using your head. I'll give you that."

We resumed walking, reaching my quarters, where he left me to gather myself, which meant replacing the tunic that had been tied around my waist, still ruing the fact that it had been one of my personal tunics and not an issued one. With some difficulty, I managed to slide the new one over my head, then with that done, I realized I was famished. My nephew had set out a large, flat round of my favorite *castra paneris* with a small jug of oil and a good-sized ball of cheese. Most importantly, there was a large hunk of roasted pork that had been cooked the night before in preparation for the assault, it being a tradition to send men into battle on a full stomach. Gnawing on the pork first, I tore hunks off with relish, realizing that, as often happened, I had not realized how famished I was until there was food available, which is a very handy trait to have for a Legionary. I washed it down with the last stock of decent wine, which I did not cut with water, telling myself that this would have to suffice until later, when I fully intended to down a spoonful of the syrup, despite how foul it tastes. I was almost finished when I heard someone approaching, and Alex came in carrying a *hamata*; I had thought I heard more than one set of footsteps, but assumed it was someone walking by.

"I don't suppose you've changed your mind," he said, but when I shook my head, he did a curious thing, stepping back out into the outer officer, and I heard a mumbled exchange.

The partition was shoved aside, and I saw one of the clerks from the *praetorium*; more importantly, I knew he was the man Germanicus used as a runner most of the time.

Since he was not a Legionary, he bowed, which I dismissed with a bare wave, then he informed me, "The Legate asks if you are capable of continuing in your role today. If not, he said that he understood, and…"

"Tell him I'm perfectly able to perform my duties," I spoke coldly, nettled by his presumption I was unfit, I suppose, "and will be there shortly."

The slave did not seem in the least surprised, which was explained when he said, "The Legate says that there's no need to come to the *praetorium* first, but that you'll find him with the rest of the Legion outside the Porta Praetoria."

"Tell the Legate I'll be there as soon as my horse is saddled," I informed the slave, who departed, as did Alex, but not before giving me a scowl that let me know exactly what he thought of what he saw as my foolishness.

Frankly, there was a part of me that tended to agree with his assessment, and this was what whispered to me that nobody would think me weak if I dropped onto my cot, but once more, the *numen* of my Avus, and the example of my father, was what propelled me outside, carrying my helmet with the new crest replacing the one that had been burned to a crisp from the heat of the fire. Speaking of that heat, although it had been many years since my skin had reacted in this manner, I did not need to look in my polished bronze mirror to know that I was almost as red as my tunic. Adding to my discomfort

458

from my shoulder and ribs was the hotness that radiated from every inch of my exposed skin, but I knew I was no worse or better off than the other men of my Cohort, and I fully expected them to be present when I rode out to join the army. Alex was standing with Latobius, still glaring at me, which I repaid by gesturing him to get on his hands and knees so I could use him as a footstool to mount, something I normally did not do, yet could not avoid at this moment. I did try to shift my weight a bit, and I felt a stab of regret at not grabbing a passing slave, but Alex did not complain, although he could not stifle the groan as my more than two hundred pounds transferred to his back, which I knew was not helped by the hobnails of my *caliga*. Once aboard, I realized I could not use my left hand for the reins, which suited neither me nor Latobius, which he let me know by arching his back, the signal he sent that, if I did not desist in my current behavior, I was running the risk of being pitched over his head, something that I could ill afford. By the time we crossed the forum, only at a walk because that was all I could bear, I had relinquished the reins and was guiding Latobius with my knees and my voice.

"I'll make a deal with you," I muttered, "if you behave and go where I tell you, you'll get two apples tonight."

With a single twitch, my horse nonetheless obeyed, reminding me that there were some creatures who were easy to command, as long as one knew the proper motivation.

True to what I had been told, Germanicus was outside the camp, along with all but two Cohorts assembled and ready to march to the southern gate, out of which still streamed a dense cloud of smoke, although I could see no flames amid the charred ruins of the rampart and gate that had been burned away. Arrayed in a single line, I saw that, while our *Aquilifer* Arvina was there, standing next to him was the *Signifer* of the Second Cohort, and this was the first occasion where I could see that they had suffered significant casualties, though not nearly as many as my First Cohort. From my quick count, they appeared to be around fifty-odd men per Century, while the Third, next to them was the exact same strength as they had been the day before. The Fourth had come with the Second, leaving the Sixth Cohort on the northern side, while Gaesorix and the cavalry guarded the western gate. The Fifth Cohort rounded out the *Legio Germanicus*, but because the First was missing, they had moved into what should have been a *triplex acies* if we had been a proper Legion.

Joining Germanicus, also mounted, he was flanked by the Tribunes, and the Legate glanced over at me, "I'm glad you're here, Pullus. You deserve to see this."

"See what, exactly?" I was slightly confused because, frankly, I was not exactly sure what was about to happen.

This surprised Germanicus, and he asked, "Didn't Vindex give you my message?" Remembering that this was the name of the slave, I shook my head, and Germanicus grumbled, "I'll have him beaten for that. But what he was supposed to tell you was that emissaries from that bastard Dodonis approached the camp. He wants to surrender."

This was welcome news, certainly, but I was not as sanguine about Dodonis' sincerity as Germanicus seemed to be, which he clearly noticed.

"Don't worry, Pullus," he assured me. "I've already warned the men to be ready for treachery, and the artillery on the hill is looking for a signal from me just in case."

Honestly, the idea of rocks raining down indiscriminately did not make me feel much better, but I was more interested in getting this over with than arguing, so I said nothing, just nodding my head in understanding. This caused him to frown, and for a moment, I was afraid he planned on making an issue of it. Instead, he gave a curt nod, then turned to order Natta to sound the advance, and we started out. Moving at a steady but slow march, I wondered why our pace was so laggardly, then I saw the small army of slaves who were coming from the direction of the river. Crossing in front of us, they headed to the southern gate, which I only understood when we drew close enough to see they were each hauling two buckets, which they began dumping over the smoldering wreckage of the gateway. Steam billowed up, informing us that, similarly to Splonum, there were still coals generating significant heat, and without thinking, I reached down with my good arm to touch my right knee, feeling the smooth scar tissue that was still an angry pink. I suppose it makes sense this was the moment when it hit me that I had suffered more during this campaign than in any other, although the wound to my left forearm, of which I was reminded whenever I glanced down at it, was still the most severe wound I had ever endured to this point in time. By the time we arrived, the remaining fire had been doused, but Germanicus did not release the slaves, sending them instead to fetch more water from the river, explaining his intention for them to stand ready to douse any flames that threatened our progress once inside the walls. While we waited, he ordered a Century from the Third Cohort forward, though not the First Century, sending them into the town to scout ahead and give us an idea of what to expect. It was the Pilus Posterior, as I recall, whose Century performed the search, and who came trotting out of the gate, his expression plain to read as he stopped to offer his report; honestly, I was only partially listening because I was more absorbed with trying to remember the man's name.

"There's nothing left inside the walls of the town below the hill," he told us grimly. "The fire is mostly out, but it's still smoky."

"Where is it still burning?" Germanicus asked, and I could see he was as unsurprised as I was when the Centurion answered, "The entire first row of buildings on the hill is still on fire, but it looks like the barbarians razed most of the buildings about three blocks up the hill, to create a firebreak. And," he finished, his face devoid of expression, which was telling in itself, "it looks like they were successful. The only building that doesn't look as if it's been damaged is the *praetorium*. Maybe," he allowed, "the *quaestorium* as well."

Germanicus seemed satisfied, which was confirmed when he dismissed the Centurion, preparing to kick his mount forward but ignoring the proper way to do such things. I held up a hand that the Centurion did not misinterpret, stopping in mid-motion as I asked him, "What about the Maezaei? Where are they? Did you see them?"

I did not take my gaze from the man standing in front of us, but I did not need to in order to see the flush of color rise to Germanicus' face at the edge of my vision, and I heard him mutter, "Of course. I should have thought of that."

"There's nothing living inside that town if it's not on that hill," the Centurion answered, suddenly looking somewhat uneasy, and if I interpreted correctly, angry, as he said, "We've come across dozens of bodies, but they're all burned too badly to know which are theirs, and…" He paused as his mouth twisted into a grimace. "…which are ours." Shaking his head, his sadness was unfeigned, if I am any judge. "We just can't tell, sir. I don't know how we're going to take care of our boys."

"We'll figure out a way." Germanicus did not say this loudly, but there was a conviction to his tone that the Centurion clearly heard as well as I did. "Now, since you've already been in there, your Century will lead the way."

Suddenly, the Pilus Posterior looked distinctly uncomfortable, and his eyes shifted from Germanicus first, then to me.

"Begging your pardon, sir," he spoke cautiously, "but shouldn't it be Pilus Prior Scipio who leads the way?"

"No." Germanicus almost spat the word. "His days of leading this Cohort are over." Suddenly, he seemed as if the notion had just struck him, and he pointed to the Centurion. "And if you perform well today, Merula, you're going to be the Tertius Pilus Prior. Is that understood?"

Stiffening to *intente*, he replied crisply, "Understood, sir, and I will obey."

He paused, but when his mouth opened to say something else, Germanicus said, "That will be all now, Merula. See to your men."

Dismissed, the now-named Merula strode back to his Century, while I fumed inwardly at myself. For the entire exchange, I had been trying to remember the man's name, and the fact that it was Germanicus who knew the name of one of the Centurions who was technically under my command was just another example, to me, of the number of ways in which I failed to live up to the expectations I had set for myself. Naturally, Germanicus was completely unaware that I was remonstrating with myself about this, and I was so occupied with my own thoughts, I did not hear him give the command for the rest of the Third Cohort to begin moving. While I do not know why I was surprised, I certainly was when, as the Third went marching by, Scipio detached himself from his Century, seemingly content to let them lead themselves into Raetinium, even if it was behind his Second Century.

I could not fault his demeanor when he stepped directly in front of Germanicus and offered a crisp salute, but this effect was ruined when, out of his mouth came what sounded like the petulant whining of the spoiled upper class boy he was when he asked, "May I inquire why the Legate has insulted the First Century in this way? I believe it's customary that it's the First Century of a Cohort who enters a conquered town."

Now, I will say I felt a bit better when I looked over at Germanicus and saw that he was as dumbfounded as I was, his mouth hanging open in shock, one so deep that he did not even seem angry.

"Are you *seriously* asking me why I'm not allowing you to enter first?" He finally got this out, then before Scipio could reply, reminded the Tertius Pilus Prior, "You not only didn't follow the planned route for the ram, you just stood by and let it be destroyed! Then," he pointed his finger at Scipio, which is something the upper classes do not care for; I cannot say I do that much, either, "you just turned tail and marched your Cohort back to leave us to fight our way through the town! You abandoned the First and Second Cohorts!"

As I was witnessing this exchange and was watching Scipio, I was reminded of another scene that, while not similar in its detail, at least had in common the manner in which Scipio was behaving. Perhaps it was way his lips formed a natural pout, or the manner in which, as Germanicus detailed his failings, the defiant manner in which he lifted his chin, but whatever it was, in Scipio I saw the Tribune Lucius Aemilius Paullus, who had been such a disaster as a leader, and who had tried to destroy the career of my former Primus Pilus Gaius Atticus. Although, I allowed to myself, Scipio's incompetence did not get men killed, or his at least, while Paullus had marched us right into an ambush at The Quarry, albeit when Urso still ran the 8th, and just the memory of this made me reach down and rub my scarred arm.

Scipio, not surprisingly, was completely unbowed and unrepentant, replying stiffly, "I did no such thing! Everything I did with my command was done in a proper manner! When our ram was unfortunately destroyed and we didn't have any way to gain entry to the town, I made the decision to take the prudent course."

"You ran," Germanicus' spoke quietly, but with an intensity, and frankly, a quality that I had not heard before, of a truly terrible anger he was just barely keeping in check, "because you're a coward, Scipio. And I'm going to make sure my father and the Princeps hear about your behavior." Suddenly, he kicked his horse forward so he could tower directly over Scipio, whose turn it was to look shocked, and from my perspective, more than a little afraid. When he reached Scipio's side, Germanicus leaned down, and while, again, he spoke softly, I certainly could hear, and judging by the expressions on the faces of the Tribunes so could they, as he said, "I'm going to ruin you, you gutless worm. I may not have had any choice when your father used his relationship with the Princeps so that I was stuck with you, but you've performed miserably. And you left us to die, Scipio, and I'll never forget it." His message delivered, Germanicus straightened up and said, loudly, "I've reconsidered! The First of the Third will remain outside the walls while we accept the surrender of the barbarians."

He did not wait for a reaction, nor did the rest of us; I barely glanced at Scipio, who stood rooted in his spot, but even in my brief examination, I could see he was shaking from head to foot. Suddenly, I felt better than I had since the day before.

If anything, the scene described by Merula was even grimmer when we were forced to confront it with our own eyes, and noses. Once a man has smelled the odor of one of his own kind essentially roasted by fire, it is one that he never forgets, yet despite being familiar with the smell, it did not help keep my stomach from lurching, though I was just able to keep my freshly consumed meal down. Neither

Appuleius nor Frugi were able to do the same, however, but for once there was no mockery of what would normally be seen as a sign of weakness; my only objection was that it was making it difficult for me. Germanicus' attention seemed fixed straight ahead over his mount's head, though I could see his eyes shifting about as our horses slowly picked their way over the charred remnants of what had been the rampart. It was about this moment that I realized Germanicus had deliberately selected the southern gate to enter, because there was no way any of us, no matter how good a horseman some of us might have been, could have forced our animals to step over the scorched and charred remains of our comrades who we had been forced to use to make our escape through the western gate. As it was, Latobius, along with the other horses, shied whenever we neared what, at a cursory examination, seemed to be a heap of smoking rubble, but invariably turned out to have at least one corpse as part of the debris. Ahead of even the Second Century, the slaves were either dumping water on the flaming remnants or performing the grisly task of dragging the dead, both Roman and Maezaei, out of our path, though it was impossible to tell the difference between ours and theirs. Because of our entry point, the hill was to our right, and we followed the street that curved around the base of the hill before turning onto the first east/west street that led directly to the forum. Being mounted, along with my height, and because what had once been single and two story buildings were now collapsed ruins, with walls that were only partially intact, I could see ahead of even the Second Century to see that, while the forum was not deserted, there was only a small party of Maezaei visible.

The instant I took this in, I turned to Germanicus and said urgently, "We should call a halt, right now!"

"Why?" He looked concerned but not alarmed like me. "What is it, Pullus?"

Pointing ahead, I tried to be patient as I explained, "There are, what, a dozen barbarians standing there? I know we killed a lot of them, but there have to be more warriors around than that." Gesturing up at the *praetorium*, which was still intact but was now completely blackened by the soot from the fire that had come within a hundred paces of it, I continued, "I don't see anything but women and children standing in front of the *praetorium*."

Germanicus' head turned in that direction, and he studied the scene for a moment, and as he did, he slowed his horse, while the Tribunes and I followed suit.

"Sound the halt," he called over his shoulder, and within a couple heartbeats, the call went out, causing the Second Century to come crashing to a stop, just a few paces from the edge of the forum. Turning to me, Germanicus asked softly, "What do you suggest, Pullus?"

"We wait until we can deploy the Third Cohort out that direction," I pointed to the western edge of the forum, moving my finger from south to north, "then ideally, I'd like the Fourth or Fifth to move to the northern edge of the forum, but facing the hill."

He did not reply, to me, but turned to Silius, and quietly ordered him to go find Proculus, whose Cohort was immediately behind us, and lead him to the position I suggested. Silius turned his mount, while the Legate ordered Appuleius to go forward and explain to Merula what he wanted done, without any mention of the disgraced Pilus Prior. Whose whereabouts, frankly, I did not even know, nor did Germanicus; the last I had seen of him, he was still rooted to the spot outside the southern gate as his Cohort moved on without him. Happy as I was to see that Germanicus had taken my suggestion, I was completely unprepared for what came next.

"Come on, Pullus," he kicked his horse forward, "we're going to go find out what's going on."

"'Going on'?" I asked cautiously, not liking that he was actually urging his horse in the direction of the forum, the path in front of him clearing itself as the men of the Third Cohort started moving, using the streets leading north as they maneuvered into their position lining the western edge of the forum from one end to the other.

He did not reply, but more importantly, he also did not slow down until he was just behind the Second Century, which had remained where it was as the anchor of the line of Centuries of the Third that was shaking out, instead of the First Century, which was now taking the farthest spot away from us in the single line, but led by their Optio.

466

Cursing under my breath, I nudged Latobius, who moved forward as reluctantly as I felt, though in a few heartbeats, I was next to Germanicus. Ideally, I would have preferred that our Legate wait long enough to send the Fifth Cohort, or even the Second, though it was being held back as the reserve, to take up position along the eastern edge of the forum, facing the Third, but I only had to glance at him to know he was not willing to wait. Indeed, once I drew abreast of him, he was about to urge his mount forward, past the Second to enter the forum.

"Shouldn't we wait for the Tribunes to get back?" I suggested, except this time, he shook his head impatiently.

"No." He did not take his eyes from the cluster of Maezaei who, to this point, had been standing there impassively watching as we maneuvered into a superior position. "Besides," he pointed out, "if they do try something, the Legion is going to need someone to command it." This was when he turned to grin at me, but I was not disposed to share it, which caused him to laugh and tease me, "Come, Pullus! You didn't want to live forever, did you?"

Then, he kicked his horse, calling out to the men in the nearest files to step aside to allow him to pass, leaving me to grumble, "No, but I don't want to die today."

Nevertheless, I urged Latobius forward and caught up to Germanicus just as he passed the first rank and emerged into the forum. He did pause just long enough for the Fourth Cohort, which had been moving at the double-quick, to arrange themselves at the far northern end of the forum, but when the Cohort *Signifer* thrust his standard in the air in the signal they were now in position, Germanicus did not hesitate. And, despite my misgivings, I was just behind him, seriously wondering how useful I could be if the Maezaei tried some sort of treachery.

As I passed by Merula, he called out loudly enough for me to hear, "Watch his back, Primus Pilus. I don't trust these *cunni*."

"That makes two of us," was all I could think to say, yet I did not hesitate in following along.

Now that he was committed to his course, I was not about to let him do it by himself, despite thinking it was a horrible idea. I did ride just behind Germanicus, mainly because he was to my right, and I wanted to keep an eye on the bottom stretch of the slope, which would have been partially obscured by his body. I felt slightly better when I saw that there was little to no chance for any Maezaei to be concealed in the charred ruins of what had once been the homes of the wealthier citizens of Raetinium, because they were still smoldering, with tiny flames just visible here and there. Once I determined that there were no warriors within bow range, I urged Latobius alongside Germanicus; this was when I examined the group of barbarians standing, waiting for us. My gut tightened, this time from anger, when I saw that it was Dodonis who was standing just in front of what I assumed were the elders and clan sub-chieftains. He looked even older than the last time we had been this close, his face drawn and haggard, but he stood there, his head erect and eyes on us, watching us approach. I was actually a bit curious about how Germanicus was going to handle this, specifically whether he planned to dismount, which I regretted not advising against before we approached. Thankfully, he gave no inclination of doing so, halting his horse just far enough from the Maezaei so that he would not have to raise his voice, but not so close that they could cross the distance between us without our having time to react. And, to my relief, I could feel Latobius' muscles underneath me, bunched and radiating the tension he was feeling, though that very well might have been a reflection of my own feelings, communicated to him through my own body. For a long moment, nobody spoke, and I stared down at Dodonis, yet for once, he did not even glance in my direction, his eyes staying steadily on Germanicus, who was no less impassive. Fairly quickly, I realized this was one of those moments where there was a quiet battle of wills going on, and I offered a silent urging to my Legate that he recognize this and not fall to the temptation of filling the silence. There is no way to know, but he either sensed my silent plea, or he had decided on his own, because his mouth was shut, and when I gave him a sidelong glance, I saw his jaws were tightly clenched.

468

Finally, something seemed to wilt inside Dodonis, because his composure, which despite my hatred of the man, I found myself admiring, crumbled at last, and it was in a barely audible voice that he finally broke the silence by saying, "I submit to the authority of Rome, and I offer the surrender of the people you call the Maezaei." He hesitated, and I understood why when he added, "I would ask what your terms for our surrender would be."

The laugh Germanicus gave held no humor, and his verbal response was no less harsh, as he scoffed, "Terms? What are my terms?" Suddenly, he caught me and, judging from the way not only Dodonis but the men around him reacted, the Maezaei by surprise, because he turned to me and asked, "What do you say, Primus Pilus Pullus? You've had more experience with these barbarians than I do. What terms would you suggest Rome offers them, given this isn't the first time they've rebelled?"

While I was not altogether sure whether he really wanted to know, or if this was some ploy on his part, I decided to answer Germanicus honestly, from the heart, and I made sure I pinned the chieftain with my gaze as I made my voice as cold as possible when I replied, "I'd put them all in chains, send them to Salona to the nearest slave market and sell every last one of them."

I felt a deep satisfaction when not only Dodonis, but those around him who understood Latin visibly flinched, their faces uniformly losing all color, which was followed by their fellow tribesmen who did not speak our tongue after my words were translated by Dodonis. Germanicus did not seem surprised and actually seemed to consider my suggestion.

Finally, he said thoughtfully, "While I understand and tend to agree, Tiberius hasn't given us specific instructions about how we're to dispose of these people." Turning to Dodonis, the young Legate actually seemed puzzled, shaking his head as he asked the chieftain, "Did you really think that you'd resist us?"

The Maezaei actually laughed, but it was one with no humor, and I heard the bitter defeat in it as he retorted, "Obviously, Legate, I did."

469

"And all this?" Germanicus swept a hand at the destruction around us. "What did you hope to accomplish with this? You'd been living here for months, and your people had settled here and taken this town for their own. So," I heard the frustration in Germanicus' voice, "why would you burn it down around your own heads?"

"Because," Dodonis replied calmly, "I gave you my word that I would, Roman. And, if I had not, no matter what happened to me after this, you would know that we Maezaei would not go through with our threats."

"No," Germanicus countered, "I'd know that you had the best interests of your people as your highest priority, and not your pride." He seemed to become angry now, and I could not tell whether it was feigned or not. "And now, you've sealed the fate of your people because you're a stubborn, prideful fool."

With Germanicus, I could not guess, but I was certain that the anger on Dodonis' face was genuine, and his fists clenched, though he was not wearing any weapons. Then, he seemed to understand that this was not the time for him to lose his composure, and I saw his chest rise as he took a breath, then he spoke.

"All I ask is that my people be spared, Legate," he said in a quieter tone of voice, and there was a pleading note in it. "Do with me what you will. And," for the first time, he turned and gestured at the men standing silently behind him, "do not punish these men too harshly. They were simply following my orders, just as your men," for the first time he looked at me, and I saw the hatred there, which I returned, glaring right back at him, "obey the orders of their leaders."

"You tried to burn us alive," Germanicus pointed out, "and almost succeeded."

If this was meant to rattle the chieftain or make him apprehensive, it did not appear to work, because he simply shrugged, then returning his gaze to Germanicus, asked him pointedly, "Are you saying that you would have not done the same?" Then, he turned back to me and continued, "Burning down a town to defeat your enemy, whether it was yours or belonged to someone else, like your enemy? You Romans would not do something like that?"

Oh, I hated the man, but this was something I could not argue with, nor did it seem Germanicus had any reply, until, suddenly, the Legate shook his head, insisting, "Not when it puts my own people in danger."

"That's because you're Roman," Dodonis replied bitterly, "and you've never been conquered by another people."

"And we never will be," Germanicus assured him, resuming his pointing, "and this should serve as an example of why." Then, before Dodonis could reply, he stopped this exchange, saying abruptly, "But ultimately, it doesn't matter. I accept your surrender, Dodonis. However," his voice hardened, and he spoke more loudly than necessary, which I assumed was because he meant for our men standing behind us to hear, "it will be under Rome's terms, not yours! Now, you will order your people to come out from wherever they're skulking about and come down here to the forum. Or," his voice dropped back to its normal volume, though while the tone was reasonable, the words were anything but, "I can promise you that we will finish what we started, and while we'll lose more men, I swear to you by your gods and mine that we will slaughter every last one of you and exterminate the Maezaei from the face of the earth."

That, ultimately, was how Raetinium fell, although the town essentially no longer existed. However, we did learn something quite surprising. It had been something of a mystery where all of the Maezaei civilians had taken refuge during the fire, because it seemed impossible that just the brick *praetorium* was capable of holding them all, even if they were crammed in shoulder to shoulder. What we learned was that, fairly recently and as part of their defensive improvements, the *Duumviri* of the town had actually dug a series of tunnels and small caverns into the side of the hill, which could only be accessed from the basement of the *praetorium*. It was there that not only the civilians sheltered, but where the Maezaei warriors who were wounded were taken, although those men who were unable to move on their own were put to the *gladius* where we found them. As far as the civilians, they were herded onto the forum, then in front of

471

Dodonis, Germanicus ordered them all bound, the youngsters and women with rope, and the men who were not warriors were put in chains. The Maezaei chieftain's face contorted with a rage that was no less powerful because it was impotent; indeed, perhaps it was compounded by his recognition that there was nothing he could do to stop it. They were allowed to sit in the forum, which the slaves had cleared of the debris, piling up the detritus of the fight and fire in several heaps around the edges of the cleared area. Despite orders for silence, which I understood even as they were given would go unheeded, there was a low-pitched but clearly audible noise coming from what turned out to be a bit more than three thousand Maezaei civilians, as it turned out that the fire had not only claimed our men and the Maezaei warriors who had been part of the delaying force, reducing their numbers by a bit less than two thousand, but the civilians as well. Speaking of the warriors, the surviving remnant of this force was easy to identify, because they looked much like I did, and the men of the Second Cohort who were present, a deep, roasted red. This did not mean that some of them did not attempt to blend in, similarly to their counterparts in Splonum, but even if they had not been scorched, just as with those in their capital, it is a practical impossibility that a man who has carried himself with the haughtiness and arrogance of a warrior can suddenly adopt the demeanor of a lowborn citizen who works every day from sunlight to dark, earning his bread with the sweat from his brow. These men were quickly rounded up, and though a couple of them tried to struggle, they were dealt with simply but brutally, with a *gladius* thrust into their body. Once these men were successfully segregated, they were put at the southern end of the forum, nearest the hill, and while we had allowed the civilians to sit, still bound of course, these men were forced to kneel, while they merited chains that had been forged by the metalworking *immunes* in preparation for this moment. Dodonis' sub-chieftains were treated in a similar manner, but for reasons he did not share, Germanicus allowed Dodonis to stand between the Legate and me, although there was almost a full section of Legionaries standing around us, with two behind, two in front and two men flanking

Germanicus and me on either side. The sun, which had been just above the horizon when we entered the former town, was now high enough in the sky that I could feel the first trickles of sweat, reminding me that I was still grimy and in desperate need of a bath, as I realized at the same time I had been awake for more than a full day. And, in a strange and painful way, the throbbing ache of both my shoulder and ribs did more to ward off the chances of me falling asleep in the saddle than any willpower on my part.

During this period, Germanicus had also sent runners to both camps, summoning every able-bodied man from my Cohort, along with Agrippa's, and although Germanicus did not explain why, I suspected I knew his reason. Dodonis was the only man not in chains, but while he was still standing erect, he was weaving with the same kind of fatigue that I was fighting, and judging from Germanicus' tightly drawn features and the dark smudges under his eyes that were present despite the fact that he had at least washed his face, the Legate's as well. Still, nothing was said between the Maezaei and my commander, nor did Dodonis attempt to engage me, which suited me perfectly. Then, perhaps a full watch after we entered the town, Merula, who had been placed in command of the search for survivors, reported that the caverns had been thoroughly searched, along with the couple dozen structures that remained at the very top of the hill, which naturally were the homes of the wealthiest inhabitants of Raetinium. The rest of the *Legio Germanicus*, save for the auxiliaries, were also present, the First and Second Cohorts now arrayed on the eastern edge of the forum. When I saw that Germanicus had clearly ordered that his command extended to the disgraced Fourth Century of my Cohort, this prompted the only exchange between us, as I turned to stare at him when I saw the standard of the Fourth crossing my vision.

"Why?" I did not even attempt to couch my question with the kind of military courtesy I should have, but I was beyond caring. "Why," I repeated, "are you allowing them to be here?"

I must credit Germanicus, because he not only did not seem surprised at my outburst, he was also completely unperturbed by my lack of respect, but all he said was, "You'll see, Pullus. And," he looked me directly in the eyes, for which I respected him, "I promise you won't be displeased."

Despite this rousing my intense curiosity, I also understood this was neither the time nor place to press him, if only because of the audience of one who stood between us, although Dodonis did not seem overly interested. In fact, he had barely taken his gaze away from the sight of his people, huddled together in their shared bondage and misery, the low moan of fear that I had become accustomed to still audible even from where we were almost a hundred paces away. Finally, once Germanicus watched as Merula marched to his new spot at the head of the Third Cohort, only then did he make any move.

Nimbly dismounting, although he took care to actually do so on the opposite side from where Dodonis was standing, Germanicus stepped around his horse to face Dodonis, but it was me he addressed, asking, "Primus Pilus, can you dismount on your own? Or do you need help because of your wounds?"

Well, I thought, when you put it that way, there's no way I'm going to answer in the affirmative, but I did manage to avoid acting altogether foolishly by trying to demonstrate how I could swing off Latobius with the same ease he had demonstrated. Indeed, I imagine I looked like an old man, but I was able to slide off my horse with only a quiet gasp that I was sure could not be heard even by the pair of rankers standing a couple paces away. Perhaps I moved more slowly than normal, but I was not hobbling as I moved around Latobius to join Germanicus, inadvertently aided when my horse decided this was the appropriate time to check the bag still slung over my shoulder for the apples I promised him earlier, and in doing so, gave me a not so gentle nudge that propelled me forward an extra step. This prompted some snickers from the rankers, further marring this dramatic moment, something that Germanicus certainly, and understandably, did not appreciate.

"You spoil your horse," he grumbled, which I could not argue then or now.

Standing to Dodonis' side, Germanicus pointed to a spot in between the Maezaei civilians, and directly in front of the kneeling warriors, who despite their chains, were guarded by men of the Third, all of them armed with javelins, ready to hurl them into the captives at the first sign of trouble. For a span of several heartbeats, it looked to me like Dodonis would have to be forced to obey, but then, slowly, he began walking. The Legionaries who had been in front of us stepped aside, turning so that Dodonis passed between them, sending him the silent message that there was nothing to be gained from fighting, while Germanicus followed behind him, and I trailed the Legate. Since there had been no discussion, I was every bit as curious as I am sure everyone other than Germanicus was about what was about to take place.

"That's far enough," Germanicus called out, and Dodonis obediently stopped, but then, when he tried to turn and face back in our direction, the Legate commanded, "No! Face your people."

Because he had partially turned, I caught a glimpse of the Maezaei's expression, and I got the distinct impression that he knew what was coming, yet instead of fear, there was a look of resignation, which in turn gave me something of an idea about what to expect.

"Kneel," Germanicus ordered, but when Dodonis whirled about, his expression changing to one of anger and defiance, instead of threatening the chieftain, Germanicus pointed past him to Dodonis' people, saying nothing else.

Closing his eyes briefly, Dodonis slowly turned around, then after a pause, dropped heavily to his knees. Once he did, only then did Germanicus stride over to stand to Dodonis' left, the spot that a right-handed man would choose for what I now understood was about to happen.

"Interpret this," Germanicus ordered Dodonis, then without waiting for any sign of acquiescence, the Legate began speaking in what I recognized as the style in which young nobles are instructed, and he had used with the Legion on a few occasions. "People of the Maezaei! You have been led to your current state by *this* man." He pointed dramatically down at Dodonis, who had now bowed his head to stare at the scorched and blackened stones of the forum, though he spoke loudly enough as he relayed what Germanicus was saying. "And

475

he lied to you! You never had any hope of overthrowing Rome!" He paused, except so did Dodonis, causing Germanicus to whisper, "Tell them, or I will pick ten children and execute them in front of you."

This wrenched what sounded like something of a sob from the humiliated Maezaei's lips, but Germanicus' promise worked, and he said the words. Whether or not they were all the right ones I could not tell, though I had picked up enough of their tongue so that I felt certain I could understand the essence of what he said, and most importantly, whether he deviated from what Germanicus had ordered him to say. Once Dodonis finished this part, Germanicus raised the volume of his voice even more, causing his words to carry a slightly ringing quality, which I assumed was due to him speaking essentially into a closed box, though the sides were the combined flesh, armor and shields of the Legion who, for the most part, were standing motionless, their faces uniformly set into hard planes as they witnessed this final humiliation of an enemy they might not have started out hating, but who clearly did by this point.

"Now you will see the fate of those who try to lure their people into the folly of rebelling against the kind and wise Augustus, and the Senate and People of Rome!"

But then, instead of drawing his own *gladius*, he suddenly turned and beckoned to me. Despite a surprise bordering on shock, I felt my legs obeying even as my mind tried to grapple with what this could mean.

"Pullus," Germanicus said this just loud enough that I, and of course Dodonis, could hear, "I think it's appropriate that you be the one to end this rebellion of the Maezaei, once and for all."

This seemed to animate Dodonis, and he started to rise, hissing, "No! Not him! Anyone but him!"

Germanicus was clearly prepared for this, because he roughly shoved down on Dodonis' shoulder before he could stand erect, then shook his head at the two Legionaries who were standing behind us as they stepped forward to secure the chieftain.

"I'm guessing that you'd prefer a clean and quick death," Germanicus said coldly, "but if not, I'm more than happy to arrange

476

one that will last for days. And" he warned, "I'll make your people watch as you piss and *cac* yourself, and beg me for mercy." Even then, Dodonis shook his head, prompting Germanicus to repeat, "For *days*."

Finally, the chieftain's face twisted into a grimace that expressed his final recognition and acceptance of his fate, signaled by ceasing his struggles, and looking up into Germanicus' face, only nodding to inform the Legate he understood. My heart had started hammering, and there was a sudden spate of sweat on my brow that I hoped was not obvious or could be explained by the redness of my skin, but I did as Germanicus directed, taking the spot he had vacated that put me in the proper position.

"You deserve this, Pullus," Germanicus whispered to me, and honestly, I was not sure why he would do so, until he added, "You suffered a terrible loss to these savages, and I know it's been a few years, but we don't forget things like that, do we?"

I forced myself to look him in the eye, just barely stopping the sudden rush of tears at this reminder of an event that, sadly, I had indeed locked away and seldom thought about over the course of this campaign, and I could only shake my head in answer. No, I thought, no, we never really forget. Titus Pullus' Gallic blade slid from its scabbard as smoothly as it always did, the handle of the weapon and my hand melding into a single unit as my fingers wrapped over my thumb, and I will not lie, I took satisfaction at seeing Dodonis flinch at the hissing sound it made. To my ears, it seemed like a sweet music as I thought, Maybe this is what the gods had in mind all along. Then, an utter and deathly silence fell over the forum; even the prisoners seemed to stop to hold their breath as I stood there, and I became acutely conscious that every pair of eyes, Roman and Maezaei, were fastened on me, and Dodonis.

It was only as I raised my *gladius* above my head, in a slightly unusual manner since this is the one type of action where the edge beats the point, that I spoke aloud, and I did so loudly enough that my comrades could hear, "This is for my brother, Sextus Porcinianus Pullus, *Tesseraurius* of the Third Century, Fifth Cohort of the 8th Legion!"

Dodonis actually turned his head to look up at me, and snarled, "And when I meet your brother in the afterlife, you Roman dog, I'll...."

Beheading a man is usually performed with a *spatha*, because its longer length adds the weight necessary to part a man's head from his shoulders with one stroke. However, I did not need one, and it was in the instant after my blade sliced through the bone and muscle of Dodonis' head, his lips still pulled back from his teeth in a hateful sneer as it went spinning up into the air, while the stump of his neck sprayed blood several inches upward like a scarlet fountain, that the thought crossed my mind; maybe that's really why Germanicus wanted me to do it, because I'm one of the few men strong enough to take a man's head off with a single stroke. This was a moment that seemed to last longer than it actually did, but the silence still enveloped all of us as we watched the Maezaei's head finally strike the paving stones with the kind of sickly, sodden thud that once one hears it, they never forget, then bounce several times before rolling to a stop at the feet of one of the two Legionaries who had been behind the prisoner. The silence was broken only after Dodonis' corpse had crumpled to one side, where it was surrounded by a still-growing pool of blood, and there was a sudden roar of approval from Roman throats that drowned out the wails of the Maezaei women. And, to my surprise, for the first time since the death of my brother, I felt, not happy, but fulfilled, as if this had been what I needed to properly appease the shade of my brother.

We never did find the body of Servius Metellus. More accurately, while there were heaps of charred bones and ash, the metal of the armor and helmets fused together in such a manner that it was impossible for us to tell which pile of slag iron with blackened bones sticking out at odd angles were Roman and which were Maezaei. That does not mean that there is not an urn with my old friend's name incised into it, sitting in a niche in my own family tomb outside Arelate. Metellus had no family; no son to carry on his name and legacy, no woman to mourn him, nor any siblings, at least who were still alive, and while this was certainly part of the reason I sent an urn containing what I could only hope were at least a few fragmented bones and ash that had once been part of Metellus to our family tomb, there was a much deeper reason. In its simplest terms, I owed Servius Metellus my life, and I never forgot that I had been the man who convinced him to leave his life of retirement and march for Germanicus. That, as far as I was, and am concerned, makes me responsible for his fate, about which I have spent many sleepless nights as I try to convince myself that Metellus had fallen to a Maezaei spear or *gladius* and not suffered the fate of burning to death. What I can say is that, while the tombstone is not just his, I do not think he would be displeased that he shares the resting place of the first and greatest Titus Pullus, along with my brother, mother and sister. Piecing everything together later was, as it usually is, maddeningly incomplete as far as the details, but what Cerrinius and the survivors of the Second Century affirmed was that, were it not for the actions of Servius Metellus and a single section of men, all of whom were essentially too old to be under the standard, the entire First Cohort, or those Centuries that were trapped within those walls, would have been destroyed.

Speaking of our lone Century who, through no fault of the men, did not even march across the bridge after we entered the western gate, the Centurion in command, Tubertus, was duly punished. That it happened just a few moments after I executed Dodonis, and at Germanicus' quiet command, while I was still standing with my blade, dripping blood and bits of tissue, meant that it was not lost on Tubertus that, if I had had any say in the matter, his punishment would have been identical to that of the Maezaei. It was only later that I recognized, and was forced to admire, how adroitly Germanicus manipulated the situation, because when presented as Tubertus was with the unspoken but obvious alternative, in the form of me standing there eyeing him with even more contempt than I had exhibited with Dodonis, and my *gladius* still ready for use, being demoted and dismissed from the *Legio Germanicus* was a punishment the disgraced man was unlikely to argue about. And, since this was done in the

479

forum of Raetinium, in front of most of the *Legio Germanicus*, it meant that his humiliation and disgrace was about as complete as it could be without actually forcing him to run the gauntlet, the usual punishment for men who exhibit cowardice in battle. The captured Maezaei were put to work cleaning up the debris that once was a thriving town, and while I never heard Germanicus say as much, I assumed he was intent on the town being rebuilt. To that end, he sent messengers to the coastal towns like Vetium, where most of the former inhabitants had taken refuge, summoning them back with the news that Raetinium was once again in Roman hands.

By the time the sun set on the first day after most of Raetinium was destroyed, the work of rebuilding was well underway, with the bulk of the unsalvageable debris dragged outside the walls. There was only one group of captives who were exempted from any form of manual labor, and that was the remaining six hundred warriors, who remained in chains, although they were moved to an enclosed pen just outside the walls of the northern camp, with two Centuries standing guard. As for me, once Tubertus was dismissed and escorted back to camp to pack his personal baggage, I was excused from further duties. Latobius took me back to camp, where Alex helped me down off his back, but before he was led away, I fulfilled my promise, producing the two apples that he had smelled, and even this simple act helped soothe me as I watched him munching contentedly. Alex was quick to use his newfound authority, and judging by the manner in which the slave he summoned hurried to take Latobius to the stables, his threat to have me thrash anyone Alex deemed worthy of punishment seemed to be taken seriously. Helping me out of my armor, once that was done, Alex left me to do something, which is the last I remember until the *bucina* call sounded the start of the next day, when I woke in the same position, sprawled across my cot. Only after breaking my fast did I finally have the opportunity for a good scraping, although I might have threatened Alex with one of the beatings he was promising the slaves when he inadvertently got too close to the stitches closing the wound on my side. As he worked, he apprised me of what had taken place during the remaining daylight watches I had been asleep.

"Scipio was caught trying to leave the camp, so he's under guard in his tent." My nephew spoke in a neutral manner, but I did not miss the satisfaction in his voice as he related this bit of gossip. "And I heard that Germanicus is seriously considering having him executed in front of the Legion."

While this sounded like an apt punishment, I am afraid that I was too jaded by this point to believe that our Legate, no matter how sincere Germanicus may have been in his desire to offer our battered Legion an example that the standard of behavior expected of rankers extended to every man, no matter their rank, would go through with it, since Scipio was simply too highly placed to be punished in this manner.

"Don't bet on it," was how I expressed it to Alex. "And," I warned him, "don't say that to anyone else!"

"I'm not stupid, Uncle Titus," he protested, and once more, I had to resist the urge to ruffle his hair, touched by his look of wounded pride that I would think so little of him.

"I know you aren't," I assured him, forced to fight the sudden surge of emotion as I looked down at him because there was something in the tilt of his head that reminded me of his father. "I just worry, that's all."

"You don't need to worry about me, Uncle," Alex said stoutly with all the assurance and pride that is the province of the young who have yet to taste the bitter ash of life's many disappointments. "I know when I need to keep my mouth shut."

"Good," I replied, a bit shortly perhaps, but during this exchange, I had been reminded of how, after a hard-fought battle, particularly when men I considered friends were lost, my emotions were always a bit rawer and exposed than normal. "Now, help me get ready. I'm going to the *praetorium* to find out what's next."

What was next was nothing, at least in terms of campaigning, which was a good thing, because the *Legio Germanicus* was essentially finished as an effective fighting force, at least as it was composed at this moment. Germanicus, on my advice, decided to plump the First Cohort back up, as we like to say, with men from the other Cohorts, but in doing so, while he brought the First back up to perhaps seventy-five percent strength, the other Cohorts were subsequently substantially reduced in strength. Essentially, until we could receive replacements, this scratch Legion was only good for routine duties, which were little more than sending out Century-sized patrols, hunting down the inevitable stragglers and small bands of Maezaei who had managed to escape, or had been out marauding while Dodonis had led the bulk of his people to Raetinium. For his part, Germanicus was alternately subdued, despondent, and fretful, depending on the latest bit of news, either from one of the patrols, or more importantly to him, from the larger world. Such were our own travails that it was easy for us to forget there was a larger rebellion going on, and from the parade of couriers, there was no way to disguise that things were not going well for Tiberius. Along with the official dispatches, there came the more informal, but no less important, unwritten messages, carried by the couriers, all men from the ranks, even if they were cavalry, which meant there was no way to keep the more disturbing news from the rankers.

"The Legions are getting restless," was how Gaesorix put it to me, back in camp from another circuit around the area. We were sharing a meal in my quarters, and the Batavian was in a somber frame of mind, moodily sipping from the cup of unwatered wine. "They're as tired and worn down as we are, and they've been chasing these savages for months without bringing them to a battle that will finish it."

Once more, I had to smile, inwardly, at my Batavian friend's unthinking echo of the term that Romans, borrowed from the Greeks as so many of our words and practices, used for the native tribes, and I briefly considered pointing out that the average Head Counter back in Rome would run screaming in terror at the Decurion for the simple fact that he was one of those barbarians. Fortunately, that was a thought that stayed within the confines of my head, and despite hearing Gaesorix use this term or something similar during our time together, I managed to refrain from ever doing so.

"Well," I commented, thinking to add a bit of perspective, gleaned from the official record of events that Germanicus made me privy to, "Tiberius has decided to go back to separating the army into three columns again. That way, I suppose he hopes to spread the men out so that the troublemakers from different Legions won't be able to get together and make mischief."

I was not particularly surprised at the scornful look Gaesorix gave me, and he emphasized his words by issuing a deep belch before he retorted, "Bah! That might delay them from causing trouble, but what they need," suddenly he leaned forward, pointing at me emphatically, "what *we* need is to beat these *cunni*! That," he finished, "is the best way, the only way to make sure the Legions don't revolt."

The idea that we were talking about the Legions of Rome essentially rebelling, as they had at Pharsalus under Divus Julius, was still not something that my mind could easily absorb, and consequently prompted me to protest, mildly, "We just did that, here."

Gaesorix did not answer me, instead giving me a level look that spoke more eloquently than anything he could have said, but rather than use words, I merely nodded that I understood and acknowledged that he meant something more decisive and less costly than what had taken place here. For, while it was true that the Maezaei were no longer in rebellion, the cost, in our blood and the treasure and property of the citizens of Rome who we were ostensibly there to protect, was staggering. Never lost on me or far from my mind was that I was far from alone in feeling so acutely the loss of friends like Metellus, and those men who, while they might not have been close companions like he was, were men under my command and who relied on me to keep them alive. It was this that created the pall that hung over the three camps, although in all honesty, Gaesorix and his men felt this more by association than through their ranks being thinned. Compounding matters was the simple fact that there was not much for the men to do at this point in time, while we licked our wounds and waited for further orders. It was now the Ides of the month named for Divus Julius, meaning that there was not that much time left in the campaign season, although given all that had taken place over the previous two seasons, this did not mean a lot. The Pannonians had certainly not shown any inclination to consider the winter as the time to rest and refit, although it was true that their actions were not large-scale, but more along the lines of their traditional mode of fighting, with raids by smaller bands of warriors. Given what we had learned about the larger situation, it was highly unlikely that we would have a quiet winter, and my personal opinion about the future of the *Legio Germanicus* aside, our Legate gave orders that made it clear he intended for us to rejoin the fight. A fight for which, I realized, I no longer had the stomach, and it was sometime in the week after the fall of Raetinium where, while I cannot place the exact moment, I made my own decision about my immediate future.

Despite my personal feelings, I did as Germanicus directed, namely replacing my Primus Pilus Posterior and Princeps Posterior, a decision that Germanicus allowed me to make completely on my own.

"Considering how Metellus and Tubertus performed," he told me ruefully, "I still have a lot to learn about judging which men are fit for command and which aren't."

This, as I had learned, was typical of Germanicus; he never tried to escape responsibility, nor did he pretend to know what he did not, which made my own decision, which was still unspoken, that much more difficult. Despite the fact I had made it, I had as yet to inform Germanicus about it, meaning that when Germanicus indicated our meeting was over, I simply saluted and returned to my quarters. I sent Alex back to the *praetorium* with a list of names whose records, the abbreviated form of them that a Legion carries while on campaign, I wanted to peruse. I did this out of a long-ingrained habit, something that I had actually learned from my father.

"You always need to have a list handy," he had explained, "because it's never a case of *if* one of the men in a command position is going to fall, it's a matter of when. So, you always need to have a short list for each spot of the men you've been watching who you think can step into that role."

These were the men whose records I had Alex retrieve, knowing as I did so that the news would shoot throughout the camp to the point that, by the time my nephew walked into our office, the men whose names were on my list would know about it. This, as I had long before learned, is one of those things over which you have no control, any more than the fact that if you jump into the air and flap your arms like a bird, you still come crashing back to the ground. And, once Alex returned, I buried myself in this routine task, trying to put out of my mind the reason I was doing it in the first place. One thing I was determined to do was not to hold it against some of the men I was considering that they were part of the contingent that had come from Rome, with Germanicus. Over the course of the time the Legion had been together, I had observed that, like with all Legions, those men who came along with Germanicus were a mixed bag of good and bad. Some of them I knew from the outset came from equestrian families, and a portion of those made it clear from the beginning that they considered themselves better than the old veterans around them. And, as often happens with young men, some of them learned that we all straddle the trench the same way, and our *cac* smells the same, particularly after sharing the same diet; a couple of those younger men were names on my list. One particular lesson I had learned from this period of time was that, while it was not absolutely essential for a Centurion in the *Legio Germanicus* to be younger, it certainly helped. I was thirty-four, and perhaps my frame of mind was affected by the maddening itch of the stitches on my side or the sharp stab of pain that struck whenever I reached for something with my left hand, but after a brief reflection, I somewhat reluctantly crossed two names off my list, simply because they were both at least ten years older than I was. What I had to balance was that, in the case of three of the remaining candidates, their record, such as it was, came only from this campaign; the only notation in their record prior to this was that they had participated in the required exercises on the Campus Martius. However, the reasons I had these names on my list in the first place was because I had either observed, or one of the other Centurions had mentioned these men's names in a positive way. Fairly quickly, with

485

one of them, I recalled that it had been Tubertus who had sung the man's praises, meaning his tablet was tossed onto the floor next to my desk. A full watch was spent in this manner, until I felt ready to summon the final candidates to speak to me personally, so that by the end of the day, while I was tired from sitting behind my desk on the hard stool, I was satisfied that I had found my men. One man in particular, while I felt confident about in my choice, I also worried that Germanicus might object, and at first, it seemed as if my fear was justified when I submitted my choices to the Legate.

"Rufius?" Germanicus' eyebrow raised, followed by his eyes from the tablet to my face. "He's your Optio, yes?"

"Yes, sir," I answered firmly, understanding that I needed to sound completely confident in my answer. "He's more than ready to be in the Centurionate."

"But," Germanicus sounded doubtful, "in the First Cohort?"

This was expected, and in response, I pointed out, "Which he's been handling from the first days when we formed the Legion. An Optio of the First of the First means that, most of the time, he's handling the Century while the Primus Pilus is off consorting with the Legate and Tribunes, holding their hands and making sure they're happy. Because," I grinned at Germanicus, "if the Legate's not happy, nobody's happy."

I would not have tried this jest with anyone else of Legate rank, but despite the bumps in our relationship, which once I had time to think about it, I recognized I should have expected as a green nobleman essentially felt his way along in their post that carries such tremendous responsibility, Germanicus and I had an excellent association.

And, as I hoped, he laughed and echoed, "That's right. If I'm not happy, I don't see why anyone else should be. It's one of the prerogatives of rank!" Glancing back down at the tablet, he compressed his lips, sighed, but then nodded, "You're right, though, Pullus. I should have thought of it that way. Although," he looked back up at me, and it was the manner in which he tilted his head that was so reminiscent of his father Drusus that I had to swallow the sudden lump as he commented, "I'm also somewhat surprised since Rufius is one of the men who came with me."

"I'm a bit surprised myself," I answered frankly, "but he's proven himself to this point, and I think he's not only capable, but he deserves the rank. Now," I allowed, "I seriously doubt that Tiberius and the Camp Prefect will keep his appointment as a Centurion, should he decide to stay in the Legions."

"No," Germanicus agreed, "I can practically guarantee that's the case. My...father," he still seemed to have trouble making that connection and thinking of Tiberius as his father, even with our attitude towards adoption and how quickly we assimilate adopted and adoptive figures into our lives, "hasn't been very impressed with the *Legio Germanicus* to this point." All traces of good humor vanished, a bleak expression crossing his features as he continued, "And I'm expecting to hear back from him any day now about what happened here. So," even in the lamplight it was impossible to miss the bony part of his throat bob as he swallowed, "I suspect that he'll be even less pleased with the Legion, knowing that we couldn't save Raetinium from being put to the torch."

This, I knew, was likely the truth, yet I still felt compelled to point something out to my Legate. "Sir, there was no way to know that Dodonis would actually carry through with his threat. And," I did not feel I was playing him falsely when I said, "I'd be willing to wager a good deal of money that, had Tiberius himself been here, he wouldn't have believed that bastard either."

Germanicus seemed torn, as if he wanted to believe my words, but could not bring himself to do so, causing him to heave a sigh and say, "I hope you're right, Pullus." Suddenly, he shook his head abruptly, as if driving this line of thought from his mind, and returned to the matter at hand. "So, Rufius is the new Princeps Posterior of the First." His eyes went to the other name, and while he frowned, it was not because of displeasure. "Quintus Fabius Pictor? He's not in your Cohort, is he?"

"No," I confirmed, "he's not. He's the Secundus Pilus Posterior."

"Agrippa won't be happy to lose him," Germanicus remarked. "He's spoken highly of him many times."

"Which is why I picked him."

This prompted what appeared to me to be a rueful smile, as he correctly guessed, "And I suppose you expect me to be the one to tell Agrippa about this?"

"That's why you're the Legate," I answered cheerfully, though I cannot say he did not look all that happy about the thought.

"Very well," he waved a hand at me, "I'll go tell him now. But," he stood up, and now he did smile, "you're coming with me."

To the surprise of neither of us, Pilus Prior Agrippa did not take the news well, and although he behaved in a perfectly correct manner, standing at *intente* as he listed all the reasons he could not afford to lose Pictor, who unlike Rufius, was not one of the men from Rome, it was easy to see he was, if not angry, then perturbed at this development. Pictor was just a bit older than I would have liked ideally; he was thirty-eight, but he had first come to my attention when, during the abbreviated games we had held before the *Legio Germanicus* marched out of Emona, he had won the wrestling crown against a much younger competitor. I certainly did not blame Agrippa for his protests, and indeed, I would have argued as strenuously as he did if the situation were reversed; but it was not, so after listening for several moments, I cleared my throat, which Germanicus correctly interpreted. As far as Pictor was concerned, his was a face seemingly designed to give none of his thoughts away, so it was impossible for me to tell whether or not he was pleased with this promotion. It was only when I thought about it later that I realized, since he was one of the veterans drawn from the settlers of the province, he obviously understood that this was a temporary change in his fortunes. Once this was done, he, and most of the *Legio Germanicus*, would return to their homes, whether it be on a farm somewhere in the province, or in one of the towns like Emona and Poetovio. And, it was as Germanicus and I were returning to the *praetorium* that I realized that I could put it off no longer; I had to tell my young Legate the decision I had made.

Which, as the gods as my witness, I was about to do, but we had just crossed the forum when a figure bustled out of the *praetorium*, and seeing us, came towards us at the run. That it was the Tribune Silius, who I knew had the duty, informed both of us that this had to be important, but it was the presence of the horse that was at this moment being led away from the front of the headquarters tent, lathered and clearly having been ridden hard, that gave me an idea of what it might be.

Saluting, Silius panted, "Sir, a courier has arrived from Legate Tiberius!"

Germanicus did not reply, to Silius at least, turning instead to me and saying grimly, "Go ahead and return to your quarters, Pullus. If there's anything you need to know, I'll call for you immediately." Puffing out his cheeks, he motioned for Silius to lead the way, then said over his shoulder, "If it's what I think it is, I'm going to want to read this alone anyway."

There is no way for me to know how I would have handled matters if I had seen the courier himself, and not just his horse, but I was happily ignorant of the man's identity when I returned back to my tent, cursing the maddening itch from my wounds, looking forward to stretching out and getting some rest.

That rest lasted perhaps a third of a watch before Alex, clearly reluctantly, entered from the outer office, touching my foot as he had learned, yet despite that, when I jerked awake, I am afraid I bellowed at him from the pain at the sudden movement.

"This better be for a good reason," I snapped, then instantly regretted it, knowing he would not have done so otherwise.

"The Legate requires your presence immediately," he informed me, something that, once the cobwebs from my brief nap had cleared, I understood would be the only cause for him rousing me.

I could only nod wearily, forced to expend my energy on standing without groaning aloud, not wanting some mouse of a *praetorium* clerk to go spreading the tale that the Primus Pilus was moaning like a Suburan whore. Standing there, I relied on Alex to inspect me, and he did so, walking around me to straighten out my tunic before wrapping my *baltea* around my waist, then handing me my *vitus*.

Giving him a grin, trying to imbue it with a confidence I did not feel, I whispered, "All right, let me see what he wants."

"And you'll tell him then?" Alex's voice was pitched at the same level, yet even so, I felt a flare of irritation that he should bring up the topic I had been avoiding for a few days.

"Yes," I muttered, "I'll tell him then."

He led the way out and did so quickly, meaning that the clerk had to leap back from the partition in an attempt to appear as if he had not been listening, and I smugly congratulated myself for whispering. I gave the clerk a glare, making it as icily menacing as I could, though I said nothing, pleased to see the color vanish from his face. Nodding in a gesture to let him know to step out of the way, I exited the tent, leaving Alex, trying not to look worried, standing in the doorway as I led the clerk to the *praetorium*. As always, I was waved in by one of the two sentries, and I could only imagine their relief that, contrary to my normal practice, I did not stop to inspect them, but honestly, I had other things on my mind. Since it was daylight, as always, it took a moment to adjust to the dimmer light, so that between this and my preoccupation, I only vaguely registered who was present in the outer partition of the large tent. Perhaps if I had taken a moment to check, I could have saved myself some unpleasantness that was looming in my near future; more likely, it would have made matters worse if I had noticed. Regardless, I did not pay any attention as I strode to where Silius was sitting at the small desk that guards the entrance to the private office of the Legate, and as I expected, he waved at me to enter immediately. As I was crossing the distance to Germanicus' desk, my eyes took in my Legate's demeanor as he sat there, but his face bore an expression that I could not recall seeing before. After returning my salute, he pointed over to a stool, indicating that I should drag it over in front of his desk, then take a seat.

Once I did, he picked up the unrolled scroll, which was telling in itself because it was not a wax tablet, waving it in the air as he began, "It's what I thought. This," he shook it, "is from Tiberius."

490

Suddenly, he stopped talking, leaving me to wait, until finally I blurted out, "Well? What is it?" Then, I was struck by a troubling thought, prompting me to gasp, "You're not being relieved, are you?"

He shook his head, then replied bemusedly, "No, I'm not being relieved." Another pause, as if he was still struggling to comprehend before he finished, "I'm being promoted."

"Promoted?" I frowned, but only because I could not see how it was possible that Germanicus could be more highly ranked than he was; however, I was thinking formally. "To what? You're already Legate."

"Maybe," he allowed, "I shouldn't put it in that way, because you're right. It's not a promotion as much as it's an…increase in responsibility, I suppose." Whereupon, he explained what he meant. "Tiberius has ordered me, or," he corrected, "us, to march from here to meet him back in Siscia. From there, I'm going to be the co-commander of one of the three wings, though I don't know which one yet."

"Us?" I echoed, suddenly feeling sick at my stomach. "What does that mean, sir?"

This startled him, and he said, "Why, the *Legio Germanicus*, of course." Suddenly, his head dropped as he consulted the scroll again. "It says that this Legion will be part of the wing that I'm being assigned to." He looked back up, a broad grin on his face that, frankly, made me feel horrible. "You know what that means, Pullus. You're not rid of me just yet," he joked.

It was when I did not reply that caused the smile to slowly fade from his face, then he suddenly sat back and asked, "What is it, Pullus? Obviously, this," he pointed to the scroll, which he had dropped onto his desk, "doesn't come as good news to you."

"It's not that, sir," I protested, then I had to amend myself, "at least, not exactly."

"Well?" His tone was turning impatient, reminding me that, when all was said and done, he was still young. "What is it, then?"

I had spent a great deal of time rehearsing the answer to this, intent on communicating to a man who, no matter how young or what his status was, I respected, and more importantly, liked a great deal.

Which, naturally, meant that I blurted out, "I'm done. Sir."

"Done?" Germanicus looked confused, which was understandable. "What does that even mean?" he demanded, then repeated, "Done?"

"It means that I'm requesting permission to be sent back to the 1st Legion, sir," I said quietly. Shaking my head, despite my resolve, I felt the familiar tightening in my chest that had been plaguing me for days whenever my mind went in a direction I did not want, but even worse, I felt the prickling of tears. "I...can't, sir. I need to get back to my old Legion. To my men."

"But these are your men too!" Germanicus cried, and seeing him as affected as I actually made me feel worse, not better. "Pullus," his voice had a pleading quality, "we've been a good team together, haven't we? Oh," he held up a hand, presumably to stop an objection that I had not intended to give, "I know we've had our bumps in the road, and I know I've made mistakes where I should have listened to you. But I *have* learned!" His expression changed then. "Haven't I?"

Why, I thought, are you making this so difficult?

Aloud, I tried to assure him, "Sir, you're right about everything you've said. And I swear on the black stone this has nothing to do with you or your command of the Legion. And," I added, "I'll tell that to any man who asks me, even Tiberius. What you did with what you were given is something that, if there's any justice in this world, you should never be forgotten for. Sir," now I was the one pleading, for him to believe me, "this has nothing to do with you and everything to do with me. I just..." I stopped, then forced myself to say it aloud, "I just need a rest, sir. That's all."

"It's about Metellus, isn't it?"

If only he had not mentioned his name, because now there was no way to stop the sudden flooding of my eyes, but it was the presence of these tears that forced me to be honest. "It's not all about Metellus, but yes, he certainly has something to do with it."

I was somewhat surprised that Germanicus did not seem to have an answer to this, meaning that the silence stretched out for a span of time, but I, for one, was determined not to speak.

Finally, the Legate seemed to give in, sighing as he said, "Very well, Pullus. If you feel that strongly about it, I won't try and stop you. Nor," he added, probably at seeing my face, "will I have any kind of adverse mark made in your record. In fact," he said, "I planned on submitting your name for a decoration, probably the *Corona Murales* for Raetinium." He seemed to think better of it, and while he gave a chuckle, there was a fair amount of heavy humor as he amended, "Although since Raetinium doesn't exist anymore, I think Splonum would be more appropriate."

Honestly, I had no idea what to say, other than, "Thank you, sir. I truly appreciate it."

Germanicus held up a cautioning hand. "That's me, Pullus. But," he warned, "that's not my father. Tiberius, as you know as well as any man, isn't one who has much forgiveness in his nature."

This was undoubtedly true, and in fact, I could have probably given Germanicus examples of this truth, but that would have put us both in an awkward position, so I remained silent.

"Very well," he said, standing up as he did so, "I'll have a clerk draw up the order. But," he warned again, "I'm not signing that order until Tiberius has been informed, and I've received his answer about this matter. That way," he pointed out, "you'll be better able to make a decision about whether or not you're willing to run the risk of whatever he has in mind for you if he disapproves."

"But," I protested, "that could take days! Or weeks!"

"Oh," he assured me, "that's not true."

However, despite my pressing him, he refused to say anything more about it; what mattered, in the moment, was that he offered me his arm, which I took, and we shared in a solemn moment where, if I am any judge, our thoughts ran along similar lines, consumed by images of fire, ruin, blood, and all the shared misery of men who have seen battle together. Then, I was dismissed, and I left the *praetorium* feeling relieved and saddened at the same time. There was a part of

493

me that felt as if I was abandoning Germanicus, and I realized that, in a strange but undeniable way, I had taken on the role of the older brother to the young nobleman, where I was as protective about his person, and his fortunes, as diligently as I had been with Sextus.

It was appropriate, and disturbing, that it would not be until after dark that, once more, Alex appeared in my quarters, although this time, I was not asleep. Instead, I was absorbed in reading a small scroll that had actually been sent to me by my father back when I was in Ubiorum, one of several that he had been sending to me over the years. These were not new titles, however, but excerpts from the scrolls written by my Avus, the originals of which still reside in Arelate, with my family. These were not random selections either; I had found them extraordinarily useful for both the practical information contained within them, particularly the description of the terrain over which my Avus traversed, years before my birth, but also because of his observations about what is, ultimately, an arcane blend of art and skill, the leading of men in battle. I specifically recall that I was re-reading about the fall of Naissus, when Titus Pullus had been Camp Prefect, and my father had won his own *Corona Murales*, because of the dilemma in which my Avus found himself, in command of an army that had not been adequately rewarded while marching for the disgraced noble, Marcus Primus. He had made the practical, but brutal, decision to unleash his battle-hardened army on the people of Naissus; I was actually reading his account of the moment when, after the fall of the city, a Moesian named Charax had been brought before my Avus who was seated on a makeshift dais, courtesy of a wound to the leg he had received, one that I knew was shared by his horse and my champion Ocelus, when a Moesian spear had passed through his thigh and into the horse's side. Specifically, I was at the part where Charax requested that it be Titus Pullus, using the very *gladius* that was even then hanging from the frame upon which my armor and helmet with the white transverse crest rested, be the man to send Charax to the afterlife when, with a clearing of his throat, Alex announced his presence.

494

"What is it?" I asked, irritated at the interruption, but the instant I shifted my attention to my nephew's face, I knew it was important, or at the least, potentially disturbing.

"Someone's hear to see you, Primus Pilus." The manner in which he addressed me, along with the tone as if he was making an announcement, served as a deeper warning.

Studying my nephew's face for a moment, I nodded, then realized I needed to say something, so I first whispered to him, "Wait." Then, after I swung my legs, not without difficulty, off my cot, I walked over to my small desk, falling onto the stool behind it before I said, "Send him in."

The sight of Tiberius Dolabella, as it always did, elicited so many different and conflicting emotions that it makes it practically impossible for me to offer an accurate or complete account of how I felt when I saw his cross-eyed countenance. And, given the fact that this time his otherwise handsome face displayed a combination of what I knew was worry and more than a little agitation made it even more difficult me to give any idea of my own feelings, since so much of my own pleasure came from the consternation of Tiberius' agent under normal circumstances. Judging from his expression, it seemed clear that I had ignited his, if not ire, then his irritation at the very least.

Which was exactly why I said pleasantly, "*Salve,* Dolabella! It's been a while, hasn't it? How are you?"

"Never mind that," he snapped, then without asking, sat down onto the stool that was sitting in front of the desk. "Maybe you can explain what's going on in that head of yours?"

As odd as it may sound, his reaction actually served to settle my nerves more than they would have been if he had presented his normal, cool demeanor, making a reasoned, logical attack on a decision that, even then, I understood was more emotional on my part.

"What's going on in my head?" I echoed him, more for the perverse pleasure of further unsettling him than any other reason. "The usual things. I've got to turn in a supply requisition because we're running low on chickpeas. And," I pretended to think about it, "we're down a few ingots of iron. We're going to need to replenish our supply."

Dolabella was nothing if he was not quick of mind, because he pounced on this, saying sarcastically, "And why would you care about it? Given that you've decided you're," his voice turned mocking and, despite my loathing of the man, I had to admit he was a good mimic, "'done and need a rest'?"

The silence drew out, and I would be lying if I said that, as had happened on other occasions, I felt a peculiar but undeniable itch in my *gladius* hand, and it began flexing as if it had a mind of its own. Normally, I tried to keep my hand under my desk when it was behaving in this manner, but not on this occasion, and I was pleased to see this was not lost on Tiberius' agent, whose one good eye was fastened on it, suddenly looking more nervous than angry.

"Yes," I replied finally, "I'm done. And I need a rest."

Now that he had heard from my own lips confirmation of what I presumed he had first heard from Germanicus, Dolabella looked, if nothing else, peeved that I did not contradict what he had heard from my Legate.

"What does that even mean?" he cried in exasperation, throwing his hands up in a theatrical gesture. "We all need a rest, Pullus! This campaign has been trying on every one of us!"

"Oh?" I shot back, nettled to put it mildly. "How many men have you lost, Dolabella? How much blood have you seen?"

This did not have the effect I had hoped, because rather than anger, or better, embarrassment, instead he returned my stare and replied quietly, "More than you will ever know, Pullus." As he sighed, there seemed to be a real sadness in his demeanor. "Not every battle against the barbarians is fought with the Legions."

Of all the things I was prepared for once I greeted Dolabella, seeing what I took to be real emotion in him about losing men in whatever private, dirty battles took place across the province that a man like him directed was not one of them. Despite being somewhat rattled, neither was I deterred, and I said as much.

"All I want to do is go back to the 1st, to my Century and Cohort" I tried to make myself sound as matter-of-fact as I could. "I've done my part here, and Germanicus has agreed to write the order to send me back to Ubiorum."

"Germanicus," Dolabella answered stiffly, "isn't the man who sent you to help him in the first place. That's Tiberius' decision to make."

"Not according to my orders," I replied, then held up the scroll, "which puts me under the command of the Legate named Germanicus Julius Caesar. And," I finished, "it's his orders that I follow."

Honestly, I did not expect this to impress him, nor did it as he retorted, "And who signed the orders making Germanicus a Legate?" Stabbing a finger at me for emphasis, Dolabella pressed, "If you think Tiberius will allow you to leave by Germanicus' order alone, you've gone mad. And," he concluded, "it doesn't seem to me that that's happened."

Then, for the span of several heartbeats, we stared at each other, but as always, I found it hard to do so when I was never sure which eye I should stare into, but despite his words, I was not swayed. And, I could see, neither was he.

Then, to my shock, Dolabella broke his gaze from mine and muttered, "Fine, Pullus. You win. And, I can't say I blame you. This rebellion has been uglier than anything I've ever seen."

I stared at him for several long heartbeats, not sure I had heard correctly, while judging that if I had, certainly there was some sort of trick that was yet to be played by Tiberius' agent.

But, nothing came, other than him saying, with a deep sigh, "I'll do what I can to persuade Tiberius that this is in his best interests, somehow." He chuckled, but it was laced with bitterness as he admitted, "Although I have no idea how. But," just as quickly, he became stern, "the only way I have any chance of doing so is if you've got something...worthwhile," was what he came up with, "...about Germanicus. Something that Tiberius would find valuable."

And, knowing this was the price I must pay, for the next third of a watch, I unburdened myself, telling Dolabella everything about

Raetinium and all that had transpired since the last time Tiberius' agent had pressed me for details. Even as I did so, I felt horrible for doing what I had to do in order to gain whatever help Dolabella could provide to extricate myself from my role as Primus Pilus of the *Legio Germanicus*.

Ostensibly, I did not depart immediately because my wounds had not yet sufficiently healed, but if I am being honest, I almost immediately had second thoughts and actually considered going to Germanicus to inform him I had changed my mind. Somewhat ironically, yet strangely fittingly as well, it was young Alex who, stepping into the role his father had played for my Avus, my father, and me, advised me against it.

"Dolabella left the next morning," was how he put it, "and by now, Tiberius has been informed. If you go to Germanicus now and tell him you changed your mind, how will either of them be able to trust you in the future?" This made sense, but it was what he said next that clinched it, as he added quietly, "Tata always told me that one thing Romans hate more than anything, it's a man who's indecisive."

This, I knew, was nothing more than the truth, yet I suppose I was still struggling with the idea of this youngster possessing a level of wisdom that was beyond his years, prompting me to argue, "So you're saying that the only way I should stay is if Tiberius forbids me to leave?"

"No," he favored me with a smile that informed me he was not falling for my trap, "what I'm saying is that changing your mind will be worse for you in the long run than risking his wrath now. Tiberius has other things on his mind besides one Centurion who's had enough and is returning to his Legion, with his direct superior's blessing."

Now, I was not quite as sanguine that Tiberius would soon forget, but I had to concede that it was a bit presumptuous of me to think that my departure from Germanicus' side would be of so much concern for arguably the second most important man in Rome. Balanced against that, however, was the insight I had gained into Tiberius' character over the previous years I had been one of the men he used to accomplish certain goals, usually by the elimination of men who he considered to be working against the best interests of Rome. Nevertheless, my instinct told me that Alex was right in his counsel, that the ramifications of my seeming indecision would be more far-reaching and damaging than actually going through with it and returning to Ubiorum.

"You're right," I finally ended the suspense, and the sight of his face, beaming at having won me over is another treasured memory, signifying the moment where I accorded Alex's counsel with the same *gravitas* and respect that I had with his father, although I did warn him, "this time. But don't get used to me listening to you."

As I hoped, he laughed and promised, "Oh, I won't."

Another reason for my tarrying was that I did not feel right in leaving the *Legio Germanicus* unsettled now that the post of Primus Pilus, however temporary it may have been, was vacated by my departure. Fortunately, I did not have to persuade Germanicus, and he did not hesitate in announcing his decision that young Marcus Asinius Agrippa, the one nobleman who had come with Germanicus from Rome whose performance was second only to Germanicus himself, would take command of the Legion. Naturally, this required a bit more shuffling, and I managed to see to it that Metellus' Optio, Gnaeus Cerrinius, was promoted to Centurion, as the Hastatus Posterior in the Second Cohort, while Veratius was moved from the First Cohort over to take command of the Second. As often happens, this created friction within the Second Cohort, namely from the Centurion who had been promoted to replace Pictor when he moved to the Second of the First, and who believed that he should have had the shortest tenure as Secundus Pilus Posterior in history, moving up to Pilus Prior two days after his first promotion. This was a moment where I was happy that I was not involved, at least to a degree whereby I had to deal with all the bickering, although Germanicus jokingly threatened to make me stay and deal with it. Yet, as always happens, something I learned the first time I was seriously wounded and removed from the daily life of my section, the life of a Century, Cohort, and Legion moves on, regardless of an individual's presence or not. This meant that, while I was not surprised, it was still somewhat saddening how quickly I became an outsider to the men of the *Legio Germanicus*; that it was at my own behest did not lessen the feeling. And, once the subject of promotions was settled, there was not anything for me to do, other than wait for the stitches to be removed, which was performed by Lysippos himself, the last of his duties where I was concerned.

"The Legate gave me very clear orders," he had waved off my protest that he surely had better things to do than this routine matter, "and I always obey my orders, Primus...er, Centurion," he corrected himself, serving me another reminder that I was no longer part of the Legion.

The wound along my rib, despite being deep, healed cleanly, in no small part because of that damned probe Lysippos had insisted on running along its length, something that he was quick to remind me about. My shoulder, on the other hand, was another matter, and his look of concern as he unwrapped the bandage made my own stomach flutter. Leaning over, he sniffed the wound, which was still open and suppurating, Lysippos having judged it too wide to stitch closed without restricting my future motion.

"Well," he pronounced, "it's not corrupt." I made no attempt to hide my relief, but he shook his head impatiently. "That's good, but that doesn't explain why it's still discharging so much pus." He pursed his lips as he considered for a moment, then decided, "That makes me think there is something still in the wound."

"Which means?" I asked, but I knew very well what it meant; I was just stalling for time to think matters through.

The physician was not fooled, looking me in the eye and saying quietly, "I think you know what it means."

"Fine," I grumbled, then opened my mouth to accept the gag, as the physician made the preparations necessary for him to rummage around in my shoulder.

Afterward, both Lysippos and Alex insisted that the procedure had not taken more than the span of twenty heartbeats before the physician fished out a scrap from my tunic that was almost impossible to see, but I did not then nor do I now believe them; I am certain that the Greek took a good third of a watch digging into my shoulder. At the time, I was quite proud of myself for not passing out, though later, as I thought about it, I realized that this was another time where my pride had gotten me in trouble, that if I had simply succumbed to the lightheadedness instead of fighting it, the ordeal would have been over much more quickly. Despite this recognition, I did not even bother to tell myself that the next time, I would not make the same mistake, because I knew myself better than that. Because of this setback, my shoulder remained sore and stiff several days longer than my ribs, though thankfully, there were no trials in my future that would have caused this to be a problem.

It was two days later when, shortly after dawn, Alex and I departed the camp outside Raetinium, me astride Latobius, and Alex riding a horse that, as both a tribute and poking gentle fun at his father Diocles, was named Lightning. And, like the long-departed Thunder, this horse was misnamed, though in his case, he did have a blaze down his forehead that looked a bit like one of Jupiter's bolts. That, however, was the only commonality the beast had with lightning, and a part of me did worry that, should we be forced to flee, whether Alex's horse would be up to the challenge. Latobius, on the other hand, was in exuberantly high spirits, happy to be traveling again, but his master was not in the same frame of mind, though it was not due to second thoughts. No, my plight this morning was that I had succumbed to the taunts and challenge of a Batavian Decurion to spend the night before my departure engaged in an admittedly abbreviated version of debauchery. This was accomplished despite some limitations; Germanicus had ordered and stringently enforced that none of the Maezaei women among the captured civilians, who were still awaiting word of their fate, could be used for our amusement, even if some of the women were willing. And, the wine supply was plentiful enough, but of a quality that it made the throat burn and the eyes water, though it was not for the quality that Gaesorix and I imbibed it. Even with our rocky start, the Batavian and I had formed a bond, and he was now a man I considered then, as I do now, a good friend. With Alex's help, I made it back to my quarters, which Agrippa had graciously allowed me to use until my departure, and I vaguely remember exchanging solemn but drunken oaths with the Batavian where we vowed we would meet again. Naturally, what this meant was that Latobius' high spirits were not appreciated, nor was Alex's excited chatter, not until midday at any rate, which coincided with the moment I was able to keep something down. My visit to Gaesorix's quarters the night before had been to say goodbye, but it was also to gather information about the route, because I had made the decision that it was in my best interests, and of course Alex's, that we not ride through Siscia, which would have been the normal route, particularly under these conditions in the province. Under the circumstances, however, I did not want to run the risk of arriving in Siscia to find that Tiberius had already returned there himself, certain that if this was the case, matters would not end well for me. Fortunately, Gaesorix had assured me, before we were in our cups, that the route that led directly north from Raetinium, up through Colapiani and Latobici territory, was safe for the two of us.

"There's nothing left of any of the bands that would cause you problems," he had assured me. "We've ridden patrols more than fifty miles in that direction, and we haven't captured one warrior, and we haven't seen signs of any either. They're either dead or they're off with one of the Batos. Although," he had added offhandedly, "I heard that they've joined forces now."

Since I had heard this as well, I did not comment on it, and I thanked him by refilling his cup and challenging him to see which of us could empty ours the fastest. Which, I had occasion to think the next day, makes it even better that there was no danger, because I doubted I could have stayed on Latobius' back if we were forced to run. Once past midday, my condition improved enough that, when Latobius, playing his game of jerking his head, did so, despite the stab of pain it caused my left shoulder, I actually kicked him into the gallop. It did not last long, as the combination of pounding head, throbbing shoulder, and aching side meant that we went no more than two furlongs before we pulled up, whereupon we waited for Alex on Lightning, leading our two pack animals, to come plodding up.

"Lightning is too clever to fall for that," was how Alex put it, though he could not maintain a straight face as he said it.

"That," I chuckled, "is one way to look at it." Grinning at him, I reached out and tousled his hair, teasing, "That's something your Tata would say about Thunder."

Instead of answering me, my nephew leaned over, speaking in Lightning's ear, "Don't listen to him, Lightning. You're a much better horse than Thunder."

This was the lighthearted atmosphere that only grew with every mile we drew farther away from Raetinium, and I could almost feel the burden lifting from my shoulders, even as there was a nagging feeling in the back of my mind, a voice that whispered I should not have abandoned the *Legio Germanicus*. And, I made a choice on that first day; I did not listen to that voice, for once reminding myself how many times obeying it had almost led to my destruction. Thankfully, that torment I was feeling at essentially abandoning the men who I had not only led, but helped Germanicus train to a level that enabled us to take not one but two fortified towns, albeit at a high cost, faded fairly quickly. Undoubtedly, especially now that I look back on this moment, I understand that this was a rationalization on my part, yet it was true that the ranks of the *Legio Germanicus* had been filled with veterans, all of them older than I was, and some of them old enough to have marched with my father thirty years earlier. It was not as if I was departing from a group of fresh-faced *tiros* who still needed my guidance, and in the more than eighteen months I had spent under Germanicus' command, I had seen him grow as a Legate under whom I would be proud to march at any point in the future. And, while I do not recall having that specific thought, I do believe that I knew even then, deep in my soldier's bones as we like to say, that I would have the opportunity to do that very thing. Provided, of course, that Tiberius did not have a man like me come visit me, as a punishment for flaunting his authority by making my own decision.

When we arrived in Emona, four days after departing Raetinium, Gaesorix had been accurate in his assurance that we would travel unmolested through the westernmost part of Pannonia. What he had neglected to mention was exactly how widespread the devastation was in this part of the province; it was pacified, but from my observation, mainly because there was nothing left to fight over. The Colapiani lands of the dead Draxo were hard hit in particular; at least, this was what I believed until we departed Emona and rode through the lands of the Taurisci. Nothing, it seemed, was left standing, but it was the relatively small and isolated flat, arable spots that arrested my attention, as all of them were still burned black, or in some cases, I saw they had been sown with large crystals of salt.

"They did the same thing at Carthage," was Alex's comment, and I could only nod as I gazed at the scene around me.

I am as proud a Roman as any man, and I carry the scars in the service of Rome that, especially after this campaign, were numerous and bespoke my dedication to our empire that no words can match, but I cannot lie; I was deeply troubled at some of the things I saw as we made our way across the northern fringe of the province. Yes, I understood, this is Rome's policy, as dictated by a man who is, at the time I write this, now a god, like his adoptive father, and when he was the man known as Augustus, there is no disputing his wisdom. Nevertheless, I could not shake the nagging feeling that, by depriving the tribes of Pannonia of the means of raising their own food, we were only borrowing trouble in the future. But, I told myself, it's not my problem anymore, which was what enabled me to continue our progress north, although leaving Emona, because of the mountains, we had to travel east first, spending the night in Celeia. From there, we continued north, alternating sleeping out in the open with nights spent in a variety of inns, some of them of the status where, the next morning, Alex and I spent a good deal of time scratching ourselves from the vermin that had leapt onto our bodies during the night. Not until we were safely out of Pannonia did I truly accept that we were safe, but once this happened, Alex and I indulged ourselves in the simple joy and pleasure of traveling and seeing new things. This was something with which I had been infected from an early age, as I sat and listened to my parents tell their children about all the places that they had visited and the sights they had seen. One memory in particular was both comforting and sad at the same time, and that was when my mother, who had begun her life as a slave of the long-dead but not forgotten Cleopatra, as part of the retinue of slaves, had been involved in what is a famous event in our world, and reminded my father that she had seen the great pyramids of Egypt during Caesar and Cleopatra's trip down the Nilus, something that Gaius Porcinianus Pullus could not claim. Regardless of this friendly competition, both Iras and Gaius had instilled in their children a love for travel and seeing new sights, and despite the fact that this was a route we had both traveled before, this time Alex and I enjoyed the sights. There were giant peaks that, even now close to the month named for Augustus, were still encased in snow and ice, thrusting up into the sky, prompting a debate between my nephew and me about how quickly either of us could scale such heights, if only to reach out and touch the sky above. This was the manner in which the many, many miles passed, as we continued north. Once across the great barrier of those mountains, we finally turned west at Radasbona, traveling through country that was peaceful, and more importantly, not filled with burned-out farms, besieged towns, and scorched fields. Granted, the natives of Raetia were not particularly friendly when they saw the two of us, and recognized that one of them was a man of the Legions, but neither did we fear turning our backs on them.

"There's a lot more green here," was how Alex put it one day, "and I haven't smelled smoke for a week." Glancing over at me, he gave me a boyish grin. "Or dead bodies. I hadn't realized I'd gotten used to it."

As morbid as it sounded, I had to laugh, both at the truth of his statement, and this sign that Alex, who I had worried about being too sensitive for a life following the Legions, had become, if not inured, then at least accustomed to some of the aspects of our world. For, dear reader, it is true that the presence of Legionaries usually means that the air we breathe is fouled with the stench of death, and the country around us has been ruined. Consequently, it never came as a surprise when, even alone or in a small party, civilians view Legionaries with a combination of suspicion and fear, the former coming from our bad habit of appropriating things that do not belong to us, particularly in the form of daughters, or even worse, wives who are lured by the appeal of living a life that is, if not anything else, different from their current state. Regardless of this, I cannot say that the looks Alex and I got, however furtive, did not stir a resentment in me, and in this I can at least say I am not alone; at one time or another, most of my comrades have expressed a similar feeling.

"We haven't done anything to them," would be the complaint, although there is always a man who can be counted on to point out that, just because it was not by us, most of civilians out here in the provinces had experienced the power of Rome's Legions in some way.

And, whenever that happened and I was within earshot, invariably I would think of Sextus Scribonius, the man for whom my brother was named, and specifically, the exchange from my Avus' account when the 10th Equestris had been confined to the Campus Martius for a period of time. It was just one of the many valuable lessons I learned from those words that, while Alex's father had actually written them, came from the first Titus Pullus. What it meant in a practical sense was that, rather than turn Latobius and trot over to some farmer, or more commonly, his son, and make an issue of his lack of circumspection at muttering an oath, spitting on the ground, or making some native sign of disrespect, I ignored them.

Another aspect of traveling north was the weather changing, both because of our direction of travel, and that with every passing day, we approached another winter.

"One thing I'm not looking forward to," Alex admitted, "is the winters up here."

"That makes two of us," I assured him, and even as I did, in the back of my mind, I wondered how the wounds I had sustained would react to the cold weather, given those were the areas that gave me the most trouble.

You're just getting old, Titus, I thought, even as Alex and I continued our conversation, while I also realized something else. Although it was normal for me to be more reflective than usual at the end of a campaign, particularly a hard one where men I considered both comrade and friend fell, I seemed to be having a problem moving on from that state to the next one, which was to begin thinking of the practical problems that face every Centurion. After some thought, I came to the conclusion that this was because, frankly, I had no idea what to expect when I returned to Ubiorum. Naturally, communication with Macer had been spotty, particularly over the last several months, so what little I did know was likely to be out of date and no longer applicable. Indeed, for all we knew, Alex and I could arrive in Ubiorum to an empty camp, as the 1st was out across the Rhenus, taking care of some problem with one of the tribes. Gradually, over the course of the more than twenty days it took for us to travel, I began thinking less and less about the things that usually consumed me in the immediate aftermath and wondering about what lay ahead. Putting it simply, over time, granted longer than normal, I stopped looking back.

Helping me in this endeavor was that, the closer we drew to Germania, the more news and gossip we heard from fellow travelers, heading in the opposite direction.

And, to my undisguised relief, what we heard from them was, "Things have been quiet for the most part."

However, it was news that was being carried in our direction, when a relay courier caught up with us just twenty miles south of Mogontiacum. It was only because we had stopped at the small station between Nemetum and Mogontiacum to allow the horses to rest and to get something to eat for ourselves when, coming at a brisk trot, another rider arrived, but from behind us. Seeing the small bronze device on his cloak that designated him as a *Dispositus*, men generally of the cavalry but who had been carefully selected for their horsemanship and reliability, I approached him as he sat on the bench outside the small station building, gulping down a cup of water.

507

Offering him the hunk of bread that I had soaked in oil, I commented, "You look hungry."

He was young, or at least younger than me, and I saw his eyes take in my *baltea*, which was at about his eye level, but it was when he continued looking up, then even before he got to my face, he suddenly leapt to his feet, spilling the cup all over himself and me.

"Primus Pilus," he gasped, rendering a salute that I automatically returned, even as my mind tried to grapple with both his reference to what was now my former rank, and the fact that his eyes had only gotten to about my chest before he recognized me. "T-thank you," he stammered, which further confused me because I forgot I was standing there with a hunk of bread in my hand. "And, yes, sir, I'm hungry."

"How did you know me?" I asked curiously, though I did remember I was holding the bread, which I extended to him.

Once I signaled him to stand easy with a wave, he began munching, so it was between mouthfuls that he answered with a shrug, "I'm stationed in Siscia right now, and I carried messages to your Legate a few times, and I saw you there. Besides," he gave me a grin that was more bread than teeth, "everyone knows Titus Pullus' grandson in Pannonia, if just because of your size." Of course, I thought ruefully, it's because of Avus and not me. Oblivious to my internal thoughts, the rider asked, suddenly becoming, if not shy, then hesitant. "Primus Pilus?" he asked, but before he could continue, I shook my head and said, perhaps a bit too sternly, "That was a temporary rank. I'm just a Princeps Prior now, on my way back to my Legion." The words were barely out of my mouth when I regretted, if not the words, then the tone, prompting me to ask a bit more gently, "What was your question?"

"Are you really as large as your grandfather was?"

Despite the stab of…whatever it was I felt at the mention of my Avus, I had to smile, since this is the most common question I am asked; besides, I had not approached this rider and offered some of my meal out of the goodness of my heart, so I replied honestly and pleasantly, "It's hard for me to say, since I wasn't grown when he died. But, according to my parents and his father Diocles," I jerked my thumb to where Alex was sitting, watching the two of us curiously, "I'm not as tall as he was, but I'm a bit broader through the chest."

"Not as tall?" he echoed in a disbelief that was almost comic, and again, his reaction was not uncommon, bursting out, "He must have truly been a giant! You're the biggest Roman I've ever seen!"

This made me laugh, and while it was not calculated on my part, I did recognize that our shared moment helped my cause.

Pointing to the dispatch bag slung over his shoulder, I asked casually, "So, what's in that bag that's got you galloping along like Cerberus is after your balls?"

For a brief instant, I was certain I had blundered, as his face immediately closed up, accompanied by a stiffening of his posture, reminding me of not only the regulations against dispatch riders sharing information with anyone not authorized to receive the information, but more importantly, the punishment for divulging that information.

Understanding how he could interpret this, I assured him, "I'm not trying to trick you, and I know that you're not supposed to share the information. But," I tried a grin on him, "I *am* Titus Pullus' grandson, and he was a Camp Prefect appointed by Augustus himself. Besides," I added, "I did just come from Siscia."

Whether it was my connection, or this last bit I do not know, but it did the trick, and he relaxed a bit. Then, with a jerk of his head, he indicated for me to follow him. Walking a short distance from the station, just far enough away to be out of earshot, he began talking, and in a short amount of time, I was beginning to wonder whether or not I could shut him up.

"Bato of the Breuci has been executed," he began, which I did not find surprising; how it happened, however, and even more importantly, at whose hands it had been was, as he explained, "by Bato of the Daesitiates. And..." I stopped him before he got any further.

"Wait," I shook my head, "what did you just say? He wasn't executed by Tiberius?"

He shook his head, replying, "No, Centurion. Apparently, he tried to seize power of the Breuci and the tribes who are aligned with them by murdering some other leader…"

"Probably Pinnes," I mused, which prompted him to nod and say, "Yes! That's the one." Laughing, he said, "You know how confusing these barbarian names are. Now," he pursed his lips, "where was I? Ah, yes. So, after Bato the Daesitiates executed Bato the Breucian, there was a revolt among the rebels." Again, he laughed. "That's something, isn't it? The rebels rebelled." While it was amusing, it was also not surprising to me in the least, but I humored him by agreeing with a laugh of my own, which encouraged him to continue, "So, the tribes who split with the surviving Bato, mainly the Breuci got to the Bathinus (Bosna) and were trapped there when Silanus and his Legions blocked their line of retreat back to their lands, so they surrendered without a fight."

It felt very much as if I had been punched in the stomach; I had abandoned Germanicus and his Legion just before it all ended?

"You mean," I asked in disbelief, "it's over?"

"Oh, no, sir." He shook his head emphatically. "It's not over. The Daesitiates and a couple other tribes refused to surrender, and they've retreated back into Illyricum. They still hold the passes, though, at least they did when I left."

"Any idea what they plan next?" I asked, but to this question he could only offer a shrug.

By this time, his fresh mount had been saddled, and as he leapt onto his horse, he called out, "Maybe I'll see you on the way back, Centurion!"

Then, he was gone and I returned to my spot next to Alex, and I resumed my meal in a thoughtful mood.

Mogontiacum had already grown substantially between my first time there under Drusus and when I transferred to the 1st, so there were no drastic changes in the town, other than there being even more shacks and whorehouses outside the walls of the camp. Presenting my signed order, Alex and I were given quarters for the night, but since we had arrived fairly early in the day, I took my nephew prowling the muddy streets of a section of town that was the off-duty spot for most rankers. My purpose was twofold; one was obvious, since it had been months of hard campaigning without a woman, although, especially as Primus Pilus, I could have had second choice of the women captives, behind Germanicus and the Tribunes, of course. However, along with my size, something else that was passed down to me from my Avus was a distaste for forcing a woman to submit; paying for them to do so, on the other hand, was another matter entirely. However, along with that, I knew this was the best place to find out what was happening downriver, at Ubiorum, despite the camp actually being located to the north, something I sometimes had trouble reconciling. As for Alex, he was still at the age where the itch a man feels is more or less constant and consumes most of his thoughts, no matter how much they might protest to the contrary, as my nephew did, though I did not have to drag him with me. He was also still at the age where he felt a bit awkward discussing his exploits afterward, something I assured him would change. Frankly, I was secretly amused at the change in his demeanor after he had been with a woman, walking with a slight but unmistakable swagger, his shoulders thrown back, although it was the broad grin on his face that was most notable. And, Alex was not the only one who was successful at accomplishing what he had set out to do, as I managed to achieve my goal of gathering information and satisfying my own needs, without having to avail myself of more than one woman, for the information, at least.

"Things have been mostly quiet," was how the first whore, whose name I forgot by the time I left the shantytown, explained it, "just a few raids by the Sugambri on this side of the Rhenus." Although she added what came next as an aside, it was this piece of information that was more interesting to me than knowing that the barbarians were behaving in their normal fashion. "The biggest problem they've been having are these rumors that Augustus is going to extend enlistments again."

This was something that I had overheard Germanicus whispering to Silius just before I left, which I assumed had been relayed to him by Tiberius in the dispatch that summoned the *Legio Germanicus*, and at the time, I had not thought much of it. Putting it simply, I believed this was more a consequence and an effect of the alarm that the Princeps had experienced when it became clear that the revolt in Pannonia was more than the standard affair of a tribe or two roaming about burning Roman farms. Having this woman, here in Mogontiacum, repeating the same thing served, at least to me, to tell me that this was more than just a passing thought on the part of Augustus. Not, I recognized then, that there was anything I could do about it at the time, but it was better to know what to expect than come riding up to a scene of turmoil and simmering tensions unaware of what I would be facing. This precaution, of course, rested on the supposition that my Century would be returned to me; Germanicus had stipulated this in my orders, but Germanicus was not Tiberius. Only when I reported to Ubiorum would I have an idea about my personal situation, and the only way to determine that was to depart Mogontiacum the next morning.

Thanks to my orders from Germanicus, Alex and I were given priority on the next military transport ship that ferried supplies to Ubiorum; unfortunately, as I feared, his name did not carry sufficient weight to change the normal schedule of traffic.

"Next week, that's the next scheduled shipment," Alex informed me, after I had sent him down to the military wharf that was essentially the same as when I was last there, less than two years before.

The same could not be said for the civilian counterpart to the wharf, which had added two more piers to accommodate the increased shipping as, little by little, Rome and all that it offered was made available to the people of this province. And, once Alex returned with the news, we made our way there next, where I found a shipmaster who was going to depart the next morning. Of course, it cost more money than I wanted to part with, but all it took was Alex clearing his throat in a silent message this would be one of those times he would not let me forget and use my parsimony to embarrass me at some point in the future, I, grudgingly, dug into my purse and counted out what I still believe was an obscenely large sum.

"Fucking bandits," I growled after I stalked away, curtly agreeing to present ourselves at the wharf a third of a watch before sunrise. "I'd be surprised if they don't try to slit our throats and dump us overboard."

Alex laughed at this, but I heard the nervous quality to it, which was precisely why I said it, hiding my amusement at the way he kept glancing up at me, before finally blurting out, "You don't think they'd try it, do you?" I gave an elaborate shrug, though I kept my eyes ahead as we picked our way past the heaps of animal dung and scraps of refuse, and the silence dragged on until he could take the suspense no longer, coming to a stop in the street. Only then, when he actually got a good look at my face, did he ask suspiciously, "Are you teasing me, Uncle?"

My laughter gave him the answer, but when I turned to resume walking back to our quarters, he stood there for some time, making it clear he wanted me to believe he was prepared to stand there. As I expected, he did no such thing, except now he had to break into a brisk trot to catch up to me, which prompted some snickers from the passersby who I guessed were imagining all manner of things about this scene.

"That wasn't very funny," he grumbled, but before we had gone another half-dozen strides, he was laughing as hard as I was.

The next morning, though, I was not laughing, and in fact, there was a prospect of bloodshed between me and the ship's master, but it was the other way around than what I had predicted to Alex.

"I'm not paying another fucking *sestertius*!" I snarled, for that was what the master had just informed me.

"You didn't tell me you had horses!" he protested. "They take space on the deck that I can't use to transport the cargo I was supposed to be taking! Now," I supposed he was trying to play on my sympathies, "I'll have to make two trips instead of one. And that's more expensive for me!" He waved a hand at the eight men, four on each side, who were sitting on narrow benches, waiting the command to begin pulling on their oars.

"They're slaves," I shot back coldly, "so you're not paying them a fucking thing."

"They still have to eat, Centurion!" he protested. "And there are other expenses! Each time I put in, I have to pay that *cunnus* of a wharf master! He's the one you should be angry with, not me! Do you know what he charges? A whole *denarius*! Just to tie a fucking rope to the pier! That's not right!" Now that his own indignation was unleashed, it began running rampant as he ranted, "And don't even get me started about what the bastard who runs the slave gang that are supposed to unload our ships charges! Before they lift a finger, I have to grease his palm with..."

"*Tacete!*" I snapped, then shook my head, partially because I was still angry, but also since I was fairly certain this had been a ploy on his part that, ultimately, I had brought on myself, and wearily, I withdrew my purse and asked, "How much more?"

For an instant, I could read the indecision on the man's face as his greed warred with his inherent sense of caution that this overgrown, scarred Centurion might just run him through, which was completely justified on his part. And, I was partially mollified when he simply asked for five more *sesterces* for our mounts and two packhorses.

Nevertheless, I was less than gracious as I shoved the coins into his hand and used my best, most intimidating growl as I warned him, "This better be the last fucking coin you ask for, or you and I are going to have a problem. Or," I added with the kind of grin I offered one my men just before I was about to stripe them, "it's going to be your problem."

Hastily, he assured me, even invoking a frankly dizzying list of gods whose names he rattled off more quickly than I could catch that he would do no such thing, and, being fair, he was good to his word. Unfortunately, for Alex in particular, this did not make me the best company, so he confined himself to leaning on the rail as the light grew, staring at the eastern bank, doing so with such an intensity that

I realized he was half-expecting some barbarians to come leaping out of the thick undergrowth. Once I had cooled off, helped by playing Latobius' apple game, which, as always, he found in the span of no more than five heartbeats, I wandered over and leaned on the rail next to my nephew, though I said nothing.

"I thought you were going to throw him off his own boat," Alex muttered, then began snickering so that in a moment, we were both roaring with laughter.

Which, I was happy to see, made the ship master, who behaved as if there was an invisible barrier between the stern of the ship and where we were standing that he could not, or would not pass, visibly nervous.

"We should be able to sleep tonight," I told Alex. "I don't think that bastard is leaving that part of the boat."

Mogontiacum had not changed that much, but we could not say the same for Ubiorum. Honestly, the place was almost unrecognizable; the most notable change was that there was now a proper brick wall, twelve feet tall, with towers and heavy, iron-banded wooden gates for the Porta Praetoria and the Porta Principalis Dextra, which was all we could see from our direction of approach. Not until we were inside were Alex and I able to see all the other changes, although not every hut had been rebuilt with brick yet; at the time of our return, about two-thirds of them were of the more solid construction. The gates were open, always a sign that we were not actively engaged with some enemy, while the inevitable town, which was situated with the camp in between it and the river had spilled around to the southern side, where there were a pair of muddy streets that terminated down at the river, while the dirt road that led from the Porta Dextra ran through the center of this section. My attention was more on the camp itself, but I did notice that, judging from the people who were moving about in this new area, this part of the town was reserved for the unofficial families of the Legion, and I mentally marked it as the first place to look for when one of my men inevitably disappeared from some duty. Leading Latobius off the ship, I barely acknowledged the shipmaster, which he appeared fine with, although Alex did stop and exchange a few quiet words, which, frankly, was something he did quite often in my wake, a habit that I found helpful and annoying in equal measure. With Alex's assistance, I had struggled into my full uniform, engendering a short debate with my nephew about whether or not I should affix the white transverse crest that would announce my most recent rank, or return to the old black of the Centurion of a Century, while the red are now for Pili Priores. Deciding that wearing the white would be presumptuous and likely to arouse the ire of Primus Pilus Crescens, particularly given the news that I also heard in Mogontiacum that he had been passed over for Camp Prefect in favor of another candidate, although the whore did not know who, after that it was an easy decision to make, since I was not entitled to wear the crest of the Pilus Prior. Despite the filth and overall cramped conditions on the deck of the ship, Alex managed to help me arrange myself and, after walking around me twice, he pronounced that I was fit to report.

"Now you just have to stay clean from the dock to the *praetorium*," he commented, which I knew as well as he did was not a simple challenge.

Somehow I managed, but even as I presented my orders to the duty Optio, who I recognized as being from the Eighth Cohort, though I did not know his name, my heart began pounding as the sweat started trickling down my back, though this was not all that abnormal whenever I was faced with a similar situation.

"Welcome back, Centurion Pullus." The Optio saluted as he said this and naturally I returned it, but I was surprised enough to blurt out, "You know I've been gone?"

The look he gave me I suppose mirrored my surprise as he answered, "Of course! The whole Legion knows you've been down there sticking it those barbarians down in Pannonia!" He glanced down then and pointed at my pink and hairless knees and commented, "But it looks like you didn't get away clean."

"Burns," I grunted, then grinned at him, "and that's just what you can see."

Whether he laughed because it was expected or he was actually amused, he did so nonetheless, then he gave a surreptitious glance at the rankers standing next to us who, while they had gone back to *intente*, were clearly listening, then said, "If you don't mind, I'll walk with you part of the way."

Understanding that this was going to be another exchange where I was expected to provide something, this time not in coin but information, I nodded my assent. Waiting until we were a dozen paces away, I had to suppress a smile at the mental image I had of the men standing behind us, muttering curses under their breath about the duplicity of officers who would not allow their subordinates to hear any of the good gossip.

"Was it as tough as we've been hearing?" the Optio asked quietly, and I glanced down at him, whereupon he added with a shrug, "We've been hearing word that the barbarians down there have been putting up a good fight."

"They have," I was forced to admit, though I sensed this was not what the Optio really wanted to ask.

When I said no more, I suppose it prompted him to ask the real question, which he offered with a whisper, "And what's happening with the Legions down there?"

Rather than answer him directly, I responded, "What's happening with this one?"

For a moment, he did not appear particularly happy that I had turned it around on him, but it was a valid question for me to ask upon my return to the 1st, and I believe he understood this.

"Not much good," he admitted. "There's been a lot of talk." Turning his head, I felt his eyes on me as he repeated quietly, "A *lot* of talk."

"There's always a lot of talk," I replied dismissively, but he shook his head.

"Not like this, Centurion," he assured me. Taking a breath, he finally asked, "Is it true that the Princeps is going to increase the term of enlistment five years?"

"Why would you think I know?" I was trying to delay him, except he was not easily put off, and as I was about to learn, he was better informed than I would have imagined.

"Because you served with Tiberius' adopted son, Germanicus," he answered, then emphasized, "as the Primus Pilus. If anyone would know, you would."

This, I understood, I could not deny, for a number of reasons, most of them involving my own *dignitas*; that what I was about to relay to him came from a whore in Mogontiacum was not something I felt he needed to know.

"I've heard...something," I admitted, "about it. But nothing more than rumors. Is that what the men are worried about?"

"Mostly." The Optio was not evasive, exactly, but there was something in the way in which he said it that prompted me to examine him more closely.

"Mostly?" I demanded. "What else is going on?"

Now he was clearly uncomfortable, and all he would say was, "It's not my place to say. You need to talk to some of the Centurions."

After that, he said nothing more, then we were at the *praetorium*, which was still essentially the same, but I was happy to see that the door had been replaced, and there was an actual latch on it that worked. Entering, I marched to the desk of the duty clerk, another of those tiny men whose sense of self-importance derives from where the gods, and the army, saw fit to assign them, and he barely deigned to look up from the tablet that, being fair, he was writing in, though I had no way of knowing whether it was a report he was ordered to copy or some lewd poem he was writing for one of the women in town.

Barely glancing up, he intoned in a bored voice, "The Tribune Laticlavus is indisposed and can't be disturbed."

Biting the inside of my cheek, I tried to be patient as I explained, "I still need someone to accept these orders so that I can properly report back."

This did cause him to look up, and the sudden change in his demeanor was both comical, and frankly, somewhat disturbing, as he actually leapt to his feet, kicking over his chair in the process.

"Ah," he stammered, "C-Centurion Pullus! I didn't realize it was you!" Nodding vigorously, the clerk, who I did recognize, though I did not have Alex with me to whisper his name, added, "You've been expected! But the Tribune was very explicit that he's not to be disturbed." Glancing about, he gave me a conspiratorial grin and lowered his voice. "He's a bit...busy, if you know what I mean." I did, although I was not as amused as he seemed to be, but then he offered, "If you want to go and report to Primus Pilus Crescens, I will make sure the Tribune knows that you reported to him before the Primus Pilus." He dropped his voice slightly to tell me, "He gets a bit touchy about things like that."

Thanking the clerk, I reminded myself to find out from Alex who he was and what my nephew knew about him, thinking he would be a good man to have on the inside of the *praetorium*; that I did not even bother trying to find out the identity of the broad striper should be informative as well. Crossing the forum, I watched as a Centurion was applying the *vitus* to a handful of hapless *tiros* who, judging from their appearance and bearing, had been under the standard no more than a couple weeks. Honestly, the bellowing the officer was doing was as sweet as any music to my ears, and for the first time since my arrival, I felt a smile forming on my lips. Maybe, I thought, things will be fine.

"So," Primus Pilus Crescens sniffed, "you're back."

I had no idea what kind of reception to expect from the Primus Pilus, but I had hoped it would be a bit better than this, and I did my best to keep this from reflecting in my own expression. Nor could he find any fault in the manner in which I presented myself, yet he seemed determined to make me stand there like a lump of meat.

Several heartbeats passed, then he sniffed again, making me wonder if he actually had a cold, before he came to what I realized then was the heart of the matter, speaking with a casualness that I could hear was clearly forced, "And I suppose you expect to come back to your former posting, with your old Century."

Without thinking, I reached down to my *baltea* to produce the scroll from Germanicus, then realized I had left it with the clerk, which forced me to think quickly, and I replied, "Honestly, Primus Pilus, I'm just happy to be back with my Legion. Anywhere you want to put me is fine."

Instantly, I saw that this was exactly the right thing to say, that Crescens had been testing me, and he rewarded me with a thin smile, leaning back in his chair to finally examine me.

"That scar on the chin is new," he remarked, which frankly, I had forgotten about since the Optio had not noticed and pointed it out. "Any others?"

Whereupon I proceeded to describe, as briefly as I could while still being thorough, all that had transpired during my time with the *Legio Germanicus*. Before I got too far, though, he stopped me, but only to have me pull up a stool, then I accepted the cup of wine he offered, which was slightly unusual. For the next third of a watch, I told Crescens of all that had occurred; the sieges of Splonum and Raetinium, leaving nothing out, other than anything that could be considered critical of Germanicus. Which, as I went on, seemed to me to be exactly what he was hoping to hear, judging at least by his air of, if not disappointment, then slight letdown when I signaled that I was finished by draining my cup.

"That," Crescens said at last, "sounds as rough as we'd heard it was." Again, he paused, and now there was no mistaking he was waiting for me to say something, if not directly about Germanicus and his performance as Legate, then something that would allow him to bring it up without it appearing as if he was prying. I continued to sit there, saying nothing, until he finally seemed to give up, saying grumpily, "As far as you're concerned, I've decided that you're going back to the Third of the Fourth."

"How did Structus do?" I asked, and while he only gave a slight shrug, his words were slightly more positive.

"He performed adequately," was how Crescens put it, then gave me a grin that was both sly and I understood his way of letting me know that there were no secrets in his Legion of which he was unaware. "Of course, I think he was helped by the beating you promised to give any of the men who Structus told you gave him problems."

I felt a slight rush of blood to my face, but I had to grin back, saying only, "Whatever works, neh, Primus Pilus?"

"Whatever works," he agreed; with my immediate future decided, he turned to the Legion as a whole. "I don't know what you've heard about the situation here."

"Just that it's been quiet, aside from the normal raids," I told him.

"That," he agreed, "is true. But," Crescens held up a cautioning hand, "there's more to it than that. I'm certain of it. I think," his voice turned grim, "the reason it's been quiet is that there are some tribes working together to start something."

Honestly, this was neither new nor disturbing, yet I sensed that an experienced man like Crescens would not be worried over the normal rumors and whispers.

"Is there anything definite that you've heard?" I asked, but he shook his head in frustration and told me, "No. That's the thing. I haven't heard anything. Which is what's troubling." Then, he said something else that did not make any sense in the moment; only later, did I get an idea why he said with an edge of bitterness that I could not miss, "I don't know why I care, honestly." Suddenly, he slapped his hand on his desk, then stood in a signal the meeting was over. "There will be enough time for you to get caught up. Now, I suggest you go report to Pilus Prior Macer. He has news of his own that I could tell you, but I'll let him do it."

Rising to my feet an instant after he did, I saluted, then left his office, wondering what the news could be, and why Crescens had said it in the manner he had.

"Perperna's gone. He transferred out."

This was the news from Marcus Macer, but by the time he got to it, night had fallen, and I had finished settling back into my quarters, pleased to see that, aside from needing to be swept out, they had clearly not been lived in since they had been reconstructed. In fact, there was still a smell of plaster, but Alex was the happiest, because these quarters were actually bigger, which meant his own sleeping space was as well, and I teased him about what he would do with all the extra room. Now I was sitting in Macer's quarters, listening to my superior and friend catch me up on all that I had missed, which was not nearly as much as I had experienced on my own.

"Where did he go?" I asked, then the more important question, "And why?"

"To the 19th Legion," Macer said with a grin. "He's stationed in Vetera now." He paused, then supplied the rest. "In the Eighth, as the Hastatus Posterior."

This stopped the cup before it reached my lips as I stared at him, thinking that he seemed serious enough, but hardly believing my ears. Actually, there were two pieces of information that interested me, though I turned my attention to the one concerning Perperna.

"He transferred into a higher Cohort?" I shook my head. "And as the Hastatus Posterior? Why would he take a demotion like that?"

At this, there was a glimmer of a smile, but it was one that was harder and a bit crueler than what I remembered from Marcus Macer before, telling me that, despite his barely mentioning it, he must have faced some trials of his own.

"Let's just say," he spoke slowly, as if measuring his words, "it was either that or have some information come to light that would make going down to the Eighth in a new Legion the least of his concerns."

"Do I want to know?" I asked cautiously, but this time, his grin was not tinged with anything deeper.

"Probably not," he answered cheerfully.

This was when I turned to the other piece of information he had offered. "But since when is the 19th all the way up at Vetera?"

Rather than answer me directly, he instead asked, "Did Crescens tell you about what's happening up at Vetera?" I shook my head, though it did not strike me as unusual for the Primus Pilus not to talk about another camp that had gone through periods of neglect. "They've enlarged it. It was supposed to be the forward base for our campaign against Marobduus, but when that didn't happen, they stopped working on it. But now the new Praetor has ordered that not only should it be enlarged, but next season, it's going to be home to at least two Legions, maybe three." Shrugging, he finished, "And it's been the 19th who was sent up there to do the work. From what I hear, it's been finished for some time, but they were ordered to stay there."

We both were silent for a moment, then after taking a sip, he turned to my Century.

"Structus struggled a bit at first," Macer informed me, and before he supplied the answer, I interjected, "Let me guess. The men from his section?"

I knew I did not need to elaborate, and I was rewarded with a nod, confirming my guess. It was not due to any brilliance on my part, and is indeed one of the most common mistakes new Optios make, thinking that their former section mates will not take advantage of his newfound authority. It was something every man who moves up into the Optionate has to face, and I had struggled with it as well, until I learned that by treating them differently I faced bigger problems from the rest of the men of the Century.

"It's all straightened out now," Macer went on, but I was not quite ready to let this go yet.

"Was it Caninas?" I asked Macer, and while at first he did not seem disposed to answer, I continued gazing at him until he gave a slight shrug, then nodded. "I thought as much," I muttered. "I should have thrashed him before I left just for good measure."

"As I said," Macer spoke easily, yet I also detected the note in his voice I had learned over the course of our relationship that signaled when he was speaking as my superior and not my friend, "it's all taken care of, and it has been for more than a year now."

From there, he went on to tell me of other changes in my Century, mainly transfers out and up to the higher Centuries, although two men had died; one of a sudden ague, the other falling into the river during a night of debauching and being swept away. The sick man had been a good Gregarius, but the other was the sort that was not much of a loss, and depending on the *tiro* that replaced him, could be an addition by subtraction to the Century as a whole.

"You have seven new bodies that arrived after you left," Macer told me, "but the last two were earlier this spring, so aside from being blooded, they at least know which end of the *gladius* to hold."

"That's good," I agreed, while privately, I was reserving judgment about these unseen replacements; what might have been good enough for Structus, or even Macer, I was not likely to think was good enough for me, but that was not something he needed to know.

"Just out of curiosity," Macer asked casually, "what did you think about Crescens?" Evidently seeing my look of confusion, he elaborated, "Did he seem…different to you?"

This is when I recalled the remark he had made, seemingly out of nowhere, which prompted me to admit, "He might have been a little…grumpy," was all I could think to say, which made Macer chuckle.

"He's always like that," he teased me. "You just forgot since you've been gone so long. No," he turned serious, "this is something new, as in the last couple of days. Nobody knows with any certainty, but Lucco squeezed some of his friends in the *praetorium*, and while they didn't know much, they did tell him that apparently he was passed over for Camp Prefect again."

"I had heard there was a new one," I mused, "but I thought that was for the Army of Pannonia, not the Rhenus."

We sat in silence for a moment, then clearly having exhausted our entire fount of knowledge about the matter, dropped the subject.

And with that, I was about to leave, but before I did, I asked offhandedly, "Who's the new Praetor?"

"Publius Quinctilius Varus," Macer informed me, and I frowned.

"I've heard the name, but I don't know anything about the man," I said, but Macer did not know all that much more than I did.

"He was supposed to have done a good job running Syria, but that was a few years ago," my Pilus Prior offered this with a shrug. "All I know about the man now is that the Princeps trusts him."

"Well," it was all I could think to say, "that must mean he knows what he's doing."

And, with that, we parted, with me returning to my quarter, preparing to start the next day back where I belonged, in a real Legion, and for the time being, away from men like Germanicus and Tiberius.

It did not take long for me to fall back into the normal rhythm of life in a regular Legion, although I was a bit disappointed to see that the new replacements were not as inept as I had imagined or hoped they would be. Nevertheless, they had to face their Centurion with the *rudis*, which was the one ritual of initiation that these men had escaped, and I must say I was pleased to see that their comrades, the veterans of the Century, had filled their heads with such tales of my prowess with a blade, even one made of wood, that every one of them was literally shaking with fear as they stepped in front of me. And now, with the new scars earned from my time with Germanicus, and the news about the grim nature of the Pannonian campaign, even the veterans accorded me with a level of respect that was gratifying. Structus, I had to admit, had done a good job running my Century, perhaps a little too good, if I am being honest, though I tried not to let this show in my time with him. Frankly, the only thing that lingered, for me at least, was the black cloud of doubt and worry that Tiberius would not forget about my show of independence. Days turned rapidly into weeks, bringing with it the change of weather, and we heard of the continued frustration of the Legions fighting in Pannonia. Sometimes, when I heard the latest gossip, I felt a twinge of regret, as if I had abandoned the *Legio Germanicus* in general, and their namesake in particular, but I suppose I convinced myself that I had performed my duty to his satisfaction. And, as time passed, I began to think that, perhaps, I had escaped Tiberius' wrath. Which, it turned out, I had, just not in the manner in which I thought, and through the efforts of a completely unexpected ally.

It was not until the Kalends of November, and we had had our first snow, although it did not stick for more than a couple days, when Alex knocked on the door to my quarters. As usual, I was reading, though I do not remember what it was, which is because the moment

I looked up from my spot on the scroll and saw my nephew's face, I knew something was wrong. My immediate thought was that he was bringing me news from home, in Arelate, and I prepared myself to hear something I had been dreading for some time. For once, my natural pessimism was not warranted, although it did not really start out that way, despite learning his presence had nothing to do with our family.

"I just got back from the *praetorium*," he began, and his young features had such a grim cast to them I suddenly saw him as he would look when he was the age I was at that moment. "I saw someone there, and I'm guessing that he'll be coming to see you."

Before I could even register the words, as he predicted, there was a sharp rap, this time out in the outer office, on the door that led into our building. Alex did not move, and I had the impression that he would have been willing to not open the door, but I nodded at him to do so, whereupon he turned reluctantly and left my room, closing the door. As he did so, I swung my legs off my cot, thankful that at least it was no longer difficult. My knees felt a bit tight from the scar tissue when I flexed them, twisting my torso suddenly could cause a twinge of pain, and I was a bit restricted with the movement of my arm at the shoulder, but these were all just part of the cost that comes with marching for Rome, which I had long since accepted. I had just come to my feet when I heard the outer door open, and since Alex had pulled my door closed, the voices were too muffled for me to make them out clearly, but there was a quality to the one I knew did not belong to Alex that gave me the first hint, signaled by a fluttering in my stomach. Then, Alex was knocking at the inner door, and I waited only long enough to move behind my desk, then sit down before bidding entry. Alex led the way, but the sensation in my stomach turned from a flutter to the feeling my guts were being twisted, even as I forced myself to sound pleasant.

"*Salve*, Dolabella." I did not stand, but I did indicate the stool in front of my desk, while at the same time telling Alex, "Pour us a couple cups, Alex."

"I don't know how you do it," was the way Tiberius Dolabella put it, "but somehow you've managed to avoid falling into the *cac* again."

As I had expected, this was not the first thing, or the second, out of Dolabella's mouth, yet despite my impatience and my long-standing antipathy towards the man, I managed to maintain at least a semblance of cordiality. And, honestly, I was interested to hear the latest developments in Pannonia, though it turned out that Bato of the Daesitiates was still behind the Dinaric Mountains, and Tiberius had commanded that the Legions go into winter quarters. In itself this was not particularly noteworthy; it was the reason why that was, which also made waiting to hear the news that impacted me personally a bit easier.

"Tiberius is worried, very worried about the Legions," was how Dolabella put it, "so he's hoping that putting them into winter quarters early and loosening the regulations a bit might help." He gave me a thin smile. "Besides, he has to go back to Rome to confer with the Princeps about the very thing the men are worried about."

"The extension of the enlistments?" It was not much of a guess, and he nodded, which prompted me to ask him, "And? What do you know about it?"

He shrugged. "Only that Augustus is very close to making up his mind about it."

"Even if it causes a revolt?" as the instant the words came out, I had to wince, but there was no other way to put it, and a measure of Dolabella's distress was that he could only look miserable as he answered, "That's what Tiberius thinks. Which is why he's going to Rome."

I was aware that I was pushing matters, especially since I knew Dolabella was not here to chat about Tiberius and Augustus, but I did so anyway. "And how is Tiberius' standing with the Princeps? Have things been smoothed over?"

Dolabella did not reply immediately, except rather than looking at me, he was staring down at the cup, a thoughtful frown on his face, before he finally gave at least a partial answer. "I think that, given

Tiberius' actions in Pannonia, the Princeps has had a change of heart. At least," at this he did look at me, a grim smile on his face, "I hope so. Or it will turn out I picked the wrong horse after all."

This proved to be the most difficult moment between us, even with what was to come, because the thought that flashed through my mind was the bitter realization that, while I was also "backing" Tiberius, it had not been by choice, but by being maneuvered into doing so, and while it might have been at the behest of the man himself, it was through the efforts of the agent of his sitting across from me. Still, I somehow managed from letting any of the sudden rush of anger that came boiling up out of my gut leak out of me in some way.

Only then did Dolabella move to the subject that was of more immediate interest to me, and that was my fate. After making his first remark about my plight, he said, "Now, it helped you that, as I told you, it was likely Tiberius would have too much on his mind, what with everything going on. But," he at least tried to sound casual, "it turns out that you've got at least one other man who's willing to stick his neck out for you. And," he added, "it's not Germanicus. Although he certainly did his part in speaking up for you."

He stopped then, which I assumed was to make me guess, but even after thinking about it for the span of several heartbeats, I could not possibly think of any man highly placed enough, aside from Germanicus, who would fit that description, prompting me to burst out in exasperation, "I have no idea who you're talking about!"

The smile that instantly materialized confirmed my guess that he was toying with me, and despite my internal admonishment, I felt my hand tighten around the cup; fortunately, I restrained from crushing it this time.

"I suppose you've heard there's a new Camp Prefect," Dolabella remarked, and now I knew he was drawing out his torment, yet I still managed to say levelly, "Yes, I've heard."

"But," he went on, "you apparently don't know who it is, because if you did, you would have already figured out who I'm talking about."

"No," I agreed, "apparently, I don't."

Dolabella looked far too pleased with himself, and it was all I could do to avoid a repeat of the episode shortly after our first meeting, when I almost throttled him to death, but at last he supplied the name.

"Gaius Sempronius Atticus."

Someone gasped aloud, and I suppose it was me because Dolabella had lifted his cup to take a sip, probably to hide his smile at my combination of astonishment and shock, though later when I thought about it, I was not sure why I found it so surprising.

"The Primus Pilus? I mean," I hated myself for sounding like an idiot, but I was still so surprised, "he's not Primus Pilus anymore, but he was the Primus Pilus of the 8th, and…"

"Yes, I'm aware of his old posting, and his new one," Dolabella was enjoying himself far too much.

Finally, I recovered myself enough to ask, "But, what did he do? For me, I mean?"

"Yes, I know what you mean," apparently, I gave him a glare that prompted him to end his fun, and he explained, "and here's what happened. Atticus heard about you leaving Germanicus, and he went to Tiberius, and persuaded him that, while you could have handled it better, you weren't wrong to leave." He paused for another couple heartbeats. "Apparently, he persuaded Tiberius that putting you with Germanicus, given your reputation with the Pannonians, was probably making the job he had given Germanicus more difficult."

I cannot say I liked hearing it put this way, but neither could I deny there was truth there, the image of Dodonis' face, turning to snarl at me in hatred even as my blade sliced off his head, leaping out at me. Nor, this thought quickly followed, was it likely an accident that Tiberius had done so, or made a miscalculation about how my reputation among the Pannonian tribes, particularly the Maezaei, would actually make matters more difficult for the young Germanicus. There is a moment, when playing the game of tables, when a good player has maneuvered his stones in such a way that the placement of just one more connects them all together and wins him the game. This is the only way I can describe the series of realizations that occurred, inside my head, with the speed of a lightning bolt going to ground. It had not been my familiarity with the ground, or the people, I thought, as a leaden ball seemed to materialize in the pit of my stomach, but how much I was hated that Tiberius had been counting on. And, I realized, it had been no accident whatsoever that the *Legio Germanicus* had been given the specific task of subduing the Maezaei. I had always sensed that Tiberius was, at best, ambivalent about how his adopted son would fare in this, his first time in the rank of Legate, but despite the resentment I was feeling as all of this came together in my mind, I also had to admire the cunning of Tiberius. Or, as I contemplated further, someone close to Tiberius who gave him the idea, and I suppose it was impossible for my face to mask all that was going on behind it. And yet, Dolabella seemed more pleased than anything else, regarding me over his cup with a slight smile.

"So," he said softly, "I see you've figured it out. At least," he added, "a part of it." Honestly, if I was still missing something, I was not sure I wanted to know any more, but even so, Dolabella, lowering his cup as he leaned forward, stared at me intently with his good eye as he warned, "Pullus, I hope I don't have to tell you that what you know, or think you know, never leaves this room, and how much danger there would be if it did."

Now, I knew this very well; nevertheless, being threatened always brings out the worst in me, prompting me to snap, "Dangerous for who?"

"For all of us," Dolabella appeared neither angry nor surprised at my outburst, which actually served to remind me that, in his own way, Tiberius Dolabella knew me well. "Not just you, but your nephew, your family. And," he added, still quietly, "for me."

He did not stay much longer after that; honestly, there was not much more to talk about, and when he left, disappearing into the night as he usually did, I was left in a distinctly unsettled state of mind. Sitting at my desk, the idea of returning to my reading was banished for the night, and I sat there brooding about what, in one visit, Dolabella had unleashed within my mind. I can only liken it to what a man who has been blind for his entire life might experience when, suddenly, for the first time, he can see clearly...and what he sees is that he is alone, on a barren island in the middle of a sea so vast that there is no glimpse of land anywhere around. Certainly, I did not have any proof that I was right in my assessment, other than Dolabella's cryptic words, which I knew was done purposely so that, should any question arise, he could deny being the man who confirmed my suspicions. Finally, when I heard the *bucina* sound the call that announced it was midnight, and knowing that the Cohort was supposed to make one last routine march across the Rhenus in the morning before winter truly set in, I told myself that, as long as Tiberius, Germanicus, and I were never together in the same place, I would be able to keep all this deadly and combustible information to myself, which allowed me to finally fall asleep.

Which, of course, meant that the gods had other plans, but that is all the time I have for now. Perhaps this record that I am leaving behind will inform those who come after me about those times, in which the young Germanicus first made himself known to Rome, and to we men of the Legions, as he rose to the challenges placed before him in a manner befitting the name that he bears. And, it is to the same Germanicus, albeit an older, wiser and more experienced version of the exuberant, brash and brilliant youth with whom I marched, that my Legion marches to now, to complete Rome's vengeance.

Aromoo
S. ST Clair
+ *people*

— Terson I'p
over Seanhell
york
3:00 PM

Made in the USA
San Bernardino, CA
08 February 2017